THE DARKEST DAY COLLECTION

The Eternal Scribe Publishing
Indianapolis, IN

MILA'S SHIFT

CHAPTER ONE

Mila took deep breaths to calm her pounding heart, anxiety eating her alive. She'd picked a table that backed up against a wall so no one could sneak up on her. The table sat on the café's patio on the far edge nearest the alley, perfect placement for a quick getaway.

Still, she felt exposed. Every set of eyes that lifted higher than their teacup or plate seemed to bore into her, questioning her, doubting her. Every Bluetooth headset made her wonder who listened on the other end of the line. And if that someone would shoot on sight.

Conversation washed over her, but she froze at the word "shifter" drifting on the wind.

A haughty feminine voice sneered and Mila caught the woman lifting a cup to her lips, so full of her own superiority. "They should all be shot."

Mila flinched, her hackles rising even more at the open hostility.

"Now, now, dear. There are no shifters near." He tried soothing her, but it was a futile task.

Mila held in her smirk.

"None near? Are you kidding?" She almost stood in her outrage, but her companion touched her hand, patting it until she settled. "A shifter could be sitting at this very cafe and we wouldn't have a clue!"

"Come now, Beatrix, the government screening is too good for that. Why, the news shows agents rounding more up every day. I saw with my own eyes one of them getting tossed into a van."

Beatrix grumbled into her cup, but her voice still carried to Mila. "The government couldn't round up their own asses."

Mila almost lost it, not sure if amusement or nerves played a bigger part in that moment. As the couple calmed, she blotted out their words. But nothing could erase the presence of two grotesque bigots sitting not three feet from her. It set her on edge, ready to run, ready to fight. She gritted her teeth, resisting the urge to beat the woman upside the head until she *really* had a reason to fear.

So when her friend, May, approached the cafe even more nervous than Mila, she raised an eyebrow.

Mila had spent her adult life on the wrong side of the law. She had good cause to be cautious. What did her law-abiding, goodie-two-shoes best friend have to fear?

Mila put on an awkward smile and called out, "Hey, May!"

Just like old times.

May's head jerked up after having scanned the tables and the street, not only looking for her, but also for a tail. Mila recognized it from experience. After all, she'd perfected the technique over the last ten years they'd been apart.

She wanted to apologize for leaving, for not explaining at

least. Instead, when her life had fallen to pieces, when she had to leave, she left a vague note to her twin in all but blood and walked out. She'd never expected to hear from her again.

Yes, Mila *wanted* to apologize, but how did one say, "I'm sorry for leaving, but I suddenly turned into a tiger, and I didn't know how to deal with that?" She almost laughed at the idea, what with the bigot at the next table.

Minutes passed with Mila lost in thought, something she knew far better than social situations anymore. May still stood behind the chair across from her, staring at Mila as if seeing a ghost.

She is, stupid.

Shaking her head at her own idiocy, Mila patted the glass surface next to her cup. "Come on, May. Sit." Though, honestly, her friend needed a bit more than a coffee and conversation right about now. Tequila shots might be in order.

May stood there, the rift between them heavy in the air. "Where have you been?"

Random abandoned buildings?

"Around," she said instead.

May scowled, but didn't push. Mila sat and stared, but the tension never left her friend's form, that awareness she knew so well feeling so alien on the other woman.

Why was May here?

And why was she so terrified?

———

Mila laughed. "Okay, maybe I shouldn't have had that second sandwich." Laughing again lightened her heart.

"Or maybe the half a chocolate cake you had for dessert," May said with a sly smile. It had taken a while, but May had relaxed little by little as they ate and talked.

It had been years since the best friends had been together. Mila had always maintained ways for the people she cared about to keep in touch with her, but never directly. She hadn't heard from anyone from her childhood in so long, it felt uplifting being a normal person for an hour.

Okay, maybe two.

"Yeah, but you can't count cake. Chocolate is a necessity, like air." A necessity she'd lacked for a long time.

May shook her head. "I don't understand how you can eat so much and not gain weight. You were like that in high school, but you haven't changed a bit, have you?"

"No, still got the metabolism from hell." Of course, May didn't know the reason for Mila's freakish metabolism. She didn't know that Mila needed excess energy to shift shape. Or that it gave her the ability to change fat into muscle. That was something she couldn't tell her friend. She trusted May, but May was an honest person, and she couldn't put that burden on her.

It was why she'd left that cryptic note, why she couldn't say goodbye in person. She loved May more than anyone else in the world, and she couldn't do that to her. Knowing May, she would have come with her, and at least one of them had to live their dream. Some days, nothing kept her going but that dream, the dream May lived for her.

May shook her head again. "I would *kill* to be able to eat that much. If I ate even a fraction of that, I'd be five hundred pounds!"

Mila stretched. "Ah, the blessings of being me."

They paid the checks, and Mila offered to walk May to her car. May had never mentioned why she'd reached out to her, and though the camaraderie had soothed them both, they remained on edge. Leaving the cafe, they turned down a small side road, tall buildings rising up on both sides like a canyon. May's car sat at the far end, she guessed. Only vehicle in sight.

Mila couldn't take the tension anymore. She had enough stress. She didn't need May's as well. "So, why did you *really* call me, May?"

May jumped and twisted sheepishly toward Mila. "What do you mean?"

"You haven't contacted me in ten years. Suddenly you reach out and you're skittish as a mouse? Something's wrong."

May wrung her hands, fidgeting from foot to foot, but she didn't speak. Mila gave her space, waiting her out. The words would come with patience.

Crashes of metal on metal, cheers, and lewd comments erupted from behind her. She turned as May's eyes grew wide. The raucous youths careened closer, pointing to the two women. Then cat calls echoed off the walls.

"Back slowly to the car, May." Mila's every nerve ramped up to a razor's edge. After ten years on the streets, she could sense trouble like a sixth sense. And these guys were bad news, big time. She started backing up, not watching where she was going, simply putting distance between her and the hooligans.

"Hey, don't leave!" one of them called.

"Yeah, we just wanna play!"

Cheers and crude gestures followed. Mila knew they were in trouble.

"Run," she whispered and turned to dash for the car. She shoved May before her and fled to the pounding beat of men in pursuit.

Her heart pounded anew, this time from exertion and fear rather than anxiety. As she ran, she focused on what she would need to survive this if it got messy. Strength. She'd need strength. She shifted every tissue she could to skeletal muscle. Years on the run, years spent hiding in old warehouses for fear of being seen, left her an expert at shifting.

As her arms pumped at her sides, she noted the increase in size and definition. It wouldn't be enough. She didn't have enough mass to get massive. But she had skill on her side. Another advantage of spending all her waking hours in a hole. She'd spent her free time practicing the martial arts she'd learned as a child and teenager.

Someone grabbed her arm and yanked it, pain shooting up her shoulder. A yelp flew from her mouth and she turned with the motion, using the guy's own grab against him and twisting him into an arm lock. She jerked her head to and fro, looking for other attackers, as the guy in her hands yelled and flailed. *Crack.* She slammed him hard on the back of the head and he crashed into the pavement.

Mila spun, searching for May, and screamed. "No!" She ran as the knife pulled from May's body, the red blood pouring out. She ran as her best friend's body fell in slow motion to the ground. Her limbs dragged at her like swimming through cement.

Mila skidded on her knees to her friend, grabbing her and pressing on the wound that pumped that life-giving liquid.

Pump, pump, pump. "You'll be okay, May. You're gonna be okay."

Wetness coated her cheeks before she realized she'd been crying. She tried to wipe the tears away, but her sticky hands smeared blood across her face.

The pace of that pumping slowed, slowed, and stopped. An eternity stretched as she waited for it to pump again, for more blood to gush out, but nothing. "No. No. She can't be." She covered her face with her bloody palms, shaking her head and denying the truth before her. "No, no, no."

After a time, the tears ceased. Numbness settled in as she rocked her friend, her other half. Soon, the numbness evaporated too, and the fog in her head dissipated, her predicament becoming clear. She couldn't call the cops. As a shifter, they would either arrest her or shoot on sight, depending on the officer. There was no ambiguity in the law on shifters. The government didn't know what to do with them, so they'd passed a law making it illegal to be a shifter.

Not like she had a choice in the matter.

Mila would never go to those camps. Even living her entire life in abandoned buildings held more appeal.

She couldn't call the cops. She couldn't report May's murder. Besides, Mila believed May wouldn't have wanted Mila to be taken. Not for her. She took a deep breath and hated herself a little. She grabbed May's keys and popped the trunk.

What else could she do?

Hours passed as she found what she needed, found the right spot, and laid her friend to rest. She thought of leaving her friend's body somewhere conspicuous, but it felt wrong to abandon her that way. She cried the entire time she dug the hole. Patting down the last of the dirt, she tilted her head to the dark sky. The same words kept passing through her mind like a marquee.

I'm sorry.

Mila sat in the driver's seat, staring at the bag next to her. When she'd been deciding what to bury May with, she'd gone through it.

May had a verified ID.

Her conscience warred with her logic. Her conscience told her it was wrong. Her logic told her May wouldn't need it anymore. What was the harm? Her conscience just kept telling her it was wrong, but her brain, her logic, kept coming up with new reasons to do it. She wouldn't have to run and hide. She could have a normal life. May was a pilot just like she'd trained to be. Nobody would ever have to know. She could have a life.

Pulling the ID from the bag, she stared at it. She stared until it almost mesmerized her, until her vision blurred, refocused and blurred once more. She knew she would do it. The ship left in less than twenty-four hours.

No one would ever have to know.

And one of them had to live their dream…

CHAPTER TWO

*H*er body felt strange, foreign, like it had a mind of its own. Her brain swam inside the cage of her uncooperative flesh. Muffled shouts and jeers drifted into her fuzzy brain. Spikes of adrenaline shot through a system that simply wanted to slump against one of these nice, comfy cars and fall asleep.

Or throw up. Her stomach lurched, threatening to unleash the countless shots of vodka she'd had that night. She held her middle, willing it to settle. *I'm never drinking again.*

Her mind flitted around like a bug in a jar. She leaned her weight against the cold, slick metal, tempted to lean her face against it, hoping the icy surface would soothe her.

"Sweetness," a slurred male voice said, making it through the murk.

She jerked up and almost fell over, catching herself against the nearest object. Her arm slammed against cold metal, pain radiating from the point of contact. A wall of men closed in, activating some far-off warning system in her psyche, like hearing an ambulance coming but not knowing where.

When had they gotten so close?

One grabbed her from behind, wrapping an arm around her waist.

Everything inside her rebelled, fighting and screaming all at once.

<hr />

Mila jerked awake, breathing hard. For a spell, she stayed in that moment so many years ago, leaving May behind, leaving her career behind. A single tear ran down her face.

Why am I crying?

Hadn't she cried out all these emotions years ago? Back then, the world felt impossible, too much to cope with alone.

Then she remembered.

May was dead.

She sucked in a shuddering breath and the tears came in earnest this time. They poured a deluge until her face burned with the emotion, her nose stuffed worse than any cold. The rivers of salty sorrow dried to an arid riverbed. A hollowed out shell, she sat there on the mattress, the once wet tracks leaving tight reminders on her skin.

Getting out of bed, Mila dressed on autopilot, falling back into the old routines with ease, but stopped dead when she reached the door to the bathroom. A part of her refused to force her feet forward.

She couldn't do it. She couldn't look in the mirror and see May's face. It would break her. Minutes ticked by where she tried to quiet the turmoil inside. After a time, she crossed the threshold with her head downcast, her—no, May's—hair blocking the view. She did what she had to, grabbed what she needed, and raced out as if her life depended on it.

Mila dropped on the bed with a gasp, needing a few more moments to center herself. "I am May. I am May Trace," she chanted again and again, tears recurring and choking her. Not capable of keeping her own company right now, she turned on the TV, hoping it could silence the pain eating her alive.

"I wouldn't say it's a controversy," the man on screen said, steepling his fingers in front of him. "It's a question of basic human rights."

"Yet, they're not human, are they?"

Mila flinched, but couldn't look away.

"Aren't they? Do we know they're not?"

"Yet it's a proven fact that they're a danger. They can change into anyone, anything. One could change into the President and just walk right into the White House, or a military base, or our schools." The screen shifted to a female leaning forward in outrage.

"First, the government takes steps to prevent that. No one can get into a secured facility without a verified ID, and many places without on site DNA confirmation. Our country *is* secure."

The woman grumbled. "But that doesn't change them from stealing other identities. No one is safe until these criminals are brought to justice."

"Criminals? Really?" The man supporting shifters balked. "You're trying to tell me that Emmaline Grayson was a criminal?" The video changed to a scene of a teenager being dragged away. She fought like anyone would, but the men easily overpowered her, hurting her. She slumped in their arms and even from the grainy footage, Mila could see blood.

"What did she, an honor roll high school student, do to deserve such treatment? What justifies stealing a child from her home, beating her, and leaving her hospitalized?"

"Come now," the woman scoffed, "that is one instance of police brutality."

The shifter supporter leaned forward. "Thirty-four percent of shifters in the camps are underage. They're children too unaware of what they are to even know to hide it."

Mila flinched, the statement hitting too close to home. She shut it off. She didn't want to hear how much the world hated her kind, how bad others had it, or more importantly, what her fate would be if she got caught.

Mila rubbed her hands on May's pants as she fidgeted in line, May's bag digging into her shoulder. *This will work. They won't question a verified ID.* She tried not to stare in awe at the giant spacecraft looming in the background. It was a veritable antique, from back when ships could still enter atmosphere. It had a MAG GRAV system, for crying out loud.

A half hour later, a woman in uniform glanced at May's ID, then up at Mila's face, which now matched May's. Satisfied, she barked a bunk and station assignment at her before telling her to report to med bay. Mila dashed off, following the guy before her. *May would want this.*

He hadn't been able to confirm the kill. Without the confirmation, he didn't get paid. He'd orchestrated that attack to make it look like a mugging gone wrong, but his lackeys fled before they knew for certain May Trace was no more.

So now he sat, scope steady and ready, monitoring each person who boarded the ship, searching for the one who didn't belong. The one who should be dead. Emergency services never found a body, and neither she nor any Jane Does showed up at the ER.

His left side had long since gone numb when his scope zeroed in on her, twitching in line.

His job wasn't finished.

Kyle Avery walked beside the captain as they ambled through the ship, discussing security protocols and the mission—in as vague terms as possible. They both knew the stakes. If this mission didn't succeed…

They passed crew members and guests, the uniforms blending into a seamless mob as intended. But as he walked by one woman, he looked behind himself and stopped, something sending all his instincts on alert. She raced away, harried like everyone else. No one was familiar with this model of ship anymore so most of the crew would struggle for a few days getting accustomed to the layout.

But something just felt *off* about her. He couldn't put his finger on it, though. Same uniform, nondescript hair, everything seemed regulation, no different from anyone else on board, but something told him she didn't belong.

"Avery?"

He spun on his heels. "Yes, Captain?"

"Is something wrong?"

He turned around, but she'd disappeared around a corner. "No, Captain." He continued walking, keeping pace with

Captain Faulk. He didn't know what to think. She had felt off, wrong, but he didn't have that gut-wrenching feeling he got when a mission went FUBAR. He didn't believe she was a threat—just a mystery.

———

Mila's gut felt like she'd swallowed acid, maybe hydrochloric acid. Or that stuff they use to dissolve mortar.

Chaos.

Medical personnel and security staff lined the walls of the med bay, standing at little temporary tables with QuiKits. Every few seconds, someone would bark out, "Next," and the line would move forward.

Mila was losing her shit. The same thing kept running through her brain. *What are they testing for?* Was it to confirm identity? But no, QuiKits couldn't do genomic identity testing. And they couldn't do identity testing onboard. The databases required to store the data would be enormous, and running that much information through secured connections took time, even today. Checking against billions and billions of bases took a long, long time, no matter how powerful your computer system.

But QuiKits *could* test for specific genotypes. It could test for shifters. If it tested that, she was dead. She wanted to open her mouth. She wanted to ask someone what was going on, what they were testing for, but knew it would spell her doom if she did.

She was a freak. Even excluding her shifter status, no one else had come onboard clueless. She didn't know their mission, didn't know their protocols, didn't know shit.

Mila hadn't served in the NSS for ten years. In fact, she'd *never* served in the NSS since she'd never finished her training.

Someone barked, "Next," and Mila realized no one stood in front of her.

She walked up to the only open station and took a deep breath, too worried to look the guy in the eye.

"Hand," he said as he busied himself opening the kit.

Mila stuck her arm out and sneaked a peek at the packaging. "QuiKit: STD Panel," it read, and she let out a breath.

Big black block letters marked every corridor, so Mila only made one wrong turn before finding her bunk. Two beds were bolted to the wall of the tiny room, one on top of the other, and two wardrobes abutted the opposite wall. Nothing else. Her arms and shoulders skimmed the wardrobes and metal bed frame as she walked down the middle. She almost hunched sideways to get around the ladder to the top bunk.

"Hi," she said to her roommate. "Name's May Trace." She'd been practicing using the name ad nauseam over the last twenty-four hours. She repeated it in her head even now. "I'm a pilot."

Her roommate glanced up before continuing to unpack. "Santos. Comms," she said.

Mila ignored the snub and unloaded her bag into her wardrobe, latching everything down.

MAG GRAV systems prevented bone loss, but paled in comparison to modern systems. They didn't produce gravity. Instead, they used magnetics to simulate the force gravity puts on your body. Any non-magnetic items would fly everywhere once they left Earth.

Mila nodded and headed off to her duty station. She had first shift on the bridge. Though everything else terrified her, she looked forward to flying. She hadn't flown in so long, she wasn't sure she would remember how.

What if she failed? Sub-space travel took skill, a skill she hadn't practiced in far too long.

But even with a sea of doubt coursing through her head, she walked to the bridge with a grin on her face.

For a military ship, slipping aboard proved no challenge at all. Once onboard, he grabbed the first person he found alone, dragged him into a quiet corridor, and snapped his neck. He took in the details, then started his shift.

As a whole, the *Orleans* might have been old and underwhelming, but stepping onto the bridge would always fill Mila with awe. It brought a huge smile to her face as she stepped into the room. There was a time she'd lived for this moment. The expansive view, the consoles, the controls, even the captain sitting in his chair looking almighty and, she was ashamed to say, hot.

After high school, she and May had trained as pilots. It had been one of the best times of her life, maybe *the* best. Flying had been her dream and her gift. They'd dreamed of shipping out together, flying side by side, even if it was a ridiculous fantasy.

But Mila had shifted before she ever flew outside simulators.

In training, she'd bested every record, but people didn't hire shifters. That drunken night ten years ago ended her life. She ran. She never stopped running.

Until now.

———

Out of necessity, Captain Tristan Faulk was on edge. He watched as each person entered the bridge, waiting for word from his Lieutenant on their status. Some personnel he'd worked with before. Others were new to him.

His attention zeroed in on a female officer who swaggered onto the bridge as if she owned the thing. She stopped, her face stretching into a smile he found contagious, then sashayed to the pilot's seat.

His gut sent him mixed signals about the girl. On the one hand, he couldn't get his eyes to drift away from how her ass swayed in those tight uniform pants. On the other, his instincts screamed that she wasn't military. Something about her was wrong. Maybe she had attitude problems. Still, he would check out her file when he got back to his quarters. And he would keep an eye on her from here on out.

On her, not her butt.

———

Mila sat, waiting for the order to take off. An effervescent sensation bubbled up inside her. She feared she would start giggling at any moment. Nothing would give her away faster than a pilot with a giggling fit.

She cracked her knuckles, rolled her neck, and stretched every muscle group she could think of. A guy next to her couldn't stop smiling at her. At least he wasn't laughing.

Mila waited as people around her went about their business. Some raced about, preparing for take off, but many twiddled their thumbs just like her.

While she leaned back in her seat, an officer—high ranked based on the amount of crap on his uniform—spoke to the captain, and took his position. The captain leaned forward and said, "Okay, everyone, final pre-flight checks."

Mila went though the motions. It had been years, but she told herself it was like riding a bike. She could do this in her sleep, even if doubt kept creeping in.

She put the panel in pre-flight mode, and ran her fingers over the controls, testing their responses. Flaps. Check. Propulsion. Check. Yoke response. Check. She continued through the checklist to the end, then turned and reported to the captain, "Pilot pre-flights complete, captain." Mila took the controls out of pre-flight mode.

Others echoed her sentiment, the echo growing with each voice. The sounds merged, building toward something. Mila almost held her breath, waiting and eager for the good part. After a few minutes, everyone had reported in.

"All right. Let's take this baby out. Communications, please confirm our flight status with the tower."

"Yes, captain," a guy several stations down from her said. He spoke into the radio, then turned to the captain. "We're cleared for take off, captain."

"Take off, pilot."

"Yes, captain," Mila said, a great big smile on her face.

Finally.

The USS *Orleans* was temperamental at the best of times. Tristan watched, almost in awe, as the pilot maneuvered the behemoth into space. She flew as if the *Orleans* were a fighter jet, not the largest ship that could leave Earth's surface, a ship so old the engines practically rattled.

Impressive.

And for a moment, he forgot his suspicion of her.

Which left room for other concerns to surface. Like the mission. He liked being a captain, running his crew. He enjoyed the responsibility, the authority. But he'd avoided this type of assignment his entire career, not that command had ever offered him one.

His thoughts strayed to the diplomats hidden among the crew. They'd been breathing down his neck since they'd arrived on board, but he'd kicked them out of the bridge, telling them he couldn't have the distractions.

Liar.

He didn't *want* the distractions.

His gaze roved back to the pilot. Her graceful arms shifted from one control to the next. Once they cleared Earth, they would enter sub-space. Faster-than-light travel didn't exist. Messages could travel faster than light, but any matter that attempted it didn't reach the other end in the same condition as it departed.

The discovery of sub-space allowed for interstellar travel. Sub-space didn't act like normal space did. Like how tachyonic particles didn't follow the same rules as normal particles, sub-space had its own unique set of rules. One of those rules made it possible to travel many light years in a matter of months.

"Entering sub-space momentarily," she said, her hands still flying over the controls.

He loved this part. Around him, the universe bent and contorted like a funhouse mirror. Then it righted itself as they arrived in sub-space, but this place brought to mind the other side of Alice's mirror. Nothing seemed quite right. Distances seemed distorted, visual range shifted. Many pilots had difficulty flying in sub-space. Many others couldn't and never received credentials for off-planet flight.

But this pilot traversed the surreal landscape of sub-space as if it were no big thing. Planets, moons, and asteroids flew toward them at speed. Sub-space seemed a compression of normal space, with distances between objects reduced. It meant navigation could be tricky if planets were close. Even hundreds of millions of miles apart in normal space could end up so close that a large ship like the *Orleans* maneuvered between them with difficulty.

But gravity wasn't a problem in sub-space. It didn't exist in sub-space the same way it did in normal space, leaving planets and stars misshapen and bloated. A pilot could come as close as one wished to a planet without fearing being sucked into its gravitational field.

He winced as they passed close to a planet's rings, but relaxed when nothing happened. The pilot never even batted an eye at the near miss. Either she knew her skills well or she was utterly insane.

His new persona didn't work the first shift. Unfortunately, his target did. At the doorway to the bridge, he leaned against a wall out of sight, but close enough to keep tabs on her. He had patience.

He would finish the job.

Once her shift ended, she followed her roommate, Santos, to the mess hall. After picking up a tray of something that vaguely resembled food, she approached Santos, the only person she knew on this boat. "Mind if I sit with you?"

Santos shrugged and continued eating.

So much for conversation.

Mila dug in. At least she could say that while it looked like gruel, it didn't taste bad. Behind her, people spouted hate, and Mila tried to ignore it, but failed.

"They're just a bunch of fucking monsters," one guy said.

"I hear they can't even enter our atmosphere. Why would we ally ourselves with weaklings like that?"

"I know, right?"

"Hello, my buds!" A guy sat down next to them, distracting her from the venom behind her.

He must work a later shift. She looked over at him between bites and realized it was the guy who'd been sitting next to her on the bridge. He had a big, goofy smile on his face. She couldn't for the life of her figure out how he had so much energy after working eight hours.

"Luke Hall, communications," he said, reaching out his hand for a handshake.

Mila, she almost said. "May Trace, pilot."

"Well, it's a pleasure to fly with you, May. That was some smooth sailing." His entire body communicated with him.

"Thanks. So, you're both in communications?"

"I'm the maths guy. She's the computer genius."

"Cool."

Mila didn't understand the TAT system. It required both a mathematician and a computer scientist to operate. If they made a mistake, it could alter the rules of the universe, breaking cause and effect.

Yeah, oops.

But on the plus side, they could send real-time messages with Earth… so long as they didn't fuck up the calculations.

Not that she had anyone to send messages to. She thought of her parents, but they probably thought she was dead.

Like May.

Mila shook her head, trying to tear the morbid thought from her psyche. She had to snap out of it. She couldn't keep doing this to herself.

"So," Luke said, rubbing his hands together, "who's up for a game of poker?"

Santos jumped right in. Mila stared, surprised at her roommate's zeal, but agreed as well.

A few hours, and a shameful sum of money lighter, Mila excused herself to head back to her bunk. Her skin crawled from the amount of social interaction she'd incurred. Sure, she kept to herself on the bridge, but she'd socialized more in the canteen than she had in years.

She passed a couple women talking between themselves as she reached her bunk assignment.

"The Incirrina just scare the crap out of me. I mean, what do they want? Nobody wants nothing for something, ya' know?"

"That's for the government to handle. Just focus on your job."

"But what if they want to invade?"

"Remember? They can't enter our atmosphere. How could they possibly invade?"

Mila entered her bunk, sighing and relaxing into the door when it closed behind her, closing off the rest of the ship.

Hopefully, her roommate wouldn't return until she'd taken everyone's money.

He was unfortunate enough to have picked someone on the worst shift for trying to catch his target alone. As soon as Trace's shift ended, his started. By the time he got off shift, she was asleep in her bunk, which had privacy locks. He'd checked, and the locks were engaged. He might have to pick another identity if he couldn't find an opportunity soon.

"So, what do you think of her? I like her," Luke said with gusto. Her money had dwindled to almost nothing in front of her. She'd never felt less deserving of her nickname, Lucky, in her life. She looked across the table to the ornery Santos's pile. It looked like a dragon's treasure. And she had the attitude to match. Pity, because if Luke were into girls, she would totally go for that dark skin and exotic eyes.

"I don't know. There's something not quite right about her."

"Ah," Luke said, waving her hand, "she's just a free spirit.

Your uptight military ass just can't handle that much awesomeness."

Santos glared at her.

———

Tristan settled into his office and pulled up the personnel files on all the pilots on board. Only one was female. May Trace. As he skimmed through the file, he got more suspicious. No demerits, no nothing. That he could tell, nothing made May Trace stand out. She'd never been in trouble, which didn't mesh with the woman he'd glimpsed today.

But, more than that, her file listed her as a mediocre pilot. Good enough for approval for interstellar travel, but unexceptional. His gut told him something wasn't right, but he couldn't put his finger on it. Trace was far too good a pilot to match her files.

CHAPTER THREE

uke greeted Mila at her bunk like a two hundred pound puppy dog. He wrapped his arm around hers and dragged her to the bridge.

When they arrived, her gaze slid to the captain as he gave her an odd look. She looked away and relieved the pilot. Throughout the shift, that moment plagued her, taunting her with the potential inner workings of the captain's mind.

She couldn't afford any scrutiny. She ducked her head, kept quiet, and resumed piloting the POS, as she liked to call the USS *Orleans*. The thing belonged in a scrap yard, not flying in sub-space.

Mila tried not to show it, but anxiety was eating a hole through her gut. She couldn't escape. She knew it. They would catch her, find out what she was, then dump her out the airlock, or shoot her. The scenarios rotated on an endless loop, tormenting her with the unknown.

I talk too much, Luke thought as she chatted up the pilot next to her. *Or maybe May's just too damned terse.* But that didn't stop her from trying to engage her neighbor in conversation. Like a teenage girl, Luke couldn't sit more than two minutes without words bubbling up her throat and spewing into existence like a bad case of food poisoning. Her mom called it "cute." She often said, "That's my Lucky," with a soft smile on her face.

Luke didn't think it was cute, though. She thought it was a pain. She'd tried, honestly tried, but every time she kept quiet, all her insecurities rose up to choke her. Like voices from her past, they taunted her, tormented her, made her feel less human. If she kept inside her own head for too long, she would go mad.

She often wondered if there was something wrong with her. She'd spent more time than she could count staring at that DSM definition, reading the signs and symptoms. But a diagnosis would be the easy way out. The military would pay for it then. "Only when medically necessary," the policy read. Or, in other words, only when you were about to off yourself.

Luke didn't want to die, not even close. She loved her life, loved being in the NSS. Most of the time. Other careers would have been easier for someone like her. Other careers didn't have communal showers or zero privacy. She shuddered at the very thought. Never again. She never wanted to be called a freak again.

"Oh my God, look at that planet," she said, distracting herself. She nudged May, but the other woman just glared at her. Luke shrugged. She would get her to warm up, eventually.

***

After a few hours, Luke managed to drag Mila from her shell. She spent the rest of her shift half paying attention to flying and half paying attention to him. Mila could fly this ship through sub-space sleep deprived, with one eye closed, and with a lobotomy, so chatting wasn't a problem.

She liked Luke. He didn't take himself too seriously, and was a tad loose with the rules. If she didn't strangle him for talking too much, she could see them becoming good friends. He was a normal person in a sea of military uptightness.

A constant litany of terrible outcomes flowing through her mind put a damper on the day, though. That and the captain's intense gaze boring into the back of her skull.

"Finally!" Luke said as he stretched. "That felt like forever."

Mila rolled her eyes at him. "Please, it wasn't any different from yesterday."

She stood and headed to the door, but someone stepped in her way.

"Can I help you, sir?"

He looked down at her name embroidered on her uniform. "Trace? We don't take slacking lightly on this ship. You're the pilot. You hold the lives of everyone on board in your hands when you're at the helm. I expect you to give your utmost when on duty. Today was unacceptable. Do you understand?"

"Yes, sir," Mila grumbled.

"Don't let it happen again," he said and stepped aside.

After they'd turned a couple corners, she asked, "Who the hell does he think he is?"

"Lieutenant Braddock. He's directly under the captain. It would probably be best to stay out of his way."

Mila smirked at Luke. "Oh, I'm fantastic at staying out of the way."

He smiled back. "I get the feeling you're gonna be *very* fun to be around."

"Always."

"What was that?" Captain Faulk said as his second in command came up to his shoulder.

"Just reprimanding a wayward crew member, sir."

"For what?" he replied, trying to think of what mistake she'd made during the shift. Or maybe it was something he hadn't seen, something she'd done behind his back.

"Not giving her position the necessary respect and attention, sir. Piloting in sub-space is not an idle task, as you well know, and I won't have pilots slacking off on shift."

"Lieutenant?"

"Yes?"

"Whose ship is this?"

"Yours, sir."

"I suggest you remember that." He stood up, and nodded to his second in command, wishing he'd had a better option. "You have the bridge."

"Aye, sir."

She kept shoveling dirt, but no matter how much she dug, it

never seemed to be enough. Beside her, May kept saying, "I thought we were sisters, twins. I thought you loved me."

"I do," Mila said, wanting to rub the tears off her face but compelled to keep digging.

She had to do it.

For May.

She had to.

"Why did you do this to me, Mila?" her friend said.

Mila gasped awake, banging her head on the ceiling. "A dream," she breathed, "It was only a dream."

She rubbed her eyes, wiping the tears away, but it didn't make the heat abate.

Or the pain.

"Come on. We'll be late. You don't need two demerits in as many days."

"I'm coming. I'm coming," he said, gasping as he raced after his friend. *When did I get so out of shape?*

His companion let out a sigh of relief as they slammed through the galley doors. "Looks like we didn't get caught. Head cook isn't here."

"See? No reason to worry."

"Buddy, they already demoted you to cook. Next step is out of the service."

"With my history? Might be a better option." He looked around. "I'm gonna go restock."

" 'Kay."

He turned and walked deeper into the galley area. The next room contained two doors for the walk-ins, a refrigerator and a freezer. He yanked hard on the lever to open the freezer. Like always, it fought him. "Come on, you stupid piece of shit." He lost his balance when the door flew open. "Stupid old-assed ship."

He entered, turning his head back and forth. Not having memorized the layout yet, he suffered under the sadist who'd arranged the galley storage for this trip. He turned around the end of an aisle and stopped, stumbling over something on the floor. *Odd.* They had to strap everything down to prevent zero gravity from making a mess. Nothing should have been paired.

The object was mostly shoved under a shelf and covered in a thin layer of ice, just like everything else. He scoffed. They had the freezer set too low. "Just my luck. I bet *I'm* gonna be the one freezing my ass off in here prying shit off the shelves."

He sighed and knelt, yanking at the obstacle, wondering who'd been too lazy to put things in their proper place. For once, it hadn't been him. He could enjoy someone else getting reamed out for a change.

When the cloth-wrapped object gave, he screamed as recognition hit. He slammed into the back wall in shock, scrambling for the handle. He couldn't take his eyes off the macabre visage. *Where the fuck's the door?!* "Fuck."

His hand slapped over cold metal, but no handle. "Fuck, fuck, fuck," but he couldn't get himself to look away, like a sick, twisted car wreck, it demanded he slow down and look.

How could he not look?

How could anyone not look?

Chills raced down his spine and it had nothing to do with the sub-zero temperatures. The plastic button connected with his palm and he smacked it hard, the door giving way under his weight. He ran out, not looking back, not that it mattered. He would never forget.

"What the hell's wrong with you?" his friend asked.

He tried to catch his breath, but he felt like he'd run a fucking marathon. "Buh, buh, buh," kept coming from his lips, not quite forming the word. He bent over, sucking in great, big gasps that didn't sting from cold. "Body," he said, "Dead body."

CHAPTER FOUR

"**W**hat have we got?" Captain Faulk said.

"Well, a dead body," the medical officer replied as he warmed his hands from the frigid air.

The captain glared at him. "You know what I meant."

"Well, someone dumped him in a freezer, so I have no way of knowing when he died, at least not by normal means like liver temp and decomposition."

Tristan pointed to one of his security officers. "Have we got an ID yet?"

"Yes, sir. He was last seen a couple hours ago."

"What?" the medical officer said, disbelief in his voice.

"What is it?" Tristan asked.

"Sir, I need to take the body back to medical, but I think it's too frozen to have been in there only a couple hours. It's hard on the outside. I don't know how much of his tissue is frozen, but I don't think that could have happened so fast. I fish back home, and it takes *hours* to freeze a fish whole."

"Do you have any idea what you're implying?" Tristan snarled.

"Yes, sir. We may have a shifter on board. And it has no qualms about killing."

"You," Tristan barked at another one of his security officers. "Find this shifter before it assumes a new identity." He turned to everyone else. "*No* one speaks of this. I can't have information about this body leaking until we catch this thing."

A chorus of "yes, sirs" echoed back at him.

He left his station to run an errand for a superior officer. With any luck, it would give him an opportunity to take out Trace.

As he walked down the corridor, an entourage of security officers pounded down the hall. He ducked around a corner as they passed, waiting. They ignored him as people often did. His eyes picked up everything. A cloud of tension hovered over them. Several men near the center of the grouping carried a bundle between them.

Trouble.

When they moved out of sight, he changed course. He had to check. He diverted to the mess hall, slipped in without a sound, and listened, waited.

Dissonant voices bounced off the old industrial walls, chairs scraped, and no one paid attention to the assassin in the corner. *There.* May Trace sat at a table near the middle of the room. He could kill her, but it wouldn't be a clean getaway. Not yet. He needed to get her alone.

He focused again on his current goal. Tucking his chin and

scrunching his shoulders, he made his way to the galley. Again, he listened, pushing the door ajar to hear better.

"You would not believe what I saw."

"I know what you saw. I saw them taking him out of here."

"It's not fair. They ordered me to keep quiet."

"Which clearly you're incapable of doing."

"Hey!"

"What? It's the truth."

"Yeah, but…"

"No but. I'm amazed they haven't canned you yet."

"Come on. It's not every day you find a dead body in a freezer."

I knew it. They found the body. Now compromised, he needed a new identity. Fast.

Mila followed Luke to the mess hall, only half listening to his idle banter. She hadn't been serious when she'd joked about her encounter with Braddock. She couldn't afford to be on Braddock's radar. That could get her killed.

Here, she didn't know how to keep a low profile, though. Usually, she just found an abandoned building and cut off all contact with others. As a strategy, hiding worked well on the run, but not so well stuck on a ship with a bunch of people who carried firearms.

She could stop talking on shift, like she had that first day. Keep her head down. Do nothing to draw attention. But was it too late?

"Whoa, what's this?" Luke said.

Mila glanced up and into the eyes of Captain Faulk. A chill ran down her spine as he seemed to stare right into her, seeing her darkest secrets. He and his battalion of security officers continued to barrel forward as she stopped in place, slack-jawed and terrified.

Oh, shit. They know.

CHAPTER FIVE

uke grabbed Mila's arm and yanked her out of the way. "Jeez, May, they almost trampled you there."

"Sorry," she said when her voice finally worked and the captain and his men continued onward, intent on whatever mission wasn't her. She let out a heavy breath. "God, he scares the shit out of me."

"Haha. Well, I've been watching him. Communications isn't as intense as piloting. I think he's attracted to you."

Her jaw dropped again. "You've got to be fucking kidding me."

He shrugged. "Just calling 'em as I see 'em."

Mila shook her head. "Maybe you should stick to comms and idle banter. Matchmaking isn't your forte."

Someone knocked at Tristan's door.

"Come in."

"Sir?" A familiar face peeked in through the gap. He walked all the way in, his stance, his demeanor, screaming civilian. "I'm concerned about the mission."

"I won't allow it to fail. You have my word on that."

"But security on board. I have concerns. I heard one of your men was killed today."

Tristan frowned at the man intruding on his limited downtime. "I assure you everything is under control."

"If this mission doesn't succeed…"

Tristan stood, his chair grinding against the floor. "I know full well the ramifications if we were to fail. We *won't* fail. We can't."

"But…"

"Is that all?"

"What's your plan?"

"I have plans to capture this assassin."

"Assassin! Are you kidding me?! There's an assassin on board?"

"We believe so. The medical officer believes the man was dead long before he was last seen."

"A shifter." The diplomat fell to the closest seat in shock.

Tristan sighed. "Yes. And if we don't find it soon, it will take another identity. It will kill again."

The civilian uttered a curse word Tristan had never heard before, then stood. "I guess I'm in the way then."

"It would be easier to do my job without repeated interruptions, yes."

"I'll go back to my quarters."

"Good night."

"Good hunting, captain."

<hr>

Mila didn't say much at dinner. Luke, his ever-talkative self, didn't even notice. Santos didn't care. After a respectable time period, she excused herself. Tonight, it was just too difficult to pretend everything was normal.

Too close. It had been too close. And she'd just stood there frozen in the hallway. If they'd actually been hunting her, they could have shot her, arrested her, anything and she would have done nothing to stop them.

What's wrong with me?

She wandered back to her room with a head full of toxic thoughts. Then someone grabbed her by the back of the neck and slammed her into an alcove, smashing her face into the metal wall. She flailed, kicked, punched, panic invalidating all her years of training. Her heart pounded away, making her stupid, jerky, useless. Her chest compressed with all she felt, most of it indescribable in the moment. But she never stopped moving.

Don't stop.

Don't stop.

Just fight.

A lucky knee found its target and he groaned, holding himself and bending over in perfect invitation for another hit. No longer on the defensive, her mind cleared. *Don't mind if I do.* She slammed her elbow into the back of his head, sending him to the floor, where he groaned again, but didn't move.

She took off, convinced he would follow at a moment's notice.

Safety.

Need safety.

People.

Anything.

She turned a corner and stumbled onto a common room. Flying through the doorway, she erupting into a space filled with other personnel. Nobody noticed as she desperately caught her breath, sucking in great gasps. Nobody noticed the blood on her face, or the darkening bruise she felt forming.

Relax.

Be cool.

Mila walked to the other side of the room, trying not to draw attention. She would be safe with an entire room of people separating her from her attacker. She sat down, shaking from adrenaline and fear. Her gaze stayed glued to the door.

After a few minutes that felt like hours, the door opened and her foe stood there, watching her, waiting. He smiled, raised his eyebrows, and ran his finger over his throat before walking away.

Oh, fuck.

CHAPTER SIX

Mila headed back to her bunk when someone she recognized as living near her left the common room. She slipped behind him and never allowed more than a few feet between them. Her heart pounding in her ears, fear kept her from wondering what he thought of her following him. She tried to move smoothly down the hall, but her limbs jerked on her joints.

What had May gotten her into? And it had to be May, right?

Once in her room, she went to bed but didn't sleep. She continued to shake, her mind running over all the fates that could befall her.

Who was he? What did he want? He couldn't have found out she was a shifter. She'd been careful, hadn't she? But May was a good girl. What could she have done to make someone want to kill her?

Hours later someone stumbled in, but she still hadn't fallen asleep. Mila didn't make a noise. She didn't look. Fear and her personal demons turned the intruder into her mysterious attacker. *Don't be stupid. It's just Santos. Nobody else can get in here.*

Could they?

<hr>

Mila woke with a start. She felt like crap. Avoiding Santos, she grabbed her stuff and slipped out to the communal showers, heart in her throat. *Oh, God. What if he attacks me in the shower?* Her pulse ratcheted up another notch. Her mind shifted the images to him attacking her, water beating down on her, slipping on the wet tiles, cracking her head. The hallway took on sinister qualities, every person, every shadow signaling her premature demise.

But she opened the door to steam and laughter. *Get over it, Mila.* It still weirded her out showering next to guys, or anyone really. The military had long stopped caring about separating men and women. After all, it wasn't possible to separate people who might enjoy the eyeful.

Mila dropped the towel and walked to a stall. Her ridiculous shower was quick and her eyes didn't leave the shower head if she could help it.

She'd discovered something new…

She hated zero gravity showers. How was a person supposed to feel clean when the water just floated and beaded up rather than flowing over you? She finished, dried off, struggling over the magnetic bands that kept her paired to the floor. Wrapping the towel back around her, she dashed out, avoiding the wall of mirrors.

Even trying not to pay attention, she registered a few odd looks in the bathroom, in the hall. She slipped into her room, grateful for the privacy. Santos had already left. She sighed.

Alone.

Good.

She got dressed, removed the magnetic bands she didn't need with clothes on, and exited feeling worn around the edges. Her face ached and swelled in places, the skin tight and uncomfortable. *Great. I look hideous. Way to stay off the radar.*

Mila returned to the bridge with her head down. She didn't want anyone to notice her face. She didn't know how bad it was and regretted not looking in the bathroom.

But then she remembered what she would see and stiffened. Bruises, she could handle, but she'd again forgotten she wouldn't see her own features. How could she keep forgetting? Her eyes misted, but she viciously shoved down the emotion threatening to choke her. She didn't need this. She had enough on her plate.

"Jeez, what the hell happened to your face?!" Luke screeched as she sat down.

She sighed. "Not now, Luke. And could you please shut up? I'm already freakish. I don't need any extra attention."

"Sorry. That must hurt."

"A bit. It'll heal."

For once, Luke stayed quiet. She turned to him, concern etching his face. He quickly looked away. She twisted her head to the other side, taking in the captain out of her peripheral vision. He seemed… on edge. That couldn't be good.

Luke tried not to stare, but her gaze flitted to May every few seconds. What happened to her? May looked like she'd gone a couple rounds with Ali. She chewed her lip, biting down on it every time she had the urge to speak up.

She told me not to. I'll ask again when we're alone.

But what if she's in danger? Luke's body stiffened at the idea. She cared about May, had from day one. When she first saw May, she saw someone with a secret, someone different. Not different like she was different, but a kindred spirit none-the-less. And kindred spirits needed to stick together.

Tristan barely noticed as the shift change happened around him. His corpse never returned for duty, which either meant his medical officer had been wrong about the time of death, or the killer had been tipped off.

There was another body on his ship.

Damn it.

He ground his jaw, all his muscles tense as he tried to keep his outer veneer calm and professional.

Another one of his men dead, and he could have stopped it. Should have. This was *his* fault.

He took a deep breath and looked up, inspecting the bridge. The pilot, Trace, jerked her head to face forward when she saw him look up. *Guess I didn't do such a good job at hiding my thoughts.*

The guy next to her kept looking at her at rapid intervals. Tristan watched the concern on the man's face and wondered why. What happened? Was there another incident?

"Trace," he called out, making her turn. He sucked in a breath. Bruises and swelling covered one side of her face. He stood and walked to her station, leaning against the console when he arrived. "What happened?"

"Nothing, sir," she said, keeping her eyes on her work.

"And I'm supposed to believe that?"

"You can believe what you want, sir. I can't stop you."

Tristan bristled, but let it slide. He figured she had reason enough to be irritable. "I believe someone assaulted you. Can you identify the attacker?"

She looked at Tristan, fear in her eyes.

"You can identify him, can't you? You should have gone to the security officers."

She returned to her work. "It's nothing, sir."

"Maybe it was nothing to you, but one of your fellow crew mates was killed. It could be the same person. You might be the only one who's seen him."

She looked back, shocked, fear surging through her frame even harder than before.

"I want to help you," he said, touching her arm gently, but she winced anyway. Clearly, more than her face had taken a beating. "Report to med bay after your shift. That's an order, Trace."

She swiveled back to her console. "Yes, sir."

***

"I can't believe we've got a shifter on board. Lousy, psycho freaks." The security officer adjusted his gun belt as they checked yet another closet. The ship had about a million of them. And that didn't even include the unoccupied bunks. "We'll never find this damn body. You know that, don't you?"

"Well, not with that attitude."

"Hey!" He slammed the door. "I didn't sign up for this duty to rummage through spare storage."

"Actually, you kind of did. Secure and investigate. That's the job."

"Oh, shut up. What's next on the schedule?"

"Cabinet 15-E."

"Come on," he said, his voice echoing his discontent. "The faster we get this done, the faster we can do something useful."

"This *is* useful."

"Whatever."

Mila spent the next few hours grinding her teeth over the impending trip to the medical unit. Whoever examined her wounds would probably look on her with pity. Then security would grill her trying to figure out who attacked her. She couldn't decide which she looked forward to more.

"Ships approaching! Fast!"

"Where?" Mila shouted back.

"Man the guns!" the captain barked.

People scrambled behind Mila, but she was in her element. The tension of her attack, of losing May, of living a lie, it all fell away, leaving just *her*. She monitored her screens, her brain processing the officer shouting out coordinates and trajectories at lightning speed, mapping them in 3D space in her head.

Move.

Move.

Move.

She grinned, loving every second as the big monster responded as well as it could to her skillful commands. She did her best to outmaneuver ships a hundred times smaller than this POS and outnumbering them God only knew how many to one. It didn't matter though. As the swirling colors of sub-space made dizzying paintings in the display, she kept moving, kept avoiding.

Her arms flew over the controls. "Fire," repeated in the background, but she ignored it, her hearing focused on a single voice tracking the enemies.

Move.

Move.

Move.

She watched as fighter ships flew out in front of her, felt the shimmy of the ship from a detonation. *Close, but no impact.* She continued avoiding the tiny ships and their attacks at the same time she tried to avoid planets and moons in sub-space. *Not the best time to battle these bozos.*

She contemplated dropping out of sub-space but nixed it. They had the maneuverability advantage whether in sub-space or real space. If she dropped out, they would only follow her, and she couldn't use her better skill against them.

She was a queen in sub-space. Mila had only done training programs, simulations, but no one ever tested higher. No one could beat her reflexes, her spatial awareness.

Move.

Move.

Move.

As they destroyed the last of the ships, Tristan stared at the back of Trace's head. She was good, damn good. She was, most likely, the best pilot he'd ever seen.

"Damage report."

He continued to ponder as he listened to the various departments reporting back the results of the attack. He vaguely registered there was no serious damage. Between the gunners and her piloting, they'd avoided every major hit.

It didn't make sense. According to her files, May Trace was a mediocre pilot. Barely good enough to receive sub-space travel qualifications. She shouldn't have been able to show off half the moves she just used.

She couldn't be May Trace, not with those skills. Did that mean the real May Trace was dead? His heart sank at the thought.

But that didn't stop him from doing his job. More lay in the balance than a pretty girl with attitude. He motioned to one of the security officers.

"Sir?"

"I want someone watching that pilot at all times."

"You suspect she might be the assassin, sir?"

"Yes."

CHAPTER SEVEN

"That was frickin' awesome, May! You're the bomb!"

Mila rolled her eyes at Luke. "I was just doing my job."

"Yeah and you nailed it. I heard the only damage we incurred was a few low caliber bullet holes."

"Well, that's good."

"Yeah, that was some impressive flying," Santos said as if it physically hurt her.

Mila turned to thank her and noticed two men following them. Following her. "Thanks," she said and spun back forward. *Shit.* She continued on, but felt their gazes on her the entire time. They had security written all over them.

What had she done to attract their ire?

As they entered the room, her shadows backed off, but kept within sight. Mila got her meal and sat with her friends, but remained hyper-vigilant.

I'm dead. I'm so dead.

Her eyes scanned the room as she shoveled food into her mouth, pretending to pay attention to the surrounding conversation.

Her gaze stopped on a man giving her the stink eye. She didn't recognize him, but she *knew* he'd attacked her yesterday.

A hand tapped her shoulder and she shrieked, spinning to meet the new threat.

"May Trace?" the innocuous man said.

"Yes?"

"The captain ordered you to go to the med bay after your shift." He glared at her.

"Busted," Luke said behind her, a grin on his face.

She gave him a glare in response.

"Come with me."

She looked back to the man across the hall who continued to give her the stink eye. She stood and her escorts rose with her. At least she wouldn't be alone.

The examination ended, but she still sat on the bed, the medical officer on a stool in front of her. "Do you have any idea why the man attacked you?"

Maybe. "No."

"We believe the man you described has been dead for several days. A shifter took his identity, an assassin."

"Oh God. Why would he attack me?"

"For new identification, I suspect."

Not likely. "But I thought shifters didn't shift outside their own gender."

"I bed your pardon?"

Shit, information I wasn't supposed to know. She scratched her head, wincing. "I read it. In an article? I mean, it's kind of logic, really. Could you imagine all your junk being different? Gone? Or having extra parts you're not used to? That would give me the willies." She shivered for good effect.

All that was the truth. Shifters didn't like to shift outside their own gender. If you were a woman, you picked female genders, regardless of species. You *could* shift into a male, but it was very unnerving. Mila imagined every shifter had tried it once in their lives, but it wasn't an experience anyone would repeat.

"Hm. Then why did he target you?"

"I don't know. I was mugged about a day before we launched. Do you think that could be related?"

"I don't know. Maybe."

"Well, I can't think of anything else. I'm not a bad person and I try to be nice. I can't imagine someone wanting to hurt me."

He nodded. "Well, be careful. And massage those bruises. It'll help them heal."

"Thank you, sir."

"Alright. Get out of here."

"Thank you, sir."

She walked out into the hall and addressed the security officers. "So, you guys gonna be following me from here on out? Because I'm kind of afraid to be alone."

"Any ideas on who the assassin is now? I was thinking May Trace. Her record lists her as a mediocre pilot, but the skills she's shown are among the best I've ever seen." *And she's suspicious as hell.* Tristan fidgeted in place. He didn't like his crew in danger. With any luck, the other man didn't notice. He needed to *act*, but what could he do?

"No," his head of security said. "She's been acting weird from day one. Whatever is going on with her, it started long before we found the officer dead in the freezer."

"Then who?" And how the hell would they stop him?

<hr>

CHAPTER EIGHT

<hr>

*D*ays after the attack, Mila couldn't get back to normal. And her minders both helped and made it worse. She appreciated their presence. Being alone terrified her, but being watched made her want to hide in a hole all over again. Stuck on a ship with hundreds of people, the claustrophobia sometimes got so bad she had trouble breathing. She wanted to escape, run, hide.

But she didn't. Even when her hands shook, even when she couldn't say a word, she continued, trying to appear as if everything was fine.

Certain times were easier. On shift, she could focus on flying. It soothed her, and for a spell, she forgot her paranoia, the attention she didn't want or need.

Same in her room. With only her and Santos, the small space served as a sanctuary. She didn't feel like her heart would pound out of her chest. The darkness helped as well. In the dark, she could imagine there wasn't a wall for hundreds of yards, miles even. It was the perfect illusion, even if she struggled to maintain it. She'd never been good at deluding herself.

Of course, her room had its own perils. She had nightmares, cried herself to sleep, and the darkness could be as bad as the claustrophobia. And every time she woke up from a nightmare, Santos would snap at her to be quiet. She'd never met a bigger bitch in her life…

"May! May Trace!"

"Huh?"

Luke caught up to Mila, puffing and shaking his head. "Jeez, your head's in a cloud lately. What gives? You're stressed, quiet. What's going on?"

"Nothing's going on."

"May, I called you about a half dozen times. How many times did you hear me, huh? And what about your hands? They're shaking half the time."

Mila shook her head. "They're not shaking half the time. Really, Luke."

"They are now."

Mila looked down. The slightest tremble vibrated through them. She clenched her fists, minimizing the shakes. "I'm fine."

"Bullshit."

"Luke."

"Don't even start, May. It may only be the beginning of this tour, but I've got a good bead on you and *this* is not you. So, what gives?"

Mila chewed her lip, contemplating what to tell him. What did she know herself? Not much. "Fine," she said, dragging him into a nearby closet and slamming the door shut.

"Really?" he laughed, the smirk no doubt plastered across his face lost to the darkness of the unlit room.

"Shut up, Luke."

"Well, if I knew this was all it took to get you in a closet, I'd have done it ages ago."

Mila punched him on the arm.

"Ouch."

"Didn't I say shut up?"

"Okay, shutting. I'm shutting up."

She sighed. "I don't know what's happening. What I do know is someone attacked me."

"The day your face looked like an eggplant?"

"Yeah, that," she said, glaring at him, "but earlier too. The day before we departed. I thought it was just a mugging. Now, I'm not so sure. I don't know what it's about, but the captain said there's a murderer on board. And I don't like the scrutiny he and his lieutenant have been giving me. A few days ago, these guys—security, I think—started following me. Constantly. They've done everything short of watch me in the shower."

"Really? Jeez, May."

"Yeah, really." Mila paused, preparing to voice something she'd been resisting herself. "What if they think *I'm* the killer?"

"Oh, May. They couldn't possibly think you're the killer."

"Luke. You don't know that. These people have never worked with me. They don't know me. They've got nothing to go by. I could work as a pilot by day, chop people into teeny pieces by night, and torture puppies on weekends as a special treat. They wouldn't know."

"May, you're getting ridiculous."

The hysteria built inside her, like a volcano ready to blow. "Luke! They're having people follow me! They don't do things like that unless they think you're suspicious. Clearly, they think I'm up to *something*." Her hands shook worse than a palsy sufferer. Her entire being screamed at her to run. She needed out. Now. "I gotta go. I need out of here."

"May, wait!" Luke grabbed her arm, keeping her from escaping. "May." He turned her around, holding onto her shoulders with both hands. "Nothing's gonna happen. I got you. We're friends."

"But my shadows."

"Aren't gonna see anything unusual. You're not doing anything bad on the ship, are you?"

Other than impersonating military personnel. "No."

"Then what's the problem? Just look at them as… bodyguards."

"Yeah?" she said, the shakes calming, her breathing slowing, evening out.

"Yeah. Don't worry. I've got your back. I won't let anything happen to you."

"Thanks, Luke."

"Anytime." He laughed. "Now, let's get out of this closet before you start getting a reputation. I mean, *I'm* fine with it, but you might not be."

Mila punched his arm again. "Very funny, Luke. Let's get to work."

Luke rolled her eyes behind May's back. *What a drama queen.* Then again, she supposed after getting attacked and having security dogging her heels, she had a *little* reason to be paranoid. She wanted to hug May, make it all better, but a hug wouldn't fix anything.

And after making that joke about getting a reputation, she was a little uncomfortable giving physical comfort. She'd never dated a girl in her life. Granted, getting caught in a closet might make her seem more normal, but she had a hard enough time maintaining a male persona without trying to fake who turned her on.

***

"This feels like the hundredth closet I've searched." He slammed the door and walked on.

"It probably has been."

"How many guys did the captain assign to this search, anyway?"

"Don't know. I imagine it's quite a few, though."

"And yet we still haven't found anything."

"I talked to Johnson last night. All they've found were two guys doing the horizontal mambo in a closet."

"Okay, I'm glad I'm not Johnson. I don't need to see that."

"See? It could always be worse," his compatriot said with a flourish of his arms.

He flipped him the bird.

***

Mila reached the bridge feeling better. Scared? Sure. Wanting to disappear? Absolutely. But mad with hysteria? Not anymore. She patted Luke on the shoulder, a silent thank you for his words in the closet. He turned and gave her a big grin and a wink. She shook her head. Leave it to Luke to lighten the mood.

She sat down, looking forward to a few relaxing hours at the helm. Strange how wielding true power, the power to shift her body into almost whatever she wanted to, made her feel helpless, alone, and scared. Wielding tens of thousands of tons of steel through sub-space, on the other hand, which required the reflexes of a Jedi Master and most people found terrifying, empowered her, making her feel in control.

As she settled in, she noticed a folded note tucked under one of the controls, keeping it from floating away. *I wonder whom that's from. Not like I have a lot of friends here. Or anywhere, really.* She unfolded the sheet and jumped out of her seat, tripping in her haste. The paper floated in midair as she stumbled back, drawing the attention of the rest of the bridge.

Her heart pounded in her chest, her breaths coming in ragged gasps, as Luke called to her. His voice reached her through a tunnel.

"May? May, what's wrong?" He hurried to her, grasping her shoulder. "May, talk to me."

"Letter," she gasped, whimpered.

Luke turned and snatched the message out of the air before anyone noticed it. He didn't read the note. He just stuffed it in his pocket and returned his attention to Mila. Mila tried to stand up straight, to slow her breathing, but made little progress. She concentrated on calming down as Luke distracted the bridge.

"She thought she saw a bug. Big bug."

Squeals rang through the room. Nobody questioned why Mila still hadn't calmed down.

Parts of the letter echoed in her head. *You are already dead, May Trace. You just don't know it yet.*

She took a final deep breath and straightened. "I'm good. Sorry, sirs."

"You're sure?" the captain said, suspicion in his eyes and voice.

What had he seen?

What did he know?

Why did I ever think this was a good idea?!

CHAPTER NINE

"So, what was in the letter?" Luke asked.

"It was a letter of intent." Mila continued walking.

"A letter of intent?"

"The letter?" She reached out, waiting for him to hand it over.

"Right." He dug in his pocket and pulled out the crumpled mess, slapping it on her palm. "So, what's it say?"

"Let's wait until we're seated and my shadows," she motioned with her head to the two security officers behind her, "are halfway to Neverland."

"Right." He kept quiet about as well as an overeager puppy, but he managed until they sat with food in front of them. "Okay, let's see it."

"See what?" Santos asked from across the table.

"Nothing," Luke squeaked.

"Yeah, because that's not the slightest bit suspicious, Luke." She rolled her eyes.

He sagged. "Sorry."

"I received a rather unpleasant note today."

"Didn't think there was a bug. You don't look the type."

Mila smiled. "Thank you."

Santos shrugged. "So, what's in the letter?"

Luke slapped the surface between them, drawing attention. "That's what I've been trying to drag out of her all day." He would never survive on the lam.

Mila unfolded and smoothed the paper as best she could and laid it out in the middle of the table, holding it down so it didn't float away. She let everyone read silently.

You are quite the foe, May Trace. I've never had to attempt to kill someone twice. Yet I have and you still live. Rest assured, your bodyguards won't save you. I can be anyone. You won't see me coming.

You are already dead, May Trace. You just don't know it yet.

-Your Assassin

"Is he saying what I think he's saying?" Santos looked up at Mila wide-eyed.

"A shifter assassin on board this ship? Holy shit." Luke paled several shades as he fell back in his seat.

"Now you know why I freaked so bad."

"But why does he want to kill you?" Santos pointed at Mila, more interested in her than she'd been the entire tour.

"No clue. I'm-I'm nothing."

"Well, clearly you're something to someone," Santos snarled.

"Well, *I* don't know who that someone is."

Luke sat up. "Seems to me, it doesn't matter who contracted the hit. What matters is catching and stopping this killer."

"Count me out," Santos said, waving her hands in front of her. "No offense. You may be my roommate, but I'm not gonna die for you."

"Thanks, Santos."

"I'm bailing." She stood and walked away, leaving a half-eaten tray behind.

"Well, I've still got your back."

But would you if you knew what I really was?

"No worries, May. I'm gonna keep you safe."

Mila peeked over at Luke questioningly for the thousandth time. "No offense, Luke, but you don't exactly seem like prime bodyguard material."

"What, me?" he said in mock shock.

"What kind of hand-to-hand training do you have?"

"Well, I'm a communications officer. What training I have, I probably forgot years ago."

"So, what you're saying is, in a fight, I'd be the one protecting *your* ass?"

"What, a pilot is any better?"

"Yeah, I've been practicing martial arts every day since I was in grade school. I could show you."

"No, no, no," he said, waving his arms in front of his frantic face. "You'd kill me by accident."

Mila shook her head. "I can assure you, I've never killed anyone."

"Good," a voice called from behind Luke.

"Luke, watch out!" Mila screamed, but too late.

A silhouette in the side corridor grabbed and slammed Luke, sending him into the wall using the same maneuver he'd used on her the first time.

"Let him go!" She dashed forward, separating Luke from the assassin to the beat of pounding boots. Years of training kicked in and she blocked, punched, kicked, blocked again, rolled, turned, ducked.

Each move in perfect sync with her attacker's, she did her best, but it wasn't enough. While she'd spent all her time away from people, this man had clearly been testing his skills on his victims.

Someone grabbed her from behind and she yelped, flailing and kicking. One bodyguard raced ahead, plowing into her assailant. He smashed through his enemy's attacks and defenses like a berserker, and before she realized the second shadow held her and not another attacker, their foe ran.

<hr>

"Go! I've got this," his partner said, the woman the captain had ordered them to follow still flailing in his arms.

"Right." He dashed after the assailant, running with ease, years of training doing him justice. Glimpsing an elbow around a corner up ahead, he picked up speed.

Come on, come on. He reached the corner. A black figure ran a few dozen feet before him. *Damn it.* He pushed himself harder, his feet pounding louder against the flooring, his breaths heaving in and out, powering his forward progress.

The dark shape took a left, but he'd closed the gap, only a dozen feet separating them. He could make out details. In uniform, but not an officer. Nothing on his shoulders. Smallish frame. Five foot nine. He turned the corner.

"Shit." He slid to a halt, darting his head back and forth as he tried to catch a similar build in the crowded corridor. After a few minutes, he picked up his radio. "I've lost him. Canteen."

<hr>

When she calmed down, the second shadow lowered her to the ground. She trembled from adrenaline, her mind taking in her surroundings for the first time. "Luke!" She dashed and slid to him, laying motionless on the floor.

Someone knelt by her side. "He's alive, Trace, just unconscious."

"Just unconscious?" Her mind tried to dash through a thousand terrible things, but the recent adrenaline surge left it running on neutral. "Shouldn't we take him to med bay? He could be seriously hurt!"

The kneeling shadow pressed his hand to her shoulder. "We've already called someone. They'll arrive with a stretcher to take him there. He'll be fine."

"Right," she said, nodding as a reflex. "He'll be alright?"

"Almost assuredly yes."

She dreaded the "almost" in that statement…

When the stretcher showed up, Mila walked beside it, straining around the bodies of the medical officers to make sure Luke would be all right. She couldn't believe it unless she saw it with her own eyes.

More security officers had arrived and she'd heard one of them order even more to head in the direction her attacker had taken off. *They won't catch him. He's probably already changed his face.* The remaining officers surrounded her on all sides, protecting her like Secret Service protecting the President.

She was too scared and numb to care.

When they finally reached the med bay, a stern doctor practically shoved her onto a bed.

"Sit."

Stay. Lie down. She wasn't sure if her sarcastic thoughts reflected in her face. By now, she wasn't sure she could move her face. The swelling and bruising from her last incident had gone down. She hadn't had the guts to look in the mirror this morning after she'd showered, but it hadn't hurt and it hadn't felt tight. Now she doubted she could smile to save her life, not that she wanted to.

"You took quite a beating, Trace."

"Thanks."

"That wasn't a compliment."

"I'm not stupid."

The doctor palpated her face, his fingers ghosting over her skin, but she winced anyway.

"Sorry."

She nodded and he continued, checking for broken bones. She knew she didn't have any. Shifters left cuts and bruises alone, but you knew when you'd broken a bone. And a shifter could fix a broken bone with no one the wiser.

She winced again as he touched a bruised rib, ignoring the pair of officers still standing guard in the room. She would have complained about the lack of privacy, but she was too tired to care. The adrenaline had definitely worn off.

CHAPTER TEN

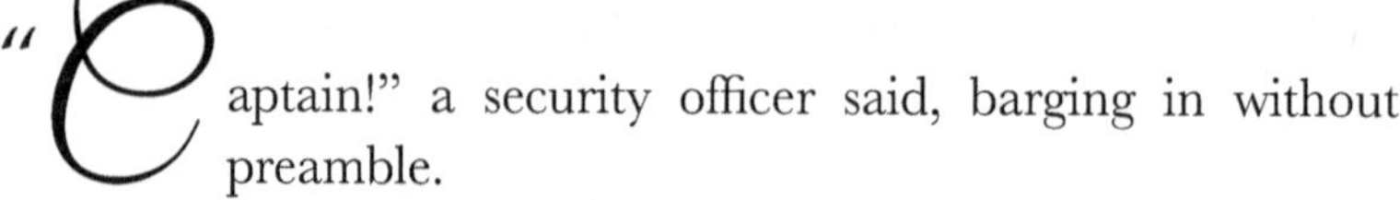

"Captain!" a security officer said, barging in without preamble.

"Yes?" he said, leaning forward, waiting for the news.

"The assassin's been spotted. He attacked Pilot Trace and Officer Hall."

His heart pounded in his chest in alarm. He jumped up and raced out. "He escaped?"

"Yes, sir. Men are searching for him now."

"Trace and Hall are in the med bay?" His boots hammered the magnetic floor plates.

"Yes, sir," the man said breathlessly beside him.

Three turns and they entered medical at a dead run. He turned and slid to a stop at one of the treatment rooms. Two security officers parted, giving him a clear sight of Trace wearing just pants, boots, and a black sports bra.

He sucked in a breath as he took in the bruises covering her arms, torso, and face. Some, newly formed, turned her skin red and purple. Others had darkened or faded to black, green, and yellow.

He ground his teeth thinking of the pain she must be suffering. *That fucker's gonna die.* He stopped, slackening his jaw and relaxing hands he didn't realize he'd clenched into fists. *Jesus, Tristan, she's just a crew member. And a suspicious one at that. You know nothing about her.*

"Report," he barked, using a commanding tone to reassert control over what must have been a serious testosterone attack.

The man to his left straightened further. "A man came out from around a corner, grabbed Hall, slammed him into a wall. Trace then attacked him before we could get to them. We fought him off and he fled down the same corridor he'd hidden in."

"Any news from the search team?"

"None yet, captain."

"How's Hall?"

"Unconscious, captain. Nothing else to report."

"Have Trace report to my quarters when she's done here." His mind entertained the double meaning there, but he stamped it down before marching off.

"ID." He stood as another in a long line of personnel handed him an ID, which he scanned. He motioned that person to move along, officers behind him directing traffic to a common area.

The next in line stepped up, handing over the ID without being asked. He scanned it and waved him on as well. Other officers were checking each person's private quarters while yet more searched every conceivable hiding place on the *Orleans*.

After the incident, the captain ordered a full ship lockdown. Anyone on shift stayed put. If you were in your bunk, you stayed there. They were trying to eliminate suspects. They were trying to catch this slippery son of a bitch.

The officer who'd lost the shifter in the crowd had rounded up everyone in the mess hall and galley, which only had one entrance. The man had insisted their foe hadn't escaped. He wasn't so sure.

They had a rough description of the shifter's last alias. Since they didn't think the shifter could create a fake ID on the fly, they searched for anyone who fit the description or didn't have a matching ID. Still, they kept everyone contained, just to be safe.

He scanned another ID as the radio kicked in. "We found another body."

I should have never come here. Oh God, I should have never come here.

Mila dragged her feet. She had no desire to spend any one-on-one time with Captain Faulk. Plus, the more time separated her from the attack, the stiffer her muscles got. Each movement involved jerking her limbs forward like a zombie. And the adrenaline crash made her want to just curl up in the hall for a nap, assassin be damned.

Mila kept forgetting she had guardians. She still had two bodyguards, but not the same two. When did the others take off?

She slowed down even further. What the hell would she tell the captain? Her brain was too sluggish to think, let alone try to deduce what only the real May Trace would have known. Why was an assassin after her?

Mila didn't need the attention. She'd taken May's identity to live her dream. She didn't want or need anyone suspecting her of murder. Anxiety and dread flooded her as her mind obsessed over everyone discovering her secret.

Mila stumbled and one of the guards grabbed her, holding her up. She caught a shared, concerned glance out of her peripheral vision, but didn't care. She just wanted to sleep. Or maybe go back to running, hiding.

They reached a set of double doors and her stomach sank. She couldn't get her legs to move anymore. *Oh God.* One of the shadows opened the door and ushered her in with his arm. Neither of them followed.

Just act normal.

He doesn't know.

Nobody knows.

Through a haze of pain, exhaustion, panic, and dread, the room seemed nice. Big. Especially by the standards of her bunk. As she expected, the place contained no decorations, no personal effects, just the bare bones needed for the space. A desk, chairs. A computer display, but no computer. Computers stayed in the No-Mag room.

Paper records were difficult to manage on a MAG GRAV ship, so there weren't filing cabinets or shelves. Probably, he only kept a few things in drawers in the desk. Cataloging the utilitarian space helped and she felt calmer, more in control. *I can do this.*

"Be with you in a minute," the captain's voice called from one of the other rooms, ramping up her anxiety all over again.

Two doors flanked the office. She focused on trying to identify from which direction his voice had come.

The right. She concentrated, closing her eyes, and heard his feet connect with the floor, coming steadily closer. The door opened and he walked through.

"How are you feeling?" He gestured her toward a chair.

She sat, her muscles shaking, trying to give out on her. Now, she had to stretch her neck back to look him in the eye, which caused her to flinch in pain. "Tired, sir. I just really want to head to my bunk, sir."

"Of course." He sat down on the edge of his desk, still towering over her.

Did he design these chairs to give a height advantage or something?

"Do you have any idea why someone would want to hurt you?"

Mila shook her head, causing a new twinge. She knew a good reason, but no one had that information. Nobody knew she wasn't May Trace, at least not yet.

He frowned. "Since you've been on board this ship, you've acted suspicious. Nervous, out of character. You have a perfect service record and yet I get the distinct impression you have problems with authority. Your record lists you as a mediocre pilot and yet you exhibit skills better than any pilot I've ever seen. You've been attacked twice on my boat, but don't seem to know why anyone would want to hurt you."

Mila's stomach sank, making her feel queasy. Her mouth hung open, shocked, speechless. *What do I do? What do I say?*

He leaned in closer, staring her straight in the eyes. The look he gave her made her want to run. She imagined him using pliers and a blow torch to get the truth out of her.

Mila pressed farther into her seat until the soft cushioning compacted her spine. She whimpered in pain and his eyes softened.

"Could you at least try to fill me in on all you can? Why have you been acting out of character?"

Her thoughts bounced around her head like pinballs, trying to find a way out, trying to figure out how to navigate whatever traps he had in mind. But when she opened her mouth, she just spilled the truth instead.

CHAPTER ELEVEN

"*I* don't know what's going on. The day before we shipped out, a group of guys mugged me and a friend of mine. I thought it was random. Then I was attacked, then the note, then attacked again."

"What note?" She hadn't mentioned a note before. Maybe they could use it to their advantage.

"Huh?" May looked up, dazed.

"What note?" He softened his voice, trying to coax it out of her.

She shook her head. "Note. Right, sir. There was a note. On my console. Today, sir."

"Can I see it?"

She dug in her pants pocket and pulled out a wad, handing it over to him. The paper had been crumpled into a ball and he tried to smooth it out against his leg. He couldn't remove the crinkles, but he could make out what it said.

He started to read aloud. "You are quite the foe, May Trace. I've never had to attempt to kill someone twice. Yet I have and you still live. Rest assured, your bodyguards won't save you. I can be anyone. You won't see me coming. You are already dead, May Trace. You just don't know it yet. -Your Assassin."

Oh, May. He looked at her in a new light, forgetting her unusual skills at the helm. He felt sorry for her, wanted to help her, protect her. She was terrified and he knew she was no killer. Someone barged in. *Thank God.*

"Captain, a body's been found."

He nodded, back in his element. "Have the two men outside bring her to her bunk."

"Yes, captain."

He looked back at her. "Nothing'll happen to you. I promise you that. I protect my crew." He winced inside saying that, considering they'd just found the body of another of his crew members.

She nodded, and he had to help her out of her seat and out the door. The inevitable adrenaline crash dragged at her, making her moves sluggish. He watched her walk away, feeling a fool for suspecting her. *Of what?*

He turned to the man still standing beside him. "Lead the way."

<hr>

"What have we got?" he said, a case of déjà vu hitting him as he entered the galley. A corpse lay sprawled across the floor between two prep stations.

"The remains haven't even cooled yet. Fresh, really fresh."

"So, it killed this guy with everyone crammed in the mess hall, one on top of the next?"

"Yes, captain. I suspect as a way of getting a new identity."

"There wasn't anyone in there or the galley without an ID, captain," a security officer with a scanner in his hand said.

Tristan nodded. "Do we still have everyone under wraps?"

"Yes, captain," his head of security, Avery, said. "They're under guard in a common room down the hall."

"Is this guy among them?" He pointed to the corpse.

"No, captain." Avery circled around and knelt by the body. "Our first assumption was that he took on this guy's identity to throw off suspicion, but my men report he's not among those individuals."

Tristan chewed on his lip, thinking. "How many people did you scan?"

The officer with the scanner studied the screen and tapped the display several times. "A hundred and twelve, captain."

"And how many people are in that common room?"

"You think he got away? Right under our noses?" Avery said.

"Maybe. How many?"

Avery touched his radio. "I need a head count in the common room."

Indistinct voices drifted to Tristan. They waited as the medical officer did what he could for the body.

The radio came back to life and Avery nodded, hanging his head. "Hundred and eleven, captain. He got away."

Mila dragged herself back to her bunk, keeping her eyes open only by the greatest of efforts. She wanted to just tumble right in bed, but her minders held her back. One officer waited with her while the other entered, checking to make sure it was safe. He exited and nodded.

She locked the door behind her, but didn't get in bed. Facing the top bunk, it might as well have been Mount Everest. She opened her wardrobe, pulled out May's bag, and fished through it, looking for a clue. But her brain refused to kick in gear, so she zipped it back up and collapsed on Santos's bed.

"So, what do you want to bet?"

"Bet?" his partner said.

"Yeah, bet. How long do you think it'll be before the captain is doing the dirty with Miss Needs Following?"

"Funny, I thought the captain ordered us to follow her because he suspected her of some wrongdoing, especially considering that first body being found." He tried to pull off a stern, professional, military mien, but his smirk came through.

He elbowed his partner. "Get real. That man is so far in denial, it should be a river."

"Okay, I'll do twenty bucks says a week."

"Twenty bucks? What am I supposed to get with twenty bucks? Grow some balls, man."

"Fine, fifty."

He smiled. "That's better." They slapped hands, but he nodded down the hall when he saw someone coming.

"I see it."

They stiffened and stood tall, watching the figure form in the distance. Female. Tall. At ease.

"Excuse me," she said as she approached.

"I'm sorry. I need to see some ID." He checked the ID. Trace's roommate. Remembering what they were dealing with, he hesitated. The killer could be anyone, including the roommate. He looked to his partner for good measure.

His colleague took up the ball. "I'm gonna have to frisk you, ma'am."

"Frisk me? Are you fucking kidding me? Let me through." She tried to shove past, but they moved in, blocking her way.

"I'm sorry, ma'am. We have our orders."

"This is bullshit," she said while crossing her arms over her chest.

They patted her down, looking for weapons, asking her to take off her shoes. They searched them thoroughly as well. Should they call it in? But the glare she gave them stopped that train of thought and they let her through. Some things just weren't worth it. Weathering a woman's wrath was one of them.

She roused to Santos storming around the small space as the last vestiges of her dream faded away. Something about abandoned buildings and cold. Mila groaned as her aches and pains woke up too. Santos zeroed in on her like a heat-seeking missile.

"You," she said, pointing at Mila with death in her eyes. "I can't believe you! What the fuck are you doing in my bunk? And what the fuck's with the psycho commandos outside the door? They tried to frisk me last night when I came back to bed. And they still didn't wanna let me in."

Mila was awake now though she wished she wasn't. Her head thudded from God only knew what, but it didn't distract her from the tight swelling of her face or the stiffness in her abused joints.

"Well?"

Santos's angry rant got the attention of the officers outside. They started pounding on the door. "Trace? Is everything all right in there?"

"Yeah," Mila said, her throat raw. "All's good."

"All is *not* good." Santos turned her back on Mila again, grabbed stuff from her wardrobe, slammed it, and pointed her finger in Mila's face. "If I find you in my bunk again, I'm gonna break you in half."

Mila didn't dignify it with an answer. Besides, what did Santos think she could do that hadn't already been done?

The woman seriously needed to take some anger management classes.

Santos slammed the door, leaving her alone. Mila slid out of bed rather than sitting up and crawled to the wardrobe. She pulled out May's bag again and looked through it in earnest.

She'd taken out things like uniforms, spare boots, and the personal products she'd added to it when she'd taken May's place. There wasn't much left. A powered down tablet, May's toiletries, a USB key, and a metal framed photograph.

The tablet and the USB key were most promising, but she couldn't use either in the bunks. Not sure if the tablet could be turned on safely, she stashed it in the bag and focused on the USB key. That needed a computer interface, so she put it in a zippered pocket of her uniform. She would get her answers after her shift.

CHAPTER TWELVE

Tristan sat at his desk, tracking his guest as he paced his office floor.

"We need to catch this assassin. What is his purpose here?" He stopped, looking to Tristan for answers.

"I've put my entire security force on it. But we're not equipped to capture a shifter. Nobody is." The government had passed a law forcing shifters into camps or prisons. But any shifter worth its salt could escape and evade those hunting it. They had it confined to a ship, for God's sake, but they still couldn't catch it.

Last night, they almost had it. Avery suspected it slipped away with the security personnel, separating out from the rest before they moved them from the mess hall to the common room. The skill this thing had at its disposal was both awe-inspiring and infuriating. The gall! Shifting right in front of his people.

"There's also the attack," Tristan chimed in, distracting his guest from the shifter.

"The attack! At this rate, we'll never get to our destination."

"We will. I told you. I won't fail."

He stared Tristan down, slamming his hands on the metal desk. "The only reason this ship isn't space trash right now is because your pilot had a lucky day. I saw her file. I read all their files. Not a single pilot on this mission should have been able to outmaneuver those ships."

He'd forgotten. Watching her fly through that attack, something didn't add up. She was just *too* good, way too good. How did she do it? Was it luck, as he suggested, or something more?

He stood and focused on the man before him, staring until he squirmed. "Just do your job. I'll do mine." He nodded to him then motioned him to the door.

Mila swallowed hard as she left her bunk. She hadn't bothered to shower today. The idea of getting naked when someone wanted her dead was intolerable. Too much vulnerability. She patted her pocket, reassured by the edges of the drive.

You can do this. You'll be fine. He's already failed twice. She nodded to her guards and headed off to grab a quick snack before her shift.

She missed Luke, who she assumed still loafed about in the med bay. Turning to ask about him, she stopped at the look of pity on their faces. She swung back around and continued down the hall. Maybe she would stop by to see him after eating.

As he went about his protection duty, he felt sorry for Trace. The military bred strong, capable personnel, regardless of their specialization. She should be confident, passing her day without care. Especially with her abilities at the wheel.

Word spread like wildfire. People from the bridge raved over how she handled herself in a crisis, how she maneuvered around the smaller fighters. Many credited her with the minimal damage they took in the attack.

Regardless, he hated seeing how she shuffled through her day, head hanging forward. She grabbed something and ate it while heading to medical. They hung back while she visited with her sleeping friend, Luke Hall, though he overhead the doctor saying that Hall had regained consciousness last night.

Next, she headed to the bridge, again with that listless shuffle. He wondered if her movements were more from her injuries or a broken spirit. She sat in her seat and stared at the station beside her where Hall should have been.

Behind her, the captain never took his eyes off her.

<hr>

Luke woke up groaning. "What happened?" Rubbing her eyes, she sat up in bed, her brain hesitant to think. Then it all rushed back to her.

Oh, that's the last time I try to act like a dude…

Looking around, her mind still didn't kick into gear. She sighed and leaned against the wall, the noisy environment settling into her consciousness. Then she sat up, her mind alarmed. "Where's May?"

The last she remembered, they'd been walking down the hall together. She never saw it coming. *She* did *protect me in that fight, didn't she?* Luke closed her eyes, shaking her head in dismay. Some protector she turned out to be. "Hello!"

She listened, waiting for a medical officer to show up. What if May was in even worse shape? What if the assassin killed her this time? Her heart tightened in her chest. Suddenly, May's fear and paranoia made perfect sense, because Luke was terrified.

She hadn't been this scared since high school when she decided to live as a girl. She still didn't like looking back on that time. People were cruel. Kids were worse. When she graduated, she decided it wasn't worth it. What was the point in living as a woman if she couldn't pass?

Gripping the sheets tighter, she waited, wondering if she should just slip out of bed and get her answers the hard way.

After her shift, Mila visited Luke again. This time he was awake and perky as ever, sitting up and giving the staff an earful.

"Luke! Glad to see you up and about!"

"Well, not about, but definitely up." He laughed at himself, but his expression darkened as he took in Mila's appearance. "You look like hell. How do you feel? I hope he didn't hurt you too badly."

Mila shrugged. "I'll be okay. I heal quick."

"That's good." But he didn't look relieved. He changed tacks and his smile returned. "The doc says I'll be out of here soon."

"That's great! Glad to hear it. I'm so sorry you got injured because of me."

He waved it off. "Nah, not your fault. Besides, what kind of guy would I be if I let a poor, helpless woman get hurt without at least trying to come to her aid?"

Mila arched an eyebrow at him. "He knocked you unconscious before you even saw him. *I* was the one wailing on him."

"Way to go, girl," he said, slapping her shoulder just hard enough to make her wince.

She healed fast, not that fast.

"Well, I'm gonna go. Get better."

"You too."

She left, guards always a step behind. Now, she just had to lose them.

Giving the security officers the slip wasn't easy. One, because she had no experience at it. And two, because she wanted it to appear unintentional.

Being alone terrified her, but she felt empowered taking some control back of her life. She got a little thrill just thinking about solving the mystery of why someone needed her best friend dead.

She lucked out. They pitied her and people underestimate the objects of their pity. It took a dash of aimless wandering and really good timing, but she caught an elevator just as it closed.

Mila exited onto a hall she didn't recognize. She wandered for a while, feeling sorry for herself and her bodyguards, who she imagined in a panic, calling in backup and a search team. She kept her head down as she made her way through the halls, looking for a computer display.

A few minutes later, she found one and plugged in the USB. She waited for the screen to come out of sleep and covertly kept an eye out for trouble. It seemed to be drawn to her lately.

She selected the file system. Audio and text files filled the drive, all organized by date. She opened the first file, dated a few weeks back and read the screen.

I overheard something today. I didn't see the people, and they didn't say anything threatening or suspicious, but they kept talking about plans and the USS Orleans.

Mila closed the file and opened the next one.

I heard those voices again. Same place, same time. Still didn't see them. I wish I could recognize their voices, but I don't think I've ever met them before. I'm certain they're up to no good.

I considered going to a supervisor, but who? And with what? All I have are suspicions.

One of them is particularly angry. Not a specific kind of anger, just angry at the universe, the kind that bleeds into their personalities until it defines them.

Mila moved on to the next file.

Okay, I'm buying a digital voice recorder tomorrow. I wish I knew where the voices were coming from, but the building is old, and they're coming from the vents. They could be anywhere.

The angry one yelled at the other for "endangering" the cause. I'm not sure I want to know what that means.

The next date was the first with an audio file as well. She opened text file, this one much longer than the earlier entries. May had written notes on her recordings. She'd left the recorder in the vent, then recharged the battery and down-loaded the audio. The entries trailed on and on.

Mila scrolled through the documents in the directory. She clicked the last one, dated the same day May texted Mila.

I've finished going through yesterday's audio and I'm shocked. The anger, the hate. I know their plans now. They're going to sabotage the Orleans.

I don't know what to do. I don't know who to trust. From the sound of their communications, they have a lot of co-conspirators. What if I go to someone and they're in on it?

I have to do something, though. I can't let them succeed. I need advice. I need help. God, I miss Mila. She has a moral compass that always points north. But will she answer my call? I haven't seen her in so long…

Mila closed the document before it went into every little minute detail of May's last day of surveillance. She leaned against the wall, wondering what to do. What *could* she do?

She would look suspicious if she said, "Oh, sorry, Captain. I forgot I'd been running secret surveillance on some yahoos plotting to destroy the ship we're on. Maybe this will help?" But maybe she wouldn't have to.

She scanned through the files again, looking for information. Names, anything that pinpointed the writer. She checked the metadata, but it only listed a branch of the military, not a specific author.

She opened the audio files, listening for her voice somewhere, anywhere. The drive contained hundreds of hours of surveillance. She couldn't listen to it all, but it didn't seem like May used any of the recordings to jot down her own thoughts.

Now she just needed a believable story.

CHAPTER THIRTEEN

Mila gnawed on her lip as she approached, knocked, and waited for the worst.

"Come in."

She eased the door open and peeked inside. "Captain Faulk, sir?"

"Yes, Trace. Can I help you?"

The captain sat at his desk, going over something on his computer display, maybe a shift report. No tension ramped up his form and for the first time since she'd arrived on board, he wasn't giving her an odd look. He seemed… normal.

"I…" She pulled in a deep breath and let it out. "You might want to see this, sir." She walked to his desk, spine straight, and reached out her hand, which held the small USB key.

He took it and plugged it into his display. For a few moments, he scanned through the contents, his expression growing steadily darker. Without conscious thought, she inched backward. By the time he looked up, her back pressed against the double doors, trying and failing to maintain a military at ease posture.

He tried to keep his voice level, calm. "How long have you had this?"

"Uh. Since before we took off, sir. The day before, in fact." She gripped her hands behind her back, her nails digging into her skin.

He stood slowly as he spoke, somewhat calm at first. "You mean to say you've had this the entire time and didn't bother to bring it forward." By the end of the sentence, he was yelling at her.

Mila sputtered, trying to get words out and failing miserably. "I… but… you…"

"Spit it out!" he said as he rounded his desk, coming even closer to Mila.

She whimpered as he came past the chairs on her side of the desk. Within moments, he towered over her. She couldn't look him in the eye. *Just pretend he's not there.* Hard to do when she was staring straight at his chest.

She started blabbering. "I didn't know what it was, sir. A friend gave it to me. I never connected it until now. But after that guy sent me that note and kept trying to kill me? It put the mugging in a new light, so I went through everything I had with me. I found the USB key. It wasn't mine. My friend gave it to me. I swear I didn't know what it was." Tears poured down her face, but she tried to keep her composure, keep it professional, even if she barely remembered what that was anymore. "I swear, captain, I swear. I just wanted to know why someone wanted me dead, sir. I just wanted to know."

Her spine grew straighter as she talked, but she also pressed against the door, defeated and cornered. Still, she tried to maintain her dignity as the captain continued to tower over her.

He sighed. "It's all right. It'll be all right. Who was this friend? What do you know about her?"

"I don't know anything about her. Not anymore. We haven't spoken in years."

He nodded and moved back, giving her space. "I see. Can you summarize the details on the drive?"

She shook her head. "I didn't go over it in any detail. When I realized what was on it, I brought it straight here, sir."

He nodded again. "Good. Very good. What do you know about it then?"

"A conspiracy, sir. She overheard something, a conversation. She knew something was up, so she bought a recorder. Near the end, she realized what was going on, and she texted me out of the blue. She didn't know who to turn to, where to go. She didn't know who to trust. She died that day."

"What?"

"In the mugging. She was killed, sir."

"I'm sorry."

Mila shrugged, even though it cut to the bone thinking of May bleeding out in that alley. "We didn't know each other anymore, sir. I think I mourned what we used to have more than the actual person."

"Any more details?"

"They wanted to sabotage the *Orleans*, the mission, whatever it is."

The captain nodded.

Mila didn't ask why. She didn't want to know. Above her pay grade.

She started to calm and looked up, realizing the captain was smirking at her. "What, captain?"

"Nothing. I was just wondering. Where are your shadows?"

"I-I… I kind of lost them."

A good-natured laugh spilled from his lips. For the first time, he didn't scare her. He moved back a few steps and sat on the edge of his desk. This time, it didn't feel threatening. It felt normal, lazy, relaxed.

"I imagine you have questions."

"It's none of my business, sir."

"But I think it is. Your life is at risk here."

"I suppose it is, sir."

He sighed. "This ship is on a diplomatic mission."

"A diplomatic mission with whom, sir?"

"With what is more like it," he mumbled. "The US government, along with a slew of other countries from the UN, are initiating treaties with the Incirrina. It's a monumental occasion. It's the first time humans have started negotiations with another species.

"But there are also some factions that have no desire to see humanity peddling to these foreign races. The mission had to be covert. You know how humans can be."

"Yeah, just look what they did to shifters," Mila mumbled, then slapped a hand over her mouth, realizing how inappropriate that comment was.

He didn't even blink. "Exactly. We aren't kind to those we consider different from ourselves."

"So, are you saying you don't hate shifters like most people do?" Mila perked up, looking him straight in the eye, not sure what she hoped for. Hell, she wasn't even sure if she would regret the question and what it might reveal about herself.

"Everyone deserves a chance. I don't believe in blaming someone for the actions of others. For example, if you were a shifter," he said, pointing to her, "I wouldn't blame you, consider you a killer, simply because another shifter on this boat is. You are not it."

"Him," she said as she nodded. "I think I could come to like you, captain." She seriously needed to install a filter on her mouth, though.

"Anyway, back to the discussion at hand. Our governments are initiating these treaties to prevent future conflicts. A lot of alien species travel the stars and not all are as peaceable as the Incirrina. This would ensure the safety of the human race."

"I understand, sir."

"Good, I have to organize a meeting. A lot of people need to know about these developments. Do you mind?" he asked, motioning to the chair in front of his desk.

Mila shook her head, seating herself as she watched the captain set up a meeting, calling people, his head of security, his lieutenant. She waited and after a few minutes, he put down the phone and motioned her to follow him.

"Where we going now?"

"Conference room. I do small meetings here, but too many people need to hear this. They'll never fit."

"Understood, sir."

He pulled open the double doors in a grand gesture you expected to see in movies and marched down the hallway, forcing the shorter Mila into a jog to keep up. They made a couple turns, then he pushed another set of double doors open, walking into a space large enough to fit a few dozen people. Lieutenant Braddock was already setting things up.

The captain walked across the room, motioning her to sit near him. When the lieutenant finished, he sat to the captain's right. When the head of security entered, he sat between her and the captain.

For the next ten minutes, people she had never seen before filed into the conference room, making her increasingly uncomfortable. All of them seemed soft, non-military, about as non-military as she did, only with less attitude. As she watched, she tried to assign traits to them, surmise their roles in life. Then it hit her… they were diplomats. Of course!

Though they wore the station of military crew members, she felt certain they were here to ensure the negotiations this entire mission aimed to achieve. Hiding them among the crew *would* be the perfect way to disguise the ship's purpose.

When the room settled, the captain stood and spoke. "We have some developments. As you know, an assassin plagues this vessel. The bulk of our security force is in pursuit of this felon.

"Through new intelligence I received only moments ago, it has become clear we have a conspiracy against this mission. Multiple people are trying to sabotage this ship and the diplomatic mission she is tasked with. We surmised, based upon new evidence, that that is the reason the assassin is on board. It was sent here to ensure we didn't learn of this plot, which was brought to our attention by Pilot May Trace."

Mila's eyes widened. She shrank back in her seat as all eyes focused on her. *Oh shit.*

"Trace? Would you care to give a report on what you discovered?"

Her wide eyes fixated on the captain who smiled reassuringly at her. She stood and stared a hole in the opposite wall. "I uncovered intelligence regarding verbal correspondence between two parties conspiring against this mission. The audio and text haven't been completely analyzed, but it's clear the *Orleans*, and this mission, were the intended targets.

"Also, since the one who gathered this information was killed shortly before the ship departed, it's reasonable to assume the two are related. And that the assassin was contracted to keep the plot secret." She looked nervously at everyone around her, then meekly sat.

"Thank you, Trace. Likely the attack a few days ago, which Pilot Trace skillfully outmaneuvered, is also connected. We believe there may be more conspirators on board."

"What?"

"What are you going to do about this?"

"Silence, please. As I said, we are currently sending much of our manpower toward the goal of capturing this assassin. We'll be having a second meeting after this one to plan strate-gies. Rest assured," he said, staring down most every person at the table, "we will do everything in our power to ensure this mission is a success." Mila noticed that he didn't stare at her or the head of security. What did that mean?

"Now, if you'll all kindly take your leave, we can get to the business of dealing with these new threats."

The room cleared reluctantly. None of the diplomats

seemed willing to leave it at that. Tension grew in the air, the urge to argue the point energizing it. Mila imagined the captain having to deal with them barging into his office at all hours, wasting his time on frivolities.

It took a while, but they all left, leaving only the captain, his lieutenant, the head of security, and Mila.

"Ideas?"

The head of security spoke. "Security's tight. We don't have the manpower for this, not with the current manhunt and security details." He discretely eyed Mila, clearly indicating he disliked the waste of resources on a lowly pilot.

"I agree," the captain said, relaxing back in his seat.

A thought crossed Mila's mind. "Captain?"

"Yes, Trace."

"How did they know where to attack? That just occurred to me. In sub-space, it's hard to pinpoint a target. Almost impossible. It takes advanced mathematics and calculations. It can't be done without a computer. And even then, we don't have to file flight plans like with Earth air travel. We could take millions of routes. So how did they find us?"

"Hm, good question," the head of security said begrudgingly.

Mila shrugged and smiled. "My best guess is someone told. Most likely via TAT. It's the only way to send long range communications. And it would have to be long range.

"It leaves two options. One, a person of no real skill sent a message, loading the message to send to the fleet that attacked us. The problem with that scenario is that the military screens messages randomly. Their plot could be thwarted before it started.

"The second would require a long range communications officer to send a message directly to the fleet. That's a pretty narrow suspect pool. There are only six officers on board."

"Excellent. Great idea, Trace."

"Thank you, captain. We should check the message directory to see which category it falls under."

"Good. Anything else?"

"We could have home base run security checks," Avery said.

"Wouldn't that take too long? I mean, doesn't it take months to run a check? And we're talking hundreds."

"True, but we don't need full reports, only affiliations. Braddock?"

"Yes?"

"I want computer specialists going over that USB key of Trace's with a fine toothed comb."

"I'll be right on it."

"And get more than one person on it. Don't forget there are wolves in our midst. We could very well be sending this information directly to the enemy."

"Of course."

"I'll take care of sending the request to home base," the captain continued.

Mila leaned forward to speak. "You should watch the communications officer as they send it. Make sure they really send it, and unaltered, sir."

"Yes, good, Trace. Thank you. And could you help me with going over the messages in the TAT system?"

"Of course, sir."

"Okay, dismissed."

And boy, did she have no idea what she would be getting herself into.

CHAPTER FOURTEEN

The captain told the head of security, Avery, to continue with the manhunt. He sent Lieutenant Braddock to his office to pick up the USB key while he dragged Mila to the bridge. She followed while her two shadows marched a few feet behind her.

People turned and looked at them as they arrived, surprised to see the captain, no doubt. Most rarely or never saw him. He manned one shift on the bridge while he had subordinates do so on the other two shifts. If something happened while he was off duty, his subordinate would call him.

That was the part she'd never understood about the old space travel shows and movies. It was always the same pilot, same communications officer, same captain. They were always in the same seats. No variation. But systems on board a space-ship had to run twenty-four hours a day. Where were the other shift personnel?

She followed him to the communications console.

"Move," he said, the officers scurrying out of his way. He started typing, his fingers flying over the display, which had an on-screen keyboard. He turned to one of the communications officers who'd fled. "I need this sent back to home base. Now."

"Yes, captain," he said while returning to his seat, where the captain hovered.

She felt sorry for the poor guy. She knew what it was like being on the receiving end of his menacing demeanor. Of course, maybe he was one of the conspirators, in which case, he deserved it.

The captain watched the officer's every move, watched the screen. Nothing would slip by him.

"Good," he turned. "Back to work, everyone. Trace, let's go."

The captain had a fondness for grand entrances. Every time he went through a set of double doors, he shoved or pulled them both open. *Dramatic much?*

He walked around his desk and sat. "Have a seat, Trace." Picking up the phone, he said, "IT." After a moment in silence, it connected. "I need a mobile computer display. Yes. Now. Thanks."

They lingered in silence, Mila's gaze drifting over a room she'd absorbed in detail on a previous visit.

The captain broke the silence. "I'm sorry if I've treated you unfairly."

"Sir?" *He's apologizing? Wouldn't have thought him capable.*

"I'm sorry." He rubbed his forehead. "Things have been… challenging, stressful, since this tour began. And, frankly, you're a conundrum. You don't quite act military, which would make me think you would have demerits in your file, but you don't. Your file says you barely qualified for spaceflight and yet you've exhibited some of the best piloting I've ever seen. I just don't get you."

Mila paused, her mind running in circles. "I'm not usually like this, sir. I love flying. It's the only time I feel a semblance of control.

"And my file says I barely qualified because I *did* barely qualify." Mila looked down, trying to pull off embarrassed. "I bombed that test and have been relegated to missions that wouldn't require a great deal of skill. I don't believe I would have been picked for this mission, sir, except no one expected you'd need a decent pilot."

"I suppose that's true." He sat back and stared at Mila, taking her in, maybe trying to piece the puzzle together. *Fat chance. That would be like dumping two puzzles into the same box, then assembling them without a picture.* "Who was your friend?"

"Friend?"

"Yeah, the one who died. In the mugging."

Mila paused, not knowing what to say. She was getting into dangerous waters. Could they verify her story? Or try to? Nobody would find a report of a mugging, but then they didn't know where she'd been when it happened.

"Mila Dragomirov. We were friends as kids. We told each other we would become pilots together. We joined the pilot program but then she disappeared. She left a note. It didn't make any sense. It had contact information. At first, I kept contacting her, hounding her, asking her why. She never answered. I never understood."

It felt good to tell somebody about herself, her story. Even if only a little. Even if she wasn't quite telling the truth.

"Maybe she was a shifter."

She laughed and shook her head. He'd guessed it in one. "Maybe."

Knock, knock.

"Yes?"

"IT, sir. Your display?"

"Come in." He nodded and smiled at her. "Time to get to work."

Mila turned on the display. "What's the directory for TAT message archives?"

The captain got up from his desk and stood behind her, indicating where to go with his finger.

"Thanks." A warm feeling suffused her chest as she gazed up at him, but she ignored it, returning her focus to the screen. "This doesn't… this can't be right. This isn't showing anything further back than a few days ago."

The captain hovered over her shoulder again, his arm reaching out as if to touch the screen, then dropping. "Come on," he said, grabbing her arm. "We're going to IT."

IT was the only place on board with no magnetic floor plates. Because of the computers and servers, it was designated strictly Zero GRAV. Which meant, as soon as you walked in, your feet lifted off and you started to drift.

The room was huge, yet felt tiny. Servers and computer towers were set up in rows, each with grab bars to orient yourself and push off. She grabbed onto the nearest bar, her computer display in the other hand as the captain pushed off in search of a geek.

Though it was usually obvious, this room served as a stark reminder that this ship had no gravity, produced no gravity. Everything, from the foods they ate to the showers and toilets, was designed around that lack. But, when walking down the hall, she found it easy to forget.

Mila smiled. She'd trained to be a pilot, but never been in zero gravity before. She laughed. "This is amazing."

"Trace! Over here."

"Coming!" She pushed off from her grab bar, aiming for the next row, using each one to push her farther. After a half dozen rows, she found the captain holding onto a chair behind a guy plugging away at a computer. "What have we got?"

"It was wiped," IT guy said.

"Can it be retrieved?" the captain asked, breathing down his neck.

"Er, Captain? Maybe give him some room?"

He turned and gave Mila a raised eyebrow, but backed off, giving the man space to work.

Fingers flew across the keys, actual keys, and a few minutes later, he said, "Yeah, maybe. If I…" Another few minutes of key clicking. "Yeah. Yes! Okay. It's not perfect, but we've got some of it."

"Not all?" Mila leaned away from her hold, trying to look the guy in the face.

He turned to her. "Sorry. This person knew to wipe it, but not enough to do a good job. Some data's corrupted, but not everything. It's not perfect, but it's what we got."

"Back it up. External drive," Mila said, paranoia seeming the better part of valor today.

"Yes, go ahead," the captain said. "If they had access to wipe it, they could see the data is back. They could try again and succeed."

The IT guy nodded and went back to his keyboard. He pulled a small drive on a wrist strap off the wall and plugged it in, then they watched as the progress bar filled up.

"Okay, now we can get to work." The captain smiled at her. She should have known that wouldn't bode well.

"What the hell was I thinking when I agreed to help you with this stuff?!" She flinched, forgetting who she was talking to.

"You were thinking it was an order from a superior officer," he said, a smirk on his face.

Mila wanted to break that smirk off, maybe flip him the bird for good measure. She resisted... barely. "How can there possibly be this many messages in the system? We've only been gone a few days."

He nodded. "And there are several hundred crew members on this ship. And shift reports, which each department sends out individually. Even if each person only sent one message so far this voyage that would be hundreds to wade through. With the TAT system, sending messages home is no more complicated than sending an email. And it takes about as much energy to send one message as two hundred."

She faked a smile. "Great. We've been at this for hours. My back feels like a pretzel." She stretched in her seat, her back popping in protest.

He laughed, and Mila wanted to hurt him even more. He stretched as well and she heard his bones and joints popping from across the room.

"I know the feeling," he said as he settled back in his seat. "How bout we take a break, grab a snack, walk around a little?"

"Yes, sir." She was at the door before he'd even stood.

"Eager, are we?"

She turned back to him, and tried not to let it show on her face, tried to remember *some* of her military training. She shook her head. "I don't know how we'll ever find this message. I mean, what if it's in code, sir? What then?"

He walked up to her and grasped her shoulder. "Even in code, some information still needs to come through. Coordinates, for example, or speed and trajectory. Numbers. No matter how it's encrypted, we know what they were sending."

She nodded. "Right, sir. Sorry, sir."

"It's okay. This is long and tedious work. You have every right to be short tempered."

"When are we quitting for the night?" she asked as they passed through the doors. "I have to fly in the morning."

"Don't worry about it. There's an officer in engineering with pilot qualifications. He can take your shift."

"Sir? Wouldn't I be better served flying the ship, especially since you've already said I'm one of the best pilots you've ever seen? We might get attacked again."

"And if we do, my office is only a minute's run from the bridge. I need someone I can trust to sort this out. Otherwise, it won't matter how good your piloting skills are."

She nodded, a little of the tension leaving her body. The captain trusted her. "Right, sir. Okay." She rubbed her hands together. "Short break, then back to work."

"Thank you, Trace."

"It's my job, sir."

"Tristan." He gave her a crooked smile and led the way to the deserted mess hall.

"Ugh, I can barely keep my eyes open." Mila closed out a message and opened the next one. She expected them to blur together soon. Or maybe she would miss something. It didn't help that the messages were a mess. The data was corrupted, all right. Some messages had half the text gone, a bunch of symbols and gobbledygook taking its place.

"Do you want to call it a night?"

Yes. "No. I think I might be to a halfway point soon." *And I really want to catch the sons of bitches trying to kill me.*

"Okay. A bit longer."

She scrolled through the message, closed it out and opened the next one. Most of the messages were boring. Things like, "Hi. How are the kids?" "How's school?" Occasionally, she came across hot stuff, stuff that equated to phone sex. She was just glad home base restricted messages to text.

She exited a message of someone talking to his girlfriend, making plans for when he got back. Opening yet another message, she read, froze, and read it again. "Um, sir?"

"Yeah, May?"

"I think I've got it."

CHAPTER FIFTEEN

Tristan did his hovering thing while she read the message a third time. It listed current position, speed, trajectory, and her name, May's name, May's shift. It said the pilot couldn't evade the attack. "They couldn't send this through home base, could they, sir? And how did they get my file? They had to have gotten my file, right?" But those files were restricted, weren't they?

"Here. Let me." He reached over her shoulder and started tapping the screen. It pulled up an information panel, detailing destination, sender, etc.

The name in the sender category blared out at her. "No." She stood up, knocking into Tristan. She shook her head. "No, he didn't do it. It couldn't be him." The display read, "Sender: Luke Hall."

"I agree. Look again."

Mila looked at the screen in Tristan's hand, then at all the details, trying to see what he'd seen. "The sent period. He wouldn't have been on shift."

He nodded. "And you can't send TAT messages from anywhere but the bridge."

She couldn't help but play devil's advocate. "But what if he posted the message on another console?"

He shook his head. "Those messages are all sent directly to home base."

"Then who was on shift?"

He looked down, checking the time again. "It's around shift change. Could have been any of four people."

"Two, actually."

"Huh?"

"Think about it. The person wiped the directory, but didn't do a good enough job to keep it wiped. So the comp sci people are out. It has to be a mathematician."

"Good thinking."

She smiled. "Anytime, sir."

One of the communications officers sat in a small room on the opposite side of the glass Mila and Tristan stood in front of. He fidgeted and twitched his way along, his gaze bobbing back and forth across the surfaces like a bobble head doll. Avery walked in before them.

"I didn't even know we had interrogation rooms on this ship." Mila looked to the captain.

"Of course we do. This is first and foremost a military vessel. In the past, these rooms have been used for interrogating prisoners of war and enemy combatants."

Mila turned to the smug man sitting in the interrogation room behind them. Each observation room connected to two interrogation rooms. *Efficient.* Mr. Fidget looked suspicious, but she would put money on the guy behind her. She didn't think anyone could sit that cool while waiting to be interrogated by the likes of Avery.

In the opposite room, Avery had started the interrogation. She'd heard his voice rising and falling, but hadn't been listening. The captain was formidable, unnerving. Avery was terrifying. All he needed was a scar running down his face.

Mila glanced at the man behind her again. A small smirk crossed his face. Chills ran down her body. She tugged on the captain's sleeve.

"Yeah?" He turned to her.

"I think Avery's wasting his time. That's the guy." She pointed to the opposite pane of glass. "He's a psycho."

He shook his head. "Psycho doesn't always equate to the right guy for the crime. Where's your display?"

She handed him the flat panel still clutched in her fist.

"Thanks. Let's see this guy's record, eh?" He typed on the screen some, swiped his finger across, then settled on something. "Psycho is probably a good description. The man has more demerits than I thought possible. Why hasn't he been booted yet?"

Mila stretched to see. "There." She pointed. "He might be a psycho, but he's the best mathematician we've got." She pulled her finger across the display. "Good God. Look at all the awards. What's this about a Fields Medal?"

"That's the foremost award for mathematicians. I only know because I've had to screen enough of them as a captain."

"What about the other guy?"

"Hold on." Tristan exited the personnel file and went about finding the other guy's file. "There's not much here. No demerits. No commendations. Nothing. Just ships he's served on, classifications, training."

"Like maybe he didn't want to get noticed."

CHAPTER SIXTEEN

Mila yawned, her eyes tearing up as she swayed in place.

"Oh, I'm sorry, May. Head back to your bunk. Get some rest. I've kept you up too long."

She looked at him critically. "Shouldn't you be doing the same, sir? You've been awake as long as I have. Why aren't you yawning?"

"Just lucky, I guess."

"Well, how about I'll call it quits when you do, sir?" She might fall asleep on her feet, but she didn't think a captain with sleep deprivation would be much help to anyone.

"Fine, come on. We'll walk you to your bunk."

"Oh, joy," she said, wincing at saying that out loud. She really needed some sleep. "You and my shadows." She slapped her hands together and stretched a worn smile on her face.

"Knock it off, wiseass."

She winked and dashed for the door. "But it's a fine ass, too."

And where the hell did that come from? Sleep deprivation was making her lose her damn mind.

"Sadly, yes," she imagined the captain mutter under his breath.

Yep, definitely her imagination.

When she slipped into her bunk, her roommate slept soundly, just a gently moving lump on the bottom bed. She groaned looking at the ladder to get to hers. Why couldn't she have gotten the lower one?

She contemplated sleeping on the floor, but nixed it as she kicked her shoes into the wardrobe, pulled off her belt, and removed her uniform shirt. In just her pants and undershirt, she slinked to the ladder, collapsing into its rungs and groaning again. The bed seemed so far away.

But she climbed, each rung feeling like a marathon. Three more. Two more. One more. Collapse. She didn't have the energy to tuck herself in. The next morning, she woke with her head propped on her arms and her legs still dangling off the bottom a good two to three feet.

She got up late. Santos was long gone. "Ow." She rolled over and rubbed her shins where they'd pressed against the metal frame all night. She stretched and her back protested with an audible pop. A yawn escaped against her will and she fell back to the bed. *I do not want to get up.*

She slipped down and contemplated a shower. She skipped yesterday, didn't she? Felt like ages ago. She sniffed a pit. *Yep, I stink.*

Damn.

<hr>

After a shower that tormented her with visions of the assassin slipping in and killing her, she grabbed a bagel and headed to Tristan's quarters, knocking on the door.

"Come in."

She peeked in, holding up her breakfast. "Probably should have gotten you one too, huh?"

"Oh, that's okay, May."

"So, what's on the agenda today, sir?"

"Avery's still working on those two suspects, which leaves Comms seriously shorthanded. Hall's the only mathematician trained on the TAT."

"Gotcha. Well, until we figure out who's innocent and who's guilty, there's not much we can do there. How's Luke doing? I kind of didn't check in on him since, well, the USB key thing." She looked at the floor, embarrassed that she'd forgotten about him so easily.

"He's fine. He's working. He's probably wondering where you are right now."

She sucked in a breath. "Oh no! He probably thinks something happened to me. I've gotta go."

"Hey, hey!" He jumped from his seat. "Relax. Don't bother him while he's working, 'kay?"

Mila rolled her eyes. "Like he's working that hard."

He smiled. "Some preliminary background checks came in. Care to help go through them?"

She pulled in a breath and thought of Luke. He would be fine, right? "Okay."

<hr>

Mila yawned. "This would be a whole lot easier in paper. We could just dump them into no and maybe piles."

Tristan looked up from his screen. "You can still do that. Just make folders in the directory."

"It's not the same. This display is a pain in the ass."

He smirked at her. "Get to work, Trace."

"Oh, now we're back to Trace, are we?"

"Well, yeah, when you're slacking."

"I'm not slacking!" But she smiled anyway. Even poring over boring as hell background checks proved entertaining with the captain, which was scary, come to think of it. She didn't want to become attached to anyone, especially him. Not with her problems. How could she get close to someone when there would always be a lie between them?

The floor shook beneath her feet, vibrating the chair under her butt. "What the hell was that?"

Tristan was already standing. "I don't know, but it can't be good."

A klaxon blared and the lights flickered before turning red. *The backup lighting system.* They looked at each other in alarm and ran for the door.

The engines.

CHAPTER SEVENTEEN

They raced through the halls, expecting the worst. The floor continued to rumble beneath their feet. *What the hell is going on?* The captain ran ahead of her, his greater height and longer legs giving him an advantage. Plus, he actually knew the way to the engine room.

Sabotage? An accident? After all, the ship *was* old. It could have just broken down, couldn't it? But her heart told her that was just wishful thinking. No. This was no accident.

They turned a corner and Mila skidded to a halt. A cloud of billowing smoke obscured the path forward. She slogged through it, coughing and holding her sleeve across her face to keep from breathing too much in. People raced past her as her eyes watered and burned. *Where's the captain? I can't see him anymore.*

She stumbled against a hard surface and yelped, flailing her arms and reaching for anything to keep her upright.

"May? Are you okay?"

Good, he was just a few feet ahead of her. "Fine." She

coughed and covered her mouth once more. "Just tripped. Be careful. There's debris on the ground. And I can't see shit through this smoke."

"Maybe you should stay back."

"Not a chance, slick."

"Slick?" She could hear the smile in his voice.

"Get moving, sir."

"Yes, ma'am," he said sarcastically.

They continued on, watching each step, shuffling forward to avoid slamming a leg or foot into debris, to not trip as she had before. Detritus covered every inch of flooring, forcing her to make a circuitous route through the hallway. They still hadn't reached the engine room.

"Shouldn't there be an exhaust fan or something?"

"Yeah. Those systems must be down, too. At least the important stuff is still operational. Actually, I'm surprised the magnetics are still working. They're controlled electronically."

"Right. And they're not vital systems, are they?"

"Nope."

And, as if on cue, she started to float. "Figures."

"Can you touch the wall, May?"

She flailed around and found the grab bars that lined the walls and ceilings of the hallways. At any other time, she gave them no regard, but she whispered a thank you for them now. Her fingers ghosted across one, then she latched on with both hands. "I'm good. Got a hold."

"Good. Let's keep going."

"Okay." She continued, moving arm over arm, afraid to let go with all the smoke. If she lost her grip, she might not find another grab bar in the blinding cloud. She coughed, sucking in more and more smoke, unable to protect her lungs.

"I found the doors. They're mangled. Like they were blasted outward."

"I'm right behind you," she wheezed. A few more movements and she bumped into his flank. "What now?"

"I'm not sure we should enter the engine room with all this smoke. It's huge and I have no idea what's left of it."

"Well, we should at least look." Mila leveraged herself to get ahead of him and held onto the doorway. "I think it's thinning." She squinted through her watering eyes as another bout of hacking coughs plagued her. She scanned around, the smoke shifting toward a few points near the walls. "I think we have depressurization."

"What?!"

"Not major. Small ones. It's clearing the smoke, which is a plus."

"Move over." He nudged Mila aside and looked over her shoulder. "You're right. This could be bad."

"I thought minor leaks weren't a problem."

"They're not, unless something causes them to grow, break open. Then this entire section of the ship would be lost. Hell, the *entire* ship could be lost."

"What do we do?"

"Follow me." And he pushed off.

115

It took forever for the smoke to clear. Mila floated and watched while men repaired leaks, patching them to regain integrity. She helped by retrieving tools and floating between engineers, but she knew nothing about the engines of the ships she flew.

Then the magnetics reasserted themselves and she screamed as she slammed into the floor.

"May? You all right?" the captain said, racing over to where she'd fallen.

"Fine," she said, getting to her feet. "Just a new cut and a sore bum." She examined the nick on her leg, but dismissed it.

"Let me see."

"You don't have to. It's just a scratch."

"May, please?"

"Fine," she said, sitting down on a large chunk of scrap.

She let him kneel in front of her and raise her pant leg, examining the cut, as she turned her attention to the state of the room. It looked like a war zone. She couldn't recognize anything. Could they recover from this? Was it even possible? She saw nothing that remotely resembled an engine. Just scrap metal.

"How are we ever getting moving again?"

"We will. Don't you worry."

She shook her head. "But this… it's devastating."

He looked around, taking in the damage. "It sure looks that way. But until the engineers assess the damage, we'll have no idea what we're dealing with."

"I suppose that's a better way of looking at it."

"Damn straight. Okay, you should be fine. Just be careful." He tugged her pant leg down and went back to helping get them limping along.

Well, at least the magnetics were operational again.

CHAPTER EIGHTEEN

"Hey, wake up."

"Huh? Wha—?" Mila jerked awake.

"You fell asleep."

She shook her head and looked around the engine room turned scrap yard. "Yeah, guess I did. Any idea on the damage?"

"Come on. Let's get you somewhere more comfortable. We're just in the way here. The best people for the job are already on task."

"Good."

The captain pulled her to her feet, and half carried her back to his office.

"Maybe I shouldn't," she said as he tried to dump her in a chair. "Maybe I should go take a shower."

"Oh, I don't care about the stupid chairs, May. Sit."

He didn't have to ask her twice. She was too tired. Exhausted and grimy. "I think I'm better off flying this POS. Being around you just wipes me out."

He smiled, exhaustion masking his amusement. "It's been another long day, hasn't it?"

"They all seem to be long days lately." She paused, too weary or too empathetic to want to continue. "So, any idea on the prognosis?"

"We're dead in the water. The engineers are hopeful. This is an old ship. The systems are hardier than they seem. They say the damage was done by some parts rupturing. But they think they can weld some of the scrap together, rebuild the engine."

"Impressive." She didn't have the energy to give it the enthusiasm it deserved.

He shrugged. "Sometimes in deep space, you have to be."

"Yeah. How long till we're flying again?"

He shook his head. "That, I don't know. We might never get it running again."

"That would mean we failed, they won."

"Yeah. I don't like it any more than you do."

"What about communications?"

"I haven't checked yet. We've been focused on stabilizing the engine room, making sure we still have life support systems."

"How long will life support last?"

He massaged his face. "Not sure on a rig this old. A few weeks?"

"Long enough for a rescue?"

He nodded. "If we can't get it up and running. And if we have the TAT. You should go. Get some sleep."

"No. I wanna help. We need all hands on deck right now."

"Yeah and you're a pilot with no ship to fly. I think you can afford to get a full night's rest."

"There are other ways I can help, sir."

"Please?"

The exhaustion in his voice made her cave. "Fine. I'll go. But you get some rest, too. You look like you're about to keel over."

"In a little while."

"Soon?"

"Yeah, soon."

A knock came at the door. "Come on in, guys." Lieutenant Braddock and his head of security entered side by side. "Sit. Take a load off."

They both collapsed, more than happy to unwind.

"I'm taking security off the search for the assassin. Our priority now is finding the conspirators. We can't let this get worse."

"I agree," Avery said. "If you want, we can put extra security on Trace." Avery's eyes lit with humor, hinting at something Tristan would not confront head on, especially not with his subordinates.

"I don't think that will be necessary."

"Of course, captain." But the amusement didn't go away. Instead, a smirk appeared.

Tristan refused to acknowledge it. "Lieutenant. You and the rest of the upper ranks. We need to get ahead of this thing. Fast."

"Yes, sir."

"I'll divide tasks out by section. Oversee repairs, everything. Report back to me."

"Yes, sir."

"Avery. May and I have been going over background reports. It's on my private directory. We've divided it out into people who might have unsavory connections and those we found no evidence thereof. I want you to bring these people in, interrogate them. I need answers. Now."

"Yes, sir."

"Dismissed."

Emergency lighting tinged every hallway red. Just before reaching his bunk for a much needed nap, four security officers stormed past him. He turned to watch them go, but kept his head down. He didn't need them to notice him, not when success was breaths away.

"Officer Fowler?" one of them said.

He held his breath. Fowler was a friend, an ally. *Be natural. Be normal.* He hunkered down and listened, opening the door to his bunk so he was half in and half out, ready to flee at a moment's notice.

"Yeah? What's going on?" His friend seemed genuinely confused.

Good. That might just save you.

"You're coming with us."

"What? What's going on? What did I do?"

They grabbed him by the arms and dragged him off.

This was only the beginning…

<hr>

CHAPTER NINETEEN

<hr>

Mila didn't bother knocking. She shoved the doors to the captain's office open and barged right in.

"Think you own the place now, huh?"

"Oh, I was just trying it out. What's on the agenda today?" She tried to overlook the shadows under his eyes.

"Going over video. I've got most of the ship working on getting various systems back up and running."

"By all means."

"I need a snack. The galley still open?"

"Of course. People need to eat. Even when things get crazy."

"Cool. You want anything?"

"Yeah, just bring me whatever."

She left the room and waited for her shadows to follow her.

They'd been at it for hours. Skimming video of the hours before the explosion, checking camera after camera. The servers and computers shut down during the explosion. They'd had to boot them up again to access the video. They were keeping a single server up while power was at a premium.

Still, they hadn't seen much. They had gone through video of the two hours before the incident which had been officially declared foul play. That was one of the first things they discovered—a simple incendiary device attached to a pipe. Just cleaning chemicals, but they caught fire and heated the fuel, causing weak points in the machines to rupture or explode.

Still, they were looking for the culprit, which meant finding who planted the device. They just had no idea when it was planted, thus hours and hours of video.

"You guys hungry?" she said over her shoulder as she grabbed some quick snacks, snatching them out from under the bands that kept them from floating away.

Neither replied.

She shrugged and started back. *Whatever.*

<hr>

"Sir! I think I've got it."

He jumped up and moved behind Mila. "Let me see."

She brought it back a few minutes and hit play. This angle showed the pipe where the device would be planted. She couldn't quite see where the bomb would be but the area before it was wide open. A man walked into the frame.

"I don't recognize him, but I don't know a fraction of the

people on this boat." Mila paused it when the man placed the device.

"I don't either. We'll get this to Avery."

<hr>

Outside his office, the ship felt ominous. They were still on emergency lighting, lending everything a red tint, and the temperature had dropped ten degrees since the incident. Mila jogged beside the captain to get her blood pumping a little faster.

They entered the security offices and the captain shouted, "Avery! Got something to show you."

Avery turned and stalked their way. "Yes, captain?"

"We rummaged through the video. Found this." He handed over Mila's display.

"Great, thank you. It needs to be enhanced. Thanks for the help, captain, Trace."

"Anytime," he said.

Mila just shrugged.

They left the offices, Mila eagerly, not wanting to interfere.

"What are the other pilots doing?"

"Running. The communications systems are mostly down. Can't call people from opposite ends of the ship. TAT's working, but we're keeping it on minimal power just to receive messages from home base."

"Guess I should be glad I got out of that assignment. Of course, if I were running around the ship, I might actually be warm." She started shivering and wished she could shift extra muscle or fat or something.

The captain engulfed her, rubbing her arm vigorously. "Any better?"

"Worlds." *Holy crap.* He felt like a furnace. She wanted to curl up into him and fall asleep.

"Good."

They walked like that, lurching along the hallway, Mila conscious of the looks people gave them. Curiosity. Surprise. Knowing smirks.

But warm trumped all, so she snuggled closer, burying her numb nose in his shirt, which made him laugh.

Then, a loud crack echoed behind her. They spun around in unison. Another crack, and the captain fell to the floor. "Tristan!" Another crack and pain raced through her chest. Mila tried to take a breath, but couldn't. She started coughing, but blood bubbled up, spilling over her lips. She sank to her knees.

A pounding noise faded into the distance. Was that her heart?

The shot cracked against the metal surfaces, hitting him and spinning him into the wall. He fell to the ground, stunned for a moment. Another crack sounded before he'd recovered his senses. He looked up, holding his injured arm as the culprit ran away wearing a security officer's uniform.

The other security officer lay on the floor, likely dead. He continued inspecting the scene. "May!" He half-stumbled, half-crawled to where she knelt, clasping her chest with shaky fingers. "May?" She collapsed as soon as his hands touched her. "Oh God," he said, seeing the terrible wound. A large hole tore through her. He pressed his hand to it, knowing on some level it was too late, but not caring, not willing to admit it.

"Don't you dare die on me, May! Don't you fucking dare!" He didn't feel the tears on his face.

"Someone? Someone help!"

He leaned over her, pressing as hard as he could on her broken chest. "Hold on, May. Hold on."

Her shallow breaths wheezed in, but never seemed to escape again. Blood pooled around his hands, her mouth, the floor. The distress he saw on her face matched his own.

When her eyes closed, he screamed, "No!"

"No, no. May, wake up." He started gently slapping her face, looking for signs she wasn't dead. But she didn't move. He couldn't even see her breathe.

He sat back in shock and waited.

For someone to come?

For a miracle?

He wasn't sure.

But he couldn't leave her.

He couldn't look at her. It hurt too much. So he didn't notice when she started breathing again. He nearly screamed when a butterfly touch glanced his shoulder. He spun around and stared gape-mouthed at her. "But you're dead."

May looked down, examining the hole in her shirt with her fingers. He watched in shock as the hole revealed perfect skin, stained with blood but perfect.

"I don't understand."

As her gaze returned to him, the color drained from her face. Fear took over and she started scooting backwards, then trying to get up. But she kept falling. Between the blood-slick floor and recovering from dying, she just couldn't stand.

"May, please."

"I-I can't," she said as she slumped against the opposite wall.

They stared at each other, neither able nor willing to end the silence. His head filled with all the possibilities, all the ramifications. He had no idea what she was thinking.

He felt like he didn't know her at all.

———

Help eventually arrived and soon medical and security officers swarmed them. Someone was bandaging Tristan's arm while a security officer questioned him.

Mila couldn't stop shaking. She didn't know what to say, so she said nothing. Her gaze kept shifting between the body and Tristan. One because she felt she was to blame for his death, the other because she feared he would be to blame for hers.

She wanted to plead with Tristan not to tell, but he refused to meet her gaze. So she waited, listening to his tale, waiting for the words that would condemn her.

But he didn't say them. In fact, he made no mention of her being hurt at all.

He's covering for me?

———

"Come on," Tristan said, pulling Mila to her feet. "We're of no further use here."

She nodded, speech still beyond her. She stumbled along, Tristan dragging her behind him by their conjoined hands. He pulled her into his office, dumped her in a chair, and leaned over her.

"What are you?"

The coldness in his voice made her face fall. Her mouth moved, but no words escaped.

He grabbed her chin, looking her straight in the eyes. "What... are... you?"

After several breaths, the truth she'd been hiding forever, the one that could get her killed or worse, slipped out. "Shifter." Nothing more than a breath, he wouldn't have heard it had he not been inches from her lips. It felt like she'd confessed some great sin. Like she'd just admitted to first degree murder.

Tristan stood back, surprised. He shook his head and stumbled, falling in the chair next to her.

After a few minutes of him staring off into the distance, jaw slack, he spoke. "You're Mila, aren't you? Your friend. Dragomirov?"

Mila nodded, numb but also relieved.

I'm not alone anymore.

He sat, contemplating for a moment. "You disappeared because you shifted?"

She nodded again. "Twenty-first birthday. We went out drinking. I got a little too drunk. Drunk enough to do something stupid, not drunk enough to forget." She looked at Tristan, but he wasn't looking at her. "I shifted into a tiger, of all things. I couldn't have picked a dog or something. I can only imagine what the news looked like the next day.

"I managed to get home, shifted back." She paused. "I just packed a bag and left."

"But you left the note for your friend. May Trace." He looked straight at her this time. "If you're here, where the hell is she?"

Mila sagged her head. How many times would the events of

that day torment her before she could move on? "She died. A mugging. Well, maybe it wasn't a mugging. Maybe it was just supposed to look like one." She rubbed her eyes until they hurt.

"You didn't answer my question."

She put her hands down, feeling like she could fall apart at any moment. Like she'd been put together with glue sticks. "I buried her." A tear fell down her cheek. She tried to steel her face, keep more tears from joining it. "Tristan, I…"

He put a hand up. "No. Stop."

"Tristan…"

He looked at her, that same cold expression on his face. "No." He shook his head. "Just give me time, May… Mila. I need time. Space."

"Okay." She stood and headed to the door on shaky legs, too afraid to look back and see that icy visage he'd worn.

When she closed the doors behind her, she ran. She kept running, not knowing if she ran to or away or where her destination would be.

When she arrived, it made perfect sense. The only place on the ship more broken than her… the engine room.

Only a handful of people drifted in and out at the moment. She'd caught it at a lull. Finding a deserted corner, she sat down among the rubble and cried.

CHAPTER TWENTY-ONE

"You know, you've been a real problem for me, Miss Trace."

Mila jumped. She knew that voice. She spun around to confront him and stood slowly. "And that's my problem why?" Her face burned from her tears, but she didn't care. Right that moment, Tristan could be deciding her fate and all because this bastard couldn't leave well enough alone.

"Because I was contracted." He stepped down from the chunk of metal he'd been standing on. "Though I was surprised to find you were a shifter like me."

She shrugged. Would he let it go if she told him she wasn't May Trace? That she was assuming a role, an identity just the same as he?

Doubt it.

"I found a present for you in the galley today when I heard you'd survived." He raised a knife to shoulder level. "I'm good with guns, but I've always been an artiste with knives. It's one of the only ways to kill a shifter."

"I'll keep that in mind." Her stance shifted, balancing her weight, anticipating the strike. She waited, but he just smiled. "Well, are you gonna kill me or what? I mean, you've already tried like four… wait. I've lost count. Not the best assassin, are you?"

Mila grinned when the anger shaded his face.

Perfect. People fuck up when they're angry.

"Aw, did I hurt the little shifter's feelings?"

"Shut up, bitch."

She cocked her head to the side. "Make me."

He charged.

She dodged the first strike, only to get sliced by the next. Her limbs moved sluggishly. *Should have gotten something to eat. I'm running on empty after the gunshot wound.*

Mila pushed his knife hand out of the way and landed a punch to his chin, but he barely responded to it.

Uh oh.

She grabbed his hand, lifting it up, keeping the knife away from her, then slammed his arm into an upright beam. He grunted, but kept his hold. She slammed it again, but her arms were growing weaker, getting cold and tingly from being above her head.

Mila ducked under his arm and ran, knowing the knife wouldn't be able to keep up. She slid behind some debris, crawled under some more.

"You're hiding? After all that bravado?"

His voice grew closer.

She waited. The engine room wasn't deserted, just not packed.

Someone will hear.

Someone will come.

Won't they?

She could feel exhaustion coming over her, a side effect of healing herself.

Someone will come.

"Come out, come out, wherever you are!"

She scrambled farther back, but kicked something in the dark under the scrap metal.

Shit.

"Gotcha."

She slid out and jumped to her feet, registering the assassin's location out of the corner of her eye. She took off at a run again, dodging hurtles, pipes, sharp edges. A piece of piping cut her arm. She bit her lip to keep from crying out as pain lanced across her.

His relentless pursuit seemed in sync with her beating heart.

He grabbed her, whipped her around, and sliced at her throat, but she pulled her head back at the last second, causing the knife to cut shallow. It hurt like hell, but she would survive.

She seized his knife hand with a shaky grip. He yanked out of her grasp with ease, making her stumble, fall. Her head slammed into something hard. *Pain. Black. Pressure.*

The assassin sat on her chest as the pain dulled. He raised his blade. Her half-insensate brain had her grasping for anything, everything. *Cool. Sharp. Grip.*

She sent it up, feeling the cool metal dig and cut into her palm. She screamed as he did, the thing going into his chest under the ribcage, slicing into her hand in three places. Shock covered his face. Metal clattered to the ground. He fell on her, causing her to cry out as the sharp debris in her hand dug in further, pressing on her sternum too.

After a while, when she managed to get the strength, she pushed him off and rolled him onto his back. She straddled him, thrust the chunk of metal a little harder for good measure, not stopping until metal met metal.

He wouldn't recover from that.

Mila stood, staring at her left palm, watching the blood pool in lines. She started to move, but stumbled. Reaching a hand out to steady herself, she screamed when her shredded palm came in contact and collapsed to the floor on her knees.

With a deep breath, she used her other hand to push herself back to her feet. Her eyes felt heavy and she could have fallen asleep right there, but she shook her head and continued.

Mila sensed movement around her, but didn't see. She heard a cacophony, but didn't understand. She just stumbled, walking steadily onward. A humorless laugh erupted from her. She probably looked like a zombie the way she was shambling along.

She collapsed against a wall next to a door she should have known she would run to and knocked three times.

"Come in," the welcome voice said.

She turned the knob, opened the door, and dropped through the doorway, landing on her face.

CHAPTER TWENTY-TWO
---

*K*nock, knock, knock.

"Come in!" Tristan said. Honestly, why did they bother knocking?

The door opened and a body fell through. "May!" He jumped from his chair, skidding it across the room, and dashed to her side, heart in his throat. "May? God, May."

He turned her over, checking her for wounds. Her throat was slit, her hand was a mess, her arms were cut. *People can't see her like this.*

He dragged her through the doorway, stood and closed the door, then looked back at her, not knowing what to do.

Tend her wounds?

Will she heal herself like she did before?

Should I call a doctor?

He rubbed his face, pacing in a small line next to her.

No one can know about her.

Mila woke in bed. A big bed. A nice bed. She rubbed her eyes, noticing her heavily bandaged left hand. So were her throat and a few choice places on her arms. She blinked her eyes open and turned her head.

Tristan sat on a chair by the bed, watching her. "Hi."

"Hi." He didn't seem as cold as he had before. She almost didn't want to hope as she let the words spill out. "You don't hate me?"

"No, I don't hate you. I just needed time. What I said before was true. I don't blame people for what they are. I blame them for who they are." He shrugged, looking down into his lap. "I don't believe you're a bad person," he paused, "Mila. Mila." A small smile curved one side of his lips. "I don't understand you, but I want to. I know you're not the assassin, and other than stealing someone's identity, I have no evidence you've ever done anything wrong. I would like to know why you did it though."

"Take May's identity, you mean?"

He shook his head, looking down again. "It's the one part I can't get past." He looked up again. "I can't understand it. I wouldn't have done it. I can't imagine anyone good doing it. It doesn't fit with how I see you."

"I didn't exactly have a lot of options, Tristan. I'm a shifter. I couldn't go to the cops and I couldn't just abandon her, the last friend I had in the world. That's why I buried her." She shook her head. "I didn't bury her thinking I would take her identity. I did it thinking I was doing the best I could. Paying her respect.

"When I looked in her bag, I found that she had a verified ID. People don't question verified IDs. I just... wanted a normal life. What I'd been reaching for when my life changed forever."

"When you shifted for the first time."

"Yeah. This was the life I had wanted, that me and May had wanted. We'd wanted it together. It just never happened that way. I thought it was something she would have wanted for me, a gift of sorts."

"What about her family, Mila? When do they get to grieve? Move on?"

Her head sagged. "I didn't think it through that far."

He laughed, shaking his head at her. "Now that *does* sound like how I see you."

She smirked at him. "So, you still don't hate me?"

"No, still don't hate you."

"And you're not going to tell."

"No, I'm not."

Things were getting interesting now. It seemed like victory was within their grasps, but their enemy was dogging their heels too. People were getting taken in left and right for questioning. Some he knew were his compatriots, others weren't. Still, even a blind man could hit a bull's-eye with luck.

He walked the halls still tinged red, rubbing his arms to keep up circulation. Couldn't they turn the heat up a bit? Honestly!

He stopped and knocked at the door he'd been looking for. The door opened, exposing a man in uniform. "I need to talk to you."

The man nodded and ushered him into the room. He closed the door and sat on the lower bunk. "What can I do for you, sir?"

"I'm sorry, but things have reached a boiling point, so to speak." His arms flew out and snapped the man's neck. "I can't have anyone knowing my involvement."

CHAPTER TWENTY-THREE

The security officer sat at a bench, trying to savor the prepackaged snack while he could. Since they'd discovered an assassin on board, he'd been worked half to death. Little reprieves like this never lasted long, often followed by long hours on his feet searching and investigating.

With the temperature plummeting and the ship dead in the water, few people were hanging around. He watched as people walked in, grabbed food, and collapsed on a bench, many times with an exhausted groan. He could empathize.

People rarely stayed long, though. It was too cold to sit still, not without curling up into something like a sleeping bag.

Someone ran into the room, hyperventilating as he bent at the waist. He straightened, but with his breaths coming in gasps, the security officer couldn't make out what the guy was saying.

He stood and walked over to him. "Are you all right? Do you need assistance?"

"Yes." He nodded, the yes more a breath of air than a word. "Found." Another couple breaths. "Body."

"Where?"

"Do you mind me asking what happened? How you got cut up?" Tristan relaxed back into the chair as she sat up in his bed.

The words wouldn't come. Looking back, she felt terrified, relieved, nauseous, traumatized, relieved. Her mind kept rebounding to the relieved part. It chewed at her gut, being glad the man was dead, that she'd killed him.

"Mila?"

She shook her head. "You shouldn't call me that."

"But it's your name. Wouldn't you rather me call you by your real name?"

A small smile crossed her face, followed by a wave of nausea. *God, he knows what I am. No one can know what I am.* She struggled to take a deep breath. "Of course, I would, but it's not safe. You'd only be able to use it when we're alone. What if you said it in public? How would you explain that? Huh?"

"I could say it was a pet name."

The smile that crossed his face made her want to smile back, then growl at him.

"What does it mean?"

"I think my parents said it meant 'dear one' in Russian," she said, reluctant to give him the ammunition.

"See? There you go. It's a perfect pet name."

She stared him down. "I still don't think it's a good idea."

"We'll agree to disagree."

"Tristan, this is my life you're playing with here."

His face fell. "I'm sorry."

He barged into the captain's office, but for once, the captain wasn't there. "Captain Faulk?"

After a few moments, a door to his left opened and Faulk walked in. "Yes?"

"Another body has been found, sir."

"Shit," he said and sagged before turning and poking his head back through the door. "Stay put."

I wonder who he's entertaining. A muffled reply came through the doorway, but he caught neither the words nor the tone of the message.

"Get some rest," the captain said, before closing the door with a gentle click and facing his new guest. "Lead the way."

Mila's eyes bulged as he closed the door on her, jaw slack. *How dare he!* Sure, she'd had a trying day. She was tired and could eat a small bison, but she still couldn't believe he'd just dismissed her like that.

"Damn it," she said as she threw the covers aside. She hadn't gotten around to telling him about the assassin. She'd wanted to tell him, meant to tell him. Mila pulled at her hair as she paced the room several sizes larger than her own.

What'll he think? Will he change his mind about me after knowing what I've done?

Her pacing picked up speed, becoming frantic, her muscles no longer able to keep up. She stopped in the middle of the floor. "I'm getting out of here."

She left Tristan's chambers in favor of her own and slipped into her own bed.

Maybe everything would make more sense after a good night's sleep.

<hr>

Tristan kept pace behind his security officer, but his mind never left Mila. He both damned and praised his job for separating and introducing them. But a ship and its crew comprised more than just one soul and he knew it. He couldn't let his feelings for her hinder him in performing his duties. Too many lives counted on him, especially now.

Tristan didn't pay attention to where he led him, only looking up when they stopped. He slipped effortlessly into captain-mode. "Report."

He hadn't seen a body yet, but his mind kept drifting to the assassin. *Another soul lost to that bastard.* Another security officer approached him, standing up straighter as he neared.

"Captain, he was found by his roommate. Broken neck. Very efficient. Clean."

Tristan nodded, his suspicions confirmed. "The assassin, then?"

"No, sir. We don't believe so."

His head whipped up in surprise. "No? Then who?"

"We don't know, sir."

"Why don't you think it was the assassin?"

"The circumstances don't fit his M.O., sir. For starters, he was left somewhere easily found. Other than once while cornered, the assassin has never left a body in the open."

"Didn't you say he was found in his bunk?"

"Yes, sir. But the body was guaranteed to be found post haste. After all, his roommate only had to return to find it. If he was taking on a new identity, he wouldn't leave it there. Also, the kill is too clean."

"Too clean?"

"Yes, sir. Military precision. The medical officer says it's classic special forces."

"You think it was someone on this ship? Someone who's supposed to be here?"

"Yes, sir. Perhaps one of the conspirators? Someone trying to cover the trail to himself?"

Tristan shrugged. "It's as good a guess as any, at the moment."

Hours later, Tristan finally made it back to his quarters. He sighed, closing the doors behind him. The long day had drained him both physically and emotionally. He thought of Mila sleeping in his bed and a smile crept onto his face. He shook his head and muttered under his breath, "You are a damned fool, Tristan Faulk."

Tristan walked across the room to his bedroom door, his steps lighter the closer he got to her. Darkness greeted him as he crossed the space and sat on the bed. But his heart sank as he ghosted his hand over the rumpled bedding, massaging the unoccupied space. She'd left. He shivered, the ship's pervasive chill affecting him for the first time since he found out the truth about her.

CHAPTER TWENTY-FOUR

Tristan arrived at Mila's bunk bearing gifts. He knocked and the door opened, exposing a woman he vaguely recognized.

Her face wrinkled into a frown. "Ugh, so not the person I wanted to see first thing in the morning." She opened the door further and pushed him out of her way, heading down the hall without a backward glance.

He stood shocked, floored by the utter lack of respect for a senior officer. "Huh." She disappeared with the slamming of a door and he turned back, knocking once more.

After some shuffling and a crash that caused his heart to jump into his throat and his fist to crush their breakfast, he heard someone stumbling on the other side. The door opened to Mila leaning half-asleep on the doorjamb. "Tristan." A small smile crossed her face and he couldn't help thinking how cute she looked mussed from sleep.

"I brought breakfast," he said, lifting the half-crushed contents to eye level.

"Oh, thank God!" she said, snatching everything before he

could blink. She disappeared into the room, but left the door open.

He took that as an invitation.

The inside mirrored any other bunk on board. Utilitarian, metallic, tiny. She sat on the lower bunk, digging into a beignet. "I still can't believe they have beignets," she said around a wad of dough.

He smirked and tried not to laugh as bits of powdered sugar floated in the air. He wiped a little powder off the corner of her mouth and sat next to her. "I'm glad you like it."

"Like it?" She swallowed and uttered the first clear words this morning. "I love it. God, beignets are amazing. And totally fattening, which is exactly what I need right about now."

"You need fattening foods?" He furrowed his brows.

"No, silly. Calories. I need calories. Fat has over two times as many calories per ounce. After having to heal myself twice yesterday, I need the calories. I feel like my stomach's gonna lead a revolt I'm so hungry."

He did laugh that time. "Well, dig in."

She shoved another beignet in her mouth, again talking around it. "So what happened?" Concern, anxiety, and fear colored her face.

"A body was found in one of the bunks."

"So, not the assassin?"

"No, not the assassin. They think someone else did it."

With a resigned expression, she put her food down. "I should tell you something. I meant to tell you last night, but that guy barged in and I was pretty freaked myself."

The more she talked, the more he realized she was still

unnerved by what happened. He rubbed her arm, trying to soothe her. "You can tell me anything."

She tried to smile, but it looked forced, the only redeeming factor being the dusting of sugar on her face. She looked away and focused on her hands in her lap. "The assassin's dead."

"What?!"

"Last night I ran off, looking for somewhere to hide, somewhere to be alone. I found a corner of the engine room where no one was working and started crying my eyes out." She snuck a peek at him, a self-deprecating look on her face. "He attacked me. I tried to fight, then to hide, run, but I was weak from healing myself. I was tired. He pinned me, but I grabbed hold of a chunk of scrap metal." She gazed down at her hand, tracing with her finger the lines where the metal had sliced deep.

Tristan became more alarmed the longer she spoke. When she said the assassin had her pinned, he nearly came out of his seat. Good God, he'd let that happen. He should have been there. He should have protected her. Instead, he'd sat in his quarters, feeling sorry for himself because she wasn't who he'd thought she'd been.

"I jammed it into his chest." Her words came harder, her voice thicker, like she was holding back a tsunami of emotion. "I killed him." She wouldn't stop looking at her left hand. "I killed him."

Tristan reached for her hand, but she wouldn't budge and he wasn't willing to force her. Instead, he put his arm around her shoulders and pulled her tight to his side. "Shh. No, Mila. You did what you had to. Nothing more. Shh." He rocked her in place.

She started to cry, and a moment's panic flooded him. He froze. *What do I do?* He pulled her into his arms, rocking her again, whispering meaningless platitudes in her ear, hoping some of it, any of it, helped.

After a spell, he tucked her into the bottom bed. Kissing her forehead, he watched her fall asleep as he smoothed her hair, wishing they weren't in zero gravity so he could run his fingers through the soft tresses. Mila had long hair, and kept it in tight styles to keep it from floating in all directions, even in sleep.

When his duty finally nagged him into action, he left to deal with the body in the engine room. He stopped to collect Avery and a few of his men, then a medical officer, not that it was needed. They knew what happened and didn't need to investigate.

"What's going on, captain?" Avery asked.

"The assassin is dead."

"Really? You're shitting me!"

Tristan looked at Avery, amused by the man's wording. "Yes, he's really dead, or at least he's been reported dead."

"Who reported it?"

"The one who did the deed." He resisted saying Mila, make that May, had done it. He didn't want to drag her into this mess. She could use a break.

"Look who's being coy!" He slapped Tristan on the back. "Come on! Out with it."

He looked over and shook his head. "Trace. The assassin attacked her again, last night. She almost died."

"Shit, man. Is she okay? I didn't hear about her going to the med bay."

"She didn't. She has a few cuts and I'm thinking the ones on her hand might need stitches, but she's okay."

Avery nodded. "Good. I'm glad. On both accounts."

"Both?"

"Yeah, that the assassin's dead and that Trace is okay."

"Right."

"Do you know how it went down?"

They arrived at the engine room, which was massive and they had no idea where the body lay. Mila hadn't been specific. "Fan out, everybody. It's probably not anywhere that's been actively worked in the last twelve hours or so."

Everyone disbanded, and Avery let Tristan's non-answer slide for the time being. But knowing Avery, that was only a temporary reprieve. Tristan didn't want to relive what Mila had been through any more than she did. He couldn't bear hurting her.

After a few minutes of search, someone called out from one of the deepest sections of the engine room. Everyone made their way there. As Tristan got closer to the scene, he started noticing blood, on the floor, on debris. Dark red from drying for hours, the stains made him relive her stumbling into his office covered in blood. His stomach sank, but he pressed on.

He weaved around pipes and more debris and finally reached where everyone had congregated. The man lay on his back, still carrying the face and uniform of a security officer. A large chunk of black metal in the shape of a narrow pyramid jutted out of his chest.

"Good riddance," someone said.

The medical officer kneeled down and checked for a pulse, not that anyone doubted the man's fate.

Avery spoke. "So what happened and where's our hero? Or should I say heroine?"

Tristan swallowed hard. "Trace is sleeping in her bunk. She had a hard day yesterday and I think she deserves the rest."

"Okay," Avery hedged, "so how much do we know about what happened?"

"She came to the engine room to be alone. Since one of her detail turned out to be the assassin and the other was dead, no one remained to watch her. I didn't expect her to just take off like that. Trace told me the assassin attacked her. She tried to fight him off, but was too weak, too tired. She ran, hid, but he found her. He pinned her to the ground. She grasped the weapon which I assume to be a weapon of convenience…"

"Clearly," Avery said, smirking.

"And stabbed him with it."

"Then how'd he end up on his back?" someone asked.

He resisted the urge to snarl at the man… barely. "I don't know. I didn't interrogate the poor woman. She's been through enough."

Before more questions could be asked, Avery came to the rescue. "Once she's fully rested, I'll ask her some informal questions, make sure her statements match the evidence, but that should be the end of that."

Tristan mouthed, "Thank you."

Avery winked and got back to business.

Tristan returned to Mila's door and wondered if he should

knock. *She might still be asleep.* He rose his fist, hesitating inches away as he bit his bottom lip. *Should I?*

Yearning won out over good sense and his knuckles rapped the door. He waited, but didn't have to wait long. Mila opened the door, a smile gracing her face as soon as she saw him.

"Hi," she said.

"Hiya back."

"Come on in." She threw the door wide and did her best to let him pass in the crowded space. "Where'd ya' go?" She turned her back to him, smoothing the lower bed's sheets.

"Taking care of the body."

She spun, alarm on her face when she looked up at his.

He smiled, hoping to reassure her. "Relax. I told them everything you told me. Avery will come by later to collect a more thorough statement, but the case is all but closed."

"Right. Okay." She sat on the smoothed bed, causing the bedding to contour around her, ruining her previous work. She looked up again. "Thanks."

"There's nothing to thank me for, Mila. I was just doing my job."

"Yeah, but your job could have just as easily thrown me under the bus."

He leaned forward, taking her hands. "I would never do that to you. You have my word." *My heart.*

She nodded and he knew she didn't fully believe him, didn't fully trust him. With a life like hers, he imagined trust had to be earned.

He looked over his shoulder, bit his lip, and prayed to be just as invisible as he always felt. He walked over to the console on the bridge. It wasn't his, but with so many people brought in on suspicions of sabotage, hardly anyone remained to man the thing.

He sat and waggled his fingers in the air, feeling at home, more relaxed, with a computer console in front of him. He went through the motions, going through screen displays, selecting the right options, then started typing.

It didn't take him long to finish his message. Looking over his shoulder again, he checked the other consoles. Most were vacant. The engines were dead, so the pilot and navigation officer were utterly useless. Standard communications were down as well so that chair also sat empty. He moved over to the navigation system, pulling up their current coordinates. Then he used it to calculate directions, distance, and time course for the destination he entered.

He returned to his previous seat, information at hand. He rubbed his hands together, praying he did this right. It wasn't his specialty. He selected coordinates, distance, speed, trajectory, and selected a setting that would have the computer err on the side of caution.

He pressed send and smiled, doing a happy dance in his seat.

Soon, it would be time for Take Two.

CHAPTER TWENTY-FIVE

$\mathcal{M}$ ila was making her way to the mess hall, a little dejected that Tristan took off to oversee repairs, when Avery stepped into her path.

"Trace," he nodded at her in greeting. "Follow me."

Her gut sank and she had that going-to-the-principal's-office dread as she slinked behind him.

Oh, shit, now what?

Avery ignored her as he walked off, taking a clear route to the security offices.

He won't put me in one of those interrogation rooms, will he?

She lifted her arm, discretely yanking on her braided ponytail, which tended to float out of reach.

He walked in and ushered her into a smaller office before taking a seat behind a desk.

"This is your office?"

"Yes, have a seat."

She sat, nervous energy revving up her fight-or-flight instinct, but at least she didn't think she would throw up if he asked the wrong questions.

He tapped the computer display on his desk. *Probably just turned on a voice recorder.*

"I have a few questions about the events surrounding the death of the man we've titled 'the assassin.' Just formalities to close the case. You understand?"

"Okay."

"First, according to the account given by you to Captain Tristan Faulk, 'the assassin' was on top of you when you stabbed him. How did he wind up on his back?"

"I pushed him off me."

He nodded. "Can you go over the events that transpired from beginning to end? I'd like to have it, for the record."

"Of course."

Trace left after her statement, leaving a bad taste in Avery's mouth. He saw the marks. The thin red line on her neck, the deep cuts on her palm. But his gut told him she was hiding something, holding something back. He didn't like it. He'd spent too many years eking out a living pulling truth from people to not spot when someone was keeping secrets.

What was she hiding? Did events not transpire the way she'd claimed? Did she seek out "the assassin" rather than the other way around? Was the dead man even "the assassin"? He didn't know and it pissed him off.

He contemplated investigating her further, but saw a universe of hurt in store for him if he did. The captain fancied the girl and being one of the few people here who outranked him, he could cause him a lot of problems. If pushed to it, the captain could easily ruin his career.

He didn't know if the captain fancied her *that* much, but he sure as hell had no desire to find out.

CHAPTER TWENTY-SIX

Mila had hardly seen Tristan the last few days. He'd spent more and more time overseeing repairs he'd already assigned people to oversee, but she could see how being idle didn't sit well with him. He didn't like being able to do little or nothing and he definitely didn't like his ship sitting in open space collecting dust.

Mila imagined him standing in the engine room, pacing like a mother waiting for a child to get out of surgery. She could empathize. She was going stir crazy herself. Flying calmed her, but she couldn't fly. The engines didn't work.

She stood, needing to move, but her room was too small, the walls closing in on her.

Mila dashed for the door, opening it to Luke with his hand raised, ready to knock.

"May!" He pulled her into a massive hug that squeezed the breath from her lungs.

She patted his back, desperate for relief. Suffocating moments passed before he let go, standing back, and without realizing it, allowing her to suck in a deep breath.

"God, May. Where the hell have you been? I've been so worried about you!"

"Around. I've been busy."

He angled an incredulous look her way. "May, you're a pilot. The engines are down. What the fuck can you do?"

"Been helping with the investigations. Maybe I can't fly right now and I have zero knowledge of the engines, but I can certainly wade through endless documents."

"Sounds terrible," he drawled. "Come on."

He grabbed her arm and yanked her through the door, her hold on it slamming the door closed behind her.

"Luke!"

But he didn't listen as he forged his way through the foot traffic of people milling around rubbing their arms or racing from place to place.

After a few minutes, he let go, dumping her in the mostly deserted mess hall. He led her to the food, collecting his favorites before falling onto a bench and slapping the table, encouraging her to do the same. She sat across from him.

At least I'm not cooped up anymore…

He leaned over the table, instantly oblivious of the food he'd collected. "So, tell me *everything.*"

She rolled her eyes. Of course, he wanted gossip.

Mila didn't eat anything with Luke. She was too busy filling him in on all the juicy details. So she grabbed a couple lunches and headed to the engine room. She would lay money on finding Tristan there.

When she entered the room, her gaze zeroed in on him. He stood tall, hands on his hips, watching over the repairs. She walked up to him and tapped him on the shoulder. Turning, he smiled at her surprise appearance.

"Working hard or hardly working?"

"Feels like both."

"I brought lunch." She lifted her selection for him to see.

"Excellent. Why don't we sit over there?" He pointed to an area out of earshot, but still within visual range of everyone.

She nodded and went to sit on some debris. "How's it going?"

"It's coming along. The engineers are hopeful. They say there's a chance they can get the engine operational again."

"That's great. Then I'll have a job again."

"Yes, you will."

The next words spilled out of her without her intent, making her want to cover her mouth to keep them in. "I missed you."

Putting down food halfway to his mouth, his lips curled at the corners. "I've missed you, too." He paused, then resumed eating, resolutely chewing before stopping again to speak. "I'm not sure how to do this, Mila."

Do what? She didn't voice it, wanting him to finish, afraid of what he would say. Would he say he didn't want to, couldn't, handle her being a shifter? In her mind, it always came back to that.

Shifter.

Freak.

Monster.

Outlaw.

"I want you, Mila. I like you. But I don't know how to have a shipboard romance, or a relationship with a subordinate. And with everything going on, this should be the last thing on my mind, but it's not. I think about you most of the time."

"It'll either work out or it doesn't. No use worrying about it."

He nodded and they lapsed into silence.

Of course, he knew her secret, which made the stakes much higher.

Too high.

<hr>

A klaxon went off, causing Mila to cover her ears, her heart pounding in her throat. It blared three times, then paused, then repeated. Tristan jumped up, grabbed her hand, and dragged her to her feet.

"Come on." Authority, and a twinge of fear, colored his words.

Mila tried to keep pace as he flew through the ship. It didn't take long for her to realize they were heading for the bridge. "What's going on?" she asked between breaths.

"Imminent attack."

"What? I don't understand."

"Comms were down, are down. We needed a warning system. Three notes means imminent attack."

"Who signaled it? I thought it was an automated system."

"We tweaked it, wired it to the radar console. And a few other places."

She nodded, but he didn't see. She couldn't keep up with him and several feet now separated them. Her heart pounded, but a smile also crossed her face. *Oh, we're so dead.*

She skidded onto the bridge, slightly less graceful than Tristan, who immediately started barking orders. She ran to the pilot's chair, testing the systems, looking, hoping.

They had sub-space, but no propulsion. "Do we have weapons?" She looked over her shoulder. No one sat at the weapons consoles, so no. *Shit.* "Can we get propulsion? Any propulsion?"

"Engineers are working on it. They'll do what they can. They know the drill," Tristan said.

Good thing, because she didn't.

She sat, waiting, her fingers twitching over the controls, her breath shaking with the need to do something, anything. She tested propulsion again. Nothing. "How far out?"

"Couple minutes based on current speeds."

Mila nodded, crossing her fingers the engineers could manage a miracle.

CHAPTER TWENTY-SEVEN

*M*ila felt a rumble and hoped it wasn't the engine room blowing up again. She checked. "Yes!" She dropped the ship into sub-space, watching as it distorted everything around her, bouncing in her seat.

Come on.

Mila urged the ship to crawl forward, not wanting to overtax the engines. She feared what would happen if she did what her entire body was screaming to do. "How close now?"

"Almost visual range, ma'am."

Mila looked around and smiled, seeing their salvation at the same time she caught sight of the first ships in her periphery. She slowly increased speed, steering the ship toward her destination. She watched as the ships got closer, closer. When would they be within firing range?

"Trace? What are you doing?" Tristan said, anxiety in his voice.

"Something they can't."

She felt a small shudder in the controls and someone said, "Impact." She picked up speed.

"May Trace, what the hell do you think you're doing? Those are gas-rings."

"And they're too small to survive gas-rings, captain. We can."

"Don't do this, Trace. The ship's old, has taken substantial damage. We might not survive it either."

"But we definitely won't survive another attack, sir."

She sped up, grinning as Tristan cursed under his breath behind her.

As she approached the gas-rings, visibility decreased. She knew she'd hit them when a large rock smacked into the shield in front of her. Visibility growing worse, she slowed as rocks clanged against their outer hull.

You couldn't avoid rocks in a gas-ring. The gas cloud made visibility all but nothing. The rock and ice from the planet's rings were like land mines in a minefield. You knew they were there, but you had no idea where. All you could do was cross your fingers and pray.

After a few minutes of pinging and clanging noises, she felt confident the POS could manage. It had maintained structural integrity. But now what?

She slowed further, but the controls felt weird for a moment, then a red light gleamed on the console. "Shit." She slammed her hand down. "Goddamn it." She leaned back and sighed. They were dead in the water again.

"M—May. What the hell were you thinking? You could have

gotten us all killed!" Tristan came to his feet, chiding himself for almost calling her Mila.

She turned in her seat and glared. She'd caught that slip.

"If I hadn't done what I did, sir, we'd all be dead. We couldn't outrun those fighters and, like you said, we wouldn't survive the impact. We had a better chance against the gas-rings."

He sputtered, fists locked at his sides, but kept quiet. His jaw clenched as he took in slow breaths, determined to be calm, professional, when he opened his mouth again. "Okay, I need an all systems check. We still have no comms so spread out. Report back here."

"Yes, captain," everyone chorused as they fled the room.

"Not you," he said, teeth still clenched.

Mila sank back in her seat, glaring at him again. "You almost called me Mila. In front of everyone." She waved her hand, indicating those that had already left.

"I know. I'm sorry."

"Sorry isn't good enough," she said as she stood. "I've told you this before, Tristan. You hold my life in your hands." By the time she'd finished speaking, she'd closed the gap between them. "No one can know."

"I know," he said, cupping her cheek.

She raised an eyebrow at him, patting his hand before moving out of his touch. "What should we do? You have them determining the status of the ship. Kind of leaves us with nothing to do."

He smiled. "I could think of a few things."

She shook her head and swatted at him. "Perv."

"Tango leader, please advise."

"Stand by, Tango one. Will inform when a new strategy has been formulated." He closed the comm and resisted the urge to rub his face. Of course, he couldn't. Not with the suit and helmet on.

The ship had been badly damaged. It had already sustained one attack and he saw evidence of further damage on another part of the ship. That pilot had to be crazy to enter a gas-ring. In perfect condition, that ship was too old to enter safely.

Granted, none of their fighters could enter either, even in the best condition. They weren't durable enough, large enough, and certainly were too damned fast. Gas-rings had zero visibility. You couldn't see the obstacles before they hit you, destroying your craft.

At this point, they wouldn't find the ship without a homing beacon.

"Tango unit, flank the gas-ring. I want full coverage. They have to leave some time."

CHAPTER TWENTY-EIGHT

*M*ila yawned, stretching out at the pilot's console. Why couldn't they have waited for reports in his office? It was a hell of a lot more comfortable.

Tristan had worn a steady path in the center of the bridge from his pacing.

"Would you relax, Tristan?"

"Relax," he said, whirling on her. "You think I should relax? My ship is dead in the water. Again. There is an entire fleet of fighters outside that gas-ring. Again. I'm not sure we can survive long enough to run out of power. Again."

"Relax, Tristan. Or you'll have a heart attack long before any of that happens, or whatever other dastardly fate you've decided we'll meet."

He glared, but it didn't look like his heart was in it. "Sorry."

"No sweat. I get it. These aren't exactly the best of circumstances here. It tends to bring out the best and worst in people."

"It only seems to bring out the best in you."

"And you're any different?"

"Do you think I've handled any of this well?"

"You've done the best you can, the best anyone could have expected." Mila saw movement past him. "I think that's our first report."

He waited, listening as his unit continued to report on the quarter hour, reporting back no change. All of a hundred fidgets and gestures had gone through his head as he sat there, but the bulky suit prevented them, driving him half mad with the urge to *do* something.

Then, his console lit up and he touched it, bringing up a map display. A homing beacon.

"Tango unit. Sending you coordinates now. Go to the edge of the gas-ring and disembark. We'll infiltrate in the suits."

CHAPTER TWENTY-NINE

"Brought you food again." Mila waved it under Tristan's nose.

He'd started supervising the repairs in the engine room again. She watched as a swarm of men raced around the room putting things to rights.

"Do you think they can manage?"

"Before? Maybe. Now? Probably not. They'd pieced the engine together before the second attack, but now even more of it's damaged."

"Sorry," she said, her head falling. If only she could have come up with another way. Something, anything.

"It's not your fault," he said, grabbing her shoulder.

Well, that's a change from his earlier assertions. "Still, I feel like I could have done better. Like maybe if I'd stopped sooner, the engines wouldn't have conked out the second time. I don't know."

"You respond well in a crisis, Mila. Don't ever doubt yourself on that front. I wouldn't have wanted anyone else at the helm today."

"Thanks. Now eat."

"Yes, ma'am."

<hr>

It was slow going through the gas-rings. The suits had limited propulsion, and they had to feel their way blindly around boulders and chunks of ice, using the homing beacon to guide them to their target.

A little farther and he saw his first glimpse of the *Orleans* since it had disappeared into the gas. Just an outline showed through the thick fog, but he saw it.

Success was within reach.

<hr>

One of the unfortunate tasks after a strike was checking the outer hull for damage. It couldn't be done from inside the ship when most of her systems were down, which meant someone had to check it visually. Outside.

Him. Him and about a dozen others. He traveled across the surface, tools magnetically clamped to his belt. He found a spot that looked weak, made his way toward it and got in close. *Better safe than sorry.* He pulled out a patch and a tool, and melted the patch in place.

He moved on, looking up around him.

It really was quite beautiful inside a gas-ring. He'd never imagined he might see something like this someday. Sure, he'd expected to have adventures, see the universe, but mostly those had been pipe dreams. It was rare to experience something that struck his heart with wonder like this.

The surrounding space exploded in colors like an aurora, but with the faintest hint of something in it. Depending on the planet, could be ice or rocks. Either could destroy a ship if hit just right.

Still, beautiful.

He furrowed his brow, looking closer at an odd-shaped rock not far off. *It's getting closer.* He squinted, remembering to lift the solar shield. *Definitely, odd shape.* It continued closer, and he wondered what could have set it adrift.

Oh, shit, he thought, as the thing took a recognizable form. Right before the projectile pierced his brain.

***

He crept to the airlock, reaching for the controls to the left of the door. Fortunately, the ship was old, and lacked any recognizable security measures. He just pressed a few buttons and the outer hatch opened. He went in, waiting for a few of his unit to follow before closing the outer hatch and re-pressurizing.

Air hissed into the room and a light turned from red to green above their heads. He nodded to his men and opened the inner hatch. His men moved out, guns at the ready. Their first priority would be taking out any hostiles quietly. He didn't expect much of the crew to be armed.

Once they were through, he sealed the way out and motioned them to a closet to the right. One dragged a man with him, having snapped his neck. They entered the small room and removed their suits.

"Second wave, ready for entry."

She checked the time. He still wasn't back yet. "Hey, John."

A man holding his helmet under his suit-clad arm turned to her. "Yeah, boss?"

"Put your helmet on again. Someone's missing."

"Ah, come on, boss. Max never reports on time. You know that."

"It's not Max. And we're missing a suit, too. Someone's still out there."

He nodded, putting his helmet back on. "Yes, boss."

John made his way back from the suit room absently. Turning a corner, he looked up, and dashed back out of sight. "Shit," he hissed. He looked over his shoulder. Nothing should be around that corner. *Think, damn it.* There had been six men. All dressed in uniforms. Not their uniforms, though.

He slipped slowly, and hopefully quietly, back the way he'd come, hoping he could alert someone before it was too late. His suit didn't help. Much more streamlined than the original space suits back in the 20th century, they were still bulky and designed for space. They tended to clomp their way along the flooring, making him curse every step he took.

Clomp, clomp, clomp.

He reached the suit room and pushed the door open, fearing he'd gone too slow, fearing they would shoot him in the back any second. *Come on. Just a bit farther.* He reached the door, opened it, and closed it behind him, leaning against it with a relieved breath.

He removed his helmet and assessed the people in the room. None were armed. "We've got intruders."

CHAPTER THIRTY

*S*ince their uniforms weren't designed for this ship, they'd had to "borrow" from the crew. Not being able to walk, having no leverage to use, could devastate their chances. Even firing guns would drive them helplessly in the opposite direction.

All dressed in the uniform of the USS *Orleans*, they traveled swiftly, grabbing people and snapping their necks with quick twists. The bodies sagged, then they dragged them to the first available space before moving on. They advanced with precision and determination, like a wave eradicating the ship of vermin.

She slipped out the back of the suit room, grateful for the second exit. Many rooms on this ship didn't have two doors. Most of the men were still removing their suits. They'd told her to run. Bring word to somebody, anybody. Damn, what she wouldn't give for a working comm right now.

She raced on, her mind consumed with the idea that the

people she'd just left behind might already be dead. They had no weapons. They were still in their suits. They couldn't escape.

Why are the corridors so quiet? There's no one here. She passed one crossing after the next, but she encountered no one. Over the last few days, she'd gotten used to people running around like chickens with their heads cut off. Now? When the engines were down and the ship's fate lay in the balance, uncertain? No one.

She turned a corner and bumped into someone. "Oh."

She stepped back, looked up, and *snap*.

"I need a break." The engineer sat, wondering if he could maybe catch a smoke. He'd snuck some cigarettes onto the ship. Technically, they weren't allowed, but he liked to light one up in the airlock, then let the smoke drift out into space once he'd closed the hatch. "I'll be right back."

He had his favorite airlock. Not far from the engine room. He always took a shortcut. Through a back corridor, it emptied out in front of the airlock in question. He rushed, his nerves on edge from too many hours on the job and not enough nicotine. He should have gone on the patch. Then he could have at least not had nicotine withdrawal.

A bit farther and he exited onto the hallway. He walked to the next door, a supply closet. He kept his smokes in there. Best not to keep them anywhere they could be found on a spot inspection of his bunk. He opened the door and a body fell out.

"Fuck!"

Tristan watched, feeling half asleep. Mila had gotten bored a while ago and had been entertaining herself with snacks she'd stuffed in her pants pockets. He found himself fascinated by the plethora of hiding places she'd come up with.

An irate voice shocked him out of his stupor. "No smoking in the engine room! Where the hell did you get that?"

"Oh, fuck off, man. I'm not in the mood."

Tristan looked over at the smoking man and stormed his way.

The man saw him immediately. "Yeah, you were the one I wanted to see."

He didn't sound sarcastic, which gave Tristan pause. "What did you want to see me about? And put that damn cigarette out."

"Not a chance in hell, cap. I need this."

Mila, finally intrigued by events, had reached his side.

"What did you have to say, then?"

"We got trouble. Found a body. And space suits."

CHAPTER THIRTY-ONE

Chaos erupted as everyone panicked around them, a cacophony filling the room. Tristan barked some word made undecipherable as it echoed off the walls. Everyone quieted, stilled.

"That's better. You, you, and you." He pointed to several people about the room, including Mila. "Come with me. The rest of you, lock this room down. Weld that door shut if you have to. No one gets in until the situation is settled. Do you hear me?"

"Yes, captain." The response rattled off the walls.

Tristan turned and ran.

"Where're we going?"

"Security offices. We need guns."

Mila prayed the entire time, even though her faith had always been a bit lacking. Not really an atheist, her faith had evaporated from disuse. But she prayed now.

There were men on board. Mila imagined them in full body

armor and carrying massive assault rifles. She imagined them shooting everyone on sight.

She shook her head and tried to keep up with Tristan and the rest of them, but she fell behind.

No wonder. Their legs are like a foot longer than mine.

She pushed herself a little harder, wishing she could just add some height or muscle and be done with it, but no. That would probably get her killed. Not worth the risk.

They reached the security offices and she skidded to a halt, slamming into the back of the guy before her.

"Watch it," he growled.

"So-rry," she said under her breath.

She waited to enter, looking in all directions around her, expecting bad guys to jump from the shadows. But there was no one. *Odd.* The others slipped in, allowing her to do so as well. She closed the door with relief.

"Arm up, everyone. Avery. Where's Avery?"

"Here, captain," the head of security said from his office door.

"Set the alarm."

"What for, captain?"

"Intruders. We're under attack."

He nodded and disappeared into his office. After a moment, the alarm went off. A single klaxon repeated over and over again.

"Will everyone know what to do?" she asked, wanting to smack herself for her own stupidity. Of course, they wouldn't. She didn't know. How the hell could anyone else?

"No, but the people who need to will. Let's move out," he said, handing a rifle to Mila.

She looked down at it, wrapping her fingers around the stock.

"You know how to use this?"

Mila shrugged. "Yes and no."

He glared at her. "That's not an answer."

She glared back. "It's not rocket science, Tristan. Sure, I've never used a gun before. Doesn't mean I don't know how."

"Just don't shoot any of my men."

"Scout's honor. I'll only shoot you. How's that?"

They marched through the ship, directing everyone they saw to the canteen. It only had one entrance. Large and easily defensible. For now, they had to lock down anywhere the intruders could permanently damage the ship.

"But what if they have explosives?" Mila whispered, keeping time with Tristan's steps beside her. He'd elected to take up the rear with Mila.

"Then we're screwed. Most of our security force is spread out around the ship investigating. Our forces are too thin and my first priority is getting my people safe, getting this ship safe."

The three most vital areas on the ship were the engine room, generator/life support room, and the bridge. They'd split into two groups, each responsible for sealing one of the remaining rooms. Tristan's group was heading to the bridge.

They reached their destination without resistance. Mila let out a relieved breath as Tristan busied himself with locking the controls and the others guarded the door.

"Done!"

He stood and they headed out. All of them exited and Tristan sealed the door.

"Will that stop them?" she asked.

"No, but it'll slow them down. The lock on the consoles should stop them, hopefully. Unless they have a better-than-average code breaker."

"So, what's the plan?"

"Retreat to the mess hall and form one."

The room had an air of panic, fear, and pain. Relegated to the fringes, Mila sat back and observed as Tristan, Avery, and Braddock put their heads together to formulate a plan. Her heart thumped in her chest as her senses, heightened from adrenal responses, pulled in every little detail. The tang of nervous sweat, the sharp smell of blood, the wide, shocked eyes, people pacing to keep from going mad, people too afraid to pace.

Chaos. Chaos reigned around her and she looked on it with a morbid fascination. Her surroundings cast a surreal landscape of human panic, distracting her from what lay out there.

She looked back at Tristan, who gave her a smile that couldn't mask the grimace beneath. He went back to his planning, leaving her to her thoughts.

How many are out there?

How many are dead?

Have they gotten into the engine room, the bridge, the generator room?

Can we stop them?

Will we complete our mission?

Will we make it out alive?

CHAPTER THIRTY-TWO

"*T*ango four, what's your status?" he called over the radio.

"Engine room still secure, sir."

"Well, bust it down, damn it!" he yelled, his voice echoing off the walls. This was taking too damn long.

"We've tried, sir. The doors are welded shut."

"Well, find something to cut it down."

"On it, sir."

"Tango nine, what's your status?"

"We've breached the bridge, but the controls are locked, sir. We need a hacker."

"Tango eight, report to the bridge." Too damned long. Should have been in and out. Covert infiltration. How the hell did they get spooked?

"Yes, sir."

"Tango twelve, have you found the rest of them?"

"No, sir. Still looking."

"Pick up the pace." He looked up and walked to one of his men kneeling on the floor. "What's the prognosis?"

"No go, sir. We need a cutting tool on this door as well."

"It doesn't look welded." He looked closer, but saw no evidence of melted metal at the seams.

"It's not, sir. Historically, life support is the most secure room on a ship. Can't risk losing life support and, with it, the entire crew. Door's locked, and from what I remember of this model, there are forty-six bolts holding this door into a reinforced steel frame. It would be easier to go through the wall."

"Well, can we? Is that a feasible option?"

"It would take hours to cut through the wall, sir."

"And the locks can't be hacked?"

The man shook his head. "Once the door bolts are in place, the door can only be opened from the inside. Those locks have no external controls."

He turned and walked away, refusing to vent his bad mood on his men. This was taking too damned long.

"Ready?" Tristan looked out at his men, every security person who made it back, plus Mila and Braddock. He hoped this was the right choice. When discussing it with his men, it seemed logical, smart, essential. But the idea of sending them out against an unknown enemy, with unknown weaponry, training, and numbers, made him ill at ease.

And bringing Mila with them made him even more so, though he suspected Mila would have verbally handed him his balls if he'd suggested she stay behind. She gave him a reassuring smile and cocked her rifle, angling it in her grip like a pro before winking at him with a smirk. He shook his head.

I hope I'm doing the right thing. "Move out."

Avery unlocked the door and men filed out in pairs, taking off in each direction as quiet as mice. Tristan and Mila left last.

"Lock it tight. Don't let anyone in."

The person nodded and he turned to Mila, motioning her to follow him. The door banged shut and she winked at him again before closing her eyes.

"Mila?" he whispered. He wondered why the hell she would close her eyes at a time like this, but then his mouth gaped as she changed. Her musculature got more pronounced and claws extended from her fingers. And he suspected that was only the tip of the iceberg.

She opened her eyes and smirked. Light reflected back and he furrowed his brow.

"Tapetum," she whispered.

"Huh?"

She smiled. "A mirror-like structure at the back of the eye. Reflects light. Boosts night vision."

"Oh. Preparing for battle?"

"You betcha."

"What if someone else sees you?"

"What are they going to see? Only the claws are unequivocal. All the rest? A person could kid themselves into thinking they remembered wrong."

"And you thought it was a risk for me to call you Mila."

"It is a risk. So is this. But I'll risk the possibility of being exposed over the possibility of being dead."

"Of course."

"Now, let's go. We've got some bad guys to beat."

"Don't worry. Everything'll be fine," he said, trying to reassure the woman beside him. He'd never seen her before, but many people here had never met before. Well, they said crises were bonding experiences…

"Don't worry? Everything'll be fine?" Her voice escalated on each sentence. "Are you fucking nuts?"

Her voice reached a shrill resonance that made him cover his ears. "Easy, woman. Easy."

"I will *not* take it easy. We are in *shit* here. *Deep* shit. There's a good chance we're never going back home." She burst into tears, mumbling things he couldn't quite understand.

"Do you have family back home?"

She nodded.

"Me too. Two girls." He pulled a photo from a pocket of his uniform to show her. "Couple of hell raisers. Both in college. Costing me a fortune."

She laughed, her tears of a moment ago giving a fragile character to the expression.

"What about you?"

"Newly married," she whispered, her voice so soft he could barely hear.

"That's nice. Wonderful."

She nodded, her eyes cast down at the photograph in his hand as she sniffed. "I'm Tira Santos."

"Nice to meet you, Tira."

Bam.

The room quieted, hearing something slam against the door, metal on metal. All motion ceased as they waited, but for what he had no clue. He imagined not a person breathed in those moments. Tira tensed, staring at the door, ready to bolt.

Bam.

They jumped, the second rap taking them out of their shock. People looked at one another, renewed panic in their eyes.

Bam.

This couldn't be good.

<hr>

Mila moved like a jungle cat. Graceful, quiet, deadly. Tristan had a hard time pulling his eyes from her as they stalked down the hallways. And so, he kept behind her.

She lifted her hand and they both stopped. Her body slipped to the side in a fluid wave, hugging up to the wall like a cat begging for attention. She slinked against the wall, soundless, coming to the intersection, rifle strapped across her body.

Her hand whipped out around the corner and spun a male form into view. Large red gouges crossed the enemy's face as she lowered him to the ground, dead. She pointed toward the corner, then signaled with three fingers. There were three more.

He nodded, waiting to follow her, rifle at the ready. She turned the corner right before him and flew at the intruders, slamming them up against the wall and onto the floor with speed and precision. He tracked every man she wasn't engaging with his rifle, ready to take him down if he thought for a second he was a danger to her.

He didn't like these tactics, but he understood them. The longer they went without the enemy knowing they were hunting them, the better.

When the last of them lay bleeding on the floor, he dropped his rifle to his side and grabbed a body, dragging it to the nearest doorway. He opened the door and dumped it inside.

"Here," Mila whispered.

He turned and took the radio from her hand. "Good idea." He clipped it to his belt and grabbed the next body.

When they had stowed the last body, Tristan motioned Mila toward a room to the right. She nodded, and they went inside, closing themselves into the darkness.

"Why are we hiding?"

"Because I want to listen to their radio and I don't want to do it while we're hunting. The last thing we need is them tipped off when the radio kicks on."

"But wouldn't they just think it was another of their guys?"

"Maybe. Maybe not. I'd rather not take the chance."

They waited in silence. After a while, Tristan started counting the number of times Mila sighed while waiting.

Thirty-six.

Maybe the team was operating under radio silence. Had they

stopped using the radios once they arrived on board, afraid the signals would be tracked, intercepted? If the enemy was smart, they would.

Thirty-seven.

But then, if they had any inkling how badly damaged the *Orleans* truly was, they would know it wouldn't matter anyway. Right that moment, they couldn't track shit.

Thirty-eight.

He chuckled to himself and thought Mila might kick his ass if she knew he was laughing at her. But he thought it was cute. She wasn't a patient person.

Thirty-nine.

The radio came to life, a distorted voice echoing off the walls after the dead silence. "Tango leader, this is Tango twelve. We've found the stragglers."

Mila's hand grabbed onto his thigh, holding on for dear life. He tried to look at her in the darkness, but saw nothing. Reaching out, he grabbed her hand and squeezed gently.

"Tango twelve, how many have you got?"

"Unclear, sir. They're holed up in what we assume is the mess hall. Door's locked, but we think we can breach."

Mila's grip tightened, this time claws digging into his leg. He patted her hand, trying to signal her to loosen up, to let go.

"Good."

Tristan crossed his fingers, hoping to hear more as he grimaced under Mila's herculean grip.

"Teams, report in with a status update."

Yes!

"Tango four. We've found a cutting tool. Working on the engine room now."

"ETA?"

"Unclear, sir."

Where the hell did they find a cutting tool? All the tools should have been in the engine room.

"Tango nine?"

"We're working on the data encryption, but Tango eight says the encryptions are much newer than this ship. It'll take a while."

They waited in silence, but no other news came through.

"I guess they haven't found the life support room," Mila said.

"Or their leader is overseeing that part of the operation and doesn't need an update."

Forty.

"Care to let go of my leg, love?"

"Sorry!" she squeaked, releasing her death grip.

His leg started to throb around the sharp pain of the punctures. "Come on. Let's go."

They left the room and Mila sucked in a breath as soon as they had better lighting. "Oh, I'm so sorry. How bad does it hurt?"

Tristan smiled. "Not so bad." He rubbed the spot, eyeing the small red dots that speckled his uniform leg. At least they weren't bleeding.

"Where to first?"

He tapped his fingers against his leg, thinking. It would take hours for them to breach the engine room or break the encryptions on the bridge. The door to the life support room was the most secure. "Back to the mess hall."

Mila nodded and they retraced their steps back the way they'd come.

CHAPTER THIRTY-THREE

The sounds outside the door only grew worse, the people inside nervously staring the door down or cowering in corners. Many of them weren't combat trained. None of them had weapons.

Then the noises outside the door grew to a frenzy, pounding, slamming, cracks of gunfire, screams. Silence.

A collective stillness overcame the room. Was it over? Were they safe? What happened to the men outside the room?

And what made them scream like that?

"Where to next?" Mila asked as she dragged the last body out of sight. She scanned the hallway, but she couldn't wipe away all traces of what had occurred with nothing more than a dragged body. Blood smeared the walls, the floor. Droplets of the red fluid hung in the air, creating an eerie tableau, playing silent tribute to the carnage.

Mila found herself oddly fascinated by the drops, wanting to touch them like she had bubbles as a kid. She raised her hand to it, but resisted the urge to touch.

"Engine room."

She turned and nodded, giving one final, mournful glance at the spectacle behind her. "Coming."

Progress was slow through the halls. They couldn't afford to be detected. At each intersection, Mila slowed, listened. With how much she'd heightened her senses, she could pick up a heartbeat at a hundred yards. Still, sound carried on the ship and their shoes weren't designed for stealth.

She waved him through yet another intersection. Tristan followed, obeying her every order. Mila smiled to herself, enjoying the reversal of roles. She held her hand up, signaling to stop. Listened, counted. She wiggled five fingers in the air. Five combatants.

From her memory of the area, they were in front of the engine room doors. She heard what sounded like a saw? Several of them paced back and forth, based on the impact of their boots on the flooring, but it was hard to tell how many. One she could only hear by breathing and heartbeat. Lounging? She focused harder. No, seated. That would give them an advantage, a slight one.

She leaned back against the wall, tugging on her hair as she thought. At that distance, she couldn't eliminate the enemy quietly. Were there other, closer, intersections they could use? She motioned to Tristan, ordering him to move away from the corner. He nodded and they retreated, finding their way to a room that offered a small noise barrier.

Yet again, they were in perfect darkness.

"What is it?" Tristan said.

"Is there a hallway that empties out closer?"

"No. That's it."

"Damn." She shook her head. "We're gonna have to use the guns."

Mila nodded to herself and left the room, slipping back to the corner. Her gaze drifted to Tristan, who already had his gun at the ready. She hefted her gun up as well and nodded before mouthing a countdown. Three. Two. One.

They turned the corner in unison like a couple badasses from an action flick. The loud cracks of the rifles echoed off the walls, hurting her sensitive ears. She gritted her teeth as she held the automatic's trigger, sending a spray of bullets down the hallway. Their opponents fell before they could even start in surprise.

The echoing silence was almost as bad. She lowered her rifle to her side, lifting her hand to her temple to rub at the headache growing there. She groaned, closing her eyes against the pain.

"You all right?" Tristan asked, grasping her shoulder.

She nodded and closed her eyes again when the movement sent sharp shock-waves through her brain.

"Headache?"

"Yeah," she whispered, afraid more sound would only make it worse.

"I'm not surprised. This isn't exactly the ideal place to fire a gun. I've got one myself." He walked ahead, tossing the rifle against his shoulder. "Come on. We've got work to do."

She mouthed okay and followed him to dispose of the bodies once again, wondering if there was a point now.

As she stood over the bodies, a radio crackled to life. "What was that? Was that gunfire I heard?"

Tristan reached over and grabbed the radio, bringing it to his mouth. "This is Tango four. We had a confrontation at the engine room. The threat has been neutralized."

They listened with bated breath, the silence filling them with dread.

Finally, the radio squawked once more. "Roger that, Tango four."

It died once more and they let out a collective sigh.

"That was close," Mila said, feeling weak with relief.

He lowered the radio, some small detail nagging at him. Something was wrong.

"Sir?"

He looked up. "Yeah?"

"Is everything all right, sir?"

"I'm not sure. Go check on the engine room."

"Yes, sir." The soldier dashed off, disappearing from sight around the corner.

He looked to the slow but steady progress on the door, then at the radio. Tango four had sounded… odd. Different. Wrong.

CHAPTER THIRTY-FOUR

*M*ila wondered what the other teams were doing as they reached the bridge. Had any of them confronted intruders? Had they gotten a radio?

The bridge was another strategically problematic place. The door was closed. No element of surprise this time. And the consoles were too far into the room. No hand-to-hand either.

As they got ready to breach, Mila caught movement around the corner, her ears still ringing too badly to hear someone approach. She dropped to a knee and raised her rifle, preparing to fire.

Tristan grabbed the barrel and lifted it quickly, keeping her from firing. She let out a breath and shifted away any traces of visible changes. Avery and Braddock. She flipped them the bird and they smiled back at her before stationing themselves at the other side of the door.

Tristan did the signaling this time. They had no idea how many men stood beyond that door, so Mila was grateful for the added support. She stood and kept her gun at the ready as she waited out Tristan's countdown, following along in her head.

Three. Two. One. Go.

She entered last, the four of them fanning out in a fraction of a second. Once again, the concussions echoed off the walls, making her blink with each sharp pop that accosted her ears.

Bodies fell, but not without a fight.

"Fuck," she said as a bullet slammed into her arm, sending her into the wall at her back. She tried to return fire, but couldn't control the gun with only one good arm, so she retreated to the hallway, praying the others came out unscathed.

The shots continued to echo in her head long after they stopped firing.

"May?" Tristan called from the other room, her ears so messed up she heard it as a whisper. She didn't hear him enter the hall and kneel in front of her.

When did I end up on the floor?

"You're shot." He pulled at her shirt, checking the wound.

"It's fine. It'll heal."

"Easy. You don't have to yell."

She hadn't realized she'd been yelling. She tried for a normal volume this time. "Sorry."

"Is she okay?" Avery said, exiting the bridge.

"Fine," she reiterated. "Perfectly fine. See? Barely bleeding." She poked at it, not bothered by the pain that flared like a good friend at the pressure. "Can we get going? We've still got bad guys to take out. We know there's at least one more group at life support."

"I like her," Avery said with a huge grin on his face.

Braddock glared at him. Well, he would never be a fan of hers. So be it.

She pushed to her feet. "Let's go."

Mila kept to the back now. She wouldn't be much use. Her head was splitting so much she felt like she could barely keep her eyes open. Just walking was giving her a migraine and she'd long gotten rid of the enhanced senses. Even her normal senses were exacerbating it.

And with her arm out of commission, she couldn't fire the gun. She glared at Avery and Braddock. Without them there, she might have been useful. Claws were better than nothing.

She could have also healed her arm if the two bozos hadn't been there. Mila rubbed her wound, digging in until gating cleared her head a little. Better her arm than her head.

Tristan turned toward her, giving her reassuring looks as they headed to the life support room. Hopefully, that was the last of them. How many more could there be?

After the second report of gunfire, he knew they needed to change tactics. He paced the hall, considering his options. Go after the enemy? But he already had men roaming the halls looking for stragglers. Call all his men back to his location? No, if Tango four's report was false, they had a radio now. The enemy could listen in on their communications.

A crack of running feet against the magnetic tiles reached his ear and he turned. The man he'd sent to the engine room rounded the corner and raced up to him. "Sir. They're dead. All of them. I found them in a room near the engine room."

"Then we assume the men on the bridge are also dead."

The man's eyes bulged, but he kept quiet.

He continued his pacing. The situation had gotten out of hand. This would require a decisive action. "Everyone. Stop what you're doing. We're heading back to the airlocks."

CHAPTER THIRTY-FIVE

They reached the corner closest to the life support room and stopped, Tristan giving orders through hand signals. Mila leaned against the wall, ignoring them and pressing even harder into her gunshot wound, causing it to bleed again. She watched as the slow flow of blood stained her sleeve a little more.

They took off as one, guns at the ready, but there were no shots. She pushed off from the wall and snuck her head around the corner. "What's going on?"

"I don't know," Tristan said, turning in a circle as if seeing the scene from all angles would make it make more sense.

"They retreated? Went back to their ships?" Braddock asked hopefully.

"Doubt it," Mila said, swaggering into the hallway behind them. "They probably have something nasty up their sleeves."

"But what could be nastier? These are the three strategic weaknesses of the ship. They haven't managed any of them."

Mila looked up at him, alarmed. "The airlocks. If they can trip the airlocks…"

"Everyone on board would suffocate," he finished.

"But they could be at any of them," Avery chimed in.

"Well, how many are there?" Mila started pacing, thinking.

"Too many for us to cover individually," Tristan said with a sigh.

"Well, do we know which airlock they came from?"

They looked at each other, growing panic setting the mood.

"By the engine room!" Tristan exclaimed. "That's where the suits were found."

"Well, let's go."

They took off, no longer caring about stealth. If they didn't get there in time, everyone would die.

***

Mila lost ground, not being able to keep up with the longer strides of her companions. Her lungs burned, her legs burned, her arm burned and throbbed, her head throbbed. She felt like her body would conk out at any moment. *Not now!* She tried to concentrate through the haze brought on by her headache. Shifters had unbelievable control over their bodies. Not just changing tissue, which allowed them to heal, but changing how their bodies functioned.

Like right now, she could really use some adrenaline and endorphins. Her head fought her, skull splitting with the pain from abused senses. Mila focused and gradually, her body rewarded her. She sped up as the pain lessened, became manageable.

She still couldn't close the gap, though. Not without doing something noticeable. But she kept on, using the pounding rhythm of their feet as a hypnotic metronome to keep her going almost effortlessly. Her mind cleared for the first time in quite a while.

They had to get to that airlock.

Tristan pointed. The suit room must be up ahead. They angled toward it, but Mila had other plans. She couldn't let the enemy get to that airlock. Suits would only slow them down. The others ran into the suit room, preparing for the inevitable.

She ran straight past and looked back. *Yes!* They didn't notice. She reached the end of the corridor and enhanced her hearing, listening for the enemy. She heard them putting on suits. Not all of them, though. Some must have been playing sentry. She returned her hearing to normal. She didn't want a repeat occurrence if she had to open fire.

Mila prepared herself, taking deep breaths. *Remember. Don't hold your breath. If the airlock opens, don't hold your breath or you'll die. They'll have ninety seconds to rescue you if you don't hold your breath.*

She shifted what she needed. Speed. Strength. Claws. And turned the corner at a dead run. Her feet pounded on the metallic plates. Otherwise, she didn't make a sound, charging like a train on its tracks toward the sentry who turned, raising his weapon. He didn't get to fire as she jumped, landing on his chest and knocking him to the ground, her claws buried between his ribs.

Mila took a fraction of a second, the blink of an eye, to reassess the situation, picking her next target from the movements he made. *That one's lifting a gun.* She charged again, raking her hand across him and throwing him into the wall. After that, each of her movements was fluid, like a ballet, one attack flowing into the next. One man after another went down. Claps of gunfire sounded, but everything missed, her movements too erratic to predict, to follow.

Then, a warning sounded, causing her head to come up. "Oh shit." A single crack of a gun echoed off the walls and the bullet knocked her back, stunning her for a moment. But the bullet meant nothing. The injury meant nothing. The doors were opening.

Mila raced to the control panel, ignoring the rest of the enemy who still had weapons and fight in them. *No!* She ran, feeling like a tortoise could run faster. She wouldn't make it. She couldn't make it. She had to make it.

The alarm gained intensity and the light above the door changed from green to red. *No!* She grabbed the man at the console, shoving him from the panel, but it was too late. The doors opened, and she latched onto the first thing in sight as the sharp pressure change caused by the opening tried to equalize the two systems.

Things, bodies, something flew by her as she held on for dear life. It was her life. If she let go, they might not get to her in time. Ninety seconds. In vacuum, she had ninety seconds before permanent damage ensued. She had to hold out, but she could feel her fingers slipping.

Her injured arm felt increasingly weak, unable to keep up even with the adrenaline pumping through her system. *Come on! Just hold on till they get here. All they have to do is close the outer hatch.* Her arm started to go numb, then slipped from the surface. One hand left. *Just hold on.* But black spots were starting to form over her eyes. Her other arm was starting to feel numb. *No! Just a little longer. They'll get to me!*

But that arm too gave up the fight and she sailed into space. *Try to breathe. No air. Try to breathe. Suffocating. Can't think.* She told herself to breathe. Count. How many seconds before she lost consciousness? Nine? Ten? Eleven? Lack of oxygen was making her head fuzzy. How many seconds now?

She couldn't help watching the ship's portal shrink as momentum forced her to drift farther and farther from help.

Sorry, Tristan.

CHAPTER THIRTY-SIX

Tristan ran into the room, racing to the nearest suit, expecting everyone to follow. Bodies dashed around him, stumbling and jumping as they tried to suit up in lightning speed when the suits were not designed to be donned in a rush. He'd zipped up and grabbed a helmet before he turned and realized with monumental dread that Mila wasn't there. "Oh no."

"Captain?" Avery asked.

"She didn't. She did," he said in a daze.

"Captain, what's wrong?" Braddock asked.

"M—," he said before stopping himself again from saying her real name. "May's gone ahead."

"That wasn't the plan!" Avery shouted, forgetting that the enemy was just around the corner.

He looked over. "No shit!" His heart raced even harder than when they'd run down the halls, fearing the worst, fearing they would be too late. Now, he knew he would be too late. For her.

Shots echoed down the hall, spurring them to action. They

waddled for the door, slowed by the suits that might very well save them, save everyone, if those doors opened.

Frustration built as they moved slowly down the hall, serenaded by the song of violence. *As long as those guns are firing, she's still alive.* He took little comfort in the thought.

An alarm sounded. Depressurization warning. "Helmets on! Now!"

They complied as they continued to make slow but steady progress. They would be too late. He just knew it. He couldn't fail her. He couldn't.

A second more strident alarm sounded and he felt the pull as the chamber started depressurizing. *No!* He made the corner, turned and saw Mila, holding onto the control panel with only one arm, her other dangling useless beside her.

He tried to pick up speed, but his progress was slow. *Just hold on.* He watched, breath coming in shallow, pained fits, as her fingers lost their grip. "No!" He reached out, but he still wasn't close enough. She drifted through the hatch and into space.

He jumped, hoping the force of the depressurization was greater than the magnetics. He couldn't engage the propulsion on the suit until he cleared the opening. *Hold on, Mila.*

Avery didn't bother trying to correct his captain, tell him not to chase after her. He had more important things to consider. Like closing that hatch. One life wasn't worth losing the entire ship.

He waddled to the control panel as it became harder and harder to keep his feet on the floor. Fortunately, the soles of the suits were designed to walk on the side of ships in zero gravity. He felt the pull, his upper body wanting to be drawn through the hatch, but his feet remained planted.

But he also couldn't move fast, no where near as fast as he wanted. If both feet left the ground, he would fly through that hatch just the same as Trace and the captain.

He reached the console and got to work, but something was wrong. He tried to close the inner hatch, but an error sound blared in his ears. *Come on.* He tried a different approach. Same sound, causing him to flinch. What the hell did they do to this thing? He wasn't a computer guy. What the hell did he know about fixing it?

But lives counted on him, on them, getting that hatch closed. He tried the outer hatch. The sound blared again, causing him to flinch once more. "Captain, what's your override password?" he demanded into the radio in his helmet.

"Mila," came the answer through the speaker.

Avery typed in the override password, mentally crossing his fingers, hoping it would work.

He got a new screen. *Different's good.* He resisted the urge to count the seconds. *How long does she have left?* He found a master override for the inner hatch and activated it.

The door closed, sealing with a hiss, and the constant pressure dragging him toward the entry ceased. He sighed. But it wasn't over yet.

"Do you have her, sir?"

"Almost."

Avery and Braddock waddled to the small viewing window in the hatch, knocking heads together before remembering they didn't need the helmets anymore. They took them off in unison, too concerned to even smirk at the comedy of the situation.

The captain had Trace in his arms now. She wasn't moving. How long had she been out there? Could it have been ninety seconds already? "I don't suppose you bothered to count the seconds," he said.

Braddock shook his head, matching worry decorating his face. They looked back, breath held as the captain held tight to their comrade and propelled as fast as the suit would take him toward the ship. *Come on. Come on.*

Right before the captain entered the hatch, Avery waddled back to the control panel, just in case the one in there didn't work. He wasn't taking any chances. *Come on.*

They stood in perfect stillness, waiting, praying.

Tristan waited as the outer door slowly closed. Too slow. He clutched the immobile Mila to his chest even tighter. *Don't die on me. You can't die on me.* The door closed and the second one opened.

He stumbled in and laid Mila on the ground at Braddock's feet. Tristan yanked the helmet off and ripped the top half of the suit off so fast he probably damaged it, not that he cared. He dived at Mila. He had to get her breathing again. Before it was too late.

He started CPR, knowing she would never make it to the med bay. They didn't have that much time. *Breathe, baby.* He counted silently, then checked her pulse. No heartbeat. *Don't do this.* He counted again, then went back to breathing for her. Time drew out to eternity as he alternated between breathing for her and pumping her heart for her.

Braddock had never liked Trace, but she didn't deserve to die like that. She'd proved her worth, repeatedly, above and beyond the call of duty. She was a pilot and yet she'd helped with the investigations, fought beside them.

A part of his mind whispered that she wouldn't be dead, dying, right now if she'd bothered to follow orders. But another part whispered they might all be dead if she had. Would they have closed the hatch if she hadn't run ahead? They would have gone against those men and they couldn't fight back in the suits.

He looked on with pity as the captain worked over her body. He felt stupid for not realizing how much the woman meant to his superior officer until he saw him crying over her just then.

As she took a breath, allowing them to breathe easily once more, his gaze was drawn to her hands, which curled under with that first breath. But he could have sworn they looked more like claws.

Had his mind been playing tricks on him?

CHAPTER THIRTY-SEVEN

"What happened?" Mila asked.

"You nearly died," Tristan said from beside her.

She opened her eyes and turned her head to him, too exhausted to even sit up. Sitting in a chair beside her bed, he looked as exhausted as she felt. "I gathered."

"Or maybe it's more appropriate to say you did die."

The pain in his eyes forced the next words out of her as if comforting him was as vital as breathing. "I'm sorry."

"Just don't do it again," he said with a weak smile that almost reached his eyes.

"Aye aye, captain." She tried to raise an arm in salute—sarcastically, of course—but both arms felt like they'd been nailed to the bedding.

He shook his head and reached for her hand, rubbing it soothingly. She closed her eyes and almost groaned.

"Is the danger over?"

"I don't know. I have security officers scouring the area surrounding the ship, but we haven't been able to find anything but dead bodies. We also have men guarding each of the airlocks. They won't get back on board," he said fiercely.

"Good," she said and fell back to sleep.

The next time she woke, she was alone. Her strength had returned somewhat and she could sit, even if it wore her out. She lifted herself upright, breathing heavily, letting the burn in her arms settle. She had a bandage on her right arm and another on her torso.

Jeez, I keep getting shot.

She could make out the whispering of voices outside her room, but no words.

As she breathed, her lungs felt worn, tired. Other than that and the bullet holes, she felt fine. "At least the headache's gone."

Without distractions, her mind kept flitting back to those terrible moments before she lost consciousness. Holding on for dear life. Her heart started to speed up. Losing her grip. She felt it pounding in her temples, making her breathe more rapidly. Breathing, but suffocating. Panic. She grabbed her chest as she struggled for breath. Her chest hurt.

An alarm sounded and people rushed into the room. They crowded around her as her world narrowed into a place where only escape mattered. Voices and movement surrounded her in a surreal amalgam of sensations, then everything became heavy, her heart slowing until she passed out.

When she woke again, Tristan was back.

"Heard you had a panic attack."

Amusement colored his voice, so she did the only appropriate thing. She flipped him the bird. He laughed and she looked over as he shook his head.

"Feeling better?"

"Yeah, strong as an ox." She flexed her arms like a muscle builder. "How long has it been?"

"A day or two."

She nodded, not letting it bother her how long she'd been out. "You find your bad guys yet?"

"We don't know if we found all of them, but we found their ships. Outside the gas-ring. The engineers think they can use the parts from the fighters to repair the engine. That is, if we can tow them back to the *Orleans*."

"That's good, I guess."

"You've got some friends who'd like to see you."

She smiled, a little excited. She'd forgotten her earlier fear. Not knowing who made it and who didn't.

Tristan got up and walked to the door, opening it for Luke, then Avery, Braddock, and Santos.

She laughed. "Half of them don't even like me."

"May!" Luke said, bouncing through the door and assaulting her with a hug.

She winced, his arm wrapping around her bandages like a vice. He didn't notice, but she breathed easier when he loosened up and leaned back to get a better look at her.

"You look good, considering," Luke said, winking at her playfully.

"Considering? I look damn good."

"Good to see you back in the world of the living," Avery said.

Braddock just looked at her suspiciously, like he expected her to do God only knew what. It unnerved her, causing a sinking feeling in her gut.

"What are *you* doing here, Santos?"

She shrugged. "Just checking to see how much longer I'll have the room to myself."

"But, of course."

"Of course."

They talked and caught up, reveling in their individual stories of daring deeds. Mila kept quiet. Everyone knew what she'd done. And if they didn't, she felt no need to tell them. She couldn't slip back into the shadows, but she had no intention of grabbing the spotlight either.

Eventually, Tristan started in on them about lazing about and not doing their jobs and the crowd dispersed. "You'll be all right on your own?"

"Yeah. Never better."

"No more panic attacks?"

"Probably not."

He paused, maybe because she hadn't given him the absolute assurance he wanted, but eventually leaned in, kissed her forehead, and said, "Until later."

No quantity of doctors, nurses, and miscellaneous medical personnel could keep Mila there indefinitely. Food and rest did her a world of good and soon she wanted, no needed, to flee the well-meaning medical staff. She slipped out of bed a few times. Even got as far as the door before someone would ask her what she was doing out of bed and guide her back to her "rightful" spot.

But she wasn't tired anymore. Other than two still healing holes in her, she was just fine. And she needed to move. Now.

Unfortunately, there were no real night shifts on a spaceship. No shift was lighter than the rest personnel-wise. So she couldn't just wait until a shift change or something. Or could she? Didn't shift changes tend to be somewhat chaotic? Maybe she could slip out when people were distracted.

She went back and sat on the bed, twiddling her thumbs and watching the clock tick the seconds by. *God, the med bay is so boring.* She needed to *do* something. Desperately.

She'd almost nodded off when she heard a commotion outside. People moving around, murmurs of voices. Shift change. She got up, and walked out boldly. *Better not to look suspicious.* Nobody noticed her. Of course, she'd already slipped on her somewhat ragged and bloodstained uniform. It was better than the alternative.

She turned and headed toward the exit, her heart in her throat the entire time. People bumped into her, mumbling "Excuse me" and "Sorry" as they went. *A few more feet.*

Freedom was in sight when someone called, "Hey, you're not supposed to be out of bed."

She ignored the voice, picking up her pace and pretending the person had been talking to someone else.

"Hey, wait!"

Mila shoved the doors open and made a mad dash down the hallway. She reveled in the feel of her muscles, in being able to stretch and work them, in the freedom of movement, the lack of claustrophobia.

Admittedly, she was still on a ship. It was still enclosed. But the long expanse of hallway felt enormous compared to being trapped in that bed, in that room, for days.

Her feet took her where they would and she found herself outside the engine room. She slipped in, noticing the lack of doors and the melted metal around the door frame. The engine room was still a whirlwind of activity as people tried to get the ship moving again.

This is even better than the hallway. She smiled and sat down, cherishing the vastness of the room. Everything would be all right. She just knew it.

"You're supposed to be in the med unit," Tristan said right next to her ear before sitting down beside her.

She shrugged. "And? You gonna throw me over your shoulder and drag me back there?"

"No. Feeling better, I guess?"

"I ran all the way here."

"Feeling that good, huh?"

"That good. People like me bounce back pretty quickly. And the injuries weren't really that bad."

"You were shot in the chest. Again."

"Getting to be a habit, isn't it?" She tried to joke, but the glare he gave her said he didn't appreciate it. "Sorry."

"It's all right. I'm probably not in the best of moods."

"What's wrong?"

"Besides you almost dying?"

She smiled. "Yeah, besides that."

He waved his hand in front of him. "We're still dead in the water. We don't know if all the enemy forces are dead. And I just got the final reports back from the attack."

"How bad?" She knew it had to be bad.

"We lost nearly a third of our crew."

Everything in her body seemed to sink, drain down. A third? She shook her head, trying to be professional, even though she'd never quite been in the military. She could have used that now. "Can we still man the ship?"

"I think so, but it'll be tight. You're the only surviving pilot, which will slow us down immensely."

She nodded, trying to work out in her head how many hours a day she could fly the ship safely. And trying to force out the images of the two pilots she'd only met in passing. The faces, smiles, sometimes haggard, kept flitting across her mind. "Are there any duty stations vacant?"

"A few, but that can't be helped. There's some overlap in proficiencies, but I'm still not sure we'll be fully covered in places."

She nodded again. "Maybe you should be going over personnel records. Planning out new duty rosters."

"Probably and I should be filling out KIA reports. I'm not looking forward to that."

"Do you want some help?"

The look on his face seemed hopeless. "Not now. You should get some sleep."

She rolled her eyes. "I've had enough sleep. I've been sleeping for days. What I need is something to do."

"You won't let me mope, will you?"

"Nope. Come on. We've got work to do." She dragged him to his feet and out of the engine room.

CHAPTER THIRTY-EIGHT

The following days passed too quickly, and far too slowly. There simply wasn't enough work to keep them from thinking of the crew they'd lost. It didn't help that Mila had assigned herself the task of filling out the KIA forms and uploading them into the TAT.

Mila worked across from Tristan as he planned the new duty rosters, moving people around to cover everything, which was impossible. She was the only person left on board with any piloting experience. She wondered how much longer until they reached their destination. How much farther was it?

She'd assigned herself twelve-hour shifts, much to Tristan's dismay.

"Nobody works twelve-hour shifts," he'd said.

But she wouldn't be moved. Twelve hours wasn't an unreasonable length for a shift, and it gave them an extra four hours of flight time they wouldn't have otherwise. She just hoped the engineers got the engine fully operational. If they only flew half the time *and* at a snail's pace, they would never get there.

But eventually, engineers reported to Tristan, stating the

engine was ready. They fired it up and the ship came off emergency power for the first time since she could remember. It was nice not seeing everything through dim, red light. They got comms back up and running next and she didn't even realize the temperature was back to normal. Not until Luke pointed it out, stretched in an ecstatic sprawl.

Mila had on a new, clean uniform. She'd viciously ripped off her bandages, declaring to no one in particular that she didn't need them anymore. She had a smile on her face, winked at Tristan as she passed his chair, and sauntered up to her place, ignoring the dirty look Braddock gave her.

Mila caressed the controls like a lover. *We meet again.* Sitting down felt like coming home. She'd been born to do this. She started the pre-flight checks. On some level, she registered the lack of people and it made her heart hurt. Only one communications officer instead of three, no one on radar. She could see the navigation officer straddling her seat to see both her console and the one beside her.

This trip has been hell.

When the checks were complete, she turned to Tristan. "Ready, captain."

"Then let's go."

She turned and took off, navigating out of the gas-ring and back into open sub-space.

Braddock stood at the back of the bridge, hands clasped firmly behind his back. He kept running the scene over and over again in his head. Had his eyes played tricks on him? His gaze landed suspiciously on their pilot, Trace. He admitted to himself that it didn't matter, at least at the moment, whether she was what he thought or not. Without a pilot, they would still be stuck.

He shifted his gaze away and to their captain, who stared moony-eyed at the probable shifter. He would get no aid from their captain, he was sure.

Days were long, arduous, but they reached their destination. Mila dropped the ship out of sub-space shortly before the alien world she knew so little of. Probably, she knew even less than the average person. She'd always tried to keep her nose down, and avoiding people and everything associated with them, including the news, had become second nature to her.

Her hands flew over the controls, docking the POS to the orbital space station above the planet covered in purple clouds. She felt a slight jerk as the ship locked in, giving her a stunning view of a purple planet.

"I heard it was caused by iodine gas in the upper atmosphere," Luke said.

Mila turned to him. "Really? It's stunning."

"Yeah, makes all the mess worth it, doesn't it?"

"Not really. We almost died repeatedly. I could make do without a purple sky."

He laughed, smiling at Mila, but the smile wasn't as big or bright as usual.

"So, want to go check out some aliens?"

"They probably don't appreciate people gawking at them."

"And?"

"I've got work to do," Mila said, returning to her responsibilities, even if it was an excuse. She would finish locking this POS up in a matter of minutes, but Luke didn't need to know that. "Go on ahead. I know you want to."

"All right. Later." He jumped up, slapped her on the back, and raced around the people leaving the bridge.

I'll never have that kind of energy.

After a few minutes, she'd set the stabilizers and powered down the engines. She turned around, but Tristan had already left. She hadn't realized she'd been smiling until her face fell. *He has stuff to do, silly.*

Tristan led the diplomats to the airlock, followed by a parade that included some of his own crew, most likely only coming to ogle some aliens. A small quiver ran through him as he opened the airlock, his mind flashing to Mila there, holding on for dear life, losing her grip, falling.

The doors slid open and he took a breath to calm himself, even if no one had noticed his distress. In the doorway stood a handful of aliens. Seeing them left his mind blank, his vocabulary failing him. They were alien in every sense of the word.

They made a writhing gesture he assumed was a greeting. The gesture seemed boneless, body and limbs rotating in a swirling pattern. It couldn't be matched by a human. He could only imagine an octopus being able to replicate the limb movements, but octopi don't have bodies like these things. He couldn't figure out how they stayed upright, but they did. His mind flitted to something he'd heard once, that their planet had much less gravitational pull than Earth.

He caught the diplomats bowing behind his back before they came forward, carefully speaking in choppy English. The aliens didn't understand much English, but they'd learned some and their speech organs allowed them to use a broader range of sounds than humans. Humans couldn't speak their tongue.

The aliens spoke up, speaking in a series of guttural tones and clicks. The diplomats replied in English, thanking them for a warm welcome before filing past him. He watched as the reduced gravity of the space station had its effect on them, lightening their steps, causing them to float just a little as they bounced along. The airlock slid shut behind them.

Now, to wait.

CHAPTER THIRTY-NINE

"*B*ack to work, everyone," Tristan barked as he turned. "Nothing to see here."

Someone laughed, but they drifted off. He walked through the halls, making his way back to the bridge. When he got there, he stood in the doorway, watching Mila stare out the windows at the planet below.

"Beautiful, isn't it?"

She jumped. "Jesus, Tristan."

"Sorry." He crossed the bridge and sat in the seat beside her.

"It is beautiful, but so is Earth."

"Yeah." Right about now, he wanted nothing more than to be back on terra firma. Earth. This had been one hell of a tour. And it was only half over.

"So, how were the aliens?"

"Weird. Big. Black. Wriggly. Friendlier than humans." He shook his head at the last one, feeling ashamed of his species. *Homo sapiens sapiens.* He looked over at Mila,

220

wondering if she considered herself human. Was she? And how much of the lore surrounding shifters was true. For all he knew, they were kinder, gentler, and more honorable than humans could ever be. "Tell me about shifters."

She looked over at him. "There's not much I can tell you. It's not like I've met a whole lot of them. I'm not that old for a shifter and I suspect the current political climate has scattered our already small community to the four corners of the Earth."

"I'm sorry."

"You didn't make policy, Tristan. You've been very understanding."

"Thanks. Anyway, I imagine, even if you don't know as much as some, you certainly know more than I do."

"I guess so," she hedged. "What do you want to know?"

"Is it true that shifters tend to be assassins and thieves?"

"Maybe, I don't know, but I doubt it's from a lack of moral fiber. In that respect, we're just like any human. Some are good, others aren't. Personally, I think it's more culture and opportunity. Keep in mind, being a mercenary wasn't such a bad thing a few hundred years ago. And many people stole because they had no other way of living. Survival is a strong instinct.

"And well, after a while, if that was their options, I think the shifter communities would become ingrained, some in normal ways, but some in less socially acceptable ones."

"How is it you don't know your own people?"

"I didn't know I was a shifter, that I would become one. It just happened one day. Well, you know the story."

"Yeah." He paused, deep in thought. "So, what can you do? What can't you?"

She smiled. "Lots." She rubbed her hands together and glanced at the door. "You know, if we lock that door, I can show you."

"Okay." He got up, and his fingers roamed over the panel, closing and locking the door. "Good to go."

Mila's smile grew bigger as she stood and held one finger up. "Shifter rule number one: we can only shift into something of the same mass. Tigers are one of the best choices for an animal, as few others carry similar bulk to humans."

She stood back by the consoles and chairs, hesitant for a second. Nervous on more than one level, she pulled off most of her clothes and shifted effortlessly into a tiger, migrating excess iron to her paws so she didn't float. Slinking to Tristan in that limp-limbed stalk large cats are known for, she rubbed up against him, her head reaching his hip and let out a gentle roar.

Tristan laughed, his hand reaching down and petting her, rubbing the top of her head, behind her ears, between her shoulder blades.

Good God, that feels good.

She sat and leaned into his hand, sending him off balance. A coughing laugh slipped from her as Tristan regained his footing. With a great yawn, she stood, crossed the room to her clothes, and shifted back to the shape of May Trace.

She ticked off more "rules" on her fingers and dressed again. "Rule number two: we can't immediately identify one of our own. Rule number three: we need calories to power a change, so if we shift, we have to eat.

"Shifting between genders is weird. I don't like doing it. It is by far the most disturbing sensation possible.

"I never have to diet. Between higher caloric need and the ability to shift fat cells into muscle mass, it's not a concern. Which is wonderful, because I love to eat.

"We tend to prefer one or a couple forms. Contrary to popular belief, we don't constantly shift from one form to the next. I spend almost all of my time in the face I've had since birth."

"What *do* you look like? I can't believe I never wondered that before."

"Okay." And suddenly, Mila felt nervous, like she was stripping down armor right before battle, more nervous than when she'd stripped in front of him. *What if he doesn't like the real me?* She took a deep breath and shifted back into herself, closing her eyes, afraid to see his reaction.

"Beautiful," he breathed.

She smiled, eyes still closed. "Not disappointed?"

"Never."

"Avery."

He looked up from his desk. "Yeah, lieutenant?"

"Can I have a word?"

"Certainly. Come on in."

Braddock walked in, shutting the door behind him. He looked around the tiny, near empty office. "What do you think of May Trace?"

Curiosity in his eyes, Avery said, "I think she's brave, dedicated, and the best damned pilot I've ever seen." He leaned forward, elbows on his desk. "Why?"

"She's rubbed me wrong from day one. There's something not right about her."

"Braddock, that something not right you're feeling is just your stick-up-your-butt mentality when it comes to military command. Ease up on the girl."

"That's not it." *Not completely.* "I think I've found her secret."

"Secret?" Nothing piqued Avery's interest like a secret.

"Yes, a secret."

"And what secret might that be?" Avery still sounded skeptical. Not for long.

"I think she's a shifter."

CHAPTER FORTY

Avery burst out laughing, pounding away at the desk as tears formed at the corners of his eyes. Little fits of laughter continued taking him by surprise but he could breathe easier as he wiped the tears from his face. "You have one hell of an active imagination, lieutenant. I wouldn't have suspected. Not in a thousand years."

Braddock puffed up, outrage turning his face red.

Holy shit, he's dead serious.

"I do *not* have an active imagination. I know what I saw."

Avery froze. *Saw? What did he see?* He raised an eyebrow at Braddock, apprehension seeping into his brain. He didn't want to believe what the lieutenant was saying. Trace? A shifter?

"The day the airlock was breached. After the captain brought her back on board. I saw her hands. Only they weren't hands, they were claws."

Avery sat back, tapping his fingers against the top of his desk.

"You do realize the implications of your testimony, don't you?"

Braddock nodded. "I do."

"She's our pilot. Our *only* pilot." Not to mention he'd started seeing her as a friend. Sitting there, staring back at Braddock, he found himself in an unprecedented position.

He didn't want to uphold the law.

***

Mila was walking back to her bunk after a long round of poker. She yawned, her eyes closing and tearing as she bumped into someone. "Oh, sorry. Avery."

"I need to speak with you privately." He looked grim.

"Sure." She nodded and let Avery into her tiny room. "Have a seat."

But he didn't. He paced a couple times before taking up a position on the opposite wall and leaning against it, arms crossed. "Don't lie to me. Your livelihood might depend on your answer."

"Okay…" Now, she was worried. *What the hell's going on?* The old anxieties fired up again and she fought a sudden urge to dash for the door.

"Are you a shifter?"

Her mouth opened, but no words came out. *This is not happening! Ten years without a single person finding out. A few weeks on this POS and I feel like half the ship knows.* Collecting herself, she said, "How do you expect me to answer that?"

"With the truth." He glared, his stance getting harder, implacable.

"Avery, I like you. Respect you. You're a good guy. But I don't know how to answer that question." She waved her hand in the air. "This whole thing with shifters is just a great big witch hunt. And I can't help thinking someone has it in for me and aimed you my way. That's what happened, isn't it?"

Mila saw the truth in his eyes. And she could guess who, too.

"Lieutenant Braddock?" Although how Braddock had figured out her secret, she might never know.

"How did you know?"

She shrugged. "He's the only one on this boat who doesn't like me, besides that assassin earlier."

"Still, Trace," he shook his head, "Braddock isn't the type to lie… or see things."

What the hell did he see?!

He stood, waiting, arms across his chest. "I'm not leaving without an answer."

What do you do when your entire life hangs in the balance? When a single person's opinion can have devastating effects and you don't know what to do? She had a strong urge to cry. She felt that pressure of emotion building up, but she dared not let it loose.

The silence built between them and in the end it was the look of disappointment in his eyes that loosened her tongue. "Yes."

He let out a sigh and his entire posture relaxed. "This is bad."

"Yeah. What are you going to do?"

"I suspect Braddock would have me lock you up, sooner rather than later."

"And will you?" She couldn't breathe, needing the answer before life could go on.

"No. I don't know what the hell we're gonna do, but I won't lock you up. In my eyes, you're a damned hero, Trace." He paused. "Is Trace even your real name?" His face paled several shades as another realization hit him.

"No, my name isn't Trace and no, I didn't kill her. That bastard assassin did. But when I showed up here, he thought he hadn't finished the job." A humorless laugh slipped out. "So many people died because of my stupidity."

"What do you mean?"

She looked up at him. "If I hadn't taken over her identity, the assassin wouldn't have been here. He wouldn't have killed all those people."

Avery crossed his arms once more, his brow furrowed. "That's not your fault. Or maybe I should say, it's the lesser of two evils. Yeah, he came here because of you. But, because of you, we learned of the plot to sabotage this mission. Because of you, that assassin is now dead. He can't kill another living soul ever again."

"Really?"

"Really."

"Braddock's still a problem."

"He's a problem we can put off for another day."

"He could send word back to Earth, tell them what he thinks I am. They could be waiting for me when we land."

"We'll figure something out. I promise."

She nodded. "Tristan knows, too."

Avery smiled. "He does, does he? Why am I not surprised?"

Avery walked beside Trace, marveling at the fact he could walk beside a shifter and not think of all the propaganda that had been bandied about over the years. "What *is* your name?"

Trace looked around, checking for people. He imagined she had to develop a cautious streak. "Mila Anya Dragomirov."

"Russian?"

"Only by very distant heritage."

He nodded. It was like that a lot in America. Many families had been in the United States for centuries, but they still clung to their ancestry. They religiously chose ethnic names, ate the food, and spoke the language of the old country to the exclusion of all others. Every aspect of their lives laid testament to a culture and land their ancestors fled from desperately. It was… ironic.

"How did you end up with May Trace's identity?"

"She was my friend. She died," Mila breathed.

"How did she die? You said the assassin killed her."

"Well, not directly. He hired hoodlums to fake a mugging. I was there. They stabbed her, then took off. It was an arterial wound. She would have never reached the hospital. Even if I'd had the wits to call for help."

"I'm sorry."

"I just wish I hadn't wasted so much time. When I found out what I was, I ran. I didn't talk to her for ten years. We should have kept in touch. We should have…"

"Stop." He jogged out in front of her, stopping her with a palm to her chest. "Don't do that to yourself. Things happened the way they were meant to. You couldn't have changed things. You wouldn't have changed things. This is how they are. This is how they must be."

Her head sagged. "I know. But it doesn't stop me from wishing things had turned out differently."

"Would you have wished you'd never gotten to fly the *Orleans*? Never met the captain?"

"No!"

He smiled at her, letting his arm down. "See? How they're supposed to be."

She shook her head. "I like how you think."

He bowed. "At your service, madame."

They spent the rest of the walk in silence. He glanced over, seeing a small smile on her face. *Good.*

Tristan jerked his head up as the doors to his office slammed open, admitting Avery and Mila in a rather theatrical manner.

"We have a problem," Avery said. "Braddock suspects."

"Braddock suspects *what*?" He looked at Mila, but she gave nothing away.

Avery looked at Tristan, then at Mila. "Yeah, I know what she is. And if we don't come up with a game plan, so will everyone else."

Mila blanched, causing Tristan's heart to clench in his chest.

"Sit." He leaned back in his chair, using his role as captain to stay calm, be what he needed to be. "Tell me everything."

"Braddock came to my office today. Told me Trace was a shifter. I didn't believe him. Actually, I laughed in his face. Asked him if he realized the implications of the accusations he was making.

"He told me that when she came back through the airlock, her hands were in the form of claws. He didn't doubt what he claimed to see. And I was inclined to believe him. Braddock has no imagination."

"The way I see it, we have two options. Option one is prove she isn't a shifter." He looked over and winked at Mila. "Option two is make her disappear. Probably, list her among the dead. There would be no body and Braddock wouldn't be able to prove she hadn't died. Hopefully."

Tristan sat, thinking. He wanted to swear up and down the hallways, but that wasn't behavior befitting a captain. It would figure Braddock would be the threat to her. *Damned tight-assed gremlin.* He should have done more than give him a firm chastisement. "I doubt either option would work, Avery. Option two wouldn't work because people remember seeing her after the big fiasco. She's our only remaining pilot. That would require too much coverup. And how the hell would we manage option one?"

"Fake DNA testing."

He raised an eyebrow at his head of security. "Fake it *how*?"

"Swap samples. All I need is a female sample, bring it in to medical for testing. Say someone accused her of being a shifter. After everything that's happened, I'm surprised nobody has done it. There's certainly enough craziness to make people paranoid."

"And you think that would work?"

"Sure. If the head of security brings in a sample, they should assume I wanted to ensure the samples weren't swapped out. You know, like trying to pass drug testing by using someone else's urine. And we have buccal swabs in the security offices for collecting DNA evidence from suspects."

Tristan nodded. That could work. It had to. "Do it."

Avery stood. "Right away," and left.

"How are you holding up?"

She let out a shaky breath. "Like my whole world is falling apart."

"I imagine. Come here." He opened his arms, enticing her.

She gave him a small smile, walked over, and sat in his lap, snuggling into his chest. "Thanks," she whispered. "I needed that."

CHAPTER FORTY-ONE

Avery felt he might jump out of his skin at any moment. He'd ordered "randomized" shifter screening, saying that after the fiasco with the assassin, it was warranted. Nobody argued as he collected buccal swab samples from a half-dozen people.

Behind closed doors, he took one of the female samples he'd collected and put it in a fresh envelop, this time changing the information. He filled out Trace's bio. Name, rank, ID numbers. Would someone be able to tell? Did they keep previous DNA tests on file? Damn, he wished he'd paid more attention to that side of the business.

He organized the stiff envelopes, wrapping a rubber band around them to keep them together. The bundle was a tight wad in his fist as he left his office. He scanned his surroundings, but nobody noticed. Everyone was on high alert after the events of this trip. There were probably still saboteurs on board, which really irked him. He felt confident they hadn't caught all of them. He wanted to catch them. Needed to.

He left the offices, his eyes scanning each and every face.

Paranoid, Avery. You're getting paranoid.

He knew it, but it didn't stop him from suspecting all those around him. He shook his head. All but Trace. He was putting his very career on the line for that woman. But he knew right from wrong. And turning her over to the authorities would be wrong. Trace, no, Dragomirov was a hero. And even if her real name would never get the recognition, he wanted to see that she didn't get punished instead.

He entered the med bay and walked up to the counter. "I've got testing to be done."

"Don't you have better things to do than give us more work?" The woman glared.

Yes, clearly this will be a walk in the park, he thought sarcastically.

He smiled, hoping to work his charms on the girl. She was pretty enough. It wouldn't be any hardship. He put his hand over his heart. "I didn't intend to make your job any harder than it already is. It's my job to protect and sometimes that means taking preventative measures."

"Like?" she asked skeptically.

"Like testing people for shifter DNA. With everything that's happened, I'm not taking any chances. Especially after that shifter ran rampant on the ship the last few weeks."

"There was a shifter on board?" she whispered, leaning forward.

"Oh yes. Nasty bastard. An assassin. Perpetrated a string of murders. He was killed, but I've got to cover my bases. You understand."

"I think I remember those. One of the officers had to bring in quite a few bodies, if I don't recall. Wasn't one found in the food freezer?"

"Yeah. He probably died before we ever took off."

"Lord have mercy."

He nodded. "Indeed. Now, any chance you could run these for me? Most of them are just checking security staff, random checks. The last one here," he flipped through the envelopes until he found the one with Trace's name on it, "is a case. Someone accused her of being a shifter. That one's got priority."

She took the bundle and glanced at the last envelope, then looked up at him, shocked. "Trace? May Trace? Who the hell would accuse her of being a shifter?"

He smiled at the mama bear protectiveness he saw in the woman across from him. *Good, an ally.* "Yeah, that was my reaction too. I don't believe it for a minute, but Lieutenant Braddock wouldn't be placated. I had to follow up on it."

"Lieutenant Braddock?"

"Yeah, but to tell you the truth, I think it's all bullshit. Braddock's had it in for her since day one. I wouldn't be surprised if spite drove his accusations and nothing more."

She nodded. "Well, that makes more sense. Honestly, Trace a shifter? She's far too sweet. It's such a pity she ended up in here so often this trip."

"Well, that's what happens when you jump in the middle of things."

"Jump in the middle of things?"

"Yeah, I mean she didn't start out doing that. When it all started, she sort of got thrust into it. A friend of hers gave her information, without her knowledge I might add, which got an assassin on her butt."

"The shifter," she said, awed.

"Exactly. But since then, she's repeatedly shown no hesitance in entering the fray, even though it wasn't her job. She helped with investigations and helped fight off the invaders who nearly killed everyone on board by opening the airlock."

"Sounds like a hero to me."

"My thoughts exactly."

"Well, Avery."

"Kyle," he said.

Her smile grew. "Kyle. I will make sure these get done. ASAP. I don't want this hanging over our friend's head any longer than necessary." She patted his hand.

"You're an angel."

"Not hardly," she said with a wink.

Avery relaxed back into his office chair. At least that was taken care of. A knock sounded at his door. "But, of course," he muttered. He took a moment. "Come in."

Braddock stormed in.

"Ah, the prodigal son returns."

"Knock it off, Avery. I outrank you."

Avery glared, his frame going rigid. "What burr got in your claw, Braddock?"

"What have you done about Trace, *Avery*? I could have you brought up on charges for not doing your job, you know."

He gave it a beat before speaking, surprised by the anger in the superior officer's voice. "You need to stop with the threats, Braddock. I *am* doing my job. Even overworked as we are, I'm still checking your rather ridiculous accusations of someone who will probably be our most decorated crew member once we arrive on Earth."

"She doesn't deserve any fucking medals. She's a damned shifter."

"Braddock, shut up," he shouted, getting to his feet. "Shifter or no, she has repeatedly saved the lives of this crew. She has gone above and beyond the call of duty. And you know what? If it turns out she *is* a shifter, however unlikely I find it, I think she would deserve it more."

Braddock stood, mouth agape.

"Because this wasn't her duty at all. She took it upon herself. No vows. No oaths. No contracts. I'll do my duty, *Braddock*. I've sent her DNA to med bay for testing. If she's a shifter, they'll figure it out. Now I'd appreciate it if you leave me and my men to more important matters, like finding the rest of those conspirators."

CHAPTER FORTY-TWO

Mila spent a lot of time on the bridge waiting. Being near her console, looking out over that odd purple planet, soothed her. *I wish I was flying. That would really soothe me.* But this first diplomatic talk wouldn't end for a few more days. It would be the first of many, Tristan had told her, but the first was often the most important.

She wasn't privy to what was going on and she didn't care. The purpose of this mission barely registered on her list of concerns right now. Instead, her mind kept flitting back to the testing she could almost feel being done. Would it work? Would they really believe the sample was hers?

"Everything will be all right," Tristan said, coming up behind her.

She jumped and turned, a smile slowly stretching her face. "Hey, Tristan." She sounded tired, even to her own ears.

"It'll be all right, don't you worry."

"I can't help but worry. Yet again, my life's on the line here. I'm getting tired of feeling that way."

"Miss your old life?"

"Yes and no. It was simpler. Safer. But it wasn't really living."

"It wasn't?"

"No, I just hid in a hole, passing my days with nothing. Certainly nothing of value, of importance. I'm doing something worthy now, even if it got me shot up in the process." She smirked at him, waving her hand in the general vicinity of her various wounds.

He walked to her, pulling her into his arms and reveling in how she squirmed closer. "You *are* important, Mila. And everyone will see that." He kissed her temple, then rubbed his cheek against her smooth skin.

"So long as Braddock's accusations don't encourage the people back home to test me again."

"They won't."

"They could. If Braddock insists again, they could."

"I won't let it happen, Mila."

She turned around in his arms, looking him straight in the eyes. "No matter how highly you think of yourself, you're not the master of the universe. There are people you have to report to, people *I* have to report to. If they ask me to get tested, my only option might be to run. And that might not be an option anymore."

"I'm not going to lose you, Mila."

Avery walked into Tristan's office, knocking this time. He chose to ignore Trace sitting in the captain's lap. "I've got the tests back. And the digits of a rather nice medical officer who just happened to appreciate my charms. Thanks for that, by the way. No red flags raised. Nobody questioned it. You should be safe."

"Thanks, Avery. What about Braddock?"

Avery crossed his arms. "Haven't talked to him yet. Not looking forward to that particular conversation. The last one didn't exactly go… smoothly. I didn't think he knew curse words."

"Well, I'm sure you can pull it off, what with all your *charms.*"

Avery shook his head and left, taking care to close the doors behind him.

"Avery," a belligerent voice snapped from down the hall.

Great.

"Yes, Braddock." He turned to the voice, again crossing his arms over his chest.

"What's the status on the Trace investigation?"

"Done. She's clear."

"What?" Braddock grabbed Avery by his shirt, lifting him off the ground. "What do you mean she's clear?"

Avery glared at the man holding him as his shirt dug into his armpits. He placed his feet against the wall and shoved, throwing Braddock off balance and onto the floor. With a single move, he flipped him, sending his knee into the other man's back. He leaned in to speak. "Never forget I'm Head of *Security.* I could wipe the floor with you, *lieutenant.* What deference I give you is due to rank alone and nothing more. Understand?"

"Yes," his opponent breathed.

"Good." He let up, standing and returning to his original position.

Braddock was slower to stand, but he glared from across the hall. Now, he stayed out of grasping distance. "I'll repeat my question. What do you mean she's clear?"

"I mean her test came back negative for shifter DNA. She's no different from you or me." And he couldn't believe he said that with a straight face.

"That's not possible."

"But unerringly true."

"It must be a false negative."

"It's not that kind of testing. There're no false positives and false negatives with DNA testing."

"It can't be! I saw!"

"Then maybe you should get yourself checked in somewhere when we get back, lieutenant." And it took great effort to hide his smile as he said it. He *really* didn't like this guy.

Braddock glared. "This isn't over."

Avery rolled his eyes. Of course it wasn't over. Why would it be over?

CHAPTER FORTY-THREE

Days passed and they started their journey back home. It was slow, but quiet. Nothing serious happened, just Avery and his people rounding up the conspirators. At the times Mila saw him, he usually wore a scowl. He tried to smile for her, but she saw it irked him that he couldn't find the last of those behind the attacks on their ship.

She doubted they would ever find them all.

Days were long, exhausting, and she went straight to bed most of the time. Tristan still tried, and failed, to keep his distance, which was all right with her. She didn't know what to do with him either. She didn't have a lot of experience with relationships.

But nothing topped when that big blueberry they called Earth entered their horizon. She laughed and shouted when she saw it. The entire bridge stopped to watch. She could feel the collective sigh. It had been a long trip. Hard. A lot of people would be glad to be home. Even with possible exposure still flitting in the periphery of her consciousness, it felt good to see Earth again.

"Ready to enter atmosphere, captain," she said.

"At your leave, pilot."

She descended, feeling the massive POS pull toward the Earth. She charted their trajectory, planning a gradual decline that would have them looping the planet twice before setting down in Florida. They entered atmosphere and soon her vision turned red from the heat of reentry.

The controls pulled at her hands like a horse wanting its head. She held firm, feeling the subtle shake as the various forces warred against one another. Clouds passed and soon she made out things in the distance. A land mass. An ocean.

She adjusted the controls, slowing them further. They were almost there.

"Luke, communications."

"Roger."

He reached over and grabbed the short range radio two seats away. "Tower, this is U.S.S. *Orleans*. We are inbound west. Requesting permission for landing."

"*Orleans*, this is Tower. Cleared for straight in on One West."

"Roger." He put the radio down. "One West, sweet cheeks."

"I'd kick your ass right now for that name, but I'm busy."

He laughed. "I know. That's why I did it."

Mila didn't even have the opportunity to glare at him. She needed to focus straight ahead. She could see the landing strip now and adjusted her controls more.

Flaps, landing gear.

She felt the pull of the landing gear as they created more resistance.

Reduce speed.

They continued their descent.

Slower.

Closer.

Almost.

Touchdown.

The ship bumped. Once, twice, then coasted down the wide runway as she applied the brakes, slowing them to a stop.

She sighed, a smile on her face.

"Excellent landing, May," Luke said.

She punched him in the arm.

"Ow," he said, rubbing the spot.

"That's for the sweet cheeks comment."

"Beast," he grumbled.

"Come on. I think it's long past time we got off this POS."

"Damn straight."

⁓

Luke bounced her way off the ship, skirting people like a fish through the sea. A grin stretched her face as she hopped off the ship, the enclosed space opening into the great outdoors. She looked around her, laughing at herself. As far as the eye could see, concrete, blacktop, and blocky buildings made up the landscape.

Well, maybe not the great outdoors…

Still, it was freeing to no longer be cooped up, no longer have a ceiling over her head or walls closing her in. She stepped away from the ship, searching for familiar faces. Her family had always been supportive, first with her differences and then with her career. That's how she'd gotten her nickname, after all. She'd told her family one time, "I'm lucky to have such a supportive family," and it stuck.

"Mom!" she squealing, taking off at top speed across the pavement. Behind her mom, her dad and siblings waited, big grins on their faces. Luke slammed into them, trying to hug them all at once and failing. "I've missed you guys."

"Welcome home," her dad said, echoed by her mom.

As she pulled away, her older brother took one look at her, clutched at his heart and said, "Gasp! You look like a guy!"

Luke threw her bag at him.

"Oomph," he said as he toppled to the ground. "What've you got in here? Bricks?"

"Wouldn't you like to know?" she said, sticking out her tongue at him.

God, it's good to be home.

The ship was a sea of commotion, everyone racing to gather their things and run into the arms of their loved ones. Mila took her time, taking the jostling she got from the people around her. *God, what if the whole crew had survived?!*

She reached her bunk with only a few bruises. Santos was already packed, her bag slung over one shoulder. "Hope I never see you again," Santos said.

"Likewise," she said with a smile.

Santos shook her head, but smiled too as she pushed past Mila and walked out.

Mila started shoving things in her bag, enjoying the weight of the objects once again. Gravity. Beautiful.

She zipped the bag, put it over her shoulder, and opened the door, only to be greeted by three men standing guard. "Can I help you?"

"May Trace?"

"Yeah?"

"You've been accused of being a shifter. Come with us."

CHAPTER FORTY-FOUR

*M*ila followed the men in abject terror. She could barely breathe. Suddenly, the same gravity she'd reveled in only minutes ago seemed amplified by the weight of the accusations against her, weighing her down, oppressing her.

She looked around her, searching, but couldn't find Tristan or Avery. Where were they? She could really use an ally right about now.

They led her into a small room with a table and two chairs, each chair on opposite sides of the table. Interrogation room. She tried to swallow the lump that had formed in her throat, but failed. It seemed determined to choke her.

She didn't sit. She was too nervous to sit. So she paced.

Time ticked by, only there was no clock. The room, the environment, seemed designed to simulate a complete stoppage of time. Was this what hell would be like? An eternity in a moment?

She continued pacing. It would be all right. They had records on the ship, DNA testing. Faked DNA testing. She would have testimony from Tristan, Avery. It would be all right.

The door opened and a man walked through. "Why so nervous, May Trace?"

She stopped her pacing. "Forgive me if I don't appreciate being trapped in a tiny room after being stuck on a ship for weeks. I'd rather hoped I'd be racing off toward my leave right about now, not pacing an interrogation room."

The man nodded and motioned her to sit as he did so himself. She did, watching him intently.

"Someone accused you of being a shifter, Pilot Trace."

"I know. We already had this investigation. On the ship."

"You did?"

"Yes. The Head of Security took buccal swabs. Had them tested. It came back normal. Lieutenant Braddock just has it in for me."

"Lieutenant Braddock?"

"That's who brought forward the accusations, isn't it?"

The man remained quiet. "I'll be back." He stood and left.

Avery waited outside the ship, watching people disembark, looking for someone in particular. He'd sent a text message to a friend, asking for a phone call. He spotted his quarry, "Faulk!"

The captain turned to him and changed course, though his head kept on a swivel.

"You won't find her," he said as the other man stepped up to him.

"What?"

"She was escorted off the ship by three MPs shortly after we landed."

"What?!"

Avery put up his hands. "It wasn't me. I can only assume it was your lieutenant. I don't have all the details yet." As if on cue, his phone rang. "I've got to take this." He pressed the icon to answer the call, "Speak."

"It's good to hear your voice, old friend."

"Likewise." He smiled. "We need to get together sometime. It's been too long."

"And yet, somehow I doubt that's why you called."

"It's not. Do you know anything about an investigation into a woman named May Trace?"

"Hold on." Clicking came over the line as his friend looked something up on his computer. "Accused of being a shifter?"

"That would be it."

"And you want the investigation terminated."

"The investigation was already terminated. We tested her on the *Orleans* and cleared her. She saved everyone on board the ship."

"I'll see what I can do."

"Thank you."

"You'll owe me for this."

Avery laughed. "Add it to my tab."

Mila's stomach growled. It felt hollowed out after a long shift, and an interminable length in the interrogation room. "For no fucking reason!" she yelled at no one, slamming a fist at the wall.

She couldn't sit still, alternating between sitting, lounging, standing, pacing, then sitting again every few minutes. Dropping her face onto her palm, she said to the empty room, "At this point, I'm too bored to be afraid. Couldn't they just bring me some fucking food? I'm half tempted to chew on the table at this point."

When did I last eat?

She looked to the door, almost daring it to open.

Tristan stayed glued to Avery's side. He wanted to tell him to fix it, but from the moment they landed, he was no longer Avery's captain and Avery was no longer his Head of Security.

"Name's Kyle. What about you?"

"Tristan." Did Kyle already know that? He couldn't remember. "How long will it take?"

Kyle shook his head. "As long as it has to. When you're calling in favors, it's best not to be picky."

Tristan nodded, but the non-answer didn't help his composure. He wanted to march over there and demand they release her. At this point, he wasn't even sure he would have cited the right reasons.

"Have some faith. We've done all we can. The military doesn't always move quickly and they aren't always just, but we've got logic on our side."

"If you say so."

If only he could make himself believe.

After what felt like three or four days, the man returned. "You can go."

"Thank God!" Mila said, jumping out of her seat. She raced out and Tristan stood there waiting for her. "Tristan!" She raced into his arms.

"Oomph. Careful, woman."

"Oh, shut up. You know you love it."

"That I do."

"Everything squared away, then?"

"Yeah. MPs got the testing we did aboard the *Orleans*. Trusted it was valid. Lieutenant Braddock is probably not going to be fit for active duty for quite some time, though."

"Why's that?"

"He keeps insisting he saw your hands, that they were claws. Since you're not a shifter, that's impossible. The mucky mucks will probably request a psych eval."

Mila frowned, relieved to be free, but she felt bad about Braddock. She didn't like him, but wasn't sure he deserved that.

"Come on," he said, grabbing her hand. "Let's get out of here."

She nodded, and let him lead her out of the blocky, institutional building. Once outside, they walked sidewalks lined with bright green grass as short as a Marine's haircut.

"After you, my lady," Tristan said with a flourish as they arrived at a big black truck at the curb.

Mila chuckled and grabbed the door, turning back to look at him. "It suits you."

"Why thank you, my lady," he said with a grin as he rounded the hood and sat in the driver's seat.

Mila buckled in, running her hand over the material, focusing on the texture against her fingertips as Tristan pressed a button to start the car. She looked out the window, at the dash, at her fingers, anywhere but at Tristan as her future opened before her.

Ten years on the run. She'd never thought about her future, only about surviving. She'd had no friends, no prospects, sometimes even no food. *I can't go back to that.*

"You're awfully quiet over there." Tristan pushed up the steering wheel and turned to her. "What's on your mind?"

She shook her head. "I don't know what to do."

"Mila? Look at me."

She turned to him, biting her lip.

"Stay with me."

"What?"

He smiled. "I said, 'Stay with me.' "

"I heard you. I can't stay with you."

He leaned closer. "Why not?"

She sputtered, her mouth flapping like a fish. "I just can't."

He shrugged, as if it meant nothing to him, but his eyes spoke differently. "Well, you can't return to the barracks. May's roommate is bound to notice a difference."

Mila blanched. She hadn't even thought of where she would live, about May having a roommate.

"That's why you should move in with me. Total privacy."

She glared. "Somehow I doubt it."

"I swear. Scout's honor." He threw up a two-fingered salute.

"Were you really a scout?"

"No, but it still counts, right?"

Mila scoffed, shaking her head. "Not really."

Then he got serious. "I won't push you into something you're not ready for, Mila. My place has two bedrooms."

"Okay."

———

"I can't do this," Mila said from the passenger seat, idly fingering the medal in her lap, feeling like a fraud. Cringing, she remembered the awards ceremony where they praised "May Trace" for her valor and for going above and beyond the call of duty. She wanted to bury it in a drawer and forget it even existed. She wanted to run to the house and hide.

"You can't avoid this, Mila."

She glared at him. "Bite me." Pointing a finger at him, she said, "And you better stop calling me Mila. Other people might not notice or care, but May's parents aren't among them."

"Sorry." His smile came too damn fast for her to believe his sincerity. He opened the driver's side door and rounded the car, dragging her out. "You're just going to have to suck it up."

She glared at the back of his head, but he just dragged her ever onward. In no time, they stood at the door of May's childhood home and a cold sweat broke out on her forehead. "I don't want to do this."

Guilt ate at her. She shouldn't have done this. She shouldn't have taken May's identity. Why couldn't she have protected May? Saved her? Why hadn't May just *told* her what was going on? Why couldn't the ground just suck her up?

Bang, bang, bang.

She glared again at Tristan. *Traitor.*

Footsteps sounded beyond the door and a moment later, it burst open. "May! Get over here." May's mother wrapped her in a big hug and Mila smiled.

Okay, just a little while longer…

EPILOGUE

Shortly after landing…

He stepped off the ship, taking in his first breath of un-recirculated air in months. It felt good, even if the jostling as he exited the ship and his frustrations over the series of events made him want to strangle someone.

Again.

He hefted his pack a little higher on his shoulder and crossed the space with strong, efficient strides. The crowd dispersed in another direction and soon he turned a corner. Even with the ship's massive size, he could no longer see it. He scowled and kept going, walking up to a black sedan.

As he climbed into the backseat, dropping his bag on the seat beside him, the driver turned to him. "How'd it go?"

"It didn't." He looked out the window as they turned a corner, the people exiting the ship coming back into view. Leaning closer to the glass, he smirked. *Was that….* "May Trace," he mouthed as three MPs frog marched her from the ship, a just outcome for someone who seemed to take a personal interest in derailing his plans.

"Don't you worry, boss. That was only half the negotiations, right?"

"Right. This was just a minor setback."

May Trace wouldn't be there next time.

He would be ready.

SUPPLEMENTARY INFORMATION

Computer Systems

While more modern hard drives and monitors do not feel significant impacts from magnetic fields, the age of the ship developed for this book and the variability in the magnetic field generated for the MAG GRAV system can result in EMP-like effects, although on a much smaller scale. Over prolonged periods of time, this can cause damage to systems from additive effects. For this reason, the NSS moved to a centralized computer system with remote access points.

MAG GRAV

Zero gravity-related bone deterioration is caused by the body not having sufficient force applied to it. The system uses electromagnetic floor plates. Ferromagnetic thread is woven in cloth throughout the ship and ferromagnetic metals are used in the manufacture of all harder surfaces. The specific strength of the magnetic force is important, as it is directly correlated to the level of bone deterioration and as such, it is important that the properties of the garments utilized are comparable regardless of size of the wearer.

QuiKit

This is a technology that currently exists (though I came up with the name). It is used in 3rd world countries to provide inexpensive testing to locals. These kits are usually antibodies bound to a paper-like substrate that will change color based on presence of molecules that will bind to the antibodies.

Shape-shifting (Physiology)

Amoeba and other amorphous organisms are capable of changing shape to escape threats and reach food sources. While it would be theoretically possible for shape-shifters to exist (though none do in higher organisms), they would need to have evolved along a separate evolutionary path.

Shape-shifters have loosely structured tissues with easy to replicate designs. Further, not all tissue types are capable of shape-shifting. Some examples include: brain and spinal column, heart, primary arteries and veins, and most of the tissue in the digestive system and lungs. These systems serve as control points to power and feed the systems and tissues as they change.

Much of the shape-shifting capability arises at the tissue level. Shape-shifters have a simplified musculoskeletal system. The hard structure of bones in shape-shifters is caused by structures in the cells themselves rather than the tissues. The cells are connected together with chemical compounds easily dissolved with an enzymatic reaction triggered by shifting. The chemical reforms once the enzymatic activity ceases. The same holds true for muscles, tendons and ligaments.

Unlike many cells in higher organisms, shape-shifter cells have cilia designed to move them against each other mid-shift. This allows cells to reform into different-shaped tissues (e.g. shorter and wider bones, longer muscle groups).

Shape-shifting (Reproduction)

An important element in this series is the idea that shape-shifters can be born from human parents and go unknown. Shape-shifters are a separate species and are not inherently human or mutants. Female shape-shifters have unique characteristics in that they are capable of reproducing with *any* species. This is handled by specialized pathways active in oocytes and early stage fetuses. Female shape-shifters produce specialized recombinases during oocyte genesis (meiosis). When the cell is fertilized, it recognizes shifter-related genes, matching them with genes in the male chromosomes (if available). If unavailable, polymerases work with the recombinase to duplicate the shifter genes into the male chromosomes, which is effective since shifter genomes do not have sex-specific epigenetic markings. During the first few weeks of growth, the fetus will use target-specific silencing methods to turn off male-contributed genes that do not work in single copy and would otherwise cause termination of the fetus.

Sub-space travel

The sub-space travel system documented in this book is an adaptation of the Einstein-Rosen Bridge. There are a great many theories as to how an Einstein-Rosen Bridge might work. Some theories postulate that it connects two points in space-time (i.e. two points in the same universe). Others postulate that it could form a bridge between neighboring universes. This concept, regardless of how it is hypothesized, is very interesting as it is the only feasible means of interstellar travel currently postulated.

I took a great deal of liberty in coming up with this method of travel, though there are other more likely scenarios such as a bridge connecting two points in space, or even a significant time difference on each side of the bridge.

The most important part of this technology is the capability of forming these bridges, which I didn't provide any details into. At present, humanity has not discovered any of these bridges, and as such, we would not be able to learn enough about them to create one. I imagine, though, once we're discovered one and studied one, learning to create and control them will be right around the corner.

TAT system

This system is a logical extension of the Tachyonic Antitelephone thought experiment postulated by Albert Einstein in 1907. Tachyons are theoretical particles that can only move faster than the speed of light. In fact, the slower they get, the more energy is required (the inverse of normal matter). For this reason, particles that work similarly would be ideal for communication between interstellar distances. Because of the risk of breaking causality, the energy applied to the tachyons is very important in relation to the distance traveled. However, if those calculations are applied adequately, it would be theoretically possible to generate instantaneous communication across any distance. Please note: Tachyons are theoretical and have largely been deemed physically impossible (i.e. have had no scientific verification), however the beauty of science is the unknown, and we will likely never know all there is to know about the universe.

TRISTAN'S CHOICE

CHAPTER ONE

*A*s Kyle Avery sidled up to the warehouse, his heart pounded. Wind howled against his face, cooling the sweat there, stealing the sound of his breathing. The thatched pattern of the gun grip reassured him, soothed him, but still, he just *knew* this mission would go balls up.

No, Avery. That kind of thinking will only get someone killed.

He shook his thoughts away, gripping his weapon tighter as he pressed his shoulder against the cold, corrugated metal at his back. Across from him, his partner, Kaufman, nodded. As a whole, he didn't like the man. He was too impulsive, too prone to leaping before looking, but he was a damn good investigator. Kyle wouldn't have gotten this far without him.

Kaufman raised his hand, counting down on his fingers.

3.

2.

1.

They spun around, slamming through the door with a jarring groan of distressed metal. Kyle scanned his surroundings gun first. They separated, sweeping the building on each outer wall, keeping their backs protected.

His hackles rose.

It was too still, too quiet, too empty. Where was everything? Along the walls, he spotted a few offices, but nothing else. No boxes, no vehicles. It felt abandoned. It didn't feel like the lair of an organization that had sabotaged a diplomatic mission, a mission that nearly took his life. If not for Mila, a shape-shifter masquerading as her best friend, he would probably be dead right now.

He frowned. This was their first lead in months, their first real chance to get these guys. He ground his teeth with the remembered frustration of not catching them. Avery and his team on the *Orleans* had worked themselves to the bone to catch all those behind the sabotage, but some had still slipped through their fingers.

"Something's not right," he whispered as he met up with Kaufman near the end of their search. They'd found nothing.

"Nah," Kaufman waved off the comment, angling his gun around the corner toward the rear offices.

Kyle followed, his chest tight as he struggled for breath. The farther inside the building he got, the more things didn't seem right. Something was off. Some detail he couldn't quite put his finger on.

A series of rooms decorated the wall they slid past. Kaufman had already checked two, swiping his gun from side to side in the doorway before whispering, "Clear," and moving on to the next.

They'd reached the second to last room, when Kaufman swept his weapon in, started to say clear, and stopped. "Oh shit."

That was all Kyle needed to hear. He grabbed Kaufman by the arm, hauling him out, and running for the door. He didn't know what Kaufman had seen and he didn't want to know.

Kaufman didn't fight him, racing out right behind him, their steps echoing off the empty walls. They had just reached the exterior door when a loud percussion threatened to rupture his eardrums, sending him flying on his face with Kaufman landing on top of him.

As pain and a ringing in his ears settled into him, he wondered, What happened?

CHAPTER TWO

Tristan sighed into the hair of the woman in his arms, enjoyed the warm weight of her pressed against him. Mila cuddled in closer to him, mumbling in her sleep, her breath feeling fantastic as it caressed his neck. Just being this close, holding her, enjoying a lazy morning with her, would be enough for a lifetime, he was sure. He could think of nowhere he would rather be.

The phone trilled, assaulting his eardrums, and he groaned, covering his face with his hand. *No.* His mind resisted getting up, leaving this moment, but all moments must inevitably end.

Mila leaned up, looking at him with amusement twinkling in her eyes. "You going to answer that?" Her smile grew, one side tilted impishly.

"No," he replied, determination in his voice. He pressed his hand tighter, as if that could make the phone stop. It almost seemed to grow in volume, as if annoyed with his inattention.

"It could be important."

"I don't care. I don't want to get up. I don't want this moment to end." A part of him feared the end, that getting up meant losing her, losing *this*.

Her smile deepened. "All things must end, Tristan."

He flailed his arm, trying to silence his cell phone with a swack. He misjudged and fell off the bed, jarring himself awake. "Wah…"

He looked up around himself, running his hand through his hair, and sighed. It had been a dream. Just a dream.

He answered the phone. "Captain Faulk."

Tristan straightened his uniform as he sat in his big, black truck, the steering wheel pushed up and out of the way. With the visor pulled down, he checked that his lapels were straight one last time before flipping it up and opening the door with a pop of sound.

The morning sun baked him in his heavy, long-sleeved jacket and pants as he crossed the parking lot to his office. A fine line of sweat formed on his brow. In front of him, the ugly, squat building loomed as his steps ate up the distance.

He stepped up onto the sidewalk, nodding his head as he passed men and women in NSS and NASA uniforms, each looking just as hot and miserable as he did. When he opened the glass doors, the burning metal handle in hand, he paused for a moment to enjoy the gust of cold wind coming from the air conditioner.

He stepped into the building, letting the steel and glass close behind him. Then, he walked to the stairs, his dress shoes clapping against the cheap floor, creating echoes against the walls. He jogged up the flight of steps to his office, his legs burning with the exertion, but it was a good feeling first thing in the morning. Hell, it was good to be in the office.

Because the nature of the NSS meant always being "on" while on active duty, leave tended to be lengthy. He'd been on leave for a couple months now. He figured he was overdue for a new mission and the call from Rear Admiral Ambrose proved it. Tristan had been asked to come in. He had a meeting with his superior tomorrow at two. In the mean time, he probably had a mountain of tasks that had piled up.

The hall he stepped out onto was quiet, but then it usually was. It was the captains' hallway and it didn't tend to get a ton of use. He passed by wooden doors with other captains' names on them before arriving at one that read, "Captain Tristan Faulk." He dug his hand in his pocket, his fingers wrapping around the body-heat-warmed key and unlocked the door.

His office left much to be desired. He spent more time in space or training than here. A scarred desk filled the center of the room, surrounded by two metal guest chairs and an office chair with strained seams. The desk was almost barren, with a phone in one corner and the computer display in its standby position flush to the desktop.

On the walls, his West Point diploma hung in the middle of the wall to his right. Various pictures surrounded it, mostly of official functions like awards ceremonies. He didn't have a single personal photo in the entire office.

He thought of his brother and pulled out his phone, but of course, there was nothing. No phone calls, no emails, no text. There never was.

There never will be.

He sat in his office looking out over stark buildings, lost in thought as he played with his pen, working up the nerve to make *the* phone call. With a sigh, he started punching numbers into the phone, then waited for the person to answer on the other end.

"Speak," the voice said.

"I have news."

"I'm listening."

"The mission has been assigned to Captain Tristan Faulk."

The line clicked, signaling the end of the call as the person hung up.

Mila woke with nothing on the agenda, yet again. It was silly, but even though she'd had no schedule for ten years, she found being on leave utterly intolerable. She felt bored, listless, and couldn't wait to be called up on active duty again. She just wanted to *do* something.

Though maybe part of it was from living a lie. She wasn't a member of the armed forces. Her name wasn't May Trace. She might have dinner with them often, but Sarah and John Trace were not her parents. She might fly a spaceship better than anyone else in NASA or the NSS, but she'd never finished flight school.

Sometimes, the mask was just too heavy.

She needed a distraction.

Mila slipped out of bed, yawning as she rubbed the sleep from her eyes. Glancing at the clock, she saw it was only six a.m. *Tristan should still be here*, she thought with a smile.

Mila had moved in with Tristan after the *Orleans* returned to Earth. He'd said it was for her protection, since he was one of the few people who knew what she was. She suspected he had other motives, but she didn't care. She liked Tristan, considered him a friend. And she was determined to keep it that way, no matter what Tristan hinted at. Being in the military, they would never see each other if they entered a romantic relationship and she just couldn't bear that idea.

And, fuck, what future could their relationship have?

Pushing the thought aside, she started moving toward the main part of the house with more vigor, hoping to see Tristan. "Tristan?"

"No, just me," Kyle Avery said as Mila turned a corner and crashed straight into him.

"What the fuck, Avery?! We gave you that key for emergencies." She grabbed him by the arm, twisting until he had to duck walk all the way to the front door.

"Jeez, Mila. Easy."

"Bye, Avery." She opened the door and pushed him through.

"Mila," he whined.

Mila slammed the door in his face, but she smiled anyway. She shook her head. She liked the guy well enough, but it was far too early for visitors. Even if he knew her secret.

Heading into the living room, she turned on the TV for the noise. A debate program came on, discussing the treaties with the alien race dubbed the Incirrina. One side waxed poetic about the benefits of befriending an alien race. The other viciously derided every comment, foaming at the mouth with fanatical glee.

With a growl, she mashed the power button. She had no patience for ignorance.

Kyle sighed as the door slammed in his face. It was hardly the first time he'd found himself checking up on Mila Dragomirov. It scared him that such a brave, and wholly self-less, woman could be destroyed so easily if the wrong information got out.

Which was why he checked on her so often. He felt responsible for her, even beholden to her, and he often felt the government didn't do enough for their heroes. If they found out about her? They would throw her to the wolves.

Of course, it didn't help that his sources indicated the saboteurs blamed her for their failures. She'd been a variable they hadn't foreseen. No one would have guessed that an utterly average pilot would save them all.

May Trace had been an ordinary pilot before her tragic death. But Mila was a different beast. Mila had a gift. She'd shown that gift with gusto during the *Orleans* mission. She'd outmaneuvered the smallest of fighters and piloted through a gas ring without taking damage. Not to mention what she accomplished outside the pilot's seat.

Still, even though she was a shifter and shifters were hard to kill, he wanted to protect her, keep her safe from her enemies, now and in the future. It was a compulsion with him.

He got in his car, meaning to go to the office. He'd spent the last couple months staring at the notes that decorated his office walls, waiting for inspiration, waiting for something to connect. When he wasn't there, he found himself in the conference room the task force had confiscated for its uses. He'd spent days on end hunting those who'd endangered

Earth's future. He scoffed. And yet, they were back to square one, scratching their heads wondering where they'd gone wrong.

Kyle drove through the base, passing the small houses in Tristan and Mila's neighborhood. Before long, the simple homes morphed into ugly rectangular buildings made of nondescript materials and no class or style.

What had he missed?

How had their targets known they were onto them? It had to be a traitor, but who? After the explosion—which left him with nothing more than a few scrapes and minor burns and left Kaufman hospitalized—he didn't trust anyone.

In fact, if he trusted anyone, it would be Tristan and Mila. Of everyone he knew, only they had a vested interest in his investigation's success—not that either of them was cleared to even know about it.

He'd been forced to keep quiet, which was normal, but now he wondered if he should clue them in. They were the only ones he trusted and he needed someone to bounce ideas off of. Of course, he could probably trust Kaufman. After all, the man had third-degree burns on his back from that explosion, not to mention a punctured lung. But he was hospitalized and drugged up to la la land. He would be no help.

So, he pulled up to his parking spot, knowing he had no one to rely on but himself. He knew deep down the task force was an utter failure. If he wanted to catch the bastards, he had to do it alone. And off the books. He had to assume any details could get back to the enemy. He couldn't have that.

The trek to his office was a short one. Down the hall and up a flight of stairs, a serviceable piece of wood and glass with the name "Kyle Avery" lettered on a plaque stood before him. It didn't even have his rank, as that would require occasional updates. Couldn't have that, now could they?

He pulled out a set of keys, fighting with the stubborn lock. Even before the explosion, he always kept his office secured. Anymore, his investigations had him looking inside the NSS, not outside, so he had to keep prying eyes off his files.

Kyle palmed the keys, shoving them in his pocket with a sigh as he looked around at his walls—walls that needed redecorating. Any leads pinned to the walls now were likely either false or compromised.

He needed to start from scratch.

Mila pulled her car, or really May's car, alongside the familiar stretch of forest, the little car bouncing to a stop on the uneven ground. There was no proper parking area, just a well-worn patch of dirt on the side of the road. She'd been here many times before and she saw herself making the trek many times in the future.

Maybe forever.

She *should* come forever.

She grabbed the flowers from the passenger seat—carnations. They'd been May's favorite, something Mila had teased May about at every opportunity. Mila hated them. They always tickled her nose, making her feel the urge to sneeze. She never did, but the nagging sensation always hung in the background, waiting for the perfect moment—a moment that never came. It always pissed her off.

Mila waved the flowers at her side, the plastic around the bouquet crinkling in her fist as she took the now well-traveled path into the trees. After several minutes of nothing but nature, her heart pounding in her chest but not from exertion, she found a small stone in front of a tree. On the stone, she'd inscribed the words, "Forever my best friend, my better half." She bought it from a place that specialized in pet tombstones. She knew a real tombstone would only throw up a red flag. Unfortunately, it was the best she could do for her friend, for the woman who had given Mila a new life the day she'd lost her own.

She placed the flowers on the stone and stood. "Hey, May. I'm going out of my mind here." Her throat tight, she paused, the words failing her. "I miss you." Her voice broke on the last sentence. "Why did it have to be this way?" Her emotions bubbled up, choking her.

Like her guilt.

She took a deep, shaky breath, hating how the building emotion made her face burn. *You will not cry, Mila.* She slapped her face a couple times for good measure. "Right. Nothing's happened since the last time I visited. Your mom is about driving me nuts with the requests to come over for dinner. Did you really visit so often?" She laughed. "Somehow, I doubt it. It just makes me miss my own mom." She sighed and kneeled again, touching the stone this time. "Why did it have to be this way?"

CHAPTER THREE

"We could have gone out somewhere to eat, rather than eating at the mess hall. The food's pitiful," Luke whined, shifting his macaroni and cheese around with his fork.

"Oh, suck it up, Luke. Nobody asked you," Mila replied, shoving another forkful of meat into her mouth. She thought it might be chicken, but it was rubbery from sitting under the heat lamps and she wasn't entirely sure.

Luke shook his head before dishing up more noodles. "You're mean," he teased.

Mila stuck her tongue out, the thick appendage coated in half-chewed protein.

"Oh, gross, May." But he stuck his own tongue out at her, giving her a view of an orange, mushed up mess.

"Classy. I can see you get all the girls."

Luke shook his head, swallowing his food. "You started it."

Mila shrugged. "So?"

Luke chuckled and went back to eating. Mila did the same, clearing out several entrees. To her, the fare in the mess hall was great. But then, between the ship's cuisine and scrambling for food in soup kitchens and stuff, anything sounded fantastic.

"So, do you know any private swimming spots? Somewhere you could swim without being seen?"

Luke looked up at her and smiled, waggling his eyebrows. "Wanting to get some skinny dipping in with the captain, eh?"

"Ugh. God, no, Luke. Get your mind out of the gutter. Jeez. You know any or not?" None of their friends ever believed that she and Tristan weren't intimate. They just assumed they were in a relationship. Probably, it was because of the looks Tristan tended to give her, which Mila felt compelled to ignore.

She cared for Tristan too much to have a real relationship with him. Yes, it sounded backwards, but being in the NSS, she couldn't report under Tristan on ship if they did. They would end up with one off planet for months while the other wallowed at home, their schedules forever off. Her mind flitted to an old movie, Ladyhawke, a tragic tale of lovers cursed to only see each other as night met the day.

She preferred seeing him every day as a friend than pursue a relationship that left her alone. Besides, what future did someone like her have?

None.

Luke smirked, not repentant at all. "I know a place."

Tristan didn't see the concrete path to his two-bedroom home on base as he continued to stew over tomorrow's meeting with

Rear Admiral Ambrose. He disliked waiting, it just left his mind running over scenarios.

What was the mission about?

How long would he be gone?

Could he bring Mila with him?

The front doorknob rattled as he turned it. He pulled at his tie as the slab of wood creaked open and he stepped through, then took off his cover, tossing it on the small table near the door.

Mila leaned out of the kitchen, smiling at him. "Welcome home, Tristan. I made sandwiches."

Looking up distractedly, he smiled, shaking his head. "Trying to cook for me, Mila?"

She shrugged. "I can try…"

She dipped back in the kitchen and he followed as she sat at the little table. It could seat four, but not with the amount of food she'd heaped in the middle. There wasn't room for four place settings now. Really, there wasn't space for *any* place settings.

"Good Lord, Mila. Did you buy out the grocery store?" Tristan's mouth hung open, gaping at the display. He stood in the doorway to the kitchen, useless as a statue.

She rolled her eyes. "No. They still had one bag of potato chips left, but I was tempted." She smirked at him as he unfroze and sat.

His mind returned to the mission briefing tomorrow. What class of ship would he need to use? What size crew did he need? What would the threat level be?

He looked up, confused for a moment. "What?" He hadn't

been listening. She watched him over the gigantic sandwich in her hands, her cheeks bulging like a chipmunk's.

Mila laughed, shaking her head. "Never mind. I'll leave you in peace."

The pile of food disappeared as the two of them ate. Mila alternated between a bite of sandwich and a handful of chips, but Tristan seemed focused on his sandwiches alone.

By the end of the meal, they'd devoured two bags of chips and about five pounds of lunchmeat. Mila ate as much as he did, sometimes more. It had to do with her shifter metabolism, though he couldn't say he understood it. Still, in moments like this, when they were alone, she let go, completely unselfconscious, eating whatever she wanted without worrying what he might think.

He liked that.

"So, Luke told me about a nice swimming hole nearby. Wanna go?"

"Uh, sure," Tristan said, only half paying attention.

"Great! I'll get changed." She pushed out her chair, dashing from the room.

"Huh?" Tristan said, but Mila was already out of sight.

Tristan stared off at the empty doorway Mila had disappeared through as muffled sounds and banging came from the other end of the house.

What is she doing?

Minutes later, Mila leaned into the kitchen, hands balanced on the doorframe and wearing a baggy t-shirt and shorts. "Are you coming or what, dipshit?"

"What?"

"Bathing suit. Do it. Now." She stormed to his side, hoisting him out of the chair with her considerable strength, then shoving him down the hall and into his room before slamming the door. "And if you don't come out in swim trunks in the next couple minutes, I'm coming in after you."

He smirked at the closed bedroom door.

If only she would...

They reached the spot largely on Tristan's knowledge of the area. Mila had spent the time since disembarking the *Orleans* trying to learn her surroundings, but there was a lot she didn't know. Remote bodies of water were one of them. And most of her adult life, she'd lived in the city of Louisville, so wooded areas were somewhat alien to her.

Following Luke's instructions, she followed a path through the woods. It curved several times before revealing a secluded pond. Trees wrapped it on all sides. The water sat clear and still as a mirror. She smiled.

She stripped to the bathing suit and ran, her feet slapping against the wet sand. "Holy shit, that's cold," she shrieked as liquid splashed her thighs, chills racing up her skin like they were running the Kentucky Derby. In remedy, she dived in head first, the icy temperature taking the breath from her. Surfacing, she pushed the stray strands of hair out of her face and looked back to Tristan, who still stood on the tiny beach. "Are you coming or what?"

He nodded, but didn't move toward the water. He seemed distracted, awkward even.

So she decided to do something new. Making sure she was

covered, she slipped everything off and shifted into a form she'd never used before—a mermaid.

It felt weird, like shifting into a man. It reminded her of when her shoes were too tight, forcing her toes to smoosh together, only the sensation went all the way up. She turned, dived, and waved her fin hard once, wondering if she'd succeeded.

Mila surfaced again, using her fin to keep her head above the surface, and smiled at the now drenched Tristan. Water dripped from his hair, nose, and chin, making her smile, but he seemed more perturbed than surprised. Did he even notice the fin? She leaned back, floating with her fin on full display, but he didn't even react. He wasn't looking at her. Instead, he stared off into space.

"Tristan!" she barked. "What the fuck?"

He jerked to her, eyes getting big as he took in the fin.

Finally.

"A mermaid?"

"Well, where do you think the legends came from? And where the hell is your head at?" She slapped the water, emphasizing her frustration.

He sighed, but didn't elaborate.

"Tristan? Please?" Her voice became pleading.

"I can't say."

Tristan knocked as he reached Rear Admiral Ambrose's office the next afternoon, his back tall as he waited.

"Enter," a man's voice said.

Tristan grabbed the handle, pushing it open with his cover held under his right arm. "Sir," he said, standing at attention and saluting as the door clicked closed behind him.

"At ease, captain." Ambrose sat tall, his yellow-striped forearms resting against the desktop. His black jacket fit snug against a body that had not gone to seed despite the short, gray hairs that covered his head. Tristan had no idea what color the hair had been, but solid silver served as a reminder that Rear Admiral Ambrose had earned every ribbon and medal on his ribbon rack.

He nodded, relaxing into a ready stance.

"Have a seat," Ambrose said, indicating one of the guest chairs with a raised arm.

Tristan sat down, the chair worlds better than his own.

Ambrose handed over a tablet that had gone unnoticed by his right elbow. "This mission is of the utmost importance."

Tristan sat taller, forcing himself to keep his thoughts hidden. *Damn, another one?* But his facial expression remained aloof as his emotions ran chaotically inside his head.

Hadn't the *Orleans* mission been enough? He'd spent most of his career happily avoiding important missions. The NSS wasn't like other branches of the military. Many journeys were NASA-sponsored, with the NSS accompanying for security purposes, or to fill in gaps in positions.

His assignments had never been "of the utmost importance." Instead, they'd been exploratory missions or ships needing overhauls. He liked it that way. Now his stomach sank in dread, suspecting those days were over. The *Orleans* mission had changed all that.

He hated the changes, but they weren't all bad. He'd met Kyle

Avery, who'd become a trusted colleague and friend, and Mila, who was that and so much more.

Still, he would have happily gone back to captaining missions where the biggest challenge was keeping the researchers from killing themselves on foolish risks.

Tristan reached his hand out, grasping the tablet in a firm, and thankfully steady, grip as he pulled it in front of him to read.

"A full paper packet will be delivered to your office by tomorrow morning," Ambrose continued, leaning back in his chair as Tristan stared at the screen.

The word "Incirrina" jumped out at him from the display and his stomach did somersaults in protest. *Great.*

"Captain Faulk, this mission is very important. Our delegates and the Incirrina are finalizing the treaty which will be a landmark event in human history."

"On the moon," Tristan mumbled, noticing the talks would take place at Kennedy Moon Station.

"Indeed," Ambrose said, nodding. "The Incirrina will be more comfortable in the lower gravity."

Tristan nodded as well, holding back a sigh as the inevitable loomed before him.

This will not end well...

CHAPTER FOUR

*T*ristan turned and walked away, wishing he could tell Mila, but he wasn't allowed. He had a new assignment, had just received it, in fact, that afternoon. Just like the *Orleans* mission, it was highly classified. Need to know only.

He sighed. He didn't want this mission any more than he'd wanted the *Orleans* mission. Considering how that had gone, his gut said this one would face a similar fate.

FUBAR.

The Incirrina were coming here, or at least to the moon. Their bodies would never handle the stronger gravity on Earth. They were to fly a short-range shuttle to the moon, carrying a minimal crew and a handful of diplomats, to the Kennedy Moon Station. There, negotiations would continue and they would finalize their political relations with the alien race.

If everything went perfectly. Tristan felt confident that wouldn't happen. Nothing about this alliance had gone smoothly. He couldn't see this being any different. And considering how badly the *Orleans* got compromised when it was top secret, he seriously questioned the NSS's ability to keep a secret.

"Hey," Mila touched his arm, the ghost touch sending goose bumps up to his shoulder.

He looked over as she finished shoving her other arm through a sleeve of her t-shirt, her doe eyes looking up at him with concern. "Heya back."

"A mission?" A sense of inevitability weighed down her words. It was a question, but she already knew the answer.

He nodded and a small, understanding smile crossed her face as she nodded in return, then ran back to the car, leaving him in the dust… and in his thoughts.

Considerations like what type of shuttle to use, what weapons to bring on board, and who to choose for the mission flew through his head. Really, the last part was a no-brainer. He wouldn't have anyone but Mila piloting, and he would have Avery on board even if it killed him. The man could handle himself and if there was some plot to sabotage the treaty, he wanted someone with that man's investigative background on the mission. After the *Orleans*, he didn't trust anyone more.

For a short-range shuttle, he didn't need much. They didn't need a dedicated communications officer, as they didn't have TAT systems on board. Nor did they need any other person-nel. They would spend a couple days on the ship, spend most of the time at the moon station, then another couple days traveling back.

As he reached the car, he looked to Mila, who already sat in the passenger seat waiting for him, a smirk and a raised eyebrow decorating her face.

He opened the door and got in. "Yeah, yeah, because running

to beat a person who's only walking is *such* an accomplishment."

That night was harder than most. As Tristan went to his bedroom, getting ready for sleep, his mind kept dancing to the fact that Mila lay only a room away. The fact taunted him, putting ideas in his head he really should banish.

She's clueless.

She doesn't feel what I do.

It'll never work.

He crossed to his dresser, opening the top drawer. Sliding his socks out of the way, he brushed his hand over a small, velveteen pouch. The texture tickled his fingertips, taunting him. He sighed, a sense of hopelessness running over him.

She's not ready.

He stepped away from the dresser, slamming the drawer closed with finality. A slight depression pressed down on him as he changed and slipped into bed, realizing that Mila's assertion that being friends would be better was right. He didn't want to admit it, often forgot, but he saw no real way for them to be together.

When they first arrived back on Earth, Tristan had suggested pursuing a relationship, but Mila had nixed the idea. She'd said she cared about him, cared about him a great deal, in fact. His heart soared at hearing it, but not for long. She followed it up with a statement that tore him up inside. She would rather see him daily as a friend than never as a lover.

He wanted to deny it, tell her they could work it out, but no matter what he said, it would be a lie. No matter how they worked it out, it would mean months apart, and he didn't like that idea any better than she did.

But something had to give.

Getting into the building was easy. They didn't even bother to lock it, except for an electronic reader that gained access for anyone with NSS or NASA clearance. He'd been given an ID for just said purpose.

And though he didn't wear a uniform, no one questioned why he walked the officers' floor. No one questioned why he searched door after door, looking for the one that said, "Captain Tristan Faulk."

Really, it was poor security, if you asked him.

After a couple more doors, he found Faulk's. He put on an act, pretending he was waiting for someone. He frowned, checked his watch, checked up and down the hallway, but really he was looking to see if anyone would see him breaking into the captain's office.

The coast was clear.

Amateurs.

He pulled his lock pick set out of his back pocket, laughing to himself that in this age of interstellar travel, the NSS still relied on pin tumbler locks.

Pathetic.

He slipped into the office with ease, closing the door behind himself with a gentle click. He turned his head, scanning the space for the perfect places. The room held little more than a desk, three chairs, and a splattering of items on the walls ranging from diplomas to pictures from awards ceremonies.

He walked to the phone, dismantling it with speed and skill, before planting his first bug, which took power from the phone line itself. Next, he powered up the computer, using a back-door login the NSS IT department used to fix everyone's computers. He pulled out a thumb drive and uploaded a program that would track the captain's activities.

Then, since the captain didn't like a lot of clutter, he had to get creative with the rest.

CHAPTER FIVE

"*M*orning, Mila. You're up early," Tristan said over his coffee mug.

Mila rubbed her eyes, glaring at him, her eyelids heavy with exhaustion. "You were banging around like two people in a knockdown, drag out fight. Of course, I'm up. Whatcha doing today?" She grabbed a box of cereal and sat down, opening it and crunching fit to wake the dead as she shoved handfuls in her mouth.

He shook his head at her. "The office."

Yet again, he had to be vague, but this time, Mila didn't call him out on it. She simply nodded and dived into her food, her curiosity forgotten. He smiled, shaking his head once again. He loved that about her. Food often trumped all with her, maybe because of all the years she'd gone without. Or maybe because she was a shifter, she needed the extra calories. Regardless, it made for a wonderful distraction mechanism.

"And you? What are you doing today?" He smiled as her cheeks puffed out with food.

"Gym." A grim look crossed her face. "And May's mom asked me over for dinner."

He shook his head with a grin. Ever since he'd dragged her there after the awards ceremony, Mila had been spending time with May's family on a regular basis. And she didn't like it. She always groaned and moaned, or just looked plain grim. If he didn't know any better, he would think they were the family from hell.

But he'd met them. Sarah and John Trace welcomed him with open arms, feeding him without complaint, fawning over "May." They complained about how she never visited, how her work kept her away for months at a time and they "never get to see her anymore." He supposed that was the problem. She wasn't May. May was dead. Every comment drove that reality deeper, spearing Mila with the reminder of the lie she was living.

Shying away from those thoughts, Tristan downed the last of his coffee and rinsed it at the sink. "Well, I'm off. Enjoy the workout." He started to leave, but then paused, smiling evilly as he turned to her to say, "And enjoy dinner."

He continued to the door, but felt the death glare she gave his back, which only made his smile grow as he walked out of the house.

Tristan settled into his office for a long day of mission prep. The air conditioner hummed in the background and something was digging into his back, reminding him he needed to put in a requisition for a new chair. His eyes glazed over as he scrolled through available short-range shuttles on his computer screen, the light glaring in the poorly lit space. Once he'd picked the shuttle, he would know how much crew he needed. Then on to crew selection and resources.

He stopped when he saw a tiny craft, only large enough for the handful of diplomats and three crew members. Perfect. It was the absolute smallest he could get away with. And, bonus, it was the same class of ship Mila used in training.

When they'd returned to Earth months ago, he'd looked up the training records of Mila Anya Dragomirov. He'd been shocked and yet, thinking back on the breathtaking flying she'd done, not at all. Not only had she broken records, she held some to this day. She was quite possibly the best pilot in the NSS and nobody had a clue.

The U.S.S. *Dakota* was an updated version of the ship she'd flown when she broke many of those records over ten years ago. He hoped that would make a difference, because he suspected they would need all the help they could get.

Hours later, Tristan sat in the office of his superior, Rear Admiral Ambrose, waiting for the man to approve or reject his mission plan. Or augment it. He wasn't worried, not until the man frowned.

Ambrose scrolled over the tablet as light seeped in through the blinds behind him, casting him in intermittent shadow. "Should you really have May Trace as a pilot? Aren't you living together?"

"We're roommates, sir. And she's a phenomenal pilot." Tristan might want more from Mila, but his boss didn't need to know that.

Ambrose touched a couple spots on the screen. "It says here

she's a mediocre pilot." He scrolled again, his frown deepening. "Barely passed deep space qualifications."

Tristan shifted in place, the chair creaking under his ass. "Yes, she told me she doesn't test well and that her testing results dictated the missions she received. The *Orleans* mission was the first time she needed more than mediocre piloting skills. She responds beautifully in a crisis, sir. I've seen that personally and that is exactly what I want on this mission. Someone I can trust to handle him or herself well when all hell breaks loose."

"Do you anticipate something going wrong?" Ambrose glared at Tristan.

He shrugged, his gut twisting just thinking about all that had gone wrong, all that *could* go wrong. "The *Orleans* mission went awry. This is a continuation of that mission. It seems only logical that any trouble we received then might follow us here. I've tried to only pick crew members I trust implicitly, but as always, there are too many variables on any mission to account for every eventuality. I would rather be prepared for FUBAR than be surprised by it."

His superior nodded, going back to the screen. "Kyle Avery is on another assignment," Ambrose said matter-of-fact.

"Can he be reassigned? I was really hoping to have him aboard."

He nodded. "I think so. His current investigation has seen some… snags."

Tristan nodded, waiting for the next comment, but none came.

He put the tablet on the desk. "Looks good. I'll get everything together. Once I've got this finalized, get in touch with your crew members and brief them on the mission. Remember, need to know only."

Tristan nodded and stood at attention. "Understood." He saluted before turning on his heel and leaving.

Mila returned from the gym and showered, but dinner at the Traces' wasn't for hours. So, she decided to do laundry. And, since she was in a good mood from her workout, she grabbed Tristan's too. Plus, she liked smelling his shirts when he wasn't around to take it the wrong way.

Yeah, yeah, well they smelled fine.

She didn't like doing laundry. Her definition involved throwing everything in the washer, then the dryer, then tossing the clothes in the bedrooms without hanging or folding.

Mila was dumping loose socks in his drawer when she found a bag buried near the bottom. She picked it up and felt the circular and knobby pattern of a ring with a decent-sized stone. She didn't open it, merely putting it back where she found it, but she was curious.

Why did he have a woman's ring in his dresser?

CHAPTER SIX

*H*e waited in his car. Waiting and waiting. He hated stakeouts. But they were part of the job, an unavoidable part. He'd been alternating his receiver between the various devices he'd planted in Captain Faulk's office. The audio crackled each time, jarring him through his headphones. The man had gone through the day working on his mission plan. He knew Faulk had chosen May Trace, the bitch who single-handedly thwarted the sabotage of the U.S.S. *Orleans*, and Kyle Avery, Head of Security from that same mission.

Tension building at the ramifications of those choices, he gritted his teeth. He hoped Faulk's superior would nix those selections. Well, at least nix Trace. There was nothing they could do about Avery. Security men were a dime a dozen in the military. But a pilot as good as Trace? They were one in a million. And they couldn't afford for her to be on this mission.

Faulk exited his office, the lines of audio changing to baseline static on his display. He put down the computer and removed his headphones. Picking up the cell phone, he dialed a number and said, "Faulk has just left the building. His office should be vacant now."

The mission should be finalized by now and finalized mission plans were always in paper format for security reasons. They wouldn't be able to access them remotely. They needed to break in. And the secure records vault would be too difficult, leaving the next best option—Faulk's office. The officer running the mission always had a copy of the mission plan secured in his office. He found that rather stupid seeing as those offices were about as difficult to break into as a teenager's locker in high school.

Faulk drove off and he followed several car lengths behind. He didn't need to be caught. It might force the mission to be scrapped. And they might not receive notice about the next one.

<hr>

Mila took a deep breath before ringing the doorbell. May's mother always told her she didn't have to ring it. But Mila wasn't family, she would never *be* family, and she felt uncomfortable walking in like that. She pressed the bell.

Indistinct shouting came from the other side, pounding feet, and May's little brother, Bryan, opened the door. "You made it. We were about to eat without you."

Mila shook her head. Bryan was always voting for eating without her. He didn't like how much food she ate. He felt like it dipped into his behemoth portions too much.

Then there were the little comments, jokes really, that he made. It was never serious, never overtly questioning her, but sometimes she wondered. Did he know?

"Well, move before I eat you. I'm starving," she said, trying to dispel the tense atmosphere.

Bryan put on airs of mock surprise. "Oh no, we'll go broke."

She rolled her eyes, punching him in the arm without any force. "Move?"

She shoved him out of the way as May's mother came barreling out of the kitchen, brushing her clean hands on her pants.

"May! Oh, it's so good to see you!"

She pulled Mila into a hug that always surprised her, it was so strong. Mila had to wait to suck in air.

"Good to see you, too," she said, her words nothing more than whispers.

Mrs. Trace leaned back, smiling at her. "Come, we made your favorite."

May's favorite, not Mila's. Granted, May and Mila had practically been twins growing up, so that distinction wasn't much of an issue. Mila would happily eat anything May had loved. Often, Mila's favorite dish would be May's second favorite and vice versa. It made the facade that much easier.

May's mother dragged her to the dining room, shoving her into a seat before taking off toward the kitchen again. "The dishes will be out in a moment!"

Mila sat at the table, wishing to be anywhere but here at the moment. She didn't want to be here, but she felt obligated. She'd taken May's identity. In a way, she'd taken May away from them, even if she'd had nothing to do with her death. Even if she'd tried to save her. And she couldn't bear to truly take her best friend from these people.

But was she doing what was best for them? Or was she

preventing them from grieving, preventing them from moving on, from honoring May's memory?

She sighed, Bryan giving her an odd look. It didn't matter. She'd chosen this path. For better or worse, she would see it through.

So although it hurt being around May's family when she missed her own to no end, she came. Every time May's mother called, she came. Dinners, family get-togethers, it didn't matter. She still came. She felt like an imposter, an outsider, but it was a punishment, of sorts, a price to be paid.

Mila deserved this.

Mrs. Trace came in with the main entrée, her husband following with a couple side dishes. Bryan sat opposite Mila, impatient as always. She laughed quietly at him. All he needed was a knife and fork in his fists to complete the picture.

Mila and Bryan stared each other down, ready to battle for the serving utensils. May's mother placed the tray on the table and Mila's hand whipped out, snatching the fork in the blink of an eye. She stuck her tongue out at Bryan, who grumbled and sulked.

Bryan reached for the side dishes as Mila served herself and they swapped when each finished. The next half hour consisted of silent eating—utensils scraping against plates, loud chewing, and shifting chairs.

As the meal wound down, May's mother started in with the weekly interrogation session. "So, what have you been up to?"

She shrugged, piling another helping of food onto her plate for good measure. The plates were almost empty, so she was out of delaying tactics. "Same old, same old." She shoveled another piece of broccoli in her mouth.

"What about you, Bryan? How's the new job?"

Bryan had just graduated college and started his new job last week.

He squirmed in his seat. "It's okay."

Probably not as fun as goofing off at college, Mila mused.

"Just okay," the mother said back, clearly intending to get the full truth, and nothing but.

Bryan nodded. "Yup, just okay."

"What did you do?"

"Just new hire stuff, reading policies and stuff. Boring stuff."

May's mother nodded, then turned back to Mila before she could cram another piece of pork loin in her mouth. "Did you do anything interesting? How are your friends, May?"

"Fine," she grumbled. "Tristan has a new assignment, so he'll probably be shipping out soon."

"Oh, that's nice. Do you know what it's about?" She leaned forward, elbows on the table, hands clasped before her.

"No." Mila crammed her mouth with more food before May's mother could ask another question, then stood. "Well, I've got to go. See you next week." She raced away and slipped out the door before anyone could stop her.

When she started her car, May's mom was standing in the open doorway, waving. Mila waved back and backed out.

A clean getaway.

A few miles down from the Traces' house, the car sputtered and rolled to a stop. Mila managed to get it off the road, but when she popped the hood to find out what had gone wrong, she saw no glaring defects. Not that she knew much about cars. Pretty much, if it wasn't smoking, she couldn't diagnose it.

Mila looked around. Trees surrounded her with no landmarks in sight. She pulled her phone out of her back pocket and cursed. No signal. She shook her head, looking up at the sky. "Really?" In this day and age, how could a single speck of Earth not have coverage. Honestly!

Without a signal, she couldn't even use the maps program to figure out where she was. GPS still worked, but without data coverage, the stupid app showed a dot against a blank grid. Useless. With a sigh, she just started walking. It would be a long walk back to civilization.

After she'd followed the road around a curve, the wild emptiness enclosed her. The leaves rustled in the wind. The night insects made their various songs. And every once in a while, she swore she heard a sound too loud to belong.

She spun around, scanning her surroundings, searching for what didn't fit. Letting out a slow breath, she hated this. It felt too familiar, too much like the life she'd lived before May visited her that fateful day. It wasn't a life she had any desire to return to.

You're being paranoid, Mila. She continued on, knowing she had miles to go. The chances of finding anyone but military personnel in the boonies surrounding the base were nonexistent.

And she wasn't afraid of any soldier.

Mila jumped when a twig broke only a few feet away. "Hello? This is NSS Pilot May Trace. Who's out there?" She tried to make her voice sound authoritative, but feared she'd failed miserably. She felt too shaky, too on edge.

Silence answered her for the longest time. She shook herself out of it when she realized she'd been standing in the road, looking like an idiot, waiting for a response. "There's no one out there, moron," she mumbled to herself.

Time passed and another noise broke through the air. *I'm being followed.* She made adjustments to hearing, smell, sight, and her various muscle groups in preparation for a fight. *What's going on?* It didn't matter. She prepared anyway. It was a reflex after ten years living on the streets.

Another few minutes and Mila stopped. "Why are you following me?" She turned, glaring at the man dressed in shades of black standing behind her on the road. He probably thought he had the element of surprise.

Instead of answering, he just shrugged and attacked. A pistol came up from his side, gripped in a steady palm. Mila jerked right just as the report echoed through the landscape, radiating through her skull, ricocheting like a small caliber bullet. She rushed in, pounding him with a fist to the stomach as she reached for his gun hand.

He hunched over with the blow and Mila turned, ripping away the weapon and flinging it into the trees. She turned back to her attacker, moving in to strike, but he blocked with an arm, shoving with his whole body since he was still curled in on himself. She stumbled a couple steps, but regained her balance and circled him, looking for an opening.

He stood slowly and glared at her before giving her a wicked smile—like he knew something she didn't. Which was precisely when a blow landed to her kidney from behind. She sucked in a breath, almost hitting the ground.

Shit, there were two of them.

Favoring her left side where he struck, she angled so she kept both in her sights. The new attacker had no weapon, which helped, but two against one was never ideal. She bit her lip, her gaze flitting from one to the other, looking for a tell. Damn, they weren't as bad as she would have hoped.

Mila couldn't win.

She forced a surge of adrenaline through her system and took off, running as fast as she could. Her heart hammered away in her ears. She sucked in breaths in even draws and exhales, but her muscles burned from the exertion, even if she refused to give in to it.

As seconds dragged into minutes, the pounding that she'd attributed to her beating heart quieted and she knew she'd lost her pursuers. She continued running at top speed until the pounding of her own feet and heart, and the loud puffs of her breath, were all she heard. She slowed to a stop and leaned over, taking in and letting out long, controlled breaths.

Mila looked back, expecting to see them gaining on her now that she'd stopped. Nothing but road and forest remained. Looking ahead, she just spotted the outskirts of the residential neighborhood on base where she lived. She picked up into a jog, heading for home.

But the experience lingered, leaving her shaken. Looking at her life so far, security was a foreign concept. She'd grown up in a loving family with a best friend who she was inseparable from, but that had quickly disappeared. She'd been attacked in a bar parking lot. She'd spent ten years in hiding, living on the street, often living by her fists. She'd been targeted by an assassin, nearly died in a conspiracy, and still lived in fear of discovery.

Would she ever truly feel safe?

CHAPTER SEVEN

The front door opened, slamming into the wall before closing with a bang. Tristan got up. "Mila?"

Mila stood leaning against the entryway, sweat soaking the outfit she'd worn to the Traces' place. Her breaths came in controlled drags, but her muscles shook from exertion.

He meant to make a joke, but it came out wrong. "Did you run all the way back?" Instead of the amusement he'd intended, concern filled his voice. As he continued to look her over, he noticed the bright red, almost purple tinge to her face and the pulse throbbing at her temple.

"Not quite," she whispered, her voice breathless as she got her body under control.

"What's wrong? Are you okay?" He walked forward, picking up momentum, resisting the urge to reach out, to pull her into his arms.

"Car died. Was attacked." Her words came out clipped, but with more force.

Tristan's face paled, his jaw going slack. "Are you hurt?" His gaze roved over her once more, looking for bruises, cuts, hell, bullet wounds. She looked okay, shaken, but okay.

Mila shook her head. Tristan sighed, relieved. He opened his mouth to ask if she knew why someone attacked her. Then he remembered the mission he'd been assigned… the mission he imagined had been approved or rejected by now. The original would have been placed in the archive vault and a copy under his office door.

"Shit." He turned, pulling his hand down his face. Somehow he knew, he just *knew*, that Mila's attack had to do with that damned mission. "I knew it would be trouble," he mumbled.

"What would?" Mila asked, her breathing finally back to normal. She stood straight, her shoulders back, hands fisted at her sides.

"We have a new assignment, I imagine. Well, I do definitely, but I'd requested you for the pilot. I hadn't received official approval by the time I left the office." He shook his head, pacing the room, a litany of curses sailing like a marquee through his brain.

"What's it about?" She stepped forward, but avoided his path, leaning a hip against the edge of the couch and crossing her arms over her chest.

He chuckled, shaking his head again. "I can't say."

She scoffed. "Since when has that stopped you when all hell breaks loose?"

He hedged, stopping his pacing and shying away from looking at her. "I can't even be sure it relates to your attack."

Mila rolled her eyes, shrugging her shoulders in a motion that emphasized her crossed arms. "Yeah, and my name's Avery."

Tristan glared, but there was no heat behind the expression. "I shouldn't say."

"But you're going to." Mila smirked confidently at him.

He nodded. "Tomorrow. I'll brief both you and Kyle tomorrow."

Mila dropped her arms, grumbled, and stomped off out of sight. A sigh escaped him, grateful that she hadn't pushed. If she had, he would have told… eventually.

The next morning, Tristan arrived at the office and found a manila envelope slipped under the door. He bent over, grabbed it, and ripped it open, pulling out the contents. A handful of papers fell out. He read through them, reassured that they matched the parameters he'd given his superior officer yesterday.

He walked around, sat at his desk, the chair groaning under him, and tossed the papers across the surface. Reaching for the phone, he dialed Kyle Avery's number and waited for the ringing to stop.

"Avery," the familiar voice barked.

"How are things on your end?" He leaned back, trying to shift so the worn out padding didn't contort his spine into a pretzel.

"Captain Faulk. Somehow, I suspect you're to blame for the call I just received from my duty officer." A slight edge tainted the other man's voice.

" 'Fraid so. I've got a mission for you. Meet me in my office at nine."

"See you then."

Mila yawned as she leaned back in the chair in Tristan's office, taking in the sights. She'd never been there before. The room was utilitarian, only the barest of personal touches. Her gaze skated over a few frames on the bare walls. "This is almost as bad as the *Orleans*, Tristan."

Tristan shook his head. "No, it's not. There's stuff on the walls. And on my desk."

"But nothing personal? No family photos?"

Tristan looked around, then down at his desktop. The sheepish look on his face was all the answer she needed.

"That's what I thought." She crossed her arms, smirking at him in triumph.

"Well, what about you, Mila?" he asked defensively.

"Tristan, I don't have an office."

"No, but your bedroom is much worse."

She scowled at him, leaning forward aggressively. "Of course, it is. I don't *have* any personal effects."

Tristan looked down, probably ashamed of himself for reminding her of her past.

Mila ignored him. She'd had her car towed that morning. An hour later, she wanted to hurt someone when the mechanic called to say it was good to go, that a connection was loose. She had to take a bus to retrieve the mechanical beast. It cost an arm and a half to repair that "loosened connection," but she had her transportation back.

A knock came at the door. "Enter."

Kyle Avery peeked in. "Reporting for duty." He smirked, and walked in, taking a seat beside Mila. "How's it been, Mila?"

"Shitty."

Avery arched an eyebrow. "What happened?"

She leaned back, crossing her arms once more, pouting. "I was attacked on the way home from May's parents' place yesterday."

"What?!" Kyle jumped up, looming over her.

"Get a grip, Avery."

He took a breath and sat back down. "What happened?"

"What does it matter? I got away and Tristan thinks it has something to do with this mission." She waved at Tristan. "Do you really think it was compromised?"

"The *Orleans* mission was. To my understanding, we still haven't figured out how. Everyone tried to be more tight-lipped this time, but the military does love their chains of command. It's impossible to keep anything quiet for long."

Avery and Mila both nodded.

"So, what's the mission?" Avery asked.

"We're taking a short-range shuttle to the Kennedy Moon Station. Diplomats will be on board, as with the *Orleans* mission. The Incirrina are meeting us on the moon and we'll be conducting the last of the treaty talks there." He looked at both Mila and Kyle. "There's a good chance this will go FUBAR. Expect it to. I have."

"This is why you asked me off the task force I've been on?" Avery asked incredulously.

"Yes, Avery. You are one of a select few I trust. You and Mila.

I will not fail at this mission and I want people around me I can count on. You've both proven yourselves."

Avery shrugged. "Well, my investigations *had* hit a dead end. Maybe I'll get somewhere now that they've taken me off the task force."

Tristan passed tablets to each of them. "These are the 'cleared' mission parameters. Keep in mind, what I've already told you, I wasn't supposed to say. The details on these tablets are all I'm authorized to give you. Understood?"

"Sure." Mila nodded. "Keep our mouths shut. And act dumb."

"Precisely."

Mila left the meeting so excited, she almost jumped up and down. Kyle still appeared on edge, but that made sense. If he was anything like her, he hated leaving something unfinished. And as a security expert, the fiasco of a threat to his mission would give him an aneurism.

They would take off in a few days, and suddenly, the unbearable need to see her family—her real family—grabbed her. She spent the afternoon pacing the living room, trying to talk herself out of it, or trying to come up with a plan to get away with it.

Fuck it. She decided to just do it. Jumping in the car, she drove the distance to her parents' home, shaking the nerves out of her hand at every intersection. In no time, far quicker than she would have liked, she found herself parked in front of their house. She turned off the engine, but couldn't bring herself to exit.

Minutes passed and her agitation grew worse and worse. Her

breathing grew shaky as a rap rattled her window. She jumped, gazing up at her father only inches away, looking in with concern on his face.

"May?" The surprise dripped from his voice.

She rolled down the window, the power windows still working because she hadn't opened the doors yet. "Hi, Mister Dragomirov," she stuttered.

"What are you doing here? I haven't seen you in years."

Not since Mila disappeared, she would imagine. "I just…" She sighed. "I just feel like it's time."

He nodded. "Come on. You're just in time for dinner."

She jerked her head, too spastic to call it a nod, pressed the button to roll the window back up, and stepped out of the car, following her dad.

He was so much older than she remembered. Gray had seeped in to pepper his hair and he'd grown a beard in the last ten years. Lines had etched his face, especially around his eyes, and his belly had grown to overlap his belt.

The house looked the same, though. Same shutters, same door, same paint job. Even the same plants in the front yard, since her mother preferred annuals.

He opened the door and ushered her in, a rich aroma wafting to her.

"That smells wonderful. I think I've missed Mrs. Dragomirov's cooking."

Dad smiled. "Well, you're welcome anytime. You were always welcome here, May."

"Thanks, Mr. Dragomirov." She sighed, following him to the table.

"Please, call me Ivan."

"Thanks… Ivan." It felt weird calling her father by his given name. She leaned over the green chair, waving to her mother, who was finishing up with dinner in the narrow room they'd always called a "one butt kitchen." "Hello, Mrs. Dragomirov."

Her mother's head whipped around. "May?! Oh my God, May!" She raced over, gripping Mila in a giant hug that suffused her with warmth and love. As she breathed in her mother's scent, a combination of flowers and cooking, she pushed aside the taint caused by May's name on her lips. "Oh May, it's so good to see you. How have you been? How long has it been? Ten years?"

She nodded. "Yeah, and I've been good. I got some medals a while back. In fact, I flew a pretty important mission just a few months ago. It was wonderful. Everything we ever dreamed of." Mila smiled, looking down, wishing May could have been there.

When she looked up, her mother looked down, the woman's thoughts probably mirroring her own—Mila/May should have been here.

Looking into Mila's eyes, she gave a painful smile, making Mila want to cry or hug her.

Or tell her the truth.

"Come, May. Let's eat."

Alyana Dragomirov waved goodbye to her daughter's oldest friend, watching her drive off. She sighed, trying to keep a tear from falling. It was both painful and precious having May over. While the visit reminded her of the daughter she'd lost, it also felt like getting a piece of her precious girl back.

Especially with how much of Mila she saw in May. She didn't remember May mimicking Mila so much. The mannerisms, the turns of phrase. Sometimes during dinner, Mila sat right across from her, talking from May's mouth. It was eerie, but maybe what she needed at this stage in her life.

If May had shown up ten years ago, talking and acting so much like Mila, Alyana would have kicked the poor girl out of her house, telling her never to come back. And yet, May had suffered Mila's loss just as much as Alyana had. She lost a daughter, but May lost her other half.

Mila and May had been like twins their whole lives. They'd done everything together. Now, Alyana felt terrible because they'd drifted apart. When had that happened? She remembered when Mila first disappeared. May hadn't taken it well and she and Sarah, May's mother, had stepped up to help her. But years had passed since she'd last spoken to May. She'd become so caught up in her own grief, she forgot everything else.

Now she suspected she'd missed out on something by pulling into herself. She should have stepped up, been another mother to May. It might have done them both some good.

Alyana grabbed the door, intending to close it. She would call May, invite her over again. She couldn't change the past, but she could alter the future. They both held little pieces of Mila in their hearts and perhaps together they could be made whole.

Back then, healing was impossible. She remembered thinking she would never stop expecting her little girl to come walking through that door. Standing in the doorway, still holding it open, her gaze skittered to the end of the road, searching the horizons as she'd done for years.

She sighed, closing the door. No, she'd never given up hope.

She still expected to see Mila come around the corner, still believed she was out there somewhere.

Would she *ever* move on?

Tristan stood in front of his open dresser, the small velveteen bag in his hand. He ran his finger over it, the material smooth on one pass, then coarse on the return trip. He took comfort in the ring's outline through the cloth.

"Whatcha got there?" Mila said.

Tristan jumped, dropping the bag, its contents hitting the floor with a couple clicks of sound, then looked on in horror as it rolled across the cheap linoleum. They both went running for it, but Mila got there first. She picked up the small silver ring with a diamond stone. She held it out to him.

"Thanks," he said. Grabbing the ring, he put it back in the bag before shoving it in his sock drawer. He closed the drawer, leaning against it for good measure, as if that would wipe her memory.

"So?" she prompted.

Damn, he did *not* want to have this conversation right now. "Family heirloom."

A sad smile crossed her face.

Double damn, that was stupid. Mila didn't have any family she could contact. No heirlooms either since she'd taken off over ten years ago with little more than the clothes on her back. Why did he bring that up?

"It must be nice having stuff like that." She turned to leave, her shoulders sagging.

"Wait!" Tristan called out, reaching with a single hand.

She turned, a heavy sadness in her eyes.

He tried to smile, but the corners of his mouth wouldn't cooperate. He sighed, looking away. How could he make her feel less alone? "My parents are dead. The only family I have left is my brother." He looked over at the frame on his dresser, picking up the wood, letting his thumb rub over the glass surface. In the picture, the Faulk boys smiled, rough housing.

Mila pressed against his side.

He stared down as a smidgeon of the sadness left her face.

"I haven't spoken to him in years."

Not for lack of trying. He never stopped trying, but pursuing a career in the military had driven a wedge between him and his brother he could never remove.

Tristan didn't know why his brother refused to respond to his attempts to contact him. He didn't know what he'd done wrong, didn't know how to fix it. He sighed, placing the photo back in its place. "It doesn't matter. We have different lives now."

He turned from the picture, looking at Mila, her expression saying it all.

She didn't believe his bullshit either.

Tristan sighed, although he couldn't figure why Mila hadn't questioned or at least teased him more about the ring. He'd expected comments like, "Planning to propose to someone?" or "Little small for you, isn't it?" But she'd said nothing. Well, not nothing, just that single comment before she disappeared into her bedroom.

He opened the drawer again, pulling out the velvet bag and let the ring fall into his hand. He'd told the truth. It was a family heirloom. It had belonged to his grandmother. He'd always kept it locked away in a safety deposit box until recently.

But a few weeks ago, he'd been at the bank, withdrawing some cash, when the urge came over him to take it out. Tristan hadn't questioned the impulse. He just did it. He still didn't know why the urge had suddenly developed to keep it close.

Looking at it now, a niggling sensation in the back of his mind bothered him. Tristan didn't want to admit it, but deep down he knew why he'd felt compelled to bring it home. His grandmother had wanted him to give that to his bride someday. He didn't intend to marry anytime soon, but when he stared at the ring, Mila filled his thoughts.

Tristan wanted her to have it. He loved her. Maybe he'd loved her since that first day when he'd noticed how fine her ass looked. They'd never dated, were nothing more than friends, but he would happily spend the rest of his life with her—if she would ever agree.

Now, he just needed to find a way.

Mila called May's parents as she looked out her bedroom window. A small patch of grass abutted a wood fence that partially blocked the view of the house behind them.

The phone rang, then Sarah Trace picked up, "Trace residence."

"Hi… Mom." She had such a hard time saying it. They weren't her parents. They never would be. The noticeable pause, so glaring to Mila's mind, went unnoticed by May's mother.

"Oh, May! It's so good to hear from you."

Mila rolled her eyes. She acted like they hadn't spoken in weeks, months even, rather than a matter of days. "I just thought I'd let you know I'm shipping out in a few days."

"Oh, we have to make you a special dinner, sweetheart. What do you want to eat?"

"Uh." What would May want? "Mac and cheese." Both May

and Mila had always been fond of the woman's mac and cheese.

"Okay." The voice on the other end grew quieter. "And what else?"

Mila racked her brain, but came up with nothing. "Meat?"

"May," Mrs. Trace chastised her.

Mila sighed. "Chicken?"

"How do you want it seasoned?"

Mila resisted the urge to growl at the woman. Why the twenty questions? Her mind went blank. "However."

"May, that's not an answer. Gosh, Mila used to do that when you two were growing up." Exasperation filled her voice.

"Teriyaki?"

"Okay. And what about vegetables?"

Will it never end?! Mila grabbed at her hair, frustrated with the other woman's apparent need to drive her insane. She wanted to say, "I don't fucking care," but figured that wouldn't go over well. "Broccoli."

"And how do you want that seasoned?"

Could she not make a decision on her own? "Buttered?"

"Okay, see you tonight, dear."

Mila sighed, relieved when the dial tone sounded in her ear. Family could be so frustrating. And it wasn't even *her* family!

Kyle found himself back at his office, the investigation he'd dedicated the last few months of his life to sucking him back, not letting go. He didn't like leaving things unfinished and this was a great big mosquito bite waiting to be scratched.

The door clicked behind him as he reached back, isolating himself in the space. It was more a hole than an office. Papers and maps were taped to the walls, a computer display waited on the desk, and a tablet sat so close to the edge, a light breeze would topple it to the scuffed industrial flooring.

As he sat at his desk, running his hands through his hair, he found a shameful comfort in Mila being attacked. Still, he worried about her, had half a mind to assign a security detail until the launch.

But someone attacking her said something. To him, it said those saboteurs cared about this new mission's outcome, that they feared Mila piloting it. It meant he had an opportunity. An opportunity to strike back, to catch these bastards and end this once and for all.

With renewed vigor, and only a couple days remaining, he started poring over information on the people who knew about the mission. Who could have leaked it? Who could have told?

A combination of excitement and boredom found Mila driving her car to the hangars in search of the U.S.S. *Dakota*. She told herself it was to get familiar with the ship, talk to the mechanical crew, learn about handling issues and any concerns she should have. In reality, she just couldn't sit still anymore and she wanted to get a head start on this mission.

After half an hour of wandering the grounds in her car, she found the hangar assigned to the *Dakota*. She parked and got out, looking up at the beautiful shuttle she would fly in a couple days.

The hangar stretched in width nearly half the length of a football field, the smell of oil and fuel thick in the air. With the wings retracted, the *Dakota* still stretched almost the entire width of the hangar. And it maxed out at a height of thirty feet. The fuselage was eighty yards from nose to rear and the engines continued beyond that.

"Hey, there," a voice called from inside.

Mila looked, seeing a man in overalls with the NSS emblem on them. She waved. "Hello, back."

The man squinted at her, then he started waving his finger at her. He could either be trying to chastise her, or trying to recall where he knew her. Mila hoped he didn't know the *real* May or she would be in deep shit.

His eyes lit up and he snapped his fingers as the pieces clicked into place. "Holy shit, you're May Trace. *The* May Trace."

Mila paused, unsure how to handle the strange man giving her an even stranger look. "Maybe." She leaned back, as if doing so would get her farther from him. She'd already taken a couple steps back without noticing.

"You piloted the *Orleans* mission!"

She nodded, letting out a mental breath of relief. At least he was referencing something she had first hand knowledge of.

"Oh, my God, you are the *bomb!*" His hands waved as he talked, emphasizing his excitement. "You saved a buddy of mine's life."

Mila shrugged. "Just doing my job."

"Doing your job? Doing your job? I heard you single-handedly thwarted an attempt to kill all the personnel on board. I heard…"

Mila held up her hand. "Stop. I did not 'single-handedly' do anything but fly the ship. Yes, I helped stop those who invaded the ship. I *helped.* I nearly got myself killed in the process, but I helped. I helped with long hours of investigating. *Helped.*" She shook her head. "I didn't do it alone. And a lot of people died." Her voice drifted to a somber whisper by that last sentence.

"I know. A friend of mine died on the *Orleans*. But more survived than died. And you were partially to thank for that."

The look in his eyes didn't make Mila think he believed his words. He still looked at her with hero worship. He'd ignored everything she'd just said. She sighed.

"I want to see the maintenance records for the *Dakota*. I'm looking for handling issues, anything I need to know before takeoff."

"You're going to be flying the *Dakota*? Oh, that's *awesome!*" He ran off, hopefully to retrieve those records she wanted. "The *Dakota* is a beaut." His muffled voice drifted from a room in the back. "She's my baby." He ran back with a tablet in hand, handing it to her. "You're gonna love her."

"Thanks." She looked around, but didn't see anywhere to sit. "Do you have somewhere I can go over this?"

He jerked. "Oh, yeah. Of course. This way." He took off again, heading for the room he'd just left. A desk and a few chairs swamped the space. Miscellaneous stains coated most surfaces. "Sit wherever you like. I'll be out with the Dakota, getting her ready for you."

"Thanks." Mila sat at one of the "guest" chairs, throwing her legs up onto the surface of the desk and resting the tablet in her lap to read. She hoped none of the stains would transfer to her clothes. She wasn't overly vain, but she didn't like cleaning either and the military did have certain standards.

Tristan knocked on his superior's door and waited for a response.

"Enter." The man's voice came muffled through the wood.

He peeked in, the light from the industrial fixture on the ceiling flickering over the office, "Hello, sir."

"Captain Faulk. Is everything progressing smoothly with the mission?"

Tristan closed the door behind him, giving them some semblance of privacy. "I suspect there's been a leak."

Ambrose frowned. "Why do you say that?"

"Because shortly after I finalized the mission parameters with you, someone attacked May Trace on the way home from her parents' house. I'm not claiming you're the leak, but at some point after our meeting, someone leaked her name, I guarantee it."

"Why do you think it's in relation to this mission and not the *Orleans* mission?"

"I suspect it's related to both. Trace hasn't been attacked or targeted once since returning to Earth. But as soon as she gets assigned to this mission, she gets attacked?" Tristan shook his head. "That's just too much coincidence. Do I think it might be related to the *Orleans* mission? Hell, yes. I would bet her actions aboard the *Orleans* were the reason behind the attack, but the impetus was her assignment to this new mission."

Ambrose nodded, then shook his head. "Damn it." He slammed his elbows on the desk. "Okay, from this point onward, no details above and beyond what's absolutely necessary go any further than you and your team. Do not tell anyone anything. No communication devices. I want your offices, your homes, everything, swept for bugs. Someone somewhere found out about this. We need to know how."

"Yes, sir."

It took most of the day for Mila to peruse the maintenance and inspection logs. Then, the mechanic kept chatting and wouldn't let her leave. She started fantasizing about doing not very nice things to him. Some of them involving claws.

By the time she got back to her car, every interior surface scalding from the afternoon sun, she was running late for the farewell dinner at the Traces' home. She sped off the base, ignoring any and all road signs. When she arrived, she was five minutes late and Bryan was standing outside the door mouthing, "You're so busted."

She responded by flipping him the bird with both hands.

She shoved him aside and entered. "Sorry I'm late."

May's mother rushed into the entry. "Oh, no worries, May. Busy with pre-launch details?"

She nodded. "Yeah, and a mechanic that wouldn't shut up." She smiled.

"Well, you're here now. I was worried the food would get cold."

Mila waved off the comment. "Mac and cheese is better that way."

"You and Mila always liked your mac and cheese cold."

Though no suspicion colored the other woman's face, it made Mila's blood turn to ice each time she mentioned her real name. Did she suspect, even subconsciously? Mila shrugged it off, refusing to worry until it became a problem. She had enough problems as it was. "It's good cold."

Mila followed her into the dining room and took her usual spot. Bryan sulked on the way to his seat, no doubt bummed that Mila escaped parental wrath for being late.

***

Once back home, Mila paced her bedroom, staring at the beige carpet underfoot, trying to decide whether or not she should visit her own parents. She wanted to, but worried it would be weird. Would they think it strange that May Trace would want to visit again so soon?

Mila didn't know and so she paced. She didn't hear when Tristan got home and she didn't go looking for him either, caught up with the problems in her own head. Time ticked by in an agitated amalgam of agonizing increments when her cell phone rang.

"Hello?"

"Oh, May! It's Alyana Dragomirov. I was wondering if you'd like to come by tomorrow for a visit. I'll understand if you can't." It was clear from her voice that she wouldn't take no for an answer.

Mila nearly laughed into the phone. "Yeah, Mrs. Dragomirov. What time do you want me over?"

"Oh, whenever you get up. And call me Alyana."

Mila could just imagine her waving it off, the same way she herself did. "Okay, I'll see you first thing tomorrow."

"Bye, May."

"Bye, Alyana."

When Mila arrived at her parents' house the next morning, she parked in the driveway. There was one less car there. Dad must not have been home. She knocked on the front door.

The door swung open instantly. "May!" Her mother grabbed her up in a breath-stealing hug. "Oh, it's good to see you."

"Good to see you, too," she wheezed through her compressed lungs.

"Come in, come in."

Mila followed her mom into the house and to the living room, where Alyana settled onto the couch and patted the seat beside her. Mila sank into the cushions, prepared for a long day of catching up.

She tried to leave several times, but each time her mother dissuaded her, encouraging her to stay "just a little longer." Eventually, the sun settled low on the horizon and Alyana demanded Mila stay for dinner. She agreed and Alyana raced off.

Mila could hear her mom ordering something for delivery and she smiled. Her mother was a fantastic cook, but she was also terribly lazy. And forgetful. Many of Mila's meals growing up had been delivered or fast food. She'd always appreciated the days when her mother cooked. They were special.

A car pulled up outside and she peeked out the window, looking through the blinds. Her father stepped out of his car, which he'd parked at the curb since Mila took his space. She felt bad, but she *had* tried to escape earlier, so she didn't feel too bad.

"Alyana, I'm home," he said as he walked through the door. "We're having takeout again, aren't we?" He sighed.

Mila stood and wandered to the entry. "Hello, Ivan."

He jerked his head to face her. "Oh, May. Good to see you. Are you joining us for dinner?"

"Sure. I mean, if you wife keeps me here any longer, someone might have to send out a search party, but sure."

He laughed. "Talked your ear off, did she?"

Mila pinched her index finger and thumb together. "Only a little."

He placed his wallet and keys on the hall table. "I wonder how long until dinner."

"She just called, so it'll be a while."

He nodded. "I know it hasn't been long since your last visit, but anything new?"

She shrugged. "I'll be shipping out soon." She paused. *You can do it, Mila. Just say it.* "My family gave me a farewell dinner."

It was still hard telling anyone that the Traces' were family. They weren't, but she had to pretend they were. She hated it. Why did she take May's identity again?

Oh yeah, because she wanted a life.

By dinnertime, Alyana was positive the woman before her, the woman claiming to be her daughter's best friend, was her daughter in the flesh. It made no sense. She couldn't fathom how it was possible, but as the day wore on, she'd watched every motion, mannerism, inflection of speech, and choice of words. May was Mila. She was certain of it.

At dinner, Alyana's mind raced with the possibilities. Only one possibility stuck. Her daughter was a shape-shifter. But no.

How could that be? She would have known, wouldn't she? How could she raise the girl for twenty years without knowing?

And where did she get it? Alyana had always thought shifting was inherited, that the skill belonged to another species that merely resembled humans or took the shape of them. But what if she'd been wrong?

Panic seized her, but she didn't let it show, continuing to eat her dinner. She let her husband carry the conversation. The topics migrated to Ivan asking about an upcoming mission of Mila's as their daughter deftly avoided answering.

When Mila cleaned her plate, she stood. "I should get going now."

"I'll see you out." Alyana jumped from her seat and jogged around her husband's spot at the head of the table. She sedately walked behind Mila, her body screaming at her to take action.

At the door, Mila turned. "It was nice today, Alyana."

"Good night, Mila." Alyana wrapped her daughter in a hug, not wanting to let her go, not after having lost her for so long.

Mila stiffened and tried to pull away, but Alyana resisted. Eventually, Mila succeeded and stepped back. "I'm not Mila, Mrs. Dragomirov. I…" She sighed, looking down and shaking her head, then looked into Alyana's eyes. "I can't replace your daughter. I don't know what happened to her. Maybe we never will."

Alyana just raised an eyebrow, broadcasting her disbelief. She didn't believe Mila's denial for a second. A moment of panic crossed Mila's face before she stuttered, bumped into the door, and jerked it open, jogging to her car. The car drove off in a squeal of tires, disappearing around the corner.

CHAPTER NINE

Mila burst through the door, slamming and locking it in a panic. She took a deep breath, and started walking to her room, her movements jerky. Her heart hammered away at her rib cage.

"What happened?" Tristan asked from the living room doorway.

Mila jerked, her heart nearly jumping out of her chest, but she clenched her jaw, ignoring him. She couldn't speak. What would she say? Tristan did so much for her, but this was her fuck up. She had to deal with it. Continuing to her bedroom, she slammed the door behind her with a definitive crack of sound. She stood at the doorjamb, unable to decide if she wanted to pace or drop on the bed and bemoan her life.

Less than twenty-four hours remained until takeoff. Mila didn't need this. She sighed and started pacing. She couldn't leave with this revelation hanging over her head. Her mother *knew*. Mila had to stop as her breaths grew shallow and uneven in her panic. Why did everyone figure out the truth? First Tristan, then Braddock, Avery, and now her mom. Why couldn't she just live her life, May's life really, in peace without everyone finding out?

She threw up her hands and sat on the edge of the bed, resigned and weary.

Life was never easy.

The next morning, Mila took off for her mother's place. It had never really been a decision. As she'd sat, staring at the wall, the idea of leaving this unsettled while she went off on mission churned her stomach until she felt like throwing up.

She stood in front of the door, frozen with indecision. The white, painted surface blurred before her eyes. Mila wanted this behind her, but she dreaded this conversation.

I'm a coward.

She could just imagine her mom fussing at her for abandoning them, for leaving without a word, for not even contacting them to tell them she was alive. She'd never seen her mother angry, but she feared her mother's reaction more than the time she got drunk under-aged and totaled the car.

After several minutes of psyching herself out, where she could have sworn eyes bored into her, she lifted her hand and knocked. She held her breath, her hands clenched at her sides.

The door opened a few moments later, framing her mother. "I was expecting you," she said as if they'd had plans.

Mila nodded and walked past her, heading for the living room. She sat down, leaning on her elbows, and not looking at the woman who gave birth to her. Footsteps shuffled on the carpet, then the other couch groaned as her mother's weight descended on it. Mila didn't speak.

Neither did her mother for the longest time. Alyana Dragomirov stared while Mila avoided eye contact. Her gaze darted to the pictures on the mantle, to the window at her mom's back, and to the doorway for a quick escape.

But before the silence grew unbearable, her mom spoke. "Why didn't you tell us?"

Mila didn't know what to say. Should she say that she'd panicked? She'd realized what she was and simply ran? Mila hadn't thought of her future, about anything, when that reality assaulted her. Partially, because she didn't believe she *had* a future. She'd believed her life ended the day she first shifted. She'd stood in her room afterward. Staring shell-shocked at the grand sum of her life in a single duffel bag, her dreams had slipped away, her life coming to an end.

When she'd shifted, she'd realized one very important thing—she would never be a pilot. The military required verified IDs, as in genetically verified IDs. Her secret would have been out as soon as she graduated. Looking back, she almost laughed. It was a miracle she'd gotten as far as she had before she had to run. Why didn't the military demand the same verification to enter pilot training? It would have been logical. Or what about school? Why not compulsory testing in elementary school, middle school, high school?

Her mind returned to the present. Of course, her time as May Trace was limited, too. Eventually, the ID would need renewal and May Trace would disappear as well. The idea saddened her and she sighed, not wanting to focus on the eventual day when she would have to say goodbye. She'd come to care about the people she'd met since this craziness began. Mila prayed that was years down the road. She squashed the impulse to pull her military ID from her pocket and check the issue date—to see how long she truly had. She hated seeing that ticking bomb waiting to explode her life to little bits.

Again.

"Mila?"

Mila finally looked up at her mother. "How could I? What would I say? Oh, Mom. Yeah, I'm a shifter. My life is over, bye?" She shook her head. "Nobody could know and I sure as shit wasn't thinking of anyone else with my life in the crapper!" She flounced back in the seat, crossing her arms, closing herself off.

A flare of anger flickered in her mother's eyes, possibly for the first time in Mila's life. "Clearly." She scoffed, hurt on her face. "How could you be so selfish, Mila? I raised you better than that." Her voice raised to a painful pitch as she continued to speak.

Mila jumped to her feet. "Selfish?! Raised me better?! I did the best I could, damn it! My life was falling apart around my ears! You expected me to take your feelings into account?!" She took a deep breath and resisted the urge to storm out of the room, and out of her mother's life. Mila didn't need this. She continued in a deceptively calm voice. "You do remember what happens to shifters in this country, right? What the consequences are if found? No, of course, you didn't. You were just being selfish."

Mila shook her head, turned, and walked out. Unable to stop herself, she walked out of her mother's home and hoped she wasn't walking out of her life.

***

Mila yawned, but on the inside, the conversation she'd had with her mother was eating her alive, leaving her mind running a mile a minute. She hated taking off like that, but she'd been so pissed. Selfish? She wasn't selfish. Mila rubbed her forehead, leaning against an interior wall of the hangar.

Tristan and Avery stood a few feet away, the shuttle waiting in the background, as they waited impatiently for the go-ahead to board the *Dakota.*

How could she leave with all this boiling inside her head? How could her mother say that to her? She wanted to call her, chew her out, apologize. She shook her head. *I don't know* what *I want.*

The diplomats hadn't arrived and the mechanics were still making last-minute checks on the ship before launch. The one from the other day kept sneaking glances her way and giving her thumbs up gestures. She tried to pretend he didn't exist.

Tristan fidgeted in place and Avery just scowled. She couldn't tell if he was unhappy the diplomats were late, that the mechanics hadn't released the shuttle, or that he'd been pulled from his mysterious mission.

She decided to break the silence. "You guys ever been to the moon?"

"Yes and so have you."

Mila raised her eyebrows. "I have?" *Really should have read May's personnel file…*

"Yes, a couple years ago, I think," Tristan said, scratching his chin.

Mila sighed. "Great, so I could bump into someone I should know, but don't. I'm so screwed." She sagged in place.

Avery shrugged. "Well, that's what happens when you steal someone's identity."

She glared at him. "I thought you were on my side."

Avery smirked. "I am. I'm just stating the obvious."

She flipped him the bird which only made him smirk some

more. It relieved the tension though, got her mind off her problems. She could kiss him for that.

An engine roared in the distance and an old muscle car cruised onto the scene. The thing had been beautifully restored and Mila couldn't help smiling. She wasn't a car junky herself, but she certainly appreciated a thing of beauty, even if it was barely street legal.

Sunlight reflected off the windshield, obscuring the occupant until the person stepped out, revealing slacks and a button-down shirt over a slim, curvy frame. A politician's fake smile crossed her face before she wandered off.

A few more diplomats had the good sense to carpool or have security bring them in carts to avoid cluttering the area. Mila stood back watching the spectacle they made as the mechanics finished their pre-flight checks.

Someone tapped her shoulder and she turned to see the mechanic she'd met earlier. "All good, ma'am. She's ready for takeoff."

"Thanks." She faced Tristan, waving a hand at the cliques of diplomats strewn throughout the hangar. "Do we have all the passengers yet?"

Tristan looked around, mouthing numbers, then shook his head. "We're missing someone, unless someone's hidden behind the ship."

Then, the high-pitched whine Mila often associated with toy cars sounded out, growing louder. A bright red insect of a car made itself known on the horizon and Mila squinted at the thing. Its engine zinged as it got closer. It raced up, stopping with a screech, and parked directly in front of the *Dakota*. A man jumped out. "Sorry I'm late."

Mila glared.

"Easy, Mila," Tristan said, taking the lead. "You can't park there. You'll have to move the car."

"And you are?" he asked, an attitude tingeing his words.

"Captain Tristan Faulk and if you don't move that car, I'm letting my pilot run it over when we taxi out."

Mila grinned. "It better not hurt the *Dakota*. I don't want car guts on the windshield."

Avery snorted, trying to suppress a laugh.

The man blanched, backing up as if he could protect his car with his body. From the corner of her eyes, Mila saw one of the diplomats—the woman with the muscle car—shaking her head at him. He raced to the driver's seat, jumped back in, and took off with another squeal of tires. He disappeared around a corner.

Mila let out a big breath. "Well, that was fun. So, he's the last one?"

Tristan nodded. "Why don't you start your pre-flight checks? Avery and I will work on getting these folks settled. Hopefully, by the time your checks are done, we'll be ready for launch."

She nodded. "Sounds good." Then, took off for the *Dakota*.

* * *

It took another fifteen minutes after Mila finished her pre-flight checks for Tristan and Avery to walk up to the cockpit and say they were ready for launch. "Did you lose one or something?"

Tristan shook his head as he took his seat to her left, buckling into the harness. "No, they're just slow. And argumentative."

"How long did it take that guy to park his car?"

"I'm not sure, but he was last on board by a long shot."

Mila nodded and looked to Avery. "You strapped in?"

"Snug as a bug in a rug."

Mila shook her head. "How *old* are you?" Mila pressed a button on her headset. "This is your pilot speaking. We're about to taxi out of the hangar. Please ensure that your harnesses are securely fastened and all loose objects have been secured before takeoff. Thanks." She changed channels on a display in front of her. "Control, this is the U.S.S. *Dakota*. Requesting permission for launch."

Silence greeted her for a moment. "*Dakota*, this is Mission Control, you are go for launch. The runway is free and skies are clear."

"Roger that, Control." She moved her right hand, gripping the throttle, and inched it forward. The engines purred around her, the big ship smoothly slipping from the hangar. A panicked voice echoed unintelligibly off the walls, followed by an irate yell. She ignored them both. She didn't care.

Once clear, she taxied to the runway, increasing speed since she had more breathing room. The engine cooed a little louder, making her smile in anticipation. When they'd cleared the buildings, Mila shoved the throttle all the way forward, a look of glee on her face. The ion propulsion engines roared to life, the high-pitched whine reverberating through the ship, barely muffled by the soundproofing, and her body sucked to the back of the seat. She laughed and whooped as the ground pulled away, leaving only a view of the clear, blue sky ahead of her.

Digital readouts showed numbers increasing at speeds unreadable by human eyes. Hell, even by shifter eyes. The sky grew darker and darker, and eventually black as pitch, with the occasional pinpoint star and the barest glimpse of Earth on the horizon.

Mila adjusted to pull out of orbit, the engines calming to a gentle wail like a fast wind through trees. She pulled up the navigation computer, setting an autopilot course to take them most of the way to the moon. It would take a couple days. Mila pressed the button on her headset again. "Control, this is Pilot Trace. The *Dakota* has left Earth's atmosphere and is on course for the moon."

"Roger, Pilot Trace. Safe skies."

"Thanks. Over and out, Control."

Mila leaned forward and changed the radio again. "We are now out of Earth's atmosphere and have a course plotted for the moon. You're free to disengage your harnesses." She turned to Tristan with a smile. "I could so do that again."

They waited impatiently as the *Dakota's* pilot, May Trace, talked with Mission Control. He tapped his foot rhythmically against the dashboard where he had it propped. Beside him, his brother sat clicking his fingernails against the nearest metal surface in a melody he couldn't for the life of him recognize. When May Trace finally informed Control that they'd left atmosphere, he jerked forward. "Bout damn time." He turned to his partner. "Ready, brother?"

His terse brother's fingers flew over the tracking display before nodding.

He waited for the *Dakota's* location to appear on the navigation screen in front of him. After a moment, a blip popped up, indicating the other ship's exact position, and he smiled. "Bingo. Let's rock this." He put on his headset, rapidly

switching between FAA channels, listening for air traffic information. With the other display, he pulled up the FAA's flight
tracking. The software allowed him to avoid other planes
without calling in a flight plan, which he had no intention of
doing. If anyone knew this ship was in the air, the mission was
fucked.

And he couldn't have that.

He'd come too far to fail now.

CHAPTER TEN

Mila marveled at the way, even harnessed tight as she was, she still felt the weightlessness of zero gravity. It was different from the *Orleans*, which had a MAG GRAV system that mimicked gravity. MAG GRAV wasn't perfect, though. Only paired objects would react to the system and the magnetic field caused problems for sensitive equipment. But on a ship like the *Orleans*, zero gravity would seriously hamper their missions.

The *Dakota*, on the other hand, was a short-range shuttle. There was no large crew and you were only on board for a few days, hardly long enough to sustain bone density decay. So, the NSS and NASA didn't bother with equipping these much smaller ships with artificial gravity. Which meant this would be Mila's first true experience with zero gravity for longer than a few minutes at a time.

She lifted her arm, feeling how it drifted with the motion. "Cool."

"You are so easily entertained, Mila," Avery said on a laugh.

She flipped him the bird and gave him a smile. "I'd much rather enjoy the little things in life than be a cynical bastard."

He shut up real quick and Mila immediately regretted the comment. She'd meant it as a joke, but before she could apologize, Avery removed his harness and launched himself toward the body of the ship.

"Damn," she said.

"I wouldn't worry about it, Mila. Avery isn't easily offended."

"Do you know him well?"

Tristan paused. "Well enough. I wouldn't have remotely considered us friends before the *Orleans* mission, but I at least consider us allies now."

Mila nodded. "Because of me."

"Yeah, because of you."

A yell came from where Avery had taken off to and then Avery's voice boomed, ringing with an authoritative tone Mila knew well.

She whipped her body around, still securely fastened to the pilot's seat. "What the fuck?"

"Shit." Tristan hit the clasp on his harness and pushed off, sailing toward the ruckus as it grew louder.

"Ah hell." She hit her clasp too. Pushing off, she gave herself enough momentum to reach the wall, then ricocheted from wall to wall in the narrow section between rooms, right on Tristan's tail.

By the time she arrived in the passenger compartment where everyone had strapped in for takeoff, the noise was bouncing off the walls. She held on to a bar on the wall, looking past Tristan to take in the scene. Most of the diplomats were still in their harnesses, seats aligned in rows like a theater, maybe hesitant to explore the ship in zero gravity.

One man made most of the commotion. He bounced from one spot to the next, like a fly stuck in a car trying to escape. His panic increased each time he touched a surface. Most of the occupants looked on in wide-eyed alarm, saying and doing nothing.

Avery kept saying things like, "Try to remain calm," and, "Sir, you need to focus. Focus on my voice." But nothing he said got through to him.

"He's probably claustrophobic," Mila said, visualizing tying him up in her head.

"How the hell did he get on this mission?" Tristan wondered.

"Oh, get a grip, Jacob!" A female voice echoed like a thunderclap, putting even Avery to shame.

Mila turned, seeing the diplomat who'd driven up in the muscle car. A smile crossed her face. *I think I'm going to like her.*

***

Sleeping arrangements were different on board the *Dakota*. They reminded her of the bunks she remembered from visiting old Naval ships. No real privacy, a single room could fit up to eight people—four bunks high set on opposite walls. The rooms were little more than closets. Outside the room, a series of small cabinets held the few personal effects they were allowed to bring.

After the adrenaline rush of the launch, and the little drama moments ago, Mila was ready for some shuteye. She moved hand over hand to a bunk in the front near the ceiling.

"You must be May Trace, the pilot," a familiar female voice said behind her.

Mila turned, holding onto the edge of the sleeping bag that served as a bed in true zero gravity. "Yes, that's me."

"Smooth flying," she said, smiling up at her.

"Thanks."

"Grace Harper." She reached out a hand and Mila shook it.

"It's a pleasure to meet you, Grace. Nice car, by the way."

Grace's face lit up and Mila half expected the other woman to tilt her head and sigh. "Yeah," she breathed, "God, I love that car."

"Gotta be terrible on fuel economy, though."

"Yeah, costs a fortune." Grace sighed. "I honestly don't drive it near as much as I'd like. Gas just costs too damn much. Usually, I drive my electric car, but knowing how long I'd be gone, I just needed to feel the wind in my hair, so to speak."

Mila smiled, thinking of the feeling when she flew.

Grace smiled. "You know *exactly* what I'm talking about."

Mila shrugged. "I'm a pilot. Do you fly?"

She nodded. "Small aircraft. Nothing like this." She scoffed. "And only earthbound. Nothing space-worthy." She looked wistful.

Mila shrugged again. "Flying is flying."

"Yeah. I wish I could fly more often, but life gets in the way, you know?"

Mila gave the woman a sardonic look. She'd just gotten off a long leave, so yeah, she knew what she meant. She gripped the bed a little harder. "You hitting the hay?"

"No, I'm just checking out the setup." Grace looked behind Mila. "This is very weird. It's like a bunch of sleeping bags secured to the walls."

Mila looked at the beds behind her. "This is pretty standard fare for shuttles."

Grace nodded. "Well, I'll leave you be. I'll explore some more elsewhere."

Mila nodded in return.

Grace smiled and pushed off, disappearing around a corner.

***

Grace left the room, leaving their pilot to her beauty rest. She'd been on her fair share of aircrafts in her lifetime, but she'd never been on a spaceship before. Though the shuttle could travel through the air, it was more like a naval ship in design. She floated past the other bedroom, making a left at the end which would lead her away from their seats during takeoff.

She took to zero gravity quickly. It reminded her of swimming, only with less resistance. Grab bars lined every wall, allowing people to keep a hold of a surface, or use them to move along. Fearing getting trapped midair, Grace played it safe, holding onto the bars as she dragged herself hand over hand.

The hallway opened up into a larger room of unknown purpose. She moved around, looking into cabinets and at strapped down items, realizing this was the dining area. Food and paraphernalia sat stored away in every nook and cranny. A diplomat she didn't know had taken up a spot at the island which served as a zero gravity table. Much like the walls, this contained little bins and whatnot for storage, but also places to strap food stuffs to it.

She moved on, continuing to the doorway on the other end. Another hallway stretched on, lined with doors. She tried the first one, but it didn't give and she spotted a keypad next to it. As she continued, she noticed every door in this section was keypad access only. Eventually, the corridor dead-ended and she had to turn back.

Nothing left to see. This would be a long couple of days.

When Mila woke up, most of the beds were occupied. She zipped herself out of the contraption and pushed off, looking for signs of life. No one stirred in this room. She passed the second bedroom, smiling as she spotted Avery and heard the sawing snores escaping his mouth. *I am absolutely teasing him about that later.* Mila turned left at the hallway, moving away from the cockpit and toward the rest of the living areas. A good push had her sailing into the dining area. She grabbed the wall, kneeling against it and reorienting herself. Another push sailed her up against the door to Tristan's office which was closed.

Not that doors would stop her. She opened it. "Hiyo, Tristan!"

"Gah!" He jerked and she figured if they hadn't been in zero gravity, he might have had a serious knock on the head. He turned to her and glared. "What is it, Mila?"

She shrugged and found a comfortable position before closing the door. "Oh, nothing. I just got up. Everything going okay?"

"You startled the shit out of me to shoot the breeze?"

She nodded. "Sure. Why not?"

He shook his head, but settled in for a long conversation.

Fidgeting with her hands, Mila said, "I had a spat with my mom."

"You mean May Trace's mom?"

"No, my real mom."

"You mean back when you first left ten years ago?"

Mila groaned. "No, today."

"You've been visiting your parents." The incredulity on his face could be seen from Earth.

"Yeah. I mean, I've been doing it as May, but yeah. I figured I could pull it off."

"Mila! The couple has known you your entire life. What the hell would make you think you could trick them into believing you were someone else, no matter what you looked like on the outside?"

Mila shifted awkwardly, realizing just how stupid the move had been. Yeah, she'd honestly thought she could get away with it. But even if she didn't think she could, she feared she would have tried anyway. At the time, the urge to see them was almost unbearable. "I…" She sighed. "I don't know what to say."

Tristan shook his head. "I'm not trying to chastise you or deride you. Trust me, I know how that can feel, wanting to see a family member as if the whole world rode on you seeing them. I'm not…" He paused, changing tacks. "What did you fight about?"

Mila sighed. "She realized what I was. She realized *who* I was. And she didn't like my answer when she asked me why I left all those years ago. She called me selfish."

"I can see how she might think that, but she's just hurting. I'm sure, once we return to Earth, she'll have a whole different perspective on the situation. Give her space and when we get back, you can try to mend the relationship."

"I'm afraid she'll decide that me being a shifter is the worst thing ever and not want to see me again."

"She won't do that. She's your mother, remember?"

"Yeah, but I've never seen her angry before, Tristan. She's always been… perfect. I mean, not 'perfect' perfect, but I've never seen her this angry. She seemed really hurt and I wanted to fix it, but I couldn't. You can't change the past."

"No you can't," Tristan whispered.

Mila left, saying something about messing with Kyle, and Tristan settled back into the privacy and silence of his office-slash-sleeping quarters. The space hummed around him as he reclined in midair. Talking to Mila about her family just made him want to contact his own, what was left of it. He couldn't remember the last time his brother had responded to one of his messages. He left voice mails, emails, TATs, but he almost never heard from Travis. And when he did answer, it was always, "Been busy. Gotta go."

Tristan stared at the computer against the wall, tempted to try again.

Pointless.

He didn't understand. Possibly, he never would. The rest of their family was gone. Tristan was all the family Travis had, but Travis seemed perfectly content to live his life alone, dedicated to his career.

When had it happened? When had they drifted apart? Had it been when their father died when Tristan started in officer training and Travis was in college? Or maybe when their mother died, when Tristan was in basic training and Travis had just graduated high school? Or maybe they'd drifted apart because Tristan was never there, that when Travis needed him most, Tristan failed to show up. Becoming a success had destroyed what family ties he had left and he couldn't help wondering if it was worth it.

But then he considered the people in his life now and thought maybe, just maybe, things were turning around. Mila made him feel the military, which he'd come to see as sucking the life from him, was the right move, the right career path, the right destiny. Mila made everything worthwhile.

Even if he could never introduce her to his parents. A memory of standing in front of their graves, a bouquet of flowers clutched in his rigid fist, popped into his head. He shook his head, trying to dislodge the depressing image. He sighed. It would be a long flight, a long couple days.

Kyle dreamed about beautiful women and catching bad guys. In his dreams, it had never been too long since getting laid. One blew in his ear. "Wake up, handsome."

He swatted at his ear, going back to what he'd been doing, which was standing over a handcuffed saboteur while a busty babe clung and practically swooned over him. Which was strange, because he would never go for such a shallow woman in real life. But it was a dream, so he went along with it.

"Your snoring is sawing through the hull, dick wad."

"Dick wad?"

The sultry vixen smirked, then sprayed something sticky at his face. "Wake up or I'll do something truly drastic."

"Gah." He jerked awake, slamming his shoulder against the wall because the sleeping bag only moved so much. "What the fuck?!"

Mila laughed. "You snore like no one I've ever seen. You are a disgrace to all mankind and I feel sorry for your roommates."

"Mila?" He readjusted in the zipped bed, and rubbed his hands over his face, his hands coming back sticky and wet. "What did you do?"

She shrugged. "Just a little wake up call when you didn't get it the first time." She laughed again and pushed off, clipping the doorframe before pushing off again and out of sight.

"I am so getting you for this, brat!"

His voice echoed off the walls, causing a chorus of groans and yawns as the rest of the compartment woke as well.

Kyle sighed. Now he needed to clean up—preferably without getting anything else messy in the process. He looked at his hands. Not that that was likely… or possible.

Mila camped out in the dining room, picking at something she thought might resemble food on the Incirrina's planet maybe, but not on Earth. "Is this baby food?"

"That's what I was gonna say."

Mila looked up, seeing the claustrophobic Jacob who'd blocked the *Dakota* with his car. It irritated her that he agreed with her. Like they couldn't possibly have similar opinions. She sealed up her meal, no longer hungry, and put it away.

"And what's with the hygiene facilities in this place?"

Mila glared at him. "It's a spaceship, not the Ritz. Get over it."

Jacob glared back, but kept quiet.

Others drifted into the dining room, one of the few common areas on the ship. The *Dakota* was only intended for short jaunts. So they had a cockpit, seating for launch and takeoff, sleeping quarters, a dining room, the captain's quarters, and storage compartments. This was the last area before you encountered locks.

As people drifted in, the noise grew louder, and the grumbling. Jacob's complaints became contagious and soon all the diplomats were complaining about the "dismal" conditions on board and the "dreadful" food. Not wanting to hear it, Mila pushed off to cross the room, grabbed Tristan's door, and slipped in again without knocking.

She found it a bit crowded. Both Tristan and Avery sat huddled in the small office, leaving zero room for Mila to get comfortable, but she didn't leave. Cramped was better than dealing with *them*. When they stared her down, she said, "I'm hiding," and pointed at the door and the space beyond.

They both smiled and nodded, understanding entirely.

CHAPTER ELEVEN

When a loud beeping started sounding through the *Dakota*, Mila wanted to jump for joy, but alas that was one downside of zero gravity—no jumping. Panicked shrieks started echoing off the walls as Mila made her way to the cockpit.

Behind her, Tristan barked out, "It's only the damn autopilot indicator. Quiet down. There's no reason for concern!"

She smiled, taking the intervening hallway in quick pushes between metal bars. Within minutes, she'd arrived, strapped herself into the pilot's seat, and started turning on the displays. The autopilot display showed they were an hour from their destination. Excellent. She put on her headset. "Kennedy Moon Station, this is Pilot May Trace of the U.S.S. *Dakota*. We are ETA one hour." She waited, not remembering how long it took communications to travel that distance.

After a few minutes, the radio crackled to life. "Pilot Trace, this is Kennedy Moon Station. We copy. You are the only ship on our horizon. We'll guide you in when you get closer."

"Roger that, Kennedy. Over and out." She leaned back and sighed.

Now, an hour of twiddling her thumbs.

"Ladies and gentlemen, we are now preparing to land on the moon. Please take your seats and engage your harnesses." Mila switched over to the station's channel. "This is Pilot May Trace ready for final approach."

"Roger that, Pilot Trace. We have you on display. Continue your heading."

"Roger." Mila adjusted settings on the ship with a fluid grace as Tristan and Avery strapped in.

"Everyone's buckled up. We're good to go," Tristan said as he tugged at his harness.

In the background, the hum of the engines and dissonant voices drifted to her.

Mila continued reducing speed. The descent onto the moon was nothing like onto Earth. With next to no gravity, the ship coasted into position, the auxiliary thrusters slowing her down and getting her closer and closer to touchdown. She saw the station up ahead; at first, a small dot on the horizon, but quickly morphing into the massive military and civilian complex that was such an accomplishment just twenty years ago. Now, it was rough around the edges, with spots of wear that resembled the speckling pattern spray paint left on walls.

She slowed the ship to a crawl, holding her breath as she approached her destination. The auxiliary thrusters reduced forward momentum further, the glow of the reverse thrusters barely visible on her screen. On the display, Mila monitored the ground architecture. Covered in craters, the moon didn't offer the best landing surface, so they didn't try a conventional landing, instead dropping like a classic Harrier jet.

When a likely spot opened up below them, Mila reduced power to the auxiliary thrusters and they drifted to the ground. With the gentlest of impacts, they touched down. "This is Pilot May Trace. We have landed and will be departing shortly for the airlock."

"Roger that, Pilot Trace. We'll be waiting."

Mila locked everything down, shutting all but life support systems off. She changed channels again. "We've now landed on the moon. Please put on your suits and head for the doors. We'll exit as soon as everyone is suited up."

By the time she'd finished the announcement, her cohorts were suiting up. Mila rushed from her seat and bounced her way to the suit locker in the back of the cockpit, but they'd already bounced their way from the room.

Mila grabbed her suit and started putting it on, thinking about the spacesuits that NASA used during the early days of space travel. She couldn't imagine having to don those clunky, bulky suits. How did they move in them? Hers was very thin, made of high yield insulated material that could handle staggering temperature variations without issue. Mila felt grateful she lived in modern times. She imagined she might not have ever seen space if she'd lived in a time where only a handful of astronauts made the cut.

She engaged the seal at her neck and grabbed her helmet, clicking it in place. With a few bouncing steps, she followed Tristan and Avery's path and found the diplomats struggling with their spacesuits. Tristan and Avery were helping some of them. One was trying to put his on backward. Mila held in a laugh.

Idiots.

She leaned against the wall, waiting for the last of them to do something so simple, a child could have done it. Honestly!

A few more minutes passed before the crew had inspected everyone, declaring them safe to exit. "Good to go," Tristan said, moving toward the exit.

Mila nodded and reached for the panel next to the door. With a handful of finger movements designed for use with the heavy gloves, she turned off life support and opened the entry door. "Ready."

Avery and Tristan started guiding the diplomats out and Mila watched as they meandered across the lunar surface. Some rushed, trying to get away as if someone were chasing them. One or two others, even without rushing, managed to trip and land on their faces. Even with help, it was hard to get them upright again. They kept flailing and panicking.

Mila shook her head as she followed them out, engaging a button that sealed the ship behind her. Though she'd never been in reduced gravity before, she flew across the surface, passing most of the diplomats and reaching the airlock at the same time as another. The person was searching the door and frame, looking for a mechanism to open it.

"Here." Mila reached around the person, flipping up a panel and pressing a green button. The airlock slid open and five people slipped in before the small space filled, a red light flashing overhead. Mila pressed the button on the inside. Air rushed in and the flashing light changed from red to yellow. Just before the inner door opened, the light progressed to green.

"Welcome to Kennedy Moon Station," a smiling woman said.

Mila took off her helmet. "Thanks. I'm Pilot May Trace." She reached out her hand to shake.

"Yasmin Cox."

"Grace Harper." Grace stood with her hand out and her helmet under one arm.

Mila turned and smiled. The person who'd reached the airlock with her was Grace, whom she'd already taken a liking to.

"Nice to meet you, May. Grace. We should file out of this hallway. Not all of you will fit. I'll show you to your bunks and station gear, and someone else will greet the next batch. This way." Yasmin turned, not even checking to ensure they followed.

Mila and Grace were the first ones to fall into step behind her.

The proximity alert came an hour ago. His hands trembled as he readied to land. Leaving Earth's atmosphere without being detected was hard. Landing on the moon undetected was almost impossible. The moon didn't get much traffic and what little it did was official, NASA and NSS. They tracked all activity around its surface. They would know if someone even came close.

But his brother could pull off the impossible. He'd done so before. He looked over at him. They'd slowed to a crawl, giving the hacker enough time and proximity to work his magic. In order for this to succeed, they couldn't be seen by the station below.

His brother nodded and smiled.

He did it. The bastard actually did it. A small smile graced his face and he reached for the controls, planning a trajectory that would keep them out of visual range at all times. It wouldn't do to make them technologically blind if they waved their asses in their faces.

He started his descent and within minutes, they settled into a crater a mile away from the Kennedy Moon Station. He clicked on one system after the next, searching for any signs that they had been seen, and let out a sigh of relief when nothing showed. "Good to go."

His brother nodded and settled in.

Yeah, now they had to wait. They'd been told to follow the *Dakota*, then hold for further instructions. His brother had set up a private communications line, so now they waited.

"Captain Faulk?" a man with an air of authority stepped up to Tristan after he removed his suit.

"Yes?"

He reached out his hand. "Commander Bennett. I'm in charge of the Kennedy Moon Station."

"It's a pleasure to meet you Commander Bennett." Tristan shook the man's hand and fell into step beside him.

"The Incirrina have yet to arrive," Bennett said as he walked, hands clasped behind his back, his gait precise in the low gravity. His boots clapped against the metal floor plates. Like the *Orleans*, Kennedy Moon Station operated with an antiquated MAG GRAV system, allowing the residents to complete their tours of duty without losing bone density.

Tristan nodded, his steps bobbing awkwardly without a ferro-magnetic uniform. "Nothing ever goes smoothly, does it?"

"No, it does not." Bennett stepped into an office, slipping behind a desk and sitting down.

"Do you have a meeting area or conference room we can use?" Tristan said as he came to a stop on the opposite side of the desk.

Bennett nodded. "Of course. It's right down the hall."

"Excellent."

Tristan walked into the bunk areas assigned to the *Dakota*. "Meeting in Conference Room A in five minutes."

Mila looked up and nodded, her thoughts on suiting up. The low gravity of the moon felt good, even fun, but wearing a MAG GRAV suit felt natural. "Can do." The room reminded her of the barracks when she first started military training—barren beds lined up in rows on each side, sterile walls, and sterile floors.

Grace smiled. "He likes you."

Mila shook her head. "Nothing'll come of it."

Grace stopped pulling on the new suit, her foot dropping to the ground with a thump. "Why not?"

"We serve together. I often have to work under him." Mila shrugged it off as she pulled her own suit up her waist.

"I wouldn't mind working under him." Grace gave Mila a suggestive gesture with her eyebrows.

Mila smacked her on the shoulder. "Get your mind out of the gutter, Grace."

"Or maybe you just don't want me thinking about your man like that." She shoved Mila in retaliation.

Mila scoffed. "Get real. He's not my man. Never will be."

Grace shook her head. "You two might not be in a relationship, but he's already your man, May."

Mila opened her mouth to speak, but nothing came out.

Grace nodded, eyebrows rising as if to say, "See? You know I'm right."

Everyone filed into the conference room. Tristan stood at the end of the table with Mila and Avery on each side. Grace sat beside her, whispering in her ear. Tristan caught his name whispered on the diplomat's lips and frowned, wondering what she was talking about.

The other diplomats were grumbling again about the living conditions or being forced to leave their personal effects on the *Dakota*.

With everyone seated around a long table, it felt cramped, the walls closing in on them. Like the *Dakota*, space was at a premium and barely a foot separated the back of each chair from the metal walls. Add to that the lack of windows and it would be easy to become claustrophobic.

When everyone sat down, Tristan glared at them until silence prevailed over the room. Mila smiled.

"The Incirrina have not arrived yet. We don't have an ETA on their arrival, so we may be here longer than we'd anticipated."

A chorus of more grumbles echoed off the walls.

Jacob stood up, but Tristan cut him off before he could even open his mouth.

"Sit. Down."

The man slinked back into this seat and Mila's smile grew. Grace snickered beside her.

"You're free to explore the moon station while we wait. I would suggest that the diplomats plan among themselves for the Incirrina's arrival and the subsequent talks. Trace and Avery will stay behind after this meeting to discuss other matters."

"What other matters?" Jacob said.

"That's classified." Tristan stared down the crowd. "Any other concerns or questions?" Silence prevailed. "Good, then the rest of you are dismissed."

The diplomats filed out. Grace trailed behind, turning back to wink at Mila before closing the door behind her. Mila shook her head. Kyle closed the door as the last of them departed.

"Did you have a concern, Captain?" Kyle asked.

"Yes. Mila, did you notice anything unusual around the time we landed?"

Mila paused, but shook her head again. "No, I was paying attention to piloting."

"Avery?"

Kyle shook his head. "What is it?"

"I thought I saw a blip on a display. It disappeared quickly and it might have been nothing."

"But it could also be something serious," Kyle chimed in, his fingers caressing the stubble on his chin.

"Indeed. I want you both on high alert."

Mila smirked. "Tristan, we have been since this mission started. We already know there's a possibility someone leaked the details."

Kyle nodded in agreement.

"I know. It's just a reminder. Keep your eyes and ears open."

Mila froze, looking uncomfortable before a smart-assed comment slipped out. "How do you keep your ears open? Aren't they always open?" She smiled.

Tristan glared and choking sounds came from Kyle's direction as he tried to hold in his laughter.

"Just… go. Report back to me if you hear or see anything suspicious."

"Aye, aye, sir." Mila saluted with the wrong hand, a twinkle of mischief in her eye as she left.

Grace waited in the hallway, leaning against a wall. "Ménage à trois?"

Mila groaned. "God, no, Grace. Is that all you think about?"

Grace thought about it and smirked. "Pretty much. That and politics."

"You have a one track mind."

Grace shrugged. "Do you want to go exploring?"

"Sure. Lead the way."

As she followed Grace through the halls, Mila couldn't believe how large the station was. She'd never seen it in person and didn't have information about improvements and expansions since she'd lived the last ten years on the run.

The complex was built in a staggered manner with the central hub built first. It was the oldest and contained all the essentials

—small living quarters, storage, kitchen and dining areas, even some offices.

The rest was designed like spokes on a wheel, each wing added as need arose. One branch held exclusively living quarters, little more than bunks and lockers for personal effects. Mila had counted a hundred and six beds in that wing alone.

Two wings held labs. They peeked in each, but other than equipment she couldn't identify, and the occasional plant or petri dish, she couldn't tell them apart. Another wing was reserved for storage. They found everything from food stores to locked armaments vaults.

The last wing held a greenhouse. She didn't recognize the setup at all and they spent some time in it.

"You should see your face, May."

"What?" She turned to Grace.

"It's just a greenhouse."

Mila shrugged. "So?"

Grace walked around. "This is pretty standard. Water recycling, hydroponics, UV irradiation, nutrient supplements, automatically rotating planters, and, of course, artificial lighting." She pointed above them where the lamps gave off a dim light similar to dusk.

Mila shook her head. "I've just never seen a greenhouse before. Never had a reason to."

Grace nodded and leaned against an upright across from Mila. "So, what's the story between you and the captain?"

Mila sighed. "You won't let it go, will you?"

Grace smiled. "Nope."

Mila sat on the floor, curling her legs up to her chest. "I really like him."

Grace sat next to her, nudging Mila with her shoulder to keep her talking.

Mila shoved her back. "Quit it."

"I will if you'll keep talking."

"Okay, okay." Mila sagged and rested her chin on her knees. "It'll never work."

"Why not?"

Mila tilted her head to look at Grace. "Because it would never work. We would have no control over our lives. At best, we would spend months, even years, apart because one or the other was shipped out. At worst, we might never see each other. If our assignments ended up staggered, one of us would be off planet while the other was on leave. We would only ever communicate by TAT. At least this way, we're together."

Grace shook her head. "You are truly depressing. You know that, right?" She held up an index finger. "If there's one thing I've learned, it's that you find a way for the things you truly want in your life. Saying you don't have time or it'll never work is just an excuse not to try. It's an excuse not to get hurt if and when it fails." She grabbed Mila's knee, shaking it from side to side. "If Tristan is someone you truly need in your life, you'll find a way to be together." Grace squeezed her knee once for good measure, ending the statement with a wry smile.

Mila shrugged, not saying anything. She didn't want to admit Grace might be right. But the thoughts drifted through her head, regardless. Maybe the problem wasn't that it was impossible, but that she couldn't figure out how to make it work. And trying to solve a problem was a whole different beast.

CHAPTER TWELVE

asmin settled in place in the Control Room, stretching her back and cracking her knuckles in anticipation of another long shift. Nothing much happened except the occasional landing, which was usually long awaited.

Nothing was scheduled.

Still, someone always had to man the Control Room. Kennedy was a military installation as well, so security was always a concern. It was easy to forget that. She was NSS and she *still* forgot from time to time. But, she always kept a sharp eye on the screens for potential threats, which was a challenge when nothing ever happened. But more than that, the Control Room held the primary controls of the station. Someone needed to be available to correct a problem, make an announcement, or sound an alarm.

She yawned, having just woken up, and anticipating a slow day. But maybe the Incirrina would show up during her shift. They had no idea when they would arrive. That would be nice. She'd never met an alien before. It would be an experience.

The radio kicked on and a gruff voice pierced the air. "This Zikka of Incirrina. See moon. Want land."

Yasmin jumped, looking at her displays, but they all showed nothing. Her head whipped around, as if that would change the fact that the Incirrina ship was within range of their radio, yet completely invisible on her screens. Her heart clenched in fear in her chest. She looked up, and her eyes widened as she saw the ship growing large on the horizon through the transparent ceiling of the Control Room.

"Moon?"

Yasmin pressed the button to communicate. "Yes, sorry. This is Yasmin Cox of Kennedy Moon Station. We are having technical difficulties with our radar. Can you get a good visual of the lunar surface?"

Silence drifted over the line before the gruff voice said, "Sorry?"

Yasmin sighed. Right, the Incirrina didn't understand a whole lot of English. She paused, trying to think of how to word it so they would comprehend. "Do not land near the station. Land at least a quarter mile from the station and a comfortable distance from the other ship. Do you understand?"

Another pause. "Yes, understand." The line went dead.

Yasmin picked up the intercom as she stared at her blank radar screens and then at the Incirrina ship growing bigger and bigger above her. "Commander Bennett, please report to the Control Room."

They had a major problem.

Bennett ran to the Control Room, his feet pounding down the

metal hallways. The kind of focus only adrenaline could give him surged through him as he went, knowing that a call like that over the intercom never meant anything good.

Within minutes, he ground to a halt at his destination, Yasmin turning to him from her seat on the other side of the room.

"What is it?" Command filled his voice and stance as he came to a stop.

"Something's wrong with our detection systems, sir. The Incirrina contacted us moments ago, requesting to land, but I never saw them on my screens. In fact, I spotted them through the windows, but not on here." She waved at the technology in front of her. Her voice had a very faint tremble to it, the discrepancy having shaken her. She pointed to the roof as she spoke, and sure enough, a large ship of alien design came closer in the background.

He scowled, advancing to the space behind Yasmin to lean over her shoulder. "Have you tried to diagnose the problem?"

She nodded. "The first diagnostic came back clean. I'm running more in-depth diagnostics now. It'll take time and I'm afraid we might not have any. We're blind, and if this is intentional, we're open to attack."

Bennett nodded, looking at the screens where several had streaming lines of data flying across. "Inform everyone that the Incirrina will arrive shortly. Do we know what airlock they're entering through?"

Yasmin shook her head. "Not really. Cameras work inside the station, but I'm not getting any signal from the airlock cameras."

Bennett's fist clenched. "Alright, contact our security personnel. I want several men at each airlock. I also want external patrols. If we can't get eyes electronically, we'll have to do it the hard way."

***

"The Brothers Grimm, do you read?" She gripped the repeater she'd smuggled in her clothes when they left the *Dakota*, the little black rectangle digging into her palm. Around her, the station was quiet, serene. She could almost pretend it was empty, that no one would get hurt.

She was kidding herself.

"Roger that, Angel," a masculine voice called back.

She knew a team waited on the other end of the line, but only one person ever spoke. They gave her a repeater that would piggyback off the station's communications system. Her instructions still rung through her mind. *Signal the team when both the diplomats and the Incirrina arrive at the station.*

"It's time," she said into the device.

She didn't know who they were.

They didn't know who she was.

It was best that way.

"Roger, Angel. We're en route."

Now she just had to keep from getting killed by the attack she'd initiated.

***

Tristan waited at the Control Room. A few minutes ago, someone had announced that the Incirrina would be landing shortly. He'd nudged the diplomats into a conference room, saying he would bring the Incirrina to them when they landed.

"Doncha just hate waiting?" the woman at the controls said.

Tristan shrugged. "When you have to, you have to. There's no getting around it."

She looked at him over her shoulder. "You're strange."

He leaned forward. "And you're impatient." Actually, she reminded him of Mila.

She rolled her eyes and turned back to her displays. "Sure, when shit's happening. It's no big deal to find stuff to fill your time when nothing needs doing. Having to wait when you want to accomplish something is just plain unbearable."

Tristan nodded behind her back. He could see her logic. Waiting to act was vastly different than having nothing to do. "There." He pointed at a display where men with guns greeted two Incirrina at an airlock. "Which airlock is that?"

She squinted at the screen. "Fifteen. It's at the end of the residential wing."

"On it. Thanks." He patted her shoulder twice before taking off at a jog, his boots clicking like horse's hooves.

He looked at his brother and smiled. "Showtime."

The other man nodded and a small smile crossed his face.

They suited up and were crossing the distance within minutes. The light cast the lunar surface in deceptive grays, its pockmarked landscape creating an obstacle course for their mission. He glanced back at his partner, his family. Everything hinged on him. Everything had always hinged on him, but he didn't mind. *It's my fault he doesn't speak.* He would happily play second fiddle until the day he died.

They reached an entrance to the station and his genius brother whipped out his gear, connecting it to the control panel. He held up a finger, manipulating his gadgets with his other hand. Air visibly escaped the airlock. They smiled at each other, celebrating the little victory.

Now for the fun to begin.

Mila had started wandering aimlessly through the station a few hours ago. She now knew every inch nearly as well as the permanent residents. She tried not to think, tried to let her mind wander, flowing over her surroundings instead of her problems. If she walked fast enough, she could forget to think entirely.

"Fucking God damn motherfucking shit!" a female voice she recognized yelled from inside the Control Room to her right.

A smile on her face, Mila stopped and looked in. It was at least twice as large as the conference room, its walls and floors equally bland, something she'd grown to expect from the NSS.

Sure enough, Yasmin sat at the controls, frantically touching keys and displays, now mumbling, "No, no, no," under her breath as she went.

Mila walked in. "Anything I can help with?"

"Gah!" Yasmin swung her chair around, clutching her chest. "Jesus, woman. Don't scare a girl like that, 'kay?"

Mila held up her hands. "Okay, okay. Sorry." She looked behind Yasmin, seeing the black displays. Earlier in the day, those same screens had shown the various corridors and airlocks. "Intruders," she mumbled. "Contact Commander Bennett. We need those cameras working. Who do you have in tech support?"

"Vaughan."

"Get him here, now."

Yasmin nodded, reaching for the communications system. She pressed a few buttons, getting more frantic with each passing moment. Mila's heart sank.

"Is it just intercom or everything?"

Yasmin turned around, her face pallid. "Everything."

CHAPTER THIRTEEN

Mila raced to the conference room where the diplomats were meeting with the Incirrina. She didn't know where Commander Bennett was, but she could find Tristan.

She turned onto the appropriate hallway and slid to a stop as she spotted Avery standing outside the room. A small smile crossed her face as she caught him with his ear to the door.

She snuck up on him, quiet as a mouse, and whispered in his ear. "I'm sure there are better ways of collecting intel."

He jumped. "Mila, don't sneak up on people like that." He glared at her, but the expression lacked heat.

She raised an eyebrow at him. "I wasn't sneaking. In fact, I was running hell for leather down the halls." *Well, except for that last bit.* She walked up to him, pushed him out of the way, and tried to open the door, but he stopped her with a hand on her arm.

"You weren't invited, Mila."

She glared at him. "Stop calling me Mila in public and let go. It's possible we have intruders on the station."

Avery stiffened, but released his grip, his arms going slack at his sides. "Where?"

"I'm not sure. Video and communications are down. I don't know how to contact Commander Bennett, so I came here, to the highest ranking officer I could find." She tilted her gaze at the closed door.

"I'll find Commander Bennett and we'll coordinate a search from here."

"Good," she nodded, her body relaxing with that burden off her shoulders.

Avery ran off and Mila opened the door. The cacophony abruptly stopped and all eyes rounded on her.

Tristan rose from his seat at the far end of the room, his face broiling with a plethora of emotions. "May, what are you doing here?"

She stood up straighter. "Video and comms are down." She needn't tell Tristan another word.

He turned to leave and the Incirrina followed. Mila's eyes widened at the sight. On the *Orleans*, she'd never seen the Incirrina. She'd stayed behind, hidden on the bridge, keeping out of everyone's way.

Being a coward, really.

The Incirrina dwarfed Tristan in both height and breadth. She found herself at a loss for words to describe them. Arms. They had lots and lots of arms and they didn't keep to a given form, either. With the appendages in constant movement, she couldn't count how many they had, and her gaze focused on them, unable to look away. There didn't seem to be a set number, or any pattern to the forms. Each individual had a unique assortment of limbs. Some looked like the octopus limbs they got their human namesake from. Others resembled claws, while others still she couldn't identify to save her life. She had no frame of reference for them.

"We help," one of them said.

Each gave the same gesture, a full body shake that Mila took as an affirmation.

Tristan faced the Incirrina who'd spoken. "Good. You and May, you're with me. Armed men should be guarding each airlock, but we need to determine if there was a breach."

"I'll come, too," Grace said, a hand up in the air, the only diplomat inclined to help.

Tristan nodded and Mila caught a slight jerking gesture from the Incirrina who spoke. Was it... irritation?

"Avery is looking for Commander Bennett as we speak. Yasmin Cox is trying to get the systems operational again," Mila said.

"Good." Tristan turned to the diplomats. "Each of you team up with an Incirrina. Head to an airlock. Ensure the lock hasn't been compromised. If you pass any permanent residents on your way, enlist their help."

"If you see someone named Vaughan, send him to the Control Room," Mila piped in, remembering the name of their tech guy.

"Yes, thanks, May."

She nodded.

"Okay, let's go."

They filed out and Tristan directed them in groups down the various wings. Soon, all that remained were Tristan, the one Incirrina, Grace, and herself.

"Do you have a name?" She looked at the Incirrina, trying not to let the alien appearance unnerve her. After all, she was hardly ordinary herself.

"Zikka." Its limbs stilled for a moment as it spoke and Mila got the brief impression of a soldier standing at attention or someone trying to stand taller.

Mila bowed in greeting, not feeling comfortable shaking one of his appendages. She just saw far too many opportunities for awkwardness with a handshake. "Pleased to meet you."

Zikka fanned out his arms and mimicked her bow. "Pleasure mine."

They followed Tristan as he moved to the last wing not assigned.

Remembering that the Incirrina had landed only moments before, she asked, "Did you see anything when you were touching down?"

Zikka kept silent for a long while, so long Mila thought maybe it wouldn't answer. "Station. Two ships."

Mila stiffened. Two ships. There should have only been one.

Tristan stopped and turned at Zikka's words. "Shit." He took off at a run, leaving Mila, Grace, and Zikka to run or be left behind.

Kyle turned the corner at a run and ran into someone, nearly knocking the wind out of himself. He stepped back, slamming into the cold, hard wall with a grunt.

"Watch where you're going!"

Kyle took a deep breath, ready to apologize and take off at full speed again. "Commander Bennett," he said with relief.

"Yes?" Bennett brushed off his pristine uniform, looking at Kyle with a hesitant eye.

Kyle stood at attention. "You're needed in the Control Room. Video and comms are down."

"What?" he roared. "When? How?"

Kyle shook his head. "I don't know. May Trace interrupted the conference to inform Captain Faulk."

Bennett nodded. "Good. Go down the residential wing. Find Ryker Vaughan. He's our tech specialist. Have him report to the Control Room."

"Yes, sir."

Bennett nodded again and ran toward the center of the complex. Kyle continued deeper into the residential wing.

Jacob sulked as he shuffled toward the airlock. Their group had branched off, heading to the two separate exits on the laboratory wing.

I hate this.

He hated spaceships. He hated the living quarters, and he hated the weird-assed Incirrina. Jacob didn't even want to look at them, let alone negotiate with them, but somehow he'd been recruited for this crap. Why had he said yes?

Oh yeah, because his boss refused to go to the moon. That's why.

Jacob sighed and let the freaky creature lead, even though he knew the station better. Jacob hadn't spoken a word and neither had the alien. He focused on the ground as he walked. He fantasized that if he stared at the floor long enough, it would go away and he would find himself back in his New York office churning out paperwork.

Jacob followed the sloshy sound as it turned a corner, then slammed into its back. Ew. He froze, then looked down, half expecting to be covered in slime. Finding himself clean, he stepped back, prepared to give it a piece of his mind, but stopped, his gaze drawn to the bodies on the floor.

He swallowed hard, forcing himself to breathe, recognizing the uniforms of the more permanent residents of Kennedy Moon Station.

Shit.

After they checked a second airlock, both with armed men standing at the ready, the urgency left Tristan. At each, he explained the situation, and told them to be on alert, that they would inform them by intercom once they neutralized the threat.

"I would say we're wasting our time, except Zikka saw two ships when landing," Mila mumbled under her breath.

Grace kept her mouth shut. It seemed odd how quiet the usually vocal diplomat had become since leaving the conference room. After all the snippets he'd overheard, he expected some snarky comment, but nothing. Grace remained reserved at Mila's side.

Tristan turned, walking backwards. "Yeah, but maybe they

haven't gotten on board yet," he said, responding to words he doubted Mila thought he could hear.

"Then how did the video and comms die?" Mila said.

He stopped. As a captain, he knew a good deal about the various systems he commanded, but he was no expert. "Can someone access them remotely?"

Mila shrugged. "How would I know? I'm a pilot."

He sighed. *Of course not.* "We'll just have to operate under the assumption that they can't."

Mila nodded, but he saw the doubt in her eyes.

Was it the best way to go about it? Tristan turned around, the women's footsteps sounding behind him up the hallway to the central area. They'd hit all the airlocks on this wing and with each step, he had the urge to prepare for the worst. His instincts had him imagining intruders at every turn. A tension set in that grew worse as they approached each corner, with the relief at finding nothing almost overwhelming as each empty corridor stretched beyond him.

I'm not cut out for this hero shit.

His heart sped up as he recalled his time on the *Orleans*, walking or running down hallways far too similar to these. Adrenaline ramped up his senses to razor sharpness, taking in every sound, smell, and sight.

As they got closer to the conference room, Mila stiffened in his peripheral vision, but he sensed nothing. "What is it?" he whispered, not taking his eyes off the hall ahead.

She stopped. "I think someone found the intruders."

Tristan turned, realizing Mila sensed something he couldn't. "What do you mean?"

Everyone else stared at Mila and it dawned on Tristan that Mila's comment was suspicious. *Shit.* Grace didn't know what she was and there was no telling how the Incirrina would act toward shape-shifters.

"I can just barely hear some ruckus up ahead. I can't tell what's going on, but from the tone of the sounds, I'm guessing someone is freaking out." She shrugged it off.

Hopefully, everyone would just pass it off as adrenaline or better-than-average hearing.

Grace leaned and scrunched up her face as she listened. "I don't hear anything."

Tristan jumped to her defense, hoping they would buy it. "May has really good ears. If she says she heard something, I would trust her."

Grace looked at Mila funny. "Well, we'd best find out what's got someone in such a tizzy."

After a few more turns, everyone could hear the person. "Jacob. Definitely Jacob," Mila said. She'd stepped up beside Tristan now, almost leading the way.

"Figures," Grace grumbled.

It took a few more minutes before they turned onto the hallway where everyone had congregated.

Tristan's voice boomed over the commotion. "What the hell is going on here?"

Silence echoed through the hall, making his ears ring after the cacophony.

Before long, Jacob started making panicked noises, mumbles that didn't make sense.

One of the Incirrina chimed in. "Found bodies." One limb angled off in a direction behind it. "There."

Tristan looked around, then frowned. "Has everyone returned?"

The crowd shifted as they looked for anyone absent.

"Where's Isaac?" a woman asked, whipping her head forward.

An Incirrina spoke in its own language, the sounds more like a machine malfunctioning than words. The diplomats understood what it said, but Tristan had to guess based on body language and the commotion it caused.

"May, Grace, Zikka. With me. Everyone else, get to the Control Room. Tell Commander Bennett, if he's there, to lock it down."

Mila groaned as a panic set in around her. She turned to Zikka and her eye twitched.

"Move out."

Despite the language barrier, the Incirrina left in an organized manner. The human diplomats took more coercion. Mila shook her head as she followed Tristan to one of the wings.

"This is the direction you sent Isaac?"

He nodded, absently touching his leg, wishing he wasn't unarmed.

Mila jogged up to his side, bumping him in the shoulder. She whispered, "Relax, you have a secret weapon, remember?" She reached in front of her, wiggling her fingers in his face.

He smiled, swatting her hand back to her side. "Focus, Mila. People have already died."

She shrugged. "It doesn't feel like a mission if someone doesn't die."

He glared at her. "That's not funny, Mila."

She stiffened and glared back. "I wasn't laughing."

Grace cut between them, throwing an arm over each of their shoulders, which was made awkward by the height disparities. "What are you two love birds whispering about, huh?"

They both glared at her.

Tristan grabbed her hand and gently lifted it off him. "I would appreciate it if you remember that I am a high-ranking member of the NSS and that that position demands a certain level of respect, ma'am."

Grace shrugged, not taking the reprimand very seriously. Of course, she could. She wasn't NSS. "So, what do you think happened?" When Tristan kept quiet, she turned to Mila. "Well?"

Mila arched a brow at her. "Do you really want to know?"

Grace nodded.

"The guy, Isaac, is probably dead. Probably, so is the Incirrina partnered with him. We're probably walking into some ambush. Probably, all gonna get injured or die."

"May..." Tristan said, exacerbated. Did she have to be so honest? He thought back to Jacob. It wouldn't take too much to cause the rest of the diplomats to fall into similar states of hysteria.

"What? It's the truth." Mila turned to Grace.

Grace had stopped moving, jaw slack as she tried to process Mila's droll comment that they might be dead in a matter of minutes.

"What? You asked."

"How can you be so blasé on the subject?"

"It wouldn't be the first time."

"That's classified, May," Tristan growled. Jesus, did she *have* a filter?

Mila yawned, as if for emphasis. "I didn't give any details."

"It's still classified."

"I don't see how classified it could be when I got medals for that mission."

Grace's eyes grew large. "You mean the *Orleans*?"

Tristan sighed. *Like wrangling cats...*

"Yeah, we lost, what, half the crew?"

"But they lauded that mission a grand success..."

"Yeah, but not before we went through a fuck ton of failures. And to appease Tristan's ethics, I won't say any more."

He scoffed, rolling his eyes at her. *Too late.* "You only gave away most of it, May."

"No, I didn't! That wasn't any more than the military already divulged. Honestly!" Mila threw up her hands, walking past Tristan at a quick clip.

Tristan picked up the pace, leaving both Grace and Zikka in the dust. "I'm supposed to be leading."

"Fine." Mila threw her hands up again. "Lead." She waved her hand to usher him ahead of her.

Grace jogged back up next to Mila. "Sorry. I didn't mean to get you in trouble with your man. Sometimes my mouth runs away with me."

Her man? A small smile crept on his face. Fortunately, no one saw it.

"It's okay. He'll get over it."

"Yeah, with a little TLC."

"God, will you let off it?"

A loud crack echoed off the halls and everyone froze. Time stood still for Tristan, a beat of confusion clouding his mind. *What happened?* Then pain surged forward, as if time had sped up, racing to full speed once more.

He looked down, his hand fluttering as he slammed into the wall with a jarring thud. His thoughts scattered, unable to react.

"Tristan!" Mila raced forward, dropping to her knees at his side.

When had he fallen?

"Tristan, Tristan, Tristan." She ran her hands all over him. Her palm came away bloody, the dark red fascinating against her pale skin. "Oh God."

A blur of movement passed over her and she looked up as Grace hit a man's hand, sending a gun flying down the corridor. It was a lucky shot because he slammed her into a wall, causing her to slide to the ground unconscious, in the next breath.

Mila surged to her feet. A fierce growl left her throat, echoing off the walls.

She attacked.

Tristan's eyes glazed over. As he lost consciousness, the last thought he had wasn't of Mila, the woman he loved, but his brother, Travis.

I'm sorry, brother.

The attack took Zikka by surprise. He'd been lulled by the constant human speech around him. Because he had trouble understanding most of it, he let it drift into background noise. The loud crack jolted him out of his malaise and he jerked to attention, readying for a fight.

May yelled and ran to her captain. Meanwhile, Grace attacked, quickly disarming her opponent before a single blow knocked her unconscious. Zikka was just about to attack when May growled, growing claws that made Zikka smile in comradery, and struck first.

Another intruder turned the corner to charge Warrior May and Zikka changed the form of his appendages to weapons and jumped into the fray.

CHAPTER FOURTEEN

Mila's heavy breathing sawed through the air as she stood over the bloody corpse of her opponent. After a few moments of cleaning the battle haze from her mind, she freaked. She spun around, staring into the peculiar eyes of the creature standing behind her. Its gaze spoke a language she couldn't hope to interpret.

"What?" she said, lifting her hands. A fine tremor moved through her muscles from the residual adrenaline.

Zikka lifted his appendages, wiggling them in a fluid movement. "Not know humans like us."

Mila continued to look at Zikka, at first confused, not understanding his inference, then fearing it. "How are we alike?" Her hands twitched at her sides.

What did I do?

"Hands. Change." Zikka wiggled its extremities in her face and she realized that the various forms of its limbs had changed.

She slapped her forehead, surprising Zikka, who reached out as if to stop her from hurting herself.

"I'm an idiot. No wonder none of your people have matching sets of arms. You can change them at will."

"Yes. You too."

"Yes," she breathed, her gut churning anew. God, if Zikka told anyone, she was screwed. "And then some." Her blood ran cold as the last of the adrenaline receded and her mind managed to hold a thought for more than a microsecond.

Tristan!

"But now's not the time." She turned, dropping to her knees in front of him. "Tristan?" Her hands hesitated over his supine form, not knowing what to do, what might hurt him.

"I'm okay," he said, giving her a weak smile.

She scoffed. "Bullshit. You need a medic. Fast." She knew *that* much, at least.

"I help," Zikka said from behind her.

Mila turned. "I've got this." Out of the corner of her eye, she noticed that the other guy still breathed. "Grab him. We'll bring him with us. We need answers."

Mila paced the room. She was too stir-crazy to wait right now. The doctor was tending to Tristan and the intruder still hadn't woken up yet. If they had communications up and running, they could at least figure out who he was or who his partner had been.

"Awake," Zikka said behind her.

Mila turned and her anger focused on their unfortunate

captive slouched on a couch in the waiting room. She stalked forward and the man's eyes rounded. A smirk grew on her face. She stopped less than a foot from him, leaning over and latching on to his throat but not squeezing.

"Speak."

His lips pursed stubbornly.

Mila's nails grew in her anger, causing the man to squeak in surprise. "I said speak."

His mouth opened and closed like a fish, but nothing came out. She growled at him, causing his eyes to grow larger, before lifting him off the couch with one hand. Dragging his body up the wall, she leaned her weight into him, partially cutting off his airway.

"I don't know anything," he mouthed. Still, no sound slipped from his lips.

Mila dropped him with a frown, causing him to collapse in an awkward sprawl. She stood upright and crossed her arms. "Let's start with a name."

He looked around the room in a panic, his gaze alarmed as his head whipped from side to side, screaming no without speaking.

Mila tapped her foot, irritated with his silence. "Can't you speak?" she said, exasperated.

He shook his head.

"Great." She turned to Zikka in frustration. "Watch him."

Zikka did the full body shake again and she entered the clinic, searching for writing tools. It was harder than she would have thought, but then they hadn't kept pens and paper on the *Orleans* either.

Mila wandered the hall, stopping the first person she saw. "Something to write with?" she asked, pantomiming it with her hands.

The man nodded and slipped into an exam room, returning with an outstretched tablet.

"Thanks," she said as she returned. She walked up to their captive. "Here." She shoved the device at him.

He caught it, clutching it to his chest, a belligerence darkening his eyes.

Mila glared right back. "Try something and I'll turn you into hamburger."

He faltered, his hands twitching on the tablet.

Mila nodded, crossing her arms. "Now, let's try this again. Your name."

"Wilhem Wolf," he wrote out with his finger.

"And your partner?"

"Niklas Wolf. Where is he? Is he okay?" His hand shook as he asked.

Mila's smirk grew. "He's dead."

Wilhem's face fell, the blood rushing from his cheeks and turning him sickly white.

Mila nodded. "Oh yes. I killed him with my bare hands." She flexed her hands in his face. He flinched backward. "Now, tell me, Wilhem. Whom are you working with?"

"No one." He tapped his finger on the device's screen to emphasize the point, little dots of black popping up on the screen each time.

Mila's eye ticked in anger and she swung her leg out in retaliation, connecting with her prisoner's shin with an audible crack. He screamed without a sound, reaching down but then jerking back as soon as he touched the abused limb.

Mila shrugged and leaned in. "What do you think? Think it's broken? I've got two hundred and five to go."

He flinched, his fingers returning to the tablet feverishly. "I swear to God I'm telling the truth. We've only communicated with one person and only my brother talked to her."

"Good, we've narrowed it down to half the human population," Mila said snidely. She leaned in, hovering over him. "You'll need to do better than that."

Wilhem gulped. "She's here."

Mila didn't speak. She just waited for him to fill the silence.

He lasted three seconds before his nerves got the better of him. "She informed us when the Incirrina arrived."

Mila stood straight, looking back at Zikka, then to the door Tristan had disappeared through on a stretcher. How many people were privy to that information? "How long ago did you receive the call that the Incirrina had arrived?"

He shrugged. "How the hell would I know? I don't even know what time it is."

Mila smacked him across the face, causing his lip to bleed. "Don't get fresh with me."

Wilhem held one hand to his face. "I'm not. I wasn't paying attention to when we received the call. It didn't matter at the time."

Mila nodded, turning her back on the man. She paced like a caged tiger. The comparison made her smile. She turned back to Zikka. "Watch him. I'll be right back."

She needed to find somewhere to stow Wilhem Wolf until they were ready to leave again.

———

They still had no news on Tristan when they locked their prisoner in a storage room, one of the few rooms with locks here.

Mila gnawed on her lower lip as she and Zikka walked back to the Control Room. She wanted to check on Tristan, make sure he was okay. The doctor said he was stable, but she needed to see for herself. Unfortunately, everyone needed to know the crisis was averted.

They turned into the Control Room and stopped. A sea of bodies had gathered. She couldn't even see the main console from her position at the door. Voices blended together into a chaotic hum. She tried to shoulder her way past people, but they were too caught up in their own individual dramas to get out of the way. Mila huffed, then barked out at the top of her voice, "Everyone shut up and move!"

The crowd stilled and all eyes turned to her.

Cool.

"Move *now*?"

She waved her hands in a gesture for clearing a path and those before her scrunched together, giving her an opening.

Mila nodded. "Thank you."

"Pilot Trace, quite an entrance," Commander Bennett said from the other end of the room. "Do you have news?"

"Yes, the intruders are neutralized. One is dead. We locked the other in a storeroom. We'll take him with us on the *Dakota* when we leave for Earth."

"I'll send security. So the coast is clear?"

"Yes."

Bennett turned to a man sitting at one of the terminals. "Send out an intercom giving the all-clear."

So, they got communications back up?

The man nodded and moments later a voice spoke overhead. "All-clear. Report to your duty stations. Repeat, all-clear. Report to your—" He stared at the electronics in front of him. "Must not have quite fixed it."

The room started to return to normal. People filed out and Mila looked up, taking in the sky above the station with awe. *What's that?* She squinted, as if that would allow the tiny speck to become larger and identifiable.

"Zikka, do you see something in the distance?"

Zikka walked up to her side. It turned its head up and paused, searching the stars. "Maybe."

Mila nodded, but couldn't shake the feeling that it wasn't over yet.

CHAPTER FIFTEEN

When the room cleared out, Mila walked up to Commander Bennett. "Did we get everything up and running again?"

Bennett scowled, checking that everyone had left. "We've got the intercom working, but we're not sure about longer range communication. And with nothing on the radar, we can't be certain that's operational either. Our systems didn't even register an error."

Mila frowned, for the thousandth time wishing she was good for something other than flying and kicking ass. She didn't know *anything* about radar. She bit her lip, thinking. "Well, one of the guys who messed it up is chilling his heels in your storeroom," she said pointedly.

The tech at the station turned, his arm bending over the back of his chair. "How old *are* you?"

She gave him a scornful look. "Thirty-one. How old are *you?*" She snorted. He looked like a teenager in the dark blue uniform.

He shifted and turned back to his console.

Mila faced the commander, that feeling of uselessness resurging. She wanted to help, but what could she do? With a sigh, she said, "I'm gonna check on Captain Faulk."

Bennett's eyes widened. "Is he all right?"

Mila's throat tightened, remembering him lying there on the ground. "Stable. He was shot."

"Jesus. Any other injuries?" Bennett started moving in agitated twitches at the news, often looking away. He checked on the computer displays behind him more than once.

"No. Shit!" She smacked her forehead. *I'm so* stupid! "I forgot about Grace." Her jaw hung open in shock as she turned to Zikka. "We left her in the hallway."

"Yes." Zikka waved his appendages around, just as agitated as Bennett appeared.

Or maybe it was just an affirmative. God, she couldn't read their body language...

"What happened to her?" Bennett said, stepping between them.

Mila shook her head. "She was slammed up against a wall. Knocked unconscious."

"She'll be okay, though?"

"I assume so." Mila shifted in place, feeling guilty for leaving the other woman lying there injured. What kind of person did that make her?

Bennett sighed, hands on his hips. "I've never had so much go wrong in so short a span."

Mila gave a wry grin, remembering the thrice damned *Orleans* mission. "I have."

Mila and Zikka returned to the hallway where the fight had taken place. Grace remained slumped against the wall where they'd left her. Mila cringed guiltily as Zikka gently lifted the woman. A moan leaked from her lips, but she didn't wake.

Mila turned to the man she'd killed, Niklas Wolf. Blood streaked across the metal walls and floor where both Tristan and Niklas had lain or struggled. Mila's gaze lingered on the place where Tristan had sat bleeding out.

Mila pushed the thought away and forced herself to turn to the large body stretched out on the floor. She stepped up, careful not to slip on the coating of tacky blood, and stared down at the man. He didn't look much like his brother. Where his brother was thin and wiry, this man was big. Even in death, he seemed menacing, dangerous, leaving Mila on edge. Wilhem looked like he couldn't hurt a fly. A scar outlined Niklas's face, blending in around his jawline and ear.

With a sigh, she bent and struggled with pulling his upper torso off the floor. "Mother…fucker…"

"I help."

Even though Zikka had Grace dangling over its shoulder, the alien helped her lift the much heavier man. She staggered as she got him into a firefighter's hold and slammed into the wall when she lost her balance.

Zikka reached out to stabilize her, but she waved him off, getting her feet solidly under her and standing almost straight. "I'm fine. I'm good. Let's just hurry before this giant breaks my back."

An odd expression crossed Zikka's face. "I hold him?"

Mila shook her head. "No thanks, but thanks for the offer. Let's just go."

———

The doctors took Grace and the dead body away, leaving Mila and Zikka waiting once more. This time, they didn't have the prisoner to distract them.

Mila kneaded her hands, her gaze drifting to the inner doors of the clinic every few moments.

Zikka broke the silence. "Is honor fight with great warrior."

Mila looked up. "What?"

Zikka's whole face contorted. "Is honor fight beside great warrior?"

"You mean me."

Zikka gave her the full body shake again.

"I'm not a great warrior."

Zikka growled under his breath and a series of clicks, whistles and grunts followed it.

Not sure I want to know what that meant…

"You great warrior. You no fear. You fight big. You win."

"Everyone fears, Zikka. Even me. I'm afraid of everything." Mila shook her head and raised her hands. "The very trait you applauded me for earlier is something to hide on my planet for fear of persecution. Some are killed for it. Others imprisoned. I do fear."

Silence settled as they both sized each other up. Mila wondered if Zikka was any better at it than she was. She must be just as alien to Zikka. But then, she knew nothing about them. "Tell me about your people."

"You not know?"

"There's been so much opposition that information is disclosed as needed." She shrugged. "I didn't need to know."

Zikka was slow to start, but Mila was patient. She couldn't imagine trying to explain humans in a language she barely understood, so it must be hard for Zikka to find the words.

⁂

Zikka had lived with the history of his people his whole life. He knew every detail of their biology like he knew his own torso, but to explain those details to the warrior woman? And in English?

He looked to May, and started his story in broken English, hoping she would understand. "Warriors once. Fight. Live. Die…" He continued on, trying his best to describe his people with the few English words he remembered.

They had once been warriors. They had lived in constant struggle on their planet alongside another species, which looked much like the humans they were negotiating with. It had been hard offering a treaty to a race that looked eerily like those terrible creatures that had once occupied their planet.

The humanoid species had been hearty, built for the most rugged of terrains their planet could dish out. But they'd never been satisfied with those places, always reaching for more—more land, more resources.

History stretched on and the fighting continued. Eventually, the Incirrina grew tired of the conflict. The humanoids stole land through subterfuge and guerilla warfare, but his people

388

had always been the stronger fighters with their minor shape-shifting abilities. In a battle, the Incirrina always won.

So, they took the fight to their neighbors. Blood soaked their purple world. They drove them back, pushing them to the harshest realms. Finally, they cornered them and gave them an ultimatum—leave the planet or perish.

They fled and his people lived in peace for a spell. But soon, rumors drifted to them. Rumors of a formidable army, a treacherous race. His leaders became nervous. They feared the rumors were true, that the terrible army wreaking havoc over the universe was all too familiar. They feared their old neighbor would return—better prepared, possibly even with allies—and fight to reclaim their planet.

They feared they would lose.

CHAPTER SIXTEEN

"I'm sure you have somewhere else you'd rather be." Someone else you'd rather be with, Mila corrected in her head, annoyed at the continued company in the waiting room. The walls had long ago started to blur together, the hard seat contorting her spine.

"Sure?" Zikka asked.

"Yeah. Go join the rest. You have work to do. You won't get it done hanging around here." *Or around me.*

Zikka stood, bowed to her, and left.

Which left Mila to wallow in her thoughts. She reached in her pocket, pulled out her ID, and stared at May's face. She knew that face so well, yet she still couldn't bring herself to look in the mirror. It always made her heart twist in her chest, made the grief and guilt rise once more like a zombie in a bad movie.

She finally looked at the expiration date. Her gaze landed on the numbers and letters, but her mind didn't really comprehend. She just stared. Eventually, she shook her head, sighed, and burned the lettering into her brain.

A year. She had a year left.

She knew it wouldn't last forever and she kept telling herself, and everyone around her, that she had no future, but focusing on that number drove it home. Her future, or lack thereof, stretched before her, and a ghost of the same panic that caused her to run so many years ago made itself known.

No. She would not let it control her this time. Shaking her head, she ground her teeth. She wouldn't run, but she still needed to make concessions. The ID in her lap loomed like a death sentence, the numbers mocking her. In a year, she would say goodbye to the NSS, goodbye to the only thing she'd ever wanted. Did it hurt more because she knew what she would be losing?

She wasn't sure.

But she wouldn't have to leave Tristan, she realized. She sat there breathless, a new path dawning on her as she waited to hear when he was all right. If she no longer worked for the NSS, she could be with Tristan. She would miss him when he was off planet, but she could *be* with him.

All this time, she'd denied them any chance, insisting it was impossible. So many reasons had run through her head. Their careers, what she was. But were they just excuses? Was she just running scared like she'd done ten years ago?

A plan started to form in her mind.

Tristan woke up to pain. His back screamed at him, taking all his focus, leaving the rest of the world shrouded behind a veil of its making. But as the seconds ticked by, the agony ebbed, other sensations coming to him. A thick pad, bandages, pressed into his back, making rest uncomfortable and awkward.

He tried to shift, but any movement in his torso or arms pulled at the wound, taking his breath away. He opened his eyes instead. Tristan lay in a room alone, a small, sterile box with medical paraphernalia on the walls and shelves.

That sterile medical scent burned his nostrils. He wrinkled his nose, trying to get away from it, but knew he would be immersed in it for a while. Nothing but the sound of footsteps outside his door drifted to him and he wondered if he should call out, tell someone he was awake.

He needn't have bothered. Moments later, a nurse came in wearing a white uniform. "Good to see you conscious," he said, pulling a tablet off his hip. He marked notes on the surface, then rested it on the bed. "Any pain or discomfort?"

Tristan snorted. He'd been shot. "What do you think?"

The other man smiled. "Thought so. Can you sit up?"

"Doubt it."

"Good."

Tristan raised an eyebrow at the man. He looked at the name tag. *Owens.*

"You shouldn't feel good enough to sit, not yet." Owens moved closer to the head of the bed. "I'm going to move you onto your side to check and change your bandages. Please tell me if you need me to stop or slow down, okay?"

Tristan nodded, bracing for the inevitable.

Owens pressed his hands into Tristan's shoulder and hip, pushing him up on his flank. "Can you hold your legs?"

He hesitated to answer, concerned that moving his arms would pull at the wound.

"I can help."

Tristan let him, feeling emasculated.

Once situated, Owens made quick but gentle work of removing the bandage. The tape pulled at his skin, feeling like it would rip right off his bones before giving up. The cool air soothed the skin as Owens walked away. In Tristan's peripheral vision, Owens stepped on the control for a trash can and dropped the soiled gauze inside before returning.

Something soothing smoothed over his wound and he groaned, then the spot went numb. As Tristan relished the sensation, Owens backed away. "All done," he said, slapping his hands together. "Would you like me to get you into a sitting position?"

"Yes."

Hands rotated him until he lay supine again, then Owens grabbed a remote attached to the bed. "Tell me if I need to slow down or stop."

Tristan nodded again. The top of the bed rose, whatever the nurse had put on his back leaving the wound a whole lot of nothing in his sensory landscape.

The bed clicked into position and Owens put the remote away. "Just press this button and someone will come running." He indicated a red button on the side of the bed.

Tristan nodded and was alone once more.

Moments later, a muffled voice outside said, "Let me know if you need anything."

Then the door pushed open too forcefully, letting a frantic Mila inside. A wild look entered her eye as she zeroed in on him. "Thank God, Tristan. You scared the shit out of us." She leaned against the wall in relief.

Tristan smiled at her dramatics. "Well, if you would miss me so much, maybe you should just marry me."

"What?!" She jerked forward, tripping in her surprise, her eyes rounded and mouth hanging open.

Shit. He sputtered, scrambling to speak. "I was joking, Mila."

"Were you?" she asked as she composed herself, looking at him like she meant to solve a puzzle.

Tristan paused, but wouldn't look at her. *Shit. Why did I say that?* "Yes."

Mila crossed the room, her footsteps tapping on the tiles and sat on the bed next to him. "Of course, it wouldn't matter if you were. So long as we're both in the NSS, this can't go anywhere."

Tristan scowled, hope surging. "So, *would* you marry me? I mean, if you weren't in the NSS?" He watched her with intensity.

"I don't know." Her gaze turned distant. "Only a year," she said under her breath.

Confusion crossed his face. "What was that?" Only a year?

She paused, fidgeting with her hands. "I only have a year left in the NSS." Her gaze remained plastered to her lap as she spoke.

"I don't understand. You love the NSS." Though she hadn't been with the military long, it was clear she was destined for space, destined to fly. He couldn't fathom her doing anything else.

She shrugged, but her nonchalance looked fake. "May's identification has to be renewed in a year."

The silence filled the air for so long Mila finally looked up at the pain on Tristan's face.

"But you love piloting." He was stuck on that thought. He couldn't imagine her *not* flying. It would be a sin. A waste.

Mila shrugged again. "We don't always get to do what we love, what we want."

Tristan didn't know what to say. He opened and closed his mouth repeatedly, but nothing came out, his mind a great void bereft of thought. Finally, he spoke. "What do you plan to do once you leave the NSS?"

"I don't know. Maybe I can find a job as a pilot somewhere where I don't need a verified ID."

"You're not going to run?" His guts clenched, breath held. What would he do if she ran?

Follow?

"No, I'm not going to run. I'm done running. I regret running the first time, but I can't change what I did. I know I couldn't have remained with the NSS if I'd stuck around, but my life would have been very different. I could have made a life. I don't know how I would have explained to everyone why I dropped out, but I could have built a life for myself somehow."

"But you wouldn't have met me."

She smirked. "Who knows? Maybe I would have met you earlier if I hadn't run. After all, my best friend was NSS. I would have probably been on base all the time." The smirk turned sad and she shook her head as if to rid herself of the morose thoughts. "There's no point dwelling on the past. What's done is done. We can only plan for the future."

Tristan smirked playfully. "Yeah. You could always marry me."

Mila's smile brightened, mischief in her eyes now. "You'd love that, wouldn't you?"

Like a rubber band snapping, he sprung forward and kissed her. His lips brushed lightly over hers, leaving them both breathless. She leaned in, putting more pressure behind the kiss. Tristan's lips curved up in a smile and she smiled as well.

Mila spoke against his lips. "Liked that, did you?"

Tristan couldn't escape the look of sadness crossing her face. What did he do wrong? Why was this so hard?

"Very much." He leaned back, drawing her into an awkward position across his chest and lap, wanting to pull her head against his neck so he wouldn't see that look again.

"This isn't very comfortable, you know."

"Sorry." He felt the moment slipping away from them, like *their* moment was slipping away. Would there be another or would they drift farther and farther apart?

Mila twisted, trying to free herself from his hold. Tristan sucked in a breath as her hand braced momentarily against his abs, sending a shaft of pain through his back even with the miracle salve.

"Sorry." She shifted her hands to either side of him and pushed herself upright. She stood and rearranged herself, then sat down to settle on his lap, her side resting gently against his chest. "Better?"

"Worlds." He wrapped his arms around her, her warmth, her closeness, making him happy. *She* made him happy.

That would have to be enough.

The first time Tristan yawned, Mila got up and told him she would see him later. Leaving the room, she closed the door with a gentle click. She looked left and right, but didn't see the doctor. Though it smelled of antiseptic, it looked like every corridor in this place. Metal plate walls, metal floors, gray as far as the eye could see.

She sighed. Knowing Tristan was fine placed her at ease. Knowing there was an abstract end in sight for their relationship problems put a hesitant smile on her face. Her mind moved on to Grace—the other person in her life who'd ended up in the clinic.

She walked down the hall away from the waiting room. "Doctor?"

A door opened up ahead and the nurse from earlier peeked out. "Done?"

She nodded. "How is Grace Harper doing?"

"Good, good. She woke up pretty quickly once she arrived here. She's got a headache, and will be sore for quite a while, but she'll be fine."

"Can I see her?"

"Sure. Follow me." He stepped out, closing the door behind him, and made a left turn at the first intersection.

Mila followed him for a couple minutes before he pointed at a door.

"This is her room. Need anything else?"

Mila shook her head. "No, thank you."

He nodded and disappeared.

She knocked this time.

A muffled voice called from the other side. "Come in."

Mila opened the door and peeked through. "Up for company?"

Grace smiled and nodded, then groaned, holding her head. "Yes, so long as I don't move, breathe, or speak."

"I bet the lights are hurting your eyes, huh?"

"You know it." She smirked, finally removing her hands and letting her head rest carefully against the pillow behind her. "I'm glad you're okay. How's Tristan? Is he okay?"

"Yeah, he's okay. He was joking about marriage so I figure he should be up and about real soon." Mila rolled her eyes.

Grace frowned, her face severe. "You know he's serious. He's head over heels for you." She shook her head, but groaned, holding it still instead. "Forgot. Head. Bad."

"Are you okay?"

"Yeah, I'm fine. Or, I will be." Grace grimaced as she lifted her hands from her head cautiously. "So what happened next?"

Mila's face blushed bright red. "Nothing," she said at least an octave higher than usual.

Grace scoffed, a sly smile forming. "Oh, you don't *really* expect me to believe *that*, do you?"

Mila shrugged. "We kissed."

"How was the kiss? Is he good?"

"Fine, until I accidentally hurt him when he dragged me onto his lap."

"Ha! You guys are like a romantic comedy."

Mila glared at her. "Can we talk about something else?"

Grace thought, leaning back against the pillows. "What happened with those bad guys? I'm sorry I wasn't more help. I only have self-defense training. It's pretty useless in a real fight."

"You did good. And one of the intruders is dead. The other is locked up."

Grace leaned forward. "Did they tell you who they're working with?"

"Not much. Not enough to identify the person, but enough to narrow it down."

Grace sighed and Mila wondered why, but Grace interrupted her thoughts.

"How are the negotiations? I assume they've started without me."

"I believe so, but I'm not sure. I'm not really involved with all that shit and I've been waiting for news on Tristan."

Grace nodded. "Could you find out for me? I'd really like to get to work if I can. I'd hate coming here in that damn space-ship and getting a concussion to be for nothing."

"It wasn't for nothing, Grace. I suspect Tristan would be dead if it wasn't for you. Thank you. No matter what else you do here, it was enough. So, thank you."

A shy smile crossed Grace's face. "Just go. Find out about the negotiations and get back to me."

Mila nodded. "Okay. I'll go. Get some rest."

Grace nodded, then groaned and held her head once more. Mila tried to contain a laugh as she left the room.

The Control Room calmed down once the crisis abated. Commander Bennett remained, overseeing Vaughan, who continued to work at getting the systems back online. Yasmin had left. With most systems down, she had nothing to monitor, and with Vaughan and Bennett there, she was redundant.

Above them, the large panels gave a perfect view of the space beyond. Pinpoints of stars decorated the canvas with a view of Earth's edge on the right side. On a normal day, a monitoring officer might spend a significant percentage of their day leaned back in their chair, looking up at the sky.

If they had, maybe they would have seen it. As it was, the non-operational systems held everyone's focus as they tried to get them to work, a steady din of voices serving as back-drop. Ironically, when paying attention to the view above was more important than ever, not a single person was look-ing. If they had, they might have seen the speck in the distance.

It was nothing, just one pixel's worth of input on a vast sky of light and darkness. Maybe nobody would have noticed it. It was tiny, maybe too tiny for human eyes to register.

But it was definitely getting bigger.

Mila opened the conference room door, but found no one there. *Figures.* She exited the room, the empty hall greeting her. She tore down the hallway for the Control Room and stormed in. The Earth's visage tickled her peripheral vision from above. The clacking of a keyboard served as the only noise. "Avery. Haven't seen you in a while."

Avery turned where he stood just behind the consoles and

gave her a smile that didn't reach his eyes. "May, I understand you found the culprits."

She nodded as she crossed the room. "Have we got the systems operational again?"

He frowned. "No. Not yet. How's Tristan? I heard he got shot."

She waved it off. "He'll be fine. What is the status on the negotiations? Grace wants to know."

"Grace?"

Mila shrugged. "She's also in the clinic. She's got a concussion."

"Oh. Well, the negotiations have stalled."

Mila grumbled, turning on her heel to leave. "Not if I can help it." They'd gone through far too much to let these negotiations stall out, regardless of the reason.

Mila dragged the last of the diplomats into the conference room by his shirt collar. "Sit," she barked.

Surprisingly, he did.

She looked around, seeing a lot of familiar faces. She was even starting to recognize the Incirrina. Zikka smiled at her and winked. Did a wink mean the same in their culture? For that matter, did a smile?

She glared at the human diplomats as they sat or stood around the conference table, shoulder to shoulder in the tight space. Somehow, she knew it wasn't necessary to chide the Incirrina. "Sit down and get this straightened. I don't care what it takes. Understand?"

Jacob rose. "But what about the intruders?"

Mila glared at him. "Did I say you could stand?"

He flinched and sank to his seat.

"And it doesn't matter, now does it? They were caught. You have a job to do here and you'll do it. Grace Harper will join you as soon as she's able." Mila looked around the room, reassuring herself that they seemed satisfactorily chastised. "Good. Get to work."

———

Kyle slipped into Tristan's room. His superior officer slept upright in his bed. He walked up and tapped him on the shoulder. Tristan woke with a groan.

"What?"

"So, what happened?" Kyle sat on the side of the bed, arms crossed.

"How the fuck should I know?" Tristan grumbled. He looked at Kyle with groggy eyes.

"Still not up to snuff?"

"Oh, fuck off." His voice was thick with sleep.

Kyle shook his head. "If we hadn't been through hell together, I might be offended by that."

Tristan sighed. "I don't remember much. I was caught by surprise. A bark of sound and then I was on the floor."

Kyle nodded. "Mila is trying to get the diplomats and the Incirrina talking again."

"They stopped?"

"Yeah, they didn't like the idea of leaving their rooms after we found the dead bodies. But, there are other things to consider."

"Like?"

"Zikka told me a woman on this station informed the intruders of the Incirrina's arrival."

"Zikka? He was with us when I was shot?"

"Yes. And when Mila interrogated the captured intruder."

Tristan nodded. "So we don't know anything else?"

"*He* didn't know anything else. But I think we can restrict it to people who arrived on the *Dakota*."

"Why is that?"

"Very few station personnel were briefed on the mission. And how many could coordinate this kind of subterfuge?"

"But then how would someone from the *Dakota* send out a message without anyone knowing? Wouldn't they have to use the Control Room?"

"Not if they had a repeater."

Tristan nodded again. "Still, we shouldn't count out the permanent residents. Who was manning the Control Room?"

Kyle paused to think. "Yasmin something. I don't remember her last name."

"Then she's another of our suspects. How many females arrived with us?"

"Six, including Mila."

"Mila didn't do it." Tristan was adamant.

Kyle smiled to himself, enjoying the protective tone in Tristan's voice. The man was so obvious. "I agree."

"Start by checking everyone's bunks for the repeater they would need to send the message."

"What if they have it on their person?" He shuddered, imagining the minor disaster that frisking or strip searching the diplomats might create. Most either had political influence themselves or worked for people who did. He didn't want to see his career go down the drain simply because he took a few necessary liberties with an investigation.

"We'll get to that when the time comes."

He nodded and saw himself out. If Mila had done her job well, he could slip into private quarters without being seen.

Yasmin yawned as she looked over Vaughan's shoulder in the Control Room. Commander Bennett had assigned her to help, but she felt useless. Vaughan had worked through system after system without finding the problems and now was going through every line of code with a fine-toothed comb. Yasmin didn't envy him.

Commander Bennett had gone off with the security team to interrogate the prisoner again. He hoped to discover how the man had shut down their systems. Yasmin didn't hold much hope in his success. Who would give up that type of information when you could have power over someone—especially when that someone held your freedom in their hands?

Yasmin yawned again, arching her back and taking in the sky above. She loved seeing the sky from space, from the moon. There was nothing more beautiful. Seeing something in the distance, she squinted. *Definitely something.* She focused on the screens, but as she expected, she saw nothing. A sick feeling twisted her gut. "Vaughan?"

He turned. "Yeah?"

"Do you see that?"

He looked up and the blood drained from his face, turning it ashen white. "Good God."

"What?" Her voice came out shrill.

"Hold on." He rummaged in his bag, pulling out an optical device and lining it up with his eye. "Still can't make out a lot of detail, but it's definitely a ship." He put the device down, as if defeated by the observation.

"Can you get radar or comms up? Either of them would help, Vaughan. We need to know who's coming."

"I know. I know. I'll work on comms. If we're lucky, we can get them on the radio and see if it's someone we know. God, I hope so."

"And if they aren't friendly, we can send a distress call to Earth."

"Not that it would make a difference. By the time they arrived, we'd be dead."

She didn't want to admit it, but he was right. That twisting in her gut gave another tight wrench.

CHAPTER SEVENTEEN

Mila walked into the clinic, hopefully for the last time before they left the station. The doctor told her Tristan could be released today, though it seemed strange to release a human after only a day. He was healing nicely, his stitches all but sealed. She entered the room to Tristan slowly getting dressed in an ill-fitting outfit, leaning against the bed for balance.

"You look silly in that."

He turned, careful of his wound. "This is all they had in medical. I'll get another uniform from the barracks after I escape from here. I'm just grateful to be out of that hospital johnny."

"Oh, come on. You looked cute in a dress." She smirked, trying not to laugh.

"It's not a dress," he grumbled.

Mila walked over and hugged him, enjoying the closeness she hadn't allowed them to have until now. She knew she was taking liberties that would only cause them problems if they were caught, but she didn't want to be apart from him anymore. The ID expiration had been an eye-opener.

Now, if I wasn't so fucking awkward... "I'm glad you're on the mend."

"Well, it's not like there was any doubt. I might not be able to shift like you can, but I'm pretty tough." He puffed up as if offended, tension from pain rimming his eyes.

Mila smiled, but figured it looked as forced as it felt. "Yeah, you are. Come on. Let's get you that new uniform. If you're a captain, you should look the part."

"Oh, man, our barracks do *not* have this view!" Mila said as she looked up at the sky, relishing her remaining time with the NSS. She knew her time was limited and she wouldn't have too many more opportunities to enjoy sights like this. She wished she could do this forever, but life didn't work that way.

Mila followed Tristan at his slow pace, making sure he was okay and wasn't in pain. She kept worrying that if she got ahead of him, he would fall, pull his stitches, and wouldn't be able to get back up again. She looked hard at him, noting the outline of the bandages under his shirt.

"It's through here," Tristan said, pointing with a hiss and flinching as he raised his arm.

"Tristan, take it easy." Mila jogged up beside him. "Why don't you sit down?" She pointed at one of the beds.

He frowned, but then nodded, sitting on the nearest one. The bed sagged, something like springs protesting his weight.

"You said here?" she asked, pointing at a storage locker just beyond the last bed as she turned to face him.

"Yes."

Mila pulled the facing doors open, looking over the shelves of matching dark blue fabric for his size. After months living together, she knew what size he wore without asking. Finding what she needed, she grabbed a full set, stuffed them under an arm, and closed the doors, returning to Tristan's side.

"Thanks," he said as he took the proffered clothes.

"No prob." She looked up, sighing as she let the view soak into her. She thought back to their walk to the station, to her first steps on the lunar surface. It was beautiful. Barren, but beautiful. Valleys and craters stretched on as far as the eye could see. The Kennedy Moon Station lingered as an eyesore amid all that natural majesty. She would never see anything like it trapped on Earth.

Neck craned at an uncomfortable angle, she took in all the little pinpoints of light and the way the Earth loomed in the background. Something large, but a good distance off, rose over the station. She shifted to improve her eyesight and jerked. "Tristan!"

He dropped the uniform in his lap. "What?"

She just pointed, not saying a word. She couldn't, having been struck speechless in that moment.

He stared. "What? What are you pointing at?"

"A ship." She didn't recognize the design. It wasn't human or Incirrina, that much she knew. "That can't be good."

He looked back where the ship was. "No, it can't."

Tit for tat.

Commander Bennett had just returned from interrogating the prisoner. His hands fisted at his sides as he ground his teeth, the frustration eating him alive. He'd gotten nowhere. The captive had refused to say anything. Instead, he'd crossed his arms, sticking his chin out at Bennett in defiance.

Tit for tat.

Throughout the session, a repeated urge to beat the information out of the man plagued him, but he was an officer. Held to a higher standard, he needed to keep his cool, set a good example for the men behind him, not let the bastard get to him. He let out a slow breath, trying to retrieve his equilibrium.

Did the son of a bitch really think he would give him what he wanted? Bennett scoffed. *Over my dead body.* They would have to be desperate and they weren't, not yet. They had time to extract the information from him. "Any news?" he asked Vaughan as he stepped up behind him in the Control Room.

"I've got the comms up and running, short and long range."

"Thank God." He sighed. "Call down to Earth. We need to inform them we're in the dark."

"Yes, sir." Vaughan touched a couple places on the console, starting the long process of sending out messages and waiting for the minutes-long reply each time. "This is Kennedy Moon Station. We're currently blind. We just got comms working, but all other first alert systems are down. We'll update you as things progress."

"We read you, Kennedy Moon Station. Awaiting your updates."

"Roger. Over and out." Vaughan ended the transmission. He turned in his seat and opened his mouth to speak, but jerked in place. "Captain Faulk?"

Bennett spun at the sound of someone running down the hall, followed by a squeaking skid as they came to a stop. "Captain Faulk? Pilot Trace? What's wrong?" What more could possibly go awry?

"Incoming," Tristan said breathlessly, grimacing as he bent, clutching his back. "Incoming ship."

"It's alien," Mila chimed in.

"Shit," Bennett swore under his breath. He looked up and sure enough, he just barely spotted a ship in the distance. "What do we know?"

"Almost nothing," Mila spoke up, scoffing. "I could tell it wasn't human or Incirrina in design, but not much else. Those are the only ships I'm familiar with. Maybe we should ask the Incirrina. They might recognize it."

"Go." Bennett pointed toward the door.

Mila took off.

Mila ran, skidding to a stop outside the conference room. She banged the door open. "Zikka, with me!"

Zikka leapt to his feet and flew around the table. Mila didn't wait for him to follow her and completely ignored the cacophony of startled voices asking her things she had no time or inclination to answer.

Zikka kept silent as they raced back to the Control Room, understanding that time was of the essence. Their loud foot-steps heralded their entry.

"There. Do you recognize that ship design?"

Zikka looked up. "Make bigger?"

Vaughan jumped up, grabbing something from underneath the workstation, and ran over, offering his device. "Here."

Zikka nodded. "Thanks." It peered through the device, holding it with an octopus-like limb, which curled around the metal tube twice. If an alien could blanch, Zikka did. A series of foreign but heartfelt words slipped from its mouth, but it didn't explain.

"Zikka?" Mila asked, touching one of its appendages gently, wondering if she'd just made a faux pas.

Zikka lowered his arm. "Sorry."

Somehow, Mila didn't think Zikka was apologizing for not answering right away.

"They bad. Very bad."

"Who are they?" Mila encouraged.

"Morg."

Mila blanched, remembering the name of the race from Zikka's story earlier. "Are you sure?"

"Yes."

"Shit." Mila turned to Commander Bennett. "We need to inform Earth, now."

Bennett nodded. "Vaughan?"

"On it." Vaughan opened up communications with Earth once more. "This is Kennedy Moon Station. We have an update."

"We read you."

"Conti—" The line cut out mid word.

Everyone in the room glanced at each other, fearing what the interrupted transmission meant. Mila prayed Vaughan just wasn't that good at his job. But as she looked at the ship growing steadily closer, a darker possibility plagued her mind.

CHAPTER EIGHTEEN

*E*veryone on the space station gathered in the only area they could all fit—an unused lab on the science wing. Mila had only seen it in passing earlier. It didn't inspire any sense of awe now. "Are you sure you're okay?" She turned to Tristan, who sat beside her. She looked, but no red circle stained his shirt to indicate he'd bled through his bandages.

"I'm fine." He patted his chest. "Good as new."

"Somehow, I doubt that," she scoffed, glaring at him.

"Silence, everyone," Commander Bennett said, his voice booming through the room. Behind him, a few NSS officers that reminded her of her shadows on the *Orleans* mission crossed their arms, looking menacing.

Security.

The cacophony changed to isolated pockets of conversation and eventual quiet.

Commander Bennett turned to Mila. "Will you?"

Mila nodded in reply, standing to her feet. "There is a ship approaching."

A chaotic cloud of voices swelled in volume once more, panic taking over.

"Silence!" Mila's voice filled the room. "The ship is alien. It likely isn't friendly." She looked around, making eye contact with everyone she could in the crowded space. "According to Zikka of the Incirrina, this race is well known to their kind. The Morg were sneaky and violent when the Incirrina lived side by side with them. They are likely no different now.

"They are coming here. We have to assume they're a threat. Our communications are down, as are radar and video.

"Now, can the Incirrina shed any further light on the situation?" She didn't expect them to say much more. It didn't look good when they brought a violent alien race to their doorstep. Certainly, it didn't bode well for the alliance between their two races.

A couple Incirrina spoke up in their alien tongue. Mila waited for the diplomats to translate.

Grace stepped forward. "They said they can't speak to the race's current capabilities. It's been centuries since they forced the race to leave their planet. But they've heard rumors about a wandering fleet of military ships."

"Thank you, Miss Harper," Bennett said.

A commotion arose once more as people realized the depth of how screwed they were.

"Quiet!" Commander Bennett yelled. Silence returned begrudgingly. "That's better." He rubbed his forehead, looking down as he thought. "Faulk, Trace, Avery, Vaughan, and the Incirrina, stay put. The rest of you, report to the barracks. We'll send word once we form a definitive action plan."

Everyone filed out reluctantly, many glancing back as they

slipped through the door. Every gaze she caught held the skittish edge of shattered confidence.

"Okay, Vaughan. Status report."

Ryker Vaughan shrugged. "Communications are still down. It might be a jamming signal."

Bennett paced for a few minutes. "Do you think it's just jamming us? Targeted? If so, the spaceships might still have communications online."

"It's impossible to know from here. The intruders' ship might have the best chances as I suspect some of the problem originated there."

Mila jerked up, ready for action. "Even if they don't have comms, they'll have radar and weaponry. We won't be blind anymore."

Bennett pointed at Mila. "Good point. Zikka, can you and your people test your ship? See if we can call out."

Zikka gave a full body shake.

"Good. Faulk, you and Trace head to the *Dakota*. Test the comms and check radar. We need to know when that spaceship will be here, what its trajectory is, you name it. The more information, the better. Avery, you're with me. We'll try to access the Wolfs' ship. Dismissed."

Mila's gaze never left the sky as she and Tristan crossed from the station to the *Dakota*, like prey watching a predator, waiting for it to strike. She was reluctant to enter the shuttle, reluctant to turn her back to a looming threat.

They jogged through the ship and Mila slipped into the pilot's chair, punching up systems one by one. "Come on, baby."

Lights blinked on, screens came online, and Mila's stomach twisted in a tangled, nervous mess.

The microphone in her helmet linked to the *Dakota's* systems, so she selected that from the digital display and crossed her fingers. She sighed in relief when the system hummed to life. She keyed in the settings to call Earth. "This is Pilot May Trace on the U.S.S. *Dakota*. Please respond."

The radio crackled, but no answer came through the line. Her stomach twisted harder. Minutes ticked by as she waited for her message to travel the distance and get a response.

"Command, this is Pilot May Trace of the U.S.S. *Dakota*. Please respond." A trembling quality entered her voice. She held her breath, waiting for a response, waiting for salvation.

Tristan touched her shoulder and she sighed, sagging in her seat.

Damn. She shook out her arms, not one to give up. "Okay, radio is down. Let's check out radar."

Tristan gripped her shoulder tighter and she switched displays, a smile crossing her face when the display worked beautifully. "Guess they only fucked up the station's radar. Good." She recorded the data to a drive, shoved it into a pocket in her suit, and stood. "Let's go."

Tristan shook his head. "The store rooms."

Mila jogged behind Tristan as they went through the seating area, past the residential hallway, past the dining area, and to the only part of the ship with locked doors. Tristan entered his codes into the keypad. The door slid open, revealing a small arsenal.

"Jesus," Mila drawled.

Tristan shrugged and smiled. "I kinda figured the mission would go balls up."

"Well, you were certainly prepared for any eventuality. Is that an EPG?" Heavy-duty, black plastic crates were securely strapped to the walls. Some were clearly labeled—like the electromagnetic propelled grenade launcher—others contained no label at all.

"Grab as much as you can carry."

Mila shook her head. "We should have recruited a few more people." Like maybe a dozen. Even at her best, she couldn't even carry half of these crates.

Tristan shrugged again. "I wasn't thinking when Bennett split us up."

Mila stretched, stepped forward, and piled two crates on top of one another. "How many can you handle?"

Tristan raised an eyebrow at her. "One?"

Mila laughed, bumping shoulders with him. "Well, I see who wears the pants in this relationship."

"Come on, let's just get going. We can do a second trip to get the rest."

"Or a third." Mila dragged the crates behind her carefully, wondering how she would get them across the lunar surface. Dragging one with each hand?

Some distance away, a behemoth ship barreled through space. Many scars marred its exterior, gifts from many fights on or near many worlds. Greed and anger had gone into the spaceship's construction and how it was used, and its appearance testified to that. Hard lines converged with angry colors—bold and unnerving when put together. When designing the battleship, no one deigned to hide its purpose. Guns covered every surface, angled in every direction.

The only concession to that aesthetic was when it entered atmosphere and the weapons retracted into the hull, but it rarely entered an atmosphere. It didn't need to. Its occupants could just as easily crush its opponents without those forays. Few ever stood in its way. Fewer still survived to see its likeness again.

Not so long ago, news had arrived and orders had been given. Their once enemy, their most hated race in a long line of those they despised, had entered into a treaty with another. They would not allow their foes any allies, any friends. That species they'd dared to befriend—Humans—must cease to exist.

The ship accelerated again, racing faster and faster toward their target.

Earth.

CHAPTER NINETEEN

Zikka's people rushed all over their ship as he stood overseeing the activity, his body vibrating with tension. A handful collected munitions, walking past the entry to the bridge with the large gray cases in hand. Several others were either compiling data from radar or attempting to get the communications systems to work.

"No go," the one on comms said in their native language, tongue clicking angrily on the last tone.

"What about the Emergency Messaging System?"

"Hold on." The man's many arms glided over the console in a manner even a dozen humans could never mimic. The ship was designed with their people in mind, curving around their forms, allowing the use of all their appendages, and couldn't be operated by less. "Yes, the Emergency Messaging System seems to be operational."

"Good. Send a message." It was better than nothing. The system couldn't reach out to Earth, only to other ships, stations, and back home. It was a broadcast signal, with no specific target. Anyone with the right equipment would pick it up. No one outside of their people had that equipment.

"Sent."

Good.

They had no way of knowing if anyone received the message, no way of knowing if their compatriots warned Earth, and no way of knowing if help would arrive.

It was better than nothing.

<hr>

"So, is there any particular reason you chose me to go with you?" Kyle Avery bent over the panel that controlled the locks for the Wolfs' ship. He pulled out a tool from his arsenal, playing it over the edges of the keypad. A blast of focused light flared in front of him. The sides of the panel started to melt and pull apart. He shoved a small pry bar in the gap, careful to split the seam but not damage the delicate circuitry. He didn't have the equipment required to cut through the door.

"I figured you'd know what you're doing."

Kyle looked over his shoulder at Commander Bennett, wondering what the man knew about him. He'd never met him before this mission and certainly no one had told the commander who Kyle was or what he was capable of. "Maybe so." He turned back to the panel, switching off the torch. With a slow, gentle motion, he pulled the edges apart, giving him a view of the circuitry in the light from his helmet. The circuit board flexed, but didn't break.

"How's it coming?" Bennett leaned closer.

"Better if you'd stop hovering," he snapped.

"Sorry."

The presence behind him disappeared. Kyle angled the pry bar so he could hold the flap open with one hand, and reached into a pocket, pulling out a pair of pliers. He inched them into the crack, careful that he didn't shadow the wires he was focused on. Settling the tool in place, he held his breath and snipped.

The door opened, revealing a stark interior similar to every ship he'd ever been on. Flashing lights and buttons decorated the small room. *Controls for the airlock.* Kyle turned and smiled at Bennett. "Guess you were right. I do know what I'm doing."

Everyone reconvened in the Control Room. Tristan came in carrying a giant black crate. Mila dragged one in, then turned around and dragged in a second. They placed them against the wall, then stepped back as the Incirrina arrived. The aliens entered hauling crate after crate. They looked around, then placed their own crates near or on top of Mila's and Tristan's. Avery and Bennett hadn't shown up.

Mila took in the growing pile of weaponry and smiled before walking up to Vaughan at the console and handing him the drive from her pocket. He was still trying to get things up and running, but Mila increasingly believed that wasn't going to happen. Whatever Wilhem Wolf had done to them was likely impossible to reverse without his help.

"Thanks, Trace," Vaughan said before turning back to his console. He plugged the device in and pulled the information up on one of the spare screens to the right. "Hmm." He worked for a few more minutes, chewing on his lip. His head bobbed back and forth between a screen with radar data, which now displayed about a million numbers, and another screen, which he used to tabulate the findings. He slid the chair back with an air of triumph. "They should arrive in three hours according to this."

Mila twisted off her helmet and rubbed her chin. "Three hours to prepare."

"We should wait for Avery and Bennett to get back to form any plans," Tristan said.

"Yes, indeed." Mila glanced at the crates lining the walls. "Weapons?"

Zikka gave a full-bodied shake. "Yes."

"Do you always travel with an arsenal?"

"Yes."

Mila turned to Tristan. "Maybe we should recruit them to collect the remaining weaponry while we're waiting on the others."

Tristan shrugged. "Want to help? We have more than we can carry by ourselves."

"Yes," Zikka said, and motioned for Mila and Tristan to lead.

They went to the closest exit and everyone geared up once more. They passed through the airlock in two batches. Mila yet again couldn't stop herself from looking up to check on the enemy ship's location while she waited for everyone else. It was a compulsion. The sick need pulled at her, like watching a car wreck on the side of the road, lights flashing on ambulances and police cars, twisted metal and debris everywhere. Even the most stalwart couldn't help but peek, even if only in passing.

"It's getting closer, isn't it?" Mila frowned at the ship bearing down on them.

Tristan shook his head. "Of course, it's getting closer."

"I mean, closer than it should be. Do you think it sped up?"

"Don't borrow trouble, May."

She nodded and sighed, but it really did seem too damn close. She was probably just being paranoid. Danger tended to bring that out in people.

The airlock opened and the rest of them spilled out. They crossed to the *Dakota*. Mila unlocked it and a stream of aliens led by Tristan flowed into the shuttle, feeling surreal, like an invasion. But it wasn't the Incirrina they had to worry about. She looked up again, but shook her head to get her mind off their impending doom.

When the last of the Incirrina passed by, she followed, making her way quickly and methodically through the ship. At the kitchen, she had to push against the wall to allow the first of the Incirrina to walk past with large black crates. She really hoped they wouldn't need all this.

Zikka stopped with a crate as he approached her, a look of concentration on his alien face. "Do you always travel with an arsenal?" It looked difficult for him to form those sounds, but she recognized the exact words she'd given him.

"Yes."

Though she sucked at reading his body language, she thought he might be happy as he moved out of sight, a steady stream of congested traffic following in his wake.

It took several minutes before there was a break long enough for her to slip past. When she walked down the hallway, she passed the first storage room, now empty of the black crates that once lined the walls. Tristan stood at the next doorway, directing people. She stepped forward. "Anything left for me?" She smiled.

"Only a little one," Tristan said, amusement tingeing his face.

Mila leaned in and smirked. *Little one, my ass.* "What is that, a nuclear bomb?" It practically took up half the room. "How did you get it in here?" It looked bigger than the doorframe.

"I don't know. I didn't load the ship."

Mila shrugged, rubbing her gloved hands together, working herself up to the task at hand. No big deal. She could do this. She grabbed the handle facing her and hefted, her muscles and back straining even with the reduced gravity. "Holy fuck, Tristan. How did anyone move this shit?" She lifted the one end and dragged it backward to the entrance.

It slammed into the doorframe. "Fuck." She looked to each side. Two inches had collided with the door jamb. It wouldn't fit. She tipped her head up and glared at Tristan. Anger and raw determination glinted in her eyes. A small smile crossed her face.

"Mila…" Tristan warned.

She pulled back, readjusted, and yanked it forward.

Crack!

The crate came free, along with a long strip of the wall. She smiled at Tristan.

He glared back. "How am I going to explain that?"

She shrugged. "Alien attack?" She turned her back and slipped the giant crate out into the hallway, slowly dragging it outside.

When they arrived back in the Control Room, Avery and Bennett had returned. Mila was last to arrive. She dropped the end of the heavy crate with a loud crack that echoed off the walls, drawing everyone's attention. "What?"

"Are we all here now?" Bennett asked.

A mumbling of answers came, but Mila was distracted. She looked at the case, curiosity getting the better of her. She flipped one latch, then the other, flung the lid open, and stood in awe, looking down at the most beautiful weapon she'd ever seen. It filled the giant crate, looked like a single clip held a few thousand rounds, and had a barrel large enough for fifty caliber shells. Didn't that technically make it a cannon?

She lifted it out by the black, metal barrel and leather-wrapped handle. It left a residue on her gloves. She grimaced. "This leather is sticky." She shrugged, figuring it didn't matter if her hands weren't directly touching it, and flipped the gun around into the proper orientation, smiling at the weight. She rubbed her face against the barrel. "I think I'm in love."

"Think you can focus a little?" Tristan said, a laughing tone in his voice.

She looked sideways at him. "Not now, we're getting acquainted."

He shook his head, leaning toward her to whisper. "It's just a gun, Mila."

She sighed. "It's not just a gun. It's a big fucking gun." She hefted it up, the business end pointing to the transparent ceiling and the butt resting on her hip. "This gun sends fear into the hearts of men the world over. This is a gun that means business. This gun is fun."

He shook his head again. "Focus for a second? Please?"

She nodded and clutched the new toy to her chest before tuning in to what was going on around her.

"Thank you, Zikka. But we can't assume help will arrive in time. Earth ships can't respond on such short notice and the Incirrina are likely too far away. We have a good arsenal here. We might be able to hold them off, if they aren't too well armed.

"Even so, we have to operate assuming we won't succeed in defending this station. We need to warn the Earth, get them prepared for a possible attack. Captain Faulk?"

"Yes?"

"Prepare to leave. You'll take the *Dakota* back to Earth, alert leadership there. We'll make sure you can escape."

A riot of sound erupted from the Incirrina. They seemed to approve of going down in a blaze of glory.

"But many of your crew aren't trained with these weapons. We're better suited for fighting them off."

"That may be true, but you're only three people and we *do* have security forces here. You have by far the best pilot I've ever heard of. She's famous for outmaneuvering those fighters on the *Orleans* mission."

"Jeez, does everyone know about that?" Mila said under her breath.

"When you launch, keep low to the moon's surface. Use the moon as cover from the approaching ship before you take off for Earth. We need you invisible to them as long as possible."

"But won't we be visible on radar?" Mila stepped forward, more than happy to fly, but practical to a fault.

"We'll work on that. We *may* have a secret weapon."

Of course! Wilhem Wolf! He'd crippled their radar from a distance. If he did it to them, maybe he could blind the enemy ship as well. This just might work.

A short while later, they gathered in one of the storage rooms to tell them "the plan." Bennett stood on a box. "Quiet!"

The room reluctantly drifted into silence.

"Good. The enemy ship is less than three hours away. Faulk, Trace, and Avery will take the *Dakota* to warn Earth. Everyone else will stay here, protect the station, and ensure that the *Dakota* escapes to give them early warning. We'll be handing out weapons to everyone in the Control Room."

Grace walked up to Mila, bumping her with her shoulder. "What's with the gun? New toy?"

Mila shrugged, hugging the giant piece of technology closer. "No. It doesn't technically belong to me, if that's what you're asking. Tristan made me heft its case all the way from the *Dakota*, so I've commandeered it."

Grace smirked. "It suits you."

Mila smirked back, posing. "You think?"

"Oh yeah. Very macho, he-woman."

Mila rolled her eyes. "Well, women *are* the stronger sex."

"Definitely." Grace spaced out for a moment. "We're all gonna die, aren't we? Makes you wish you'd done things differently, doesn't it?"

"Yeah." Mila's mind drifted to her relationship with Tristan. Or lack thereof. She shrugged it off. "You're not gonna die, Grace. It'll be fine."

"If that ship comes to the moon, we're dead. Most of us have never held a gun before, can't fight, and would probably pee our pants if we found ourselves in a life or death situation. We're as good as dead." She shook her head and sighed. "I shouldn't have agreed. I shouldn't have made that stupid call."

Mila didn't know how to respond. Grace had some valid points. The Incirrina seemed well trained, even enthusiastic about the upcoming conflict, but a hum of manic tension grew as reality sank in. "There's going to be a panic."

"Yeah." Grace leaned farther back toward the wall, as if trying to keep herself from the center of the room, where she might get trampled once everyone flipped out. "We'll be lucky if we don't end up killing each other."

"Well, it's the human way, isn't it?"

Grace smirked, but there wasn't a lot of energy behind the expression. Mila hugged the weapon tighter.

<hr>

Wilhem sat down at the console in the Control Room, cracking his fingers with a grin. He looked around, but dour faces surrounded him. He frowned. *Spoilsports.* He hadn't honestly expected Commander Bennett to return to his little prison, begging for his help. He'd expected to be carted off to the *Dakota*, dragged back to Earth, then locked up for treason for the rest of his life.

Possibly, in a hole.

He'd tried to hide the smile that wanted to burst out when Bennett returned. It wasn't easy. He was surprised, though, when the commander spoke.

"How did you shut down the radar remotely?" Bennett had said.

He'd shrugged. *Like I'm gonna tell you.*

"I'll give you what you wanted."

What did he *really* want? Wilhem had waited, raising an eyebrow in question. He had all the time in the world. He'd suspected the commander *didn't.*

Wilhem used that to his advantage.

Bennett had shuffled his feet before speaking again. "An alien ship is coming. We need to shut radar down so the *Dakota* can escape to the Earth without being noticed. We need your expertise."

Wilhem's gaze darted from screen to screen, his brain automatically organizing the information into a logical pattern that flowed and shifted in his mind. He smiled. Sabotage an alien ship's radar without any knowledge of their systems or programming, all from a distance?

God, he loved a challenge.

"Why would you turn to a life of crime? You're clearly gifted. You could have done anything."

He turned, taking in the grunt who'd spoken, and shrugged. It was better than the poorhouse. He returned to his screens irritated. He hated people questioning his life choices. Like he had a choice. Some people just didn't.

CHAPTER TWENTY

"Uh, Tristan?"

Tristan turned. "What is it, Mila?"

She pointed up, a slight tremble in her hand.

He looked and his mouth dropped open. The spaceship hung huge in the sky, only minutes from landing. "Run!"

They took off, Mila resting the giant gun against her shoulder as she tried to maneuver the uneven ground. The lunar surface dipped and rose, making her progress jerky and slow. The other ship would land any minute now. They were out of time.

"We're not going to make it." Mila's voice came out in jagged puffs.

"Of course we'll make it. We have to." Tristan didn't sound so sure. He sounded on the brink of panic himself.

Mila scoffed, but didn't argue. She didn't have to say it for it to be true. The enemy could see them on radar. How could they possibly escape?

The ground reverberated with the force of the enemy's landing, nearly knocking them off their feet. No, no, no. The distance between them and the *Dakota* felt like miles as the surface calmed, leaving an eerie stillness. They reached the shuttle and Mila slammed her hand against the keypad.

Mila spun as the door opened, taking in the monstrosity that loomed over the *Dakota*. Her lips thinned to an angry line. "Not on my watch." She stepped back, lifted her gun in both hands, and aimed. She took a deep breath before pulling the trigger.

Surprised by the lack of noise, the recoil pounded into her. She gritted her teeth as the massive cannon attempted to topple her over. Her eyes grew large as the round hit the side of the alien ship and exploded, taking out a gigantic hole in their hull. A big grin crossed her face and she leaned the gun up, wishing she could kiss the barrel. "I think I love you. I'll call you Vera."

"Jesus Christ, Mila. Will you hurry?" Tristan barked from the doorway.

She settled the weapon back on her shoulder and raced after him. "Coming. I'm coming." The huge grin wouldn't go away.

Tristan shook his head. "You have issues."

She shrugged it off. "I'm going to miss things like this when I leave the NSS." She ran past him and rested the gun in the locker where the suits were stored for the crew. Then she raced over, pressing a bunch of buttons on the console. The *Dakota* came to life. "Come on, baby. A little faster."

Tristan and Kyle raced to their seats, buckling in without even waiting for life support to kick on so they could remove their suits.

With the systems cycling on, Mila followed suit, cinching the straps in place, and not bothering with the usual pre-flight checklist. They didn't have time. If they were lucky, Wilhem Wolf had shut down the enemy's radar and the ship couldn't chase them with that giant crater in its hull. At worst, it would shoot them out of the sky, giant hole be damned.

"Okay, here goes." Mila took the controls and pulled, feeling the gentle throbbing of the engines as they lifted off the ground. *I will not think about the giant battleship sitting spitting distance from us.* She angled for outer space, turned in the opposite direction, and prayed they wouldn't be shot in the ass.

"You've got this, Mila. We trust you." Tristan's voice soothed her.

Nerves edged in, increasing the tension caused by even a normal takeoff. They would make it. She chanted the words to herself over and over, hoping if she said them enough times, it would make them true.

The moon's surface flew past below them. Mila followed the plan. *Use the moon as cover, then jet off for Earth.* The shuttle shuddered wildly, controls dragging to the right. "What was that?"

"Just ignore it." Tristan's voice was no longer soothing. Instead, he sounded like he wanted to have a death grip on something.

Something banged against the hull, vibrating through her skull. To the left. Mila looked. She couldn't help herself. She passed clouds of lunar dust and just *knew* they were being shot at. "Shit, shit, shit." She started moving the shuttle in a zig-zag pattern above the surface. The ship shook. Debris tinged off their hull.

Mila held her breath and turned the *Dakota* so it hugged the edge of a crater, the high sides hopefully protecting them from the enemy. Time passed in creeping increments as she piloted farther and farther from their foes. She let out a sigh of relief when several minutes ticked by without another shot. "I think we've lost them."

"Good, now take us home."

She tugged on the controls once more, and the moon pulled away from her horizon, the blue and white expanse of the Earth taking over her vision.

Home.

Grace cringed as everyone filed into the Control Room, packing in like sardines and jostling each other. Commander Bennett, men and women in NSS uniforms, and the Incirrina stood at crates against the wall, handing weapons to each person as they approached. The doorway was just wide enough for one to enter and one to leave. Once they received their armaments, they left to suit up and prepare for anything.

The *Dakota* had just launched. She glanced up at the clear ceiling, wondering if she could spot the *Dakota* from here, but no. Nothing marred the view of Earth as her chest tightened with emotion. The stakes were so high and suddenly she felt lost.

Jarred from her reverie by someone poking her in the back, Grace advanced, grabbed the weapon with a fragile smile, and tried to keep her nerves from consuming her. She tried not to let her previous fight undermine her confidence. A flashback of an arm knocking her into a wall assaulted her brain. She shook it off. Grace didn't know what she was doing, felt hopelessly under-skilled, but their lives depended on standing their ground. She prayed silently as Commander Bennett placed the cold metal rifle in her bare hands. A sense of numbness settled in that had nothing to do with the sensation seeping into her palms. She forced an awkward smile as she headed to the lockers near the airlock.

The gun felt like a dead weight in her hands, haunting, death-ly. Grace propped it up and pulled out her space suit. Jacob came around the corner as she slipped her first foot through the leg hole.

"What business do I have holding a gun, huh? This is clearly mismanagement! There should be more security on this station. What were they thinking?"

Grace sighed, trying to ignore him. She had no interest in getting in a fight with Jacob when they had a fight for their very survival looming. Soon, they could very well end up as rotten corpses stuck on the lunar surface.

Great, now she was getting morbid.

"What do I know about shooting a gun? I should give someone a piece of my mind, that's what."

Grace sighed. "Oh, shut up, Jacob!" she said as she hefted the suit up her hips.

Jacob sputtered for a few beats, but then a man Grace didn't recognize stepped forward.

"I know your voice." He pointed at her, waving his finger, trying to place her.

Grace froze.

"Angel!" The same scratchy voice echoed off the suddenly quiet corridor, powerful in spite of its low volume. "You're Angel!"

Grace's face blanched, but held out a hope that no one would know what that meant. She stared at the man in horror, real-izing he must be one of the Brothers Grimm they'd captured.

Commander Bennett walked into the hallway, his grim coun-tenance cold as he loomed over her. "You? You're the one that called in the strike?"

All the warmth left her body and her response stuck in her throat. Her life was over. She'd been caught. The worst mistake of her life and did she get a chance to learn from it? No.

Around her, aggressive voices multiplied. Bodies shifted in her periphery. Anger, betrayal, and revenge glittered in one set of eyes after the next.

The man who'd outed her stepped in front of her. He slapped his hands together, a loud *crack* echoing off the walls.

People didn't seem inclined to pay him any mind, though. He'd attacked the station, nearly killed Captain Faulk. The angry horde grew closer, the frenetic energy of the mob mentality amplifying with each moment.

Grace tapped him on the shoulder, causing him to turn around. "I don't think they'll listen, but thanks for trying. You might want to move so they don't go through you to get to me."

A tragic look crossed his face, but he stood his ground. "Everyone, stop!" His ragged voice boomed even louder than the clap, reverberating off the walls, and Grace couldn't believe the small man had managed to make so much sound.

The noise level dropped and some even backed up a step.

Wilhem nodded, crossing his arms over his chest and glaring at everyone.

Grace stepped forward, touching his shoulder. "I know you're all angry, that you all feel betrayed, and you have every right to be."

A chorus of agreement rose in the air, the energy level in the corridor growing.

"But this isn't the time. There is such a thing as the lesser of two evils." She pointed to herself and to Wilhem behind her. "Yes, we've wronged you, but there is a much greater threat out there, one we all have motivation to overcome."

She motioned to everyone around her. "Everyone here has their lives on the line. That makes us all equal, on the same field. If we want to survive, we need to work together. We can't let our differences break us apart before we can stop this threat. For all you know, either of us could end up saving your life or vice versa. We need each other. Until they're stopped, we need each other."

Commander Bennett stepped forward. "Grace is right. We don't have the luxury of revenge right now. Too much hangs in the balance. If we can't stop or at least slow the enemy down here, Captain Faulk and his crew might not have enough time to warn the Earth. It might be too late. Don't forget that it isn't just our lives we're fighting for here." He pointed to the airlock. "Billions of lives ride on what happens next. Don't let them down."

***

Mila leaned back, letting out a sigh of relief. They'd made it. The moon was at their back, the Earth before them, and as far as she knew, they'd received no damage in the attack.

"How fast can we get back?" Tristan asked.

"If I push the engines, we might run out of fuel, but I might be able to shave it to a day."

"Really?" Tristan sagged in his seat.

Mila nodded. "But we could run out of fuel doing that. This ship is designed for short jaunts, not speed. Up to a space station or the moon. That's it. We should check our fuel stores before considering burning that high."

"Okay, Mila, go check. Avery, check for damage from the attack. I need to know if we have anything to worry about. Anything, no matter how small."

"Yes, sir," they said in unison, before getting up from their seats.

Mila stripped out of her suit, putting it away in the locker. Avery settled in to pull up sensor data, looking for damage to the hull. Even minor damages at these speeds could be catastrophic.

Mila left, heading for the maintenance hall. While the consoles in the cockpit had fuel gages, they weren't accurate. Good enough for day to day use, but not when you might plan your fuel usage down to the last ounce. They couldn't afford any inaccuracy here. That would leave them stranded and they might not get their radio back.

She passed the empty weapons room, then a couple more doors flew past before she stopped at the end of the hallway. It opened into a space with displays, buttons, and lots and lots of electronics she didn't recognize. She went straight for an undersized door to the right.

The door read "Fuel Tanks," and warning signs screamed out at her.

Gas Under Pressure.

Radioactive Materials.

Mila pushed it open, bending to slip through. Dim red light tinged the surfaces of the room. Mila faced the wall to the left of her, touched a display to bring it to life, and selected "Drop Explosion-Proof Shielding." A humming sounded behind her and she turned around as the cylindrical metal sheaths dropped to expose the clear tanks of xenon gas.

She pushed off, running her hand along the analog pressure

gages. There were external monitors, but analog was more accurate. Mila jotted down the first number and moved on to the next, methodically recording the pressure from each tank. She flew to the back where tanks with heavy, permanent metal shields sat. Her heart rate pumped up a few notches at the bright yellow radioactivity warnings screaming at her. She hesitated, unnerved by the proximity to the fuel for the nuclear reactor, but it was safe. Mila wrote those numbers down as well, then floated back, reactivating the shielding.

"Okay, done." She turned, almost slamming her head on the low doorway she'd just entered. "Oh, that was stupid." She shook her head and dipped to make her way through, holding on for good measure.

***

The captain of the Morg battleship looked on as repairs continued on the damaged hull. Bright lights from tools lit up the space as the metal heated neon orange, sealing the jagged hole. They'd managed to seal off that section before the entire ship lost atmosphere, but a dozen good men died in the process. He glared, angry about the delay, but it would be much worse to need a quick exit and be trapped on the surface.

A man walked up to him. "Sensors are still down. We're not sure where the shuttle went."

He growled, resisting the urge to backhand the man. "It went down to the planet, that's where it went. Don't be an idiot."

The soldier meekly slinked away, annoying him further. Pathetic ingrate. If that was the kind of men he had on this ship, no wonder he'd found himself stranded on this gods-forsaken rock.

He wandered up to a man overseeing the repairs. "How long?"

He jumped, clearing his throat. "Um, not long before we're space-worthy. There's still a gaping hole, but we'll be ready in case of emergency."

"Good." He turned on his heel, taking off for the other end of the ship. He found his second in command in the bridge. "We attack now."

<hr>

Grace fiddled with her rifle from where she sat against the corridor's wall. Wilhem Wolf sat next to her, almost hip to hip. A buffer of precious space isolated them from the rest of the warm bodies in the hallway.

"So, I didn't catch your name," he said, his voice even rougher than before.

"Grace, Grace Harper."

He nodded and smiled, reaching out his hand. "Nice to meet you. Sorry it wasn't under better circumstances."

"I never thought my life would end up like this. Considering what I have to look forward to, considering what I've done, I'm not even sure I care if I live through this."

He shrugged. "Your life isn't over just because of one mistake." His voice cracked on the last word.

She glared at him. "I'm pretty sure people would see it as treason. It's a bad mistake." She sighed. "My life is over. I'll be lucky if I don't end up with a death sentence. They still execute traitors."

"American?"

"Yeah."

"Didn't they get rid of the death penalty?"

She slouched into the wall, as if the weight of her worry weighed her down. "Yeah, but I always thought treason was a special case. Like the same rules didn't apply."

He shrugged, wincing as he pointed to himself. "German."

She smiled at him, shaking her head at how that one word said so much. "You have a way with words."

"Have to," he whispered, barely audible.

"And yet *I'm* the diplomat."

"Not anymore," he mouthed, frowning. He laid a gloved hand over hers on her lap and the determined look in his eyes said it all. *None of this defines you.*

Then she remembered what he'd said before. *Your life isn't over just because of one mistake.* She narrowed her eyes at him. "You are entirely too wise to be a criminal."

Wilhem shrugged, rolling his eyes.

A cacophony of repetitive claps and screams echoed off the walls, causing everyone to jump in their seats. Everyone looked to their respective leaders, looking for guidance.

"Follow me," Commander Bennett said, picking up his rifle and taking off down the corridor, waiting for no one.

Grace got to her feet, helping Wilhem as she grabbed her own rifle. "Ready?"

Wilhem shook his head, mouthing, "No."

"Good enough."

They followed, the first people to move, heading into almost certain death as if they weren't terrified.

Grace raced back up the hallway toward the noise, heart in her throat, her footsteps pounding a constant rhythm. Commander Bennett skidded to a halt at the corridor that connected the wings.

Another scream and a couple cracks of gunfire echoed off the walls to the right. He chased the commotion like a flash. Grace took off after him, vaguely registering Wilhem at her side. She didn't know or care if anyone else had taken up the pursuit.

How long could it go on? How many were in that hallway? What if they all died? She took comfort in the recurring gunshots and screams, knowing it meant her compatriots still lived, still fought.

Commander Bennett slowed to a stop in front of them, holding up his fist in a signal she'd seen in plenty of movies. She stopped beside him, barely breathing, too afraid to make a sound. Bennett knelt low, bringing his rifle up to shoulder level, just like in the cop shows.

Grace raised her own rifle, pretending she didn't see the slight tremble of the barrel as she held it aloft. Bennett turned the corner, letting off a burst of gunfire. Grace jumped behind him, pulling the trigger right alongside him. Her ears rang with the continued assault and she marveled as the weapon barely jerked in her hands, having nowhere near the kick she'd expected.

Raising the gun to eye level, she tried to aim at someone she didn't recognize. He looked surprisingly human, yet wore a uniform unlike anything she'd ever seen.

Crack!

She missed, but he dodged and stopped firing at those trying to escape the assault. Several bodies ran past her, unarmed, bleeding, trembling with fear. She pushed them out of her mind as soon as they escaped her sight.

Crack!

She hit someone this time, the man in the alien uniform going down in a spray of blue blood. Grace turned, looking for her next target, but the enemy was regrouping and they seemed better armed.

Their foes let out a volley of shots that sounded like hail hitting a tin roof in the middle of a hurricane. Everyone ducked behind a corner. Grace's breath came in ragged gasps as she clutched the rifle to her chest, trying to squeeze as close to the wall as possible.

"Munitions check," the commander barked.

Grace stared down at her weapon, but she was stumped. "How?"

He showed her. Popping his clip from the gun, he pointed out the indicator on the stock and slapped it back in place with a click drowned out by the gunfight.

Grace checked her weapon, saw she had fewer bullets than she would have liked. She would have liked about a million, but had more like twenty. That wouldn't last very long. Grace looked to her right, where others stood plastered against the wall, shaking or crying. Wilhem grinned at her, a steady soul in a sea of people not trained for this.

Grace turned to the commander. Grim determination set his jaw. He wasn't looking at them. He had more important things on his mind.

Grace leaned out as far as she could without risking her own neck. A big gun, almost as big as the one May Trace had been carrying, sat abandoned on the floor in the heart of the kill zone. "What's that?" she asked.

"Looks like a rocket or grenade launcher," a male voice said over her shoulder.

Her eyebrows rose. She looked back at the terrified huddle, then at her gun with a measly twenty rounds left. *We're all gonna die.* A lull in the shooting settled over the corridor, like the station was holding its breath. "Here, hold this for me." She threw the rifle at Wilhem.

He caught it automatically.

Grace didn't wait to see if he had a good grip on it. Now or never. She dashed out into the open hallway, bending to grab the weapon. Voices called out to her, but they blurred into the background. She turned, lifted it onto her shoulder, and hoped she was doing this right. She pressed the trigger.

Something big and nasty took off from the barrel in a cloud of white smoke. The enemy freaked, ducking for cover, but there was none. Grace twisted around, opening her mouth to tell everyone to run, but they didn't need to be told. Everyone had already started running for the end of the hallway, knowing what was coming next.

The explosion boomed in her ears with the screeching of twisting metal. The force of the blast pressed into her, debris hitting her as she ran away. She silently thanked God for the heat protection of the space suit or she might have been cooked alive.

Everyone reached the main corridor winded, an alarm blaring in their ears.

"That was really stupid, Grace Harper," Commander Bennett said, bent over and trying to catch his breath.

"Yeah, probably. It seemed like a good idea at the time." Grace's mind felt fuzzy and she wavered on her feet. Pain started to throb through her middle. "I think I was hit by some debris, though." She looked down and stared in shock at a rapidly spreading red circle coating her suit. It was growing so fast. She turned to Wilhem. "I told you I wasn't going to make it."

CHAPTER TWENTY-ONE

The bridge of the Morg ship went abruptly quiet, the background sound of military chatter silenced. Everyone in the room froze for a single beat of time, then the captain raced to the viewing screen as a poof of smoke drifted from the enemy station. "Zoom in on that." He pointed at the smoke.

A woman responded, doing as he asked, and the display zoomed in, showing a large hole where an airlock used to be. He narrowed his eyes. Wasn't that where the infiltration team had entered?

The room became sedate as people edged away from him. Everyone knew not to go near him in one of his moods.

"Was that—"

"Yes, sir," a man said, jerking ramrod straight.

"How many men did we send?"

"About three dozen, sir."

He glared at him, trying to remind himself it wasn't the soldier's fault. "Double it. I want that station *crippled.*"

It was bad enough they'd let a shuttle escape. The moon station served as humanity's early warning system and they'd already failed to keep Earth in the dark, but he couldn't fail on the second front. The station also served as a repair facility for ships that couldn't enter the planet's gravitational field. Crippling it would be a first strike against the unsuspecting species. Without the station, any heavily damaged ship would be out of the fight permanently.

Wilhem caught Grace in his arms. "Grace?" His voice wavered, cracked. He shook her, but she didn't move after she collapsed to the metal beneath them. He laid her gently on the floor, his hands uncertain on what to do. An uneasy silence hovered over the group.

"We need to shut off this wing," Commander Bennett said, the only person not shocked stupid by the series of events. "Jacob, come with me."

Jacob jerked out of his shock, nodding before picking up his rifle and following the commander out of the area.

Wilhem looked down at Grace again, shaking his head as if to deny her state. "You didn't deserve this," he mouthed, unable to speak the words.

And with the great gaping hole in the station, he wouldn't dare take off their suits to check for life signs. He *knew*, but it was a reprieve, an opportunity to kid himself, to live in denial a little longer.

Wilhem had hardly known her, but he felt certain she was a good person. Certainly, a better person than him. She'd regretted her decisions and not just because she'd been caught. And she didn't think twice about running out into the open hallway, right in the line of fire. A bad person wouldn't do that, a criminal wouldn't do that.

I *wouldn't do that.*

<hr>

Jacob followed Commander Bennett in subdued silence. Grace's death had stunned him almost as much as her betrayal. She pissed him off and constantly set him in his place, but he couldn't deny that, occasionally, he needed it. He'd never wanted to be here and he took it out on everyone around him. Now she was dead and he'd made the last days of her life harder than they needed to be. He couldn't take that back.

Bennett turned a corner, reaching the doors that would seal the wing off from the rest of the station. This sector wasn't essential. Which was lucky, because he bet they wouldn't be able to repair it for some time.

Maybe *ever* if they didn't win.

"Shit," the commander said, stomping for emphasis.

"What is it?" Jacob said, resting his rifle on his shoulder to look, but it didn't take a genius to see the problem. Debris had slammed into the surrounding walls, but one piece had lodged into the door's tracks, mangling the bottom edge and preventing it from closing. A red light blared on the instrument panel to the right.

"Can it be fixed?"

"Maybe, but not quickly." Bennett stomped his foot.

Jacob raised an eyebrow. "What do we do?"

"Check that the station is safe. There's an emergency procedure for when the airlocks fail."

"I'll go to the Control Room."

Bennett nodded. "Thanks."

They ran in opposite directions. After a few minutes, Jacob skidded to a halt in front of the Control Room. He pressed for entrance, but got no response. He slammed on the door. "Hey! What the hell?"

No one answered and a sinking feeling settled in his gut. It dawned on him that the hallway was now open to space. The commander's boot had made no sound.

No sound.

No oxygen.

No nothing.

The doors wouldn't open.

And they only had whatever oxygen remained in their suits.

Yasmin flinched as an explosion rocked the station. "What the fuck?" she said, turning in her chair toward the noise.

Beside her, Vaughan flurried into action, his hands running over the display.

"What happened?"

He scoffed. "How should I know?"

Yasmin frowned, but kept her mouth shut. He was just as in the dark as she was. She looked behind her again, her eyes widening as she noted the red light on the panel display. "Vaughan." Her voice trembled as she stood and crossed the room.

"Not now."

She crept closer, a part of her not wanting to know what that angry beacon meant. Her mind blanked, forgetting every safety policy she'd read, every procedure drilled into her skull.

An angry buzz came from the panel by the door, making her flinch. It happened again and again, then a loud bang rocked the room and she jumped.

"What was that?"

Yasmin turned to Vaughan where he sat twisted in his seat. His heavy breaths assaulted the air, the only noise in the still space. She didn't have any answer, so she swung back to the door, half expecting it to bite her. The distance dragged on, taking longer and longer to go shorter and shorter distances, until she finally reached the display.

She stared, but she knew after only a glance. There were no controls now, nothing, just big red letters spelling out, "Emergency Lockdown."

"Vaughan," she said, her voice shaking even more than before, "check station integrity."

"We're on our own," Jacob said as he reached the others. He focused on his breathing as it fogged his vision, the exhales impossibly loud in his ears, all too aware that the air he breathed was all he had.

On the way back, he'd debated running versus walking, wanting to get there fast but not sure if it would be worth the oxygen consumption. In the end, selfish shortsightedness won out and he walked.

Smoke had started clearing, the red glow of fire gone, snuffed out by the lack of oxygen.

In front of him, Bennett stood, hands on hips as a group of people milled around.

"What about the airlock?" a whiny voice said from the floor.

Bennett shook his head, looking down on the person. "No go. The explosion damaged it. There's a great gaping hole in the station now."

Damn, Grace really did screw us. He immediately felt guilty about the thought. She gave her life to *save* them. It may have been misguided, but he couldn't forget that.

Bennett shifted his hands around him. "You," he said, moving his arm in an arc to one side, "search for any loose metal pieces. You," he picked another group, "look for tools. The major areas of the station will be in Emergency Lockdown but closets will not. We need welding tools."

"How the hell are we supposed to recognize welding tools?" a man said, throwing his hands up.

Bennett faced away from him, but he could practically *see* his glare from the tension in his shoulders. "Just start looking for tools." He looked around. "Does anyone have welding experience?"

One of the Incirrina lifted an arm.

Bennett nodded. "Good. Hopefully, we can find something to use. The rest of you, come with me. We need to remove that obstacle from the door."

<hr>

"I got it!" Yasmin yelled over her shoulder. She lifted her hands in the air in triumph.

"How?" Vaughan said. He stepped up behind her, looking down at the display.

"Maybe you're not as good as you think."

He glared at her and she laughed. It felt good to rile him up. Things had been too damned tense.

After discovering the Emergency Lockdown, the Command Room started to close in on her and it took everything she had, every opportunity for distraction, to keep from losing her shit.

"Well, we can't help, but at least we can watch."

Yasmin looked down at the displays before her, where she'd pulled up surveillance footage of the hallways. On one, a panicking mob banged against a locked door, yelling to get in. There was no audio, but the video caught the way one person's mouth opened wide through her helmet.

Another showed a group opening closet after closet, though she couldn't imagine what they were looking for. On another screen, people collected debris while the smoke dispersed.

She kept her gaze from the display showing a ragged hole in the station. It made anxiety ramp up in her every time she caught it out of the corner of her eye.

Instead, she focused on the display she'd set up in the middle. It showed Commander Bennett surrounded by a group of people as they examined the blast door connecting the lab wing to the station's core.

Kennedy Moon Station was designed modular, with blast doors at regular intervals so additional wings could be added with ease. It allowed them to build new structures without compromising the core. But it also let them close off sections in case of emergency.

That door should have slammed down the instant the explosion rocked the station. Even from the small screen, she spotted the narrow gap between the door's edge and the floor.

"It must be jammed," Vaughan said.

"Yeah," she replied, not taking her eyes off the tableau. Her gut twisted. If Bennett's team didn't get that blast door down, they would die in here. Though maybe Vaughan could override the emergency protocol. Did they have space suits in here? She knew they didn't have food.

Or water.

"I'm going to work on comms."

"Okay," she said, but she didn't give a damn about comms right now.

Little by little, the lab hallway emptied. People dropped debris just inside the door as an Incirrina held some type of tool. Three people gathered around the door.

Yasmin held her breath. Were they?

They leaned back, putting all their weight into what they were doing. After a few moments, others joined in, grabbing onto the three and trying to pull them back, using their own body weight to help.

Time ticked by as nothing happened and the people on screen struggled in vain.

Then, pop! Yasmin jumped in her seat as the entire group fell backward, tumbling onto one another. "Phew."

The door slammed down. Yasmin spun around, excited, but the excitement died as the light on the panel continued to glare bright red. "What?"

She turned back, squinting at the screen. "What's wrong? Why hasn't the lockdown lifted?"

The Incirrina with the tool stepped forward as Bennett directed another to approach with bits of scrap. The bright flare of an arc welder whited out the screen, messing with the camera's auto-exposure for a moment. Yasmin watched as the person held the metal in place while the Incirrina welded it to the door.

Her focus was so complete, she jumped when a loud *thunk* echoed across the room. She jerked around, sighing a breath of relief.

The red light had turned green. The lockdown was over.

CHAPTER TWENTY-TWO

---

*B*ennett stood in the large Control Room once more, saddened by the reduced numbers before him. Some faces were missing because he'd sent them away—like Faulk, Avery, and Trace—but with others, if they weren't here, they must be dead. He'd worked with many of them for years.

Damn, I wish I were military...

He cleared his throat. "Attention!" He didn't have to say quiet this time. No one was chatting. He wasn't the only one who'd noticed the absences. "I'm sure all of you know about the attack." He paused. "Grace Harper died saving our lives."

He couldn't imagine many would make the decision she had. He was simultaneously grateful and mad as hell. She'd saved their lives. He felt certain of that. They were pinned down, without adequate firepower to hold them off. But she also blew a giant fucking hole in his station, which just pissed him off.

"There's a breach in the lab wing. We've locked down that sector." Bennett couldn't blame her, though. He *refused* to blame her. She'd given her life and he figured that bought a bit of forgiveness. He would eat his anger, let it stew, and unleash it on the enemy. *They* deserved it. *They'd* caused this.

He paused for effect, looking at all of them. Fear, hopelessness, and despair filled the room. "I've decided we'll take the fight to them." He pointed off in a random direction. He wasn't sure where the ship was, but it didn't matter.

I'm really *not cut out for this.*

What am I doing?

"There are brave men and women here. We have weapons. We can fight. Together, in one group, we can stop them." He didn't really believe what he was saying, but he tried to put feeling into his words, make them convincing. He didn't need to believe it. *They* did. "We'll be collecting at an airlock at the opposite side of the station from the ship, giving us time to plan out the attack and maneuver into place.

"We can do this." He pumped his fist, speaking with more determination than enthusiasm.

Mila leaned back, glaring at the screen in the *Dakota's* cockpit, her right eye twitching. "I hate math."

Tristan hovered over her. "But you figured it out. I checked your calculations. Looks sound. How long till we get there?"

"A day and a half." Mila sighed. She wanted to be there *now*. But alas, the world didn't work that way. "I guess it's better than three days."

Tristan squeezed her shoulder. "You did good."

She shrugged and entered the rest of the course information. "Done. We'll get a warning when we approach the Earth."

"Good. Now, go take a break. I think you could use it."

She nodded, unbuckled from her seat, and drifted up before pushing off. As she settled against a wall, she looked back at Tristan and tried to drag in a settling breath. Her entire body felt tense, as if her muscles would tear under the strain. They needed to get back yesterday, but this was the best they could do. "Do you think we'll get comms back once we're farther from the moon?"

"Maybe," Tristan said as he buckled into one of the seats. "I'll continue trying to connect with someone over the communications system." He turned around. "Now, get some rest."

She nodded again and pushed off down the hall.

She just hoped distance would make a difference. If they had to wait almost two days to warn Earth, it might be too late. Mila feared it was already too late for the people of the Kennedy Moon Station.

Bennett organized everyone into groups of eight—large enough for a coordinated assault, small enough to pass through the airlocks in one shot. Each team had a leader, usually security, someone he would direct as they advanced. He would lead the first group.

I'm not ready for this.

He stepped into the airlock along with five other humans and two Incirrina. One was Zikka, the only alien he'd learned the name of. He suspected it was their leader, but he wasn't sure. Zikka seemed to carry a sense of authority.

He greeted Zikka with a small smile and a nod. He hadn't noticed its space suit before, but it seemed strange. What material was it made of? It didn't look even remotely similar to anything he'd seen on Earth. It looked almost… liquid.

"Everyone ready?"

Everyone bobbed their heads, too subdued for speech. The Incirrina showed the most life, raising their various appendages in the air with gusto. Bennett nodded and pressed the button to open the exterior door. It opened, air rushing out with a hiss, and he led them outside.

He waited, nerves making his heart throb in his chest, as one group after the next left the airlock. When he thought they'd all exited, he signaled for them to follow and crept along the metal walls, keeping in the shadows of craters and the station. The moon made for a wonderful landscape for stealth—a pro and a con for placement. As they moved forward, slipping from one concealed spot to the next, he felt confident they could sneak up on the alien ship looming before them without being seen.

Bennett had to crane his neck upward to see the entire battleship. It sat parked, a monstrosity of military might. It was foreboding and he could imagine it would send fear into the hearts of his already skittish army.

We are so screwed.

He sighed, but edged closer, checking back frequently to make sure no one had stopped, no one had frozen in terror or trauma. The Incirrina crossed the lunar surface in movements that reminded him of the slithering of snakes. They must have been a sight to see in action on their own planet. All's the pity that their anatomy wouldn't allow them to step foot on the higher gravity of Earth.

They drew closer to the enemy craft and Bennett slowed, waiting for his people to catch up. Finally, he stopped, with only a single crater's edge blocking them from their destination. Most of the suits blended with the dusty landscape, making it difficult for them to be seen from above. He even felt grateful that the metal surfaces of their gear were powder coated to prevent reflections, which would have given them away.

Bennett turned back, but couldn't stop himself from flitting his gaze over his shoulder to check the ship. He wasn't military, but putting his back to an enemy freaked him out.

When the last of the groups entered the crater, he motioned Vaughan and Wilhem to the front. "Can you crack it?" he asked as they came up beside him, leaning against the dusty ground.

"Are you kidding? I don't know anything about that kind of stuff," Vaughan said, indignant. "I could fix it if it was broken, remove a virus from the software, but just… not that." He shook his head.

Wilhem pushed forward, a cocky grin on his face that spoke volumes. He stretched his arms out in front of him, cracking his knuckles. With one last glance behind him, he motioned to his eyes then around them.

Bennett nodded at the request to watch Wilhem's back, but the hacker didn't wait for an answer. Jumping over the edge of the crater, he made a mad dash for the ship. When he arrived, he plastered himself to its hull, then inched to the panel. Bennett waited impatiently as the criminal worked his magic, praying those skills would come in handy once again. He tried to reassure himself that the man had already blocked the alien ship's radar, so there was a good chance he could do this as well.

The door slid open to the side and Wilhem spun to face the others, pausing before giving them two thumbs up. Bennett checked in all directions, stood, and motioned everyone to follow. He raised his rifle to ready and charged through.

The Morg Captain paced the bridge, glaring at the viewing screen every few minutes. He'd sent out a second wave of men to the station. They'd better succeed or he'd gut them himself.

A series of pop-pop-pop sounds came from somewhere behind him and he froze. "Report!"

Everyone scrambled to answer, but it didn't please him. This whole mission was going south. He could feel it.

Someone turned around from their terminal. "Intruders on the lower level. A lot of them."

Shit.

Tristan pressed the button once more. "Control, can you read me?" His voice sounded tired, worn, discouraged. Hours had passed since they'd left the moon and there was no telling when a message would get through. He might not be able to get through. For all he knew, it wasn't a blocking signal, but something that permanently damaged the system, like an EMP, only focused toward communications.

He looked out the screen, the Earth deceptively large, and sighed, wishing he wasn't the only one up here. Mila was sleeping, curled up in one of the bunks, while Kyle prepared a report for their superiors. Tristan had argued that it was *his* job, but Kyle claimed he was better qualified, being the security and investigation expert. Tristan suspected the man just didn't want to be stuck in the cockpit, speaking and pressing a button every few minutes, bored out of his skull.

He pressed the button again. "Control, can you read me?" This time, it left his lips in a monotone.

Bennett turned a corner of the enemy ship's hallway and opened fire. The percussions of the gun echoed off the eerily dark walls, piercing his skull even through his helmet. His ears wouldn't stop ringing and he wondered snidely if the damage was permanent. He could barely hear a damned thing.

Jacob stood to his left, rifle at the ready, pulling his trigger, and taking down enemies with a raw determination he hadn't thought the man was capable of. When the last alien fell, Jacob advanced at Bennett's side and he felt better knowing the other man had his back. And how weird was that? This was the same man who'd whined constantly, making him cringe.

As they moved forward, careful of cross corridors, Bennett glanced back, ensuring no one was hurt, that they left no one behind. A solid wall of Incirrina filed in after him, disturbing smiles on their faces. They were enjoying this. Bennett wasn't sure whether that was good or bad.

Tristan sat staring out at space, the Earth overwhelming the view in front of him. Exhaustion consumed him, both emotionally and physically. He shuddered to think this might be his life now, moving from one disaster to the next.

He pressed the button for the comms, "Control, can you read me?" Leaning back, his body felt heavy in spite of the zero gravity.

Looking behind him, cold metal walls stared back, making

him feel alone. Maybe he shouldn't have sent Mila off. It would have been nice to talk to her. But then, he always wanted to be around her.

But she *doesn't.*

His thoughts drifted to sitting in that hospital bed, proposing to her. Though he made it a joke, he'd been dead serious. Until he saw that look on her face. She'd looked horrified and his heart shriveled up in his chest. He shook his head, wanting to hit something. Why'd he have to love a woman who would never love him back?

"Those look like deep thoughts," Kyle said from behind him.

Tristan swiveled around, trying to mask his feelings, put on his captain face once more. "It's nothing."

Kyle scoffed as he floated forward, grabbing onto the back of a chair. "Bullshit. Mila has you wrapped around her little finger and you know it."

Damn, Kyle saw it too?

"Don't worry, she still seems clueless."

That's the problem. "What do you want?" he said dejectedly.

Kyle shrugged, his muscles pulling against his flight suit. "Do you need a reprieve? I imagine we'll be trying to reach out to command for quite a while."

"No, I'm good," he said, running a finger lightly over the comm button.

Then a percussive boom rattled the ship. Tristan reached out, grabbing the console as if that would do a damned thing. He looked over at Kyle. "What the hell was that?"

A klaxon blared overhead, the light tinting red and flashing to the beat of the warning siren.

CHAPTER TWENTY-THREE

The Morg unit ran straight at the ragged hole in the side of Kennedy Moon Station. Debris littered the area and they ignored it, knowing some of it had once been friends. At least no recognizable body parts stood out as they flew past.

As they advanced, the blackened, distorted walls became structurally sound, then only streaked with soot. A large, formidable door stopped them in their tracks.

"Get this open, now," the man in charge barked.

People scrambled, collecting supplies, and examining the thing between them and certain victory.

The inner workings of the station waited just on the other side. If they could scrap the station, they could swing the coming battle in their favor, not that anyone on their ship would be in that battle. Their battleship was too badly damaged.

"I need this done yesterday!" He stood, legs spread apart, arms crossed over his chest, glaring at his men to speed them up.

Tristan's heart froze for a moment as he stared at the Dakota's control panel, his mind utterly blank in response to this catastrophe.

What the fuck happened?

His ears continued to ring with the constant obnoxious noise that would not let them forget their lives hung in the balance. "Avery, check station two." Tristan shoved over to station one, looking for error codes, hoping the system knew what the hell happened.

It might not. If the explosion damaged sensors, they would be blind.

"Right," Kyle said, pulling himself over the seat back he still gripped to work the controls.

"What the hell was that?" Mila said from the door behind them.

Tristan turned from the display he'd just loaded up. Mila floated in the doorway, holding the metal framework with a white-knuckled grip. "An explosion, I assume. Check the fuel room."

"Right," she said, nodding before pushing off in the opposite direction.

Tristan returned his attention to the console. *Come on, damn it.* The red light made reading the screen difficult. He squinted as he navigated the options, checking system after system, sensor after sensor.

In his mind, their list of tasks grew longer and longer as he noted sensors with faults, sensors with warning codes. Damn.

"I can't feel the engines," Kyle said beside him.

Tristan stopped, turning to his coworker and friend. "What?"

Kyle looked up and around. "I don't feel them. There's no vibration."

Tristan settled his hands on the console, closing his eyes, trying to block out the harsh red light and loud warning sound. A foul smell like burning rubber drifted to his nostrils.

Silence.

He held his breath, waiting, hoping.

Nothing.

"We're dead in the water."

"Over here," someone called. "I think this is an engine room."

Bennett turned, looking behind him. One of the engineers stationed with him had fallen behind, standing ten feet back at a door he'd looked through, then quickly assessed as "not a threat." He motioned everyone to move, then peeked through. How had he missed that? He was no engineer, but now that he stopped to look, it did sort of resemble an engine room.

Dark and sinister like the rest of the ship, with bold sharp angles, the space hummed. Mammoth equipment filled the area with barely enough room between to traverse. Parts moved overhead, speaking to whatever mechanism the enemy used to power this beast.

"Anyone have any suggestions?" He turned to the group.

The Incirrina were standing guard, watching the hallway for potential threats. The rest looked to each other, hoping someone else would speak up.

Wilhem raised a hand. He slapped his chest, pointing at

himself and Vaughan with a smile before giving them a thumbs up.

"You've got this?" Bennett asked.

Wilhem nodded, but Vaughan didn't look so sure as he followed.

<hr>

Mila's heart pounded away in her rib cage, leaving her movements jerky as she tried and failed to pull and push herself smoothly to the fuel room.

Come on, damn it. Come on!

God, she felt so slow and every time her muscles locked up on the grab bars, slowing her down, she wanted to scream.

Why did this keep happening to them? Why couldn't anything go smooth?

She reached her destination after an eternity, the cold, harsh edge of the doorway biting into her palm as she whipped herself around the corner and dived in. For a moment, her mind blanked, just staring at the warning signs on the tanks, the room, the door.

She moved to the first tank, hesitant as she stared at the explosion-proof shielding. Did she dare? What if another explosion happened? It could happen, right?

Mila shook herself. Honestly, the xenon tanks weren't even the biggest danger. Conversely, the heavily shielded tanks in the back with yellow radioactivity signs made her want to run.

She pulled up the display to her left, dropping the shielding with an audible *thunk*. She let out a breath. *So far, so good.*

Moving forward, she checked each tank, running her hands over the smooth, clear surfaces. No cracks, no damage.

Good.

She went to the far side of the room. She couldn't drop the shields on these. The contents would slowly kill them if she did. Still, she inspected them for any signs they'd taken damage, that they had something to worry about.

Mila sighed when they seemed unharmed. Slapping her hand against the wall in relief, her breath locked in her chest when her hand made contact. She looked on in horror, her eyes tearing as the heat radiated into her bones, almost burning in its intensity.

Too hot. Way too hot.

———

"Move." The Morg captain shoved one of his subordinates out of his chair, sitting down in his stead. He typed up a quick message, getting angrier with each word. A status report and he wasn't at all happy to be sending it.

They'd yet to cripple the station, their first wave of soldiers were dead, a giant hole breeched their outer hull, and an unknown number of humans had infiltrated the ship. Still, it needed to be done. His superiors needed to know.

He sent the message, looking up at the wary faces around him. "What are you all gawking at? Get back to work!"

———

Wilhem and Vaughan stood up with wicked grins on their faces.

Wilhem spoke first, his voice barely a whisper as he

talked with his hands as much as his mouth. "Let's move before this blows." He picked up his rifle and started running, not waiting for Bennett's command.

"What did you do?" Bennett asked as they ran past him.

"Well, I can't be sure," Vaughan said, out of breath and yelling over his shoulder, "after all, it's not technology I'm familiar with, but it's probably like removing the cooling rods from a nuclear reactor."

"What?!" Bennett stopped in his tracks, mouth dropped open. "Are you fucking nuts?" He started running again, this time with renewed vigor. "Please tell me those engines aren't as powerful as a nuclear reactor."

"I wouldn't know," Vaughan said, gasping, his brain stuck on a litany of *oh shit, oh shit, oh shit.*

"Oh God, we're all gonna die."

Wilhem shrugged with a smirk as he tried to keep up, the dark walls blurring in his periphery.

They didn't even bother worrying about their guns, everyone just focused on running as fast as humanly, or inhumanly in the case of the Incirrina, possible.

The leader of the group of Morgs let out an angry puff that fogged his helmet. They'd switched to plasma torches, the brilliant arc of heat and light blinding in its intensity. He had no idea what the humans did to the door, but no amount of hacking would open it. Some of the best computer experts in their race and they couldn't open a fucking door.

According to his tech expert, it should be opening. He thought he'd even felt the lock mechanism disengage, but the door didn't open. It simply wouldn't respond and for not the first time, he wondered why they weren't just blowing the station sky high.

Oh yeah, because their battleship didn't have those types of munitions on board. From what he'd heard, they'd used the last of their large bore ammunition attempting to take out the shuttle that escaped.

He shook his head. Sloppy, just plain sloppy. If he'd been in charge, they'd have shot that ship before it even took off *and* decimated the moon station with the large bore cannons.

But he wasn't in charge. He was stuck leading a team trying to cut through a several-foot-thick door with a handful of high heat torches.

"What's the ETA?"

"Honestly? I have no idea," a man with a torch said, not turning from the task at hand. "If we knew more about the door's manufacture, maybe I could give a more useful answer."

"Well, we don't, so stop wishing for the impossible."

A jarring thump rumbled through the wall he leaned against and he perked up. What was that, a bolt?

<hr>

Something slapped against the wall behind Tristan, snapping him out of his focus. He spun around, staring at Mila as she heaved breath in the doorway, her face red with exertion.

"The reactor's overheating," she gasped, her eyes rounded in fear, an expression he rarely saw even in the direst of circumstances.

"Damn," Kyle said beside him.

Tristan angled back to his display, punching through menus on the smooth surface. "Damn," he whispered. The reactor sensors said, "Cannot Connect." He turned to Kyle then Mila. "Let's move." His voice boomed over the more strident alarm, sending them both into action.

He bumped against Kyle as they both rushed to the door simultaneously, Mila floating ahead. He barely saw the ship around him as they headed to the sealed maintenance rooms.

What happened? What exploded?

Why?

Tristan didn't presume to know, but the sense of time passing, of time running out, built as they moved.

Ahead of him, Mila sailed into a door that read, "Maintenance." Her hand touched something and she said, "Damn."

"Move," Tristan said, coming up behind her moments later. Everyone had access to the maintenance corridor, but just their luck, the explosion must have triggered a lockdown. She moved aside and he typed his master code in the panel. The moment dragged on and he feared *this* system was down too, but it beeped and a *thunk* heralded the lock disengaging. He pushed it open and pulled himself hand over hand through the space.

At the end of the corridor, a door read, "Coolant Room." He shoved the door open and froze. Like the rest of the ship, the light flashed red. The ever-present klaxon muted by his abused ears. In front of him, though, was their doom.

His heart pounded in his chest, sending adrenaline surging through him as the reality of the situation became clear. The coolant system had ruptured. Around them, debris and gel floated in the air, the coolant tanks that kept the reactor at ideal temperatures were nothing but a mangled memory.

His body grew cold with dread. He thought of the Kennedy Moon Station with all its residents, the diplomats, the Incirrina. They were doomed. They would never reach Earth, never warn them of the danger.

Tristan turned to Mila and pulled her into his arms, taking comfort in her body heat.

I failed.

CHAPTER TWENTY-FOUR

*S*he yawned as she stumbled into the engine room, ready to start her shift. Lacking in both stature and skill, she'd always been a disappointment. Useless in a fight, her parents had always shaken their head, lamenting not having a big, strapping boy.

But all's the better. She'd managed to settle into a nice quiet life maintaining engines. She liked it and knew she hadn't been built for war—physically or mentally. Just the thought of picking up a gun made her shudder.

Looking up at the vast space holding her babies, she smiled, letting a happy sigh escape her. "Hello, my cuties. How have you been? Have the mean men been abusing you since I've been gone?"

She walked over to the first of the engines, checking on gauges, displays, fittings, the works. She ran her hands over every surface, as if getting a bead on their statuses by touch alone.

When she stopped in front of the last one, her hand froze, her face falling in shock. "No." Her gaze dashed over the surfaces, a startled whimper slipping out. "No, no, no, no."

Someone had tampered with it. Her hands followed the rewiring, trying to figure out what they'd done to her baby. When she reached the end, she sucked in a breath with an audible squeak. "Good gods."

She turned and raced across the room, flipping a cover up and slamming her hand over a button she thought she would never have to press. A loud klaxon started sounding and lights flashed in a distinctive pattern, warning people to evacuate, that a critical engine failure was imminent.

Even she couldn't be sure when it would blow. Much as it pained her, she wasn't going to sit around trying to fix it and get herself blown up in the process.

The Morg captain sagged with a sense of resignation as everywhere around him, men and women started evacuating. Feet pounded the floors beneath them and panicked voices rang out, echoing off the ship's walls. They didn't even stop to wait for orders. They just fled. Apparently, a reactor melt down trumped his bad attitude.

He stepped up to the console and quickly typed another message.

They'd failed.

And yet they might still succeed. He still had his men. They could still take out the station. But it had now become a suicide mission.

"Sir, another message came through from the advance ship." The man turned around in his seat, facing the superior officer.

The officer walked forward, chest puffed out, arms clasped firmly behind his back. He shook his head. "I should have known better than to send that incompetent louse. All ships, advance."

"Aye, sir." Every voice on the bridge echoed the same words and the space broke out into a flurry of movement and voices as they scrambled to coordinate the fleet.

They passed carefully through an asteroid belt, edging closer and closer to their target. They didn't need to take out the moon station to win. His kind just believed in destroying an enemy totally. The humans didn't have a chance.

"What do we *do?*" Mila said, panicking behind Tristan outside the Coolant Room.

Tristan turned to her, surprised by her tone. Mila never panicked. He'd watched her fly her way out of the worst of circumstances without batting an eye. He'd seen her fight off intruders with speed and grace.

Now a fine tremble ran through her, her face open with fear. Avery waited in the doorway, seemingly calm but severe, giving nothing away.

They both looked to *him.*

Shit.

He returned to the impossibility before them. They couldn't call out for help and while inertia would keep them going, they couldn't land. They could wait and hope they could get a message through, but since they couldn't slow down either, what would happen when they approached Earth?

Their normal speed in space was over 10,000 miles per hour. His breath locked in his chest, the impossibility of the situation bearing down on him. They couldn't land at that speed. It wouldn't just kill them, it would destroy everything around them.

But without the engines, which required power to ionize, what could they do? They couldn't slow down, couldn't brake, couldn't steer. He looked at Mila again, but for once, she was silent. They were relying on *him* to save them.

Double shit.

He was no engineer, but he knew that if the reactor continued as is, it would be game over long before they reached Earth. He stared at the flying chunks of metal and blue goo. Turning off the reactor would do no good, at least, he didn't think so, though maybe it would prevent it from heating any further. But then how could they get it to cool down without coolant.

"Venting into space?" Avery said, startling Tristan out of his trance.

"What?"

Avery crossed his arms, the gesture losing its impact with him floating like that. "You were mumbling about cooling the reactor. Sealing the reactor room from the rest of the ship then opening the surrounding vents should help. There are no other means of cooling off on a shuttle." He pointed at the shell of the coolant tanks.

He nodded. It was as good an idea as any. "Do it." He forced his captain's voice through even though he didn't feel it.

Avery saluted and pushed off, disappearing out of sight.

Mila stared him down, the panic gone from her face now. What did she see? Did she see how scared he was? Did she see he had no clue what to do next? "If we reach Earth without being able to slow down, we're dead."

He didn't want to agree with her, even though it was true. He didn't want to voice it. "We need power going to the engines. We don't have that."

"Don't we?" She raised her eyebrows.

He frowned at her. What did she know? "What?"

She smirked and shook her head, clearly enjoying the moment. In a sing-song voice, she said, "Not everything runs off the reactor."

His eyes rounded. Of course! The reactor charged their capacitor, which powered most of the systems. It was inefficient to do with the engines, but not impossible. "We need to reroute power."

She nodded.

"If we're not careful, we could kill ourselves."

She smirked, then nodded again.

He shook his head. "God, you're crazy."

She grabbed his arm and urged him out. "Where?"

He pointed and they floated away. Mila opened a door with "Electrical" written on it. Inside, he looked around, daunted by the sheer volume of the problem. Dozens of boxes lined the walls, each with countless circuit breakers in them. In the middle of the room, cages filled with matted tangles of cables ran in aisles. "I think we're in trouble."

CHAPTER TWENTY-FIVE

The soldier holding the cutting torch jerked as the second bolt on the uncooperative door gave out. The Morg leader contemplated sending some of his men to another entrance. There had to be a better way. Of course, the enemy wouldn't expect them to come through an access point they deemed impenetrable. And he suspected busting this door open would damage the integrity of the station. With the airlock blasted to the gods themselves, he bet this metal barrier was all that kept the atmosphere from being sucked out onto the moon's surface.

He turned and paced some more, too frustrated with the agonizingly slow progress. Gods damn it! He was a soldier! He didn't have the patience for this shit. Okay, so being an officer, a little patience was in the job description, but this was getting ridiculous.

He confronted the first person he saw. "Can you think of a way of speeding this up?"

She shook her head, an alarmed look in her eyes.

"Anyone else?"

Everyone avoided eye contact. He started pacing again.

It was hopeless. Tristan stared from the doorway to the Electrical Room, overwhelmed by the nightmare before him.

"Come on!" Mila said, slapping him on the arm. "Read the labels."

Tristan nodded and moved to the right wall, opposite Mila. He slapped his hand against the cold metal of an electrical box wondering what he was doing here. What business did *he* have rewiring a ship?

Fortunately, everything was labeled. He ran his finger over letters etched into the metal, disregarding each label he came to, hoping *something* would call out to him. He moved from one panel to the next. With each panel, his stomach sank deeper and deeper.

Would they ever find what they were looking for?

Did they even *know* what they were looking for?

"I think I found it," Mila said from the opposite corner.

Tristan whipped around, hope floating inside him like a deflated balloon. He moved to her side, zero gravity making the passage unbearably slow. Touching her shoulder when he reached her, he leaned over and looked at the tag in question.

RR IPT In

He frowned at it, wondering what the hell that meant. What did Mila see that he didn't? Then again, the entire panel appeared different from the rest. Every label included the words, "IPT In." The box itself was bigger, looking like a beast compared to the other more standard electrical boxes. It made him suspect this one ran more power through it.

He flipped it open. The breakers were like nothing he'd ever seen before. Checking around its edges, he noticed the lines out fed in a different direction from the other boxes in the room.

Tristan's hand rested on the lever to the right. He hoped it would disconnect power so they could operate safely. "Mila, we need tools."

"Where?"

"Last door on the left before leaving the Maintenance Corridor."

"Right." She nodded and pushed off.

Tristan pulled the lever down and the breakers tripped with an audible *pop*. He looked around him once more. They could probably cut the lines leading up to remove the link to the reactor, but they needed to create a bypass.

Mila returned moments later, a bag of tools clutched to her chest.

He turned to her. "I don't suppose you have a degree in electrical engineering?"

She scoffed. "Tristan, I didn't even finish pilot training."

He nodded grimly. "I'll cut the connection to the reactor. Find a way to reroute to the capacitor."

"Right."

Tristan grabbed something big, sharp and vaguely plier-like from the bag floating between them. He held his breath, resisting the urge to close his eyes as he rested the blades against the thick bundle of wires at the top of the box.

Snip.

He breathed out. Nothing bad had happened. So far, so good.

"Hey, Tristan, I think I found something."

Tristan turned to Mila, who had slid a panel aside on the back wall near the floor, exposing a compartment behind the room. "What is it?"

"Well, all the cables in those central cages feed here." She waved vaguely through the hole she'd entered.

He grabbed onto a cage, using it to draw himself lower to look inside. It was dark, giving him nothing but vague shapes. "Do you see anything we can splice?"

"Yeah, I think so. I see a bundle with really thick wires. Maybe that leads to the capacitor."

Tristan looked around. "Mila, we need something to bypass with."

She peeked her head out, glaring at him. "I'm not stupid, Tristan. There's cable in the bag."

Tristan flung his hand at the bag just barely out of reach before he caught a handle, dragging it closer. Sure enough, a big coil of high gauge wire rested near the bottom. "You'll have to work in there. I won't fit."

She sighed. "I know. How do I get myself in these messes?"

He grinned. "Just lucky?"

Her middle finger flew out of the hole this time and he laughed.

"Here," he said, handing her wire strippers.

"Thanks."

Time dragged on as he handed her item after item, the uncertainty eating at him as moments ticked by.

"I think I'm getting the hang of this," Mila muttered, breaking up the silence. "Shouldn't be long now."

More lengths of wire flew out the hole. Of course, they still had to connect them to the severed connections at the box.

But what if this didn't work? What if the wire was too thin? What if they caused a fire? What if it was too little, too late?

Mila crawled out, pushing Tristan aside. "I'll get these too," she said, smacking the box.

He nodded, handing her the wire strippers once more. She moved efficiently this time, much more efficiently than before, possibly from experience. Or just better lighting and space. With each moment she worked, he felt more confident they would make it.

"Done," she said, pushing back from the panel, then frowning. "Though, we need to secure or remove this door. If it's loose during landing, it could cut off power to the engines and kill us all."

"We will, but you sure it'll work?"

She shrugged. "Only one way to find out."

"Well, that was a rush," Wilhem said, his voice scratchy. A broad grin stretched his face as he tried to suck in gulps of air.

Man, I can't wait to see something other than this station's metal floors and walls.

Hell, even his own ship was less monotonous than this military installment. He winced, remembering how his brother would stick shit to the console. His chest constricted in pain.

"You're a nut," Vaughan said between wheezes.

Commander Bennett sucked in a breath, wishing he were anywhere but here. "All right, everyone. It isn't over yet. That ship's gonna blow any minute now, and we have no idea how big the blast will be. You know the drill. Diplomats, follow me. You too, Wilhem."

People scattered in all directions, leaving two dozen humans and aliens waiting in the corridor.

"What's the plan?" Vaughan asked.

"Follow me." Bennett took off, not even looking back to ensure everyone followed.

They jogged from one hall to the next and Wilhem lost all sense of direction by the time Bennett stopped, ushering them inside a relatively empty room.

"This is one of the most reinforced locations in the station. It should withstand a blast."

Hopefully. "What about the rest?"

"They have specific sites they report to, places closer to their duty stations. Those areas can't shelter a lot of people. That's why we came here."

The most horrific screeching sound known to man silenced everyone, reminding him of the death throes of some tragic monster. For the longest time, they continued to hear clanging and sponging noises as debris fell on the station.

"Do you think it's over?" someone said.

"Not even slightly," Bennett mumbled under his breath.

The Morg team froze at the door they were working on when the station rattled around them. His HUD flashed red letters as the pressure drastically increased before dropping off again. *What of the gods was that?*

He turned, walking to the bend in the hallway. Running figures were silhouetted against a red-orange backdrop of flames that dogged their heels. His lungs seized in his chest as the blazes spilled closer, then let out a breath of relief when they started to trickle backward, the lack of oxygen extinguishing them. Whatever blew up, it had been filled with oxygen and big.

He turned back around the corner. "Back to work," the leader said as he shook himself out of his reverie. He knew what had exploded. If he kept his men occupied enough, maybe they wouldn't realize.

She sat in her little closet on the Kennedy Moon Station, waiting for the worst of the explosion to pass so she could get to work. Anxiety that had been ramping up steadily higher for hours now slowly drained, leaving her exhausted.

Still, she glanced around. Compressed gas canisters lined the walls, securely locked in place with heavy chain. Caution and warning signs in red, black, white, and orange sat sentinel above their respective dangers. At least if the worst happened, her death would be quick. She imagined an oxygen tank exploding, or a chain breaking and a canister impaling her. Maybe a tank would leak and put her to sleep before suffocating her.

She glared at the liquid nitrogen tanks. She would start with those, not relishing what those monstrosities could do to a person. Checking the valves, looking for damage, she moved on, making sure each tank had no weak points, wasn't leaking, that the chain was firmly in place. Basically, that none of them would kill anyone any time soon.

The tanks were used by the laboratories, which were out of commission because of the gaping hole. Still, they served as one of the greatest dangers on the station.

After she'd finished inspecting the last of the canisters, a loud pop echoed off the walls. She froze, anticipating her inevitable demise, but nothing happened. She opened an eye and peeked out, but nothing appeared out of place. Odd.

If it wasn't here, where had it come from? She exited the compressed gas storage room and looked both ways, looking for signs of movement or some indication of what the noise had been. She didn't think it was a good sound. To her mind, it sounded like something breaking.

She walked toward the defunct laboratory wing, figuring if anything broke, it would be there. Turning a corner, her mouth fell open. A red aura rimmed the edge of the door between the central station and the lab wing. Her breath froze in her chest as she noticed the spots where the metal had melted around the edges. Her lungs burned and she gasped a breath.

She ran in the opposite direction, running for Commander Bennett. She had to tell him someone was trying to break into the station.

His fellow crewmates had scattered in all directions when their ship blew. Pain lanced his side where debris had hit him moments ago, but he barely paid it any mind. His thoughts flashed back to racing through the corridors, dozens of them rushing to don space suits even as the countdown to destruction loomed, unknowable and imminent. Many didn't get their space suits on fast enough. As he scanned the surrounding chaos, he knew many more never made it off the ship. Chunks of the battleship littered the ground, but so did broken bodies.

As he walked along in shock, his heavy breath fogging his helmet display, he passed corpses that had been ripped apart in the explosion. Some were burned, unrecognizable as anything other than meat. Others were sliced to ribbons, caught in the blast radius and killed by shrapnel.

The area outside the Kennedy Moon Station looked like a war zone. Debris littered the lunar surface—some of it metal, some of it *not*. Around him, people walked in a daze, while others tried to herd everyone into a single location. Some of the suits were damaged, but there was nothing to be done about it. And a person wouldn't die because of a small tear in a space suit.

People cried out, their faces stretched tight as they yelled, looking for their friends. But with ears ringing, sounds muted from the blast that had rung over their comms for the briefest of moments, and comms now out of commission, only silence answered.

A young woman raced into the room just off the Control Room as Commander Bennett and Zikka sat huddled, planning what to do next. All heads turned to her as she stood there, face white as a sheet.

"Someone's... trying... to break in," she gasped.

Bennett jumped up and clasped her shoulder, seeking to reassure her. She trembled under his palm. "It's all right. You did good. Now, can you tell me any more details?"

She nodded and sucked in a large breath, the air wheezing through her nose. "The door to the lab wing. I think they're trying to go through it with torches." Her arm flailed behind her.

"All right," Bennett said, looking down at her, rubbing her shoulders. "You did good," he whispered before stepping back and clapping his hands, raising his voice with authority. "Looks like the break is over."

CHAPTER TWENTY-SIX

*Z*ikka stepped through the airlock along with his fellow men and the human security personnel. He and Commander Bennett had decided that he would lead a small group of Incirrina and humans. The station was currently blind and there would likely be survivors of the ship explosion wandering about, but they had no clue how many had survived. Or how much of a threat they would be. For all they knew, there could be an army outside their doors.

He waited for the rest of the men to leave the airlock, then motioned for them to follow, with several individuals watching their flank. They hugged the station's wall as they progressed forward, determined to go unnoticed. The building's shape worked to their advantage, the spokes masking their progress.

"Sounds" rang out, the vibrations from the ground unintelligible from this distance. He sank to the surface, pressing his appendages against it to get a better feel for what awaited them. In his periphery, his people did the same while their allies looked on in confusion. The humans didn't have the same sense for vibration and the Incirrina's suits amplified it when needed to phenomenal levels. At this setting, he could detect a single step on the moon a mile away.

He focused. Chaos reigned just over the ridge to his left. Many steps, hap-hazardous and harried, raced across the surface, aimlessly. It would work in their favor.

They slipped past the jagged edges of the station where Grace's rocket had taken out an entire squadron. The walls were scorched black, twisted and mangled in places. Debris littered the ground, and Zikka motioned for everyone to be careful, and not to make a single noise. Vibrations would carry through the corridor's metal walls and they did not want their enemy to know they were coming.

Zikka kept an appendage touching the wall, listening. The echoing vibrations of their quarry drifted down to them—shuffling feet, metal banging on metal, the hiss of a torch. Zikka moved toward them with a grace his race was infamous for. The humans stumbled along in relative clumsiness. Though fairly quiet and nowhere near loud enough to alert their foes, they were still graceless buffoons by comparison.

The scorch marks faded and disappeared as the tension in the hallway grew. Weapons were raised. Gaits were slowed. Zikka came upon the first of the enemy. The Morg wasn't even facing him. He reached out, wrapped a tentacle-like arm around the man's neck, and snapped it, holding him aloft until he could rest the body without it disturbing the stillness.

He nodded for the others to proceed. Bodies passed beside him on his left as he finished lowering the dead soldier to the floor. He smiled as his men dispatched the enemy with practiced efficiency while Bennett's crew tried desperately to keep up.

Zikka moved forward, trailing behind until a single shot broke through the corridor, the feel of ammo hitting metal walls sending shock waves up to his core.

"Fall back, fall back!" one of the humans yelled.

A storm of gunfire cut through the air. A human fell to the ground while others managed to duck behind the corner. One man kept leaning around the corner taking potshots at the enemy. The vibrations through the walls and floor were too intense to sense if any of the shots hit.

They were pinned down, but so was their enemy.

<hr>

By the time the first crack of gunfire echoed through their recently reactivated comms, everyone's ears had stopped ringing and the Morg officers had restored a semblance of rank and order.

They stilled, turning to look at the large hole in the station.

"I forgot about the unit sent to infiltrate the station."

Another nodded. "Maybe we should send reinforcements. If an enemy team went in after them, they would be sitting ducks, cornered."

He peered over the mass of people, most of whom weren't soldiers. "Assemble a team and send them in."

"Yes, sir."

The captain stopped the man. "I'm coming, too."

"Are you sure, sir?"

He glared. "I'm tired of this getting fucked up every time I delegate. Yes, I'm sure."

"As you wish."

Bennett jerked when he heard the first crack of gunfire, followed by a barrage. The reports reverberated off the walls, shattering the stillness. People around him responded, clutching guns or gripping those closest to them.

That doesn't sound good.

He waited for the battle to end, for the last pummeling rounds to drop into silence, but silence didn't return. He glanced at the door, wanting to check surveillance in the Control Room, but as he scanned the skittish people surrounding him, he knew he couldn't.

"Shit," Bennett said under his breath. "All right, everyone. It looks like Zikka's team needs backup. Let's move!"

Most stood, gripping weapons and setting their shoulders with grim determination. Some, however, huddled closer together, but Bennett ignored them. They were useless to him. He stepped from the room, leading them into battle.

The last man fell, slumping against the wall. Creaking and shuffling broke the stillness, which felt empty without the constant barrage of gunfire.

"Good job," Zikka said.

They hadn't lost too many people, thanks to favorable placement. The Morg had nowhere to hide and his allies had been able to fire from around a corner. It could just as easily have gone the other way. Fortunately, there were no rooms, no doorways, that close to the central hub. Many of them managed to duck into other rooms when their enemy opened fire. Their foes had not been so lucky.

A skittering followed by a clang came down the corridor, barely discernible over the soft vibrations of Zikka's men as they checked their fellow fighters, ensuring no one needed medical attention.

"Quiet," Zikka whispered fiercely.

Everyone responded in an instant. Vibrations echoed and amplified. With his suit, he was sensitive to even the faintest tremor. A steady rhythm reverberated back to him.

"Someone's coming," one of his people said in a voice that barely carried to the group.

"Yes," Zikka replied.

"Feels like they're marching."

Zikka nodded, but didn't say another word, making a gesture for everyone else to do the same. He motioned for half the men to take positions in the labs down the hall, as they'd done earlier. The rest, he directed to wait around the corner, hoping it would be enough.

Time slowed, passing as easily as hot, humid air through your lungs. Some fidgeted while others tensed and relaxed their grips on their weapons as if overeager to be let loose. The time for action would come soon enough and his people knew those times quite well. Perhaps, too well.

The battle didn't start with a single shot this time. The enemy turned the corner, but didn't see Zikka's forces from their places of cover, even if Zikka saw all of them from his. He nodded and everyone opened fire.

He'd again gotten a taste for warfare.

The first wave fell in a bloody mess, not even putting up a fight.

Commander Bennett led those who would follow along the edge of the station. He imagined they followed the same path as Zikka and his team. Some were in a state of shock, moving on autopilot. He hoped he wasn't leading them to their deaths. Others, like Jacob, took to the challenge and danger with an alacrity he would have never credited them with.

They didn't bother with stealth as they rounded the ragged hole in the station. They ran down the corridor, kicking debris out of their way as they went. Guns raised and ready for battle, Bennett prayed they wouldn't be too late.

Zikka peeked around the corner, only half registering the bloody tableau as he sent off a volley of shots before taking cover once more and waiting. He looked behind him, checking his weapon.

Some of his men had fallen, too many men. He couldn't see all the humans from his position. Many of them had taken up positions farther forward. Zikka sighed and took comfort in the vibrations of battle raging through the walls, reminding him they'd not yet lost the fight.

Then the melody of the battle changed, turning into a wild frenzy, rising above the constant cacophony of war. What happened? He rounded the corner once more, pulling the trigger as he investigated.

Some of the enemy faced the wrong way, firing in the opposite direction. He shot them in the backs, their bodies falling one by one to the hard floors.

He turned again, leaning his back against the wall.

Why?

Bennett ran around a corner, his finger jerking the trigger as the enemies' backs appeared in front of him. He gritted his teeth and laid down on the trigger after that first, surprised shot, killing half a dozen soldiers before they'd even had time to react.

Jacob came up beside him, taking down a few more before the enemy turned, guns raised. Jacob pushed him out of the way as the burst of gunfire showered the hall in their direction.

"Thanks," Bennett said.

"No problem," Jacob replied, waiting for the perfect moment to fire once more. He glanced back to Bennett, a smile on his face. "A dozen down. God only knows how many to go."

Bennett shook his head, amazed that this was the same man who'd bitched and complained without end not even days before. He squatted, moved around Jacob, and initiated another assault as more of his people came up behind them. Some froze, backs plastered to the wall, their weapons trembling in their hands. Others looked to him for guidance. He just jerked his head toward the enemy. What did he know, after all? He wasn't military. Few of them were.

"Hell," Jacob mumbled, barely audible.

Bennett turned, seeing the other man clutching his leg, blood seeping out from between his fingers. He pushed him to the ground, placing his hand over Jacob's to apply more pressure. "Is it bad?"

"I don't know." Jacob said, a stunned look crossing his face.

They lifted their hands, but with the suit on, it was hard to tell.

The battle raged on around them. They pressed down harder. "It'll be fine. The battle's almost over, anyway."

Jacob nodded, but doubt filled his eyes.

***

Minutes passed and the battle petered out. Zikka's men left their places of cover, advancing through what had once been the enemy line, taking out the stragglers with single, well-placed shots. Mangled bodies tripped them up as they continued forward.

Eventually, they passed the last of the enemy. Zikka turned to his men. "Check for signs of life." Those that understood his language complied instantly. Before him, humans came out of their positions, their weapons dropping to their sides. The humans behind him advanced on their fellow man, smiling in greeting at their saviors.

Conversations were exchanged as they checked who made it and who didn't. Zikka waited for his men to report back. A couple cracks reverberated off the walls. Not all the enemy had been dead. He nodded in approval.

***

Bennett and Zikka led their people out of the hallway and onto the lunar surface, where they hesitated. How many of the enemy still lived? Had they sent everything they had or did more wait just over that ridge, ready to end their lives if they should attempt to cross.

Bennett crept forward and settled in, looking over the edge at the people who populated the crater. "So, what do you think?"

Zikka dropped beside him. "No weapons."

Bennett looked closer. "You're right." He didn't see a single weapon. The aliens cowering before him appeared just as dazed as some of those in his own ranks. Certainly, none seemed trained to deal with what had happened. "Should we round them up?"

Zikka wiggled an affirmative.

"Alive?"

"Yes."

Bennett nodded, then they both waved their men to advance as they stepped over the ridge, their weapons raised, ready to create carnage. They advanced like a tide, falling on the shell-shocked enemy in a formidable wave.

As they flowed over their foes, most huddled together, frantic eyes darting around as the humans and Incirrina surrounded them. Others ran, their suits hampering their progress. Zikka waved and several of his men gave chase. Bennett looked on in awe as they dashed over the moon's surface with a grace that made humans look like bumbling toddlers. It hadn't occurred to him until that moment that this was closer to their native gravity, that their bodies were *designed* for this. One of the Incirrina tackled an enemy, sending him to the ground in a cloud of lunar dust.

Minutes passed as they held their position. Bennett felt like a bully holding a gun to these people. They shook in fear with no weapons. Not one of them seemed like soldiers, like a threat. The Incirrina returned, dragging or carrying the runners and dumping them unceremoniously with the rest.

Bennett stared down at them, surprised by how *human* they looked. There were differences, of course. Their skin tone was different, though he could barely see it through the gear protecting them from the harsh realities of space. Their space suits, deep black with hard edges much like the rest of their technology, were both menacing and strange. He gestured to Zikka. "Do you know their language?"

"Maybe. No comm."

Bennett frowned, but realized without common communication units, they wouldn't be able to speak to them, not out here. He turned to his men. "Return to the station. Lock them up. Don't let any get away."

Bennett settled into a seat in the Control Room. They'd locked up the enemy in one of the storerooms, the same one they'd used when no other space was large enough to fit everyone. Now he had his people scouring the station, checking for damage.

The diplomats and the Incirrina had returned to their talks, more determined than ever to finish. As Zikka had said, "Need now more. Both sides do."

From what Bennett had gathered, they were nearly done. Jacob had joked that they would probably be done before Bennett's people managed to check the station for needed repairs.

"Ha!" Vaughan said, standing up from his position under the desk. "Got it!"

Wilhem shook his head, tapping his screen, which Bennett couldn't see.

Vaughan glared at him. "Don't call me Rick."

Wilhem ignored him, tapping some more.

"That's because you caused it," Vaughan said through his teeth.

Wilhem grinned, smugness leaking through.

"So, communications and radar are back up?" Bennett cut in, determined to prevent the fight he saw coming.

Vaughan faced Bennett, momentarily forgetting Wilhem. "Yeah. Everything should be good now. I'll contact Earth to update them on our status."

"Good. Then let's check the radar for anything significant."

Wilhem nodded, giving a sarcastic salute as Vaughan chattered in the background. Wilhem turned to the displays and paled, before turning back to Bennett. "We might have a problem."

Bennett walked up, leaning over Wilhem's shoulder. "What is it?"

Wilhem pointed to a spot on the screen covered with a whole bunch of little dots. He shook his head, lifting his palms to say he didn't know.

"I think they're ships," Vaughan said, his voice frail.

CHAPTER TWENTY-SEVEN

"I need a nap," Mila groaned, pushing toward the door at the rear.

Tristan smiled from his seat at the *Dakota's* control panels, amused by her impatience. He shook his head. She would never change, would she?

He returned to the task at hand. The engines had power, but he hadn't heard from Kyle yet and he still needed to run through diagnostics again. They had a chance now, but would they make it?

The arc of the Earth before him drew his gaze, making it feel imminent, impossibly close, as if they would reach it at any moment. It was a false hope, though.

His hands hovered over the controls. Why did this keep happening? He had over a decade of smooth sailing under his belt, over a decade of missions without any hiccups, any conflicts, any challenges. He glared at the door Mila had disappeared through. It all started with her.

He shook his head again. *No, it hadn't.* That was a coincidence.

Mila had nothing to do with how FUBAR the *Orleans* mission became.

"Those are some deep thoughts," Kyle said behind him.

Tristan snapped out of it, not even realizing he'd drifted into a trance staring at the Earth. He spun to face Kyle. "Status?"

"Reactor temperature is dropping. We'll have to close the vents before entering atmosphere or it'll burn out the systems."

Tristan nodded. "Good."

The comms crackled and they both tensed, breath held. A distorted voice came through the speaker. "Kennedy... Station... Please respond." Words were garbled in the middle, making it difficult to understand.

Tristan picked up the microphone. "This is the *Dakota*. Go head, KMS."

"We read... *Dak*... Can't reach... at Command. Transmitting..."

A data link flickered on the screen before him and he waited. With the comm transmission so fucked up, they might not receive any files intact. What were they sending?

"Receiving, KMS," he said into the microphone, the cold metal fisted tight in his hand.

Only static responded.

The last person stepped back after he signed the treaty, placing the stylus cater-corner over the device holding the all-important document. A sense of accomplishment rolled over the room, making everyone stand a little taller as they stared at the black square against the long, gray table.

Jacob had lost track of time as they worked out the details, the battle putting a fire under their butts. As he looked around, he knew. They *all* had something to fight for. It lit their eyes, fear with just a dash of determination.

"I don't know about you guys, but I'm not willing to wait and risk this all being for nothing." One of the human diplomats walked back to the tablet and picked it up. "I'm sending a copy to leadership on Earth." She faced Zikka. "I suggest you do the same with the Incirrina."

Jacob's pessimism leaked in, tainting the moment. Could they even *send* to their leaders? Would the signal go through?

Zikka nodded at the other diplomat. "Of course."

She handed the device over to Zikka, who sent the treaty to his own leaders. Since his human comrades came from a great many countries, many of them also took turns sending the document to their superiors.

Jacob sat up carefully in his seat, cognizant of the wound he'd barely allowed the doctors to patch up. It wasn't bad, just a graze, but it hurt like a bitch. When did he become such a badass? "Well, I guess on to the next little fiasco."

"Control Room?" Zikka asked.

Jacob nodded. "Commander Bennett said there's trouble."

Zikka nodded back, said a few quick words in his native tongue, accentuated by the occasional staccato click, and led his people from the small quarters.

Jacob stood, taking his time as the movement pulled at his wound and jerked his head toward the door. People would come or not as they pleased, but he didn't expect much from them. He hadn't expected so much from himself, but you never knew how you would react in a crisis.

"Command, do you read?" Tristan drawled with a yawn as he stared up at the cockpit's ceiling, tracing the seams with his gaze.

The line crackled, causing him to jump to attention in his seat. He waited but nothing else happened. Still, it had been the most he'd heard coming though that damn set of speakers in hours. He wasn't sure how long it'd been since the KMS transmitted to them. His chest tightened once more with the significance of the data they'd received.

God, we're so fucked.

"Command, do you read me?" he said more stridently, holding his breath for an answer.

It crackled again, then a distorted voice came through. "This is Command. Identify yourself."

He sighed, relief coursing through him. "This is Captain Faulk of the U.S.S. *Dakota*. We have an emergency situation. A hostile alien ship has landed on the moon. Communications and radar are intermittent."

He didn't mention the image that kept popping into his head. He prayed the data was just a radar glitch. He knew what it *looked* like, but the *Dakota* didn't have the facilities to analyze it. He couldn't be sure.

God, I hope I'm wrong.

"We read you, Captain Faulk. Please hold."

The line went dead and Tristan hoped it was because the man on the other side was scrambling to send aid. Lord knew everyone at the station needed it.

A few minutes passed and the voice broke the silence again,

this time without static. "We're sending a ship now. It was en route for minor repairs."

Tristan sighed again. "Thank you. Myself, Pilot Trace, and Lieutenant Avery are on our way back to Earth."

"Please provide the status of the other passengers attached to your mission. According to departure logs, ten individuals departed on the USS *Dakota*."

He shook his head, even though the man couldn't see him. "The situation necessitated an immediate takeoff. Before departing, we unloaded our weapons cache for use by station personnel. A hostile enemy craft was on approach and landed immediately before our departure, firing on us as we launched. Immediate assistance is requested for the remaining personnel."

"Affirmative. What's your ETA?"

Tristan looked around, suddenly wishing Mila hadn't wandered off to take a nap again. "Less than a day?"

"We'll see you then."

The line cut out and Tristan wished he could call the moon to tell them help was coming, but he'd failed to open a comm with them since.

Was it too late?

CHAPTER TWENTY-EIGHT

---

*T*he summons had been urgent.

Kennedy Moon Station under attack. Assemble crew at once.

The words still rang in her skull. Every member of her crew waited in fear for the members of the station. Would they arrive too late? What was the threat?

They'd been told just enough to get their asses in gear, but little else. She had no clue if command didn't *know* more or if they just weren't saying. It could go either way. She frowned, hating the bureaucracy. She had no patience with it, had no interest, either. It was a miracle she'd managed to pull herself up to the position of captain.

After too long racing to the rescue, her chair dug into her back and butt, making her want to pace. She felt too idle, too useless. She'd never been called out on a rescue mission before. Usually, they were sent on research missions with NASA. There was little need for military in space, but try telling military command that.

Yet again, her thoughts drifted to the attack on the moon

station. It was unexpected, taking her by surprise. What would she find when she got there?

"We're approaching the moon, Captain."

"Good," she said, nodding her head.

Through the view screen, the pocked surface of the moon grew, but it didn't look the same as usual. She'd been there countless times to drop off personnel or perform repairs. Sometimes, they used the moon to run simulated missions and battles. The celestial body proved useful for practicing maneuvers and fleeing attacks.

Today, though, dark marks scorched the ground. Beyond the sprawling complex of the Kennedy Moon Station, a monstrosity lay scattered across the moon's surface. As they grew closer, it became clearer. A large hull, looking disturbingly like someone's chest after a facehugger broke free, sat next to the station with detritus littering the ground. The station, itself, looked worse for wear, with a ragged hole in one of the wings.

"Reach the station on comms."

"Aye, Captain." The little woman got to work. "Kennedy Moon Station, this is USS *Utah*. Please respond."

The radio crackled, but came to life moments later. "This is Kennedy Moon Station."

"What is your status?"

She held her breath, waiting, hoping.

The radio crackled again, the words garbled but decipherable. "Sealed off lab wing. Enemy contained. Threat neutralized."

She let out a sigh of relief. *Thank God.*

Then the radio crackled once more. "Unknown ships on the horizon."

———

Mila sat in her seat in the cockpit, waiting on final approach vectors. Tristan and Avery had both strapped in. Soon, they would all be on solid ground. They would be back on Earth, where gravity settled you, made you feel substantial, at home. She loved flying, but there was nothing like home.

"U.S.S. *Dakota*, this is Control. We are sending landing trajectories now."

She looked down and the approved flight path popped up on her screen. "Roger, Control. Received."

"Transmission confirmed, *Dakota*."

Mila turned to her friends. "Ready?" A sly smile crossed her face. This was the best part.

"Just don't enjoy it too much," Avery said as he gripped the armrests a little tighter.

"Almost as good as takeoff," she mumbled as she changed their angle, causing the vista to flare red as they entered the atmosphere. The heat from reentry tinged her view, making the landscape before her waver.

This ship was more than capable of handling the heat.

They angled downward and Mila monitored everything, checking temperature, speed, horizon, geo-positioning. She made minor tweaks constantly as they grew closer and closer to landing. It was fun, but complicated.

Because shuttles entered atmosphere at thousands of miles per hour, they looped Earth multiple times. Planning the gradual decrease in speed without overshooting your destination was a skill unto itself.

But like a carefully choreographed dance, the forest around base came into their view as she turned on flaps and dropped the landing gear. She held her breath, anticipation always getting her in this last moment.

Closer.

Closer.

Touchdown.

The wheels bumped against the tarmac once, twice, before coasting to a stop. Only the tower and runway graced the view before them as they stopped. Mila popped the clasp on her harness and stood, letting out a sigh and a smile as the solid weight from Earth's gravity pulled at her bones.

"A good feeling, isn't it?" Tristan stood beside her, massaging her shoulder with one hand.

"Especially after a rough assignment." Her sigh took on a different quality. "But the shit isn't over." She reached out, fisting the radar data she'd downloaded from the Kennedy Moon Station's transmissions—radar data on the fleet of ships approaching. The information would help determine how long until those ships would arrive. Mila just hoped it would be enough.

Tristan nodded sadly. "Yeah. Let's go." He turned and led them to the door.

Mila opened it, exposing the crowd that had gathered. A man with a whole slew of shit on his uniform stood at the front of the group. Behind him, green trees stretched just outside the range of the hangars and runways.

Home.

Clark NSS Base.

"Rear Admiral Ambrose." Tristan snapped into a sharp stance.

"At ease, Captain." Ambrose came forward and shook Tristan's hand. "Follow me."

Mila sat down across from Avery in the conference room. Tristan took one end of the table. Rear Admiral Ambrose sat at the other. Tristan had spent the last few minutes briefing the admiral on the situation while Mila plugged in the data drive to put the information up on a big screen.

She looked up. "Ready."

"Go ahead," Rear Admiral Ambrose said, motioning toward the screen that covered most of the wall.

Mila inserted the cable into the display port. A series of beeps sounded as the computer processed the request. Then the screen went black for a moment before popping up on both the small computer and the much larger wall display.

Tristan pointed at the enlarged visual. "Twenty-four hours ago, Kennedy Moon Station contacted us. The transmission was unintelligible, but they managed to send this data. As you can see, a fleet of ships was at the edge of the asteroid belt. Trace?"

Mila nodded, changing to the next time point.

"This was a transmission from twelve hours ago."

Mila advanced it again.

"Six hours ago. We'll need the data to be analyzed by an

expert to determine when the fleet will arrive at Earth and if that is their destination."

Rear Admiral Ambrose nodded. "We received word from Kennedy Moon Station about this."

Tristan turned in surprise. "They've got full communications back up?"

"Yes and no." Ambrose didn't offer more.

"Is everyone all right?"

"They haven't provided a full report or been able to transmit any data. To the best of my knowledge, they're still evaluating their status."

Tristan nodded. "Are they still under threat?"

"No, the enemy ship was destroyed. All remaining enemy combatants have been secured."

Tristan nodded again. "Good."

But the wall display loomed, taunting them, a constant reminder of the greater threat bearing down on them…

CHAPTER TWENTY-NINE

*A*fter meeting with Rear Admiral Ambrose, Tristan, Mila, and Kyle sat alone, waiting for analysis of the data. Tristan leaned back in his seat, taking it all in as Kyle paced the length of the narrow room and Mila fidgeted in her seat.

She slouched with a groan. "I hate this."

Tristan's mouth twitched, resisting a smile.

"I'm *bored*." She stood, running her fingers along the table, then moving to the wall to play with the seams of the display.

"It takes time. It's a lot of data you gave them."

She turned and glared at him. "But why stick us in this room while they do it?"

Tristan shrugged. He knew why, but didn't think Mila would appreciate his commentary. She seemed intent on her foul mood. He knew the severity of the situation, what the information meant. He knew what it would take to face the upcoming threat.

Tristan also knew humanity wasn't known for putting their differences aside.

———

Elias Evans, captain of the U.S.S. *Texas*, yawned, leaning back in his chair as he stretched. A pregnant moment drifted over the room as the occupants waited for him to fall from his precarious perch. His feet rested on a console, looking like a light breeze would knock them off, and his back more than his butt kept him in his seat. Fortunately, breezes were rare on a spaceship. The captain settled back into a relaxed stupor, releasing the sense of anticipation in the air.

Manning one of the ships that couldn't exit Earth's gravity, the ones that had to be built in space, was always a boring prospect when docked. It meant having only the barest of crews and being stuck with a whole lot of repairing and inspecting of systems.

The radio came to life, shocking the group into stillness. "U.S.S. *Texas*, this is Command."

"We read you, Command. This is the *Texas*." The woman who'd been running tests on communications spoke up, sending the message home in her normal soft, breathy voice.

"The *Texas* is ordered to stand at ready. Additional crew will be arriving shortly. Make preparations for launch."

The captain slapped his boots down with a resounding clap that made everyone jump. He stood, crossed the room, and smacked his hand on the communications console, activating the microphone. "What's this all about, Command? We were told the *Texas* was down for a six month overhaul."

Silence answered them for a moment before Command

responded. "You'll be informed once more detailed orders are available. That is all. Over and out."

Travis sat back in his chair, trying desperately to focus on the numbers on the screen. If he could finish the financials soon, he could jump in his truck and hit the water before it got dark, get some decent paddling in.

Unfortunately, Last Frontier, his outdoor goods shop, didn't run itself. And the computer work was his least favorite part of running his own business, a business his brother never understood.

Travis frowned, shaking his head. He hadn't thought of Tristan in ages. He leaned forward, dropping his chin onto his hand. Memories flitted into his mind of the years before their parents died, before Tristan went off to basic training. He remembered laughing with him, roughhousing, getting into trouble.

He chuckled. His brother had always been too strait-laced for his own good. He invariably came along, insisting he had to keep his younger brother out of trouble. In the end, they would both return home with their tails between their legs.

When had it all gone wrong?

Except he *knew* when. His chest tightened with emotion. It had been hard watching his best friend leave for basic training, but standing there as they lowered their mother's coffin into the ground had done what nothing else could.

He remembered Tristan standing tall and foreboding in his dress uniform while their father fell apart, cracking down the seams. He remembered the anger. Anger that their mother was taken from them. Anger that his father couldn't keep it together. Anger that his brother left them. Anger that even standing only feet away, Tristan felt worlds away.

Travis never talked to him again.

Pulling himself out of his thoughts, he admitted to himself that the anger had long since vanished, leaving only an emptiness where his family once resided. He should reach out. He should connect with his brother once more, but the gaping chasm between them seemed impossible to cross.

Sure, Tristan tried from time to time. Occasionally, Travis received calls, texts, emails, but he never answered. And the more time passed, the harder it became.

He sighed. "Useless."

Returning to his screen, he tried to focus once more on the accounting software, but the data made little sense in his mental state. With a frustrated sigh, he pushed back his chair, walking out of his crowded office and into the main part of the store.

He passed kayaks on his right, paddles lining the spaces between. To his left, shoes of every variety ran on shelves. He walked past them, stepping into the front where clothes filled racks on the floor and specialized gear hung on the walls.

At the register near the middle of the space, the cashier stood with her hands covering her mouth, shock on her face as she gently shook.

"Uma, what's wrong?"

She dropped her hands as she turned to him, a look of horror on her slack-jawed face. She looked around, her movements slow, listless, before finding the remote on the counter and hitting a button.

The TV's sound popped on and grew in volume. "According to satellites, an unknown disturbance darkens the sky outside atmosphere this afternoon after various military bases across the country flurried into action earlier today."

The image changed, showing a commotion at the Clark NSS base south of Louisville, the base his brother was stationed at. On screen, space shuttles rocketed off in the distance, the sheer number of them alarming.

The newscaster continued. "Speculations continue as to the nature of the events that caused the mass mobilization of military bases. Branches mobilizing included NSS, Army, US Air Force, and National Guard. Rumors abound that militaries in foreign countries are also mobilizing, though we have not been able to confirm."

The screen changed again, returning to the reporter. She pointed up at the sky, seemingly at nothing. "You can't see it, but at this moment, our satellites have detected interference from an unknown number of larger structures amassing just outside Earth's atmosphere. We cannot say if they are human or alien or what threat they may pose.

"At a time when Earth is attempting its first treaty with an alien race, this development could spell disaster for humanity."

Travis reached out and grabbed the remote, hitting the power button with too much force. The screen died, an after image haunting him. He turned to his employee. "Store's closed for the day. Go home."

She nodded and dashed away to clock out. His gaze returned to the TV and he thought of his brother.

"Tristan."

The Clark NSS base erupted in activity. Men and women grumbled as they drove onto the base, irritated at their leave being cut short. Every few minutes, the chest-vibrating growl of a short-range shuttle broke through the air, its familiar shape shooting out across the sky.

Luke sat in anticipation, waiting for the phone to ring, telling her her assignment. She tried to keep out of the way, but foul moods ran rampant on the base at the moment, everyone either too rushed or too angry to make any attempts at politeness.

Eventually, after the tenth time someone bumped into her in their hurry to get where they were going, she trudged into her room and slammed the door. She sighed and leaned against the smooth, flimsy surface. Across from her, the window gave her a bird's-eye view of the chaos the base had become in the blink of an eye.

She massaged her phone in her pocket, the flat shape soothing her. "Man, I wish May were here." But May was on assignment. Had been for days.

I should be too.

She frowned, pushing off from the door to sit by the window, looking out over people nearly trampling each other in the rush to act.

What the hell was going on?

CHAPTER THIRTY

*M*ila settled on the break room's couch with a sigh after having spent more time than she cared to admit pacing the hallway. She took a deep breath, but hated the waiting. They hadn't been told if they would join the fight, but at least the meeting left her feeling they had a shot.

And planning was still progressing as she sat on her ass feeling useless. Countries were coordinating, armies were amassing, and every few minutes she heard another short-range shuttle launch or land.

In the history of Earth, preparations like these had never been attempted. Instead of fighting each other, they fought for something a hell of a lot more important—their world. How many ships would be up there once they all launched? She didn't think it would be a hundred—nowhere near—but she had to believe they had a fighting chance. But even if they lost the battle in space, millions of troops waited on Earth and a hundred ships couldn't defeat that, no matter how many soldiers each one carried.

"Thinking deep thoughts?" Tristan's voice invaded her musings.

She looked up. He stood against the doorjamb, holding it up with his shoulder, a gentle smile crossing his face.

"We should be *doing* something."

He shrugged, pushing off from the doorway. "Not everyone can join the fight. There are only so many spaceships and there're a hell of a lot more active members of the NSS than can be deployed at once. You know that."

Yeah, she did. Like any well-organized force, the NSS trained enough men and women so all the ships could be fully manned, even accounting for leave. Which still left people on base, twiddling their thumbs. "I don't like not doing anything." Especially after the action of the latest mission. She had energy to burn, had too much momentum to sit here tapping her foot against the wood flooring.

He sat down next to her, wrapping an arm around her and pulling her into his shoulder. "I have a feeling there's going to be plenty of action for everybody."

He kissed her hair and she let herself snuggle into his chest, letting his warmth calm her, comfort her.

Just this once.

Admiral Brad Lewis, Commandant Commander of the United States Space Command, could really use a smoke. He stepped out of the war room, looking up and down the hallway with chipped checkered flooring and dirty white walls. They'd taken a five-minute recess and his hand twitched at his side.

Enough time for a smoke?

He sighed, no. With a shake of his head, he patted the cigar in his breast pocket and resigned himself to a coffee instead. Not the same, but better than nothing. The day was shaping up to be long and frustrating.

He rubbed his forehead as he walked down the hall toward the break room, hoping none of the other blowhards followed him. He felt a headache coming on. Maybe the caffeine would help.

As he approached the open doorway, two voices drifted to him, dashing his hopes of a few moments in peaceful quiet. His steps slowed, reluctant to join them until he recognized them—Captain Faulk and Pilot Trace.

"What if we can't stop them in space?" Trace said, her voice holding an air of desolation.

Brad scoffed, insulted she would think so. They *would* stop the invasion in space.

"We have enough ground troops," Faulk said. "They'll hold it off."

Trace sighed. "I'm so fucking useless on the ground."

Faulk chuckled. "I've seen you fight, Mila, you're not useless. Pilot or not, you're the only reason the *Orleans* mission succeeded."

Mila?

"Any shifter could do that."

Shifter? Did she just say what he thought she did? Was Pilot May Trace a shifter? Brad's eyes rounded as he settled against the wall, letting it hold him up as that bombshell detonated in his brain.

"I don't know about that."

Trace chuckled. "You know, the military should recruit shifters. Experienced ones? They're practically unstoppable in a fight."

Hmm. Brad pushed off, Trace's words ringing in his head. Recruit shifters? Interesting.

But how?

"Come on." Travis slapped his palm on the steering wheel, his hand stinging against the leather. His entire body hummed with tension as car horns blared around him. Gridlock surrounded him as he reached Louisville, cars bumper to bumper as they impatiently crossed the Ohio River.

His mind wandered as he stared off to the left, imagining himself walking over the Big Four Bridge. The sky had begun to change as the sun set and constantly changing colors already lit the bridge for the night.

He'd always hated driving into Louisville, hated how the bridges bottlenecked the travel between the two states. He scoffed at himself. *Yet another excuse for why he never saw his brother.*

But it was only that, an excuse. As the traffic creeped forward, he looked ahead again, now able to see shuttles taking off from the base. Still over an hour away, streaks of light marred the darkening sky, beautiful and yet ominous.

Please be okay, Tristan.

Chaos reigned around Travis as he pulled up to the gates of the NSS base. He tapped his fingers on the steering wheel as his urgency intensified. Four cars sat ahead of him, waiting to enter. From the sticker on the car in front of him, base employees.

A soldier at the security checkpoint waved a truck through, holding her rifle at the ready as she approached the next vehicle. She leaned in, her voice muffled by the window and the distance. She took an ID from the driver, slipped it into a tablet strapped to her side and handed it back, nodding before letting the vehicle through.

Would Tristan be home? Travis scoffed at himself for even thinking it. He hadn't bothered to call his brother. Well, he had, but he never got past staring at the phone with Tristan's number programed in.

He'd chickened out.

Somehow, it was easier to drive the three goddamn hours to the base than to make one stupid phone call. But he was here and the soldier waved to him, ushering him to the gate.

"ID?" she said, waving her hand for it.

She looked down and frowned at the ID. "You're not military personnel." She stared at him with a suspicious glare. "Says here you live in Indiana."

He nodded. "My brother lives on base. Captain Tristan Faulk."

"Hm," she grunted, unimpressed, but she slipped his ID into her tablet all the same. She typed a little, then glanced up again. "What's the reason for your visit?"

He frowned. What else would it be? "To visit my brother."

"Your brother's currently deployed."

Travis stared up at the sky. The sun had set, but a boom shook the air as another shuttle took off, breaking the sound barrier a split second after launch. "I figured as much. I wanted to surprise him when he got back."

"Could be a long wait," she said, doubt in her voice.

"Doesn't matter. He's waited long enough."

The phone call had jarred Mila awake and as she stood outside the private office, she blinked her eyes, attempting to wake up. She resisted the urge to slap her cheeks. A symbol portrayed by an eagle and shield surrounded by pinpoint stars in a black circular background graced the door. Below it read "Admiral Brad Lewis, Commandant Commander, United States Space Command."

"Come in," a voice said through the slab of wood.

She took a deep breath, then turned the knob and pushed through. The door opened into a no-fuss office. She could imagine papers strewn over every surface in an older time. Instead, a desk and three chairs comprised all the furniture. Other than a handful of awards on the walls, the only décor was a desk lamp, more functional than aesthetic.

"Sit." He motioned to a no-nonsense chair meant for visitors that didn't in any way allude to the high rank of his position.

Mila hovered over the seat, trying to decipher what the superior officer wanted, but his face gave nothing away. The air conditioner hummed rhythmically in the background, like a backdrop to some standoff.

Didn't he have more important things to do than bother her?

He leaned forward on his elbows, his intense gaze almost making Mila squirm. His gaze spoke volumes, as if he could peel all her secrets from her, so long as he had enough time in her presence. Mila resisted the sudden urge to run for the hills. He didn't know anything.

How could he?

"So," he said finally, his voice almost echoing in the room, "do you have any contacts in the shifter community?"

Mila froze, alarm surging through her. *Fuck.* She scoffed. "Why would you honestly think I would have connections in the shifter community?"

Admiral Lewis raised his eyebrows at her, pausing for emphasis. "You don't?"

Mila's mind raced in circles, trying to find a way out of this trap. What could she do? What should she say? She sucked in a deep breath, but it did nothing to calm her nerves. "Why are you asking, exactly?" She leaned back, trying to portray nonchalance, but every muscle pulled taut.

"I'm seriously considering your proposal." He leaned back as well.

Her thoughts pinged inside her head like pinballs. She could almost hear the bells going off as they collided off the walls of her mind.

What proposal?

What was he talking about?

What the hell did she get herself into this time?

"Of course, it's not entirely my decision. After all, I have no command over ground forces, but others are considering it as well. The military is more open minded than one might assume."

"So, your compatriots are considering using shifters in the coming fight..."

"Yes."

"And what will happen to those who helped after the dust settles?"

"I can't say for certain. I'm not involved in those types of policy decisions. But I certainly wouldn't punish a patriotic citizen brave enough to take up the good fight. People like that deserve our respect, not our condemnation."

Mila nodded, staring him in the eyes, trying to read him. She didn't know what she was looking for, maybe sincerity, conviction. Seconds ticked by as she hesitated, uncomfortable making a decision for not only herself, but countless individuals she'd never met, a community she'd never wanted a part of.

Finally, she reached out her hand, waving her fingers. "Give me the phone."

The admiral nodded and tossed a portable phone at her.

Mila caught it and tapped in a number from memory. She hadn't had many chances to use it, but she would never forget it. She'd crumpled up the paper, torn it up, even thrown it away eventually, but the number itself remained burned into her brain. The line rang two times before being picked up.

A male voice barked over the small speaker. "What?"

Mila looked at the Commandant Commander across the desk from her. "It's Mila. We have something to discuss. The fate of the world hangs in the balance."

CHAPTER THIRTY-ONE

The Incirrina ship approached radio range, but received no response from their human allies. "Do we have anything on radar?"

"There are a lot of ships amassing near the Earth's orbit."

He stepped forward, looking closer at the navigational display. It showed all obstacles in their path. Currently, a rock satellite awaited them to the right. They would fly past it on their way to Earth. In the distance, the outer curvature of the Earth graced the larger view screen with bright yellow dots speckling the intervening space. "What's our ETA?"

"Maybe an hour, sir."

Good. They should be in time. "Alert the other ships to be prepared for the worst."

"Yes, sir."

Outside the walls of the ship, several dozen other Incirrina spaceships rocketed toward the Earth, toward their allies, responding to the distress signal they'd received. They *would* arrive in time.

"Okay, Mi… May, what's so all fired important?" Tristan grumbled. Behind her, a hangar loomed.

Kyle and Luke rounded a corner. They looked around, then focused on Mila, waiting for an explanation. Kyle raised an eyebrow at her, his stance speaking to impatience.

Mila glanced up at the sky, then smirked at Tristan.

"I don't like that look." That look spelled trouble. She only got that look when she was flying. Specifically, she got that look when she was flying like mad, when everyone else was holding on for dear life or reaching for the emesis bags.

Her grin grew, the other two coming closer with confused looks on their faces. Kyle's morphed to concern as he nudged Luke beside him. "Hold on to your seats, boys," he said under his breath.

Luke snorted, lifting his hand to his mouth as he bent slightly.

Tristan's expression turned to worry. "I *really* don't like that look."

"Come on," she wheedled, grabbing his arm and racing toward the hangar. His feet dragged, but she pulled him along, anyway. "I've got a plan."

He put his foot down as they approached a shuttle. "Am I going to like this plan?"

"No, but do you really want to leave your fate in the hands of others?"

"Shit."

CHAPTER THIRTY-TWO

"Good God," Captain Evans whispered under his breath as the enemy stretched before the USS *Texas*. Tension held the bridge as the moment of battle approached.

He swallowed hard, anxiety digging into his gut. Countless dark, ominous ships loomed before them. While they were little more than blobs on the main screen, he'd zoomed in on his personal display.

Damn.

Each ship was huge, bristling with jutting edges that he just *knew* were weapons.

Had other ships arrived yet? He switched screens, checking the radar, reassured by the dozens of symbols dotting the screen around them while more exited atmosphere.

Would it be enough?

He glanced up and out at his crew, who looked uneasy, scared. The NSS had never encountered a threat like this before, never fought a battle like this.

He needed to *do* something, *say* something. As he sat there, the tension on the bridge built, his people looking around them with uncertainty. The enemy ships on screen grew, a dark cloud on the horizon, intent on destruction.

A red haze flashed over the main screen and he flinched. He took in a long breath, letting it and his own tension out.

"For Earth," he whispered, a sick feeling settling over him.

Then he leaned forward, speaking with authority he didn't feel, "Fire."

Mila dropped into the pilot's seat, a wicked grin on her face. Asphalt and government buildings took up the view before her.

"I don't like that look," Tristan said.

"Neither do I." Avery's words were barely audible as Luke squealed and the wind howled eerily just out of reach.

Mila's smile grew as she punched the throttle on her right. The small battle shuttle jumped forward, startling everyone but her.

"Damn it, May. Nobody's belted in yet."

Mila didn't even bother to shrug. No time for that. The ship surged, rocketing toward the stars, and her grin only grew.

She lived for this.

"May, what the hell?"

Out of the corner of her eye, Tristan picked himself up off the flooring and almost crawled to his seat, holding on with a death grip.

Mila cocked her head, dropping the throttle back as Earth's gravity started to lose its hold on them. "Well, I don't know about you, but I have no intention of letting those fuckers attack Earth. Not if I can help it."

"May, this could be considered theft. You could get court marshaled for this."

She shrugged. "It's not like I'm really a member of the military, now am I?" She thought of that conversation with the Commandant Commander. Her gut twisted at what she'd done. She'd outed herself. She'd admitted to what she was.

Or might as well have.

Regardless, she had no future with the military now. It didn't matter if they threw her in jail. It didn't matter if they threw her in one of those damned camps. She thought of her parents, May's parents, May's brother, the brother Tristan had never reconciled with, even her goofy friend, Luke.

I can still save them.

The front window reflected a ghost image of the people around her. They looked at each other in uneasy ways, uncomfortable with her speaking aloud what they'd known for so long.

"This isn't about secrets or military service. This is about protecting what's ours. And Earth is definitely ours." With a hesitant glance at the sub-space controls, she activated the drive, dropping them into sub-space for a move that was both highly theoretical and bat-shit crazy.

"May…" Avery said, his voice edgy with concern.

"I am seventy-five percent positive this will work, but I'll need you on the guns, Avery."

He stood up and dropped in a seat next to her. "Seventy-five percent isn't exactly reassuring." His hands caressed the triggers.

"Ready."

Avery nodded, arming missiles.

"Steady."

Mila's face hurt from grinning so much as she lined up the shuttle just where she wanted it. If her assumptions were correct…

"And drop!"

They dropped out of sub-space, right behind a series of enemy ships. A sea of dark marks blotted out the blue and white orb of the Earth, then Avery opened fire.

"Sir, we've got incoming," Yasmin said as she turned in her seat. Above them, shadows passed over their view of the Earth. The comms crackled again, garbling another distress call from a ship in the combat above. She faced the station beside her. "Damn it, Vaughan. Can't you fix this damn thing?"

He threw his hands up in the air. "I'm trying!" He glared at the outlaw who smirked knowingly.

"You could help, you know," she growled at Wilhem.

He just shrugged.

Behind her, Bennett started a broadcast. "All personnel report to duty stations. Expect incoming damaged ships and injured personnel."

The comm crackled again, but she could make out the words this time. "This is the USS *Ohio*. We've sustained significant damage." It fizzed out and Yasmin gritted her teeth in frustration. "...full evacuation."

Yasmin leaned forward, mouth to microphone. "This is KMS. I hear you *Ohio*. Is your ship stable?" She waited, wondering what the nature of the problem was. Lots of things could force an evacuation, some relatively benign. Others? Not.

"...life suppo..." came through, garbled but enough that Yasmin could respond.

"I hear you, *Ohio*. Get the ship as close to KMS as you can and get all personnel evacuated in space suits."

She didn't get a response.

***

Captain Evans flinched as two ships gave up the ghost. They exploded outward, fire spewing from the hull as it cracked apart before being snuffed out by the vacuum of space.

The silence disturbed him. On Earth, such a spectacular display would have been accompanied by an epic burst of noise, loud enough to threaten eardrums. But here, where sound didn't carry, nothing.

Then it all came crashing back. Men and women shouted from their duty stations, calling out trajectories, warning of enemy movements. At the comms stations, officers called back and forth between other ships, coordinating attacks. But even as he stood there, taking it in, more and more voices went silent over the comms.

Elias stepped forward, gripping the back of his seat. Tension settled over the crew, matching his white knuckles as he looked down.

He struggled to find the words. His crew needed him, needed his guidance, his resolve, his strength, but he didn't feel strong in that moment. He felt out of his depth, out of his element.

This wasn't supposed to happen.

They weren't supposed to be here.

The Incirrina ships slowed as they came up behind the enemy, cloaked against discovery. Before them, a battle raged, ships fighting against ships, large bore arsenals wrecking havoc in the vacuum of space.

"Strategy?" another captain's voice asked over the radio.

"Focus on battleships being attacked by our human allies. The damage from both sides with hasten the enemy defeat."

"Aye, sir."

For a moment, silence filled the room, even the smallest squeak of someone shifting in their seat heard like an alarm going off. He stared at the carnage before him, dread and excitement filling him both.

The captain on this ship, and leader of the rest, stood tall, his appendages still at his sides, a symbol of confidence and steadfastness.

"Fire at will."

A constant unease settled into Tristan's gut as the battle wore on. Several human ships had already been destroyed, but they'd managed to take out quite a few of the enemy as well.

Hope surged, though it fought a fierce battle with the anxiety eating him alive.

Mila handled the little shuttle with grace, reminding Tristan of the *Orleans*, when she'd outmaneuvered those fighters. He shook his head.

Get your head in the game.

He fired again as Luke squawked into the comms, coordinating with other ships. The straps of his harness dug into his shoulders as he leaned forward into the weapons controls. The rubber grips bore into his hands, his thumbs sore from pressing down on the trigger.

He didn't know how much time had passed, but it felt endless.

"Oh, we've totally got this," Luke said in his buoyant voice. He bobbed in his seat until a sudden evasive maneuver had him holding his mouth as the scenery spun madly.

The world hovered momentarily as Mila smoothed out her flying. Tristan held his breath, his thumbs hovering over the triggers.

Then everything exploded around them.

"What the fuck!" Mila said as she jerked on the controls, causing the shuttle to careen to the side.

Small parts of the enemy ship flew straight at them as Mila fought to avoid them.

What the hell just happened?

Then those fragmented bits took off, the telltale signs of engine ignitions flaring behind them as they rocketed forward. "Fire! Fire now!" Tristan cried out.

Luke yelled over the comms as Mila evaded and Tristan and Kyle fired.

There's too many.

They caught a few of them, but there were just too many. The larger ships were no match for these small fighters, their weapons systems incapable of even firing on them.

Too damn many.

The enemy fighters streaked around the human battleships, ignoring them all, heading straight for Earth.

CHAPTER THIRTY-THREE

Captain Evans stood almost paralyzed, the bridge still and quiet, as if time had stopped. Before them, the enemy ships blew apart without any action on their part, splintering into thousands of pieces. He couldn't speak, couldn't move.

The shrapnel exploded in all directions, slowing almost to a stop, before engines flared and they raced forward.

"All battle stations, fire!" he yelled as the situation dawned on him. "Fighters, launch."

The bridge sped up, spiraling into chaos as everyone tried to respond to the new threat.

The crew scrambled to react, but they had been fighting large battleships. Their controls were set on their highest yield weapons. Precious moments passed as they switched to more appropriate guns.

Evans held his breath, leaning forward, but then the ships flew straight past them and out of their primary view. He looked around. "What just happened?"

One officer turned in his seat. "They're heading to Earth."

***

"Oh, no you don't," Mila yelled.

Tristan looked over at her, alarmed as she jerked hard on the controls, turning them around. Earth loomed in front of them now, the racing enemy fighters zooming toward home.

They sped up, following the fighters.

"May, don't you dare." The shuttle wasn't designed for fighting in atmosphere, though it could fly in it no problem. For a moment, he questioned how he could love such a madwoman, but the thought flew from his head as quickly as the ships flying around them. "You're going too fast."

Ahead of him, Kyle crossed his chest, looking up as if pleading with God. He didn't blame him. Mila was a brilliant pilot, but this was madness. The ship rumbled, shaking them in their seats as it hit Earth's atmosphere, but she didn't slow down. He wanted to yell, scream that she would kill them all, but his voice kept silent.

"Get ready, Avery," she said, rocketing through the air at breathtaking speeds.

"Absolutely."

"Fire," she said, never slowing as Kyle opened up a barrage at the enemy before them.

He flinched as they passed through the explosions of their enemy's demise, the smoke turning their visibility to zero. "Mila," he drawled a warning.

The engines roared as Mila accelerated further.

"Bullshit. There's still more of them." Minutes ticked by as she continued to pick up speed, lining up a repeat approach on their enemy. "Ready."

The streaks of enemy ships showed up again and they tensed. Tristan held his breath, tempted to close his eyes, but he would never dare. He wasn't in control this time, but it didn't matter. He couldn't shy away from this, from her.

Please, just let us get through this.

Boom!

Travis jerked his head up as dark spots streaked across the sky trailing fiery tails.

Boom, boom, boom.

As each slowed below the sound barrier, another boom shook the air. He stood up, a sick feeling settling in his stomach. Above him, the sky grew darker and darker, as if those shapes had started amassing nearby.

You're at a military base, stupid. Strategic target.

He swallowed hard, his hand reaching for the doorknob behind him without thinking. It was locked. Still, the cold metal grounded him, keeping him from freaking out.

His brother was the soldier, not him. He wasn't trained for this.

As moments ticked by, the situation became clearer. Ships slowed overhead, all menacing black angles that landed just out of sight, dropping below the trees surrounding the base.

He swallowed hard again, a fine sheen of sweat forming on his brow.

I'm so dead.

The shuttle slowed, but Tristan kept his grip firmly on the trigger, firing at each black ship that entered his field of vision.

"They've landed," Luke said.

An incoherent radio response nagged at the edges of Tristan's consciousness as he focused on targeting the enemy.

"Jesus Christ, they're pouring out like a flood," Luke said.

In the distance, Tristan spotted landed ships outside Clark NSS Base. Trees framed the picture as black dots vomited out of the back of one of the ships, flooding toward the base. Then the earth seemed to move toward the enemy and he frowned, trying to make sense of what he was seeing.

Mila laughed. "Rot in hell, fuckers!" She yelled, flying in a straight line to allow Tristan and Kyle to mow down as many of them as they could before they flew past.

Kyle laughed beside him. "God, I love this woman!"

Tristan glared at him, but then had to brace himself as Mila turned the shuttle. The ship struggled against gravity as it made the tight maneuver it wasn't designed for.

"Another round boys. And try not to hit the friendlies," Mila said as she leaned into the controls.

Tristan looked back at the battleground, finally realizing what the moving ground was—humans in camo gear.

They roared forward, the engines whining in the low atmosphere. Before them, their weapons kicked up clouds of dust when they missed their targets then sometimes splitting the enemy in half when they hit.

To their right, a ship blew up and Kyle roared, his hands flying up from his controls in triumph.

"Avery!" Tristan barked, reminding him of where they were, what was at stake. They didn't have time for a victory lap.

Kyle nodded, gripping the trigger once more, his face fierce as he pressed his triggers again.

Chaos reigned down below and with pass after pass, he had a harder and harder time firing without endangering their own men and women. The enemy stood out like a sore thumb, their black gear better suited for blending in space.

Time dragged on, each second seeming to grow longer and longer the more the battle raged. And as the battle continued on, he grew more and more focused on precision.

The world was at stake.

CHAPTER THIRTY-FOUR

ith a single pop of their weapons, the battle ended, the final enemy falling to the ground, almost in slow motion. Tristan held his breath, waiting for the inevitable twist, for a ship to come out of nowhere, an alien to come out of the woods, or an ordinance to detonate. Something.

But silence, stillness, reigned in the aftermath.

Below them, a bloody path of destruction littered the earth. Craters from their weapons served as counterpoints to the slaughter, empty spaces devoid of all, including vegetation.

Below them, men and women in and out of uniform wandered around. Some injured, some not. Mila turned the shuttle, dropping the landing gear with a thunk that jerked the small craft before she maneuvered a vertical landing next to the battlefield.

Tristan sighed, letting out the breath he felt like he'd been holding since this all began. The tension left him. He looked over at Mila who had a conflicted expression on her face. She tried to smile, but it didn't quite work.

"You sure you don't want to find another fight?" Kyle joked, smirking at her.

"I think I've had enough fighting for one day."

<hr />

It's not like I'm a real member of the military...

Those words rang through Luke's head as she stood facing May while the others left the shuttle. May glared backwards as she struggled with her harness.

"Luke?" she said, her gaze stopping where Luke remained planted in the middle of the space like an idiot.

I'm so stupid. How did I not see it? How did I not know?

She wiggled in place, her mouth sealed shut, but she had to say it. May had opened up, left herself vulnerable. It felt *right* being open with her in kind. She *owed* it to her, her friend.

"I'm trans." She looked out the viewscreen at the battlefield that lay silent before them.

The ship ticked into silence as May released her harness with a click. She faced Luke, a determined look in her eye.

Luke turned from the carnage. It took time to gather the courage to meet May's gaze. "My family calls me Lucky."

May smiled, her lips tilted rakishly on one side. "Lucky, huh?" She reached out her hand. "Mila Anya Dragomirov, at your service."

Luke looked down at the hand, then stepped forward, pulling *Mila* into a hug. Mila's warmth seeped into her, making her feel everything would be all right.

"He or she?" Mila asked against her ear.

"She," she said, choking up as she pulled her friend in tighter, tears burning her eyes.

Tristan stepped onto the ramp of the ship, Kyle close at his heels. He cleared his throat, which tickled at the smoke and dust in the air. The smells of gunfire and blood played counterpoint to the gory tableau before him.

For a moment, he couldn't move. He'd spent most of his military career on spaceships, never seeing conflict, never seeing the carnage a true battle left behind. He felt unprepared, innocent, as if he'd led far too sheltered a life.

Kyle slapped his shoulder, breaking the spell. He turned to him. A knowing look settled on Kyle's features, telling him all he would ever need to know about his friend's history.

He's seen far worse.

Kyle slapped him again, then pushed him down the ramp. Behind them, footsteps cracked against the metal panels.

"Jackson!" Mila shrieked, causing Tristan to spin in place on the dusty ground.

She picked up speed then ran across the field. Stopping in front of a man out of uniform but covered in the effects of battle, she reached out her hand. "It's good to see you."

He gripped her forearm, nodding with a smile. "And you. What are the chances, huh?"

"How did you fare?"

"I don't believe we lost anyone. The military was better prepared than I would have hoped."

A dark looked crossed Tristan's face.

Who *was* he?

CHAPTER THIRTY-FIVE

*E*verything felt surreal as Tristan drove back on base with Mila quiet in the passenger seat, the only sound the gentle hum of the engine. Tristan gripped the steering wheel, feeling lost as the identical homes passed by him.

Throughout, Mila didn't say a word, her silence eating at him. His silence ate at him as well.

What will happen to us, to her?

He had half a mind to turn around and never return, settle somewhere they would never find her, never take her away. He couldn't bear the idea of losing her.

Twilight dimmed his community, creating a shroud that masked everything, leaving a quiet serenity to a place that had known chaos only hours before. It didn't feel right, didn't feel normal.

What was normal now?

His gaze darted up to the sky, but only the navy blue of the rapidly approaching night touched his vision. He didn't detect any enemy ships, even if he could almost *feel* them bearing down on his flesh.

Tristan slowed as he approached his house, frowning as he spotted a dark figure huddled on his front stoop as he turned in, pulling to a stop.

"We're home," he said absently, his arm reaching out to Mila to hold her back as she reached for her seatbelt.

"Tristan?"

"There's someone here." His voice was barely above a whisper.

Mila leaned forward in his periphery. "Do you know who it is?"

He shook his head. He couldn't see the person in any detail, but as they spoke, the figure stood, triggering the motion sensor over the door. The bright light cast the man in shadow, further masking his identity.

He stood there for several moments longer before stepping down, taking the path toward their car.

"Tristan?" Mila said, her voice soft and hesitant, a gentle caress in the gloom.

He didn't speak, his hand going to his hip, which was naked of any weaponry, their mission complete.

"Tristan, he's your brother. Travis," Mila sounded surprised.

Tristan turned to her, then to the shadowed form that loomed closer. He couldn't make out any details, but he trusted Mila. She was capable of things he could never pull off. "You're sure?"

His heart thudded painfully in his chest, afraid to hope. He hadn't seen his brother in years. He'd thought their relationship was doomed, destined to wither away and crumble into dust.

"Go," she whispered, pushing him toward the door. "Go to him."

He looked over at her, observing her cheeky grin.

She pushed again. "But I'm taking the car. You blocked mine in and I have my own battle to fight."

He laughed, putting his hands up in surrender as he popped open the door and exited. As he watched, she hopped in the driver's seat and revved the engine, taking off in the last vestiges of light.

His muscles froze. He had no excuse left not to turn and face his only remaining family.

"Brother?" Travis said behind him, his voice so damn hesitant.

Tristan turned, seeing his brother for the first time in years. Shadows still hugged his features, but he made out familiar elements, recognizing little bits and pieces he saw in the mirror every day. He reached forward, grabbing Travis in a hug, burying his face against his neck. "Brother."

<hr>

Mila stood in front of the door. She'd knocked, but it was late. Maybe her parents weren't home. It could happen. She hadn't called ahead. She'd come here on a whim. Seeing Travis there, knowing Tristan could finally bridge that gap, she'd felt the urge to resolve her own familial issues.

One way or another.

The door creaked open, her mother holding its edge. The other woman stood hesitant, an unnamed emotion on her face.

"I'm not selfish," she said, her voice cold, fists tight at her sides. She stared at the ground, not able or willing to look at her mom while she spoke, the words they'd exchanged ringing in her ears. "I can't change the past, nor would I dream of it." She looked up, her eyes damp with emotion. "And I *refuse* to pay for those decisions!

"If you can't deal with that..." *I walk.*

She didn't get it all out before her mom latched on in a suffocating hug.

Mila stood frozen, even confused.

"You're alive," her mother gasped. "I was so scared."

Mila softened, forgetting the words, the threats, she'd prepared for this moment. She pulled up her arms, wrapping them awkwardly around her mother's frame. "I'm here. I'm here, Mom."

Tristan sat at the kitchen table across from his brother. Travis. He still remembered the gangly teenager from their mother's funeral. He remembered the irresponsible youth who couldn't be bothered to wear a suit at their father's burial.

Those were the last times he'd seen Travis.

And now they were together... and he didn't know what to say. What *could* he say? *Why didn't you answer? Why did you ignore me all these years?*

Everything that popped into his head felt wrong, so he shut up, waited.

Travis looked down at the table. He had grown up, filled out, but he still wore a t-shirt and jeans, so hadn't grown up *too* much. "I saw a news broadcast." He spoke to the tabletop, not meeting Tristan's gaze. He shook his head, scoffing. "I don't even know what happened, just that the military were called up. I had to come. I couldn't not. I didn't care that you wouldn't be here, that you would be out there fighting."

Travis shook his head. "No, that's not right. I cared. I've always cared. I've just been too much of a coward to break the silence." His fists clenched on the table which groaned under the force of his emotions. "I'm sorry. I'm sorry I was such a stubborn ass. I know it wasn't your fault, none of this was. I was too immature to deal, then the distance just felt too far to bridge."

Tristan scoffed and his brother's head popped up. "It's never too far. Never." He stared his brother down.

A humorless laugh slipped from Travis's lips. "Yeah?"

Tristan nodded. "Yeah."

<hr>

Tristan sat on the couch staring at the TV, seeing but not really watching, as the front door creaked open. He looked up and smiled as Mila peeked her head in. "Is it safe?" she said, a smile on her face.

"Yeah, Travis left."

She frowned as she closed the door behind her with a click. "How did it go?" She walked forward, leaning against the doorway to the living room.

"Good." The TV droned in the background.

"Good." She nodded, pushing off the wood molding and dropping on the cushions right beside him. She looked over at him. "I'm glad."

"And how did your 'battle' go?"

"Good." She nodded again.

Tristan held his breath as her bodyweight slowly curled into him. He didn't move, not sure what was happening, not wanting it to stop. He turned back to the TV, but couldn't follow the broadcast, only barely registering as an Incirrina posed with world leaders. A marquee at the bottom said something about "First Human-Alien Alliance."

"We did it," Mila said against his shoulder.

"What did we do?"

He caught a smile pulling her lips up, but she didn't look at him. "We saved the world."

EPILOGUE

Kyle stalked past holding cell after holding cell, a specific person in mind. Metal bars passed in his peripheral vision, proof positive that sometimes tried-and-true methods were best.

Voices called out into the desolate landscape, bickering back and forth, cursing in multiple languages. He recognized three of them.

As he approached his target, his mind ran over the reports by the personnel on Kennedy Moon Station, kicking himself that he hadn't seen it. How could he have fucked up so much on this case? How could he have missed it?

He shook his head, slowing as he drew close. He just couldn't understand her. Why did she do it? Why did Grace betray them? Damn it, Mila had become friends with her near the end and he *knew* that woman didn't trust easily. He ground his teeth. It pissed him off that she'd violated that trust. He shook his head again as he stopped just out of sight of his prey to compose himself. He just didn't understand her.

Wilhem, on the other hand, he understood. Some things were

universal and one of the most universal was that money could buy *anything*. He stepped forward, jaw and fists clenched tight, glaring down at the human filth lounging on a cot in a dark corner.

He stood there, relishing this moment, the moment before everything changed. Nothing was more powerful than the imagination and he'd always excelled at capitalizing on that. A cold smile tilted his lips as he tipped his head just slightly to the side.

"Let's talk."

SUPPLEMENTARY INFORMATION

German Hand Gestures

In this book, a German man uses the thumbs up gesture
multiple times. In Germany, a thumbs up actually means the
number 1. However, because he knows his audience is American, he uses this gesture for clarity of communication.

MAG GRAV

Zero gravity-related bone deterioration is caused by the body
not having sufficient force applied to it. The system uses electromagnetic floor plates. Ferromagnetic thread is woven in
cloth throughout the ship and ferromagnetic metals are used
in the manufacture of all harder surfaces. The specific
strength of the magnetic force is important, as it is directly
correlated to the level of bone deterioration and as such, it is
important that the properties of the garments utilized are
comparable regardless of size of the wearer.

Shape-shifting (Physiology)

Amoeba and other amorphous organisms are capable of

changing shape to escape threats and reach food sources. While it would be theoretically possible for shape-shifters to exist (though none do in higher organisms), they would need to have evolved along a separate evolutionary path.

Shape-shifters have loosely structured tissues with easy to replicate designs. Further, not all tissue types are capable of shape-shifting. Some examples include: brain and spinal column, heart, primary arteries and veins, and most of the tissue in the digestive system and lungs. These systems serve as control points to power and feed the systems and tissues as they change.

Much of the shape-shifting capability arises at the tissue level. Shape-shifters have a simplified musculoskeletal system. The hard structure of bones in shape-shifters is caused by structures in the cells themselves rather than the tissues. The cells are connected together with chemical compounds easily dissolved with an enzymatic reaction triggered by shifting. The chemical reforms once the enzymatic activity ceases. The same holds true for muscles, tendons and ligaments.

Unlike many cells in higher organisms, shape-shifter cells have cilia designed to move them against each other mid-shift. This allows cells to reform into different-shaped tissues (e.g. shorter and wider bones, longer muscle groups).

Sub-space travel

The sub-space travel system documented in this book is an adaptation of the Einstein-Rosen Bridge. There are a great many theories as to how an Einstein-Rosen Bridge might work. Some theories postulate that it connects two points in space-time (i.e. two points in the same universe). Others postulate that it could form a bridge between neighboring universes. This concept, regardless of how it is hypothesized, is very interesting as it is the only feasible means of interstellar travel currently postulated.

I took a great deal of liberty in coming up with this method of travel, though there are other more likely scenarios such as a bridge connecting two points in space, or even a significant time difference on each side of the bridge.

The most important part of this technology is the capability of forming these bridges, which I didn't provide any details into. At present, humanity has not discovered any of these bridges, and as such, we would not be able to learn enough about them to create one. I imagine, though, once we're discovered one and studied one, learning to create and control them will be right around the corner.

TAT system

This system is a logical extension of the Tachyonic Antitelephone thought experiment postulated by Albert Einstein in 1907. Tachyons are theoretical particles that can only move faster than the speed of light. In fact, the slower they get, the more energy is required (the inverse of normal matter). For this reason, particles that work similarly would be ideal for communication between interstellar distances. Because of the risk of breaking causality, the energy applied to the tachyons is very important in relation to the distance traveled. However, if those calculations are applied adequately, it would be theoretically possible to generate instantaneous communication across any distance. Please note: Tachyons are theoretical and have largely been deemed physically impossible (i.e. have had no scientific verification), however the beauty of science is the unknown, and we will likely never know all there is to know about the universe.

Incirrina Limbs

Incirrina limbs are capable of minor shape-shifting abilities due to their unique physiology. The mechanics are similar to muscular hydrostats or hydrostatic skeletons. A complex network of muscle and connective tissue directly below the skin serves to drive the movements and shape while a liquid core provides constant hydraulic pressure. During movement, muscle fibers shift around the liquid core. During shape-shifting, the connective tissue lattice expands, creating weak spots where the limb must bulge, and compresses, creating dense spots where the limb must *not* bulge. Because each segment of connective tissue can expand or compress independently, very complex shapes can be created.

TERRA'S FATE

PROLOGUE

"*L*et's talk," Kyle Avery said, looking down at the human filth lounging on a cot in the corner of the holding cell. He clenched his fists, jaw tight with frustration and anger.

Springs groaned as Wilhem Haus shifted on his bed, glancing out at Kyle from the deepest shadows. His face dipped in and out of the prison's dim light. It was a dark hole, a cesspit meant only for the foulest criminals.

Then again, what could you expect when you literally betrayed the entire world?

Kyle leaned against the opposite wall, playing at a nonchalance he didn't feel. He had devoted months to finding the culprits, to putting them behind bars. They'd tried to sabotage two separate missions he was on.

Wilhem was the first real lead he'd had. He wouldn't let it go to waste.

So he waited.

From his personal experience, people tended to hate two

things: silence and stillness. Kyle excelled at both.

With arms crossed over his chest, he waited. Wilhem lounged as if enjoying a warm day at the beach, soaking up the rays, arms resting behind his head. He'd had little interaction with the criminal at Kennedy Moon Station, but suspected this was par for the course.

His gut churned as he let his mind drift, remembering recent events. The klaxon of an alarm, the red emergency lighting, racing to save their lives, to save everyone's lives. He half smelled the taint of the battlefield—smoke, death, and cordite.

Really, those were the scents of his life.

Time drifted like a lazy river. Kyle stared his prey down. A menacing omen of death that had no qualms or remorse, he did what needed doing, no more and no less.

Kyle didn't check his watch or fidget or otherwise give away his perception of the passage of time. He just stood against the wall like a statue, a deadly harbinger come to punish the prisoner for his crimes.

"I miss him," Wilhem whispered, his gruff voice echoing in the dead air. That voice had seen better days, almost painful in its gravelly, chainsaw tones, and yet so quiet a pin drop could silence it.

Kyle continued in mute stillness, letting the prisoner fill the void.

Wilhem glanced up, his eyes shining from the darkness, broadcasting his pain. "I'm not a bad person." He sat up and stared at his hands in his lap. "Just practical. It was a job." He cleared his throat as his voice got so bad it was barely decipherable. Then he looked up at Kyle, staring him dead in the eyes, a determined strength flooding them.

"It's not over yet."

PART ONE

"There is nothing more frightful than ignorance in action."

— Johann Wolfgang von Goethe

CHAPTER ONE

ot so long ago…

Terra Wilson glared at her computer screen, pen caught between her teeth as the television chirped in the background. She had a vague impression of a debate about shifters, though she couldn't for the life of her figure what the argument was about? What's there to debate? Shifters were dangerous. Everyone knew that.

But shifters weren't her problem now. She just had the TV on for the noise. No, her problem was this stupid job website and that stack of bills taunting her from the entry table in the other room.

It had been months since she'd been "let go." Most of the time, she was lucky to find listings she qualified for, but nobody called her for an interview. It was like living in a vacuum, devoid of all stimuli.

She hated it. She just wanted to work.

Sitting back and sighing in disgust, her mind warped back to that last day, standing in her boss's office, shellshocked as he imploded her world.

"I have to let you go," he'd said, his face deadpan.

"But why?" she'd whined, at a loss for what she'd done wrong to deserve this. It must be a mistake. She could fix this. She had to.

He'd sighed, looking put upon, a spot on his temple throbbing as he leaned back. "You're just not a good fit. I'm sorry."

From the tone of his voice, it had sounded like that was the tip of the iceberg, but he didn't say more.

It still plagued her.

Months had passed since she lost her job. Terra found herself becoming a bit of a hermit. She'd never had many friends, but being short on cash, she didn't have money for midweek lunches and bar crawls. It left her lonely, isolated, stir-crazy even.

As she smoothed her hands over the new suit, one she really couldn't afford, she stared up at the bland, blocky building. Excitement ran through her, causing her hands to shake even as the institutional gray dimmed her eagerness.

Was this what she had to look forward to?

Was this *really* what she wanted?

When she'd answered the call from NASA of all places, she couldn't believe it. NASA! Sure, it was just a secretarial position, but still. It had to be better than the ongoing series of boring office jobs she'd held until now.

But craning her neck up at the painted cement-brick facade and mirrored windows, she wondered. *Is this what I want?*

She shook herself. It didn't matter. It was a job. She reached out, her hand connecting with the surprisingly cold, metal handle as she pulled the door open, her sweaty palm sticking against the surface.

A cold blast of air smacked her in the face. She flinched and froze in place, handle still gripped firmly.

She stepped inside, her muscles stiff from the long drive to the flight academy outside Clark NSS Base where NASA and the NSS trained their pilots side by side.

NASA's outdated red, white, and blue emblem stood out against the gray wall over the receptionist's desk as the receptionist/security guard eyed her suspiciously.

Terra stepped forward, her heels clicking against the cheap sea foam green and white checkered floor tiles. "I'm Terra Wilson. I'm here for an interview," she said as she approached.

He looked down, his closely cropped hair not budging a millimeter as he checked something on his desktop, then nodded. Looking up, he pointed behind her. "Take a seat. They'll be with you shortly."

"Thank you." She turned around, staring at the weird blue sectional as she moved on autopilot.

This is it.

Finally.

Terra sat in the waiting room, the hard plastic chair dimming her high. In her lap, her fingers once again ran over the surface of the envelope. The wording still caused effervescent joy to bubble up inside her.

"I am delighted to offer you the position of staff secretary..."

Her face stretched into a smile and she squirmed in place, her seat groaning under her. She tipped her head up, trying to push down her excitement.

Gotta get through this first.

She'd already submitted her information for the background check. Now, she just needed to pass the drug screening and ID verification. Piece of cake.

Only, she didn't like doctors' offices, and they'd insisted on the base physicians for the testing, which meant another lengthy drive with her nerves jacked up to eleven.

Around her, men and women in uniform sat or stood, looking far more composed than she did. Across from her, a nurse worked behind a clear partition, ignoring the lot of them.

A door opened to her left, just registering out of her periphery. "Terra Wilson?"

She jerked, shifting her gaze to the man in puke green scrubs and dirty white sneakers holding a clipboard. A tired, frustrated expression had settled over his face.

Terra stood, offering him the paperwork NASA had emailed her. He grabbed it and slapped it against his clipboard, beckoning her onward with a jerk of his head.

She slipped past him into a bland hallway filled with government and health posters interspersed with lock boxes next to closed doors.

"Put all your belongings in the box," he said.

She didn't bring much, just her car keys, ID, and paperwork, the couple of items appearing pitiful in the large box.

"Here," he said, handing her a urine cup.

Terra didn't listen as his voice droned on, giving her instructions and restrictions, no doubt. She stepped into the bathroom, closing the door behind her. As she stared at the toilet, relief coursed through her. Thank God her period ended yesterday. She couldn't imagine giving the ornery bastard a cup full of bloody urine.

She smirked. Then again...

She imagined his face bright red and uncomfortable with the blazing proof of normal body functions.

"Hurry it up in there," he barked.

She rushed through her business, handing off the warm cup as she exited.

He jerked his head again, leading her to the next room, where a chair with a single arm rest waited. He smacked the seat. "Up you go."

She did, and he pulled on a pair of gloves, wiping her inner elbow with something cold before palpating her skin, searching for a vein. She flinched as the needle went in, but he didn't even notice.

Can't look.

"All done," he said, pressing a gauze pad to the place where she'd felt the pinch, then smacking a bandaid on it. "Now git."

She jumped up, turning back to him at the door. "When will I hear..."

"How the hell would I know?" he snapped as he removed his gloves.

She flinched then dashed out, glad to be rid of him.

Bastard.

Terra sat, watching TV. On screen, personalities debated the pros and cons of treaties with alien races. She had a hard time focusing on it, though, even when the one foamed at the mouth with each comment. Instead, her mind filled with worries and what ifs.

Standing up, she paced her living room, needing to burn off her nervous energy. She shook out her hands, but it did little to relieve the tension. "It's just a stupid job."

Except it wasn't. The months of unemployment loomed behind her, like an unstoppable force trying to bury her. The job market had been a vast, toxic wasteland, devoid of all prospects, all hope. Once the initial excitement had faded, Terra had been almost paralyzed during the interview, even if only for a secretary position. But she'd gotten through it, and now it was down to waiting on background checks, drug testing, and ID verification.

She'd never needed an ID verification before, but government usually required it. Terra wasn't worried. She'd never done drugs, or anything noteworthy, in her life. She'd lived at home, reading books, and volunteering at the local animal shelter because she couldn't afford a pet. Hell, she'd never done anything more radical than sipping wine at a bar with friends.

"There's nothing to worry about. Just relax." She sighed and looked around her little apartment. From here, she could see every room in the place. No curtains covered the windows nor decorations hung on the walls because she still hadn't decided if she wanted to stay. In her bedroom, boxes stacked to the ceiling, and in here, a TV, table, and recliner made up the contents.

How depressing.

A sharp ring sung through the air.

"Coming," Terra grumbled under her breath, "Better not be another evangelist or magazine salesman…"

With economical efficiency, she opened the front door, holding it in place with her right hand. Two stern men in dark suits stood at the doorway, a white panel van at the curb. "Can I help you?"

Dread curdled in her gut.

She opened her mouth to ask another question, but they snapped like vipers, latching onto her biceps in a vise-like grip that hurt. "Hey!"

But they didn't say a word, simply turned around and started toward the van.

"Hey! Stop it. Let me go!" She struggled in earnest, kicking wildly, yanking at her arms to wrench them from the men's hold, even biting at them, but the white, mechanical beast grew ever closer, its maw open to swallow her whole. "No! No, you can't!"

Then the large, boxy vehicle loomed before them. Panic gripped her. Her imagination, never the best of companions, chose this time to pop up an image of her rotting in a ditch somewhere. "No!"

In the next moment, she latched onto the edges of the side opening like a cartoon cat refusing to take a bath. For an interminable moment, Terra held herself on that edge. Tension, panic, and fear kept her frozen. Fate pushed her onward.

She lost her grip, and the door slid closed with a resounding thud.

"No!" she screamed, slamming her closed fists against the contoured metal. "Let me out!" Her throat protested at the abuse, rubbing raw, but she didn't care. Again and again, her fists landed against the door with resounding tones that echoed through her body. Her face burned with emotion as her hands started to hurt.

Then light flooded the interior, and the vehicle rocked with the weight of the two suited men. Terra turned and slammed against the wire mesh separating her from the front seat, but it did no good. "Let me out!"

But the van started up, ignoring her pleas, and jerked into motion, sending her sprawling across the back. Pain twinged her side as she fell on something. It didn't matter. Nothing mattered.

She slid backward, scooting into the farthest, darkest corner. Tears slid down her face, losing control of her emotion as everything else fell out of her grasp.

Why were they doing this to her?

What did they want with her?

The men drove on, and before long, the overpowering emotion faded into numbness, and her brain kicked on again. Terra took a deep breath and re-evaluated her surroundings. They took a turn, and she held onto the wall.

She sat against the back door. Too dark in the windowless enclosure, her hand drifted, feeling out the environment, looking for an out. She put a second hand into the task, brushing her fingertips along the back wall for handles. Didn't vans usually have back doors?

Systematically, her hands ran over every inch, top to bottom. About halfway up the wall, her fingers fell into two holes. She explored the holes, hoping for a latch or lock mechanism, but frustration got the better of her.

With a huff and some hair wringing, Terra shifted back to the side door, hoping maybe they hadn't bothered to lock it. But even she knew a certain level of hysteria drove that hope.

After all, they'd removed the interior rear door handles and installed a screen to separate the front and rear of the vehicle. What were the chances they forgot to lock a door?

Terra held her breath as she reached for the handle which showed up as a dark line against the lighter metal, just enough to tantalize. Just enough to give her a little hope in the dim lighting. She grabbed on, yanking hard, but it wouldn't give.

"Gah!" she cried out as she yanked on it a few more times for good measure, but still nothing. Slumping against the wall, all hope slipped away. A hole opened deep inside her chest, devouring her whole and leaving her ready to cry again.

But this time, the tears didn't come. She stared at the roof above her, a roof she couldn't see anymore than she could see God in heaven. Terra sighed. *God only gives us that which we can handle,* she reminded herself. *I've got this.*

If only she knew what *this* was. Who went around kidnapping people in broad daylight, dumping them into panel vans wearing dark suits? It made no sense. One expected nefarious beings to slink around in the dark of night, skulking in the shadows, but these bastards had been bold as brass. They'd walked up to her apartment like they owned the place and took her away as if it were their God-given right. It made no sense.

Unless…

Her blood ran cold, her heart seizing in her chest. An image from a news program a few weeks ago flitted through her head. In the broadcast, two men in suits had dragged a kid away from his home. The kid had been a shifter.

But she couldn't be a shifter, could she? None of her family were shifters, and everyone knew shifters were a bunch of criminals, stealing and defrauding their way through life, not a conscience among them.

But she'd done nothing wrong. She was innocent. They couldn't do this. She had rights. She was a law abiding US citizen. There must have been a mistake. A mix-up in a lab or something.

Nodding, reassured by that logic, she sat back and waited, certain she would be vindicated once they arrived at their destination, and they would apologize for the inconvenience. Yes, that was what would happen. She just had to be patient.

CHAPTER TWO

Kyle walked into the task force headquarters, a small conference room on Clark NSS Base. It left much to be desired, but a fire burned in his gut demanding satisfaction. It was early morning and a couple people looked like they hadn't had their daily dose of caffeine yet, their eyes drooping and movements sluggish.

The strong scent of coffee permeated the space, dimming his optimism. He'd never been one to rely on stimulants to get him through the day. He'd served in too many places where coffee was a luxury that just wasn't available.

Kyle stepped farther into the room and dropped into a seat at the long table. As he waited for the first session to start, his fingers worked a steady beat against the table's mystery-material surface. The tap-tap-tap counted down the seconds as more people filed in, taking their seats.

He paused, stilling his hand as he focused on himself. His tense jaw and shoulders telegraphed his inner landscape. He took a slow, deep breath, releasing the tension and keeping the focus there while he waited.

I hate this.

Kyle wasn't accustomed to waiting on others. He usually led the way, giving orders, or ran solo, following each lead to its natural conclusion. Sitting here waiting for the bureaucracy to get their shit together didn't sit well with him. He wanted to *act*, not sit on his ass listening to people debating *how* to act.

Why am I even here?

Kyle frowned, turning his attention to the cheap wood door to his right, but knew he wouldn't budge. He was a soldier through and through. He would follow orders.

And his current orders were to take part in this task force to capture the individuals or group behind the sabotage of the *Orleans* mission. He'd looked forward to taking action, to catching the bastards. It still chapped his hide that he hadn't caught them all while he headed security on that mission. He saw it as a personal failure, one he meant to rectify.

A man at the other end of the room cleared his throat, drawing everyone's gaze. "Thank you. You've been called here to operate in a task force to identify and capture the culprits behind the recent *Orleans* sabotage." He touched a display on the table's surface, and the walls along the long room lit up, showing a slideshow. "*Orleans* Mission Debriefing" was written across the wall in large letters.

The screens changed and the task force leader droned on, Kyle mostly zoning out, his mind processing the information but not needing a recap of events he'd lived personally. He remembered the fighter attacks, the engines exploding, and running through the ship trying to stop the intruders. He remembered interrogating personnel to find who'd betrayed them to their enemies. He remembered rounding up suspected and actual conspirators.

After the slideshow ended, the leader gave out assignments and partnered up field operatives.

"Avery, you're with Kaufman."

He looked up, scanning the room, catching sight of a soldier who vibrated with intensity. Kyle frowned, suspecting he wouldn't like the man.

"That's it. Dismissed," the team leader said, clapping his hands together.

Everyone got sluggishly to their feet. Kaufman made a beeline for him, and Kyle scowled.

"This is gonna be fun," Kaufman said, beaming at him.

Kyle's scowl grew.

Terra yawned as they came to a stop. The long drive nearly lulled her to sleep, and all her nervous energy and panic had long ago melted away.

When the doors opened, she didn't even move. She just blinked as the sudden light pierced her eyes after so long in darkness.

"Move it," one of the men said.

Terra crawled gingerly to the door, the hard metal digging into her knees. As she got close, he grabbed her arm and dragged her out. Not caring when she collapsed to the ground, he started moving before she even got her feet under her.

"Slow down," she said, trying and failing at first to get her footing. After a few false starts, her feet started lagging far enough behind that they no longer folded under her. She pushed up, stood, and finally managed to keep up with the impatient bastard.

Around her, tall fences topped with razor wire stretched into the distance. Green grass served as visual hope with its festive color, but the inner fence and foreboding, dreary block buildings negated that effect. The man not currently pulling at her arm opened a door in front of them. They entered a poorly lit entry room with even poorer decorations and a single desk, staffed by a stern woman. Her face and body language said she'd seen it all and didn't give a shit anymore.

"New one."

"Obviously," the woman behind the desk said, rolling her eyes. "Name?" She looked down at her computer, fingers hovering over the keyboard.

"Terra Anne Wilson."

This is a mistake. Don't they know this is a mistake?

She typed it in, chewing on her lip as she went. "Yup. One sec." Her fingers flew, and she clicked a few times with the mouse, then she pointed at the wall to the right. "Have her stand against the wall, facing this."

Impatient Bastard dragged into place, letting go when her back hit hard against the drywall. Terra grunted in surprise. She glared, but it had no affect. He'd already turned his back, chatting quietly with his compatriot.

"Hey, eyes front," the other woman said, startling Terra.

She looked toward the woman, but with a waggle of the woman's index finger, Terra shifted her line of sight farther left, where the camera lens waited.

Flash.

Her vision went white for a moment. She covered her eyes,

wondering when the afterimages would go away. Clicking resumed as the battle-axe at the desk did whatever they paid her to do.

Terra wanted to ask why she was there, why they'd taken her, but she didn't. No one here would care. No one here would help. No one here would listen.

Patience.

She just needed patience.

They're just doing their jobs.

They don't know any better.

She needed someone in charge, like a caseworker or something. Someone who could review her situation and have it overturned. Clearly, this was a mistake. It should be obvious.

So she stood, back pressed to the wall, feeling like a criminal getting a mug shot, like her life had just flushed down the drain.

And waited.

Terra forced herself not to struggle as two men in uniforms hauled her out of the administration building, bumping her carelessly onto the grass before disappearing behind closed doors once more.

She wheeled around to snap at them, but the door clicked closed, the lock dropping in place with a thunk. Her stomach churned as she looked up at the forbidding edifice.

This isn't over.

She tried to draw comfort from that thought, but it was difficult. Her heart slammed away in her chest, leaving her breathless in panic. She shook herself.

No, this isn't me.

Shakily, she stood, pushing off with her hands against the sharp grass. It did little to reestablish normalcy. What did she know of normalcy? She'd spent the last few months in desperate search of a job, constantly feeling at sea, like the ground was shifting under her feet. Now, she didn't even have that unsteady sensation to ground her. She had nothing.

"It's okay," she reminded herself. "This is just a moment in time. I'll find someone to listen to me. I'll get out of here." She shook her head. "It was just a mistake." But what if she couldn't get anyone to listen? What if she couldn't get them to see their mistake?

Still standing in front of the administration building, she turned to take in the camp. A series of long, one-story cinderblock buildings occupied the opposite side of the yard. To her left, another cinderblock building, square and two-story this time, spat out people at regular intervals. A couple children ran screaming out, the door banging behind them as a woman caught it, easing it closed. A chill ran down Terra's spine as she took in the expression on the woman's face— haunted. In the background, a child wailed, crying out for its mother.

Maybe I'm not the only one they made a mistake with.

She eased across the courtyard between the buildings, uncertain what to do or where to go. She wanted to dash back up to the administration building at her back and bang on the doors until she got someone's attention, but that probably wasn't the best solution.

And what is?

Terra ambled to the two-story building, keeping a close eye on her surroundings, feeling lost. At the edges of her consciousness, she recognized the walls of her cage—chain-link fencing with barbed wire topping it.

I don't belong here.

There had to be someone she could talk to, someone she could convince. But as she surveyed her surroundings, taking in the dozens of men, women, and children wearing drab, gray t-shirts and pants, the unrealness of the situation hit her. How could all these people be shifters? They didn't look like criminals, they just looked like normal people.

She'd always known shifters were devious, but to see this place, it brought that understanding into a different dimension. Chills ran down her spine once again. She could have passed any one of the people here on the street, at the grocery store, at the gas station, and not even batted an eye. How could anyone keep themselves safe with a threat like that?

Clearly, the government isn't doing enough.

Stiffening her shoulders, Terra entered the square building. The doors opened onto a hallway. On the wall, a sign pointed left for "Cafeteria" and right for "Rec Room." No one occupied the hall.

Terra turned right, running her fingers feather light over painted cement blocks in the wall, focusing on the crevices and divots, if only to not focus on other things.

At the end of the hall, a door sat open. Behind it, people milled around, but no one smiled. A couple people sat reading on a threadbare couch. Beside the couch, a bookshelf held a pitiful array of old, worn books and a few games. On the other side of the room, four people occupied a table and chairs, playing cards. No one seemed interested in the game. Children's toys, all worn and depressing, spilled out around an old wood toy chest.

"You're new," a woman said to her left. She walked up to the door where Terra stood, a hesitant smile on her face meant more to reassure than express emotion.

"What is this place?"

The woman gave a knowing, sardonic smile. "It's the land of misfit toys."

Terra gave her a dark look, not in the mood for snark. She needed answers, not attitude.

The woman's face lost all humor. "This is a shifter camp."

Terra bristled, even if she'd already guessed that. "I'm not a shifter."

"Yeah, you are. Every person here has the genes to shift. You're not the only one who had no clue. Most people don't." She rolled her eyes, but the glance back at the sad corner of children playing spoke to deeper emotions.

"They don't?" How could that be? Shifters were dangerous, criminals. Everyone knew that. That's why they needed to be locked up, for the common good.

The other woman shook her head and scoffed. "The government doesn't tell you that little factoid." She looked down, her expression turning sad. "Like you, I didn't have a clue. I went around blissfully ignorant of the ticking time bomb in my own body. My kid tested positive, so they tested both me and my husband. My daughter and I ended up here. My husband is still out there somewhere." She seemed to fold in on herself before speaking again. "My husband's still out there somewhere."

Terra didn't know what to say. What could one say to that? The single sentence held a world of pain, and her mind revolted against the idea. *Not my government,* it said. *Not here. Not America.*

America was the land of the free. How could this happen? But denial reared its head again, and her determination to clear up this obvious misunderstanding came back good and strong. She hadn't expected to meet another like herself here, someone wronged, displaced, but that didn't change the facts. Someone *had* made a mistake. She just needed to get them to see it.

"There are about fifty men and woman, ranging in age from eighteen to sixty-five, plus an additional seventy children, again of varying ages," she droned on.

The statement struck Terra frozen to the spot. "Why so many children?" Her mind again reeled against her views of the world she lived. *Not here. Not* my *America.* It didn't make sense. It defied all logic. Children were innocent, wheren't they? They weren't criminals, not like the adults.

The other woman scowled, but shrugged. "I think some private schools have bowed to parental pressure and started testing students at admission. Nobody wants their kids in a school with shifters." She rolled her eyes. "Nobody considers that *their* child could be the shifter."

Terra opened her mouth, but no words came out. The woman had unfolded a tragedy before her eyes. She couldn't unsee the small children playing in the corner. No part of her could justify that.

"I'm Terra," she said, feeling like the woman had earned that much.

"Oh, sorry. Name's Macey." Macey shook her head. "You'd think I had more manners than that."

"It's okay. Who administers all this?" There had to be someone she could talk with to fix this. The government *lived* on bureaucracy, and even if things moved slowly, if you found the right channels, you could right the wrongs.

"Don't bother. Nobody leaves here. You're gonna have to accept that. You're a shifter. You belong here."

Terra glared at her.

"Oh, don't give me that look. Everyone goes through that phase. First, they're in denial, then they assume someone must have made a mistake. Eventually, there's acceptance, but that's usually a while down the road, and the rest of us have to suffer through all your shit in the meantime. Trust me. Just let it go. You'll be happier in the long run."

Terra turned, not willing to listen. Macey said nothing as she walked away. Retracing her steps, she continued beyond the sign that had directed her to the Rec Room. *I should at least* see *the cafeteria.* After all, she would need to eat at some point before she gained her freedom.

At the end of the hall, the cafeteria consisted of long tables and benches in parallel lines with a counter at the far wall. The empty room brought home a loneliness she didn't want to feel, didn't want to see. In that room, she saw the predicament of every person here.

But not her. She would *not* stay here. No matter what. She would be free of this place, one way or another. Turning around, Terra walked back to the administration building. She *would* talk to someone, and she *would* straighten this out.

At the door, she paused. She twisted the handle, but it wouldn't budge. Made of glass, she could peer in, but only empty hallway filled the other side. Walking away, she followed the outline of the building, peeking in windows as she went, but each either revealed nothing of value or had shades drawn. When she reached the corner, she turned only to walk face first into wire fencing.

"Well, shit." Terra tried to peek around the fence, but saw nothing but more concrete. "Macey was right."

She collapsed against the fence, the metal protesting with a rattling noise as she fell to her butt, hugging her knees. It didn't matter if some bastard had made a mistake, did it? There was no opportunity for appeal, no court system, no nothing.

How many people like her were trapped in these camps? Terra thought back to every time she'd reacted in fear or felt vindicated when a shifter wound up in custody. She felt betrayed. What had gone wrong with the country that they could steal the lives of innocent people and nobody protested, nobody questioned it?

Except she'd been part of the problem, hadn't she? She'd never questioned it. She'd never protested. Hell, she'd approved, chatting with friends and bemoaning the dangers of shifters and how they should be locked up for the greater good. She laughed, no humor in the noise.

Karma's a bitch, isn't it?

CHAPTER THREE

Two days had passed since they stole Terra from her home. By now, she'd wandered the entire camp, checking out every inch of the surrounding fences for weakness, looking for any opportunity for escape. She found none.

Then again, she wasn't exactly an escape artist. She'd spent her entire career working in office settings. It didn't teach a person many survival skills. Terra could type a hundred words a minute, answer multi-line phones, and use every program in the Office suite like an expert. But ask her to escape a government installation or survive in the wilderness? She didn't know the first place to start.

Now, she almost wished she *were* a shifter. That might have come in handy. She knew almost nothing about them, but she figured a shifter could have escaped this damned place if they wanted.

But what could they *do*? She knew they could wear another person's face, but was that it? Could they do more, like shift into an animal?

She imagined shifting into a bird and flying away from here.

The currents would lift her up, taking her away. The sun would beat down on her feathers and a sharp cry would pierce the air as she screamed her excitement.

But she wasn't a shifter. She was an ordinary person. This was all a big, horrible mistake, and she needed a plan, needed to convince someone, *anyone,* of her innocence.

Or escape. She could always escape.

Terra sighed. She'd spent the morning sitting under a tree, watching life go by. She couldn't think of a better solution, and the longer she sat there, the better the idea seemed. But if she really wanted to escape, she needed to learn the patterns of her prison.

Patterns, then resources. That would be next.

For now, though, she just watched and waited.

And tried not to cry. She'd gotten to where every time she saw a child in here, her chest would tighten up. Then a uniformed man walked through the door of the administration building holding a toddler, the little one clutching him like a vise, screaming and crying for her mother.

Where was her mother? They hadn't separated her from both parents, had they? The idea horrified her.

No one followed. The child continued to scream. The man tried to separate himself from her, but the kid held tighter, pigtails flailing back and forth as he jarred her little body. Finally, he managed to dump her on the ground, then stormed back inside, the little child's cries unable to move him.

Terra jumped up and ran across the distance, sliding on her knees the last couple feet to the child. "Shhh." She picked the kid up, cradling her to her chest and rocking her back and forth. "Shhh. It's okay. I've got you."

The cries continued, but eventually tapered off. First calming to occasional sobs, then hiccups, then sporadic sniffs. Finally quiet, she looked up at Terra with wounded, curious eyes.

Terra hadn't noticed before, but tiny fingers seized her in a clutch that almost pinched. The girl's death grip cut off her air, but she didn't complain. "What's your name? I'm Terra."

She sniffed a couple more times. "Annie."

Terra smiled. "That's my middle name. Terra Anne."

A hesitant smile crossed her face before freezing and starting to fall off again. "Where's Mama?"

"I don't know, Annie. I'm sorry."

The sniffing returned, and her lower lip started to quiver.

Terra held the girl tighter, tucking Annie's head into her neck. "Don't worry, Annie. I'll make sure nothing happens to you."

Annie nodded, buried her face in Terra's neck, and quieted, her hot breath puffing against Terra's skin as she rubbed the toddler's back in long, slow strokes.

Children had a separate bunkhouse, but Annie refused to release Terra, so she'd eaten dinner with Annie glued to her side and paused uncertainly when it came time for bed. She walked down the middle of the women's dorm, military-style bunks lining either side of a central aisle. She approached the opposite end, where an open door waited, through which she could make out a utilitarian bathroom. Tiny showers ran the left wall, while toilet stalls lined the other. Just a couple sinks stood guard around the entrance, and no mirrors covered the plain walls.

"Annie, you have to let go now."

"No!" she moaned, gripping tighter to the soft, gray fabric of Terra's t-shirt, causing the material to dig in painfully.

Terra sighed. "You have to potty and brush your teeth." She probably needed a bath, too, but Terra had no clue how to accomplish that. She remembered always sitting in the bath-tub growing up, but the building only had showers. How was she supposed to give a toddler a shower?

"I don't wanna!" Annie slurred, running the words together.

"It's bedtime." Actually, it was well past the little girl's bedtime, seeing as Terra was ready for bed herself, so Annie should have been asleep hours ago. Terra hefted her up a little higher against her hip and turned to look her in the eye. "You remember what I said when we met?"

She nodded shyly.

"What did I say?"

"That you wouldn't let nothing happen to me," she mumbled into Terra's shoulder.

"That's right. Well, I'll add one more. I won't abandon you. You can go to the bathroom and brush your teeth, but I'm not going anywhere. I'll be here for you. I promise." Terra tilted Annie's chin up, putting a serious face on. "And I never break my promises."

"I see you've made a friend," Macey said, a smile in her voice.

"Shh," Terra responded, not even bothering to open her eyes. Annie lay on her chest, and each movement made her worry that she would wake her. They'd settled down to rest hours ago, but she didn't trust the girl's stillness.

After a shower, Annie had resumed clutching Terra's gray

uniform in a death grip. The shower had been a long, unpleasant endeavor with Annie flailing and shrieking the entire time, leaving Terra soaked to the skin. Terra had changed her clothes then settled on her bed with Annie, but she couldn't sleep.

Quiet breaths, squeaking bed-frames, and the occasional snort or snore broke the silence of the women's dorm. Terra didn't dare to move, though, afraid either the movement itself or the protest of the bed beneath her would rouse the fitfully sleeping Annie.

"How's she doing?"

Terra half-opened one eye, scowling at Macey, haloed by the floodlights peeking through the tiny windows behind her. "Too soon to tell," she whispered. "She's clingy right now, but children are resilient."

Macey nodded. "See you at breakfast."

Terra nodded as Macey walked away, but a surge of panic tightened her chest, leaving her breathless.

Now what?

———

Terra hefted Annie onto her hip and approached the buffet. "What do you want for breakfast, Annie?"

Annie sucked her thumb, her head tilting as she perused the offerings. "Nana!"

"Okay, what else?"

She pursed her lips.

"How about some eggs?"

The little girl frowned.

"Come on, eggs are good for you."

But her charge didn't respond, choosing to bury her face in Terra's neck again.

"Anything else?"

She shook her head again.

"Okay, I'm going to get you a banana, eggs, and some hash browns, okay?"

Another nod.

Terra paused, biting her lip, realizing she didn't have enough hands. "Well, that summer waitressing had to come in handy sometime." She filled Annie's plate halfway, then another for herself. After only a couple days, she'd resigned herself to the garbage they called food. Still, food was food. She tipped one plate half on top of the other, then slipped her arm underneath, balancing one on her palm and the other on her forearm.

Returning to the table, she swore under her breath. She forgot drinks. Sagging in place, she glanced back at the drink station. The cafeteria had become crowded, the cacophony of human voices playing harmony to the jostling bodies pushing between each other and inanimate objects. She had a new respect for parents worldwide.

"Let's go get something to drink, huh?"

CHAPTER FOUR

Kyle scowled when his partner beamed at him, a mischievous grin that didn't bode well for anyone. His teeth stood out in stark contrast against his darker skin and an ebullient energy pervaded his large form. Kyle wanted to grab him and hold him back by force, but knew from several weeks' experience that it would do no good.

If Kaufman weren't a fucking fantastic investigator, Kyle would have ditched his ass ages ago. Unfortunately, the bastard was actually useful. He saw patterns in information Kyle could never have hoped to find and picked up minutiae from interviews Kyle often missed.

Kyle excelled in getting people to talk, tracking them down, not studying nuance. He was a sledgehammer. Kaufman was a computer. It meant Kyle always told his partner to stay in the observation room when interrogating someone, but they didn't have that option out in the field.

Unfortunately, Kyle couldn't avoid bringing Kaufman into the field. Today, they needed to talk to personnel from the *Orleans*. They were working their way through a list, going from bunk to bunk at Clark NSS Base.

The stark hallway reminded him of every ship he'd ever served on.

Kaufman walked up to a steel-gray door and banged on it, making Kyle flinch. The door protested with a hollow sound before shuffling started on the other side.

A crack opened at the doorframe, and a groggy eye peeked through. "What do you want?"

"Hi, how ya doing today?" Kaufman bounced, smiling his thousand-watt smile.

Kyle grabbed his bicep, pinching it in warning. Kaufman backed off. "Neil Nussbaum?"

The eye narrowed. "Yeah?"

"You served on the USS *Orleans*, correct?"

"Yeah," he said, dragging out the syllable.

"Tell us what happened," Kaufman jumped in, not able or willing to help himself.

Kyle resisted smacking his forehead. It was going to be a long day.

Something's not right here.

The thought had plagued her for a while now. Terra still hadn't given up hope of escaping or convincing someone to realize their mistake, much to Macey's consternation, but most days, taking care of Annie distracted her.

It had been a couple weeks since Annie entered her life, and on some level, she suspected the little girl had saved her. She kept Terra grounded, giving her focus and purpose when she started falling apart at the seams.

She sat in a chair she'd pulled up to a window in the Rec Room, looking out over the courtyard. Annie sat on the floor playing with toys that had seen better days, but she didn't seem to mind. They still clacked and rang with energetic sounds that grated on the adults in the room. As long as Terra didn't leave, Annie acted as if nothing were wrong.

People meandered across her vision, living as best they could inside these wire fences. In the weeks after her arrival, she'd classified her fellow prisoners into a variety of categories, though she couldn't figure out what differentiated them.

First was filled with people like Macey. Maybe a bit haunted, they'd accepted their fate, but weren't really broken. They were often sad, but they went about their days with a tenacity that reminded her of factory workers in Charles Dickens era stories.

Next contained people like herself. They were the newest. They would rattle the fences, bang on the administration building doors, and yell at the top of their lungs, crying out to be heard, to be saved. She felt embarrassed lumping herself in that category. Looking at it from the outside, it seemed like yelling into the wind—fruitless and an annoyance to everyone around her. Still, the impulse came to her on a regular basis, and she caved to it more often than not.

The last category unnerved her, though. They were the traumatized, the zombies, the broken. They would stare off into the distance, not really seeing you, not really seeing *anything*. They shuffled about, devoid of life, waiting to die.

The thought of becoming one of them terrified her.

"I'm hungry," Annie whined, pulling on Terra's hand.

Terra looked down, smiling at the little imp affectionately. "Well, you're just gonna have to wait. I don't have anything on me."

The girl pouted, then sagged on their joined hands, her legs folding beneath her.

Terra held in a laugh, amused by the counter-productivity of the toddler's impulse. "Do you need me to carry you?" Terra loved her and suspected she had from the moment she set eyes on her three weeks ago.

Annie scowled, standing up once more, then dashing forward, dragging Terra along by her hand. "Let's *go!*"

Terra did laugh this time, but kept to her sedate pace. After all, there was no need to rush. They would get there eventually, and there were far too many hours in the day here at the camp.

Suddenly, a group of men in uniforms spilled out of the administration building. Terra flinched and picked up Annie, holding her to her chest as she hid behind the nearest tree. She watched as the men walked up to a woman in the courtyard and grabbed her by the arms. She screamed, fighting back.

In Terra's arms, Annie cried out in answer to the woman's fear. Terra held the little girl tighter, running a hand over the back of her head. "Shhh."

At the other end of the yard, the men lifted the woman and hauled her off, but she didn't stop struggling. She flailed and kicked, catching one man in the chin. His head snapped backward, but the other caught her wild leg and contained it as they continued inexorably toward the administration building.

The door closed behind them and an eerie silence settled over the crowd. No one spoke, no one moved, but all too quickly, the moment ended and people went about their business like nothing had happened.

Did this happen often?

What *had* happened?

Why did they take her?

Terra spotted Macey leaving the women's dorm and called her over. "What was that? Why did they take her? What did she do?"

Macey scowled and stared at the place where the woman had disappeared. She shrugged. "She must have shifted."

Terra was taken aback, her mind slow to click back into gear. The shock she'd felt only a moment ago dissipated, this logical explanation and cause easing that underlying fear of the unknown that had gripped her only moments ago.

She looked back at the doorway they'd retreated through, and guilt tickled the edges of her mind because suddenly it didn't really bother her that they'd taken the woman away. After all, she'd deserved it. You couldn't control your genes, but you could certainly control your actions.

And nothing could make *her* shift. Not in a million years.

"Watch me!" Annie said, bouncing in place.

Terra had become a surrogate mother for her, sort of adopting her. She couldn't believe they'd been here for weeks, that it was approaching a month. Having Annie beside her made it so much easier. "Show me." She leaned over, giving her a smile.

Annie scrunched up her face, making Terra smile even harder, then her blond locks cascaded into a rich red. "I'm like you!" She bounced and giggled, tugging at the two braids Terra had made that morning.

Alarm flew through Terra, and she tucked Annie into her side, hiding the new color from view. "That's great, Annie, but maybe not in public." She looked around, but didn't see anyone. Letting out a sigh, she ruffled Annie's hair. "Now, I want to see your beautiful hair again, okay?"

"Oh-kay," Annie moaned, and the color changed back as easily as rain falling from the sky.

"Good girl." She picked up Annie, bringing her to a spot under one of the few trees, and sat down. "How'd you do that?"

Annie shrugged. "I just did."

Terra frowned, resting her chin on Annie's head, holding her tighter as anxiety swelled inside her, choking her. She tried not to let it show, but feared Annie would sense it. Children were unbelievably intuitive. Her hand rubbing down Annie's back soothed them both, but nothing could silence the implications of what Annie had just done.

Annie knew how to shift. And being a child, she wouldn't have the self-control hide it.

Her heart pounded in her chest, remembering the woman being dragged away only a few days ago. More importantly, she remembered how that same woman had walked like a zombie just this morning as they'd shoved her out into the camp.

What had they done to her? An image popped into her head of two men dragging Annie away as she screamed, "Terra!" over and over again. She flinched, her muscles seizing up, and ducked her head closer.

Not her.

"Promise me you won't do that again in public. Okay, Annie?"

Annie squirmed, separating herself from Terra enough to look up at her with those big, brilliant blue eyes, and said, "Okay, Tewa."

Terra smiled, her heart melting at the mangling of her name. She kissed her on the forehead. "Don't worry. We'll still let you shift, but it has to be a secret, okay?"

Annie nodded. "Okay."

"Good girl."

Terra rocked Annie, her brain running in circles as her mind scrambled to figure out how she could protect her.

———

Terra sat with her fingers teasing the fabric of her pants as she watched Annie play, the girl's squeals and laughter tinkling through the air. Her mind ran in a repetitive loop.

Annie can shift.

The thought plagued her, haunting her. What could she do? What *would* she do?

She didn't know.

After that little discovery, she'd walked Annie into the Rec Room. Annie kept checking behind her shoulder to make sure Terra hadn't left, which broke her heart a little each time it happened. She had to protect her. She just *had* to. But how? Terra didn't know squat about security, but it seemed airtight here. The dual fences alone would have been enough to keep her in or out under normal circumstances.

But these weren't normal circumstances. She had something to lose, and that made all the difference in the world.

"Well, you look pensive." Macey sat down next to her, raising her eyebrows in question.

"I am."

"I hope you're not trying to figure out how to escape again."

"I am." What other choice did she have? She didn't trust people who could lock away a toddler. She would have to escape, but how?

Macey sighed, shaking her head in Terra's peripheral vision. "I told you already. Give it up. No one's leaving this place."

Terra turned to her. "Well, certainly not with that attitude." Standing, she walked away. She made a beeline for the exit, then the fence, walking along it as she thought.

The administration building was a no-go. It was the only exit she'd seen, but no one left through there. Between the height of the fences and the razor wire, climbing wouldn't do either, especially not with Annie, which left digging or cutting. What tools could cut through fencing? Something strong and sharp, she imagined, but she doubted she could get her hands on anything like that. She would be lucky to find a kitchen knife in this place.

Which left digging, although how she would manage to dig under the fences with no one the wiser, she had no clue. She could dig with her hands, but it would take time. Someone was bound to notice not only the mound of dirt next to the fence, but the dirt on her as well.

Plus, as she walked along the barrier to the outside world, she noticed things on the top of some fence posts that just might be cameras. If they were, this just got a hell of a lot harder.

So, they had to escape in one shot, digging underneath two fences without being seen. Terra came to a point at the corner of one of the buildings used for sleeping quarters. At this spot, the building came within a couple feet of the fence, so close Terra had to squeeze through.

Stepping forward, she entered a mostly enclosed area. The fence arched out to the right, and the three residence buildings hugged together on the left, so close a baseball bat would have trouble getting through. On the fences, nothing that could be cameras waited, and nobody had bothered to install any lighting.

With deep woods beyond the chain link, this area would be pitch black after everyone went to sleep. How long could it take to dig two trenches? Could they get it done by dawn? She didn't know.

But maybe she could use Annie's shifting to their advantage. Could Terra shift to dig faster?

Terra looked down at her hands, the digits shaking as she tried to come to grips with a reality that still wouldn't click in her head. How could she possibly learn, from a child no less, how to shift if she couldn't even bring herself to believe she had the ability?

She didn't know, but she had to try.

CHAPTER FIVE

Terra left the secret space, walking out into the open.

"Tewa!" a little voice cried.

Terra jerked her head up. Annie was running at her, arms outstretched. She tripped and wailed. Terra sped up into a jog and crouched down next to her. "What's wrong, Anna Banana?"

Annie sniffed. "You left." She rubbed her eyes, giving Terra her best pouty lip even after Terra called her by the nickname that always made her smile.

"I didn't leave. I went for a walk." Terra leaned in. "Where do you think I'm gonna go? Do you see any doors? Any gaps in the fence? You're stuck with me. And even if I were to get away, I'm taking you with me. That's a promise. And you remember what I said?"

"You never break your promises."

Terra nodded. "That's right. I don't." She caressed Annie's cheek. "Don't worry, sweetie. I'm not going anywhere. You're

gonna be stuck with me when we're both old and wrinkley."
She reached down and started tickling Annie's tummy.

The girl squealed, rolling onto her back and giggling so hard she could barely breathe.

"I'm gonna get you, and you're gonna be stuck with me for all time." She leaned over and blew a raspberry on the girl's now-exposed stomach.

The squeals picked up in tempo, followed closely by bubbling laughter that made Terra forget all her troubles.

After Annie'd calmed down from her giggle fest, Terra took her for a walk. Annie gripped her hand like she wanted to squeeze all the blood out of the extremity, but Terra tried to ignore it.

They made their way behind the residence buildings. "Whatcha think, Anna Banana?"

Annie looked up at Terra, her face scrunched up in confusion.

Terra laughed. "It's out of the way. You can do whatever you want back here and no one will see. Completely private."

"Yeah?"

Terra nodded and crouched down to Annie's level. "I want you to be yourself. Always."

Annie's eyes lit up, and she looked around the space with new enthusiasm.

"Do you know what it means to be a shifter, Annie?"

Annie turned back and shook her head.

Terra frowned. "Truth be told, neither do I. How about we

figure it out together? Can you tell me how you changed your hair before?"

Annie frowned, concentrating in a way that made Terra want to hug her. "*I* don't know. I just wanted my hair to look like you and it did."

"That's it?"

Annie nodded and smiled, the expression stretching to encompass her entire face, exposing dimples on each cheek. In the next moment, her hair flowed into a red color to match Terra's.

Terra smirked at the little imp as she bounced away, dancing along. *I wonder what* she *sees.* "Is it just that simple? Want it and let 'er rip?" Terra closed her eyes, tried to clear her mind, figuring doubts would only prevent her from succeeding. She needed the purity and innocence of a child.

She snorted. Good luck with that. She'd never even figured out the whole mindfulness thing, her mind constantly drifting and thoughts bouncing around like pinballs.

Shaking her head, she started over.

Clear mind.

Picture what I want.

What do I want?

Eyes drifting open, Terra watched Annie run around, trying and failing to do cartwheels. *I want her hair color.* A mental image popped in her mind of the pale blond tresses with little bits of reddish highlights. She opened her eyes but didn't feel any different.

This was stupid.

I'm not a shifter.

I was right all along.

This was all a huge mistake.

I'll never get us out of here.

Annie landed on her butt, legs sprawled out in front of her. A giggle like bell chimes rang out into the air.

Terra laughed, and Annie turned to her.

"Your hair!" Annie jumped up, charging forward. She grabbed a short lock and yanked, pulling it just far enough from Terra's skull to expose the blond.

"Fuck me," Terra said, reaching and touching a strand, then realized what she'd said. "Shit." Eyes going wide, she zeroed in on Annie, but the little girl seemed more interested in Terra's hair than the vulgarities coming out of her mouth.

Thank God.

<hr>

The next day after breakfast, Terra and Annie returned to the little field. Annie ran and played, oblivious to all but being a happy little child.

Terra shook her head. "How does she do it?" After such a short time, Annie had recovered, feeling secure and light of heart. Meanwhile, Terra couldn't go anywhere without heart palpitations. Every moment put them one step closer to discovery. And really, they did seem to run this place like they didn't expect anyone to shift, even though its sole purpose was to house shifters.

Terra stared down at her hand, wondering what more she could try. What was her next step? She'd pulled off the change in hair color yesterday so effortlessly. Disturbingly effortlessly. What if she did it by accident? What if Annie did?

The problem was she didn't have a plan. When did she ever? Terra had lost her job and felt lost at sea. She'd ended up spending a month feeling sorry for herself, moping around the house and watching entirely too much TV before she finally started looking for work. She couldn't let that happen this time.

Except she did, didn't she? She'd let herself get absorbed in caring for Annie instead of trying to leave. She'd forgotten her goals, forgotten to gather intel. It didn't matter now.

"How are we going to get out of here?" She looked down at her hands again. The easiest way would be to shift into an animal good at digging. Terra shook her head. "And why not?" She didn't know tons about shifters, but if they could shift into other people, maybe they could shift into other animals.

"God, why didn't I take more biology classes in school?"

All she could remember was a chunky-looking animal with funky claws. Terra tried to visualize that in her mind, imagining her hand morphing into a claw, but it was like there was this disconnect between her brain and shifting. She opened her eyes.

Nothing.

What did I do yesterday? What's different?

Terra chewed her lip, feeling useless.

I am *useless.*

I'll never save us.

I'm not a real shifter.

She shook her head, trying to dislodge the thoughts, wishing she'd spent more time learning meditation. It would have come in handy now.

What the hell did I do differently yesterday?

It had been so easy. She'd pictured her hair, and it just happened, without even feeling it. But not today. Maybe it was her faulty memory. Maybe she just couldn't visualize what she wanted. Maybe she just didn't *want* it enough.

Or maybe I need to just stop second-guessing myself.

But it was *so* hard to see herself as a shifter. It flew against everything she knew about herself, everything society had told her. Terra was a good girl. She obeyed the law, paid her bills, didn't cheat on her taxes, and sped no more than ten miles above the speed limit. She tried to be a good person.

On some level, she just couldn't rectify that notion with her concept of a shifter. In her head, a shifter was a con artist, stealing identities, breaking and entering. Though, now that she thought about it, the things running through her head reminded her of the perception of the Romani throughout history, and most of that was utter bullshit. Maybe this was too?

Even in her head, the question held so much doubt. Except, as she looked around, she couldn't unsee the chain-link fence and utilitarian buildings—the *prison*—set aside for people who had done nothing except *exist*. You didn't need to do anything wrong to come here. You just needed to be born with the wrong genes.

And how is that any different than how the Holocaust started? She didn't know how this would end, but she shivered thinking of it going in that direction. If it did, living in one of the camps, she would be the first to know... intimately.

Terra shook herself, dragging her mind from those dark thoughts, and focused on Annie instead. The girl laughed and played, chatting away as she pulled at the grass around her.

Terra smiled, letting the love she felt for the little girl chase away the toxic thoughts she'd been wallowing in.

Maybe I can do this. For her.

She focused in on that hazy image of an animal's claws. When the thought wasn't clear enough, she closed her eyes, scrunching up her face in focus, forcing herself to concentrate, to think of nothing else. Then, a sensation like things crawling under her skin invaded her, and she gasped, looking down where her hand had stopped in mid-transition. Skin still tan in color, her nails had elongated, the palm a little wider. It didn't look much like she vaguely remembered, but it was something. She looked at her other hand, this time trying to hold the image of her normal hand with her eyes open.

Nothing happened. She scowled and tried not to panic. "Deep breath." Closing her eyes, she tried it again. The crawly feeling returned, and when it stopped, she looked down and laughed, wiggling her fingers experimentally. "It worked."

Checking on Annie, she found her picking weeds and making a bouquet. Terra shook her head. Kids.

She flexed her fingers once more, paying close attention to how each of the joints functioned and moved. Closing her eyes, she let out a slow breath, focusing the image in her mind. The same creeping feeling returned, but she squeezed her eyelids more tightly closed, focusing harder on her goal. The creeping left, followed by a tickling along her skin, which soon left too.

Terra peeked one eye open, letting out a breath of relief when a fully transformed hand sprang out of the end of her arm. She flexed her fingers, a little weirded out when an extra finger off to the side just sat there taking up space. Her arm ended in a furry, wide palm with six short fingers, each with thick nails longer than the fingers themselves. She could move all but the new finger the same as she ordinarily would. The last one, she didn't know how to move. Maybe she'd screwed up. But the big, broad hand *did* look like it would be good at digging. Maybe it would be enough.

"Wow, Tewa!" Annie grabbed her clawed hand, yanking it this way and that and sticking her face inches away from it. "How'd you do that?"

Terra shrugged. "The same way you changed your hair."

Annie's eyes grew big and round.

"But I wouldn't try it. Practice with some simple things like changing your hair and growing or shortening your nails for now. Okay?"

Annie nodded. "Can you dig with that?"

"I don't know, Anna Banana. Why do you ask?"

Annie shrugged. "It looks like a mole hand."

Mole, of course. That was the name of that stupid animal. "Do you want to watch me try with the other one?" She wiggled the fingers of her left hand in the air.

Annie nodded with exuberance, plopping on the ground with legs crossed.

Terra closed her eyes again, pulling the image of the hairy claw with a wide palm, six digits, and long, thick nails. Again, a creeping sensation crawled up her hand that made her want to shake it out, followed by a tickle that soon faded. When it stopped, she opened her eyes and waggled her newly formed hand in front of Annie, who applauded with high-pitched giggles.

Terra looked at her two modified hands, which weren't identical. *It must depend on the accuracy of the image in my head.* Her left hand was wider, but her right hand had longer nails.

"Dig!" Annie said, bouncing in her seat.

"Okay, okay." Terra smiled down at Annie, digging her fingers into the earth experimentally. The dry brown soil under the grass gave easily to her hands. When she tore her hands away, she left a small but significant hole. With another pass, she pulled even more earth away. She laughed. "This is fun."

She put real effort into it, removing great big handfuls of dirt each time. It flew out behind her, Annie cheering her on. When she finally stopped, she'd dug a hole as deep as the length of her arms. She looked up and laughed. Annie had decided to play in the dirt with her. Dirt covered her from head to toe.

Terra wiped a smudge off the girl's cheek, then chuckled and shook her head when her own dirt-covered claws only made it worse. "I'm gonna get us out of here, sweetie."

"Okay," Annie said. She didn't get it, and that was okay too. Better if she never understood this place.

"Let's fill this hole back in."

"Aw," Annie said, tilting her head to the side and sagging.

Terra leaned forward. "If we don't fill it back in, then we can't play again tonight."

"Tonight?"

"How would you like to play in the dark?"

Annie thought about it for maybe a second. "Okay."

"Okay. Let's fill this hole, clean up, and get something to eat."

And tonight, they would be free.

CHAPTER SIX

$\mathscr{I}$t was a good idea. Kaufman had come up with it, reminding Kyle just how useful the bastard was. He glared over at the man lounging in a guest chair on the other side of the room, a tablet resting in his lap.

They'd come up empty while interviewing members of the *Orleans* crew. Kaufman had suggested a few people to monitor more closely at the task force meeting a couple days ago. Unfortunately, there was no reason for any of these fuckers to slip up, so Kyle didn't have high hopes of that going anywhere.

But then Kaufman sailed into the office this morning beyond excited, a sardonic grin stretching his face. "Guess what," he'd said, nearly bursting to speak.

Kyle had been exhausted, seriously questioning his aversion to coffee, thinking it was too damn early to deal with his partner. He'd needed at *least* a couple more hours to wake up first. "What?"

"I have an idea for new leads." Kaufman had dropped into one of the guest chairs, looking smug.

Kyle had jerked his head up, grateful for a new lead, a new angle. "What?"

"The fighters."

Kyle had frowned, his mind not connecting with Kaufman's words.

"The men who infiltrated the *Orleans*?" Kaufman had hinted.

"They're dead."

"True," Kaufman had pointed a finger, "but according to the reports, we don't know if they *all* died. We also have their ships and we can gather personal accounts to identify them. Your security team will cooperate?"

Kyle had scoffed. "Of course."

"Good."

It *had* been a good plan. Surveillance footage from the *Orleans* was unreliable at best and eye witness testimony even more so. Still, security personnel were trained to be observant.

Also on their side, sub-space technology and pilots were hard to come by. He supposed, in theory, someone rich enough could get their hands on ships. Or, he shuddered, someone unscrupulous enough could order NSS fighters to attack one of their own. That possibility always left him feeling a bit cold inside.

He stared at his monitor. His office's solitary window sat behind him, making it difficult to view the screen. Through the closed glass, engines rumbled, coming and going from the parking lot it overlooked. Occasionally, he could make out the mumble of voices. It distracted him, making him want to find a quieter place to work, but no place was quiet on a military base.

Tension and frustration gripped him as he squinted at the

display, trying to ignore Kaufman. It *was* a good lead, so why did it feel like the lead was fighting back? The task force started weeks ago. A dozen men and women worked diligently to bring the responsible individuals to justice, and yet where were they?

Nowhere.

Just fucking nowhere.

Terra hunched over her bed where she'd placed Annie for an after dinner nap. Darkness had set in hours ago, and all the women in the building had fallen asleep. Terra had made the excuse that she wanted to read while Annie took a nap. No one questioned it seeing as Annie tended to latch onto her like a leech, leaving Terra little time to herself.

"Wake up, sweetie," she whispered, rocking her gently.

Annie mumbled and curled up tighter into the blankets.

Terra smiled and decided not to bother. She lifted the still sleeping child into her arms. Walking back to the entrance, she was conscious of every breathing body she passed, every soul who could wake up and ruin this for them. She didn't think anyone would stop them from escaping, but no one had to *try* to thwart them. They only had to draw the wrong attention.

She held her breath as she went along, turning her head one way then the other, expecting someone to catch them at any moment. Someone to the left groaned and rolled over. Terra gasped and nearly jumped, then froze in place, waiting for the inevitable. Her heart hammered away in her chest, ready to bolt, but nothing else happened. She let out the breath she'd been holding and took in another, pulling the air slowly through her lips to avoid making a sound.

Not that it mattered. They were all dead to the world, and Terra reached the door without incident. She hefted Annie onto her hip, opened the door, and started rocking her as if trying to get her to sleep. Anyone paying attention would realize Annie had her head resting on Terra's shoulder and wasn't making a peep, but hopefully the ruse would work for anyone watching on video.

She walked around the fence, continuing to bob Annie up and down. Every once in a while, Annie would make a little groan and curl up tighter to her side. When they reached the corner of the building, Terra slipped through and dropped the ruse, dashing out of camera range, then set Annie down, letting her curl up on the ground.

Terra closed her eyes and took a deep breath, pulling up the image of claws once more. The now familiar sensations returned, and she didn't even bother looking when they stopped. After only a couple times shifting, she'd already come to know what to expect, at least with this little transformation.

She kneeled down and dug her fingers into the soft soil next to the fence, pressing her hands down, then ripping them back past her hips. She repeated the action again and again, her hands growing cold with the damp earth surrounding them. Over and over, she displaced the dirt, her hole growing bigger until she had to kneel inside it to go further.

Now, she began alternating hands, curling to the side to avoid her claws as she threw the earth behind her. The hole continued to grow. Once she started going under the fence, it grew more difficult. She had a harder time pulling the dirt away without it refilling the hole or hitting her body instead of going behind.

Mud caked her hands now, matting the fur there. Instead of soft dirt, clumps of mud came up with each pass, the deeper ground saturated. Her progress slowed, but soft, fluffy earth started falling down from the surface on the other side. Through the fence, she could just barely see an ever-increasing hole out of the corner of her eye, which gave her a headache to watch.

After a few more moments, a big fall of soil covered her arms, leaving a gaping hole on the opposite side of the fence. She sat up, shaking out her arms, which had grown sore from the unusual exertion, especially her forearms, which felt ready to snap. *Maybe that's why moles have such short arms…*

Terra patted down the loose soil in the bottom of the hole and leaned under the fence. Yes, she could get under it no problem. Turning away, she rocked Annie again, being less careful this time to be quiet. "Wake up, Annie. It's time to go."

Annie groaned again, but this time she opened her eyes, rubbing them with two tiny little fists.

Terra laughed, because she'd gotten dirt all over Annie in her digging and the girl had spread it across her cheeks in the motion. "Ready to go?"

Annie blinked her eyes, sat up, looked at Terra, and giggled.

"What?" Terra smiled.

"You're covered in dirt."

Terra tilted her head toward the hole she sat in. "I've been playing." She reached toward Annie. "Come on. In you go."

"Where are we going?" Annie said as she awkwardly climbed in, then skittered under and up the other side. When she clambered back out again, mud formed a single skid down the front of her shirt and pants.

"Anywhere," Terra said and followed suit. "Anywhere."

Jackson stood against a tree, hands in his pockets, chewing his lip. He'd come by this monstrosity every day for a week. At times, he'd glimpsed both adults and children walking inside the enclosed areas, separated from the outside world by twin rings of chain-link topped with razor wire. He scoffed. There was something very wrong with a society when it grew suspicious of children.

He'd been tempted more than once to just burn the camp to the ground, but that would leave a lot of innocents in jeopardy. *His* people could never do such a thing. He shook his head. What was wrong with these people?

Best not to think about it. It would only upset him further and accomplish nothing.

"Night would be best." The place seemed minimally staffed, but *did* see the occasional vehicle arriving throughout the day. At night, it became a ghost town, and the spot directly in front of his perch even more so. None of the flood lamps reached that particular point, leaving Jackson and forty feet of fencing in complete darkness.

And based on the wireless scanner he'd brought today, they hadn't even bothered to put up cameras in this location. Around other portions of the compound, his scanner picked up Wi-Fi-connected cameras with motion detection and night vision options. Even if he killed the lights, the cameras would still catch him.

"Could it be a trap?" he said, scratching his chin. It seemed too obvious a gap in the security to be accidental. Yet why would they bother? They couldn't know his people were here.

They were off the grid, nomads mostly. Nobody knew they existed, and they liked it that way. It was safer. You would never find *them* in a bloody concentration camp.

Which was about when a gray-clad figure inside the compound stepped into the shadowed region not covered by light or camera. He could have easily missed him, but the gray of his clothing was just a tad too pale to fade into the darkness. "This is interesting."

The person placed something on the ground, then planted himself near the fence. Jackson could tell he was moving, but not what he was doing.

"What the?"

The man remained there for some time. Jackson just barely made out movement behind him, but couldn't identify it. It seemed to fly through the air, though. As time passed, the man got harder and harder to see, until he disappeared, only his gray satchel on the ground visible in the non-existent light.

"Huh." Then it dawned on him. "He's digging." Jackson laughed. "Clever bastard." And at the rate he was going, the guy would clear both fences in less than half an hour.

The digger popped back out and reached for the gray package. The package moved, then rose. "That's a person." His anger flared again. "A child."

Both disappeared into the hole, then surfaced on the other side. The process repeated on the other fence, and Jackson crept forward. Minutes ticked by as the man again disappeared into his own ditch. Jackson reached the edge of the tree line and waited. He wanted to meet the first person he'd ever heard of to escape the shifter camps.

The two crawled out, then the man picked up the child,

hoisting it onto his hip, and unknowingly walked toward Jackson. While Jackson's eyes were adapted to the darkness, they were almost upon him by the time he saw them clearly.

"You're a woman!"

She screamed.

CHAPTER SEVEN

Jackson reacted instantly, covering her mouth and grasping the back of her head before she could pull away. The scream had barely started by the time he acted, and he prayed it would be mistaken for an animal noise. "Quiet. You don't want them to hear us." Her breaths heated his palm, a damp sensation in direct contrast to the cool, dry air around them. She breathed through her nose, the noise impossibly loud in the stillness of night.

She nodded, her hair shifting against his hand with the motion, and he let go. He looked down at the child—a girl if he could judge based on the long, blonde hair—and noticed the woman's animalistic claws. "Clever. Very clever."

"I couldn't leave her in there." Her voice was quiet, hollow.

Jackson blinked, taking a moment to decipher her statement. "You didn't escape for yourself." He saw her in a new light now.

"No." She looked behind her, then turned back to him, her face twisted in worry.

"You're right. We should get out of here. Follow me." He

turned, walking deeper into the woods, but stopped when he couldn't hear her follow. When he looked back, she hadn't moved. She still stood just barely inside the tree line, clutching the little girl in a death grip. The light from the camp back-lit her, casting her in shadows even his shifted vision couldn't quite compensate for. It was almost as if, even after escaping it, the shifter camp continued to create a dark stain on her.

He shook himself, disgusted with his fanciful thoughts. *She's just scared.* He could practically see her muscles shaking. She needed somewhere safe, somewhere *away*. He could provide that. She'd saved herself and a child. The least he could do was bring her to safety.

"Why should I trust you?" she said, breaking him out of his reverie. Her voice quavered, speaking to her emotions.

He reached out a hand, shifting it to match the shape of her own. "Because I'm like you."

***

Terra sighed and hefted Annie a little higher on her hip. After digging under those fences, her forearms burned and felt like jelly, but she figured Annie would just slow her down if she let her travel under her own steam.

She was too tired to be surprised by the man's revelation. It probably didn't help that she could barely see an inch in front of her face. Whatever he'd tried to show her, it had definitely not been a human hand. She'd only caught a glimpse of something wide and stubby.

With nowhere better to go, Terra followed the man blindly into the dark, dark woods. After the second time tripping and nearly doing a face plant, he stopped and scooped Annie up, offering his other hand to Terra to guide her. Annie was so tired, she didn't even make a token protest.

As they ventured deeper into the woods, dark objects and outlines became a great black void. "How can you see anything? There's no light out here."

"We don't need much light to see. I just shifted my eyes to better adapt to the darkness."

"How?"

He stopped and based on the way their joined hands shifted her arm to the side, he'd turned to her. "Some species of animal are much better adapted to the dark than these human forms. Envision the eyes of one of these creatures and you should be fine."

"One of those creatures?" She closed her eyes, even if it wasn't necessary when she couldn't see her own nose, and imagined a wolf's eyes. She imagined the light reflected off the backs, making them shine in the night. When she opened them again, she still couldn't see for shit, but she could make out the outlines of the trees and roots underfoot. She looked to him.

"Good. Are you ready to go on?"

Terra nodded, and he tugged on her hand, continuing to pull her forward. Once she could see, they made quick work, moving through the darkness like wraiths, graceful as wild cats.

Well, he moved like a wild cat. Terra moved like a water buffalo, but she didn't manage to trip after shifting her eyes, which was something at least.

Before long, the light grew shades brighter, and the trees opened up to a dirt road with an SUV parked there. "Get in," he said.

Terra paused, an image of her bloated body rotting in a ditch somewhere floating through her head. "How do I know I can trust you?"

He turned to face her. She could see him much better now. Tall, he stood at least half a foot taller than her, with broad shoulders and features etched in shadow. In the dark, she couldn't tell his hair color or ethnicity. She couldn't even read his expression to gauge his trustworthiness.

He sighed, running fingers through his hair, still holding Annie with the other. "My name is Jackson. I'm a shifter, and I'm not going to harm you. We aren't like the people you're used to dealing with. We look out for each other, protect each other. You're safe with me."

"Okay," she said, and walked up to the passenger side door of the vehicle. "I'm Terra."

<hr>

Jackson rounded his SUV and opened the back door with one hand. With slow movements, he lowered the little girl to lie on the bench seat. She curled into a ball, oblivious to the world and him. His chest grew tight, a warm emotion washing through him at the sight. The door closed with a barely audible click, and he climbed into the front seat.

The automatic overhead light gave him the first real glimpse of the woman beside him. Terra. Like the kid, dirt and mud caked her everywhere, even her hair, and even in the better lighting, he couldn't tell what color it was.

Against the darker contrast of the smudges, her skin shone through white as milk. She sat uneasily, shoulders still, watching him with suspicion. Still, those gray eyes captivated him. Behind the skepticism lay layers of determination and strength that spoke well of her.

He couldn't imagine what she'd been through. While outcasts, shunned or vilified by the world at large, he'd never been abandoned, never been betrayed by the people he trusted, and he supposed that was how she must feel. He turned away from her and started the car. The sooner they arrived at his people, the better. Nothing he did would make her comfortable or trust him right now.

That would take time.

And he was a very patient man.

They didn't say another word as he started onto the dirt road. Strangely, the silence was both awkward and comfortable. He felt relaxed around her, like he could trust her, even though he knew nothing but her name and that she'd escaped a shifter camp. But he suspected he could grow to like her very much. He saw signs that she held traits he admired a great deal.

Just the fact that she'd rescued the girl said something about her. He didn't know if the child was hers or just a child she'd bonded with at the camp, but it didn't matter. She'd risked not escaping at all rather than leave the girl behind. He didn't hold humans in high regard and didn't believe many of them would do the same. Altruism was a rare trait among their kind, one squashed into submission by their callous ways.

And yet, in spite of all this, he couldn't figure out what to say to her, how to reach her. Occasionally, on straightaways, he would turn toward her, intending to speak, but no words came forth.

But even those moments were short-lived, instantly replaced by a sense of calm and focus. He shifted his attention back to driving. The rest would come with time.

The decision to join Jackson in his car was the hardest decision Terra had ever made. The vehicle loomed in front of her like some dark monster, waiting to devour her, and she was the hapless victim willfully walking to her death. When she climbed in and nothing happened, she took in and let out a calming breath, telling herself que será será. There was no point worrying or freaking herself out over it.

Terra buckled in as Jackson laid Annie on the backseat, and they took off in silence. At first, fear and anxiety overwhelmed her, but no one could maintain that level of stress indefinitely, and she relaxed, turning her curious gaze to her mysterious ally.

She knew nothing about him other than his name and that he was a shifter. He could be a serial killer or a good Samaritan. Uncertainty was a bitch, and as she absently scratched her hand, the sharp claws scraping against the skin, she realized she'd never shifted them back to normal. Looking down, her hands shook, the odd shape, the hair, the claws leaving a queasy feeling in her stomach. Still, she hesitated to shift them back. She would have to close her eyes. While intellectually, she didn't think Jackson would jump on her the moment her eyes were closed, a deeper, more animal part of her resisted showing vulnerability.

The clock on the dash changed from 11:58 to 11:59 before she closed her eyes and concentrated on returning them to normal. *What if I can't do it? What if I screw it up? I'll have useless, mangled hands for eternity.* She shoved the thought ruthlessly aside. *Even if I did mess it up, I could always fix it later, with practice.*

She looked over to Jackson, suspecting he would be more than happy to help her. He seemed like the type that would be a good, patient teacher. She closed her eyes again, took a deep breath and pictured her normal hands. Long fingers, medium length nails—a little uneven from breaking them—and narrower palms. She focused on the feel of them changing back and opened her eyes, smiling at the familiar shape that had returned to them.

They traveled slowly on back roads, mindful of divots and potholes. Jackson would slow further when he turned onto side roads that were much higher or lower. By the time he stopped the car, the clock had reached 12:28. The headlights revealed yet more trees and dirt road. Out in the distance, a glimpse of something white or cream gleamed.

He killed the engine and rotated in his seat, his arm wrapped around his headrest. "Welcome to my home."

Terra looked around and frowned. What home? "Where?" she whispered.

He smiled at her, probably an indulgent expression. "Through the trees there. But I warn you. Don't expect what you might be accustomed to."

"What should I expect?"

He paused, then shrugged. "Home?"

Terra laughed, careful not to wake Annie.

"Come on. It's late. Probably no one's awake, but I can show you around a bit." He popped open the driver side door. Terra held her breath as he reached into the backseat for Annie, afraid he'd wake her, but Annie curled into his side as she often did with Terra.

He came around, opened Terra's door, and offered his hand. "Come on."

Terra grasped it, feeling it for the first time with her own. Warm and big, it gripped her securely, firmly. She gripped him right back and followed him along the path. Around the bend, more cars lined the road, the first a white truck that must have been what she'd seen gleaming earlier.

They continued to walk, and Terra started to flag, counting cars to keep her mind focused. It had been a grueling day, and she just wanted to collapse somewhere soft and pass out.

After she'd counted ten cars, the path opened into a small field containing an entire village of RVs and trailers. Some had tents between them. Billowing cloth and decorations made the place feel alive, wind chimes welcoming them home. Jackson pulled her to a unit on the left, opened the door, which wasn't locked, and ushered her inside.

He led her down the narrow central aisle to the end where a bedroom lay, bed in disarray. "You can sleep here tonight. There's a bathroom there if you want to get cleaned up." He pointed to the left where an accordion door covered a hole in the wall. He set sleeping Annie down on the bed and closed the door behind him without another word.

Terra looked back, a little puzzled at the closed door. Her brain was too tired to even puzzle out why she was puzzled.

CHAPTER EIGHT

*T*erra woke to sun shining down on her head. She dragged the covers up, groaning, unwilling to greet the day just yet. The comforter and big, soft bed swallowed her up, encouraging her to dally.

Then a small hand latched onto her shoulder, pulling at her. "Tewa!"

Terra blinked her eyes open to the dirtiest face she'd ever seen. She laughed. "Hey, sweetie. You need a bath." She touched Annie's nose with a single finger, smearing some caked-on mud.

My God, she's a mess.

She sat up and paused. Instead of the expected cot in bunk-style housing, a tiny bedroom with built in storage surrounded her. She and Annie sat on a wide bed, a vibrant, multi-colored quilt bunched around them. Then Terra remembered last night. Escaping, deciding to go along with Jackson. She didn't really remember this room, but then she'd been half asleep and in the dark at the time.

Oh shit. What the fuck was I thinking?

Her hands bunched the comforter, her jaw locked. *Don't let it show. Don't scare Annie.* She forced her muscles to relax, but her mind still ran in panicked circles. *What was I thinking?* She'd never done anything so stupid in her life.

Why the hell did she get in the car with him? She knew better. That was serial killer stupid. She almost deserved to be turned into a skin suit for that level of stupidity.

But as she inspected the small but neat room, she could admit that at least *this* hadn't ended badly... yet. She wouldn't hold her breath, though. She'd thought she was safe at home and look how well that turned out.

Returning to the task at hand, she glanced at Annie once more. Terra was mostly free of dirt, having taken a shower right before sleep, but Annie had covered herself and the bedding with mud. She went to lift Annie up, but even the act of stretching out her arms hurt. She was definitely paying for the digging she'd done yesterday.

But looking at their surroundings, it was worth it. She reached out to Annie, her arm twitching in protest. "Let's get you a bath."

Jackson woke with a kink in his neck. Not wanting to disturb Terra or make her uncomfortable, he'd slept on the couch. It was too short for him and didn't have linens since everything was in the bedroom, which had seemed the most logical place for them until now.

He got up and stretched, his neck protesting with sharp pain every time he rotated it to the left. He let out a deep breath, focusing on that area, and the tightness and pain receded at about the same time his stomach started growling.

Usually, he would make something up quick and go about his business, mooching a larger meal off one of the older, motherly women later in the morning. They were far better cooks than he, but he figured Terra would be starving when she woke after her adventure last night, and children rarely tolerated waiting for their meals.

Jackson opened the cupboard doors and stared at the offerings.

Terra stepped out of the bathroom to the smell of something burning. She raced across the room, threw the bedroom door open, and froze at the image before her. Jackson stood at a stove, waving wildly at the smoke billowing from something in front of him. She assumed it was a pan, but the smoke was so thick she couldn't tell.

She ran forward, grabbed the pan's handle, only visible once she nearly ran into it, and pushed Jackson out of the way. In one movement, she turned on the water at the sink next to the stove, and held the pan under it. Steam hissed and billowed from it for several moments, but soon the water poured over nothing more than a charred mass and a black pan. She dropped the pan in the sink with a clatter of metal on metal and turned off the water. Smoke continued to sting her eyes, so she turned to the stove, flipping on the fan to pull the smoke away before shutting off the burner.

Terra faced Jackson, but his gaze was elsewhere, drifting down her body. She glanced down and her face turned red. Having nothing clean to wear, she'd rummaged last night and found a large t-shirt, too tired to care. Now, she stood in Jackson's "kitchen" wearing a shirt that barely covered her ass and exposing legs that hadn't seen a razor in weeks because "it wasn't like anyone was gonna see it."

Boy, major mistake. She wanted to race back into the bedroom and slam the door, but she held firm, if a little rigid, in place. She didn't know if fear or sheer stubbornness held her there, and it didn't really matter. It took several moments to work up the guts to look him in the eye, and when she did, she did so with conviction.

Or maybe stubborn determination.

Terra couldn't read his expression. Was he embarrassed? Amused? Upset that she'd borrowed his shirt? Turned on? Or maybe shocked by the quantity of thick, dark red leg hair that made her look like a mutated monkey.

Annie saved them both from the moment of awkwardness with a plaintive, "I'm hungry." She plopped down on the couch with a huff.

Jackson smirked. "Well, I would offer, but you can see what happened the last time I tried to contribute."

"A lot of fast food?"

He shook his head. "You don't generally see our kind eating fast food. We fend for ourselves." He shrugged. "I can cook a few simple things, but sometimes they end in disaster, as you can see. Usually, some of the others cook extra, so I eat there. We all contribute, so it balances out."

Terra nodded. "Why don't you find me a pair of pants, and I'll try to make a meal out of whatever you have around."

"Sure, I'll be right back." He walked away, leaving the RV.

Terra turned to Annie. "Let's see what we've got to work with here." She opened the cabinets as she went, finding small quantities of plates, silverware, bowls, cups—more than adequate for a bachelor who apparently never ate in—along with a single pot and pan and some very basic staples: bread, rice, potatoes. A few bananas and a couple apples sat on the counter. In the refrigerator, she found very little—a few eggs, leftovers in an old Corningware dish, and a few varieties of cheese.

Terra tore a banana off the bunch and handed it to Annie, then started pulling ingredients out of the fridge and cupboards. Except, there was only the one pan… and Jackson had managed to burn it to a crisp. She picked up the pan and scratched at it with her fingernails, but while black char came off, it just revealed more char underneath. There was no way she could clean that before Annie died of hunger.

She grabbed the pot instead. It wouldn't be the first time she'd improvised in the kitchen.

Jackson returned with a stack of brightly colored women's garments in hand. Well, actually, they were piled so high he could barely see, but Jemma, their most skilled seamstress, was as generous as she was a busybody. She wouldn't let him leave until he'd spilled whom the clothes were for, where she was from, and how he'd come upon her.

So now he juggled a week's worth of clothes for both Terra and the little girl he still hadn't learned the name of. Jemma had tried to dump more into his arms, but he'd protested. He couldn't even open the door as it was.

Jackson awkwardly cradled the clothes while he reached out to grip the handle. He turned it, conscious of how tilting his arm caused the pile to lean precariously. He had to back away down the steps, pulling the door with him. Then came the rapid shuffle to anchor the door against his body, which almost sent the entire pile tumbling to the floor.

"You should have asked for help," Terra said, catching the door above his head and holding it open.

"Thanks." He walked around her, trying not to look down at the long legs peeking out of his shirt.

"You didn't have to get so much." She threw out an arm and stabilized the top of the pile.

He shrugged. "That's Jemma for you." He placed the pile on the entry table, grabbed a skirt and handed it to Terra. "Here."

"Thanks." She waved the material, revealing it, before pulling it on. She motioned at the kitchen table, where the girl sat eating with her fingers. "Grab something to eat. I made plenty, I think."

Jackson looked over at the table. He hadn't noticed it before, but multiple plates stacked high with food sat off to the side. He sat down across from the girl. "So, I didn't get your name last night. I'm Jackson."

"Annie," she said, mumbling the name around a mashed, yellow lump rolling around her mouth. Based on the offerings, it could be any number of things.

Jackson loaded a plate with cheese, scrambled eggs, toast, and an apple and dug in.

Terra sat down at a plate of food with a single bite taken out of a piece of toast. "Annie, you can't just eat banana."

Annie scowled, but snagged a piece of toast and went at it like a lion tearing into its kill.

Terra rolled her eyes, but dug into her own food.

Jackson just watched them, a little mesmerized. For a moment, it was like a tableau of a happy family at the dinner table. He forgot that they probably weren't a family, and the events that had brought them together were not happy ones, certainly not for those two.

When she finished eating, Annie jumped up, saying, "All done," revealing that she too wore one of Jackson's t-shirts.

"Sit down, Anna Banana," Terra said, pressing down on her shoulder.

Annie huffed, dropping like a rock onto the seat.

"You can wait until everyone finishes."

Jackson smiled, memories of his own mother's admonishments, however dim they might be, surfacing briefly, the memories fuzzy with age.

Annie watched the two of them like a predator waiting to pounce. Probably, that was an apt comparison.

When they finished, both Terra and Jackson stood and Annie leapt out of her seat. Jackson reached to the table covered in clothes and chose some children's garments for her. "Here, Annie. What do you think?" He held out a crazy rainbow of colors, an eyesore to most, but he knew children often liked the bright colors.

Her eyes lit up, but she hesitated, looking up at him askingly.

He pushed the clothes toward her. "Go ahead. You can change in the bedroom."

She squealed, grabbed and hugged them to her chest, and raced off. Seconds later, she slammed the door with youthful exuberance.

"She's so adorable," Terra said, turning back to smile at him.

"Yes, she is."

"I still can't believe how well she's bounced back. When she arrived at the camp, she was screaming for her mother, crying and clinging to the man bringing her through the administration building. I tried to comfort her even though I still hadn't come to terms with my own stay there, and for a while, she refused to be separated from me.

"She would latch on, clinging to me, not giving me a moment's peace." She smiled. "That first night, she fell asleep on my chest, still holding on as if her life depended on it. Even though she's away from that place, I fear she'll still panic if I'm not nearby."

"She'll adjust. Children are amazing that way. They can recover from things that would destroy an adult." He sat down again at the table. "So, you sort of adopted her?"

She shrugged and leaned against the back of the couch. "I guess so. I couldn't leave her there. Especially not when she started shifting. I mean, before that, I definitely wanted to escape, but I didn't try in earnest until she came up to me excited to show me her new hair color. Until then, I was just coping. After that, I was afraid."

"You did good. And you'll fit right in around here. You both will."

She gave him a wry smile. "I don't even know where *here* is."

"I guess the best way to describe it would be a shifter caravan."

Terra blinked, a surprised look on her face. "Everyone here are shifters?" She blanched.

He nodded. "Did you think most shifters lived among humans? We aren't human, Terra, even if some can reproduce with them."

"Only some?"

"Women always can. Sometimes men can too if one of their parents was human. But most men in shifter caravans can't. I don't really know why. It just is."

Terra nodded. "What do you do here?"

He smiled at her. The question was just so innocent, so guileless. "We live. It's a simpler life, but I think it's better. We look out for each other, something humans haven't done for a long time." He scowled, but vanquished the bad mood. He didn't need it.

"That's all a little vague."

"I suppose it is. I can give you a tour and introduce you around once Annie gets changed. If you want, you can also change your shirt. Jemma provided enough for a week or more, so you don't have to wear what you slept in."

Terra nodded, grabbed a shirt from behind him, not even bothering to look at it, and closed herself off in the bedroom with Annie.

CHAPTER NINE

Kyle rubbed his bare chin, trying to make sense of the information they'd gathered so far. He stood in his office, enjoying the quiet. They'd taped a wall of data with strings and pins to connect everything together.

He couldn't say it made a hell of a lot of sense.

But then, neither did any of the task force meetings he'd been to. Each time he went, he sat back as people argued back and forth, picking apart the evidence, pushing for their own direction in the investigation. Each time, the same thought rolled through his head.

We're falling apart.

As he looked back at the wall, he had to admit the sub-space pilot lead had been a good idea, giving them good leads, but he was still missing something. Unfortunately, two days had gone by and they were running dry again.

He paced along, skirting the corner of the desk which came too close to the wall, but not really taking in the details. He stopped at the far corner by the door, staring at the list of components, passing his finger over the words.

His mind started to click into gear, slowly but it was starting. A hint of an idea, but an idea nonetheless.

A knock cracked against his door, jarring him out of his thoughts. He nearly jumped out of his skin. "What the fuck?" He glared at the door, then sighed.

"Come in."

Kaufman slammed the door open, a huge grin on his face. "How's it going?"

Kyle scowled, irritated with his partner. He tried to retrieve any whispers of the epiphany he'd been on the cusp of, but it had dissipated like smoke in a breeze. "Do you have anything?"

Kaufman's face fell, showing one of his rare moments of somber expression. "No. I checked in with the task force, but frankly," he nodded at the wall, "ours is more detailed than theirs. Any ideas?"

Kyle scoffed and leaned against his desk, crossing his arms. "Just trying to pull something out of my ass, that's all."

Kaufman barked a laugh. "If anyone can do it, you can." After only a second, the serious look returned. "What were you looking at last? Maybe I can give you a fresh set of eyes?"

Kyle pointed at the list. "Be my guest."

Jackson waited for the girls to get changed. A list formed in his head of things he had to do. He had to set up the second bedroom, which usually served as his office. He would be sleeping in there for the foreseeable future. But first, he needed to give Terra and Annie a tour of the caravan, introducing them to everyone.

Then there were his normal duties. He needed to check on their supplies, see if they had everything they needed, balance the books on the caravan's finances…

He sighed.

Terra would need a place among their people. He didn't know what she was good at or what she did for a living before. No doubt, it would be useless here. Most things were, but he was sure she would adapt.

Terra stepped out in a black short-sleeved shirt and vibrant skirt that reached her ankles. Behind her, Annie spun into view, her skirt flying out around her to the music of her giggles.

"Are you two ready for your tour?"

Terra nodded, and Annie latched onto her arm, a shy smile on her face.

They left his home, Jackson several paces ahead, walking backwards, and the girls trailing behind. He couldn't help noticing the distance between him and the girls, and his heart sank. Was she afraid of him? Nervous? She'd been closer in his trailer, but then again, there was no space in the trailer. In there, keeping a distance was a couple inches at times.

"Wow, pretty," Annie said, jumping up to swat at the colorful fabric that served as decoration around the caravan. It was made of thick dyed wool, and served a wide variety of purposes, including acting as shade, a tent, partitions, and wind and rain barriers.

Terra noticed too, but she kept her own council, not even responding to Annie.

He wished he knew what she was thinking.

Everything seemed so much *more* in the light of day. Last night, the caravan had been awash in subtle shades of gray, but now the colors assaulted her. Terra fell back a few more steps, overwhelmed after weeks of nothing but gray and a lifetime of her own preference for earthy greens and browns.

Here, they'd unabashedly declared, "We are who we are and the hell with what anyone else thinks." She tended to agree, but she also slowed a bit more with each step.

What am I doing?

As she scanned her surroundings, the thought plagued her. She didn't know what she was doing, but more than that, she didn't know what she *should* be doing. Should she be grabbing Annie and running away again? Should she stay put, gather intel?

Jackson watched her, and again she couldn't read his expression. He almost seemed *more* unreadable now than last night.

I don't belong here.

The feeling only grew as they moved around the caravan. No one else showed their faces, leaving them in a sea of stillness that reminded her of post-apocalyptic movies. Sure, she'd woken up to Jackson burning breakfast, but it wasn't *that* early. The sun still tinted the sky above the trees in vibrant colors, but it had done so for a while now.

The caravan was eerie, quiet and isolating in a way even the camp hadn't been. She felt *other*, different, like a sociologist stepping into a foreign village, invading the culture and tainting it.

I don't belong here.

She listened hard, but couldn't hear anything at first. Then chirping birds and insects serenaded the empty world, sounds she'd rarely experienced living her whole life in cities. Still, no human noises came to her, at least none she could recognize. Had anyone been awake when Jackson left to find clothes for them?

"It's a little early at the moment, but the central resources and storage are up ahead. The community is always set up around them. That's the laundry, that's raw storage, and that's the community hall. Other than that, there's just individual residences."

"What's raw storage?"

"That's where we store raw materials. Wool, shelf-stable food, cloth, and such. Anything that needs refrigeration is stored in the community hall."

"Oh, okay."

Jackson turned to the larger trailer and attached tent he'd called the "community hall." Off to the side, a portable grill/smoker waited to be used, filling the air with the lingering scent of smoke. He pulled back the tent flap, ushering them in. Inside, folding tables and chairs filled the tented space in haphazard fashion. Everything could be moved or folded away for whatever purpose the community had.

They walked through the sea of foldable furniture to the entrance of the trailer. There, it looked to have been gutted. Multiple chest freezers took up the space to the right and bare walls to the left. The entire facing wall was designed for cooking for the masses. Several full-sized refrigerators, three stoves, and plenty of counter space to prepare. The other wall just held straps, probably to store everything while traveling.

"The caravan has lots of meals that start right here. The freezers mostly hold deer meat, but we'll keep frozen bread and vegetables if there's a danger they'll go bad. If you need anything, it will either be here or the raw storage trailer."

Terra nodded as Annie let go of her hand to check out the refrigerator and said, "Where are the bananas?"

"We don't generally store bananas. We don't grow them, so we have to buy them and they don't store well."

Annie pouted, crossing her arms.

"You just ate, Annie," Terra reminded her.

"I like bananas." Her expression didn't pick up at all.

"I know you do."

"Don't worry, Annie. Someone goes shopping at least every few days. We can't produce everything we need. We make a lot of excess to sell so we can buy everything else."

"Jackson, is that you?" a male voice called from behind them.

"In here."

A large man stepped up to the door, shoulders taking up the doorway and making Terra shrink back. He nodded at Terra and winking at Annie. "You gonna be able to help today?"

"Sure. I'm just showing Terra and Annie around."

"Well, it's a pleasure to meet you two ladies. I'm Micah."

"Likewise, Micah." Though friendly, he alarmed her, making her want to run. Without even realizing it, she found herself almost climbing Jackson where before she'd been giving him a wide berth.

Jackson had finished his tour in the community hall which slowly filled as the morning dragged on. There were only a few dozen people in the caravan, and by midmorning, most of them had passed through the tent. As a whole, his people were loud, colorful, and energetic, often leaving him exhausted. Today wasn't so bad.

Terra stayed glued to Jackson's side the rest of the morning with Annie within a finger's distance at any given time. Annie seemed more willing to explore, her eyes wandering wildly, watching everyone with anxiety and awe. She observed the children who ran screaming into the tent with the most intensity, but didn't budge, staying plastered to Terra's leg.

By noon, he'd introduced them to everyone, and he really needed to help Micah with his animals. He looked over at Terra apologetically. "I have some work to do. Do you want to stay here or go back to the trailer?"

Annie looked around but didn't speak. A bunch of children were on the other side of the tent as several women working on various crafts watched. He could see her yearning.

"Back to the trailer should be fine," Terra said, not meeting his eyes.

Jackson nodded, expecting that answer. Terra wasn't comfortable with the people here yet, but she would be in time. He felt confident in that. He would make sure of it.

CHAPTER TEN

yle pulled to a stop a couple blocks away from the warehouse. Outside, wind howled, and cans rattled and loose paper fluttered as the weather beat at them, pushing them across the expanse of pavement. He ducked his head, looking out through the windshield at the property in question. It was nondescript, without any signs or emblems to indicate ownership. In good repair, it was definitely large enough for the suspected purpose, but the entire place was quiet, eerily so.

"You're sure?" He turned to his partner, who dwarfed the sedan's passenger seat. Then again, a supermodel would probably overflow that seat.

Kaufman nodded. "Regular shipments of regulated sub-space engine components, but not among the companies contracted with the NSS or NASA."

Kyle nodded back, but still felt like they were missing something. Maybe it was because this just seemed too damned convenient. It hadn't even been a day or two since Kaufman stared at that list of components and came up with the idea. Shouldn't this warehouse have been harder to find?

"Come on, let's go." He popped the door open, the piece of contoured steel fighting him as the wind caught it and pushed back.

"Well, this is a damned ugly day to be in the field."

He glanced over at Kaufman, who stood behind the passenger door, squinting into the wind. Kyle shrugged. He'd had worse. "Come on." He closed his door, pulling his gun from the holster. The thatched pattern of the grip pressed into his palm, grounding him.

His gut churned as he approached, Kaufman at his side.

Something's not right.

He shook out his left arm, trying to shake off the uneasy feeling. It wasn't helping, and he needed to keep his focus.

The building didn't have windows on the front, just long sheets of corrugated metal and a single door, so they approached quickly, sidling up to opposite sides of the door. He looked at Kaufman.

We should have called for backup.

But it was too late now.

Terra peeked out the window of the trailer, ill at ease after the morning in the community hall. There was something off about this place. She couldn't quite place it, but she had this nagging Stepford Wives impression.

Granted, nobody she'd met was perfect, but everyone was just a bit *too* friendly and accepting, especially of someone they didn't know. It made her nervous. Nobody was that nice without a reason.

Annie bounced onto the couch. "Tewa!"

"What, Annie?"

"I wanna play."

"What do you want to play?"

Annie paused. "I don't know."

"You want to play with the other kids."

"No, I don't."

"You can tell the truth, Annie. It won't hurt my feelings." She changed tack. "What do you think of this place?"

"I don't know." Annie shrugged, her entire body moved by the action.

"Annie…"

The little girl didn't speak at first. She did her adorable "I'm thinking" look where she pursed her lips and looked up at the ceiling.

Terra watched her expressions closely, shifting slowly from contemplative to sad. "You miss your parents, don't you?"

Annie nodded without looking Terra in the eyes.

"Oh, Annie." She pulled the girl onto her lap, holding her close. "I don't know if you can go home." Or if you'd be wanted. How many broadcasts or news articles had she encountered where parents denounced their shifter children saying, "I don't know where it could have come from. It wasn't us."

Annie buried her face in Terra's neck for the first time in days, sniffles assaulting the air.

Terra held her even tighter. "It'll be okay."

Terra had put Annie down for an afternoon nap, leaving her alone with her thoughts. It wasn't a pretty place to be. She considered going for a walk, but the idea of running into anyone sent chills down her spine.

I shouldn't have come here.

But where could she go? Where else was there? She couldn't return to her apartment. Sure, it was on auto-bill pay, and the lease wouldn't end for another few months, but then what? She couldn't get a job. She'd had a hard enough time finding work *before* this whole fiasco. Returning home just delayed the inevitable.

Sitting at Jackson's table, she looked out at the world beyond, seeing nothing but blurs of brown and green. Her nails idly tapped the cheap surface, clicking sharply like a metronome for her mind.

I just want to forget.

Boy, wasn't *that* the. truth. She would have done *anything* to forget everything that had happened. It still felt surreal, like a movie she might have watched once. Things like this didn't happen to people in real life. They just didn't.

This isn't happening.

She shook her head, trying to dispel the weird feeling that had settled there. Children rushed past her window, their voices muted. She smiled, their happy faces tugging at her heart-strings. One looked back, taunting the others, then spun around and shifted, becoming a dog and taking off at even greater speed into the trees. She flinched, looking away, but not before the rest of the group followed suit. She turned back to the packed earth outside as the last of their dark tails, one with a white patch on the tip, disappeared into the woods.

Terra could have done without the reminder. She didn't want to think about shifting. She just wanted everything to go back to normal.

A sick feeling invaded her gut, made worse by the happiness only moments before. It swirled and grew, making her swallow hard. She needed to keep it under control. She breathed slowly through her nose, but it didn't help.

I don't belong here.

I'll never belong here.

Terra bit her lip as, newly revived after her nap, Annie rushed ahead, running down the path leading to the community hall. Once there was a good distance, she would always look back, impatiently urging Terra onward. If that didn't work, she would hurry back, tugging on Terra's hand. It was adorable, if a bit exhausting.

And did nothing to dispel the feeling of exposure as Terra stepped farther away from Jackson's trailer. She wanted to hide, spying on the world with a jaded eye, ready for the next blow. She didn't have that luxury, unfortunately.

Seeing Terra lost in her thoughts, Annie raced back and yanked Terra's hand again, beaming up at her. "Tewa, Tewa. Look what I can do!" She shifted, turning into a little dog, letting off a happy woof.

Terra froze, her heart seizing in her chest. *No.* She dropped to her knees, staring Annie dead in the face. "Shift back." A desperation surged through her.

She can't do that.

It's not safe.

They could never return to the human world, the *real* world, if Annie kept shifting. It would be too dangerous. She wouldn't be able to protect her.

She shook her head as Annie returned to her little girl form and clutched Annie's arms in both hands. "No, Annie. You can't do that. Don't you remember?"

Annie pouted, her entire body sagging. "But everyone else is doing it?"

Terra gave Annie her sternest expression while her heart pounded away. "Just because everyone else does something, doesn't me *you* should."

"Isn't it safe here?" Annie's voice turned quiet, shaky.

Terra sighed, pulling Annie into a hug. "I don't know, Anna Banana. I just don't know."

That evening, Terra sat in the trailer, alone with Annie. Jackson hadn't returned yet, and the sun had started setting on the horizon above the trees. On the couch, Annie was nodding off, but still determined to stay awake, to play some more.

"All right, Anna Banana. Time for bed." Terra stood, scooping up the little girl.

"No!" Annie protested, squirming in her arms, but even those protests were half-hearted, not having the energy to be believable.

She dropped Annie onto the bed to start their nightly ritual. Before long, the space grew quiet. Terra sat alone and idle, listless without Annie to occupy her time. She glanced around. What should she do? What was there *to* do?

She glanced at the dirty dishes in the sink, but nixed the idea.

It would make too much noise. A walk across the trailer revealed a bedroom/office on the other end from where they'd slept. The room was tiny and neat, and Terra felt like an intruder just standing in the doorway.

She decided to straighten up their chamber instead. Crossing the trailer, she peeked, but Annie was dead to the world. So long as she wasn't too loud, she wouldn't disturb her. She shouldn't make a lot of noise picking up clothes, and at least she would leave the place as she'd found it. But then she paused, wondering at the wording in her head.

Did she intend to leave? Was she just waiting for her moment again? It would be hard. She doubted Jackson would stop her, but if she did leave, where would she go? She couldn't go back to her old life. That bridge had been burned. Was she just yearning for what she could never get back?

She walked into the bedroom and changed her mind. She needed to do a load of laundry. The sheets from last night were heaped on the floor covered in mud, and she now remembered that hers and Annie's dirty clothes were lying on the bathroom floor.

Terra scooped up the bedding then grabbed the clothes from the bathroom, dumping them together and wrapping them into a ball. She picked them up and dropped them near the door. She thought about walking to the laundry and cleaning them, but anxiety gripped her. Just this afternoon, she'd been walking behind Annie, feeling watched, judged, isolated, and out of place.

Terra stared out the window. Could she slip out and clean them without being seen? But that would mean leaving Annie alone. She looked at the sleeping girl, gnawing her lip in hesitation. She stood there for the longest time, standing on a precipice.

She couldn't keep stalling, waiting in limbo for a solution to smack her in the head. That was how she'd dealt with her problems for weeks now. First firmly believing that if she could only reach out to someone in authority, she could make them see reason. Then allowing herself to get so absorbed in caring for Annie that she didn't do much more than exist, certainly not thinking about the future.

It had to stop. That wasn't any way to live. Terra stared out the window again. Her mind and body danced on an edge, pushing and pushing. She could barely breathe. Like the rest of her, her breath snagged in her lungs, stuck.

On an impulse, she grabbed the door handle, gripping it in a white-knuckled hold, the cold metal pressing almost painfully into her flesh. She closed her eyes, embracing the sensation, the reality of it. It balanced her, centered her, and she took slow, deep breaths.

She glanced back at Annie, sleeping peacefully on the couch, and leaned against the door, hand still firmly on the handle. She smiled and looked away. Somehow, they'd become a family of sorts. And if Terra could get over herself, she felt Annie had a real opportunity to be happy here. That meant more than anything else, didn't it?

For Annie.

She scooped up the bundled laundry, twisted the knob and quietly slipped out. Scanning left and right, no one waited, poised to hit her with a helpful or friendly greeting. She felt certain she would run away from the next person who said, "Hi," to her. She'd grown up in a city. People just didn't greet strangers. It was an unwritten rule.

Terra hefted the bundle over her shoulder and set off, head tilted down to avoid eye contact with anyone she might encounter. Maybe they wouldn't notice her. Maybe they would assume she was just one of the people they'd built a community with.

One could hope.

No one paid her any notice until a small robot, hobbled together with a variety of parts from defunct equipment, maneuvered up next to her and said, "You should twist the cloth before grasping it to get a better grip. You should carry it over your shoulder to better balance the weight load."

"What the fuck?" Terra said, whirling around to face the disturbingly human voice. The deep baritone made her think some tall, burly man had snuck up on her. Instead, she faced a two-foot tall robot, which peered up at her with an innocent look on its face.

Terra backed away, moving toward the laundry, but it followed her, hopeful as a puppy dog.

"I'm Timmy," it said as she stopped.

"Good for you." She picked up her pace, but the little-robot-that-could easily matched her. "Knock it off."

It pouted. It actually pouted. How the hell could it make facial expressions?

Terra sighed. Somehow, the tiny Frankenstein's monster of a robot was almost as adorable as a puppy when it pouted. She about-faced, trying to ignore the thing as she reached the laundry and opened the door, not looking down as it wandered past her.

Two washing machines lined one wall, sitting opposite some counters and shelves loaded with handmade laundry detergent. Terra dropped her bundle on the counter and started loading the nearest washer.

"For maximum efficiency and to reduce the probability of the washing machine going off balance, you should…"

Terra glared at it. "I don't care, Timmy." She finished loading it and added the soap.

"You should use 25% less soap to improve effectiveness and prevent irritation and sensitization."

Terra looked down at Timmy and scowled. She suspected this little monster would be the bane of her existence…

CHAPTER ELEVEN

I should have listened to my gut.

Kyle stood outside a hospital room, hesitant to enter. He should have called in the task force, should have been more cautious. Hell, *he* was the responsible one in the partnership. It was his fault.

He pushed the door open and forced a smile as he entered, his gaze focusing on the occupied hospital bed. A beeping from the monitors serenaded the room and behind him, voices made announcements over the intercom.

"Dude!" Kaufman said, a drugged up smile on his face as his head lolled to the side. "If it takes that much effort, don't bother."

Kyle frowned, scratching at the bandage on the back of his hand. He'd escaped the explosion with minor scrapes and burns. The doctors had shoved him off after only a few hours in the ER. Kaufman, on the other hand, had come in with burns on his back and a punctured lung.

Now, he lay on his stomach, pupils dilated wide as he stared into the distance. Unfortunately, his partner had uneven burn patterns, a combination of second- and third-degree burns that meant he could still feel pain, thus the drugs.

Kyle sat down in a chair next to the bed. "Any news on your prognosis?"

Kaufman shifted, like he wanted to shrug but couldn't. "Just getting touched by lovely ladies on a regular basis. Not so bad."

Kyle scoffed. "About the healing, moron."

"Don't know. Lung is good, but they want to wait and see if I'll need skin grafts or not." He tried to look nonchalant, but the meds left him without any guile.

Kaufman was scared.

It had been a week since the explosion, a week of Kyle filling out reports and attending debriefings. Nobody blamed him, even applauding him for getting his partner out alive, for calling in emergency services. He'd received pats on the back, been called a hero.

Kyle didn't feel like a hero. He felt like a failure, a fraud. He could have done more, *should* have done more. Over the last week, he'd racked his mind, trying to figure what he could have done better, how it could have made a difference.

"Hey," Kaufman said, his voice unusually strong, unslurred. "Don't."

Kyle looked up, surprised at his partner's severe tone. "Kaufman?"

"Not your fault."

"I don't care, Timmy!"

Yep, Terra had been right. Timmy had become the only bad spot in a life that had turned around surprisingly fast. She'd tentatively fallen in love with the culture here. And after a brief acclimation period, she'd accepted the rapid welcome of the community, even if it still weirded her out from time to time. A lot of the women had taken her into their confidences, and the older women had taken her under their wings, trying to teach her new skills or recipes.

She and Annie still slept in the master bedroom while Jackson used his office to sleep in. It had a bed, but was normally tucked away. Terra made meals for the three of them, and Jackson encouraged Terra to take on the administrative tasks of the caravan. She'd been hesitant at first, not feeling she had the right, that someone who'd been there longer, who could more easily be trusted, should do it. She wasn't a member of the caravan, hadn't proven herself, had no real connections to it. What right did she have to take on such an important role?

Jackson'd had a logical answer for every protest. He'd been handling it by himself, and while he managed, it was a lot to keep track of. Eventually, she caved. Not that she minded. She enjoyed retreating into the office and working on paperwork. She often did it when she felt overwhelmed.

"Terra, pay attention," Jackson said, drawing her focus back to the conversation at hand, specifically him trying to teach her to shift.

Terra didn't want to shift. She didn't see where she *had* to. What difference did it make if she didn't? As far as she was concerned, she could go the rest of her life without shifting and it wouldn't change a damned thing. Jackson didn't quite see it that way, so she changed the subject. "It's his fault," she said, pointing at the diminutive robot.

Jackson tried to look stern, but a smile cracked his lips. Behind him, people poured out of the community hall, chatting away.

"Tewa, Tewa, look!" Annie said, running at them at full steam.

Terra searched out the little girl and smiled when she caught sight of her. "Anna Banana!" She opened her arms, then squawked when Annie shifted into a baby wild cat and pounced on her, dropping her to the ground. "Wow, easy on the claws, baby girl." The little cat's claws had dug into her, not doing damage but pinching like a bitch.

Her gut churned as Annie sat up and rubbed her head against the underside of Terra's chin, purring in a ratcheting pattern as she went.

She forced a light tone to her voice. "Now, where did you come up with this one?" Annie had shifted into new and interesting animals every other day. Most times, Terra flinched, unnerved and dismayed by Annie's continued attempts at shifting.

Annie looked around, then shifted back into a little girl. "Caleb showed me pictures of one on his phone."

Terra sighed. Caleb, teenager and tech genius, had designed Timmy the annoying robot, wanting to make an AI that would grow emotional attachment to people. When he wasn't trying to fix Timmy's more colorful character traits, he often showed the children pictures of animals they could try to shift into. Sometimes it worked well. Other times, he had to bring the little one to their parents to soothe until they were calm enough to shift back.

Much to Terra's chagrin, Annie was a genius at shifting, taking to it like breathing air. Terra had no interest in trying in kind, though. She didn't even want Annie to try, but good luck getting a toddler to cooperate when there were big kids doing the same thing not feet away. It was a losing battle. Terra made a motion with her head indicating Jackson should head off, and he smiled at them.

She knew the conversation on shifter lessons wasn't over, but she didn't mind. She had Annie and an entire community to support them, and while they were all shifters, very few of them shifted on a regular basis. When they did, it was often in minor ways, like improving night vision, stamina or coping with body image issues, which were flat out scary in shifters.

A couple people here changed by little bits every day. She had a hard time recognizing them, and she suspected being able to change their appearance so easily just fed whatever syndrome they had.

Terra stood, bringing Annie with her.

"You should lift with your legs and keep your back straight to avoid stress injuries."

She kicked him, sending the little bot flying a couple feet. "Oops, so sorry, Timmy. Didn't see you there. You should be careful where you stand."

Terra smiled. "Hey, Jemma," she said as she entered the community hall.

"Oh, Terra," the other woman said, wiggling in her seat at the other end of the tent.

Terra looked around, but didn't see any sign of Timmy. She'd given him the slip that morning and had every intention of keeping out of sight of him for as long as possible. "Any new projects?"

"Nothing special." Jemma waved at Terra to sit down across

from her. "I've been trying to decide what to do with this beautiful weave."

Terra leaned over the material, soaking up the riot of color. It was beautiful, if not exactly Terra's style. "Does anyone need anything specific?"

"Not really. I mean, the kids always need something new. Hand-me-downs only get so many uses, especially around here." She winked. Jemma had already replaced all the clothes Terra and Annie had been given. Terra helped, mostly by fetching whatever item Jemma wanted. She didn't exactly have a knack for sewing...

"Maybe something salable? What sells well?"

Jemma thought for a moment and nodded before leaning into her work.

Terra felt superfluous and wondered what more she could do. Most of the time, she felt useless, incompetent among these craftspeople. She scanned the tent, but other than Jemma, who was absorbed in her work, precious few were here at the moment.

Terra stood up without saying a word and walked out of the community hall. A stiff wind hit her as she exited and she huddled in on herself until it died. She hadn't noticed it when she entered, but little islands of yellow, orange, and red had pushed in on the verdant leaves surrounding the caravan.

How long had she been here? When did that slight chill hit the air? It felt like only yesterday the weather had been sweltering, oppressively hot, but it was always like that, the weather as changeable as a pregnant woman's mood swings.

Deciding on an action, she rotated on one foot and ambled back to Jackson's office. She felt more comfortable and useful holed up in there anyway. Everyone here was nice, but she still felt like she didn't belong, like an outsider, and that "Stepford Wives" impression had never quite left the back of her mind. Everyone was just too nice, too accepting, and until the dark underbelly showed itself, she wouldn't be able to get comfortable, to relax.

Terra opened the door to the trailer to silence. Annie had asked to spend the day playing with friends, and Jackson was off helping one member or another. She hadn't really paid attention, and she didn't really care.

She sat down at the desk, noting the pile of papers that hadn't existed the day before. Honestly, Jackson could learn a thing or two about organization. She picked them up and placed them in the intake tray.

And froze.

If you asked her what had sparked the moment, she couldn't have said. To this day, she still couldn't figure out what it was, but it hit her like lightning. The other shoe. The dark underbelly. It hit with the force of a Mack truck.

Here she'd been recovering, getting back the optimistic person she'd been before all this happened, trying to find ways of adjusting, and she'd completely spaced. She'd been so focused on the now, on Annie, that she'd blanked out anything else, no matter how critical. Again!

How could I have forgotten?

How could I have been so thoughtless?

So selfish?

Terra stood up, knocking the chair back with a screeching groan that toppled it to the floor. She didn't bother to right it as she jogged out of the trailer. By the time she hit the bottom step, she took off into a flat run, zeroing in on the first citizen she could find.

She didn't know who the leader of the caravan was. He'd been described as old and wise, bringing to mind an old man with a long, gray beard. So far, she hadn't seen anyone matching that description. In fact, not a single soul in the entire caravan looked a day over fifty. But she *did* know Jackson, and she knew damn well he knew about the shifter camp. He'd helped her get away from there, for fuck's sake.

"You," she barked, reaching some poor, unsuspecting person, "Have you seen Jackson?"

He nodded, a nervous expression flashing on his face as he pointed off into the distance. "He's helping do some repairs on a generator. Can't miss him."

Terra didn't dignify it with a response. Jackson had an ass-chewing coming, and she had every intention of delivering.

CHAPTER TWELVE

Jackson knelt on the ground in front of the nonfunctional generator. It had been repaired ad infinitum. He very much wanted to scrap it, but they needed it. Caleb hadn't yet come up with the solar generators that would make this piece of junk defunct.

He reached in, adjusted a pressure valve, and pulled his grease-smudged hand out again. "All right, try it again."

The other man yanked, pulling the cord to start it up. The engine puttered before going quiet again. He tried it two more times to the same effect before shaking his head.

Jackson nodded and reached in again, scouring the parts for anything that might indicate why the generator wouldn't start.

"Jackson!" a shrill voice screamed, causing him to jump and scrape his hand against the inside of the generator as he jerked backward.

It took him a moment to realize the voice he'd heard was Terra's. He turned around, surprised by the aggressive expression on her face as she stormed his way. "Yes, Terra?"

She stepped up to him, but didn't speak, dragging in several deep breaths. Anger rolled off her, making him tense up. Finally, she took one deep breath and spoke. "I need to speak with you."

"Go ahead," he said, wondering if he really wanted to hear. He'd lived long enough to know better than to invite a woman's ire.

She glared at the man next to her, who turned tail and ran, smart enough to flee this conversation. "The camp." She didn't say anything else. Just those two words.

"What about it?" He wasn't sure what she was getting at.

Several expressions crossed her face, none of which he could identify. None of them looked good, though. "We just left them there!" She flailed her arms up and down.

"So?" None of the others had the good sense to try to escape. As far as he was concerned, that camp and its inhabitants were nothing more than unfortunate neighbors.

Anger flared again across her face, her body tensing. "What do you mean, 'so'?" She lunged forward as if to hit him, but no blow landed.

He shrugged. "It's none of our business."

Her eyes rounded. "What do you mean 'it's none of our business'? Of course, it's our business. They're shifters too."

He shook his head. "They're a bunch of untrained shifters, raised in a society of fear, anger, and prejudice. They aren't much better than humans." *With unfortunate genes.*

"There are children there." This time her voice turned cold, and Jackson suspected he was about to lose big time.

"Look around you, Terra. *This* is our home, not that camp, not the human world you come from. You're. Not. Human.

Stop acting like one. Do you see space for all the people in that camp? We can't support them.

"And then what? Attract the attention of the US government? Do you think they'll ignore us stealing their prisoners? Of course not. They'll hunt us down. Rescuing them puts everyone here at risk."

"You rescued us. You took us in." Terra's voice was quieter now, a sad, unreadable expression on her face.

"That's different."

"Is it?"

He nodded. "You're strong. You escaped on your own. And even though you risked not escaping at all, you brought Annie with you."

Terra stood before him, pensive, relaxing into a blank expression he didn't entirely trust. "I can't believe you, Jackson. You helped me, accepted me, supported me. You gave me food, clothing, and a place to live, to belong. I saw the community here, the acceptance." She shook her head, this odd almost smile on her face. "I knew it was too good to be true. It was. You're not accepting. You're even more prejudiced than the people you shun."

She whipped around, looking back at him before taking off. "I don't care if we can support them here. Anything is better than being imprisoned for nothing more than genes you were born with. If you won't rescue them, I will."

Jackson stood up, reaching out his arm to call her back, but the word lodged in his throat, silenced forever.

Terra dashed away her tears with hands jerky and rigid with

emotion. How could he? Better yet, how did she not see it? What had she missed? She racked her brain, trying to find that one clue, that one puzzle piece that made it all fit.

She threw up her hands. "Why the hell was he waiting outside the camp if he had no intention of rescuing us useless, bigoted shifters, so far inferior to his people?" But she thought she might know, and it spoke worse of him than that entire conversation did.

He saw them *all* as threats.

He'd been scoping out the enemy and stumbled upon her instead. When he judged her and found her worthy, apparently far more worthy than the others he left to their fate, he brought her home.

Terra shook her head, disgusted with him for his attitudes and herself for not seeing it sooner. What had she been thinking?

Clearly, she hadn't been.

And God, the rest suddenly made so much sense now. Why she'd been accepted so readily. It hadn't been generosity or goodness. No, they saw her as one of them, an insider, and not an "other" to be shunned and hated. By escaping, she'd run their gauntlet and come out the other side.

She sighed and kept going, staring down at the packed dirt path, kicking the few leaves that had already fallen. Wind rustled the trees, sending more leaves to flutter to the ground. She walked past Jackson's trailer, not really sure what she was going to do. What could she do? Well, she planned on rescuing the others. That much was certain. But she couldn't risk Annie so she would have to leave her here.

For now.

Annie couldn't stay here in the long run. As soon as she rescued the others, she was collecting Annie and leaving this place. It ripped her guts out even thinking about it, but she couldn't leave Annie to be raised here surrounded by bigots. She would rather uproot the poor girl for the third time in a manner of weeks than do that.

Terra had reached the line of cars before she realized that it had taken them a while to get here by vehicle. She couldn't imagine how long it would take to walk. In front of her, Jackson's black SUV loomed, and Terra had a moment of conscience before reassuring herself it would be fine. After all, she was only borrowing it.

Jackson had sat down on Philippe's front step hours ago. He'd needed his friend's counsel somewhat desperately, but Philippe kept his own schedule, and one could never truly know where the bastard was from moment to moment. He liked to hunt and often returned with a great big buck dragging behind him. Sometimes, he hunted in human form. Most times, he did not.

He also enjoyed fishing. Again sometimes, in human form, most times, not.

Jackson frequently join him, a certain peace settling over him at returning to such a basic, primal part of himself. While this form was his most comfortable, the one he felt most himself in, it helped ease his burdens and stresses to slip free and let out a little aggression on a more worthwhile pursuit.

And it didn't get more worthwhile than feeding the caravan.

"You look like you could use a hunt," his friend said, his deep voice rumbling the words, making him think of the bear form Philippe preferred when fishing.

Jackson glanced up. "Hello, old friend."

Philippe waved the greeting away. "If you don't let it out, it'll fester, and you've already got a hell of a lot festering in that rickety old carcass of yours."

Jackson smirked, shaking his head. "Rickety, huh? You look a hell of a lot more rickety than me."

"This?" He pointed to the wrinkles on his face with his massive paw. "That's just wisdom. It's supposed to accumulate over time. I notice you have precious few."

It was a common joke between the two. Jackson, though much older, preferred the form of a human in his twenties. It felt comfortable to him, right, and Philippe often razzed him for it. Conversely, Philippe wore his age proudly, or at least some of it. He appeared somewhere closer to forty, with fine lines, roughened skin, and little bits of gray speckled throughout his dark hair.

Philippe sat on a stump he used for chopping wood and crossed his arms. Splinters of wood, uncut logs, and bark surrounded him. "Speak."

"I'm not a dog."

"Woof," Philippe said, smiling. "We're men. We're all dogs. And shifters worse than others." He winked.

Jackson looked away, staring at the rough-hewn railing of Philippe's porch, unable to meet his friend's gaze. "Terra took off."

"What'd you do?"

He jerked his head back. "What do you mean?"

"Well, clearly, you did something. Or maybe *didn't* do something."

"Why do you assume it was me? Why couldn't she have been at fault?"

Philippe looked at him, doubt in his eyes. "I've met the woman. Skittish as a mouse, but sweet as can be. She's got a light in her. It's been doused, but all it'll take is a little TLC, and it will be bright enough to light even the darkest night again, I have no doubt."

Jackson grunted, not liking the direction of this conversation all of a sudden. He stared at his trailer, his mind momentarily entertaining the idea of walking away, but he wouldn't, couldn't. Especially not with a friend like Philippe.

"Why did she take off?"

"She was upset that I hadn't rescued the others at the camp."

"And why didn't you?"

"You know why! We can't afford the exposure. And what would we do with them once we saved them? Bring them here? We're self-sustaining here, but not nearly *that* well off. What if the government tracked us back here? What then?"

Philippe shrugged. "Then we leave."

Jackson scoffed. "This is our home. Sure, we don't spend all our time here, but it's still home. Do you really want to put us through the risk of finding a new site for the summers?"

"No, of course not, but it wouldn't be the first time, and it would certainly be worthwhile. Do you honestly think anyone here would begrudge the change if it meant freeing all those people?" Philippe watched him for a few moments, the intense gaze making Jackson nervous. "But that wasn't the entire argument, was it?"

"She said I was prejudiced."

Philippe laughed, nearly falling off his log.

"See," Jackson said, waving his hand at his friend. "It's laughable. I'm not prejudiced."

"Jackson, my friend, you've been prejudiced for decade upon decade. It's only gotten worse with age. Each new experience around humans only reinforced that hatred, blinding you to all the good humanity is capable of."

Jackson's jaw dropped, floored by the words coming out of his friend's mouth. Sure, he wasn't the most accepting person. Leading a community like he did meant having to make the hard decisions, having to be cautious, skeptical. But he made those decisions, and sometimes he made assumptions because he couldn't afford to give someone the chance to hurt his people.

Better safe than sorry.

"I do have to make decisions that may appear that way, but I have no choice," he admitted aloud. "With the camps out there just waiting for one of us to fuck up in public and the general hatred flung at our kind constantly, how can I not? It's the only way to protect our people."

"And yet you can't fight prejudice with prejudice. It only breeds off itself. Besides, I think you have somewhere you need to be, don't you?"

Jackson nodded, uncomfortable with the realization that he might have handled things wrong for too long. He stood up and ran to the cars, ran in the only direction he suspected Terra would go.

CHAPTER THIRTEEN

"*S*he stole my fucking car," Jackson said, flabbergasted by the empty space where his car had been.

A deep laugh roared behind him, and he looked back and glared. Philippe had followed him.

"What do you want?"

"To help," his friend said, holding up a couple bolt cutters in one hand and an airsoft rifle he used to scare away critters in the other. "Though I'm thinking we'll need my truck as well." He glanced back at the green pickup a few cars back.

"What's with the toy gun?"

"Oh, this? Shooting out cameras."

Because why wouldn't you try to shoot out surveillance equipment with a weapon that was only accurate inside the viewing range of the camera… "I'm thinking we won't need it."

Philippe furrowed his brows.

Jackson scrambled for an excuse. "They'd surely come investigate when the camera went down."

"Oh yeah, you're right. Well, no matter. I'll just leave it in the truck." He walked back, opened the door, and tossed it behind the seat.

For all the man was helpful, and Jackson trusted his counsel implicitly, he often had an almost comical innocence about him, not quite seeing through the simpler, less philosophical problems.

"Whatcha standing around for? Get in the truck." Philippe slammed his door.

Jackson shook his head, but jogged forward, eager to be on his way himself.

Terra sat against a tree, using the woods as cover, waiting for nightfall. She'd been there quite a while now and the more she waited, the more the same thought kept drifting through her head.

I should have planned this out better.

She had no idea how she would get in and out without being seen, nor how she would convince and wrangle dozens of men and women to follow her. *I'm not a leader!* But she had to be. For this, she had to lead them, and it was starting to freak her out.

Deep reds and oranges now tinted the sky, and she was no closer to coming up with a plan.

"Do you have a plan?" Jackson said from over her shoulder.

She jumped. How did he know?! How did he *find* her?! "Of course."

He nodded and sat down next to her. "Well, I figured you might need some help. I'm sure you've got a plan, and you can get in and out. You've done it before. But coordinating so many people *will* be easier with a few extra hands."

"Precisely," another deeper voice said behind them.

Terra spun around on her butt, not an easy thing to do, and took in the bearlike beast of a man before her. There was something paternal and warm to him that made her want to like him, to trust him. It warred with the part of her that still felt burned and scarred by the realization about Jackson and the caravan by association.

"I brought the bolt cutters," the bear said, lifting them in both hands, the handles on them as long as her arms.

"Great. Thanks," she whispered.

"I assume your plan is to wait until nightfall? Until it's dark?" Jackson said, drawing her attention.

"Yes. It'll be a lot easier to stay hidden, but I'm not sure how to get the others out undetected. The only gap in the cameras—at least a few weeks ago, I don't know about now— is that area behind those buildings. I figure so long as there's no light once night settles in, then there're no cameras. I don't see anything right now, but I could have missed something."

Jackson squinted, turning his head back and forth. "No, I don't see any either. Or any lights for that matter. It doesn't look like they tried to fix their system after your escape."

Terra scoffed, shaking her head. "Classic government red tape."

"Probably."

Terra turned back to the fence a few feet in front of her. She had mixed feelings about Jackson being here. She was grateful for the extra help. At the same time, she resented him not choosing this path on his own. How could he think so much less of these people that he would refuse them the common decency everyone deserved, whether they be people or animals?

It had to mean something that he was here. It just had to. A part of her simply couldn't accept the possibility that she'd been so wrong about him. Then she remembered the argument earlier today and went stiff with rage. "Who's looking after Annie?"

"Oh, Caleb is," Jackson said, before returning to his conversation with the friend he still hadn't introduced to her.

Great. God only knew what she would return to with Caleb watching her. Probably, a baby animal. Hopefully, not anything too dangerous. She looked to the duo behind her. "So, um, you didn't introduce yourself."

Smooth, real smooth.

The other man laughed, not at all insulted by her abrupt and rude observation. "Name's Philippe."

"Terra," she said in reply.

"I know. We may not have been introduced, but I've seen you around and it's easy to learn the name of a new person in a community our size."

"True."

"Well, I'm this knucklehead's best friend."

"Hey!" Jackson protested, not putting much effort into it.

"Aren't you a bit old…" she started but stopped at Philippe's laugh.

"Girlie, you gotta re-align your perceptions. I'm the baby of the two of us."

Terra looked skeptically at Philippe, then at Jackson.

"We're shifters, darling," Philippe said as explanation, which she supposed it was.

"So, you don't age?"

"*We* don't age," he corrected, pointing to include her in the statement. "Not if we don't want to. It's usually instinctual to keep ourselves at whatever condition we're comfortable with."

She frowned at him, not quite buying it. It *did* make sense on one level, except cells still aged. "But you obviously look older than him."

"True, but then, I like this better. I feel more mellowed out this way."

She could see that. Not everyone felt the need to be their best, just look at the number of overweight people in the world. "But then shifters would have been outed ages ago. I mean, I was raised among humans. One of my parents had to be a shifter. Why did they age, but you don't?" It still didn't make sense to her that she was a shifter. She'd shifted before, but a part of her still rejected it, pushing it away.

"Mother."

"What?"

"Most likely, your mother was the shifter. I don't think humans have figured that out yet, but generally only female shifters can reproduce cross-species."

Terra nodded, thinking she might have heard that already. "But why did she age then, if she was a shifter?"

"Because that's what she was comfortable with."

"That doesn't make any sense."

"Well, how comfortable would you be not aging when

everyone around you does? Besides, controlling how you look is a skill, one people raised by humans haven't learned. It's rare for them to shift at all, let alone be good at it."

That silenced her, and she turned away, noting that the sun had set, and while it wasn't dark yet, it was well on its way there. "Maybe another fifteen minutes."

Jackson nodded, shifting in his seat. "Philippe, hand me one of those bolt cutters. We might as well get started. If we're careful, they won't have any chance of seeing us from this side."

"Are you sure that's wise? Is it worth taking the risk? It's just another fifteen minutes." Terra stood, unsure as she looked at the fencing. "Maybe we should wait. Just in case."

"It'll be fine. Look there. That's the closest security camera. With its arc, it won't reach this far. It can't."

"What if it's not whatever model you think it is?"

Jackson smirked at her. "Trust me, I got a *really* good look."

"How? You must have been really close."

Philippe, standing behind Jackson's back, answered by waving his arms around like a bird's wings.

"Never mind."

Jackson crept up to the fence, letting Terra and Philippe come or not as they saw fit. They both followed close behind, Terra nearly bumping into the other man in her unease at starting this before full dark. Really, what would another fifteen minutes have hurt?

Jackson reached the chain link and placed his bolt cutters against the wire, Philippe stepping up beside him to do the same. They made quick work of the task, making a hole big enough for a person to get through one pop—pop—pop at a time.

They crept at speed to the second fence, repeating the process and producing a hole just slightly larger. When they passed through, Terra on their heels, they glanced up at the sky, measuring how much light remained. Terra could still see her fingers in front of her, so she figured still too much. They stood around again, waiting.

Philippe paced the dead space behind the buildings, impatient to get going. After all, who would want to sit around twiddling their thumbs in the middle of a break-in? "What about these windows?" He pointed to the tiny windows high on the walls of the buildings. Big as he was, he could reach it, tapping the glass lightly, making Terra cringe.

"Who could possibly fit through those?"

Philippe looked at the window, then at Terra assessingly.

She didn't like that look. She didn't like it at all. "Whatever it is, no."

"You could fit."

"No, no, I couldn't."

"It would take some shifting, but I'm sure you could do it."

She jabbed her finger at the window a child would have trouble getting through. "How could I possibly fit through that?"

"Shift into a shape that is narrower and taller. Should do it." He nodded, happy with his assessment.

Terra wasn't. She'd refused to even *try* to learn to shift since arriving at the caravan. She had no confidence that she could pull this off, nor did she want to. If they thought it was such a good idea, they should do it. Opening her mouth, she intended to tell them off, but with one good look at them, she closed it again. Each was big and tall already. They would have to shift into a giant to be thin enough. That, at least, she'd managed to glean. When shifting, mass always stayed the same.

She walked up to the window, examining it closer, racking her brain for an image to hold in her mind. Small, but not as small as she'd initially thought. *Think tall. Think tall.*

Moments ticked by without anything happening. She started to second-guess herself.

What am I doing?

This isn't me.

She turned toward the fence, contemplating turning back, walking away. Was Jackson right? Was this none of her business?

She tried to visualize herself as tall and thin, picturing a model from the neck down, one of those anorexic beauty symbols that gave most women complexes. But her mind protested, pulling back, and the creepy-crawly feeling never ran over her skin like it did when she escaped.

"No," she shook her head. "I can't do it." She retreated from the building's back wall.

Jackson stepped forward, reaching out for her shoulder. "Yes, you can."

"No," she hissed, jerking out of his reach. "I'm not *like* you."

"Easy," Philippe said, pulled Jackson back. He stared up at the window. "It wasn't the best plan, anyway. She might have been able to get through, but the people we're trying to rescue couldn't, so it's a moot point."

Terra felt vindicated as she looked at the window, then at the other buildings that served at dormitories for her kind. Her kind. *Her* kind. It didn't seem real, her mind shying away from it, skirting around saying the actual word. But she had to get them out of here. They would have to move in unison. The faster they got everyone through those holes in the fences, the higher the chances of success.

"One challenge to consider—there are more children here than adults. We can probably organize and wrangle the adults easily enough, but the children will prove difficult. They'll either be tired and sluggish, little hellions, or rebellious," she said.

Jackson stepped up to her shoulder. "How many of the children are small enough to fit through the windows?"

"I have no idea. I'm not even sure I saw all the kids. I was told there were about 75 children and 50 adults, but those numbers could have changed." She shook her head again. "This is like one of those nightmare logic puzzles. I suspect most of the children will fit through the window, but what do we do with them while we're collecting the others. The adults would be invaluable keeping track of so many kids. But if we get them first, how do we do it without raising an alarm?" What they needed was a bigger hole.

Terra faced Jackson. "Can we remove the window? Enlarge the hole?" The buildings were made of cinderblocks. "If we break the mortar between the blocks, we can get everyone through the opening."

"That'll make a lot of noise. It might bring security."

Terra stood there, tapping her foot. Too bad they didn't have access to a hardware store. She knew certain types of acids could dissolve mortar, which would certainly be quiet, but they'd already cut the fences. They couldn't risk leaving without the others. "Could we grind it away rather than try to break it?"

"That would take forever."

She turned to Jackson. "We have all night."

CHAPTER FOURTEEN

*J*ackson and Philippe spent the night chiseling away at the wall with shifted fingernails while Terra talked to the adults and older children through the windows, telling them what would happen next. Small noises of distress rose from the open windows, quiet enough only they could hear.

It was slow work, something Jackson wasn't even 100% sure he could accomplish. His arms burned from the steady progress they'd made, but they'd managed to enlarge the holes on the dorms for the children and the women. Terra had ushered women to the children's dorm so that when the time arose, they would be ready to grab kids and flee. She'd offered to help with the windows, but they'd both refused. She could help more by keeping the people as calm as possible. Terra had a big heart, so it came naturally.

Besides, the look in her eye told Jackson her heart wasn't in the offer. She didn't *want* to shift, didn't want to *be* a shifter. He *knew* that, and yet he kept hoping to see a change, a spark that told him he'd been right that first night when he found a strong, clever woman in the woods rescuing a child.

Refocusing on his task, Jackson's hands protested as the last block groaned. The sound of rough stone sliding echoed in the dead silence of the night. He flinched just as he had every time their work had cried out into the dark. They paused, cinderblock in hand, listening for any signs of failure.

Nothing.

They removed the last stone and waved at the men inside. They filed out one by one, their gray outfits standing out against the pitch black. Philippe ushered them toward the children's dorm, where they disappeared. A few minutes later, Terra stepped out and nodded to them.

They were ready.

Terra waved at the occupants of the dormitory, and people ran out in a flood, most carrying small children. Terra vanished from sight as the crowd between them became a solid wall from the buildings to the tree line.

It took too long.

That same thought kept running through his head.

It's taking too long.

We'll get caught.

He didn't even have Terra's reassuring smiles as he couldn't see her. For all he knew, she was gone.

Philippe slammed a hand down on his shoulder, the big bear of a man's version of comfort. The abused shoulder smarted, but he looked up at his friend and nodded.

Time dragged on, insensitive to his state of mind, but finally the last stragglers lurched from the hole, and Terra came into view once more. She slipped into the building, causing him to suck in a breath, before coming back out again with a smile and a thumbs up.

They took off at a run behind the large group, Jackson grabbing her hand as soon as they got close enough. She smiled at him, nerves showing in her brilliant gray eyes.

They ran, the forest swallowing them up, and didn't stop until they reached their vehicles, a dark SUV and a faded green truck sitting side by side.

"We did it," Terra said.

The loud crashing noises of less than graceful shifters dashing through the underbrush serenaded them. Slowly, he registered a dozen people slipping out of the trees around their vehicles, waiting for direction, orders.

Relief flooded him that not all those they'd freed had sought them out, looking for guidance, but a dozen still stretched their numbers greatly. How the heck would they find room for the lot?

"Macey!" Terra jogged up to a woman.

Macey shook her head. "I thought I told you no one gets out of there."

"Yeah, not with that attitude." Terra smiled, maybe at an inside joke because Macey smiled too, her face stiff, like she'd forgotten how.

"Well, everyone, let's go. It's gonna be a tight fit," Jackson said as he waved them to the vehicles. A lot of people would be taking a ride in the truck bed.

Terra sat on Philippe's front stoop as the first flush of dawn tinted the sky, looking out at the new "tent" they'd set up at the edge of the caravan. No one had space for twelve extra people, so it was the best they could do at the moment. Macey and her daughter were staying with Philippe in the trailer behind them. The two had protested as there was only one bed in the tiny trailer, but Philippe had insisted, stating, "I can sleep anywhere." Terra couldn't help imagining him as a bear and tended to agree.

"We shouldn't stay here," Jackson said, cutting into Terra's inner world.

She had to admit, being so close to the camp had given her the creeps at times, but she didn't see any other way. Was there somewhere else for the group to go?

"The season's not over," Philippe cut in from his spot on a log in the yard. "We'd leave crops unharvested, and correct me if I'm wrong, but isn't the other site usually rented out this time of year?"

Terra blinked and resisted smacking her forehead. She was an idiot. She'd been managing all the paperwork and finances for the caravan. She'd wondered about the rental agreements and AirBNB, but she hadn't thought anything of it. She chided herself now for not figuring it out. After all, it was a caravan. Caravans migrate. "There's a rental agreement through the end of the month, but the AirBNB account is shut down after that."

Jackson scowled, not liking that answer.

"Where else can we go?"

Jackson scoffed. "You know? Once upon a time, we could go wherever we wanted. Now, finding somewhere large enough to settle an entire caravan is like pulling teeth. You can't just park it anywhere. People will call the police, tow you, even arrest you. I don't know what the world's coming to."

Terra smirked. She'd never noticed before, but Jackson was a lot older than he appeared.

"There's nowhere to go, Jackson," Philippe said, his voice calm, soothing.

"I can look into rental spots, places we can reserve last minute that'll fit us. It's not ideal, but it gives us an option. We should be prepared to leave at the drop of a hat. We should also have someone monitoring the camp, watching for any signs they might search the area, might find us."

Jackson nodded and stood. "I'll get someone on the recon. Terra, find us a place."

Terra returned the gesture and headed back to the office. Looked like they had a plan.

Over the next few weeks, they stayed on high alert. Terra didn't notice whoever happened to be on surveillance at any given moment, but tension thickened the air, keeping everyone on edge. She wanted to forget about it. After all, this level of stress didn't help anyone. But her mind kept wandering back to that little plot in the mountains she'd found.

Some people adapted readily to their new environment. The children, as always, had it the easiest. They thrived on meeting new people and the colorful clothes Jemma handed out like candy. Beth, Macey's daughter, handled it worst of all the kids. She didn't interact with the others her age, and she drew even further inward when she watched men playing with children. Did she miss her father?

Terra knew that Macey missed her husband. Of the adults from the camp, she adapted the poorest as well. A female construction worker and male carpenter managed the transition best. None of them trusted easily, but most felt more secure when they could contribute meaningfully to the group, feeling they were earning their keep.

But every day, Macey only grew worse, not better. At first, Macey had been happy to see Terra, and she'd watched as a weight lifted off Macey's shoulders. But little by little, a cloud settled over Macey's mind. She tried for Beth's sake, but either Beth could read her mother's mood, or they were simply in the same state, each feeding off the other.

She sat on the steps of Jackson's trailer, staring at Philippe's shiny silver bullet. She couldn't imagine even two people living in the thing, but then she'd been surprised by how comfortably she and Annie had managed in their new home.

In the distance, children giggled and squealed, a constant sound here at the caravan. It was a jarring, but welcome, contrast to her old life, more apt to hear yelling, car horns, slamming doors, and thumping music than happiness of any kind.

Her hand rested on the wood step, picking at splinters as she thought.

What could she *do*? She felt she needed to do *something*, but what? Macey and Beth hadn't left the trailer today, even though it was past noon. Based on the size, she couldn't imagine keeping a child cooped up in there comfortably, which meant they were probably lazing about, wallowing in their individual miseries.

What would happen if they were left like that?

Terra didn't want to know.

CHAPTER FIFTEEN

*K*yle sat, frowning at the phone.

What the fuck?

He'd just returned from the hospital again. Kaufman had been in recovery for weeks now. This time, he stepped into his office only to receive a call from his duty officer.

"You've been removed from the task force," she'd said, her stern military mien even more abrasive over the phone. He'd drank with the woman before when off duty, so it was always a bit jarring when she pulled on her military mask, changing from an energetic, positive person to a badass who'd just as soon bite your ass off as look at you. She was so laid back when off duty, almost a pushover, but she would lay you out if you tried anything.

The words still rung through his head.

You've been removed from the task force.

Why? He didn't understand. The conversation had been short, just those words and a statement he would be contacted with further instructions.

Was he in trouble after all for the explosion? Was he about to be punished?

He swiveled his chair, staring out the window, but not really seeing anything. The air conditioner kicked on, whirring to life. Details filtered into his brain.

Metal window frame.

Dirty blinds.

Reflections in glass.

He let the details blur and settle into nothingness until the phone ringing jarred him out of his reverie. He spun around, snatching it up.

"Avery," he barked into the phone.

"How are things on your end?" Tristan drawled.

Kyle sneered, a slight edge in his voice. "Captain Faulk. Somehow, I have a feeling you're to blame for the call I just received from my duty officer."

" 'Fraid so. I've got a mission for you. Meet me in my office at nine."

Kyle sat up straight, intrigued. "See you then."

———

"Jackson," Terra said in a sing-song voice, slipping up behind him as he went about making the colorful tent a little more fit for its residents. It was dark inside the tent, even with the main flap open to let in light. A large, open enclosure, it provided little privacy, with pillows and blankets that served as sleeping bags on the dirt floor. It wasn't ideal and with the weather threatening to change, would not do for long. They still had a week before they could move.

Jackson kept frowning down at the area, like it offended him. She'd come to realize he took his role very seriously. He felt compelled to take care of those in his charge, and these new people from the camp were definitely in his charge.

Whether he liked it or not.

He sighed and turned around. "What is it, Terra?"

"I'd like to take Macey to see her husband. I know she missed him while at the camp. I think it's worse now."

Jackson shook his head. "That's a bad idea."

Terra fidgeted in place but held her ground. "She needs closure. Maybe it'll be a happy reunion, maybe it'll be a train wreck, but I don't think she can move on until she gets that."

"And what if she wants to stay with her husband?" Jackson spread his arms wide. "They can't exactly go about their normal life, now can they?"

"They can stay here."

"Oh, no." He shook his head. "There are no humans here, and I intend to keep it that way."

"Jackson!"

"No."

"You're such a fucking bigot."

"I'm not, and I said no. That's final."

Terra scowled. This wasn't over.

"I don't know how you talked me into this," Jackson said, glaring at the building across the street, his arms crossed as he sat in the driver's seat. The building *screamed* human, with its quaint, well-manicured lawn, well-trimmed bushes, and perfectly coordinated paint job. Everything was clean, everything was quiet.

It gave him the creeps.

On the radio, a talk show debated back and forth about the mixed feelings in the populace regarding the Incirrina and the treaty mission to the Kennedy Moon Station. Some chimed in with how great it was, that it would bring Earth into a new era, that it would make the world safer to have allies on other planets. But for every caller insisting it was good, another called spouting hate, that the Incirrina were freaks, monsters, that they would turn on us. They asked how we could trust creatures that had nothing in common with us, no common history, no common experiences.

And it only got worse from there.

Jackson grumbled about it not being any of their business, turned off the radio, and glared out the window again. Just as well, Terra had grown increasingly agitated with each minute they listened to that garbage.

He didn't like seeing her like that, but wondered why it upset her so. Did it remind her of her own prejudices? Or did it remind her of being taken away? He somehow didn't see her as being terribly introspective. She seemed to focus more on the problems of others.

Case in point: driving God only knew how long to sit outside a human's house so that her friend, Macey, could get closure.

He couldn't believe he'd agreed to this, but Terra had been persistent, like a terrier latching on even though their feet had long left the ground. It didn't even take twenty-four hours for him to fold. Bundling the three of them in his SUV, he'd driven off into the human world, a place he'd never wanted to visit.

He just wanted to get back home.

Macey ran her sweaty palms over her pants, rubbing them over and over, afraid to knock on the door, afraid of the unknown. Had he missed her? Had he mourned her? Had he looked for her? She didn't know, and it ate away at her insides.

She checked the driveway, confirming yet again that he was home. A big, silver electric SUV sat on the pavement, waiting on its owner's pleasure. It was the same car, the same car they'd driven out on date nights, the same car she'd watched take off every morning when he left for work. But she wasn't the same, and she very much doubted he was either. Could they find their way back to each other? A nagging feeling in her gut said no.

She hated her gut right about now.

Macey could feel the caravan leader's stare, egging her on, demanding she get on with it. It only made her more nervous. She turned around, and yep, his glare practically melted her to the brick steps. She didn't like him. There was something wrong with him. But Terra was a friend, and her friend seemed to like him, so she would let those feelings go as best she could.

She and Terra didn't see eye to eye, but the woman had an inner strength she couldn't fathom, let alone experience herself. Macey had adapted, accepted. Terra had rebelled, fought, fled. Where Macey had given up, Terra had searched for an out, for a solution, and she'd succeeded. It made Macey feel small, weak, and in awe of the other woman.

She needed to channel a bit of Terra right now. Terra wouldn't stand here on this doorstep pondering her naval lint.

She would charge up to the door and bang on it like there was no tomorrow.

Macey lifted her hand, hovering over the painted wood. Another moment passed. She wondered if she was doing the right thing, but then she thought of her daughter. She'd become a ghost, not even recognizable as the happy little girl she'd been before they'd received those terrible test results. Macey raised her chin and knocked. Moments later, footsteps rang out on the hardwood floors, and Macey held her breath.

This was it.

The door opened, and she smiled. He looked so handsome, his hair tousled and his eyes sleepy, like he still hadn't had his morning coffee. That perfect moment didn't last, though. Recognition crossed his face, and hope surged through her.

Only to get crushed a moment later. "What are *you* doing here?"

She gasped. "What?" Her words came out as soft as an ephemeral spirit.

He shook his head. "How are you even *here*? You're supposed to be locked up like the monster you are."

Her heart sank. "But, we're married. We have a family."

He shook his head again. "I don't have a family. And I *certainly* don't have a wife." He slammed the door, the loud bang striking her like a slap.

Macey stood there for the longest time, not knowing what to say, what to do. What was there now? She'd never imagined in a thousand years, even with all her doubts and fears, that he would treat her like that. *I don't have a family.* The words reverberated in her skull, stinging each time they struck their mark.

She turned around and stumbled back to the SUV, her world in a tailspin.

What now?

Terra worried about Macey the entire way back to the caravan. Her friend didn't say a word, didn't make eye contact, and looked destroyed. She knew the conversation had not gone well. She didn't listen in, but she'd watched, and it didn't take eagle eyes to see the facial expressions that passed across her husband's face. He'd looked disgusted, like he hated her. That had to hurt.

They reached the parking area and Jackson turned off the engine, giving a heavy weight to the moment as the silence settled into their bones. Terra exited and ushered Macey from the car. Macey barely noticed the guidance as they made their way to Philippe's trailer, where he had a deer carcass stretched out over a table. With efficient movements, he cleaned the animal and dumped parts destined for the community hall in a cooler and offal in a bucket on his other side.

"It didn't go well." He stood as he spoke, his voice gentle and kind as they approached. He peered down at Macey with sympathy.

Terra shook her head, not sure if speaking it out loud would break her friend.

But Macey surprised her by lifting her chin high, drawing in a deep breath, and facing Philippe before saying, "I'm a widow."

Terra looked at her friend in surprise, taking in the shut-down, haunted look in her eyes, but kept her counsel. She supposed it was as good an option as any. Certainly, it should allow Macey and Beth to mourn what they'd lost and move on.

If they *could* move on.

***

After they returned, everything seemed to fall into place. The new members of the community were adjusting, and Philippe had started making overtures toward Macey, who, while not completely open to them, wasn't closed off to them either. Philippe had been trying to connect with Beth as well and making more progress. Though she was still hesitant, Beth accepted him better than her mother did. Probably, she was so starved for a father figure that, even in her own quiet and reserved way, she welcomed what he offered.

All around Terra, people she knew and cared about were adapting, healing, but she just couldn't settle. Every day, she was eaten away by the things she'd heard. She'd lived in a bubble for far too long, first with her own willful ignorance, then at the shifter camp, then here at the caravan. She kept drifting into these mindsets where the outside world didn't matter, where it couldn't affect her. Then, every time her nose was pushed into the shit brewing in the world, she was shocked, motivated to act, and sick with the thought of how she'd lived until that point.

But it wasn't just her. Jackson did it too. His attitude bothered her. "It's none of our business," she griped under her breath. Was it, though? Sure, she understood and could even accept that sometimes you had to make change where you could, that sometimes a problem was just too big. Terra wasn't a leader, didn't know how to motivate people, and certainly didn't know how to initiate change.

So what could she do?

What *should* she do?

And would it make any difference?

She huffed as she stormed into the trailer, stomping into the office. On the wall, a dry erase calendar marked a day only a few days away when they planned to move to the next site.

Had it been that long already?

But it had been weeks since they'd rescued the others from the camp. They still had patrols watching for retaliation. She kept expecting something bad to happen, for people in uniforms to storm the caravan, rounding everyone up.

Terra collapsed into her chair, a padded folding job that wasn't comfortable, but didn't take up space when Jackson slept. She stared at the paperwork that needed her attention, at the computer for accessing the accounts and records. She wanted to be productive, useful, but her heart wasn't in it today.

To her left, a solitary window had its room-darkening curtains drawn open, letting in light. It also revealed a straight path to the community hall with the temporary tent peeking out behind it. Near the community hall, adults chatted while children ran in furred forms, more appropriate to the cooler weather. She flinched, hating her reaction yet again to facing the nature of this place.

She dragged her hand over her hair, pulling for good measure. Why couldn't she get her head around this? Why couldn't she accept this? "Gah!" She slammed her hands down on the desk, the flimsy material complaining ominously at the abuse.

Terra froze, hoping it wasn't broken, but it held and she let out a sigh of relief. She shook her head, resting her forehead on her palms.

"What am I doing?"

CHAPTER SIXTEEN

Jackson pulled the squeaky door to his trailer open, an action he took more and more pleasure in nowadays. It felt good having people to come home to, even if they weren't always there when he returned.

His head was filled with planning for the move now, his people packing and securing community resources behind him. Still, having Annie's things strewn over the couch or leftovers Terra'd cooked the night before waiting in the fridge put a lightness in his heart, drawing him from his thoughts.

So when he walked through the door and Terra stepped out of the office, he smiled. He couldn't help himself. It just made her scowl at him, though.

"Something wrong?"

What happened?

Where was Annie?

Was she okay?

Terra crossed her arms at him, shaking her head for good

measure. "We can't just hide in this little oasis you've created for us, Jackson."

He stilled, confused. "What do you mean?"

"It's none of our business?" She looked at him as if he should know what that meant.

Did she mean the shifter camp? Sure, he'd said that, but he'd also helped her free the others. She couldn't be mad at him for that, could she? He still wasn't sure it had been a good idea. He still had people monitoring the surrounding areas, expecting the government to find them, to come down and scoop them all up.

It was a mistake. You know it was.

Yet, he would have done it again, wouldn't he?

Terra didn't wait for an answer. "You say that about everything, everything outside of your self-imposed walls. Shifters in camps? Not our problem. Treaty with the Incirrina? Not our problem."

He stared at her, incredulous. "And what would you have me do?" he said, throwing up his hands. He felt powerless for the first time in ages. He didn't know what Terra wanted from him, didn't know if it was something he could even provide.

Her face fell, and he wished he'd kept his mouth shut. "I don't know. Something. We need to do something."

After that conversation, they didn't talk. It ate at Terra almost as much as when her bubble had popped, forcing her to act, to rescue the others from the shifter camp. She wanted to talk to Jackson, almost apologized a couple times, but she couldn't give the words voice. After all, she didn't mean them. She was sorry it had put distance between them. Even worse, Annie felt that distance, worried about them, tried to bridge the gap, which about killed Terra, but she wasn't sorry she'd said what she said.

It needed to be said, even if he didn't want to hear it.

She dropped onto Philippe's front stoop, wondering if the big guy would be around any time soon. Then again, Macey would be just as good. She couldn't decide if she needed Philippe's quiet wisdom or Macey's resigned realism right about now. Either would be welcome.

She got neither. A bear lumbered up to the front of the house, cocked its head at her, then ambled up to her and plopped its massive skull on her lap.

Terra looked at it wide-eyed for a moment before dropping her hand on its head and running her fingers through its long, brown fur. It rumbled in appreciation, and she smiled. "Maybe *this* was what I needed."

Jackson hated himself a little at the moment. Annie had started chasing him around, asking lots of questions, most of them having to do with why he wasn't talking to Terra. The girl was voracious, like a terrier, and completely adorable. Today, she was following as just that, a terrier, an improbably large terrier, but a terrier nonetheless.

He looked behind him. Yep, she was still following. Jackson kept adjusting his stride so she could keep up with him. If only Terra's needs were so simple. He didn't know how to please her. He didn't know how to fix this, but he'd broken them, and he needed to do the mending.

Around him, tents had been dismantled, outdoor furniture

were being stowed, and trailers closed up. At this rate, they could leave for the new site tomorrow morning, but his gaze did little more than run over the proceedings disinterestedly. In the past, he would have helped each person as he saw a need, directing them to higher efficiency.

Moving was always an exciting time, but he preferred to be settled, to watch as the life returned to the caravan, as their lives bloomed and stretched over the land, overtaking it in all their color and vibrance.

So watching it all packed away and broken down left him a little hollowed out this time.

Buh-rringg.

He jumped, the sound of an old telephone ripping him out of his funk, saving him from yet another downward spiral. "What?" he barked into the cell phone.

A voice he hadn't heard in some time came through the line. Many years ago, he'd offered a hand to a shifter who was strong, capable, but in the end, untrusting. She hadn't been ready for what he offered that day, so he'd given her his number, telling her he would be there, anytime.

He never expected to hear from her again, so her voice on the phone now was jarring, shattering his world without even trying.

"It's Mila. We have something to discuss. The fate of the world is in the balance."

PART TWO

"Vanity and pride are different things, though the words are often used synonymously. A person may be proud without being vain. Pride relates more to our opinion of ourselves, vanity to what we would have others think of us."

—Jane Austen, *Pride and Prejudice*

CHAPTER SEVENTEEN

*T*he door to the trailer opened, and Terra peeked out from behind the office door. Jackson stood in the doorway, holding it open. She was tempted to ignore him, return to her paperwork, but the look on his face stopped her. "What is it?" she said, standing up from her chair.

"I just got a call." He stared down at the phone in his hand, rubbing it absently with his thumb.

"What about?"

"Someone I met years ago. She's asking for my help."

She? Terra tamped down on the moment of jealousy. "What's she want?"

"She wants shifters to help save them from an alien invasion."

And she saw it, the purpose, that nagging feeling that made her fight with Jackson in the first place. She didn't know what this would mean, what would happen, but she knew they needed to act.

Then her mood turned dark, reality setting in. "And you don't want to do it." She glared and pointed a finger at him, furious over his obstinate insistence on non-involvement. How could he be so heartless, so cruel? How could he turn his back on billions of people as if they were nothing?

Not our problem.

His constant refrain popped into her head, working her into a lather, her frustration spilling out her mouth without thought. "You know, you might not trust humans, but those fuckers won't stop at the humans." She spread her arms wide. "These shifters you love so much, that you hold in such high regard, share this planet with them. We have to get along, we have to share. Sometimes that means putting aside our differences and past mistakes."

She scoffed. "But you don't want to get along. You just want to bury your head in the sand and hope it all goes away. I mean, they're still packing up out there, aren't they? You're *still* planning to pick up and leave, as if that'll solve *any* of our problems."

Her mind flitted to the camp, and she shivered. Was this a mistake? She couldn't go back, not to her old life, not to the camp.

"I could be sentencing everyone to the same fate as you." He looked torn, devastated, shaking his head. "I couldn't do that."

"Or you could be sentencing them to death." She shook her head in turn. "You're not a government, Jackson. You're just one man. You can let the others know what's going on, but you can't force them to help. This isn't on your shoulders."

"You want to hear them out."

"I do."

Terra wrung her hands, butterflies wrecking havoc on her stomach as she sat in the passenger seat, Jackson driving them to the meeting. It felt like Jackson had told her about the call only moments ago, but they'd been on the road for over an hour.

She let out a deep breath, telling herself that it would be fine. But they were meeting the military, and she struggled to make herself believe her own assurances. Her mind flashed back to getting screened for that secretarial job, to the puke green scrubs. She didn't know why that detail stuck in her head, but it did. That was the last time she'd been on a military base. That moment changed her life forever.

Then inevitably, her thoughts skipped to the day she'd been taken, men in suits dragging her out of her home, dumping her into a van and driving away. The hopeless certainty that it was a mistake. The helpless need to escape.

That hopelessness burned off into righteous anger, her heartbeat pounding in her ears. How dare they! For nothing more than the genes she carried, they locked her up and stole her life. No one had that right, but they used their fear to justify violating the very laws and rights they'd founded their country on.

But then, according to the laws, she wasn't human, so it didn't count.

Bullshit.

Her hands curled into fists at her sides, pressing hard into her thighs. Around her, shades of green whizzed by, intermittently interrupted by speckling shadows as light seeped through the branches of the trees they passed through.

"You could have stayed behind," Jackson said, taking his eyes off the road and looking pointedly at her fists. "I could handle this on my own."

But something inside her rebelled at that thought, unwilling to let him go alone, needing to have his back. "I'm fine," she said, but she was anything but fine.

<hr>

Jackson sat at a large conference table, Terra deceptively meek as a mouse at his side. He hated how she almost cringed at them like a prey among a pack of predators, and yet a seething, impotent rage bubbled under the surface. He wanted to take her away from this place, bring her back home where she could be safe with Annie.

His mood had soured during the long drive to Clark NSS Base as Terra's mood remained dark, fluctuating between fear and fury seemingly without pause or reason. To make matters worse, his skin crawled at being surrounded by so many humans, especially since they knew what he was.

He'd had his dealings with humans in the past, but always with the added armor of their ignorance of his true self. It kept him confident and allowed him to go about his business feeling assured that he and his people were safe from those he did business with.

Now, nothing was certain. He couldn't hide from the military, the government, any longer. Once he returned to his caravan, they would know, would follow his movements using all resources available to them. He'd lost his greatest armor —anonymity.

Bodies continued to stream into the room, settling into their places, chatting idly while sipping coffee. No one smiled. The air hung heavy with the seriousness of current events.

Then an older, sterner gentleman in a stark uniform marched in, walking to the head of the table. "Let's begin," he said as he took his seat. He steepled his fingers. "I'm told we have a shifter named Jackson here." He pivoted his head, zeroing in on one of the only civilians in attendance. "You understand the situation?"

"I doubt I've been fully briefed."

He nodded. "An alien military force is on approach to Earth, estimated to arrive in a matter of days. This force likely outmatches our military might in space and as such the battle will likely extend to ground forces. This is an event unlike any in human history, and as such, we are considering non-conventional approaches to the problem."

"You want to use shifters in the fight," Jackson said, his voice dark with anger.

Terra gasped at his gumption, and he clasped her hand, rubbing his thumb across the back.

"Yes, if they would be willing."

Jackson stalled, trying to sooth Terra with his touch. A part of him felt paralyzed, knowing that his next words would change the fate of shifters for all time. It was terrifying and thrilling at once. Terra's presence at his side encouraged him to jump in with both feet, but he hesitated. She would judge him if he refused. He knew that. She might even leave him, which left his chest cold and empty. But how would it affect his people?

He imagined his people, shifters, bleeding out and dead on the battlefields, fodder for the aliens' cannons. But he also imag-ined children running from their homes, screaming as they were gunned down. He had no illusions about the stakes. He glanced over at Terra, who curled into her seat, a fine tremor running through her, her anger having fled, consumed by fear.

There was no decision, was there?

"I can't guarantee any of the shifters will join the fight."

Terra looked over at him, her jaw slack.

"We don't have military or commands like you do. We are more like nomadic tribes than anything that organized. I can spread the word, coordinate, but I can't force anyone."

Jackson paused, not sure what he wanted to share. He didn't trust these people, had no faith in humanity or even their own self-interest. They would shoot themselves in the foot if they thought his kind were a threat. On that, he had no doubt. They'd done it countless times throughout history.

He leaned back, squeezing Terra's fingers without realizing. She patted his hand, smiling at him ever so slightly. That attempt to reassure him settled him. It reminded him of the responsibility he had, the custodianship he had over the people in his caravan, and over those he would soon be contacting to garner their aid.

He leaned forward, steepling his fingers like the big honcho had been doing from the start. Though the oldest and highest ranked human here, and as such the most respected, he was still a spring chicken next to Jackson. "I'm sure you know more than I can imagine about my people. You've probably experimented on those you held hostage over the years."

A few men squawked as if to object, but Jackson didn't let them.

"But I'll provide a few highlights, nonetheless. We are very difficult to kill when in reasonably good health. If we are to help, we will need significant quantities of calories and nutrients readily available. We will need all the resources that any soldier would receive, including weaponry and body armor."

A general across the table from him leaned heavily on his elbows. "But with your natural talents, wouldn't that be a waste of resources? The humans are a lot more vulnerable and will need those things more."

"Humans are not more vulnerable than shifters. Shifters can recover from injuries humans cannot, but they will sustain just as much damage, feel just as much pain. And before you say it, while we can do considerable damage with hand to hand combat, it still pales in comparison to an automatic rifle.

"What's more, most of us have no formalized training, which means we'll need some orientation before stepping onto the battlefield."

Some of the faces around him closed up into scowls. He suspected those opposed to this didn't like the direction this conversation was going. Tough.

Jackson stood, glanced to Mila, who'd made the call to bring him here, and nodded his head. She looked better than the last time he'd seen her ten years ago. They'd had the occasional conversation in that time, mostly in couched "theoretical" terms where she would ask about the experience of being a shifter, never willing to admit it openly.

She'd developed into a strong, confident woman. Though a slight uneasiness remained in her eyes, she didn't show it anywhere else. And the rampant paranoia from their first meeting was completely gone. "Keep in touch," he said before pulling Terra to her feet, turning his back to everyone, and walking out.

CHAPTER EIGHTEEN

"Wait up!" Mila said as they walked out of the building, her voice breathless from running after the two shifters. She jogged up beside them and smirked. "You know, that wasn't the end of the meeting, right?"

Jackson shrugged, as stoic as ever. She'd met him over ten years ago after she'd shifted for the first time. He'd reached out a helping hand, and she'd repeatedly swatted it away, too scared to see a good thing when it was right in front of her.

Not that it made a difference. He'd still helped her, saved her life, and she never forgot his number, always keeping it in the back of her head just in case.

I bet he never expected me to join the military.

And yet as she stood before him, she couldn't believe her eyes. He looked just the same, like a mountain that measured time in eons rather than years. Mila shook her head. "You haven't changed a bit, have you?"

"Not much," he said, his chin stuck out as if he were proud of that fact.

Mila turned to the woman at his side. "And you are?" she said, offering her hand to Jackson's compatriot, a striking redhead who acted shy as a mouse. She seemed calmer now that she'd escaped that insufferable meeting room. Mila couldn't blame her. After her first shift, being in a room full of military officers would have sent her into apoplectic shock.

"Terra." She grasped Mila's hand in a firm if slightly damp handshake. "Nice to meet you."

Mila just grinned. "Since you asked for an orientation, have your people call here for orders. The suits are still working out the details on coordinating ground troops between countries, but we can direct them to their nearest military base for gearing up and debriefing." She handed Jackson a card.

Jackson shook his head. "You never really needed us, did you?"

"Oh, I did, but good luck getting me to admit it." She smiled, no longer afraid. Ten years ago, she saw Jackson as a threat, someone to run from, to fight. "But thank you for offering. I may not have accepted, but thank you."

Terra had never realized how influential or connected Jackson was. He had seemed completely comfortable sitting in a room filled with humans he hated, barking orders at them. High-ranking officials at that.

They'd taken a roundabout way of returning to the caravan, spending three times as long getting home as getting to the base. She suspected he didn't want to be followed, but she didn't see how it was possible to avoid it. If the government wanted to follow them back to their people, they certainly had the resources to do so and without them the wiser.

Sitting in Jackson's small office, she marked off the next person on her list. They'd started as soon as they got home. Over the evening and next day, the list grew, tallying who Jackson had called, who'd agreed to help, and who was staying the fuck out of it.

She'd expected Jackson to be unable to withhold his constant hatred for humanity. She'd expected it would ooze into his voice, into his word choices, discouraging his equals from helping Earth, but the list of those agreeing to fight was growing.

Even so, Terra felt time slipping away. They only had days until the alien force would invade Earth, days to coordinate, to prepare. How could they ever succeed?

But she wouldn't tell Jackson that. She'd pushed him into this course of action and she needed to see it through, have faith in him, in their people. She refused to think of the consequences should they fail.

And yet the image popped into her head, anyway. Ships and flames filled the sky as missiles and bombs launched on both sides. The sky grew dark with death and the air filled with the sounds of terror and the smell of smoke and decay. She shivered, hating her active imagination, which had always thrilled in taunting her with worst-case scenarios.

Not now!

"Next?" she asked Jackson, putting all her effort into keeping her voice and face light. She smiled. He didn't need her negativity now.

Philippe sat on his front stoop, staring out over the packed-up caravan, holding Macey and Beth as they clung to him.

Around the caravan, the children were reserved, the adults resigned. None of them could have predicted Jackson's announcement last night when they returned, least of all Philippe. He'd known the man for years, had coached him on some of his worst tendencies many times over. He'd never expected the man to actually overcome some of them, especially not in so wholehearted a way.

At the announcement, many people shouted in anger, others in fear. Some had not even heard the news of the imminent alien invasion. One advantage of living in the middle of nowhere was they could choose to ignore the world around them. They could let the outer world pass them by and simply live.

Some were angry because Jackson had taken that away from them. Right here, right now, they couldn't simply let the world pass them by because he'd dragged it to their doorstep. He didn't demand that they fight, but he also didn't let them bury their heads in the sand either. They had to make a choice, and for once, Philippe was conflicted.

Ordinarily, he would have stepped up without a second thought, even without people knowing he was a shifter. He saw it as a duty, one he took pride in. Unlike Jackson, at least the Jackson he'd always known before, he saw clearly how the outside world could encroach on their oasis, dash their little utopia against the rocks. He had no illusions now about what would happen if the aliens landed on Earth.

But with the girls in his arms, he hesitated. Their small bodies shook with the terror and uncertainty of the near future. He needed to protect them, and he wasn't sure how to do that best. If he left, fought, he could keep them safe, but they would be alone, with no one here to comfort them. If he stayed, they would be comforted, but what if some of his people died because he didn't have their backs?

He felt trapped, and he pulled them closer to his sides.

What do I do?

Jackson stepped out of his trailer, taking a deep breath and stretching. It had been a long day, just over twenty-four hours having passed since the meeting with the military. "I don't care, Timmy!" Terra yelled. Somehow, Timmy had snuck in without him noticing. He hid a smile as Terra's grumblings filtered out through the thin walls. The little robot had been criticizing her organization techniques and providing feedback. The battle between woman and robot had raged pretty much from the day she arrived. He was curious to see how it would end.

Before long, the fight dissipated and the sounds of splashing and laughter drifted to him. Terra was giving Annie a bath. He looked down at his watch. He would have to start calling numbers overseas soon. They couldn't stop simply because it was getting late. Already, he felt sleep deprivation dragging at him. But the longer they took to call, the more people would be in danger, the harder it would be to organize the shifters.

Stepping off and down the lane, he wandered with his hands in his pockets. He was wound up, anxious. He didn't like it, but he didn't want to let Terra down. This was all for her, for Annie. But that wasn't to say he didn't see her point. She was right, of course, not that he would ever admit it. They shared the Earth with the wretched humans, and like it or not, they needed to defend it too if they wanted to survive.

"Ho there," Philippe called out, waving him over.

"Hello, old friend. You look troubled."

Philippe huffed, a self-deprecating smile pulling at his lips. "I find myself in a quandary."

"Oh? I thought *I* was the one always in need of *your* guidance."

Philippe laughed, the expression almost reaching his eyes. "I think we can leave off your neuroses for a spell."

"Then what's the problem?" Jackson sat down on a stump in the front yard, the uneven edge and splinters digging into his ass. He shifted in his seat, but it didn't help.

"I don't know what to do."

"What do you want to do?"

Philippe sighed. "That's the problem." He glanced back at his home, his shoulders slouching in defeat. "I can't do both."

"Tell me."

He looked Jackson dead in the eye. "I love Macey."

Jackson stared at his friend, not sure how to respond. "That was sudden."

"I imagine no more sudden than your love for Terra."

Jackson kept his mouth shut. He had no room to talk. He *did* love Terra, would do most anything for her. How stupid was that? "Then what's the problem?"

"She's fragile, jaded, hurt by her past. The pending invasion has only made her more so. I want to comfort her, protect her, but I want to fight as well, protecting her and *everyone* else."

Jackson nodded. Philippe had disappeared repeatedly over the years when he saw a just cause. He knew how the other man's mind worked. "Then ask her. Ask her what you should do, what she needs. She may tell you she needs you here, she may not be able to verbalize it, or she may tell you to go. You won't know until you ask."

Philippe shook his head, a great grin on his face. "When did you get so wise?"

"I reckon I learned it from you."

CHAPTER NINETEEN

Terra hated this. She'd started this mess, and now she would have to live with the consequences. She wanted to say stupid things like, "Do you really have to go?" and "Don't leave me." Instead, she stood tall, Annie hugging her leg as she tried to serve as a symbol of strength for the others left behind.

She stood in the center of the caravan, hard-packed earth unmarred by the brightly colored fabrics that had littered it before. It felt empty, like an uninhabited house. In every direction, she could see well beyond the trailers to distant fields and meadows. Trees still closed them in, but a far ways off.

She turned back to the gathering, running her fingers gently through Annie's hair. Both men and women hugged their friends and loved ones goodbye. Almost half the settlement, not including those rescued from the camp, had volunteered to fight. In a couple days, the battle would begin. How many of them would return home?

To her left, Macey clung to Philippe while he hugged Beth with both burly arms. He buried his face in the girl's neck, taking in a shuddering breath. She couldn't hear what they said, but it rang true in her heart. It was what she wanted to do as well.

But she didn't, because she needed to set an example. She didn't want to, but she had to.

That didn't stop Annie from racing into Jackson's arms and screaming, "Don't go!"

Terra gave him a lopsided smile as he picked up the little girl he'd adopted just as much as she had.

Looking Annie in the eyes, he said, "I'm coming back. Don't you worry. That's a promise."

Annie nodded, but buried her head in his shoulder. She sniffed and broke Terra's heart. She walked up, rubbing the girl's warm back through her clothes.

"It's okay, sweetie. He said he's coming back, and he will. What about all the other boys and girls who have mommies or daddies leaving? Don't you want to help them, be strong for them?"

Annie sniffed again, lifting her head from Jackson's shoulder, then looked around, seeing the whole scene for maybe the first time. She nodded, her face red and puffy from crying.

Terra smiled, proud of her. She rubbed her cheek with the back of her hand. "That's my big girl."

Annie smiled and rested her cheek on Jackson's chest.

"When do you have to leave?"

"We should probably already be gone, but this isn't easy for any of them. Many have never left the caravan, even for shopping."

She nodded. "But they'll have you. I have faith in you. You'll see them through this. I know it."

"And you'll see those left behind through this." He caressed her cheek, smiling at her, but it left her cold inside. "Be strong. They're going to need you."

"Jackson, I'm not a leader. I've only been here a short while. Why would they listen to me? Why would they *look* to me? I'm no one." She felt on the brink of hyperventilating, panic rising to choke her.

"You're mine."

She stilled. "Really?" she said, doubt edging her voice. She'd never been overly fond of the whole he-man, alpha crap in romance. You couldn't just declare a woman yours and be done with it, but she did like him, even if he drove her nuts sometimes.

"You're everything I want, everything I never knew I needed. And you're everything *they* need to get through this."

She shook her head, not wanting or willing to believe what he was saying. *I'm not a leader. I can't do this.* But he believed in her, had faith in her, and whether she liked it or not, he was leaving her responsible. She sighed. "Okay, but don't blame me if this place is a mess when you get back. Don't forget you're the one who left me in charge."

He smirked. "I'm sure I'll never hear the end of it."

"Of course not."

Jackson leaned in and pressed a feather-light kiss to her forehead. His dry lips were like angel's wings against her skin, begging her to hold her breath in the hopes that it would last a moment longer. "Until we meet again," he said, handing Annie off to her and walking away.

"You couldn't just say goodbye, could you?"

He turned around. "Goodbye is an ending. This isn't the end."

He walked toward the cars, disappearing out of sight as the lane curved between the trees.

<hr>

Terra turned around, hefting Annie onto her hip. Around her, the people left behind milled about, not knowing what to do with themselves. She couldn't blame them. The caravan was packed for the move, and the entire place felt empty without the others. She had spent the last day or so doing nothing but helping Jackson reach out to his contacts all over the world, calling shifters to the cause. Now she felt listless, uncertain. He wanted her to help his people while he was gone, be a leader, but she didn't know how to do that.

I don't want *to do that.*

That's not me.

She rubbed Annie's back, the little girl holding the folds of her shirt in a death grip. Terra didn't know how to be a leader, but she sort of knew how to be a mother. "Well," she said, releasing a big breath, "that was a bit rough." She smiled, knowing nothing she said would reassure them, but maybe she could distract them, like distracting a child from an injury or illness.

But how? The thought plagued her, leaving her frozen in place as she continued soothing Annie in her arms.

"I'm hungry," Annie whined, attracting her attention.

"Are you?" Terra said with a smile.

"It's well past breakfast," Jemma said, moving up toward

Annie to bop her nose. The girl giggled, smiling a reward at Jemma.

"Come," an older woman said, clapping her hands. "We'll need to unpack the community hall."

Terra let out a sigh, relieved to have the burden of leadership taken from her shoulders for a while longer. As the caravan broke into action, she once more felt like an outsider, like she didn't belong. She put Annie down, letting her dash off to play while Terra hovered near the crowd of men and women who'd stayed, fruitlessly trying to find some way to help.

"Come on, children," a voice called off to the side, drawing the kids out of the way of the adults.

Terra stopped, watching as the woman started up a game that involved a lot of running and shrieking. As she stood there, everyone moved in concert, like a choreographed dance, working together without getting in each other's way. Everyone had a role. No one hesitated.

Everyone except me.

The call came at the wee hours of the morning. He rolled over in bed, grumbling to himself as the phone's shrill voice continued to assault him. "I'm up. I'm up."

He slapped his hand against the phone, triggering speakerphone more by habit than sight, and plopped back on the bed, rubbing his face with both hands to wake up. "Speak."

The person on the other end of the line hesitated before beginning. "This is *him?*"

He scoffed, wondering when he would stop having his time wasted by fools. "You're the one who made the call."

The voice hesitated again, and he contemplated going back to sleep. He looked over at the window, but no light leaked around the room darkening curtains.

"I have news of importance to the movement."

He sat up, resigning himself to having his sleep cut short. "Speak." He didn't like repeating himself.

"The military is planning to use shape-shifters."

He slammed his hand down on the wooden nightstand.

Those leftist sons-of-bitches.

CHAPTER TWENTY

---

*O*nly hours after leaving the caravan, Jackson stood next to Philippe as they filed into the supply office at Clark NSS base, both of them still as boards. Soldiers called out directions, asking them to form lines, provide identifiers, accept uniforms, armor, weapons. Jackson waited at the head of the line, accepting each item without pause. He noted a patch on the shoulder of the uniform—a chimera with the words "Shifter Division" written underneath.

"Is this necessary?" he asked the man barking orders.

The man stood up straighter. "It's so the medics know what to do with the wounded. From my briefing, I was informed that shifters can heal fairly quickly with sufficient nutrients. Is that not correct?"

"It is."

He nodded. "The insignia is intended much like a diabetes bracelet—to inform medics what medical resources you need."

Jackson nodded, seeing the logic in the design, and moved on to collect the rest of his gear. Once finished, another soldier urged them down a side hallway and into a briefing room. Jackson and Philippe entered and sat at the front, waiting for the briefing to start.

Around them, their people trickled in, arms filled with gear, uncertain in this new environment. Many of them had lived largely rural or agrarian lives. This high tech, structured lifestyle didn't appeal to him, and made everyone else nervous and unsure of themselves.

Before long, the room roared with murmurs. A man of authority walked to the front of the room and cleared his throat, snapping his heels together to get the attention of the group. The crowd dwindled into silence as he dead-eyed them, demanding quiet, demanding respect.

"Better," he said, hands held behind his back as he started to pace. "You all know why you're here. In three days, an alien force will meet our space fleets above us. We are here to ensure that by then, you are prepared in the event they cannot repel the enemy."

The look in the man's eyes told Jackson all he needed to know. The officer didn't want to be here, thought this was a waste of time. He looked down his nose at the shifters who had agreed to come out of hiding, out of anonymity, in order to help protect their world. Jackson scowled, feeling an unfortunate similarity to the man. It left a bad taste in his mouth.

"I have to make you cretins ready for battle so you don't get good men, soldiers, killed." He glared at them, pivoting his head. In his gaze, he managed to broadcast that he thought he would fail. "You'll be split into squads. Each squad will be lead by a human military officer. You will follow his or her orders as if they are your own thoughts. You will not doubt. You will not question. You will not hesitate. Do I make myself clear?" He waited.

The room fell silent. Then it echoed with a dissonant, "Yes, sir."

"Good. At the back of the room is a group of officers. I will call each of your names. You will stand then file out after the officer by the door. That officer will own your ass until this clusterfuck is over. Do I make myself clear?"

"Sir, yes, sir," they said, this time almost as one organism.

"Good."

***

Terra sat down at the table in the newly set up community hall for breakfast, her "council" around her, helping her. Her hands flexed over a hot cup of coffee, the fumes and warmth soothing her. It was early and quiet, a sense of hesitance and anticipation in the air.

Yesterday had gone better than she'd hoped. They'd kept busy, though it was hard since they'd been planning to leave that day. Everything was packed. There were no crops to tend, no crafts to work on. A few of the adults wandered off to recheck the vehicles, make sure they were in good shape to travel. Others went off to hunt. The rest stayed behind with the kids. They'd managed to wear the children out last night, so they fell into a deep sleep as soon as their precious heads hit the pillows. A few had nightmares, came awake screaming for whichever parent or family member had walked away, but it could have been worse. It could have been much worse.

Terra zoned out as the men and mostly women discussed how to proceed until the others returned. All she heard was the murmur of voices, some deep and rumbly, others soft and gentle. Her gaze roamed as she took another sip of her coffee. They'd only done the bare minimum of setting up the community hall. They'd stacked the tables and chairs against the wall of the trailer, only setting out what they needed, and hadn't bothered with the tent that usually rose above it all. It gave them room to cook, sit, and eat.

As her gaze continued to roam, it stopped on Philippe's trailer, making her think of her friend. Macey was handling things better than she'd hoped. She and Beth were staying in Philippe's place, "looking after" the trailer as she'd put it yesterday. She doubted that was the real reason. But she didn't say anything. They were coping. That was all that mattered.

Terra was having a harder time. It had taken all she had not to cry herself to sleep last night, and the only thing that stopped her was Annie's little body sleeping so close. It would disturb the little girl, and she couldn't bear upsetting her. Jackson had asked her to be strong, but she didn't know if she had it in her. Every time she had an opportunity to be an example, to step up, to lead, she froze, doubting herself and her place here.

And what place is that? You can't even bring yourself to shift.

She was a fraud, an imposter, and these people deserved better. She couldn't even bring herself to open her mouth to speak, but she had to.

I have to do something.

But what could she do? "What else can we do to keep everyone busy?" she asked, trying to shake the melancholy. They needed to keep together, keep busy, and she needed to stop fretting over the chasm between herself and the caravan. They needed to forget about the others. The volunteers were safe for now. The enemy wouldn't arrive above for another couple days. There was no reason to freak out yet. They had time.

———

Jackson brought the rifle to his shoulder, taking aim. He took a deep breath in, feathering his finger over the trigger. With a breath out, he squeezed, a bullet punching into the middle of the target almost at the same moment the weapon bucked in his grip.

"Good," the sergeant in charge of their group said. "Again."

It was the first day of "training" and he stood elbow to elbow with other shifters at Clark's outdoor firing range. Behind the range, trees darkened the distance while blocky buildings rose tall on each side.

Pop. Pop. Pop.

Beside him, more guns fired, causing him to flinch each time even through the sound dampeners hugging his ears. He lifted the gun again to fire, a scowl forming on his lips.

Jackson and Philippe had ended up in separate groups. He didn't like it, wishing he could have his friend's back, but he kept his mouth shut, focusing on the task at hand. If they wanted to make it off the battlefield he knew was coming, they would have to focus, prepare. They didn't have long, only a few more days, and it was nowhere near long enough. Not at all.

Philippe dwarfed the small woman commanding their squad. But that didn't faze her. She barked out commands all day, running through drills until they managed to follow orders without thinking, without hesitating. He slowed, trying to keep pace with the much shorter stride of the officer leading them in a circuit around the base. Soon enough, though, he found himself almost stepping on her heels again.

She looked over her shoulder, unleashing her rage on him without a word. He would get an earful when they stopped.

Again.

It didn't matter. All that mattered was protecting Earth, protecting their loved ones. He thought of Macey and Beth, and he started to speed up again. This time, he stepped down hard on the officer's heel. She growled and stopped, yelling some unintelligible command to halt the procession.

"Drop and give me a hundred," she commanded, pointing at the ground as she glared at him.

Philippe dropped to hands and knees, his fingers curling into the prickly grass, and started the series of push-ups. It didn't bother him, didn't serve as punishment as it was intended. He felt bad that he'd stepped on her foot. But he'd never had to work as a team with someone so small before. In the past, he'd been grouped with men just as big as he was, fighting just as fast, just as strong. He'd never had to worry about stepping on *their* heels.

Terra stepped out of the trailer. It should have been just another day, but as she looked up, her stomach sank. It had been three days since the others left and she'd known it was coming, but she still wasn't ready. Her hand flexed on the edge of the door as red streams like meteors or shooting stars streaked across overhead. A patchy darkness blotted out the sky, hiding the sun from view except for the occasional rays peeking through.

It had begun.

CHAPTER TWENTY-ONE

The radio crackled through the little shuttle, a constant background cacophony of battle, a reminder of what they fought for, who they fought with. Panic and determination bled through the airways, telling tales of which ships were doing well and which were losing.

Mila tuned it out, focusing on the fight in front of her. That was all that mattered now. She couldn't draw her attention away from the ships around her, keeping them one step ahead of the enemy. She dropped them into sub-space again, a dizzying swirl of colors as they jetted across to what should be the side of another enemy ship. *Hopefully.* "Ready," she called as Avery flexed his fists over the weapon controls. She sent them hurling out of sub-space with a flick of her wrist. The small shuttle shook with the barrage of ammunition being launched.

She smiled, smoothly shifting around the enemy. Then alerts triggered from behind her. "Shit," she said. "Craft approaching at six o' clock." Her hands flew over the controls, and she plunged them back into sub-space. They needed to get out from between two enemy forces. They would be road kill otherwise.

Coming out behind the new fleet, she hesitated, holding off Avery, as a message came over the radio in an automated translation, "This is the Incirrina battleship *Cirri*. We have received your distress call and are coming to your aid. We repeat, this is the Incirrina ship *Cirri*. We have received your distress call and are coming to your aid."

Luke tapped on the comms. "This is Communications Officer Hall of the Earth forces. Welcome to the fight."

As Mila glanced at her friend, she hoped they could understand him, but what did it matter? They weren't here to kill them.

We just might win this thing.

The Incirrina quickly drove the enemy toward the human ships, forcing them to take heavy fire. Cheers rang over comms as the tide of the battle changed before their very eyes. The darkness lit with weapons fire, pummeling the enemy from all sides. Adrenaline surged as the excitement of anticipated victory choked her.

A grin crossed her face.

We're got this.

Resistance proved more than they'd anticipated. The Morg officer frowned as his fellow ships failed around him, succumbing to the enemy. The damned Incirrina had arrived, determined to aid their hopeless allies. It wouldn't work. They had planned their vengeance for too long to be thwarted now.

But the battle in space was lost. An alarm blared, making him flinch as voices careened against each other in a discordant din that spoke less of confident authority than generalized panic. He scowled as he took in the view, ships battling against ships. He knew a lost cause when he saw it.

"Authorize the ground assault."

They hadn't seen *anything* yet.

Mila's mouth gaped as the enemy's ships seemed to explode before her eyes all at once. It defied sense, reason. Small chunks of the formerly massive vessels flew out, careening through space between the remaining battling spaceships. "Shit."

A moment later, the chaotic spray of metal shrapnel converged, streaming in a single direction—toward Earth.

Tristan leaned over her shoulder, "Fire at the pieces," he yelled.

Space lit up with weapons being discharged from dozens of ships hovering over Earth. Mila held her breath, gracefully avoiding the line of fire of any other ships while allowing Avery to fire at the impossible to hit specks.

A few exploded, but most accelerated, plummeting toward Earth, toward their friends and family, their homes.

God help us.

Something has changed, Jackson thought as he stared upward. Before, the ships amassing above had blotted out the sky with their bulk, the occasional flare of burning detritus streaking overhead. Now, the sky erupted in a display of fiery streaks to rival any Fourth of July celebration.

"They're coming."

Beside him, someone nodded right before a siren blared, calling everyone to their duty stations. Jackson took off at a run across the base, thinking of Terra momentarily before pushing her and everything else from his mind.

Today, they fought for Earth.

Jackson hovered in a transport vehicle, cradling his rifle, waiting impatiently to arrive at the coming battle. They hadn't left the base yet, the diesel engine still idly rumbling away to his left. Others in his shifter unit surrounded him as their officer sat in the front seat and out of sight, awaiting orders.

He looked out the back of the transport, but saw nothing but concrete and grass. He wished Philippe were there. The man had seen more battles than he could count, always following his conscience wherever it led. He would know what to say in this moment.

Without him, though, Jackson's nerves tensed, binding him up in anxiety and anticipation. His hand flexed harder over the barrel of his gun, feeling the cold metal compressing his flesh.

"Moving out," their leader's voice yelled over the engine.

The truck jerked to a start. *Where are we going?* He didn't know, and he wouldn't get any answers if he asked. Of course, in a way, he *did* know. They were going to the enemy, to where they'd landed. Soon they would spill out and take up the fight, spilling blood and taking lives. His heart sped up, and he turned to face the back, watching the base pass them by.

Before long, they slowed, and he recognized the area around the gate.

Then a rain of gunshots assaulted the air and competing voices drowned out the truck's engine.

"We're under attack," someone yelled.

"Fire. Return fire," the officer said.

Jackson stood and ran from the truck, turning in the direction of the gunfire.

Boom.

He flinched as heat lambasted him. Swiveling his gunsight, he found the security booth in flames, taken out by something big.

"Spread out! Spread out!" the order came, and the shifters reacted instantly, not needing to be told even once.

After all, standing out in the open was suicide.

He ran for the nearest cover, a copse of trees fifty feet from the fences. It felt like a lifetime, but moments later, he curled behind a tree, pressing into the rough bark as he sighted his gun around the trunk to locate the enemy.

Holes riddled the cloth cover of the truck, and the security booth continued to burn, but otherwise, nothing moved in the clearing between the trees flanking the gate.

We shouldn't have used this entrance.

After a few days on base, he knew it middlingly well. While he'd passed through at the booth currently on fire only days ago, another had no trees near it, preventing the possibility of an ambush.

Somebody fucked up.

Not that it mattered. He squinted, trying to spot hostiles in the quiet that settled over the *wrong* battlefield.

We don't have time for this.

He shifted his eyesight, needing to see better, needing to speed this up. For all he knew, aliens were landing as they stood here with their thumbs up their butts. He thought of Terra, of Annie, of his caravan. He couldn't let them down.

Scanning the opposite trees, he caught the telltale glint of sunlight on metal and opened fire.

CHAPTER TWENTY-TWO

"Mila, don't you dare," Tristan called.

Kyle glanced over as Tristan ran for his seat and flopped down, fumbling for the straps as Mila rocketed forward in the mad crazy style that reminded him of old school fighter pilots. She had a gift, careening around the ships with a single-minded intensity that he'd always respected and admired.

Still, as Earth loomed before them, his hands couldn't help flexing over the armrests as Luke whined in a seat to his left.

"You're going too fast," Tristan complained.

"No, I'm not. I think this is just right," Mila said as she continued to accelerate, pushing him back into his seat.

Kyle crossed himself, struggling to remember the prayers of his childhood as the ship rumbled, shaking them in their seats as it hit Earth's atmosphere. But she didn't try to slow down. He wanted to scream, but wasn't sure if it was in excitement or sheer terror.

Maybe both.

"Get ready, Avery," she said, rocketing forward at breathtaking speeds.

"You expect me to fire at these speeds?" But he gripped the controls anyway, his hands trembling.

"Absolutely."

He shook his head, but dragged in deep breaths, trying to focus.

Lines formed on the horizon, and he realized they'd looped the Earth. Small pieces of the enemy crafts streaked before them, lined up perfectly to be picked off by a decent shot.

"Fire," she said, never slowing as Kyle opened up a barrage at the alien menace before them.

Kyle grinned, wanting to laugh as his foe proved only too easy to hit this way.

God, this woman's brilliant.

The shuttle they drove wasn't intended for fighting in gravity, in atmosphere. It could be slow and difficult to maneuver. By accelerating, slingshotting around the Earth, she removed those deficiencies from the equation. They were like a missile locked on its target, destroying everything in its path.

He whooped as ships exploded before them, smoke turning visibility zero. Kyle tensed, waiting, ready.

"Mila," Tristan drawled a warning.

"No worries. I've got this." And she did. The main screen switched over to an alternative viewing option, showing obstacles in infrared. They passed straight through and out the other side.

The engines roared as Mila pushed the little shuttle further.

"Mila, no. That's enough."

Kyle tuned out Tristan's bleating, focusing on the task ahead.

"Bullshit. There's still more of them." Minutes ticked by as she pushed the ship harder, lining up a repeat approach on their enemy. "Ready."

"Ready," Kyle said, gripping the controls as his heart pounded an excited tempo in his chest. This time, it was anticipation that made his hands shake.

The streaks of enemy ships showed up again, and they all tensed.

The cockpit echoed as Kyle fired.

Fuck, yes! Take that!

Jackson stepped out of the transport vehicle that had seen better days, looking up. He didn't know what he expected, but little had changed. Fire still streaked the sky. The enemy still hadn't landed.

After the firefight they'd just left, he'd half expected to arrive to a bloody battle, but they probably weren't delayed more than ten minutes in total. He forgot how quickly battles tended to end.

As he hefted his rifle to his shoulder and jumped down, stepping up to the military officer leading them, he wondered who they'd been. Why did they strike? They'd been human. He knew that much. But why attack a military convoy on their own soil?

Or were they from another country? Were they an enemy of the United States? But then why would they choose *now* to strike, when working together meant more than ever?

They're human. That's why.

He'd long given up trying to understand the self-destructive tendencies of humans. They made no sense, were counterproductive, and he'd washed his hands of them long ago.

Still, now he was in the middle of their bullshit once more. Around him, the humans prepared for the inevitable, though he couldn't say he understood their logic. With hand gestures, he and his people were ordered behind the human troops as the sound of guns being checked and boots coming down hard on the ground filled the air.

He looked to the officer, a frown on his face, not liking the direction things were going. Meanwhile, his people looked to *him* for guidance. By his best guess, the military had estimated the ships would land a few miles outside the base, had coordinated troops to intervene, and evacuated civilians. As they'd driven up, he'd seen people racing in the opposite direction, running for their lives from a force they had no hope of escaping.

As he glanced around, encouraging his people with a look, he noticed that all his men and women waited behind the lines while the human soldiers stood before them, ready and waiting for the enemy to land. Their officers told the shifters to hold, to wait for their command. Jackson had the sneaking suspicion that a command to fight would never come, that they would rather their own people die needlessly than risk relying on shifters to save them, to defend them.

He scowled, not liking the nature of his thoughts or the reinforcement of those thoughts that stood in a line before him. While Jackson had never wanted to help humans, saw their flaws evident again and again in the actions they perpetuated against shifters and anyone they saw as "other," he'd shoved his prejudices aside for the greater good. It seemed not everyone had been so magnanimous. He didn't like it.

With a look, Jackson gave his people reassurance, encouraging them to follow the human leaders… for now.

The last of the enemy ships landed, their occupants flooding out, a sea of locusts on human soil. Human troops and war machines opened fire from below as Mila changed her game, and Avery did the same. Jets and bombers flew circles around her, taking out as many as they could. She shivered as soldiers fell, good men and women willing to die for their countries, for their families.

From above, she could differentiate the aliens from humans, but nothing else. The aliens crossed the grounds like a dark cloud, poisoning everything in its path, leaving death and destruction in its wake. The humans, on the other hand, blended into the environment, their camo uniforms designed for the terrain. Even the tanks blended somewhat with the landscape.

She circled again and again, feeling like a sitting duck, waiting for the enemy to start firing on her. The sluggish controls frustrated her, holding her back, and she wished she was still in space, where this bird could really fly. But the aliens had brought the fight here, to their home turf.

A proximity alert blared as a shot passed alarmingly close to her left wing. "Shit. Hold on."

Jackson waited, almost growling in frustration for the orders he feared would never come. Would they wait until all the human soldiers fell before calling on them? With each moment, his guilt ate at him, gnawing at his gut to do something. His people looked to him, their faces increasingly worried, anxious. Waiting didn't sit well with them either.

His ears rang from the constant barrage as he scanned the battlefield, reducing his hearing even as he enhanced his vision to see the distance and details better. It didn't look good. The firepower the aliens used plowed straight through their body armor. His allies took some down with them, but it took two or three times as many shots to down one of the enemy as it did one of their own. The tanks and jets could do significant damage, but it was a danger close mission, which limited their options. He glanced back at his people. "Fuck it."

Jackson took off at a run, increasing musculature and adrenaline as he lifted his gun to his shoulder, sighting along the barrel. He started firing before he even got close. *Pop. Pop. Pop.* Three enemies went down from perfectly fired rounds into the center of their foreheads right below the edges of their helmets. The thin edge of the trigger dug into his finger, keeping him grounded.

A round pummeled his shoulder. He grunted, gritted his teeth, but pushed on as he forced the wound to heal, to close. *Pop. Pop.* One more enemy dropped, another falling into his buddy, but staying on his feet. In his peripheral vision, his shifters followed his silent command, following him into battle. Sprayed dirt hit the side of his face as large artillery struck the battlefield once more. He flinched, but kept going.

His uniform stuck to his skin where he'd been shot, the blood hard to forget even when the wound had already healed. Flashes of light blinded him as an explosion erupted ahead, small but taking out a handful of the enemy. Jackson blinked, shooting blindly for a few moments until his vision cleared.

Like a a shifting tide, everything changed. His shifters dragged the fallen humans out of the line of fire, protecting them with their rifles and their bodies when necessary. A shifter dropped, not getting up right away. A retreating human grabbed him, pulling him up over his shoulders and dragging him to the medical tent.

Jackson turned his focus forward.

Pop.

<hr>

Terra trailed behind as the last of them entered the caves. When the ground assault had seemed imminent, they'd picked up and left, heading here, where they hoped they could hide in safety. She thought of Jackson, who was currently or would soon be fighting them.

What was I thinking?

Why did I push him into this?

Anxiety gnawed away at her as she gripped Annie, comforted by her presence.

"Please be safe," Terra whispered under her breath. "Come home to us."

Ahead of her, one of the elders said, "Alright everyone. Settle down and let's set up our camps."

Terra stepped into the chilly entrance of the cave system, pulling her jacket closer around her shoulders as the briskness hit her all at once. In the dim light, people huddled together as children cried.

In the distance, the engines of distant jets and spacecraft roared, upsetting the sanctuary they prayed this out of the way place would be. Terra held Annie's hand tighter, tempted to lift her into her arms, as the little girl stared up at her in question. She looked down. "Everything'll be just fine, sweetie. I promise."

She just hoped she could *keep* that promise.

<hr>

Jackson's mind kept flitting back to Terra. Was she safe? Was she scared?

Stop it.

He refused to dwell on that. He had people here who needed him. Especially since the human officers were useless to them. They'd yelled at their backs when the shifters dashed forward.

Did other shifters around the world face the same?

It didn't matter.

He alternated between fighting on the front lines and falling back to direct his people. As time passed, a rhythm developed. Men and women fought for a spell, using all the skills at their disposal to take out the aliens while trying as best they could to avoid fire.

But the enemy were thick before them, their black armor like an ever-shifting sea, and operating at this level was exhausting. Each of them grew tired, took shots they couldn't avoid, got sloppy. When that happened, he called them back, directing them to the medical tent where they could refuel and patch themselves up if need be. Some had to be carried off the field, but fortunately not many.

If they could keep this up, they might have a chance.

Maybe the world *would* have a chance.

CHAPTER TWENTY-THREE

The silence took Terra by surprise. For hours, the air was filled with explosions, roaring engines and cracks of gunfire. The caravan huddled together, distracting themselves as best they could, but they feared making noise as much as they feared for their loved ones. If they were too loud, would the enemy find them, capture them, kill them?

It ran through most everyone's heads, and the hours of constant sonic barrage mixed with the drifting scent of violence kept them on edge. So when it ended, they all stopped breathing, their bodies tense, waiting for it to start up again.

It didn't.

For a while, her ears rang with the remembered cacophony, but before long she caught the dripping of water. Deep shadows flickered around campfires which barely chased away the bitter cold and illuminated only enough to reveal the dreary grays of the cave walls.

Annie peeked out from under her arm, looking up at her with hopeful, trusting eyes. "Is it over?"

She smiled down at Annie, but the expression pulled at her, difficult in the wake of the uncertainty. The battle had ended, but who won? Was Jackson safe? Were the others?

Uncertainty surrounded her, every face asking, "What now?"

In a quiet voice, she said, "We'll stay here. Until we have news of what happened, we'll stay here." Shifting in her seat, she looked around. "Who's got the radio?"

Terra had made sure they brought a radio, figuring in the aftermath, it would be their only source of information. It wouldn't work in the cave, unable to get a signal, but she'd also brought headphones, and if they were careful, they could reach the mouth of the cave without risking exposure.

"I have it," one woman whispered, raising her hand as if they were in school.

Terra nodded, standing up and carefully crossing the uneven floor of the cavern. "Thank you," she said as she accepted the radio from the other woman's hands. "I'll see if there's any news."

Many people nodded, and she took a deep breath. "Annie, stay put."

Annie's lip pouted out, shuddering in that way little kids had of manipulating adults. "But…"

"No buts," she said, kneeling down on Annie's level. "I don't know if it's safe out there, kiddo, okay?" She touched the girl's cheek. "I need you safe."

The girl sniffed, but the woman she'd taken the radio from rested her hand on Annie's shoulder. "I'll keep her safe."

Terra nodded, smiling in thanks, and walked gingerly across the rocky terrain, careful not to trip as she exited the dim environs of the cave system. As she stepped closer to the outside world, a stiff wind brought with it smoke and warmth.

At the edge of the cave, she knelt down behind a bush, unnerved by the flames tinting the sky orange in the background. She plugged the headphones into the radio and clicked it on, scanning channels for news. For anything.

White noise filled her ears, interspersed with music from stations too far away to hear clearly. She kept scanning, but didn't hear anything resembling news. Switching to AM, she started again. Voices this time, a talk show declaring the end of the world. She moved on. More music. *Keep going.* Then she recognized something useful. NPR. She fiddled with the dial until it came in semi-clearly.

"We're still getting reports from correspondents around the world." Static crackled, blocking out words, obscuring them into nothingness. "The alien forces have been defeated in some places while battles roll on in others. Please, stay in your homes or shelters."

That was all she needed to hear.

It wasn't over.

Jackson stood surrounded by his people in the quiet that signaled the end of the battle. It lasted for a few heartbeats before his ears adjusted, returning to normal. Then the real aftermath of war greeted him. Blood, death, and weapons' discharge tickled his nostrils while the cries and moans of injured soldiers drifted on the breeze. Smoke dispersed, revealing more clearly the ground covered in black.

Bodies.

His stomach twisted, hating the necessity. He'd lived a

peaceful life, even if he'd lived with hate in his heart for far too long. At least he could say that hate had never turned to violence. He had no idea why they'd attacked, why they'd singled out Earth to conquer. It didn't matter. It was simply tragic. A waste.

Around him, his people waited for orders. "Search for wounded and bring them back to the medical tent. Once that's done, secure the enemy survivors." He didn't know what the human militaries would want them to do if there were any survivors, but international laws dictated they be taken as prisoners of war.

His mind strayed to Terra once more as he dropped his rifle to his side, and finally he didn't have to push the thoughts away. No enemy waited on the horizon, no one was in danger. He didn't know if more enemy forces would show up, but for now, there was a moment of peace. He wanted to go home, hold her, pick up Annie, see his people safe and sound.

Jackson turned and walked to the command tent. Stepping up, he saluted. "Is there any news?"

The man with the most bars on his uniform looked up at him and glared. "If you were military, I'd court marshal you for that stunt you pulled today." He stared hard at Jackson, but an understanding crossed the other man's eyes, gratitude. He would never admit it, but he was grateful for Jackson breaking rank, saving his men. "We're hoping to hear soon."

"Jackson!" Mila said in surprise as her gaze landed on a familiar face in the background. She stormed down the landed shuttle's ramp.

Jackson pivoted, orienting himself to her calling his name.

Mila picked up speed. She jogged across the expanse, glad to see him in one piece, even if they'd never really been friends. "It's good to see you," she said as she approached, reaching out a hand.

He gripped her forearm, nodding. "And you. What are the chances, huh?"

"How did you fare?" Mila wasn't sure she wanted to hear if shifters had died. They weren't her friends, she didn't know them, and she'd never connected with any shifters, always keeping herself aloof, but still...

"I don't believe we lost anyone. The military was better prepared than I would have hoped."

A dark look crossed his face, and Mila wondered what it meant, what he didn't say.

Again, she wasn't sure she wanted to know.

Terra stepped from the cave again, radio in hand. The smoke had cleared, and the world around her had returned to the natural serenity she expected. Blue sky rose over the trees that, more and more, were emblazoned with fiery colors. She plugged the headphones into her ears and turned the device on. A commercial played, trying to con people into buying the latest extravagance, which she found especially satirical in the current situation.

After a few minutes, the commercial ended, and the announcer spoke up. "There are continued reports of isolated pockets of fighting, but some areas have been cleared of the alien threat. These areas include: the US and Canada, Europe, and China. We have received no reports from Central or South America and sporadic reports from Africa and the

Middle East. Asia has mostly eradicated the threat, but there is still fighting in most countries on the continent.

"Around the world, reports have been consistent, though the information remains unclear. In all accounts, a few squadrons of soldiers, often times the second string, proved the key to the victory.

"These brave men and women were often seen fired upon, injured, and in many instances, they continued to fight long after their compatriots fell. Many war correspondents claimed that these individuals seemed to move at speeds they'd never seen before, returning to the battle even after grievous injuries.

"Some have theorized that these brave heroes were, in fact, shape-shifters or possibly the result of military experimentation. We'll keep you apprised as more details come through."

Terra clicked the radio off, wrapping the headphones around it. *Shifters.* She had no doubt. She didn't think hard on what this could mean for them. What did it matter? What mattered now was they could leave these frigid caves.

Tucking the radio under her arm, she ambled into the cave toward her people, not bothering to be quiet this time. There was no need. It was over. "Come on, everyone," she said as she approached. "The coast is clear."

There was hesitation, the moment stretching as they absorbed the news, then everyone stood, the children jumping to their feet and shrieking in delight. Terra smiled, stepping up to help people collect their belongings.

When would Jackson return home?

CHAPTER TWENTY-FOUR

*M*ila wrung her hands, wanting to bolt as she stood in front of the office door for the Commandant Commander United States Space Command, Admiral Brad Lewis.

Remember: No more running. You promised.

She'd received the summons as she was returning the battle shuttle.

Report immediately to Admiral Lewis's office.

The words still chilled her. She stared at the bold letters on his door, trying to con herself into bravery. Many people thought she was brave, but it was easy to be brave in the heat of the moment, when the enemy was breathing down your neck.

She shivered, feeling her courage evaporate. Everyday bravery was an entirely different beast, though. In those things, she'd always been a coward. So reaching up her fist took monumental effort, and she hovered there, her knuckles inches from the door's solid mass. Fear and anxiety raced through her, a nameless villain defeating her from the inside out. A villain who had defeated her more times than she could count.

"Fuck it," she said, smacking her knuckles against the surface a couple times, her heart pounding in her throat.

"Come in," a familiar male voice said from the other side.

Mila took a deep breath, embracing the "fuck it" she'd just said out loud. "Sir?" she said as she entered, standing tall with her hands behind her back.

"Sit."

Sitting made her even more nervous, at a disadvantage. It would be harder to flee, to fight. Not that she was thinking of doing either.

Don't kid yourself.

"What's your real name?"

Mila froze, ice rushing through her veins as the careful house of cards she'd built tumbled around her. She'd been caught. It was over. She would never fly again.

I should have known this was coming. Of course, he knows. He asked me to call Jackson, didn't he?

Oddly, despair filled her instead of the expected fear. She thought of Tristan, the future she'd never truly believed they could have. They wouldn't now, no matter how much he wanted it.

Would they lock her up? Send her to one of the camps? She couldn't remember, but impersonating a member of the military was a few years in prison, wasn't it? Maybe Tristan, her friends, would visit her. The thought made her heart lift a little.

For the first time, she realized just how tired she was. Mila had been running for so long. She didn't want to run anymore. She didn't have the energy. "Mila Dragomirov," she said, sealing her fate. She wouldn't run. Not again.

I promised, didn't I?

But he only nodded at that news and started typing away at his computer. "Mila Dragomirov. NSS Pilot Program. Passed sub-space qualifications with record scores." He sounded impressed and turned to her. "I'm assuming you took over for the USS *Orleans* mission." He paused, looking her dead in the eyes. His stare asked a question his lips didn't speak.

"Yes, sir. She died in a mugging shortly before the mission began."

He didn't seem surprised, which she found odd. Almost no one knew about the mugging. "You'll be properly rewarded for your actions, Pilot Dragomirov, and I'll start the paperwork to have your records transferred from the Pilot Program to NSS active service."

Mila's mouth fell open, not capable of believing her ears. Rewarded? She wouldn't be punished? She wouldn't have to hide, to lie? "Come again?" Her voice squeaked on the last syllable.

He stared her down, his face an expressionless mask. "You're dismissed."

She nodded, floating up from her seat and out the door. Her mind operated on autopilot, not seeing her surroundings or registering where she went. She arrived at her front door without remembering any of the steps in between. She could have been hit by a car and wouldn't have seen it coming.

Slipping inside, her footsteps pounded on the flooring.

"Are you okay?" Tristan said, suddenly there, holding her shoulders, searching her eyes for answers.

She looked up at him and smiled. It felt like a shroud had been lifted from her, one that had covered her for over ten years. "Yeah, I think I am," she said with wonder.

Mila stood in the hallway, uncomfortable in her new uniform. She rubbed at the nametag where "Dragomirov" was spelled out in neat lettering like a blazing billboard crying out, "Shifter! Fraud!" She resisted the urge to cover it with her hand.

It had not even been a day since the battle to defend Earth ended. Hell, there were probably still pockets of fighting around the globe. It felt strange to be standing in a dress uniform in a crisp, clean government building while what sounded like hundreds of voices murmured in the background.

"Mila," Jackson said.

She turned, surprised to see him once again. They'd spoken over nothing but phone calls for ten years and now seemed to bump into each other at every turn. "Jackson. Good to see you again."

He walked up to her. "Do you know what this is about?"

She shook her head.

He glanced down, his eyes widening. "That's not the name that was on your uniform the last time we met."

She looked down, rubbing the spot again, a smirk on her face. "No, it's not."

"They know?" He looked sad.

"It's a good thing. I think."

He arched a brow at her, not saying a word.

She turned her back on him. Having enough cynicism for the both of them, she didn't need his to amplify it. From her position, she could see the podium where microphones sprung out like branches on a tree. The media swarmed in the audience, eagerly talking amongst themselves, chatting with friends or sharing suspicions about the press conference's topic.

Mila didn't have a clue. Though, looking at Jackson, she figured shifters had to play some role. Otherwise, why ask two shifters to attend?

From her right, a parade of people stormed down the hall, and a couple Secret Service agents ushered her out of the doorway, giving them room to pass. She just barely recognized the President from passing TV broadcasts on the streets.

What the fuck? She'd been called to a press conference being held by the President?

Her eyes rounded and mouth gaped just a bit.

"You're catching flies," Jackson said, leaning into her ear.

That brought her back in a blink. She snapped her jaw shut and turned, glaring at him. That he was right just made it worse.

"My fellow Americans," the President said into the microphones, silencing the crowd. Behind him, a line of men sat, mostly in military dress uniforms. "Our country, our species, our *world* has just survived a monumental occasion. In the last few days, we fought off a military force not of this Earth, fighting alongside allies of different countries, different species, even of a different planet. We worked in harmony, without prejudice."

Jackson snorted. Mila jabbed him in the stomach with her elbow, glaring at him again for good measure.

"By this cooperation, we won the day, saved our world, protected our families, our liberties, our lives. Without the assistance of those different from us, those we haven't always seen as equal or seen eye to eye with, we would have failed, would have lost.

"This day, I give thanks to the Incirrina, who unfortunately cannot be here in person, the countries of the world that looked past their differences in favor of a common goal, and the shape-shifter community, who stepped forward in spite of the risks to their own freedoms and liberties. The courage those young men and women showed in volunteering for combat, fighting for countries that had stolen their freedoms and imprisoned or even killed them, cannot be understated.

"As such, I thus avow that I intend to enact laws to give shape-shifters the same rights as any American citizen and resolve the issues that their abilities make in society. What's more, starting today, all shape-shifters currently in camps will be released, with reparations and redress to follow."

He turned to the doorway where Mila and Jackson stood, urging them to come forward.

The President smiled. *Fuck, what's his name?* "Shandor Jackson, when called, you rallied the shape-shifting community together, serving as a liaison, leader, and soldier in the war against the alien menace. For that, the world will forever be in your debt." He shook Jackson's hand, earnestness in his gaze.

Shandor? His first name is Shandor?

Then he zeroed in on Mila. *Oh shit.* Her palms started to sweat, and she resisted the urge to rub them against her pants. "Pilot Mila Dragomirov has repeatedly shown selfless courage in the face of unthinkable odds, putting her life and liberty on the line for others. On board the USS *Orleans*, she flew beyond all expectations to protect her crew and fought against an invading force to repel them when they threatened not only the crew but also the mission, a mission which contributed to the alliance that helped save our planet. She was also instrumental in the mission which finalized our alliance with the Incirrina and brought the early detection required to organize forces against the threat to come.

"During the battle to save Earth, she also piloted a battle shuttle into the fight above, taking out countless enemy craft, and continued the fight in atmosphere even though her craft wasn't designed for that type of combat. For that reason, the United States, the world, owes her a debt, and she will be awarded the Medal of Honor in formal ceremony next week for her gallantry."

The President lifted his arm in salute. Her mind blanked, shocked, but she lifted her arm in return, her chest tight with emotion.

Holy shit.

It's not over yet.

Those words rang through his head as Kyle stared Wilhem down where he sat on the cot in the prison cell.

It's not over yet.

Kyle waited, waiting for an explanation, waiting for answers. From the information he'd gathered, an incident years ago had destroyed Wilhem's voice, leaving it the scratchy, barely audible mess it currently was.

It also meant the criminal wasn't accustomed to speaking. His contacts had told him his brother, Niklas Wolf, had been the talker, the one people negotiated and conversed with. Wilhem was the brains, the skill, to Niklas's brawn and mouth.

So he didn't expect the fucker to open up easily or use a ton of words.

The battle was over, they'd won, in spite of the Wolf brothers' interference, but it would never truly be over for Kyle until he got his "man." He couldn't rest knowing there were traitors out there, people willing to kill, to sacrifice even the human race, to see their mysterious ideals met.

Kyle even wondered if the attacks on the shifter units might have been the same group. He'd heard about those events second hand, but security men did love to talk, especially to a compatriot stuck in the hospital. It was amazing how he could show up at Kaufman's bedside and get the scoop on half the active investigations in the NSS.

So he knew that while those attacks had been poorly organized and manned, they'd been well funded. The weapons recovered had been top notch, expensive. They'd had access to a few weapons not available to the general public, which made him practically drool at the investigative opportunities there, but it wasn't his case.

He refocused on Wilhem. Moments had ticked by in silence since Wilhem's latest statement, but Kyle didn't move, didn't rush him. He just glared.

Wilhem laughed, the sound cracking in his damaged throat, and shrugged. "I can't help myself. It's what I do."

What's he talking about?

Kyle resisted the urge to frown, leaning into his patience, his determination to get this bastard to crack.

"After receiving the job, I hacked the clients. I like to know who we're getting into bed with, know if we're likely to get stabbed in the back." He looked up at Kyle and shook his head. "They've got a hard on for your pilot like you wouldn't believe. They hate her for foiling their plans, blame her."

And she did it again, didn't she? She helped stop the sabotage on the moon and then got praised for it in a press conference just that morning. They attacked her shortly before the *Dakota* mission, didn't they?

And what the hell's gonna stop them from doing it again?

PART THREE

"Hell is empty and all the devils are here."

–William Shakespeare

CHAPTER TWENTY-FIVE

*M*ila sat, staring at her food for once instead of eating it. The announcement from the press conference continued to rattle around in her head. Though she couldn't remember the exact words, the President's face, or who attended, the words "Medal of Honor" kept rolling through her mind on a marquee.

"Well, this is a sight," Tristan said as he strolled in behind her, sidling up to the table. "Are you sick?"

She looked up, seeing the concern etching his face, and laughed. "No, I'm not sick. Just distracted."

He sat down across from her, his fingers tapping against the wooden tabletop, drumming away in a steady beat. "Must be *some* thoughts."

"Yeah." Her focus shifted internally again.

Medal of Honor.

God, how the hell did this happen? She didn't deserve a medal. She deserved to get thrown in prison for impersonating a member of the military.

Heavy hands wrapped around hers and she jerked her head up. "You *are* worthy, Mila."

She smirked. "It's gonna take me a while to believe that."

He patted her hands and leaned back again. "Of course, but don't forget. We all believe in you. We have from the start."

Mila stuffed something soft and chewy in her mouth to keep from talking. She knew the next word to pass her lips would likely start an argument.

Bang.

They both jumped in their seats, looking up at each other in question. "What the hell was that?" she said, turning to face the noise.

The back door.

"I don't know." He stood, turning toward the sound as well.

Then, men in black swarmed the room, brandishing weapons.

"Shit!" Mila yelled, jumping to her feet as she flipped the table and knocked Tristan to the side as a gun zeroed in on him.

Then the gun arm pivoted, targeting her. "No fucking shifter's getting the Medal of Honor," the man growled, a sneer on his lips.

Fuck.

Kyle stopped with a squeal of breaks in front of Tristan and Mila's place. As he turned in his seat, an uneasy feeling settled in.

It's too quiet.

Was he too late? Too early? Maybe Wilhem had been wrong?

Then he castigated himself. Wilhem didn't *know* they would attack. He didn't know their plans, though he imagined if he'd asked, he could have gotten the bastard to hack their systems and get specific information.

He cursed under his breath. That's what he should have done. He should have convinced him to help gather intel under the supervision of a cybersecurity expert, monitoring his web traffic. Instead, he'd gone off half-cocked, dashing off to check on his friends at even the *hint* of danger.

So fucking stupid.

When had he lost his edge?

Crack.

Kyle jumped, jerking his head toward the house as the single gunshot reverberated through the neighborhood. He popped his seatbelt and jumped from the car, not even bothering to close the door as he barreled forward, trampling the grass in the front yard as he ran for the door.

He burst through, stalling just inside the entrance. In the front hallway, everything looked normal. All was quiet again. Should he call out? What if there were still hostiles inside? He pulled out his pistol and lifted it into the air, then systematically searched the house.

To the right, the living room was clear, empty and undisturbed. He stopped in a doorway to the left. Mila stood in the center of the dining room with a gun shaking in her hand. She was covered in blood with drops plopping onto the ground from the fingertips of her left hand.

Around her, food was strewn everywhere, the table flipped on its side and riddled with holes. Blood soaked the floor, and he counted at least two bodies not moving.

"Is he? Is he?" Mila stammered, trying to finish a sentence but seemingly unable to complete the thought.

"Mila? What happened?"

Where's Tristan?

And then her stuttering sentences made sense. Kyle spotted a set of legs peeking out from behind the table and holstered his gun, dashing forward. He squatted at Tristan's head. Tristan looked pale and wasn't moving. For a second, Kyle wasn't even sure if he breathed.

"Is he?" Mila said once more.

"I don't know."

Then Mila collapsed, her body thumping against the floor. Kyle jerked to his feet, torn.

What the hell do I do now?

Kyle paced the waiting room of the hospital.

Mila will be all right.

That thought was easy to believe. Mila was a shifter. A little food, and she'll be right as rain.

Assuming they can get her to eat.

After the initial panic had worn off, he'd called 911. Tristan was bleeding, but breathing. He did the best he could to staunch the bleeding before checking on Mila. She was in better shape. Injured, but he didn't fear for her life. He quickly returned to Tristan's side, putting more pressure on his wounds and reassuring himself that Tristan still breathed.

So he wasn't too concerned about Mila, but Tristan was

another story. They'd immediately sent him through to surgery.

A doctor in a white coat stepped into the room. "Kyle Avery?" he asked.

Kyle jerked to attention, approaching with a click of heels as if he were responding to a superior officer. "Yes?"

"Ms. Dragomirov is awake. She should be released later today. You can go see her now. She's in room 103."

"Thank you, doctor."

He nodded and disappeared through the swinging double doors.

Kyle approached the nurse's station adjacent to the waiting room. "Where's room 103?"

The man at the counter pointed down the hallway to his right. Kyle followed the directions, startling when he entered the room only to be faced with someone he didn't know.

The patient smirked. "New girl's in the bed next to me."

"Thanks."

"Avery?"

Kyle walked past the curtain separating the two beds and stood at the foot of Mila's hospital bed. "The one and only."

She tried to smile, but the expression trembled, too much effort for her to manage.

It surprised him, so contrary to everything he'd known about her from the moment they met. She was strong-willed, stubborn, and courageous. She did what needed doing and sometimes bent the rules to do so. Seeing her so badly shaken disturbed him. He sat down on the end of the bed. "Hey, you okay?"

Her shaking hand went up to brush her loose hair back. "Yeah. I will be. Any news on Tristan?"

He shook his head. "Not yet. I'm sure he'll be fine."

She nodded her head, then stared out the large picture window. "They did it because of the Medal of Honor."

"What?"

She still didn't look at him, dropping her shaking hand to brush over the ugly hospital johnny. "They said no shifter would get the Medal of Honor."

Kyle leaned forward. "Can you tell me what happened?"

"They broke in through the back door. I pushed Tristan out of the way, then the guy pointed a gun at me, fired. He winged me and I attacked, managed to knock the gun from his hand. We struggled. There were gunshots, but I don't remember more than the sound of it. I knocked that one out and charged the other, struggled for the gun, then it went off." She turned to him. "Did I kill both of them?" She looked distant, almost haunted.

"I don't know. I didn't check. Didn't care."

She nodded and turned to face the window again, not saying another word.

Kyle stared at her, wondering if the same organization was responsible for this attack as for the *Orleans* and *Dakota* mission sabotages. But then, prejudice against shifters was practically a national pastime. It could be anyone who decided she didn't deserve the honor.

Except, his mind nagged him with a teasing thought; she wasn't the only shifter acknowledged at that press conference. Shandor Jackson might not be receiving a Medal of Honor, but the President had certainly made a spectacle of him.

Jesus Christ.

He stood up, but Mila didn't even notice. "I have to go." He left the room, pulling out his cell phone to make some calls.

Maybe Mila wasn't the only target.

Terra felt lost as they returned to the caravan site. Around her, the trailers and such stood sentinel, like abandoned buildings long after the residents had died or moved away. It was eerie. So was the hesitant way everyone entered, almost afraid to return to normal life, almost like they *couldn't.*

Then again, the others, the volunteers, still hadn't returned.

Will they return? Will the military, the government, let them?

She rubbed her face, not liking the direction of her thoughts.

My fault.

If they never returned, it would be all her fault. *She'd* convinced Jackson to volunteer, to organize the shifters. *She'd* told him they needed to step up, to do their part to save the planet. Had she been wrong?

She didn't want to believe that. She wanted to believe Jackson would come around that bend any moment now with the rest and her own failings would be forgotten, lost to the passage of time.

Annie was bouncing about, smiling and trying to get the other kids to join in her play. Some looked to their parents in askance, uncertain in the face of all this change. Others were still being gripped by their parents like a lifeline. But that didn't stop Annie. She dashed forward, glad to finally be free of that miserable cavern.

Terra couldn't blame her. It had been cold, wet, and dreary, perfectly matching everyone's mood as they waited to hear their fates. Now, she watched the blue, cloudless sky, but her mood still felt gray. The sky felt wrong, like it was acting out of character.

Then a sound. Footsteps came from the area where the caravan parked their cars, and her heart jumped in her chest. She glanced over, her feet taking her a few steps closer even before she registered the impulse.

Annie, having heard the same sound, squealed and raced forward, eager to greet everyone returning. Terra smiled, finally feeling like all was right with the world.

Then a shadowed figure stepped from the trees.

I don't know him.

"Annie!" she screamed, but it was too late.

More men in black surged from the woods, raising their weapons, and Annie was right in front of them.

*T*erra curled her arms around Annie as fear consumed her. All around her, the caravan sat on the cold, hard earth while men in black patrolled.

What are they waiting for?

She didn't get it. That scene continued to play out on repeat in her head. Annie running across the ground, kicking up leaves as she raced to who they all thought was Jackson and the others returning from battle. Then the men appearing, deadly efficient and well-armed. Annie sliding to a stop at one of their feet as Terra screamed, but they'd barely paid her any mind.

Instead, they'd stormed forward, corralling the adults, yelling slurs and curse words when they didn't move fast enough. Panic and pandemonium reigned as they were pressed together, body slamming against body as they fruitlessly try to escape their captors. Only they'd caged themselves instead.

Why did they attack?

That thought kept plaguing her. It didn't make sense, and her mind kept coming back to it, probably to escape everything else. If she kept wondering *why*, she didn't have to see the looks the others were giving her. If she kept wondering *why*, she wouldn't have to think about what would happen to her, to Annie, to them all.

But she couldn't escape the pleading glances. Where before the caravan had readily taken over, falling back on old habits and skills, glazing over Terra's inadequacies, now they looked to *her*. Faced with something they'd never imagined, couldn't cope with, they looked to *her*, a washed up office worker. They looked to *her* as a leader.

Can't they see I'm a fraud?

What was Jackson thinking, leaving her in charge? She couldn't do this. She couldn't lead them. She couldn't even save herself. How could she possibly save them?

I'm a hypocrite.

As she continued running her hand through Annie's fine hair, watching the men in black pace back and forth with guns hugged to their shoulders, she had to admit it.

I'm a shifter who's biased against shifters.

God, had she even been able to admit that to herself before? Had she ever managed to say, even in her own head, "I'm a shifter?" She couldn't remember but feared the answer was no. She looked behind herself at the others. A woman whimpered somewhere in the huddle while children hiccupped in anticipation of tears. Fear and trauma stared back at her, serving as the perfect mirror to reflect who she really was.

I'm a monster.

Terra looked around with sad eyes. People shifted on the hard ground as the armed men loomed nearby, their voices indistinct. Her own inner turmoil darkened the situation, leaving her feeling at sea. It's not happy or comfortable to realize you're the bad guy in the plot, that *you're* the one who needs to change, needs to grow, needs to evolve. It was so easy to just assume someone else was in the wrong, that your own problems have outside sources. No one wanted to admit they'd fucked themselves up.

But I let it happen, didn't I?

By listening to the media, the news, by not thinking for herself, by being in denial and not honest with herself, she'd let this happen. Even when Jackson tried to encourage her to learn to shift, she'd refused, burying her head in the sand. Even when Annie started shifting with alacrity, she'd remained in denial. Hell, she'd tried to stop her.

I've got to stop.

She couldn't live in the dark anymore, couldn't hide from her problems and herself a moment longer. Studying her surroundings, something jumped at her.

We outnumber them.

The fact nagged at her consciousness, like a loose stitch on a knit sweater.

We outnumber them.

The bad guys had guns, but *they* had superior numbers. If they could just overpower them, they could get free.

But how? She was no military mastermind, had never been in a fight in her life, and knew her own abilities about as well as a toddler learning its first steps. She struggled to piece together what she knew about shifters, about the skill sets of those who'd stayed behind, and came up blank.

God, I am a fraud.

But an urgency was building in her. They needed to *do* something. They needed to act. They couldn't wait around, hoping for a rescue, hoping for a hero. This was the real world, and the real world didn't work that way.

God helps those who help themselves.

And Terra was done letting someone else act for her.

CHAPTER TWENTY-SEVEN

Terra sidled up to one of the older women, continuing to hold Annie in her lap. She glanced over to where the armed assailants stood. Maybe a half hour ago, they'd drifted off, convening in small groups around the huddled captives, just out of earshot of normal hearing.

Of course, they were shifters and "just out of normal hearing" didn't mean jack shit. Not that she was listening. She had other plans in mind.

She slid over until her outer thigh bumped up against the woman's. "We need to act." Her voice didn't raise above a whisper and she didn't look at her. She'd chosen her to speak to first because she didn't know who she could rely on. She needed someone who knew the others, knew what they were capable of.

"What do you suggest?" the woman said, her voice trembling from nerves and age.

"Not sure yet. Need to rally the forces first, figure out what we've got."

The woman nodded.

"Most of the fighters left with Jackson." Her voice started to smooth out as she spoke, confidence and purpose easing her. "We don't have much in the way of weapons. Maybe a knife or two."

Terra frowned but tried to mask the expression as soon as it formed. It wouldn't do to give away the game before they even got started. She studied the nearest cluster of armed men. They stood in a loose group. One smoked, a plume billowing into the sky as he sucked hard, the end flaring bright red. None looked this way.

She turned back to her partner in crime. "We outnumber them. Do you think we can take them without weapons?" She glanced over at the woman again, who frowned.

"I want to say yes, but I just don't know. If everyone was here, I would say absolutely. Philippe alone would have been a wonderful asset. He often shifts into a bear and has fought in many wars he felt had merit. But with those here? I just don't know."

Terra bit her lip, chewing on it with worry. Then, Annie tipped her head up, an adorable confused look on her face. "I'll fight, Tewa. I have claws!" She lifted and curled her hands, looking adorably fierce.

A grin curved her lips before she froze.

I have claws.

Every last one of them was a shifter. They could shift into animals with built in weapons. Claws, talons, fangs, you name it.

A plan began to form in her mind.

764

Terra sat back, her nerves wound tighter than a tourniquet. Before her, two foot tall Timmy was ready to initiate the plan. As she looked around, her team was just as tense, primed for action. It had taken time to organize everyone, maybe an hour in the seemingly unending crawl of captivity, but they were ready now. Everyone knew their parts.

I can't believe I'm using a robot in this plan. This is crazy.

Yet, this was the best she could come up with. She wasn't a tactician. She wasn't a soldier or leader. Give her some paper-work and she could take it on like a boss, but give her a life or death situation and she was hopeless.

Timmy sidled up to the nearest throng of baddies. He proceeded forward on his little legs, wobbling on parts not made for their final purpose. When he stopped, he looked up, focusing on one of the armed men. His simulated voice broke the silence. "You should cup the butt of your rifle to your shoulder to minimize probability of musculoskeletal damage."

"What the fuck?" he said, backing up and staring down at Timmy. "What the fuck is this?"

Another laughed, pointing at the man in question. "Man, that little bucket of bolts *owned* you."

More masculine laughter welled up, all directed at Timmy's target.

"Shut up," he said, pulling his weapon tighter to his shoulder, though, noticeably, doing exactly as Timmy instructed.

"Did the wittle wobot teach you to hold your wittle gun?"

"Shut. Up. Asswipe."

"Hey!" a voice barked from the opposite end of the clearing. "Knock it off." He marched across the space, his steps pounding the dirt.

Terra pivoted her head, monitoring the other men. They started shifting toward the spectacle, helpless to resist the ass chewing about to go down. She turned to her partners in crime and nodded.

The huddle erupted into fur and sharp claws, surging outward seemingly in all directions. Moments later, gunshots cracked through the air. Terra tried to shift as blood splattered the ground around her, but she couldn't focus, couldn't visualize anything in that moment.

She stood there, paralyzed and worthless, as the others struck, attacking with determination. Long, thick limbs swiped out, hitting men so hard they collapsed. To her left, an enormous cat pounced, knocking a man onto his back.

Come on, just shift. Anything.

She stared down at her hands, willing them to *do* something, but her mind was blank. Then a single image popped into her brain, the only time she'd ever really shifted, and her hands changed, forming those digging claws she'd made when she escaped.

Good enough.

She raced forward, coming up behind a man who was being corralled by a large wolf. Pulling back her arm, she walloped him, the dull claws scraping against his back, leaving deep furrows. He screamed, whirling around, but then the wolf pounced, ending him with a rending bite.

Terra turned, looking for another target.

"Enough," that same authoritative voice snapped.

Her gaze zeroed in on the voice, and she froze. He stood in the middle of the fray. Bodies thrashed around him, but he remained still, holding a small, squirming body in one arm as another held a gun to her head.

"Annie!"

CHAPTER TWENTY-EIGHT

---

*T*erra dropped her hands to her sides, frozen by terror as Annie continued to squirm in the monster's grip.

"Let me *go!*" Annie shrieked as she ground her little nails into his arm and wiggled like she intended to squeeze out above the confining limb.

Around her, the fighting died down, shifters on four legs retreated, sidling up behind Terra, showing a constancy and loyalty she didn't deserve. Someone whined, the animalistic sound making her want to pet the person, soothe them. She didn't dare move a muscle, afraid what the man might do next.

"That's better," he said, ignoring Annie's struggles. "Men?"

With an alarming speed and coordination, the armed men raised their weapons, training them on the shifters. The sharp double click of a dozen guns cocking at once split the air, making her jerk in place.

My God, we're gonna die.

She wanted to close her eyes tight, wait for the end, but Annie was staring at her, pleading silently. She couldn't abandon her.

Then, over the man's shoulder, she spotted movement. Terra blinked, not understanding what she was seeing. She wanted to squint and crane her neck to get a better look, but resisted. She refused to give herself away if it was help arriving.

Although, who could possibly be showing up to help? They were far from civilization. Nobody came out here. It wasn't like a hero would just pop in and check on them.

It could be Jackson, the others, returning.

Her breath seized, that hope surging like an unbearable pressure, obliterating her. It *could* be Jackson. Hadn't they been wondering when the others would return? The battle was over, at least the one to save Earth. Unfortunately, another battle loomed ahead of them. She glared at the man holding Annie, but it didn't even faze him.

Without moving her head, she took in her surroundings, trying to see those around her, trying to form a plan. She still couldn't tell if she'd imagined the movement in the woods. Hell, it could have been a deer for all she knew.

We're on our own here.

Terra had to believe that. She couldn't wait on a rescuer, a hero, to save them. She had to act, but how? What? As she focused back on Annie, that tightness in her chest grew, choking her.

I can't fail. I just can't.

Then, over the bastard's right shoulder, Jackson stepped out of the trees. Relief surged through her, grateful to not be alone. But he was over there, too far away to make a difference. Around him, more people in camo slipped from the trees and underbrush, forming a thick line.

Wait. She mouthed the word at Jackson and he froze, holding an arm up to stop the others. They dropped into a crouch, pulling their weapons in tighter, ready on her signal.

A weird calm settled over her as she first looked at Annie, her beautiful precocious Annie, then at the enemy leader who continued barking orders as Terra's mind wandered off, forming a plan.

She stared him down, not afraid, as the plan solidified in her mind.

You might be in danger.

Jackson had received that call just a few hours ago. He didn't know the man, had never met him, but something about his tone had resonated with him from the first moment he answered the phone.

He'd hoped Kyle Avery was wrong, that his hunch was unfounded, but as they drove to the caravan's site, they passed big black SUVs lined up along the dirt road. Jackson's hands had flexed against his steering wheel when he'd spotted them.

Those shouldn't be here.

They were in the middle of nowhere, far from popular sites to get lost in nature, and those three big SUVs could easily carry eight people a piece. He'd driven past, craning his neck to see, but his stomach sank, churning away with anxiety.

Are they okay?

He didn't even want to think about it, instead turning to face ahead, toward what they would be facing. As many as two dozen mercenaries could be at the caravan *this* instant, threatening his people, Annie, *Terra.*

His heart seized in his chest, and for a moment, he had trouble breathing.

Dear God, no.

He drove at recklessly fast speeds down the rutted road, his head smacking a time or two against the ceiling when he hit a rut too hard. The entire time, he reminded himself his caravan could take care of themselves.

Except for Terra.

The thought latched on just as he started to convince himself that everything would be all right. Unfortunately, Terra could barely shift, had only done it a couple times, knew nothing about weapons or fighting. She was smart, resourceful, and strong, but she was no fighter.

He hit another rut with a thunk of the suspension as the SUV bottomed out, smacking into the ground, and slowed. They were getting too close. If there *was* a danger, they couldn't afford to let on that they approached.

He pulled over and waited, checking the rearview mirror as more vehicles stopped, and people disembarked. He spotted Philippe's pickup truck and the military transport truck stopping behind him, then opened his door, stepping down on the hard, dusty road.

To his left, rocks skittered across the lane as people and cars disturbed them. Philippe and Avery closed the distance, stopping in silence. He waited for direction. This was Avery's show, the military officer stiff and silent as dry fall leaves rustled and fell around them.

Minutes passed, and their entire group closed in, a tense anticipation thrumming through them.

Avery nodded and finally spoke. "The site is at the end of this lane?" He pointed down the road, asking Jackson.

"Yes. Less than a mile."

"We continue in silence. You know the terrain best. What is your suggestion?"

Jackson frowned. "We should follow the path until shortly before it opens up onto the caravan site. It takes a sharp curve right before that, which will keep us obscured until then."

"Not travel through the trees and underbrush?"

Jackson shook his head. "We should avoid that as much as possible. There are too many dry leaves. It would be difficult to go unheard."

Avery agreed, and Jackson wondered what type of assignments he'd run in the past if that hadn't occurred to him. "We stop just within the tree line. Do *not* be seen. I'll evaluate the situation and direct you accordingly."

Around him, mumbled voices and movements telegraphed everyone's assent and they took off, letting Jackson lead once more. Philippe slipped in beside him, speaking in a whisper. "Do you think Macey and Beth are okay?"

Jackson almost stopped in place, his steps losing their steady rhythm at his friend's question. He couldn't honestly say. He'd paid little attention to the two since they'd arrived at the caravan, only really noticing how much Philippe seemed enamored of them. His mind had been filled with Terra and Annie, but Philippe's charges, hell any of those they'd rescued from the shifter camp, were even more vulnerable.

It was unlikely any of them had ever shifted before. For all intents and purposes, they were human, with human sensibilities and faults. Like humans, they'd grown soft, forgetting the very survival instincts and skills that would have helped them now. He didn't want to tell his friend that, though. Philippe was already worried. Jackson didn't need to add to it.

Before long, he spotted the curve in the road and slipped off the path, edging around wild bushes and underbrush. Despite his best efforts, leaves crackled under his feet and he winced, but continued onward. He advanced, watching his feet, but had to jerk his head up constantly to make sure he didn't walk into an ambush or something.

Wouldn't that *be just my luck?*

Finally, he stopped and crouched at the edge of the forest, staring out from behind an especially dense thicket. He wanted to curse. A group of men in black with guns poised stood with their backs to them. In front of the guns, the people they'd left behind waited to die, some in human and some in animal forms.

Avery came up to his side. "Damn, they're shifters, aren't they?"

Jackson glanced over his shoulder at the whispered comment. "Yes."

"It just... never occurred to me. Mila's only ever shifted parts of herself before. Remarkable."

Jackson ignored the comment. He knew damn well Mila had fully shifted. So did Avery, if he knew her. He gathered she'd been living in another person's skin for a time. "Strategy?"

Avery craned his head, looking off to the side. "Wait until everyone's in position and sneak up behind them."

"That's a lot of distance."

"My men can make it, can yours?" Avery smirked, a challenge in his eyes.

Jackson didn't dignify it with a response.

Moments passed, then Avery signaled, and they surged forward, stepping out into the open. Immediately, he spotted Terra. She stood stiff, tension pulsing through her form. Then her gaze locked on his, and her mouth moved, forming a single word.

Wait.

Jackson slapped an arm out, holding Avery back. The man glared at him, but motioned the others to stop too. Avery stared him down accusingly, but Jackson didn't know how to explain. He didn't understand himself. He looked back at Terra. She appeared frozen solid, but the longer he watched, the more her face transformed, a plan forming.

What is she up to?

———

Terra stared down at Annie, ignoring Jackson and the line of men forming at the tree line. She knew what she had to do, what *they* had to do.

This will work. It has *to.*

"Shift," she whispered.

Annie froze in the man's grip, not reacting for a moment. Terra nodded, giving her permission for the first time.

And hopefully not the last.

Annie smiled, then shifted into a cougar, her little voice crying out in a sound that was a mix between a sheep and a bird chirping. The man jumped, losing his grip on the little wildcat who quickly dropped to the ground on all fours and dashed behind Terra, losing herself in the group of shifters.

Terra pounced, not even thinking as she leapt at the cold-hearted bastard who would use a toddler as a shield. For the first time, the shift came effortlessly to her. She didn't have to imagine something in her head. She didn't have to focus. Her body *knew* what to do and took over, ready to protect her little girl.

She slammed into his body with full force as he screamed. They crashed to the ground with a jarring thud, and she screamed in his face, though the sound didn't register. He froze, eyes wide, not even breathing as movement blurred in her periphery.

***

Jackson looked over at Avery, who stood tense as if a single thread held him in place. When Terra pounced, turning into a cougar and tackling one of the men in black, they didn't need a command. They acted.

Startled by Terra's transformation, Jackson fell behind a few steps as the others surged forward to join the fight.

She shifted.

He couldn't believe it. With all the times he'd tried to get her to shift, she'd finally done it.

She shifted.

He shook himself, noticing his allies racing across the empty distance, and rushed forward at full speed, trying to catch up. They spread out, forming a solid line behind the threat, as the people they'd left behind took Terra's attack as a rallying cry, her wild screams piercing the air.

Though he had a gun strapped across his body, he didn't use it, not with innocents in the line of fire. As he surged up behind a black-clad body, he let a wicked cross loose, spinning the man around, lining him up for a perfect shot to the throat. He went down in a sprawl of limbs as predators attacked all around him, swiping with paws or biting down with strong jaws to subdue.

He tipped his head up, searching for Terra. Standing on four legs, she'd abandoned her unconscious foe as she spun around, chirping for all she was worth. The high pitched, almost birdlike sound, made him smile, until he realized she was looking for Annie.

Jackson stepped up to Terra, adding his eyes to the search, but didn't see the little girl he'd come to know and love anywhere on the battlefield.

And it *was* a battlefield. Though few gunshots burst through the air, blood and death littered the ground as clashes of bodies surrounded him.

Where is she?

He wanted to call out to her, but he held the words in, afraid of drawing attention to their search.

Terra chirped again and dashed forward, Jackson on her heels. She cuddled around a small cougar and Jackson smiled, then took his gun off his shoulder, using it as a blunt weapon to protect his family.

A body bumped against the back of his lower leg and he looked behind him, finding Terra covering his back, swiping at anyone who came near. Annie hid mostly underneath her, chirping adorably at each person who approached.

It didn't take long before the fight ended, leaving military and shifters the only ones standing. Some of the enemy lay on the ground unconscious while others sat huddled, cornered by his allies.

Avery barked out orders as the bad guys were secured. Someone ran off for the tree line in the direction they'd left the vehicles. Jackson stared at Terra and Annie and smiled, kneeling down to their level. Annie pounced on his lap, chirping at him happily, while Terra leaned into him, likewise happy to see him. He pulled them close, digging his fingers deep into their furs, relieved to find them both safe and unharmed.

———

After the fight, the caravan had slipped off to the periphery. Some were shaken, keeping out in the open where they could see a new threat coming. Others just wanted the familiarity of home and disappeared into their respective trailers. Those they'd rescued from the shifter camp seemed mostly unnerved, skittish. They watched the soldiers with skepticism and fear, but they had nowhere to go, so many of them huddled together, taking comfort in each other.

Jackson had retreated with Terra, Annie, Philippe, Macey, and Beth to the space in front of Philippe's trailer. The group gathered around a small bonfire that just pushed back the sharp, chill air that spoke of the winter yet to come. The flames crackled, little sparks dancing in the air around them.

Terra and Annie remained in cougar form. Annie bounced around the fire, occasionally staying put just long enough to get a few pets before bounding off again. Beth looked after her with yearning.

Terra lay next to Jackson, but facing the area where Avery still interrogated the men they'd captured. At least, he did with the conscious ones. He'd ordered the unconscious ones to the transport truck they'd pulled up into the clearing. Now, a couple men guarded it in case the captives awoke. Her tail twitched back and forth, her body a tense spring of silent menace. He kept a hand on her neck and shoulders, reminding her of his presence.

Or maybe holding her back.

When Avery waved the last of the prisoners to the truck,

Jackson stood, patting Terra on the back. He'd hoped she would stay behind, but she rose to her feet, following beside him like a dog heeling. He walked up to Avery and reached out his hand. "Thank you."

Avery took it, shaking it with a palm rough with grit. "Any time."

"What now?" he asked as Avery released him.

The military officer smirked. "Now I round them up."

Jackson frowned.

What did that mean?

CHAPTER TWENTY-NINE

Kyle walked into a swanky office building, pushing the swinging glass doors before him as a team of men followed behind him, ready to do his bidding. He didn't foresee a challenge here, but the building was high profile. Then again, so was the entire damned case. They needed a win, desperately.

And nothing spelled victory like a corporate suit being frog marched out of his own headquarters by a half dozen badasses in uniform.

He didn't bother with the front desk. In full-blown misogyny, a woman in a low-cut blouse stood from her seat, squawking as he ignored her to head for the elevators.

"Hey! You're supposed to sign in first."

He walked to the first elevator, pressing the metal "Up" button, and stepped back to wait. His team filled the lobby around the bank of elevators, leaving the few people passing through or stopping to take an elevator uneasy. They stood at parade rest with pistols at their hips, a stark contrast to the rest of the people flowing through the area. They were like a mountain surrounded by running water. Unmovable. Unstoppable.

The elevator dinged, and they slipped in together. The space was large, but they barely fit. Kyle pressed the button for the top floor and smirked.

He waited impatiently with his hands pulled behind his back as the car rose, dragging down on his body with each foot. When it dinged again, he stepped out, moving to the right without even glancing at the open central floor plan flanked by offices. He continued onward as people in fancy suits, mostly men, glanced at him, alarmed.

He stopped at the last office, which had smoky glass double doors and white lettering etched onto the glass reading, "Stewart Xavier, CEO."

Avery pushed the doors open, revealing a secretary on the phone. Another woman in a low-cut shirt, her mouth hung open. The phone drifted away from her ear as she sat there. He ignored her and rounded her desk, aiming for the door behind her.

"Hey, you can't go in there," she said in a high-pitched voice.

He grabbed the door handle and pushed it open, stepping into the enormous office. Behind the desk, a man in a shiny suit stopped in mid-action, then put his phone down and knitted his hands together. "Can I help you?" he asked, his tone acidic.

"Stewart Xavier, you are under arrest." Kyle pulled out the card from his back pocket, a card that had "Miranda Rights" on one side and "Article 31b Rights" on the other. He didn't usually arrest civilians, so he didn't have these rights memorized. "You have the right to remain silent. Anything you say can and will be used against you in a court of law. You have the right to an attorney. If you cannot afford an attorney, one will be provided for you. You can decide at any time from this moment on to exercise these rights. Do you understand each of these rights I have explained to you?"

Mila slipped into the hospital room, a tote bag pulled tight to her side. As the door closed with a hiss, she half expected a nurse to come charging in to confiscate her bounty. When nothing happened, she sighed and crossed the room, dropping onto the edge of Tristan's bed. The bag landed in his lap.

"What's this?"

"Fuel," she said with a smirk.

He peeled open the canvas, hamburger and fry fumes bursting out. "Thanks." He dug in, starting with the burger.

The room quieted as he ate, conversation replaced by a TV reporter reporting the news. "In national news, the National Space Service arrested individuals from the terrorist organization, MEGA." Mila turned around, the mention of the NSS catching her attention. "MEGA, short for Make Earth Great Again, was responsible for sabotage and attacks on the Incirrina Treaty missions. It is also implicated in a group of attacks on shape-shifters throughout the United States."

On screen, Avery and a half dozen MPs walked out of a set of glass doors, dragging a man in a fancy suit to their vehicle. The prisoner appeared outraged, puffed up with his own superiority complex. Behind him, Avery looked confident and proud.

"Good for him."

Tristan swallowed hard beside her. "Oh?"

She pointed at the screen. "Avery finally got his man."

Mila stood against the backdrop, trying to keep a straight face. It was hard to stay stoic when she just wanted to grin from ear to ear, but she didn't want the tech to have to take the photograph again. The camera flashed, and she blinked, splotches of color blinding her for a few moments.

With a nod, the person led her to a workstation at the RAPIDS site. "Place your hand on the panel."

She did, and after a few clicks from him, the panel lit up like a flatbed scanner. "Ow." She resisted the urge to pull away from the pinching stab to her fingertip.

"That's the genetic ID sample," he said, not looking up from his display.

Mila sat, squirming in her seat. She didn't have the patience of Job, even under the best of circumstances. Here, she was on the cusp, a tipping point in her life, and she couldn't wait.

A machine hummed in the background, and the man got up. He returned with a small rectangle in hand. Mila leaned forward, subconsciously reaching for it even if her hands stayed in her lap.

"Here you go," he said, handing it over.

Mila looked down, strong emotion choking her. "Thanks." She stood up, not able to take her eyes off the little bit of plastic.

A verified ID.

Her eyes teared up as she moved toward the door. She ducked her head, but otherwise did nothing to hide her emotion.

"Pilot Dragomirov?" someone called from behind her.

She turned around, blinking away the moisture, her new Common Access Card clutched to her chest. "Yes?"

"I have a couple messages for you. They're to be hand delivered."

Mila reached out, taking the two envelopes. "Thanks."

He saluted, then about-faced and left.

Mila was torn. She didn't have enough hands to hold the ID and check the contents of the envelopes. It took all of a moment for her to shove her ID in her pocket and open the first one. Her mouth dropped: A federal pardon for impersonating a member of the military. When the Commandant had confronted her about her identity, she'd been terrified, and as a huge weight lifted off her shoulders, she realized she'd still been worried. But she needn't worry any longer. She sighed, all her muscles relaxing at once.

Next, she opened the other envelope. Inside was an invitation to a formal Medal of Honor ceremony to be held in D.C. For her. She clutched it to her chest, shaking her head, a little smile on her face. Sure, the President had said he would, but that was a press conference. That could have easily been posturing. This was real.

She still couldn't believe it, though. Walking out of the building, she stared at it, trying to process the news. She'd expected her stint in the military would be limited, a brief bout of happiness before she lost it all again. She'd wanted to grasp as much of the experience as she could, make the most of every moment. Mila never expected *this*.

CHAPTER THIRTY

Mila waited in her living room, pacing erratically as she rubbed her sweaty palms on her pants. Tristan sat on the couch, cool as can be. She growled at him. "Why are you so calm?"

He shrugged. "Because we'll get through this. We can get through anything." He smirked, taking the edge, the intensity, off the statement. He'd just been released from the hospital earlier that day. His movements were still a bit stiff, but he insisted he was fine. She didn't quite believe him.

They're coming.

The thought slipped into her head, and her anxiety ratcheted up again. She couldn't do this. She wasn't ready, but would she ever be?

I hope so.

The doorbell rang, and she jumped, turning to the open doorway.

Tristan got up with a wince and touched her shoulder, the small gesture calming her slightly. "I'll get it."

Mila held her breath, lost in that moment. She'd agonized over how to handle this. What face should she show them? What would be the least shocking? May's face? Mila's face? She'd been on TV, but maybe they'd missed it. Maybe they hadn't seen.

It had been Tristan who suggested her current course of action. She stood in jeans and a blouse, uncomfortable in the casual attire. She wanted to be in uniform, wearing that armor to protect herself. Maybe she could go get changed? Her uniform spoke to who she was: pilot, soldier, Dragomirov.

No, someone was already here. Of course, she couldn't change.

Change. She scoffed. The irony. She would change all right.

May's parents walked through the door, a little puzzled.

"May, what's going on? Why are you so nervous?" May's mother said, walking up and rubbing her upper arms, trying to soothe her. The gentle look in the other woman's eyes nearly broke her.

She couldn't do it. She couldn't take the woman's daughter away from her.

But this was a lie. They deserved to know.

"Have you seen Mila? Talked to her?" May's father said, touching his hands to his wife's shoulders, providing that strength and support.

"Yeah, I have."

"Is that what this is about?" the other woman said.

Mila sniffed, whispering, "Yeah," under her breath.

The doorbell rang again and Tristan, standing in the living room doorway, slipped out gingerly to answer it.

Moments later, Mila's parents walked through the door. Mila's eyes watered, but she held herself back. Did her father know? Did her mother tell him? She'd asked them here because she needed everything in the open, but also because her mom had always been friends with Mrs. Trace. She'd hoped her presence would soften the blow.

"May, are you all right?" her mother said, voice rising with alarm and concern.

"I have something to tell you guys."

Alyana looked into her daughter's eyes, and just like when she figured out Mila had been masquerading as May, she figured this out too. She saw her daughter's difficulty and relaxed, voicing the words that lodged in Mila's throat like a rock. "You're Mila," she said, confident and calm.

"What?!" May's mother squawked, her head rotating between Mila and her mother. "No, she's…" But she stopped, pain crossing her face.

Alyana went up to her friend, hugging her tight. "You knew. Deep down, you knew just as I did."

Mrs. Trace nodded against her friend's shoulder. "I didn't want… I couldn't admit…"

"I know, I know." Her mom turned to her. "What happened?"

Mila paused, unsure what she wanted to know, so she changed forms, unable to bear the pain wearing May's face was causing the couple in front of her. She spilled it all. She told them about shape-shifting for the first time, about running away. She told them about meeting up with May after ten years, about the mugging, the *Orleans*, everything. At times, May's mother gripped her friend tighter, emotion getting the better of her, but they kept quiet, let her finish.

Moments passed in silence after she finished speaking. She

looked at them, trying to read their emotions, their thoughts from their faces, their body language. Not that she was any good at that.

After a while, they settled, pulling away from each other, and Mila realized that Tristan had come up behind her, reaching his arms around her middle. She lifted her hands, clutching his as both sets of parents turned to her and Tristan.

Mila gnawed at her lip, afraid of what they would say. Would they condemn her? Hate her for her lie? For not giving them the opportunity to grieve?

May's mother sniffed, rubbing a finger under each eye. "You've always been like a daughter to us." She shook her head. "I never imagined. It must have been awful."

"We can have May properly buried," Mila blurted out, not being able to take the kindness, the acceptance.

But the other woman only nodded, then came up to Mila and hugged her.

Mila stood outside the East Room of the White House in her dress uniform. She felt exposed, even more so than when she'd participated in the press conference. At least the press conference a week ago hadn't just been about her. This *was*.

"Breathe," the President said beside her. "Just breathe."

She sucked in a huge breath, the influx of oxygen settling her nerves. "Thanks."

He nodded. "Are you ready?"

No, but it didn't matter. She still couldn't believe she'd spent the last hour in the Oval office talking to the President in casual conversation. They'd chatted about her life, about what she'd been through. He never once judged her, not for any of it. She didn't vote for him, but if he were up for election, she would. He was a good man.

Music swelled from the room before them, and the door opened.

An announcer said, "Ladies and Gentlemen, the President of the United States accompanied by Medal of Honor recipient Pilot Mila Anya Dragomirov."

The President nodded, and Mila started walking. All around her, people held up cell phones, taking pictures and videos as she and the President passed through the middle of the crowd. With each step, having such a powerful, important man behind her made her want to run, triggering long outdated survival instincts.

They moved to the front of the room where a dais took center stage. They faced the audience, the President on her left. She stood at attention, hands behind her back, using that stance, that familiarity, to give her strength.

Before her, her family and friends sat in the first and second row. Tristan, Mila's parents, May's parents, Kyle Avery, and even Luke Hall and Jackson. She took strength from them being here as well.

The music ended, and a man in uniform walked up to a podium to her left. "Let us pray.

"Almighty God, today we honor an American soldier deserving of our nation's highest respect. She deserves this admiration for the bravery, valor, and heroism she has displayed…"

Mila tried not to listen, growing increasingly uncomfortable with all the grandstanding and the sincerity with which he spoke her praise. She wasn't used to it, and she didn't like it. She just wanted to run and hide, forget this ever happened.

The man finished his prayer with an "amen" then the President stepped forward, started talking. "We all know of the terrible events that lead to this day. The whole world was made aware in those hours of our vulnerability to threats that we, as a whole, never once speculated on. But it is because of men and women like Pilot Mila Dragomirov that we can continue to speculate, even plan, for our future.

"Because of her, we won that fight, can keep fighting. Because of her, more good soldiers were not lost. We can not honor her enough for the risks she took, the dangers she faced. We thank you." He turned to her, bowing his head.

"I would like to welcome Mila's family and friends, many of whom she's served with. I want to also thank and honor Pilot May Trace, who discovered a plot to sabotage the USS *Orleans* and, not knowing who to turn to, reached out to a friend, thus starting Mila on this path and changing hers and our lives forever.

"I would like to welcome the members of the Medal of Honor Society," he nodded at a group of current and former soldiers to the left who wore their medals around their necks, "who are welcoming their sister soldier into their ranks today. We are very proud of all who have served so gallantly."

He turned back to Mila, smiling. "When I first met Mila, I had no idea the depths to her character or struggle. When I talked with her, she often said things like, 'I didn't want this,' or 'I don't deserve this.' She insisted anyone would have done the same. By then, I already knew about her past, about how great a risk she'd taken as she served.

"Mila, as a shifter hiding among the military, could have lost her freedom at any time, yet she never let that stop her, risking her life on board the USS *Orleans* to save her crew even though she didn't have the training. She refused to leave her fate and the fate of the entire crew in others' hands.

"She ran ahead and fought off a half dozen men so her team would have time to suit up, to survive when the airlock was opened, so they could close the hatch and save the rest of the crew. Sucked into space, she nearly made the ultimate sacrifice for that difficult decision.

"At the Kennedy Moon Station, she was involved in the early warning required to coordinate forces, taking off even though the enemy ship could have shot them out of the sky.

"On Earth, she was the one who suggested and coordinated the alliance with the shape-shifter community, a move that could also have led to loss of her freedom, a freedom she had exercised when she ran away ten years ago, risking a life on the streets rather than one in the shifter camps.

"Now, if the military aide would please come forward."

Two men stepped into place. One held a warm wood case with a glass window in front of his abdomen as he faced the crowd, standing to the left of the President. The other went to a podium behind them. "The President of the United States of America, authorized by Act of Congress, March 3, 1863, has awarded in the name of Congress the Medal of Honor to Pilot Mila Anya Dragomirov, National Space Service, for conspicuous gallantry and intrepidity at the risk of life and liberty above and beyond the call of duty."

He continued on, repeating much of what the President had already said. After a spell, he became quiet and the man to her left handed the medal to the President, who then posed with her for a picture. Applause rang through the room as everyone stood. Mila smiled down at Tristan, who gave her an ear to ear grin.

"Thank you all who have served, as members of the military or not. Thank you, Mila. God bless you. God bless America."

The room broke out in applause once more, and Mila turned to the people that mattered most, not wanting the praise, and certainly not needing it.

Terra stood in her old apartment, feeling a little shellshocked. She still couldn't believe she was doing this.

I'm saying goodbye.

Most of her apartment was now in boxes or had been donated. Annie gamboled around, giggling and playing a game only *she* could fathom. Terra's heart constricted in her chest. They'd been trying to find Annie's parents but no luck so far. She honestly couldn't decide if she hoped to find them or not. She loved Annie and couldn't bear to lose her. And yet, what about Annie's parents? Were they now pining away for the child they'd lost?

Unfortunately, things were still risky for her kind. The Shifter Rights and Identification Act had just been proposed in Congress and while it was a step forward, until it passed, her place in society was tenuous at best. The President had promptly shut down the shifter camps, released the captives, and promised restitution, but that didn't stop prejudice or discrimination. It didn't stop people from thinking of her and the rest of the shifter community as subhuman. It didn't protect them from being singled out.

A chill ran up her spine, and she suddenly just wanted to return to the caravan. They'd decided to wait, again, to move to the new site so she could close out her old life. Also because Mila had invited Jackson to her friend, May's, funeral. Terra never met the woman who'd passed, but she suspected Jackson needed outside perspectives, so she'd encouraged him to go, feeling that fostering a friendship with the military pilot would be good for him.

"All done?" he asked, coming up behind her.

She faced him and smiled. "Looks like it." She turned back to the boxes. It was still quite a lot, and Jackson's trailer was tiny. "Where are we going to put all this?"

"Don't worry about it. We'll figure it out."

She shook her head. "None of this stuff matters."

"It's yours. Thus it matters."

"I could leave all this behind and be completely happy. I just want to go home."

He beamed at her. "Home, huh?"

"Yeah."

He leaned in, a mischievous glint emerging in his eyes. "Well, just for that, I'm going to teach you a new trick when we get 'home'."

She grinned ear to ear, her body thrumming with excitement. "Really?"

"Oh yes."

She laughed. "I can't wait."

Kyle pulled at his collar. He never met May Trace in life and couldn't see how attending her wake made any sense, but Mila had invited him, almost begging him to come, so he stood at the back, wondering when it would be over. The wake hadn't officially started, so people milled around, drinking and munching on cookies. He let the sea of people wash over him, the din of overlapping voices nothing but white noise.

Before long, people started wandering to folding chairs set up in rows in the middle of the room. Kyle sat down and spotted Mila and Tristan entering through a side door, hands clasped together. He smiled, then they spotted him and made a path through the crowd, aiming straight at him.

He tensed.

"Avery, I'm glad you made it," Mila said, smiling at him. The smile didn't quite reach her eyes, speaking to the conflicted emotions she still dealt with.

He shrugged, not knowing what to say. What *did* you say to a woman who stole the decedent's identity and buried her in the woods?

She touched his arm, gaining his attention once more. "I was hoping you might say a few words?"

"What? I didn't know her."

"Yeah, but we were all touched by her in some way."

He frowned, but nodded. She needed the support. So be it.

"Thanks." She patted him again and dragged Tristan up to the front by his hand.

A few moments later, a male voice spoke up. "Well, I didn't expect to see *you* here."

He spun around, spotting Shandor Jackson, the shifter targeted by MEGA. "Or you."

Jackson shrugged, the action lifting his woman's arm by their joined hands. "Mila invited me."

Kyle looked around. "Did she invite everyone?"

Jackson chuckled. "I have no idea."

The two sat next to him. The woman reached over Jackson, offering Kyle her hand. "I'm Terra, by the way."

"Kyle." Her grip was surprisingly firm as they shook hands. "Did you know her?"

"No," she shook her head. "Just showing support. I did meet Mila, though."

He nodded. "I think we all have."

Up ahead, a man in black stood at a podium next to the closed casket. Clearing his voice, the room quieted, and the stragglers settled in their seats. "We are here to honor the life of May Trace, pilot in the National Space Service, and beloved daughter and friend."

Kyle tuned out as the officiant began a prayer. Before long, the man stepped down, disappearing off to the side as a middle-aged couple stepped up with tears in their eyes. May's parents. They spoke of her as a child, of her dreams and fantasies, of her skills. They talked of her friends, especially Mila. After a few minutes, the mother broke into tears and the two returned to their seats, settling into the first row where another woman hugged her and rocked her back and forth.

A few more people talked about May's life before Mila approached the podium. Her eyes looked glassy with her tears, her voice thick with emotion. "May was my best friend, my twin, my other half. We did everything together." She shook her head as emotion built, choking her. "She died doing what was right. I'm sorry. I can't."

She dashed back down to the front row and nobody said anything, understanding entirely. Then Kyle's name was called, and he stood, walking down a central aisle. When he reached the podium, he looked down at the others and froze.

I shouldn't be here.

Any one of these people could have spoken to May's life better than him. He didn't know her, had never met her. What could he possibly say to honor her life?

His hands gripped the worn wood as he took a deep breath. "I never met May Trace, not the real one. The first time I saw who I thought was May Trace, I knew something was off about her. Not a threat, but not honest either. I guess, deep down, I always knew that woman was a shifter in disguise, Mila." He held out his hand at Mila in the audience.

"What I do know about her is that she was a mediocre pilot, but in spite of that, she never gave up. She never quit, even when her friend disappeared." He felt grateful for the research he'd done into May Trace before he'd known she was a shifter. It was coming in handy now. "She lived her life serving this country with integrity. This is what got her killed, but never forget that. As far as I'm concerned, she was just as deserving of the Medal of Honor as Mila Dragomirov was. She not only identified a possible threat, she took measures to record it, documenting evidence that would later serve vital. When she didn't know who to trust, she didn't freeze up and bury what she knew, figuring she couldn't do anything about it. No, she went outside the system, going to someone she *could* trust for advice.

"May Trace died a hero, trying to protect this country." He saluted her. "And with her actions, she brought people together, creating alliances that have served to protect the *world*. I salute you, May Trace. Thank you."

Jackson sat next to Terra, an arm over her shoulders, pulling her close to his side. Annie squirmed next to them, waiting for the announcement. It was expected that the Shifter Rights and Identification Act would be passed today, should have already been passed. Months had gone by since that press conference. Jackson had been the face of shifters to a lot of people ever since, and Terra had nagged him until he made good use of it.

The President had promised that day that he would make changes, but Jackson had never had faith in promises, especially from humans. It was Terra, though, who pushed him to take action, to lobby for changes, alter public opinion, instead of hiding in the shadows hoping the world would pass him by. It hadn't taken much for him to agree.

He smiled, playfully rubbing the top of Annie's head, to which she scowled at him, the look adorable on her youthful face. These two had changed him. For the better, and he was grateful for it. His old self wouldn't have done half the things he'd done recently, and he couldn't help thinking that was tragic.

What had he been doing with his life? He'd lived so long and yet had hidden more than anything, isolating himself and his people when he could have done so much more.

Now, they were back at the caravan site where he'd first welcomed Terra and Annie, and he'd never felt a sense of home like this before. Somehow, it was so much bigger than it had ever been before. They still lived off the land, off their skills, but they didn't fear the outside world as they once did. Surprisingly, Terra had taught him that.

He pulled her closer to his side, reveling in the warmth and companionship. He refocused on the TV. On screen, C-SPAN showed the congressional floor, and the ticker at the bottom changed. "SRIA passed in Senate 66-34."

They were finally safe, protected.

Free.

MAY'S NIGHTMARE

May Trace tossed back another round, laughing as the bar's oppressive noise bolstered her. It smelled of unwashed bodies, but this far into a bar crawl, she didn't care.

Then a scream rent the air. She swam through the drunkenness, her body moving on autopilot to the door. Limbs and torsos attached to drunken fools bounced against her as she floated to the door. The music distorted like she was underwater.

Another scream hit her, but it barely surged above the music and carousing. No one reacted.

How can they not notice?

Her head spun as she pivoted, taking in her surroundings. Some part of her was hammering her brain with the need to get outside, to help, to save… someone. But who? And why was everyone partying like nothing had happened? It made no sense.

But her brain couldn't latch onto the concern. It dissipated like so much smoke. She turned to the door. It looked like an ordinary door. Stained wood, gouges, a pull handle at waist-height. It looked dark and foreboding, growing with each moment she approached.

Before she knew it, her hand clasped the door, cold, sticky metal imprinting her hand. She couldn't move, though. As she stared down at the handle, her body both liquid and frozen at once, she just stared at the dirty brushed nickel.

What's on the other side?

Part of her didn't want to know. A part of her wanted to turn her back, sidle up to the bar, and order another drink. That was the easy choice, but it wouldn't be the right one, now would it?

Mila would do the right thing.

Mila…

That's right. I was looking for Mila.

May gripped the handle more firmly and pulled it open, exposing an empty parking lot. The door slammed shut behind her, and the world fell into deep silence. Not even a cricket disturbed the eerie calm.

No, not empty.

Something lay on the pebbled parking lot. She approached. Rocks scattered underfoot, disturbing the peace. A part of her disjointed thoughts shied away from the lump of darkness. A bulb flickered, sending that lump into intermittent shadow. She continued to advance, unable to resist its draw.

The light flickered again.

I know that… that…

She held her breath, but her feet pushed her forward without her command, driving her to a reality, a fate, she didn't want to confront.

It can't be…

Her breathing picked up, and she started panting. She wanted to look away, but her head wouldn't turn. Hell, her eyelids wouldn't even close.

Why can't I look away?

Why?

The word echoed in her head. *Why? Why? Why?* Her hands rose to her head. She wanted to pull at her hair, cover her ears, but they just hovered there, useless.

Why?

Her face fell as unnamed emotion tightened her chest.

Dread. It's dread.

I don't want to see this.

Why can't I turn away?

The light stopped flickering, finally giving her a clear view of the only other inhabitant in the parking lot.

Mila.

She looked peaceful, almost sleeping. She didn't even appear hurt. Maybe she was okay.

Then she rolled over, staring up at May. A red circle bloomed on her chest as blood started to bubble from her lips. "Why didn't you save me, May? Why did you leave me to die?"

May screamed as she came awake, breathing hard as the

horrible image remained branded on her brain. Her entire body shook as she took each settling breath. "Oh my God," she groaned as she sat up and raised her hands to her temples, trying to rub the nightmare from her mind.

"It's not real. It didn't happen. There's nothing I could have done."

But a part of her didn't really believe that. Ten years ago, while she'd been drunk out of her skull, Mila Anya Dragomirov, a woman she'd known her whole life, a woman who'd been her better half, had disappeared.

Why?

Even outside her nightmares, that question still plagued her. She'd managed to move on with her life, but the *why* still eluded her. *Mila* had been the perfect pilot, the model soldier. *Mila'd* had the bright future. May had just been along for the ride, and Mila's disappearance had nearly destroyed her.

So why would someone who'd just passed sub-space qualifications, who was about to graduate from pilot academy for the NSS, just up and disappear? Why would someone like that, with family and friends who cared about her, abandon everything?

With one last breath, she dropped her hands, staring despondently at the other end of the room. It was just an empty wall, just a pale gray meant to help mask the appearance of stains. As her gaze roamed the room, her mind further escaping the grip of her ongoing nightmare, the absurdity of her surroundings hit her.

She had one roommate, a woman she didn't really know, who had decorated her half of the room with fake floral bouquets, glass tsatskes, and lots of color. Even when off on assignment, like she was now, her space contained more life than May's.

May had self-combusted after Mila disappeared. Eventually, she'd trashed her own things, sometimes screaming her pain as she threw anything that reminded her of Mila in big trash bags.

There hadn't been much left. Even years later, her room still looked like a scene from a pre-furnished apartment.

When did I stop living?

The chime of her cell phone rang through the air, but she didn't even flinch. She stared at the smartphone on her nightstand for a moment before picking it up. The solid weight and smooth metal and glass grounded her after the recent attack from her scarred psyche.

She checked the screen.

CO Fuckface: Report to my office.

Her commanding officer. Her head sagged. Couldn't she get a coffee or breakfast first? What was with the early morning meeting?

Do I even want to know?

Do I even care?

<hr>

May straightened her collar as she stood outside her CO's office. She sniffed a couple times before knocking.

"Come in," a female voice said from the other side.

May stepped through, ready and waiting for yet another ass chewing.

"Close the door and have a seat."

"Yes, ma'am." The cheap door felt weightless as she snapped

it closed. She turned and sat in one of the two guest chairs. The room was cramped, but had the advantage of two windows letting in plenty of light.

The extra light, however, had the unfortunate side effect of highlighting the room's other deficiencies. Like the scuff-marks on the desktop, wrinkles in the carpeting where it hadn't been stretched properly, and a suspicious stain on the other guest chair's seat.

Her CO, Commander Parker to everyone else, propped her elbows on her desk and folded her hands together. May leaned back as yet another exasperated expression crossed the older redhead's face. Fine lines and little bits of gray at the temple spoke to her age, but she wore it well.

Parker sighed, her head sagging a little before lifting it again to stare May down. "What can I do to make you try harder? I know you're capable of more, Trace. What's it gonna take for you to step up, to stop going through the motions? What's it gonna take for you to take charge of your own life? You have so much more inside you. I know it. I just need you to see it."

May shook her head. "That was Mila. She had the bright future, not me."

"You sell yourself short. And until you see that, you'll keep sabotaging yourself." Parker looked down, grabbing a manila envelope from her desk. "Here, take it. It's your next assignment."

"Yes, ma'am," May said, reaching out for her orders as she stood. "And I'm sorry I can't live up to your expectations. I wish I could."

Her CO sighed. "I wish you could, too."

———

When she wasn't deployed, May's day always started with office work. In that way, it wasn't much different from a job in the public sector. Paperwork still needed to be done, they still needed to do continuing education on the latest technology, safety, and whatnot. At her desk, she stared at the envelope, too apathetic to open it at first. What did it matter? Job after job, mission after mission, it all blurred together after a while. When did it end? When did it matter?

Maybe I should just quit.

She had, what, another year on her service contract? But then what would she do? This was all she knew, all she'd ever known. She'd followed Mila blindly, enamored with the other girl's passion. Hell, she was swept up in it. Before she knew it, she'd settled on a path for no other reason than her best friend wanted it.

That's no way to live.

May opened the envelope as the office came to life around her, coming dangerously close to a paper cut as she peeled back the flap. She skimmed the orders. Most of it didn't matter, just a bunch of legal jargon meant to sound officious. Usually, she could sum up her orders in a few words. Like she could summarize this one with a single sentence: May Trace will pilot an upcoming mission on the USS *Orleans*. There were dates, times, protocols she needed to complete before boarding, but what did it matter? It was always the same.

She put the paperwork down and sighed, leaning back in her chair. Around her, people chatted and greeted each other, avoiding the start of another work day. Coffee fumes permeated the space, filling her head with a tension she couldn't deal with.

I need to get out of here.

Pushing up from her seat, she scanned the nearby cubicles, but nobody was paying attention.

They never do.

She left her desk and walked away with purpose.

Nobody needed to know her purpose was escape.

May slipped into her little hidey-hole, a storage room on the second floor with a single arrow-slit window. This was where she always fled when she needed to escape. It wasn't much, just a narrow room with wire shelves lining the long walls. She leaned against a shelf at the end. The metal dug into her back as she angled her head to see out the window.

Below, people milled around chatting or hurried from place to place. She liked people watching. She often imagined what they were thinking, what their lives were like. Maybe the angry-looking Major had a fight with his wife this morning. Maybe the two women laughing on the sidewalk were talking about a recent adventure at a bar.

Funny, but she never conjured up anything spectacular when she fantasized about their lives. She never came up with wacky things like international spies or jewel thieves. Was she just that banal? Or did she crave normalcy so much she recreated it in others?

Turning away from the window, she shook her head in disgust. "Damn." She couldn't even escape in her own thoughts.

What am I escaping, though?

With a sigh and a frown, she looked back out the window. Too bad she didn't know the answer. Maybe if she *did,* she could actually *fix* herself.

"It's all Mila's fault. She broke me." Her face grew hot as those old emotions built up, trying to choke her. She shoved them down ruthlessly, forcing them into submission. She refused to let them drown her again. Even if she decided tomorrow to quit and never look back, she would not let grief control her. Not again.

A footstep sounded, loud in her ear, and she jumped, whipping around to face the intrusion, but the room was empty. Her heart hammered away in her chest and she pressed her hand against her rib cage to settle it.

What the hell?

This was her *sanctuary.* Nobody ever came up here. The nearest office was halfway down the hall. The only rooms nearby were a few utility closets, a server room, and an out of service bathroom. No one should be near enough for her to hear.

Once her initial spike of fear abated, curiousity welled up in its place. Who could be up here? And why? A small smile crossed her face as she leaned away from the shelving unit at her back, taking a couple steps forward without even realizing.

"Do you think anyone spotted us?" a male voice said, tinny and distorted.

May jumped again, then froze, startled by the surprisingly clear words.

That didn't come through the door.

Moving along the narrow room, she panned her head around, searching for the source. Anticipation squeezed her chest, leaving her breathless.

"Don't be paranoid," another voice said, this one more gravelly, older. "Nobody knows."

"Right."

There.

There was a vent up near the ceiling, a square metal grate. The voices grew louder as she approached it. Where could they be coming from, though? A neighboring room? She tapped her bottom lip, thinking.

"If anyone finds out, we're dead," Mr. Paranoid said.

Dead?

Her curiosity grew, and she leaned closer to the vent even though she could hear just fine.

"*Nobody* will find out. There's too much at stake and they've planned for every eventuality."

Mr. Paranoid scoffed, and she imagined him shaking his head. "*Nobody* can plan for *every* eventuality. That's impossible."

A sharp crack echoed through the vent, and May startled, banging against the shelf at her back. Bottles of cleaner rattled, and she whirled around, settling them. Her heart leapt in her chest. She waited, convinced they'd heard her, convinced they would come running. Guilt assailed her for eavesdropping. But behind her, the conversation continued.

"Enough," Mr. Hardass snapped. "This *is* happening. *Nothing* can stop it."

May's hands flexed against the shelves as she turned back to the grate.

What the hell were they talking about?

CHAPTER TWO

May went through the rest of her morning distracted. She should have been preparing for deployment in a couple weeks or working on continuing education, but she couldn't focus, the mysterious conversation consuming her.

Hell, she couldn't even remember eating lunch even though her stomach was uncomfortably full.

What were they talking about?

What was going to happen?

What couldn't be stopped?

She still had those questions spinning around her head when she pushed into the training center.

You'd think military service would be exciting, but mostly it was the same thing day after day. Mornings were filled with paperwork in the office then the afternoons involved either training or shuttle runs to space stations or vessels in low Earth orbit.

Which was probably why she couldn't get that conversation

out of her head. Nothing that interesting *ever* happened in the NSS. They didn't fight wars in space, didn't have battles. They were glorified babysitters, making sure nothing happened to NASA scientists out in the great beyond. So, a mysterious conversation in an empty part of the base? That was more intrigue than she'd experienced since her best friend disappeared.

And nowhere near as traumatic.

But life couldn't be all intrigue. Today, May was scheduled for the simulator. She wasn't exactly looking forward to it. She wasn't good at the simulators under the best of circumstances, and she was hardly focused today. At least, she wasn't sched-uled for a full bridge simulation, which meant she wouldn't have an immediate audience to her spectacular failure. No, she would just have CO Fuckface giving her disappointed looks tomorrow when she called May into her office again.

Entering the building, it looked a lot like any other military hallway, but it wasn't. The drab space lacked any windows, lit only by harsh overhead lighting and the red LEDs of the biometric scanners next to each door. May walked down the hallway until she stopped in front of "Pilot Sim 4." She pressed her palm to the reader and the light turned green, letting her in.

Inside, the room was identical to a shuttle's cockpit. The screen was dark, but just enough dim overhead lighting bled across the surfaces to illuminate the console and a series of chairs. She'd been in enough shuttles that the familiar layout soothed her, settling her mind as she took her seat at the pilot's station.

Even the ever-present questions and curiosity abated, though a low level anxiety remained. Was it caused by the very real possibility of failure or the ominous nature of that conversa-tion she'd overheard?

With a deep breath, anchoring herself in the moment, she slowly reached back and grabbed the harness. Clicking it into place, she tugged at the straps and tilted her head back. "Computer, May Trace, Pilot, signing in."

"Identification and voice print recognized. Proceed with pre-approved simulation?"

"Proceed." Damn. What did they have planned for her this time? She hated these fucking things. At least the shuttle runs were easy. All she had to do was complete pre-flight checks, launch, leave atmosphere, and dock, then report back home. Easy.

Simulations were never easy. They were always intended to test your reflexes, test your emergency response training. May rubbed her bottom lip, then started with her pre-flight checks. She went through the list knowing it would probably be one of the last easy things until the simulation ended.

"Pre-flight check complete. Are we go for launch?"

"Go for launch, Pilot Trace."

May ignored the rest of the spiel as the computer droned on. It spouted all the random crap that might actually be important if this were a real flight, like runway numbers and how many other shuttles were waiting to launch.

But this wasn't a commercial airport, and this wasn't a real flight. The simulation only had one runway and there was never any traffic. Launch was the calm before the storm, always relaxing her just enough to fuck her up.

Today, however, was different. She didn't feel calm as her back pressed into the seat, the G forces plastering her body to the padding. The anxiety grew, her hands vibrating against the controls as she took deep, calming breaths, but the simulated forces made every inhale a struggle.

What's it gonna be this time?

The sky on the screen darkened as she approached the edges of the atmosphere and soon only her harness held her back. Her hands relaxed only slightly on the controls as she approached the ship she needed to dock with.

Under normal circumstances, a communications officer would contact the ship or space station while she piloted. In one-man simulations, it was all on her. "USS *York*. This is Pilot Trace requesting permission for docking."

"Pilot Trace, permission granted."

The ship was one of the newer models, a big monstrosity that, if real, would have been built in space, hooked to one of the space stations by an umbilicus. They were beasts and even individual parts baffled the mind when you saw them up close. Many of the parts were built in Kentucky, then floated down the Ohio River, dwarfing the barges they sat upon.

In pilot training, she and Mila used to grab a bottle of vodka to watch the boats float down the river when one of them had a hard day. Suddenly, she really wanted to do that. She wanted those moments back, that feeling of camaraderie as they downed swigs of cheap booze and laughed off their troubles.

When was the last time she'd felt that carefree?

May shook her head.

Focus.

You have a job to do.

She was approaching the docking station too quickly. Of course, she was. Why would she ever do what she was supposed to do? She was the fuckup, the loser. She was the one who always followed, never lead. Never exceptional, never remembered unless she screwed up.

Hell, even her parents seemed to prefer Mila to her.

It should have been me.

She shook herself again, engaging the reverse thrusters and the automatic dock targeting. American ships and space stations all used the same system. Sensors told the shuttle how to automatically adjust its trajectory to line up. She just had to get close enough for the sensors to communicate without ramming the ship.

Sounds easy, right?

She snorted.

A klaxon blared. "Error. ADTS is offline. Sensors cannot be detected."

Fuck.

Wham.

May's knuckles collided with the punching bag, causing the stand to shift a couple feet until it slammed into the corner. The bag swayed wildly until she grabbed it, settling it back in place. She rubbed her right knuckles, which were chapped an angry red and starting to look bruised and swollen.

She should stop, but threw a quick jab at the bag with her left hand instead.

I knew. I just knew it.

Simulations never went smoothly.

Probably why I always follow afternoon training with PT.

She licked her dry lips, salty with sweat, and fired three more quick jabs at the heavy bag, sending it wobbling all over until she had to settle it again. Nobody was in the gym so, unfortunately, there was no one to hold the bag for her. She loved being in the gym on her own, but it *did* have its disadvantages.

With sweat dripping down her back and forehead, she dropped her hands to her sides, flexing her fingers open and closed to work out the stiffness. Her mind drifted back to the simulation and the botched docking.

"Fuck." She spun around, looking for something to empty her mind, to help her forget. "Who's gonna be my next victim?" The room was filled with exercise equipment. Treadmills, weightlifting machines, free weights, mats, all reflected off the mirrors lining the walls.

May zeroed in on the elliptical and climbed on. She'd once nearly passed out on one of these because she wasn't monitoring her heart rate closely. She'd pushed herself so hard, her vision went dark. If she couldn't forget on there…

An image of an exploding docking port popped into her head. She shoved it aside, pushing herself into focusing on the movement of her arms and legs.

That was tomorrow's problem.

CHAPTER THREE

---

*M*ay stood in front of CO Fuckface as she received the ass chewing she'd wholeheartedly expected. Her mind zoned out as the older woman's face turned as red as her hair. She leaned heavily on her hands, glaring at May.

It was nothing she hadn't experienced before. May didn't even know why she bothered. She would never live up to Mila's example, and her friend had been gone for ten fucking years.

How could she live up to a ghost?

She couldn't, so as Fuckface continued to yell at her about failing to dock her shuttle without ADTS in the simulation, her mind drifted, remembering the curious conversation. What was *that* about? Why were they hiding up on the second floor? What didn't they want others to hear, to see?

Her body coiled with tension, wanting to go back to her hidey-hole in the hopes that she might overhear the duo again. Maybe they'd met there before. Maybe they would meet there again, but how could she catch them? It wasn't like she knew when to expect them. Did they meet on a consistent schedule, or did they use some convoluted system out of an old spy movie to decide when to meet? She had no idea.

But I want to find out.

"Dismissed."

Her CO sounded exasperated yet again, but May barely noticed as she left the office and returned to her cubicle.

I need a plan.

This was not the plan.

Leaning on her fist, elbow on the desk, she stared down at the Unassisted Docking SOP without seeing the words. Coffee fumes wafted to her from a distance, but even the distant stimulant couldn't get her brain focused on the mind-numbing document in front of her. *No one* was meant to read this stuff without falling asleep.

Read it until you can "recite it word for word," Fuckface had said. Well, that was never going to happen. May rolled her head, catching the movement of other personnel out of the corner of her eye. Why couldn't she feel the same sense of purpose she saw in others' gaits? What was she missing?

Dropping her head to focus back on the document, she searched for where she'd left off, but couldn't remember and just started at the top of the page again.

I'm gonna be at this all day.

But then, wasn't that the point? Fuckface was punishing her for screwing up. May frowned. It wasn't even that much of a screw-up. When was the last time assisted docking failed? Never? While still in development? She scoffed, but continued trying to read.

This is pointless.

May pulled away, leaning back in her chair to stare up at the ceiling.

I don't need to know their schedule if I record them.

The thought popped into her head out of nowhere, all thoughts of productivity forgotten. What would she need, though? She wasn't exactly a spy or a cop. She also wasn't technologically gifted.

This is gonna suck, isn't it?

May tapped her lip, trying to think of the best way to proceed. She couldn't exactly go through hours of recordings, could she? She'd heard of triggered recording, but that seemed awfully complicated and well outside her ability.

If she could only do some research… She stared at the computer, knowing IT monitored everything. Would they know? Would they care?

It was burning a hole in her bag.

She'd gone to an electronics store on her lunch break. This far from Louisville, there weren't a ton of options, just a few small stores that mostly sold cables and adapters. There were a grand total of two recorders at the store. Neither of them had voice activation as a feature.

On the upside, her research that morning had panned out. With luck, she could use the software that came pre-installed on her home computer to search for sections of recording that were louder than others. It looked easy enough on the website.

Anxiety gnawed at her gut, though. She thought of all the times she'd screwed up in the past.

What if I get the recordings and can't find anything?

What if there's nothing to find?

She checked both ways as she exited the stairwell, the unreality of the situation hitting her. Here, she'd taken this same path countless times in the past, never once wondering who might see her. Now? She couldn't help wondering. Would she get caught? Who might be watching? Would it matter if they were? What was really going on?

The questions plagued her as she patted her bag and turned toward the storage closet. Hard cardboard and plastic pressed against her fingers, calming and ramping up her nerves at the same time. She couldn't decide if she was excited or terrified.

She reached the closet without incident, her palm gripping the cool metal and sticking as she turned the handle.

God Almighty. What am I doing?

She closed the door behind her, resisting the urge to rest against it to take her breath.

You're better than this, May. Man up.

She raised a fist to her face, muffling her laughter. Man up. Right. Dropping her things on the nearest shelf, she pulled out the recorder and the scissors she'd grabbed from her desk on the way up. She tore into the packaging with increasing frustration as the adult-proof plastic refused to give up its prize.

"Stupid shit," she muttered under her breath as sharp edges dug into her fingers. She pulled, the plastic stretching and tearing where scissors couldn't get a decent angle. Finally, the recorder slipped free, dropping onto the floor with a clatter.

May bent down and pressed the button on the side of the device.

Please start up.

The screen powered on and she smiled.

Didn't break it.

Standing up again, she placed it on the shelf and pulled the instructions from the packaging to read. She glanced over most of the information, searching for features she cared about, like power save modes and how to keep the recorder from turning off automatically.

When she was ready, she put the paper down on her bag and picked up the recorder, fiddling with the settings. Holding it away from her, she whispered. "Testing. Can you read?" A couple button presses and she replayed the recording, each word coming through crystal clear.

Good.

Crossing the room to the vent, she pulled the screwdriver out of her pocket to remove the cover. A little thrill ran through her as she prepared to plant the listening device.

Listening device... Am I a badass or what?

A few minutes later, the vent cover slid out of place, letting her place the active recording device. She slid it back, loosely replacing the screws to make access easier next time.

For a few moments, she just stepped back and stared, just barely able to make out the little black box between the white slats. She couldn't believe she was actually doing this.

Why am I doing this?

And what am I going to hear?

CHAPTER FOUR

---

*L*ast night sucked.

May walked up to her desk the next morning with anticipation gnawing at her insides. She wanted to go check the recording, but why bother? Sure, she could go upstairs and download the recordings real quick, but then what? She couldn't review them until tonight, anyway.

Patience, girl. Patience.

So instead, she sat at her desk, struggling to focus on the reading assigned to her. The plan she'd come up with yesterday meant she wouldn't go upstairs until near the end of the day. Fuckface had her stuck at a desk until further notice. Her one reprieve was emergency training in the late afternoon, which would distract her, but that was hours from now.

She needed to get out of her own head. Reading certainly wasn't helping. Especially not *this* reading. She pushed the tablet away in disgust, leaning back in her chair. The mottled ceiling provided no distraction.

Fuckface was making a mistake.

The epiphany came to her as her mind tried making patterns out of the marks above her. She had a mission coming up, a mission she needed to prepare for. How could she prepare if she wasn't even training? Snapping forward, she stared at the screen. Page 3 of 29 shouted back at her, taunting her.

She shook her head, wanting to throw the mobile device. She knew how to do an unassisted docking, for fuck's sake. There was a very big difference between *knowing* and *doing*, though. She was good at the knowing. She *sucked* at the doing. *That's* what she needed to work on, not rereading an SOP for the thousandth time.

Not that Fuckface would agree. She sighed and pulled the tablet back toward her. She would have to resign herself to the reality that she needed to keep reading the dry document until her eyes bled.

Or until CO Fuckface said to stop.

* * *

"Okay, that's it for today. Good job, Trace."

May stood taller, hands clasped behind her back. "Thank you, sir."

"Dismissed."

At least, there was *one* thing she was good at. She always excelled at emergency training. NSS Training was different from other branches of the military. They still did combat training, but survival training was replaced with "emergency training." Basically, it encompassed what to do in case of various emergencies. Life support failure. Engine failure. Leaks. Loss of artificial gravity. Stranded on foreign worlds or moons. You name it. Emergency training was more diversified, encompassing every possible scenario a soldier could experience on a mission in space.

It was never dull, always varied. She loved it.

And now she could check the recorder.

What would be on it? She practically skipped as she headed back to the office building. The light was dimming as the sun set, engines interrupting the silence as people drove home. Some tore out of the nearby parking lot with a squeal of brakes. May turned as a flash of yellow gunned it around a corner, disappearing out of sight. She smiled and focused back on where she was going. *The office. The recording.* Usually, she would be heading to PT right about now, but she didn't have the patience for that today. She would do it after reviewing the data… maybe.

Swiping her badge, she entered the building. This door opened onto the stairwell, so she jogged up to the second floor, again checking both ways. By this time of day, everyone was downstairs getting ready to leave. She needn't worry about being spotted, but better safe than sorry.

She slipped out of the stairwell and into the closet. Looking up, she immediately spotted the little black device waiting for her. She approached. She'd left the screwdriver on a shelf below the vent, hidden behind a box of pens.

As she retrieved the device and downloaded the data, she wondered what was on it. Did the men show up again? What did they say?

Excitement and anxiety ratcheted up inside her as the download finished and she plugged the recorder into her power bank to recharge. Once everything was set to rights, she slipped from the room and headed home, almost holding her breath as the unknown stretched before her.

"Never thought my computer was this slow," May mumbled as she stuffed a few overly salty fries in her mouth, waiting for the data to download to her computer.

She'd grabbed fast food on the way back to her room, a room she, thankfully, had to herself at the moment. She grabbed a couple more fries from the paper bag, the salt crystals forming a glove around her fingertips. Fry fumes wafted up to her, making her swoon.

94% complete.

It took everything she had to keep her breathing and heart under control as she waited. Swallowing, she reached for the cup of soda and sucked hard on the straw. Over-sweet liquid filled her mouth as the status window on her computer reached 100%.

A slight smile tipped the edge of her lips as she set the cup down and leaned forward, ready to work. She opened the recording in the audio editing software.

On screen, a single track showed up with lots of space below for additional tracks. A large information pane took up the bottom third of the window. The graphic display for the track was mostly a single red, flat line. It was condensed so far it was hard to see any detail, so she used her fingers to zoom in until she spotted the first peak. She tapped right before it and hit the triangular, red play icon.

After a momentary pause, the now familiar voices filled her room. A chill ran down her spine.

"Where are you on your end?" Mr. Hardass said, his tone a threat in and of itself.

May could practically hear the other man swallow nervously.

"It's progressing." Mr. Paranoid's voice trembled, barely avoiding stuttering.

Heavy breathing came through for a few moments. What were they doing? "I don't have to tell you the importance of this mission, do I? The fate of all humanity lies in the balance. If we fail, the world will never be the same."

"We won't," Mr. Paranoid said, sounding almost confident for the first time. "The *Orleans* mission will *not* succeed."

May froze, staring at the screen as the recording continued to play, but she didn't hear another word. The voices flowed in and out of her brain like so much background noise. Her mouth gaped, and she had a hard time breathing.

The *Orleans* mission.

Were they talking about the ship she was set to deploy on in two weeks? She shook her head, pushing back from the desk. "It can't be. It just can't."

May stood and started pacing the room, her mind in turmoil. Who *were* these people, and why did they want that mission to fail? What was so special about it? She'd read the mission briefing. Nothing alluded to anything that could impact the entire world.

What the hell did they know about her mission that *she* didn't?

CHAPTER FIVE

The next morning, May went upstairs to retrieve her power bank, then headed to her desk, finding a note from her CO asking to meet. She dropped the power bank on her already overcrowded desktop. A pile of papers, pens, and highlighters covered the surface while a tablet set awkwardly on the heap, ready to fall to its demise.

Without pause, she detoured to her CO's office and knocked on the door. "Ma'am," she said as she entered.

CO Fuckface leaned forward on her elbows, hands clasped before her. "I'm considering putting you back on the training rotation again. Are you prepared for that?" Her CO's face spoke to her doubt.

"Yes, ma'am."

She nodded. "Don't let me down again, please. I believe in you. You have a lot of potential here. You're not a hotshot, Trace. Hotshots take unnecessary risks. They burn bright, and they burn out just as fast." She shook her head. "You have the potential for more."

"Thank you, ma'am."

Her CO leaned back, reaching for her coffee cup as she relaxed into her seat. The ceramic mug scraped against the wood as she picked it up and held it a breath away from her lips. A look crossed her face that May couldn't quite identify. Tender? Combined with the minuscule streaks of gray highlighting her red hair, pulled back in a matronly bun, it made her think of a mother. "Don't disappoint me, okay?"

That was the last thing she wanted to do.

"Yes, ma'am," she said, standing taller, straighter.

"Dismissed."

"Thank you, ma'am."

May turned tail and ran back to her desk. Today was one of those days when her CO didn't deserve the nickname of Fuckface. It didn't happen often, maybe more because of May's issues than anything else, but she knew it wouldn't last.

She sat down at her desk, and maybe because she wasn't being forced to, she started reading the manual docking SOP without any issue. Her mind still drifted to the recording on a regular basis, though.

It frustrated her that, despite having no reason to believe someone was listening, the most overt comment they made was mentioning the *Orleans* mission just once. She looked down at the mission briefing again after she finished reading the SOP one last time.

Had she missed something? Was there something else in that briefing, something to warrant this kind of attention? She scanned the information in more detail.

She would be on a piloting rotation for a Titan Class spaceship. They were old, among the first equipped for sub-space travel. They used a MAG-GRAV system, which would suck.

She hated showering in zero gravity. It was such a pain in the ass.

Still, the choice of the ship, along with picking a pilot like herself, told her a lot about the mission. Specifically, it couldn't be all that important or sensitive. Titan Classes were flagged for low priority missions or travel that required the spaceship land since most modern ships couldn't.

The captain, as well, was a pretty modest officer. She'd never worked with him before but, from what she'd heard around base, he'd never taken a high priority mission in his life. He was a career officer, perfectly happy with easing his way along until retirement. She doubted he would take an important mission.

Flipping the page, she moved onto the mission objective. All it said was, "Exploratory."

She frowned. That *did* seem odd. She'd been on plenty of exploratory missions, mostly NASA expeditions requiring NSS support, read plenty of those mission objectives. Frankly, whoever wrote NASA mission briefs was a bit of a windbag. They often wrote everything from where they were going to the scientific names of the native fauna and flora.

Which meant NASA didn't plan this trip, the NSS did. But why would the NSS run an exploratory mission? May leaned back in her chair, tapping her lip thoughtfully.

She could only think of two scenarios: evaluating potential military threats to future missions, or they were lying about the purpose of the mission.

She could believe the former. If NASA provided a list of places they planned to go, and the NSS didn't know what potential risks there would be in those areas, she could see it. But it was months and months before NASA had a budget review, when they would need to survey their current and future projects. Why would they be releasing that information now?

The second option made her blood run cold, because while the first was plausible, even reassuring, the second explained the two men conspiring in that small room upstairs.

And if they were keeping their mission objective secret, maybe the rest of the peculiarities made sense, too. If they didn't want anyone to know how important this mission was, they wouldn't want to assign the best ship, the best pilots, the best captain. They would want to make it look low priority, unimportant, an afterthought.

So what were those two planning? What made this mission so important?

May pushed off from her desk in a huff. Shoving to her feet, she stormed off to her favorite spot on the second floor. As she slammed the door open, her gaze immediately darted to the little black object behind the vent. Her mood tanked.

She closed her eyes, face scrunched up as she blindly approached the window at the opposite end. When her fingertips touched cool glass, she opened them, looking down on the world below.

It wasn't the same.

She looked out over the military personnel going about their days, but failed to reclaim the former peace her escape provided. Her mind couldn't shut out the recorder at her back. Hell, even her body stood braced, waiting for voices to break the silence.

She found her finger tapping her lower lip without even realizing it. Suddenly, every person who passed below was a reminder of the stakes. They'd said the *world*. They'd said the world would never be the same. All of humanity. Everyone below was a potential victim. She didn't know what would happen, but she was starting to get scared.

"What do I do?"

<hr>

May kept a journal now on her personal tablet. She kept notes as she listened to the recordings, then isolated the sections with speech.

It didn't amount to much, though. Not yet. Mr. Hardass was cagey as hell, and Mr. Paranoid acted like a scared rat most of the time. They talked without going into specifics, as if knowing someone was listening.

Which was just paranoid. Crazy talk. They didn't know. They *couldn't*. But that didn't stop her from thinking it, didn't stop her from paying increasing attention to her surroundings. She listened for voices, breathing, footsteps. She checked behind herself frequently, looking both ways before entering a hallway.

May could admit to herself that it was excessive, unnecessary, but she couldn't seem to stop herself. Even immediately after telling herself there was nothing to fear, she would check for threats all over again. She jumped at the slightest sound, now. She couldn't help it.

Why couldn't she get that earlier excitement and curiosity back? Wasn't this still exciting? Wasn't there still a mystery to solve?

But it wasn't fun anymore. The stakes were too high, far too high for a nobody like herself. She wasn't prepared for this, couldn't handle it. Not at all.

The only time she felt comfortable, safe, was when she was in her room alone. Even then, though, reviewing the recordings left her on edge. Time was slipping away. How many days had passed already? Would she snap before the mission commenced? It sure felt like it. And yet, it had been two days since she heard the recording. Two days since it stopped being an adventure for her.

"What am I doing?" She looked out the window of her room and felt completely alone. "I'm not equipped for this. Why did I even start this? I should have just told someone."

May pushed back from her desk and lay down on her bed, staring up at the ceiling with hands clasped on her stomach. She tried to relax, but the feeling simply wouldn't come.

"I can't keep doing this."

May held her head in her hands. It had been a hell of a day. She didn't remember much of her day, just going through the motions, mostly.

"I'm paranoid." She shook her head. "How did this happen?" Leaning back, she looked up and sighed. "This isn't me. I'm not this person. I'm just an uninspired pilot with a CO who likes to nag me all the time." She laughed, shaking her head again. "I don't go around playing super-spy, that's for damned sure."

And yet, sitting at her desk, she couldn't resist swiping the display into the vertical position, couldn't resist downloading today's data. She felt compelled, driven forward by a force she'd didn't understand. Even with anxiety trying to eat her alive, that force shoved her forward, pushing her toward a fate she couldn't possibly fathom.

"Can't stop now, can I?" She chuckled, but it came out humorless, flat.

She wasn't sure she wanted to stop.

May scanned the audio, searching for speech, searching for clues. She jotted down notes each time she found something, but like always, they didn't say much of importance. There was a ton of insinuation for every spec of useful intelligence. Not that she knew what to do with any of it.

Then she heard a word that stopped her cold. All her muscles froze up, and she threw her hand forward, stopping the playback. She moved the cursor back a few seconds and replayed that last section, hoping she'd misheard and knowing she hadn't.

Mr. Paranoid's squeaky voice came through.

Funny, she'd always thought Mr. Hardass was the scary one.

"I don't know if I can do it, sabotage, I mean."

"You will," Mr. Hardass said, the threat clear in his voice. "Because the world is on the line. Do you want to let everyone down?"

CHAPTER SIX

I'*ve got to tell someone.*

As May walked to her office building the next morning, that thought kept plaguing her. She *needed* to tell someone, but whom? Those two were meeting in a secured building on a military base. They could be anyone. If she told the wrong person, what would happen?

Nothing good, that was for damned sure.

If it was just Mr. Paranoid, she wouldn't be so concerned. He reminded her of a weasel. It wouldn't take much for him to back out. In fact, Mr. Hardass seemed to be the only thing keeping him on track.

And that was the problem: Mr. Hardass. She had no doubt that he would see this through to the bitter end. His voice alone could send chills down her spine when he spoke of their plans.

Sabotage.

She couldn't say it. She could barely think it. Who would even contemplate sabotaging a spaceship? The *Orleans* was a pretty big ship, would have hundreds of people on board. A lot of people could die.

"It's too much." May stood in front of the outer door of the offices just staring at the badge reader. "I can't do this." She took a step back involuntarily. "I can't do this."

She turned around and walked away, pulling out her phone as she went. She sent a text message to her CO. "Not feeling well. Won't be in today."

It was sort of the truth.

Just thinking about the conspiracy made her sick.

My palms are sweaty. My palms are never sweaty.

Those thoughts meandered through May's skull as she walked mindlessly around the base. She didn't go home, feeling too listless to sit still, and yet every idea that popped into her head got summarily rejected. PT? Too confining, too pointless. Her mom's place? Too many questions. A friend? Who?

Damn and didn't that hurt. She had a roommate, had family, but friends? She didn't pull up a single face in that category. Well, except for Mila, but she didn't think that counted, not anymore. Mila was probably dead by now.

Then again…

She pulled out her phone, unlocking it and bringing up Mila's entry. It included all her information from ten years ago: name, title, address, phone, email. But it also included one more item: a second phone number. She'd never called it, probably never would. At this point, she was too afraid nobody would answer or that it would be a wrong number. What were the chances Mila even had that number still?

She could still see that note in her mind's eye, feel the raw pain as she realized her best friend had abandoned her. Why? Even after all these years, after all the time she'd spent moving on, the question still haunted her. Why? That was the part she could never understand. Mila'd had everything in front of her. May still couldn't believe that *she'd* become the military pilot and *Mila* had become nobody.

How is that for irony?

Pulling herself out of her thoughts, she looked up and stopped. She was in front of the security building. Her mind started turning in a more productive manner once more. She stared up at the edifice.

I need to tell someone.

And who better to tell than the Head of Security?

And May just happened to remember his name from her orders. Kyle Avery. Just like the captain, she'd never worked with him, but security personnel usually either had an office or cubicle in this building, so it was a place to start.

May stepped inside.

A man in uniform sat behind a desk with lots of monitors. "Can I help you, ma'am?"

"I'm here to see Kyle Avery."

The man nodded, looked him up, and rattled off directions that went in one ear and out the other. Feeling like an idiot, she nodded and headed for the stairs. She'd managed to catch the floor number and that it was a ways down the hall, but that was it.

Hopefully, it wasn't too far.

May jogged up the stairs, ignoring the railing as dust bunnies floated in the morning light coming from the landing above.

Her boots pounded on each step, echoing up the stairwell. Before long, she was breathless and pushing open the door to the correct floor, assuming she'd plucked at least *that* detail from the directions.

The hall was poorly lit and littered with wood doors every few feet on both sides. Each door listed a name, but no rank or position. Her gaze glanced over each nameplate, reading and moving on when it wasn't the right one. She stopped and turned when faced with another stairwell in front of her and another hall to her right.

It was a bit uncanny walking down that hall. Though each door held a name, they felt disembodied, unidentified, like there was no unique person assigned to each room, just a faceless automaton. Which, of course, got her thinking about walking automatons chasing her down these same hallways.

Like I need new nightmare material. Reality is bad enough.

Finally, she spotted the name Avery on the right and stopped in front of the door. But now that she was here, she didn't act. Instead, she stood there, arms stuck at her sides as a nameless anxiety rose inside her.

This is the moment.

She told herself that, trying to psych herself up, but it didn't work, her body remaining firmly plastered in place.

I never knew I was such a coward.

But she wasn't a coward, was she? She'd gone on countless missions, flown countless ships. She'd never flinched, run, or backed down on the job before, so why now?

Because I don't know who's involved.

"Shit," she muttered, turning around to pace. The walls blurred around her, a sea of fuzzy gray as she sped up, her emotions driving her faster and faster. She didn't know who was involved. *Anyone* could be, even the Head of Security.

And really, how could any sabotage get off the ground if the Head of Security was *not* involved? He would man an entire team of security specialists, could control the direction and breadth of any investigation. He could choose to ignore signs of something being wrong or disappear evidence.

And if he wasn't involved, he would be the single greatest threat to the sabotage. He had access to every camera, every personnel file, every transmission. Again, he ran an entire team of security specialists, ready and willing to put an end to any threat.

He could be her greatest ally or worst enemy, and she just had no way of knowing which.

I can't take that risk.

May walked back to her room in silence, feeling defeated more than ever. After opening the door, she threw her keys on her desk. They clattered and nearly fell off, parts of them dangling off the edge. She didn't care. She sat on the bed and dropped her head into her hands.

"What am I gonna do?"

It seemed so hopeless. She just wanted to return to being oblivious. She wanted it done, to go back to blindly going through her life, going through the motions, having her CO fuss at her for squandering her potential again.

Her CO.

She liked to call her CO Fuckface, but she was a good woman. Smart, strong, and a bit of a mother hen, but she couldn't see her going along with sabotage. She was a servant leader, willing to do or be whatever you needed to get your ass in gear. Frankly, May was surprised the woman hadn't resorted to kicking May's ass by now. She probably deserved it.

Maybe I can tell her…

May had a challenge in front of her. She'd called in sick to work, but she still wanted to get today's recordings, which meant returning to the office. If she got caught, it might raise questions she really didn't want to answer.

And yet, she made it upstairs without any issues other than a pounding heart and an anxiety overload. Her hand slipped on the door handle when she reached for it. She had to wipe her palm on her pants just to get in the closet.

She let out a sigh of relief when she was finally away from prying eyes. "I am not built for this."

Pushing off from the door, she crossed to the vent and started removing the grate with her screwdriver. Like always, it made little metallic noises as the tool connected or the grate shifted in place.

"Did you hear that?"

She froze, banging against the grate as she tried to keep it still. For a moment, she even stopped breathing, hoping they would forget all about it.

"Maybe it was just the HVAC?" Mr. Paranoid said, sounding hopeful.

Yes, let's go with that. HVAC.

"That wasn't the HVAC. Feel this? No airflow. No airflow means no noise."

"Then what was it?" Mr. Paranoid's voice trembled as his hopes were dashed.

"Don't you mean who?"

"You don't know it was a person."

Mr. Hardass didn't respond right away. "Are you willing to risk it if it is?"

"No?"

"That's right. Whoever it is, we need to find them and silence them."

A moment later, a door slammed.

"Oh my God," she breathed, looking to her own door. "They're gonna find me." She scoured her surroundings, but there was nowhere to hide. It was a fucking storage closet, for crying out loud. All it had were shelves and boxes. And none of the boxes were big enough.

Backing away from the vent, she reached for the door, but stopped herself. They could be just outside waiting for her. She could be walking right into their arms.

...find them and silence them.

What did he mean by that? How would they silence her? She knew what her imagination was voting for, and it was nothing she wanted to experience.

May backed up, crossing the length of the room in a handful of steps until the cool surface of the window pressed into her back. She whipped her head back and forth in desperation, settling on a small cubbyhole to her right. It was just a small space between the wall and the last shelving unit. She could easily see the door once she squeezed her bulk into the space, but she had no other options. It was that or say, "Here I am, just kill me now."

She tried to control her breathing as she sucked in her gut, her everything, trying to appear smaller. Each breath shuddered in and out of her, making small noises that, in her terror, might as well have been cymbals clashing.

Then the door creaked open, and she stopped breathing mid-breath. She stood there, expecting to be caught at any moment.

I'm so dead.

"Anything?" Mr. Hardass said.

"Yeah, come check this out."

Oh, God, no. They've found me.

CHAPTER SEVEN

oe opened the door to the storage closet, heart pounding in his ears. He half expected a ninja assassin to come flying at him as he opened it. Muscles tensed, he pushed the door further, exposing boxes and metal shelving.

"Huh," he said as the door slid open. A vent up high on the wall was missing three screws, the last one holding the grate precariously. Still in motion, it swung gently, just moments from stillness.

"They couldn't have been gone long," the bastard behind him said.

He didn't know the man's name, nor did he want to know. Sometimes, he wondered how he got himself into this situation. How did he get mixed up with people like this? The man was ruthless, calculating, and a cold feeling in Joe's gut told him he would be dead in some senseless accident if he ever tried to back out.

Otherwise, he would have backed out ages ago.

It had all started so harmlessly. He loved his country, respected humanity. He'd joined the NSS because he wanted to protect the planet. United We Stand and all that.

But, frankly, the Incirrina scared him a little. He didn't trust them and didn't want them anywhere near his planet. He would be happy if he could just forget there were alien species out there. They had enough enemies here on Earth to deal with.

Solve problems at home first.

That was what he always said in the meetings. How could the people of Earth even think of alliances abroad when they couldn't get their own house in order? Wasn't that pure madness? A lot of people agreed.

When had those innocent bitch sessions turned into sedition, subterfuge, and conspiracy? When had everything gone so heinously *wrong?*

He didn't know, but he was trapped. So far, all he'd done was talk, but would that change anything in the grand scheme of things? Would he get any less of a sentence because he didn't act when he withheld information vital to national security?

All it takes for evil to triumph is for good men to do nothing.

That was him, all right. Doing damned nothing, nothing at all.

He should have been spilling to the nearest superior, ending this whole beast before it grew any bigger, but he was too much of a coward, too selfish.

"There," he said, pointing at the vent, where something dark peeked through the metal slats. He stepped forward and pushed the metal aside, the hard edges pressing into his soft fingertips.

A little black recording device sat on the flimsy, metal ventilation duct. He pulled it out and hit stop, turning around to face his partner in crime as icy fingers squeezed his insides. "Someone's been listening in."

"And they have evidence."

———

May released a slow breath as the door closed once more. Her body wanted to collapse to the floor as she leaned hard against the wall, the surface jamming against her shoulder blades.

"Jesus Christ," she breathed, taking another deep drag of much-needed oxygen. "I thought I was a goner there."

Turning her head, she stared at the now closed door and the empty space where Mr. Paranoid had been only moments before. Her entire body was shaking as she pushed away from the wall. "Thank God it was Mr. Paranoid." She was confident Mr. Hardass wouldn't have missed her if his partner hadn't blocked the door.

The room felt different in the aftermath, somehow surreal. Or maybe she just felt detached after that shock to her system. She crossed to the vent, but as expected, the recorder was no longer there.

"God, this was stupid. What was I thinking? I am *not* a hero. This is not me." She spun around, blinding registering shapes surrounding her without identifying them.

She just wanted out, wanted this to be over with. What was she thinking? This wasn't a game. This was serious, life or death. Her finger and lip trembled as they made contact, the digit running a feather-light touch over that smooth surface. She tried to calm down, tried to control her breathing, but she failed.

I can't do this.

<hr>

I'll be in touch.

Those were the last words Joe's partner had said to him before ditching him yesterday.

I'll be in touch.

He didn't know if that was good or bad. Frankly, he didn't know what to think anymore. On the one hand, he wanted everything to be over. He wanted back to his normal life. On the other, he feared a normal life was impossible and the only way out was through.

He *really* didn't want to go through with this, though.

And the look on his partner's face had made him very much fear for the owner of that recorder.

He stared blindly at the computer screen at his desk. Automatically color-coded lines of code blurred together in the program he'd been working in. He couldn't even focus on his work. Having arrived at work hours ago, he'd accomplished nothing. He couldn't wait for the day to be over with.

Around him, his coworkers chatted about the latest video game, trying to one up each other, but he didn't process the words, only the confident posturing in their voices. It was just background noise.

He rested his hands against the keyboard, laying them flat when he just couldn't bring himself to work. His fingers ran over the smooth surface, index fingers hovering over the raised bumps on the J and F keys.

"This was never supposed to happen like this." He had the sinking feeling that people were going to die. He didn't want that on his conscience. But what could he do? He rarely knew what his partner was up to. How could he stop him?

And what would happen to Joe if he did?

CHAPTER EIGHT

May sat down at her desk at work, staring at her computer screen. She was still a bit dazed from the close call yesterday.

I can't keep this up. This isn't me.

She turned her head, staring off in the direction of her CO's office. What could she do, though? She felt trapped, stuck, and it was driving her nuts. She wanted to just forget all about this, but she couldn't. Could anyone?

I need to tell someone.

Unfortunately, she still had the same problem—she didn't know who to trust. Anyone could be involved, and if she went to the wrong person, it wouldn't end well for her.

So, who could she trust? Who could she *truly* trust? She could name them on one hand: Mila, her family. None of them could help.

Who could she trust on base? She'd already nixed the Head of Security for the mission. He could be innocent, but if he wasn't, he was the last person she would want to cross.

She rocked her chair, the springs squeaking in protest as she stared up at the ceiling, hypnotizing herself with the water stains. Although, they looked suspiciously brown to be made from water…

Her computer chirped, and she snapped back into action, waking it up. An email from her CO.

Her CO.

Her hands froze on the keys. She had a hard time believing the woman could be involved in something so malevolent. She was nice to a fault, always trying to lift people up. That is, when she wasn't giving May a tongue-lashing for her latest failure. But even then, it wasn't out of malice. Could she have what it took to be party to a conspiracy?

May looked back toward her CO's office once more, her hands resting on the edge of her desk, ready to push to her feet. The door was open, welcoming. She sat poised on the brink, trying to convince herself to act.

She's not involved.

There's no way she's involved.

She's too much of a mother hen.

May stood up, kicking her chair out of her way as she crossed to the opposite side of the room. She hesitated near the office door, just out of sight.

Last chance, May.

She knocked.

"Come in."

May pushed through her fear. "I'd like a word in private, ma'am."

"Of course. Close the door."

"Thank you, ma'am." May folded her arms behind her. Her hand twitched, the open posture leaving her feeling vulnerable.

Her CO, Parker, smiled at her benignly, leaning back in her chair and letting May come to her words in her own time, her face and posture open and welcoming.

May leaned against the door, the solid pressure grounding her just enough to speak. "I have reason to believe the *Orleans* mission may be compromised."

Parker leaned forward, the barest hint of alarm entering her expression. "In what way?"

May bit her lip. "I think someone's going to try to sabotage it."

"Who? Why?"

She shook her head. "I don't know. I overheard something. I overheard two people talking about the mission, about sabotaging it. They were pretty circumspect, but I got the impression it was larger than just the two of them."

Parker leaned back in her chair again, looking increasingly troubled. "This is very serious. Have you told anyone else about it?"

"No. I didn't know who to trust."

Parker smiled. "But you trusted me."

"Yes, ma'am. You're my CO, and you've got integrity."

"Thank you." She leaned against her desk, folding her hands before her. Her knuckles grew white with tension. "Is there anything else I should know? Anything else I should pass along?"

"I have recordings. Of their conversations."

"Good. That's-that's really good. That's hard evidence, not hearsay."

"If you like, I can head home and make you copies."

"Absolutely. Go now. Report back to me as soon as you have them."

———

May practically ran back home for the recordings. As the audio files copied, the progress bar crawling onward, she paced from the wall to the side of her bed.

"Come on, already."

Why was it taking so long? She stopped and stared, but her nervous energy wouldn't let her stand still for long. Now that she had an action to take, she wanted to take it… yesterday. Every moment that passed seemed too long, too much.

Why hadn't she thought of telling her CO before? Of course, she should inform her CO. Who else could she tell? But even with her faith in the woman, a nagging feeling lingered in the back of her mind, taunting her with what ifs.

What if the wrong person found out?

What if she made the wrong choice?

What if there was no right choice?

What if she couldn't stop this?

She ground to a halt as the progress bar disappeared. "Thank *God.*" She yanked the thumb drive from her computer and dashed for the door, crossing the base's campus without seeing her surroundings.

What felt like moments later, she knocked on her CO's door.

"Enter."

May pushed the door open and held out her open hand, the small drive cupped ominously atop it.

"That's it?"

May nodded.

"So much in such a small package." She chuckled, but the expression of amusement was fleeting, quickly replaced by a stern, serious look. "Don't worry, Trace. I'll see that this gets into the right hands."

"I believe you."

And yet her gut still churned with anxiety.

It took him all day, but Joe finally settled on a course of action. He couldn't go head on against his partner. That would be suicide, but it occurred to him he might have an ally out there —the owner of the recorder.

And he still had it in his possession. Joe rolled the small black device in hand as he contemplated his options. He knew what he *could* do. He was just trying to figure out what he *should* do. It wasn't a simple thing. He refused to get himself killed over this, which meant he had to keep his inquiries quiet. Nobody could know, which just kept returning him to the one option he didn't want to take.

I promised I would never do that again.

She would understand, though, wouldn't she? If he was potentially saving lives, it was worth the cost, wasn't it? And yet, it felt like an excuse, a cop-out. It had nearly destroyed his life when he was a teenager, and she'd made him promise.

It had seemed such an easy promise when he was a teenager, so simple. Like a light switch being flipped. So, he'd turned his talents to better uses, went to college, joined the military.

She would be proud of me now, wouldn't she?

And yet here he was, screwing it up all over again.

How had that bastard known?

That's what kept messing with him. Nobody should have known. Those records were sealed. They shouldn't even exist anymore, right? How could anyone have known what he did when he was just a stupid kid?

But it didn't matter how he knew. It only mattered that he did. It only mattered that Joe's life, his future, was on the line.

"I should have said something." He scrubbed his hands over his face as he sat at his desk. "I shouldn't have let him control me like that. All I did was make things worse."

A noise that couldn't be called amusement leaked from him as he admitted to himself that he'd made things *much* worse. He'd let this happen. He'd played himself.

And now I have to pay the consequences.

Or did he?

As he stared at his computer screen, he knew he could get away with it. Really, it was the *only* way he could safely find his future ally.

His hands moved to hover over the keyboard. He'd looked up the recorder. It was sold in a couple nearby stores and some online retailers. He needed to know either if someone bought one locally or if one was shipped to base. Then, he could narrow it down.

He just needed to hack into sales records to do it.

I'm sorry, Mom.

Parker entered her superior's office, the thumb drive held firmly in her fist. She was generally an optimistic person, but she felt a little nervous right now. This was potentially huge, and she was just a paper pusher.

She stood taller as she came to a stop, feeling ill at ease in the fancy environment.

I really should decorate my office better.

Being in here always made her feel insecure. It wasn't fancy, per se, but the entire atmosphere screamed, "Important!" The walls were laden with pictures of him rubbing elbows with important people mixed with frames and window boxes of his various accomplishments. The desk and chair were nicer than hers, too. Behind him, pictures of his family filled surfaces strategically, each one pristine with pristine people portrayed.

"Ah, Parker. You said it was urgent?"

"Yes, sir." She offered him the drive.

He leaned forward, his short nails scraping her palm as he picked it up. "And this is?"

She took a deep breath. "It's a recording between two individuals that may be conspiring to sabotage an upcoming mission."

"Which mission?" he asked, his gaze focused on the side of his computer as he plugged in the drive.

"The *Orleans*, sir."

He stopped mid-motion, his expression showing a certain level of shock and something else she couldn't quite name. Determination? "That's serious."

"Sir?"

He shrugged her off. "I'm afraid I can't divulge the details, but thank you for bringing this to my attention."

"Permission to speak, sir?"

"Proceed."

She took another deep breath. "I have several subordinates on that mission. Is there reason for concern?"

"I'll take care of it. Dismissed."

"Yes, sir."

He removed the drive from his computer without listening to the recordings. He didn't need to hear them. He knew what they would say. He knew what they were about.

Picking up his phone, he dialed the switchboard, asking to be redirected, taking the extra steps to eliminate records of their connection.

"Yes?" the man on the other end said by way of greeting.

"We have a problem." He rocked back in his chair, rolling the drive in his palm, the hard plastic brushing against his skin in a soothing manner. He stared at the closed door, thinking of the woman who'd just left. Red hair pulled back in a tight chignon popped into his head. Parker. Good woman. A pity, really.

The other man intruded on his thoughts, snapping him back to attention. "What type of problem?"

"A Katrina," he said, using their code, Katrina being one of the most memorable hurricanes to hit New Orleans. It was apropos.

"The regular place?"

He nodded, even though the other man couldn't see it. "I'll meet you in one hour."

CHAPTER NINE

*J*oe found her. In the end, it was a lot easier than he remembered it being. Then again, in the intervening years, he'd completed high school, a computer sciences degree, and spent years working with computers for his job. So it wasn't really that surprising, was it?

Still, a small amount of pride surged through him as he watched the woman leave the barracks. He'd found her. It hadn't even taken that long.

Of course, that brought with it a whole new set of problems. He'd already nixed leaving a note at her room. That was almost guaranteed to freak her out. So how should he approach her? What would he say? Had she already told someone about them?

Shit.

He hadn't thought of that. What if even now his voice was being passed up the ranks, ready to court martial him?

Don't think about it.

It was hard to do, but he pushed it out of his mind. One thing at a time. First, he had to figure out how to approach her without fucking it up. But without knowing her state of mind, how could he possibly know what would work? If he did this wrong, he could send her into a paranoid tailspin or even get himself shot. After all, this *was* a military base. It was possible.

She seemed pretty relaxed, though. He followed her at a safe distance, and she didn't pivot her head, just focusing on the path ahead of her. Also, her shoulders weren't raised, and her gait was smooth, fluid.

What did that say about her? Had she told someone? Or was she overconfident, focused on some goal? He had no idea.

She approached the side door of a building, and he jogged ahead, holding the door open for her after she unlocked it. "Ma'am," he said, nodding his head.

"Thanks." She nodded back and entered.

He swiped his own badge out of habit and continued into the building. She beelined straight for a cubicle, sitting down at the enclosed desk. He walked straight past, pretending to have a specific destination in mind even though he had no business in this building.

But now he knew where her desk was.

He could have pulled the information from military sources, but that could be dangerous for him. It was one thing to hack into some stores. It was another entirely to hack military databases.

Unfortunately, she was one of many military personnel that didn't have permanent desk assignments. Spending so much time deployed, it wasn't practical to assign a desk to her when she didn't need it, so the military had moved to a desk sharing policy. Personnel were expected to pack their desks up in lockers when they deployed, then their CO would assign them a desk once they returned. It worked well, but it also meant it wasn't easy to find a specific person's desk unless you worked in that department.

But now he'd found it.

If only he knew what to do next.

<hr>

Crossing his arms, he waited impatiently at the assigned location. He didn't take kindly to waiting and absolutely *hated* tardiness. Unfortunately, beggars couldn't be choosers, and when dealing with a group held together by philosophy rather than productivity, there were no guarantees on who you would be dealing with.

And the situation didn't make him any more patient. His mind resurrected an image of the little weasel holding up a voice recorder in that tiny second-floor closet two days ago. He couldn't believe they'd been recorded. How could he have been so sloppy?

It was just an accident. Dumb luck.

The thought didn't reassure him as much as he'd hoped, though. He still had a problem, a problem that would be solved as soon as this guy bothered to show.

Finally, a small blue car pulled up, and he pushed off the side of his own vehicle, dropping his hands to his sides. "You're late," he said as the car door opened.

The man checked his watch. "Not *that* late."

Late enough.

"We have a task for you."

The man shrugged. "What's the task?"

He leaned into the open back window of his car and tossed a manila envelope at the man. "Details are inside. Destroy it ASAP."

He scoffed. "What do you think I am, an amateur?"

He simply glared at the man before turning his back and opening his door to leave.

Behind him, papers ruffled. "What's she done?"

He turned back. "Got nosy." Not that it was any of his business.

The other man gulped hard, his Adam's apple bobbing as he nodded and backed away.

He drove off without another word.

Returning from a bathroom break, May spotted a blank envelope on her desk. Leaning her hip against the edge, she ran her finger under the lip, the paper sharp against her skin. Pulling a single piece of copy paper out, she tossed the envelope to the side and froze.

Her heart rate accelerated, breath coming harder without even realizing. She jumped to her feet and looked around, searching in all directions. Who'd left the note? How could they possibly have known it was her?

She stared down, rereading the words. "I know you placed the recorder in the storage room upstairs. Let's meet. I'll contact you soon."

"This can't be happening." How did they find her? And what was with the letter? Who sent it, and why?

She grimaced as she returned to her desk. Sitting down with a groan of springs, her fingers automatically moved to her lip, rubbing back and forth, as her other hand crinkled the sheet of paper.

This was supposed to be over. She'd passed the recordings onto her CO. She was supposed to be done with this. Tension building inside her, she growled under her breath, her frustration getting the better of her.

Okay, calm down.

She took a deep breath, letting it out slowly.

What do I do?

Should she tell her CO? But what could her CO do? It wasn't like the note was signed, and while they could check the note and envelope for fingerprints, there was no guarantee one of the culprits sent it. All it mentioned was her recorder. There was nothing illicit there.

Still, I should keep her informed.

May walked to Parker's office and knocked on the door, but got no answer. She looked around her, shifting her weight from foot to foot. The area was surprisingly empty, quiet.

Now what?

May walked back to her desk, trying to think of a plan of action. There was no way she was meeting this person. Not a chance. Everything about the note gave her the creeps. He could be an assassin or a stalker, but either way, nothing good could come of meeting him.

Laying the note on her desk, the envelope resting beside it, there was nothing special about either. The note was hand-written on cheap paper he'd probably snatched from one of the printers, and the envelope was just a standard letter size envelope. She pulled out her phone and took a picture of them.

Just in case.

Then she sat down and fired an email at her CO. She didn't go into specifics, just that she had an update on her current orders. She leaned back and nodded. Yeah, it looked plenty official and vague enough that it gave nothing away.

Now, she just had to get through the rest of her day.

<hr>

He looked both ways as if checking for traffic. It was a habit borne of repetition.

Blend in.

Give nothing away.

He walked through the parking lot, focusing on looking like he belonged. He was wearing a uniform, so he certainly looked the part, but the better part of avoiding suspicion was not what you wore but how you wore it. Confidence went a lot farther than a good uniform ever could. Given enough confidence, you could talk your way almost anywhere.

As he approached the car, he didn't feel an ounce of nerves. This was business as usual. If someone were to stop him, he would have a plausible story to tell, and they would go their separate ways, none the wiser to his nefarious plans. He stopped behind the dark green sedan, double checking the license plate against the memory of the file he'd been given.

A match.

He walked between the two cars, dropping to his knees as he pulled a tool from his pocket. Laying down, he reached under the car, snipping a line. Liquid drained onto the asphalt.

Sitting up again, he took a container from his other pocket. It had a nozzle like a can of WD-40. He sprayed into the front and rear wheels. When satisfied, he moved to the opposite side of the car and repeated the act.

Finished, he sat up, using the rough asphalt under his palms to get to his feet, careful not to leave fingerprints, and walked away.

Parker entered her office at the end of the day to check her emails one last time before going home. Most of the messages could wait, but when she spotted an email from May Trace, she read it right away. She stood up straight, hurrying to May's desk, but as she figured, the pilot wasn't there. She would have to catch her in the morning.

 Walking back to her desk, she shut down her computer and closed up for the night. She stood there for several moments, her mind in turmoil.

I hope everything's okay.

The launch was rapidly approaching. She didn't want to believe something might go wrong. Even worse, if something went wrong, and she could have stopped it.

I'm doing everything I can, aren't I?

God, she hoped so. She took a deep breath as she left her office, locking it behind her. The office building was empty at this time of the day. She'd stayed late again. Her husband was going to fuss at her. He didn't like her working long hours. It was a near constant refrain in her house.

You don't get paid to stay so late.

Parker couldn't really argue with that, but what could she do?

She felt responsible for the men and women under her command. She couldn't leave without ensuring they were all taken care of, could she?

Not that her husband saw it that way. He saw her throwing her life away, giving the military time they hadn't earned.

You only have one life, baby.

She smiled as she exited the building, crossing the parking lot to her little car. He was probably right. She really *should* cut back, but then she always said that. She never seemed to pull it off. Her husband often said you needed a pitchfork to pry her away from work.

Spotting her car, she changed direction. The parking lot was vacant but for a handful of cars, so she didn't need to stick to the aisles. The sun was low on the horizon, casting her environment in warm tones, but also pricking her guilt. She should have been gone hours ago.

I hope he didn't make dinner.

It would be cold if he did, which would make him even grouchier. She stopped with her hand resting on the door handle, suddenly a little hesitant to head home. She didn't want to walk into a fight when she opened the door, and the possibility left her a little anxious.

Stop borrowing trouble.

She opened the door and dropped to the seat, the steering wheel hot as she pressed her hand to it while starting the car. It hummed to life, and she pulled away, leaving the parking lot at such a crawl, she didn't need to hit the brakes once.

Parker turned the wheel with her fingertips, the leather scorching her sensitive skin. The sun streaked across the windshield, blinding her momentarily before the window adjusted for the lighting.

Just a few more minutes, baby.

She smiled, shaking her head at herself. Just moments ago, she'd dreaded the possibility of a fight. Now, she couldn't wait to get home. Without thinking, her foot came down harder on the accelerator, pushing the car faster.

Her turn coming up, she pressed the brake pedal, but nothing happened. Parker frowned, glancing down and pressing it again. Nothing.

What the hell?

Her foot lifted off the gas, the car slowing, but not fast enough. She pulled the parking brake, but flinched as a loud screeching noise assaulted her ears. "What the fuck?"

Her hand jerked off the brake. She was still going too fast for the turn ahead. The parking brake hadn't helped at all. She pumped the brake pedal. Still nothing.

The turn was approaching. She would have to skip it, just go straight. She could walk home if she had to, or maybe call for a ride. It would be fine. She just had to let the car cruise to a stop.

Parker passed through the intersection. The car was taking far too long to slow down.

The next intersection was a light.

The light was red.

There was a car coming.

Oh God.

CHAPTER TEN

May arrived at work a little earlier than usual the next morning, eager to talk with her CO about the note. She went straight to her CO's office, but the woman wasn't there. The door was closed, locked.

"That's weird." She was always here early. May checked her watch, but it only confirmed what she'd expected. Her CO *should* have been here already.

She shuffled to her desk, uncertain of her next step. When she looked into her cubicle, she spotted another note on her keyboard and froze.

Damn, another one?

This was it. He'd said he would send another note, this time with meeting instructions. She didn't want to open it, though. She sure as shit didn't want to meet with him.

Crossing the space, the office eerily quiet this early in the morning, she picked up the envelope, flipping it over in her hand. It was just like the last one. What did it say? What did he want?

She ripped the envelope open, jerking the paper out. A location, date, and time were scribbled on it.

Below that, it simply said, "I'm on your side. It must end."

What did he mean by that? On her side? Was he part of the sabotage? Or was he like her? Did he find out and feel compelled to prevent it?

It doesn't matter.

May was done with this. She'd turned the recordings over to her CO. She would turn these over as well. The launch was less than a week away. She had more important things to focus on right now, like getting her affairs in order.

Fortunately, she lived on base, so that was an easy enough thing. She'd left her computer on last night, so she got started with getting her mail stopped and making all the rest of the arrangements necessary for deployment.

Halfway through her preparations, an email came through from command. She opened it, not even noticing the subject line.

Oh God.

She read the email over and over again, her mind refusing to process the information, instead registering words here and there.

Parker.

Died.

Car accident.

It couldn't be. It was too much of a coincidence. What were the chances that her CO would die in an accident so soon after she'd told her about the sabotage?

Non-existent.

It just couldn't be an accident, which meant she'd been killed, murdered. And if they were willing to kill for this thing, May just might be next.

And with the launch days away, they didn't have long to act.

May entered the gym as if on a mission. She'd been a bit lax in her PT lately, but right now, she needed to let off a little steam. Zeroing in on the heavy bag in the corner, she crossed the space in long, ground-eating steps. She didn't even wait to square up before throwing her first punch, a sound of confusion and pain escaping her as she let it fly. The punch was wild, wide, glancing off the edge of the bag, but she didn't care.

My fault.

All my fault.

Squaring up this time, she gave the bag a quick jab with her right, then followed up with her left. Before long, the bag was swaying chaotically, forcing her to steady it. She pulled in a long shuddering breath as she gripped the smooth leather. She stared at a spot where the bag was worse for wear, the leather cracking under the abuse of many, many fists. Her breathing slowed, returning to normal.

"Again."

This time, she tried to be in more control as her knuckles started to hurt. She hadn't wrapped them, hadn't put on gloves. She didn't participate in organized fights, so practicing bare knuckles made more sense. After all, if she needed to defend herself, they wouldn't give her time to wrap up, and hesitating because of her hands could get her hurt or worse.

She focused on force, on hitting the center of the bag, stabilizing it every few punches, but the feelings of guilt and responsibility wouldn't go away. The self-recriminating thoughts waited on the sidelines, ready to strike as soon as she relented.

All my fault.

Should have acted sooner.

But then maybe she would have died sooner?

Or maybe not. She didn't know, and that was killing her. She'd gotten her CO involved, and now the woman was dead. That kind, motherly woman was dead.

Because of me.

Because of me.

<hr>

Later that day, May stood outside the meeting location. It was public, thank God, so the risk was lower. He wouldn't kill her in a public place, would he? She hoped not. She prayed she wasn't making the second worst mistake of her life.

The first being getting her CO killed.

She didn't know why she'd decided to meet him. Had she developed a sudden death wish? Did she want to die? Or did she feel so guilty about her CO that she was willing to take any chances to make that death *mean* something?

It was a little café with outdoor seating. As she stood on the sidewalk out front, she wondered where he was. Most of the tables were occupied, but more seating waited inside. He could be any of them. Hell, for all she knew, he could be a woman. She didn't know intrinsically that the writer was a man.

May adjusted her pants, the hard metal of the gun at her back digging into her spine. She never carried a gun, but today it seemed prudent. If he tried something, she could fight back by any means necessary. She also had a knife in her pocket.

Just in case.

A man waved from a table at the edge of the patio. She stared at him. Was he waving at her? Could this be the man she'd come here to meet? He looked a little tense, wearing a collared shirt that he tugged at with his other hand.

He looked her in the eye. Yes, that was him. May crossed the distance slowly, taking his measure. He didn't *look* dangerous. He was a little skinny, with a tight military crop haircut, and a pair of glasses sticking out of his breast pocket.

She reached the seat across from him, but didn't sit.

"Thank you for coming."

She didn't speak. What could she say? She didn't trust him.

He swallowed hard and looked away, idly playing with his coffee cup.

"What do you want?" she said when he failed to fill the silence.

He looked up again and shrugged, his hand flexing hard against his mug. "Like I said in the note, I want it to end."

She gripped the back of the bistro seat, the wrought iron cold against her palms. "Not exactly specific."

He scoffed. "You expected me to be?" He leaned forward. "I want this to end, but I sure as fuck don't want to die in the process."

"And what do you want with me?"

"You've been recording our conversations."

She stiffened. Damn, this was bad. Which one was he? But even as she had the thought, she knew. He was Mr. Paranoid. The voice was different, the lack of nerves changing the timbre of his voice, giving it a smoother character, but it was definitely him. "And you want my help?" she said through gritted teeth.

"I *need* your help. I'm too close to this thing, too likely to get noticed. But you? You're not associated with this. You *could* go unnoticed." He shrugged one shoulder. "And me meeting with a woman, especially in a place like this, looks more like a date than something clandestine."

She pulled out the chair and sat. He had a point. This *did* look more like a date spot than anything else. Although, she could definitely imagine a spy movie set in Paris having a drop in a small, outdoor café.

Then again, that was Paris, not Kentucky.

"What do you want from me?"

He sighed and took a sip of his coffee. "I don't know. Have you told anyone?"

Sharp guilt sliced through her chest. "Yeah."

"And?"

"She's dead."

He paled, leaning back in his seat. "How?"

She composed herself, taking a deep breath. "A car accident. Last night. I don't know the details."

He nodded slowly. "That could be them."

"They would do something like that?" She wanted him to say no. She wanted the accident to have nothing to do with her, but she didn't really believe it.

"I don't know for certain, but I think so. The guy I was meeting with? There was something about him. I have no doubt he would kill."

"He's a soldier, isn't he? Aren't we all trained to kill?"

He hemmed. "Well, maybe, but this was different. There's an avarice, a ruthlessness, when I look into his eyes. He'll do whatever he feels necessary."

"Mr. Hardass," May muttered under her breath.

"What?"

May shook her head. "Sorry, that's the nickname I gave him."

He smirked. "And what was my nickname?"

"Mr. Paranoid."

He snorted. "Okay, I guess I deserved that. So, what was your next move?"

"I didn't have one. I thought once I told my CO, it would be over. I thought I was done with this. Now, she's dead because of me. I can't live that down, not ever."

He reached across the table, but stopped midway as if wanting to comfort her but rethinking it. "You don't know that."

She scoffed. "You don't really believe that."

He hesitated, not denying it. "So, what do we do now?"

"You're the one who came to me."

He looked down. "Yeah, I did. I didn't think much further beyond that, though. I just thought I needed to act."

"I know the feeling, but it has to be the right action, doesn't it?"

"Yeah."

"So, what *can* we do? I tried telling someone, but that didn't end well. I'm not sure I could risk that again, not unless we *know* the person isn't involved or won't get killed." May tapped her lip, thinking, then she looked at the guy across from her, a man she didn't even have a name for. "If telling someone is our plan, the way I see it, there are two major factors in play. First, they need to not be associated with your organization. Second, they need the clout to stop this directly."

He leaned back, looking nervous. "What are you asking of me?"

"Well, I don't know. I'm just a pilot. I'm not a spy, not security. I don't know how to run an investigation." She paused, something forming in her head. How did he find her? He knew she'd recorded them. The only evidence she suspected she'd left behind was maybe the recorder, fingerprints, maybe surveillance video? May smiled. *She* might not know the first thing about running an investigation, but it sounded like he did.

"But you?" she said, speaking to her inner thoughts. "You were able to find me with almost no information. It seems to me that you could find this out no problem."

"Oh no," he said, waving his hands in front of him. "I'm done with that. That was the last time."

"You said you wanted this to end." She leaned forward, folding her hands together in front of her like she'd seen her CO do a thousand times before. She breathed through the pain that thought created.

"I do."

"Then you're gonna have to do something. And it seems to me

that you're the perfect person to run the investigation. I'll help, but you need to lead. I don't know what I'm doing."

"God help us."

That night, Joe stared at his computer, the NSS logo on the desktop blurring before his eyes as he leaned back in his chair and tried to think. The dark room closed in around him, the only light coming from the monitor. It left him feeling claustrophobic and alone. He'd wanted to recruit May so he wouldn't have to stick his neck out. How had she convinced him to continue with his hacking? How was it he kept breaking his promise to his mother?

It didn't matter. It needed to be done, and she was right. She didn't have the skills to do it; he did. He snapped his chair upright once more and got to work. First, he needed a comprehensive list of those involved in the plot, but how? Was there even a list? And even if there was, it needed to be somewhere he could access remotely and cleanly. He wasn't about to stick his neck out on this. He had to protect himself.

As a starting point, he wrote down what he knew, *who* he knew, just to get his brain going. When that didn't help, he moved on to something that was maybe a bit easier—finding who they could contact to stop the plot. The list couldn't be that long, could it? The person had to have a significant amount of influence and command, able to set things in motion quickly and, preferably, quietly. There were too many eyes on this, too many ways this could go wrong.

And it absolutely *couldn't* go wrong.

CHAPTER ELEVEN

$\mathcal{M}$ ay reached her desk and smiled down at the envelope sitting there when she arrived the next morning. She knew who it was from, but this time, he'd written her name in a flowing script on the envelope with hearts surrounding it.

She snorted and sat down, ripping the note open. Several names filled the top of the note in a list. Below it, he'd written, "These are our best prospects. Don't meet them yet, just observe, then meet me at the café tomorrow with your opinion."

Opinion? What the hell did that mean? Did he forget she didn't know what she was doing?

Well, if she needed the information by tomorrow, she would have to get started ASAP. She stood and slipped out of the office. Nobody noticed, not with their CO dead and no one yet assigned to replace her. A memorial service was planned, but not until after May shipped out, so she wouldn't get to go.

She wasn't sure how to feel about that. Should she be upset that she couldn't pay her respects to a woman who'd always treated her fairly, who'd always tried to make her into a better version of herself? Or was it just? After all, she was responsible for the woman's death. Attending her memorial service felt a bit wrong when she thought of it that way.

Stepping out of the building, the warm sunlight crossed her face, blinding her for a moment. She covered her eyes and lifted the note, rereading the names. She recognized several of them, even knew where their offices were, but she didn't see how she could observe them, let alone get a meeting with them. Hell, one was a Rear Admiral. She bet he was too damned busy to meet with lowly pilots.

May pocketed the note, the paper crinkling as she stepped forward.

"How the fuck does he expect me to get all this done by tomorrow?"

He frowned as he stared at the barracks. He'd been suspicious of his partner ever since they found that recorder five days ago. Eventually, he'd started following him. And the more he followed, the more suspicious he became. He had nothing concrete, nothing to bring to the higher ups, but his gut told him the man had betrayed them.

Unfortunately, proving it would be difficult. His associate was a computer specialist, which meant the true proof would be on his computer, information he would be hard-pressed to access. He wasn't a computer person, probably wouldn't know what he was looking at even if he found it.

But his gut had never been wrong before. The last few times he'd met with him, the little bastard had been cagey, not looking him in the eye. The guy was always a weasel, but this was different. He could feel it.

And he wasn't willing to take the chance.

Fortunately, he knew the nerd lived on the bottom floor, even knew which room, so he might just be able to find the evidence he needed. He crossed the tightly trimmed grass until he was close to the outer wall. Wearing a hooded sweatshirt, he looked like he was just out for a jog, allowing him to go unnoticed. He trotted along beside the building, his gaze darting to the side every time he reached a window.

Bingo.

He jogged past the window he'd been looking for, and his partner was indeed at his computer, which meant it was unlocked. This was his chance. He changed direction, angling for the entrance. Once inside, he started stretching like he'd just finished a long run. His muscles pulled taut in that warm, tight feeling that always felt so good after a hard workout. He pushed his hood back, checking the room numbers, counting down to his destination.

At the correct door, he stretched his quads, making it good for anyone who might be watching. Finally, he dropped his leg and knocked.

"Coming," the voice said from within.

His hand reached into the pocket of his hoodie. When the door opened, he pushed through, lifting the weapon and slamming it down. His victim dropped like a log, a trickle of blood running down his face. He turned, closing the door behind him with a gentle click.

Turning back, he smiled. The computer was still powered on and logged in. He sat down and rubbed his hands together.

Now, to find the truth.

It wasn't easy, but May had done it. She'd watched each of the targets, observing their behavior, how they interacted with the people around them, even how others interacted with them. She didn't know what else to do. How was she supposed to know who to tell?

I need someone like Parker, like my CO.

She needed someone who would do the right thing, regardless. She needed someone who would feel the urgency and do whatever it took to save everyone. A heavy breath escaped her as she reached the barracks. She needed to get changed out of her uniform to meet at the café. She didn't think arriving in full military togs would send the message they wanted to send.

But as she approached, several MP vehicles and an ambulance were parked outside. Lights flashed, tinting the atmosphere with anxiety and urgency.

What happened?

Other than the vehicles, the area outside seemed deserted as she scanned her surroundings. She pushed into the building to chaos. People crowded the narrow hallway, chatting excitedly and basically being nuisances. In the background, she saw an MP, but couldn't tell what was going on. Clearly, someone had been hurt, but who and why? Was it just a medical emergency? But then why were the MPs called out? Did someone get attacked?

"What happened?" She addressed a tall man wearing sweats.

He turned to her, having to tip his head down to look her in the eye. "Someone was beat to a pulp."

"What? Who?"

He shrugged. "Don't know."

May frowned at him. She wanted to snap at him for getting in her way. After all, how the hell were they supposed to get a stretcher through here when it was wall to wall bodies?

"Excuse me," she said, leading with her shoulder to get past. People stepped aside begrudgingly, but she lived here, damn it. She had every right to get to her own damned room.

"I heard it was Joe," a feminine voice said.

"Joe? Computer Specialist Joe?"

May glanced over as the first voice, a woman she knew only in passing, nodded. "Yup, Joe Wilder. I heard he was beat so bad, they couldn't even recognize him."

"Who would beat up a Computer Specialist?"

May moved on. *It's not important. It's none of my business.* Some poor bastard got pummeled. She had more important things to focus on right now.

Like her meeting with that guy at the café.

She unlocked her door, looking over her shoulder toward the sea of bodies farther down the hall. They'd never had violence like this at the barracks before.

"I wonder what happened," she mumbled under her breath right before she stepped inside.

When May reached the café a half hour later, he wasn't there. She frowned, but took a seat on the patio, ordering a coffee while she waited. Time passed, her coffee growing cold.

She watched as people came and went, oblivious to the turmoil within her, too absorbed in their pointless personal dramas. It all seemed so small by comparison. Hell, even her own dramas of the past seemed small. After all, while Mila had left her, she'd left a note. It wasn't some big mystery. There was no reason to think she was hurt, no reason to think she was dead. She just left.

Put into perspective, it seemed silly the way May had let that event define her life the way she had. She didn't know why Mila did it, but she had. And it didn't matter. Their lives were connected. They weren't entwined. Her leaving didn't end May's life, even if it felt like it at the time. She'd lost all motivation, and it seemed until this wake-up call, she hadn't recovered it. Not once.

"Ma'am, we're closing up soon."

May's head jerked up, staring unseeingly into the face of a young woman with a waitress apron on. A chill had entered the air without her realizing and as she looked up to the horizon, she realized the sun was setting, the sky tinted deep oranges and pinks.

Had she been sitting here for hours?

"Thank you. I'll be on my way."

He'd never shown.

May returned home in a daze. Had she been punked? Was he just playing her? Why did he stand her up?

Or did something stop him?

That thought alarmed her more than a little, especially as she approached the barracks, remembering the MPs and ambulance that had overwhelmed the parking area the last time she'd approached.

Could that have been him? The man who was attacked? It would certainly explain why he never showed.

May hurried back to the privacy of her room. The door sounded impossibly loud as she closed it. The room felt unfamiliar as she stared at it, her reality twisted by the events of the last two weeks.

"Now what?"

I need to know if it was him.

She crossed the room and dropped in front of her computer, pulling up the military roster. "What had that name been? It was something ordinary." She tapped her lip as the cursor blinked in the first name field.

"Joe." Wilder. The surname flowed into her brain on the cusp of his given name. She typed Joe for the first name and Wilder for the last.

No hits.

"Joseph maybe?" She changed the first name and got a hit. She got some basic information not available to the general public, including deployment status, work assignments, and housing.

It was him. The man she'd met stared back at her wearing a military uniform in the picture. Military housing right down the hall from her, Computer Specialist, currently not deployed.

And someone had just beat him to a pulp.

Now what?

CHAPTER TWELVE

The next morning, May lay in her bed staring at the ceiling. She didn't know what to do. She was running out of time, and certainly, the ceiling didn't have any answers for her.

Sitting up, the sheets still covering her legs, she tried to think. Nothing had gone right since she first heard those two talking, disrupting her hidey-hole.

For a moment, she contemplated going to him, seeing if he was awake. How bad was he hurt? It was possible he'd been released already. Or he could be in a coma. She had no clue.

But she very much doubted he could help her now. She'd gone to her CO. Now her CO was dead. She'd partnered with this guy, a guy on the inside. For all she knew, he might be dead, too. She thought of the list he'd given her. It still waited in her pants pocket from last night, dumped on the floor without a care. She could go to one of them, but her stomach twisted, a part of herself certain that would simply sign the person's death warrant.

So, what could she do? She played with the edge of the sheet, running her finger along the seam, trying to think. What could she do? She knew she couldn't stop this by herself. She didn't have the clout. And without knowing how to safely warn someone, how could she act?

She needed advice. Unfortunately, the only person that came to mind was Mila. May had always told the other woman everything. They'd been like twins growing up, planning their lives together. They'd gone to pilot training together. Hell, they'd been a breath away from graduating side by side. Mila had set records on her sub-space qualifications, for crying out loud.

Then she'd disappeared, never to be heard from again.

Not for lack of trying, though.

May froze, remembering the note her best friend had given her. At the bottom had been a phone number, a number she'd kept, always simmering in the background like a live wire ready to fry her. She'd never called it, too chicken to find out why her friend had abandoned her.

"She probably doesn't even have that number anymore," May said to herself, shaking her head.

And yet, wasn't that just another cop-out? Wasn't that just another in a very, very long line of excuses? She'd let so many things keep her away from her best friend for so many years. "No more excuses."

Except, couldn't she be putting Mila at risk, too? But then, Mila was off the grid as far as she knew. Nobody, not even Mila's own parents, knew where she was. If anyone was safe to talk to, it was Mila. And she wasn't trying to rope her friend into this. She just needed advice. She needed Mila's unwavering moral compass. Mila always knew what to do.

Except for ten years ago.

That thought stalled her out. It *did* seem out of character, running like that. Mila had always faced her challenges, laughing in the face of adversity. She was the type to bow if someone called her a bitch. She was brave, so why did she run?

May pulled out her phone. "I'm not gonna chicken out." Tapping her contacts, she scrolled to the Ds, to Mila Dragomirov, and tapped the text message icon. An empty screen popped up.

No message history because you've been too chicken to reach out.

Her thumbs hovered over the screen, trying to decide what to write. What did you say to a friend you hadn't spoken to in ten years? Sorry? Hope to hear from you soon?

In the end, she tapped out a simple, if cryptic, message. Short and to the point.

I need you. Let's meet.

May took a deep breath as she exited her car around the corner from the café. She'd had trouble finding a parking spot today, having to park at the end of an alley behind the restaurant. Only another day or so remained before her deployment. She was running out of time. She felt nervous, on edge, like she would jump out of her skin if a trash can tipped over.

Since Joe's attack two days ago, she'd half expected someone to come after her. Maybe on the way to or from work, or an accident like her CO's. Every time she entered her car, she was afraid to start it, afraid to start driving. So many things could be sabotaged in a vehicle. First, you had good old bombs. Pressure plates attached to the driver's seat, detonators attached to the ignition. Hell, you could even get fancy and attach it to the speedometer like in that old movie.

Then there were the more pedestrian acts, like sabotaging the brakes or locking the accelerator in place so the car wouldn't slow down.

So many ways to die by car. It really was just a glorified lethal weapon.

May turned the corner, the bistro tables now in view. It should have been a relaxing sight, a nice morning meal with a friend sitting out in the sunshine, but it felt too crowded. Too many people to overhear, too many chances to risk it. The crowd was loud, chaotic, like a thousand whispering voices that would go silent the moment you spoke. And while the sun was shining, it didn't seem to warm her. Instead, a slight breeze left her feeling chilled to the bone.

Her hands shook at her sides as she scanned the tables, wondering if Mila had already arrived.

May had never expected to get a response from her friend. She'd expected that screen to remain with the single line of text for all time. But later that night, she'd received a response.

Mila: When? Where?

May: ASAP. Café outside the base.

Mila: Tomorrow morning.

That was it. Just four lines on the screen, but it was enough. She had her friend back. It seemed amazing that even after ten years of separation, all it had taken was a single text that said, "I need you," and Mila had come running. She didn't know where Mila had been, but it must have been close for her to show up the next morning.

"Hey, May!"

That voice. She would know it anywhere. It was Mila. Her head jerked up, scanning the tables once more. There… in the corner. She looked older now, though she couldn't say how, exactly. Maybe it was the tension in her shoulders or how she'd positioned her chair up against a wall.

Minutes passed. May didn't even realize she'd crossed the distance, standing behind a chair across from Mila. She just stared, momentarily forgetting her paranoia, the fact that she'd been watching her back ever since her CO died.

Mila shook her head and patted the glass tabletop. "Come on, May. Sit."

But she couldn't. She just… couldn't. How could she sit when Mila sat there as if nothing had happened, as if they'd seen each other just yesterday? "Where have you been?" All the pain rose up inside her once more, fresh as the day Mila left. It choked her, strangling her worse than ever.

"Around."

May scowled as Mila just sat there, staring. As her pain fled, her paranoia returned. She wanted to laugh.

Was it really paranoia, though? She resisted the urge to look over her shoulder, check the street. After all, she didn't know who she was looking for. She didn't even know what Joe's partner looked like, for crying out loud. Being this tense, this on edge, didn't do anyone any good.

May stared down at Mila and tried to let go of the anger, grief, and pain that had bubbled up to choke her paranoia. It wouldn't serve her now. Now, she had a job to do. She needed advice, and she knew the café wasn't the best place to discuss it.

She glanced over toward the alleyway. Her car was at the end of it. In that car were her recordings and her tablet. She was going to show them all to Mila, tell her what was happening, ask for her advice.

But right now? She needed to fix their relationship.

She needed her friend back.

"May I walk you to your car?" Mila said as May put money on the table for the check.

She turned to her friend, smiling at the convenience of the offer. She'd had every intension of offering Mila a ride, anything to get her in an enclosed space where they could talk. Mila had just made it that much easier.

They'd reconnected over breakfast, soothing the hard edges they both felt. Now, she had one last thing to do before they could part. They left the café's patio and dipped into the shadow created by the tall buildings on either side of the alley. At the end, her car loomed, waiting with the evidence.

Soon.

"So, why did you *really* call me, May?"

She jumped, lost in her thoughts, and twisted sheepishly toward Mila. "What do you mean?"

"You haven't contacted me in ten years. Suddenly, you reach out, and you're skittish as a mouse? Something's wrong."

May wrung her hands, fidgeting from foot to foot. She didn't know what to say, and the weight of both her CO and Joe's fates squeezed around her throat, silencing her further.

Mila being Mila, she waited her out, knowing she would speak in her own time.

Crashes of metal, cheers, and lewd comments erupted in front of her and May looked up, her eyes rounding. A bunch of boys blasted into the alley, pointing at her and Mila, their cat calls echoing off the walls.

"Back slowly to the car, May."

Mila didn't have to tell her twice. Her steps were already creeping backward from the moment she first saw them. Wouldn't it just figure to get caught up in a huge military conspiracy only to be attacked by hoodlums?

"Hey, don't leave!" the leader said, laughing as he gamboled closer.

"Yeah, we just wanna play!" a boy behind him said.

They cheered and thrust their hips, making it obvious what they wanted.

"Run," Mila whispered.

May glanced over, but Mila had already turned to dash for May's car.

Damn, she's fast.

As if on cue, the hoodlums surged forward like dogs after fleeing prey.

May grunted, afraid to turn her back to them, but she ran anyway, pushing herself like the hounds of hell were on her heels. From the sound of it, they were.

She'd only run a couple steps when someone grabbed her hair from behind, yanking her backward. Pain seared through her scalp, and a choked scream escaped her lips as she fell. Her stomach flipped as her body recognized she was falling, and she couldn't catch herself.

Crack.

Her head hit the unforgiving ground, arms slamming hard

into the rough pavement. Her skull pounded, and she closed her eyes, groaning as that pain became her entire focus.

"Bye, bye, girlie," one of them whispered by her ear.

May gasped as pain and pressure assailed her gut. She couldn't figure out what it was at first. It hurt, and tears streamed down her cheeks.

Why am I wet?

"No!" a voice screamed from a distance. She couldn't quite put a name to it, but she knew that voice. Who was that? Why were they screaming? She tried to wrack her brain for the answer, but her thoughts kept drifting like clouds on a breeze, impossible to catch.

More pressure on her stomach and she grunted, but it didn't seem to make any sound. "You'll be okay, May. You're gonna be okay."

But May wasn't sure she believed that. She felt really cold. Really, really cold. And she couldn't seem to lift her arms.

So cold.

She tried to work her lips, to form words, but they wouldn't cooperate.

I'm sorry, Mila.

<hr>

EPILOGUE

<hr>

Mila stared down at the tombstone of May Trace, her best friend. She might be dead, they might have spent ten years apart, but May would always be her best friend.

So much time had passed since the day she'd watched May die. So much had happened.

Because of May meeting her that day, Mila had taken her place aboard the USS *Orleans*. Because of May, they'd prevented the sabotage planned for it. Because of May, humanity was now allied with the Incirrina.

And because of May, they'd prevented an invasion of Earth that would have surely meant the end of the human race.

A chill ran along her arms and down her spine. She wanted to blame it on the wind, but the trees and grasses were stubbornly still around her.

Mila stood in full dress uniform, her cover firmly on her head as she stood at attention in front of the newly placed headstone. They'd buried her officially a couple weeks ago. So many people had spoken at May's wake. So many people had been touched either directly or indirectly by May.

A tear leaked from one eye and ran a cool trail down her cheek.

"Thank you, May." She lifted her hand up in salute, trying to hold back the sniffles that threatened to ruin the moment. "You are a hero and a friend. You will never be forgotten."

DID YOU ENJOY THE BOOK?

IF SO, YOU CAN MAKE A **BIG** DIFFERENCE…

Reviews are among the most important tools in my arsenal for getting my books in front of readers like yourself. I'm just one person. No matter how much I shout, my voice can only carry so far.

But do you want to know what does carry?

A crowd.

When one voice joins another who joins another, that matters. *That* gets heard.

Let your own voice be heard by leaving an honest review. It only takes a few minutes, but makes a major difference not just to me as an author, but to readers like yourself who are trying to decide on their next read.

Thanks again!

Danielle

ABOUT THE AUTHOR

Danielle Forrest is a Paranormal SciFi author and Medical Laboratory Scientist based out of Indianapolis, IN.

She has dedicated her life so far to two things:

Science & Books

So it really shouldn't be a surprise if science finds its way into even the most fantastical examples of her writing.

Sign up for her mailing list at www.theeternalscribe.com to get access to exclusive content and updates.

facebook.com/theeternalscribe

twitter.com/theternalscribe

instagram.com/theeternalscribe

goodreads.com/theeternalscribe

amazon.com/author/danielleforrest

bookbub.com/profile/danielle-forrest

ALSO BY DANIELLE FORREST

THE DARKEST DAY SERIES

Mila's Flight

When she shifts for the first time, an unsuspecting shape-shifter runs away to live on the streets. But after a mysterious man enters her life violently, she'll die if she doesn't stop running from her problems.

Mila's Shift

Hiding from a government bent on eradicating her kind, a paranoid shape-shifter steals her dead friend's identity to board a military spaceship, but when the captain discovers her secret, she must learn to trust again or no one will survive.

Tristan's Choice

After he receives orders for a new mission, an unambitious space ship captain transports diplomats to the moon for a historic treaty negotiation with an alien race. But when an alien ship attacks, interrupting the talks, he must warn Earth or everyone will die.

Terra's Fate

When a child in her care shifts for the first time, a prejudiced shape-shifter in denial must escape the shifter camp imprisoning them both. But when an alien invasion looms, threatening what little peace she's found, she must accept herself or lose everyone everything.

www.ingramcontent.com/pod-product-compliance
Lightning Source LLC
Chambersburg PA
CBHW060739210726
48292CB00012B/9